The vampire stepped elegantly out of its coffin. Its bare feet made no sound on the wooden floor.

Fisher wrinkled her nose at the smell. 'Dirty stinking bastard. Lying down or standing up, it makes no difference. Let's do it, Hawk.'

Hawk nodded slowly, and then sprang forward, swinging his axe double-handed at the vampire's neck. The creature put up a spindly arm to block the blow, and the axe bounced off, vibrating as though it had struck an iron bar. Hawk's hands went numb from the impact, and it was all he could do to hang onto the axe. Fisher thrust at the vampire with her stake, using it like a dagger. The vampire avoided the blow easily, and knocked Fisher sprawling with a single backhanded blow. She lay where she had fallen, her head swimming madly. There was an inhuman power in the creature's slender frame. Fisher clutched desperately at the wooden stake, and struggled weakly to get her feet under her. The vampire looked down at her and chuckled suddenly – a low, filthy sound.

HAVEN
OF
LOST
SOULS

Simon R. Green

No Haven for the Guilty © Simon R. Green 1990
Devil Take the Hindmost © Simon R. Green 1991
The God Killer © Simon R. Green 1991

The right of Simon R. Green to be identified as the
author of this work has been
asserted by him in accordance with the
Copyright, Designs and Patents Act 1988.

This edition first published in Great Britain in 1999 by
Millennium
An imprint of Victor Gollancz
Orion House, 5 Upper St Martin's Lane, London WC2H 9EA

To receive information on the Millennium list, e-mail us at:
smy@orionbooks.co.uk

A CIP catalogue record for this book is available
from the British Library

ISBN 1857989007

Typeset at The Spartan Press Ltd,
Lymington, Hants
Printed in Great Britain by
Clays Ltd, St Ives plc.

Contents

No Haven for the Guilty

Some things can never be forgiven

1

A Hidden Darkness

Haven is a dark city.

The narrow streets huddled together, the plain stone and timber buildings leaning on each other for support. Out-leaning upper storeys bowed to each other like tired old men, shutting out the light, but even in the shadows there was little relief from the midsummer heat. The glaring sun scorched down on the sprawling city, driving all moisture from the air. The streets were parched and dusty and thick with buzzing flies. Being a seaport, Haven usually got all the rain it wanted, and then some, but not in midsummer. The long days wore on, and the baking heat made them a misery of sweat and thirst and endless fatigue. The days were too hot to work and the nights too hot to sleep. Tempers grew short and frayed, but it was too hot to brawl. Birds hung on the sky like drifting shadows, but there was never a trace of a cloud or a breeze. Haven at midsummer was a breeding ground for trouble. The heat stirred men's minds and brought forth hidden evils. Everyone watched the skies and prayed for rain, and still the long dry summer dragged on.

Hawk and Fisher, Captains in the city Guard, strolled unhurriedly down Chandler Lane, deep in the rotten heart of the North side. It was too hot to hurry. The grimy, overshadowed lane was a little cooler than most, which meant the heat was only mildly unbearable. Flies hovered over piles of garbage and swarmed around the open sewers. The squat and ugly buildings were black with soot from the nearby tannery, and the muggy air smelt strongly of smoke and tannin.

Hawk was tall, dark, and no longer handsome. He wore a black silk patch over his right eye, and a series of old scars ran down the right side of his face, showing pale against the tanned skin. He wore a simple cotton shirt and trousers, but didn't bother with the black Guardsman's cloak required by regulations. It was too hot for a cloak, and anyway, he didn't need one to tell people he was a Guard. Everyone in Haven had heard of Captain Hawk.

He didn't look like much. He was lean and wiry rather than muscular, and he was beginning to build a stomach. He wore his dark hair at shoulder length, swept back from his forehead and tied with a silver clasp. He had only just turned thirty, but already there were a few streaks of grey in his hair. At first glance he looked like just another bravo, not as young as he once was, perhaps a little past his prime. But few people stopped at the first glance; there was something about Hawk, something in his scarred face and single cold eye that gave even the drunkest hardcase pause. On his right hip Hawk carried a short-handled axe instead of a sword. He was very good with an axe.

Captain Fisher walked at Hawk's side, echoing his pace and stance with the naturalness of long companionship. Isobel Fisher was tall, easily six feet in height, and her long blond hair fell to her waist in a single thick plait. She was in her mid to late twenties, and handsome rather than beautiful. There was a rawboned harshness to her face that contrasted strongly with her deep blue eyes and generous mouth. Like Hawk, she wore a cotton shirt and trousers, and no cloak. The shirt was half-unbuttoned to show a generous amount of bosom, and her shirt sleeves were rolled up, revealing arms corded with muscle and lined with old scars. She wore a sword on her hip, and her hand rested comfortably on the pommel.

Hawk and Fisher; partners, husband and wife, guardians

of the city law. Known, respected, and mostly feared throughout Haven, even in the lower Northside, where the very rats went round in pairs for safety. Hawk and Fisher were the best, and everyone knew it. They were honest and hard-working, a rare combination in Haven, but more important still, they were dangerous.

Hawk looked about him and scowled slightly. Chandler Lane was deserted, with not a soul in sight, and that was . . . unusual. The afternoon was fast turning into evening, but even so there should have been people out selling and buying and making a deal. On the lower Northside everything was for sale, if you knew where to look. But all around, the doors and shutters were firmly closed despite the stifling heat, and the shadows lay still and undisturbed. It was like looking at a street under siege. Hawk smiled sourly. If his information was correct, that might just be the case.

'There's going to be a full moon tonight,' said Fisher quietly.

Hawk nodded. 'That'll bring out the crazies. Though how anyone has the energy even to plan a crime in this heat is beyond me.'

'You do realise this is probably nothing more than a wild goose chase, don't you?'

'Not again, Isobel, please. The word is he's hiding right here, at the end of this street. We have to check it out.'

'Three months,' said Fisher angrily. 'Three months we've been working on that child prostitution racket. And just when we're starting to get somewhere, what happens? The word comes down from Above, and we get pulled off the case to go looking for a vampire!'

'Yeah,' said Hawk. 'And all because we raided the Nag's Head. Still, I'd do it again, if I had to.'

Fisher nodded grimly.

The Nag's Head was a hole-in-the-wall tavern on Salt Lane, just on the boundary of the Eastside slums. The upper floor was a brothel, and the word was that they were interested in acquiring children. Cash in hand, no questions asked. Child prostitution had been illegal in Haven for almost seven years, but there were still those with a vested interest in keeping the market open. Like many other places, the Nag's Head kept itself in business by greasing the right palms, but one man had made the mistake of trying to buy off Hawk and Fisher. So they had paid the place a visit.

The bravo at the door tried to bar their way. He was either new in town, or not particularly bright. Hawk gave him a straight-finger jab under the sternum. The bravo's face went very pale and he bent slowly forward, almost as though bowing to Hawk. Fisher waited till he was bent right over, and then rabbit-punched him. The bravo went down without a murmur. Hawk and Fisher stepped cautiously over him, kicked in the door, and burst into the Nag's Head with cold steel in their hands.

The staff and patrons took one look at them and a sudden silence fell over the crowded room. Smoke curled on the stuffy air, and the watching eyes were bright with fear and suppressed anger. Hawk and Fisher headed for the stairs at the back of the dimly lit room, and a pathway opened up before them as people got hurriedly out of their way. Three bravos crowded together at the foot of the stairs with drawn swords. They were big, muscular men with cold, calculating eyes who knew how to use their swords. Hawk cut down two of them with his axe while Fisher stabbed the third cleanly through the heart. They stepped quickly over the bodies and pounded up the stairs. The upper floor was ominously quiet. Hawk and Fisher charged along the narrow landing, kicking open doors as they went, but most of the occupants were long gone, having disappeared down the fire escape at the first sound of trouble.

One of the prostitutes hadn't been able to get away. Hawk found her in the last room but one. She was dressed in torn silks too large for her, and wore gaudy colours on her face. She was chained to the wall by the throat, and her back ran red from the wounds of a recent whipping. She sat slumped against the wall, her face pressed against the rough wood, crying softly, hopelessly. She was almost twelve years old.

Fisher joined Hawk in the doorway, and swore angrily as she took in the scene. The chain was too heavy to break, so Hawk levered the bolt out of the wall with his axe. Fisher tried to comfort the child, but she was too frightened to say much. She'd been abducted in the street two years ago, and been brought to this room. Her abductors put the chain around her neck and locked it, and she'd never been out of the room since. Both Hawk and Fisher told her she was free now, but she didn't believe it. *There's a man who comes to visit me*, she said quietly. *He was here today. He'll never let me go. You can't protect me from him. No one can. He's important.*

She didn't know his name. No one ever told her their name.

Hawk and Fisher never did find out who he was, but he must have had influence. Only two days later, the child was stabbed to death in the street. Her attacker was never found. Hawk and Fisher were officially taken off the case and sent to join the other Guards searching for the supposed vampire that was terrorising the Northside. They raised hell with their superiors, and even talked about quitting the Guard, but none of it did any good. The word had come down from somewhere high Above, and there was no arguing with it. Hawk and Fisher had shrugged and cursed and finally given up. There would be other times.

Besides, it seemed there really was a vampire. Men, women, and children had been attacked at night, and occasionally bodies were found with no blood left in them. There were dozens of sightings and as many suspects, but none of them led anywhere. And then a lamplighter had come to see Hawk, and there was no denying the horror in his voice as he told Hawk and Fisher of the dark figure he'd seen crawling up the outside of the house in Chandler Lane . . .

'All the Guards in Haven, and that man had to choose us to tell his story to,' grumbled Fisher. 'Why us?'

'Because we're the best,' said Hawk. 'So obviously we're not afraid to tackle anything. Even a vampire.'

Fisher sniffed. 'We should have settled for second best.'

'Not in my nature,' said Hawk easily. 'Or yours.'

They chuckled quietly together. The low, cheerful sound seemed out of place in the silence. For the first time Hawk realised just how quiet the empty street was. It was like walking through the empty shell of some village abandoned by its people but not yet overgrown by the Forest. The only sound was his and Fisher's footsteps, echoing dully back from the thick stone walls to either side of them. Despite the heat, Hawk felt a sudden chill run down his back, and the sweat on his brow was suddenly cold. Hawk shook his head angrily. This was no time to be letting his nerves get the better of him.

Hawk and Fisher finally came to a halt before a decrepit two-storey building almost at the end of the lane. Paint was peeling from the closed front door, and the stonework was pitted and crumbling. The two narrow windows were hidden behind closed wooden shutters. Hawk looked the place over and frowned thoughtfully. There was something disquieting about the house, something he couldn't quite put a name to. It was like a sound so quiet you almost missed it, or a scent so faint you could barely smell it . . . Hawk scowled, and let his hand fall to the axe at his side.

Vampire . . . revenant . . . that which returns . . .

He'd never seen one of the undead, and didn't know anyone who had. He wasn't altogether sure he believed in such things, but then, he didn't disbelieve in them either. In his time he'd known demons and devils, werewolves and undines, and faced them all with cold steel in his hand. The world had its dark places, and they were older by far than anything man had ever built. And there was no denying that people had disappeared from the Northside of late . . . and one person in particular.

'Well?' said Fisher.

Hawk looked at her irritably. 'Well what?'

'Well, are we going to just stand here all afternoon, or are we going to do something? In case you hadn't noticed, the sun's getting bloody low on the sky. It'll be dark inside an hour. And if there really is a vampire in there . . .'

'Right. The undead rise from their coffins when the sun is down.' Hawk shivered again, and then smiled slightly as he took in the goose flesh on Fisher's bare arms. Neither of them cared much for the dark, or the creatures that moved in it. Hawk took a deep breath, stepped up to the front door, and knocked loudly with his fist.

'Open in the name of the Guard!'

There was no response. Silence lay across the empty street like a smothering blanket, weighed down by the heat. Hawk wiped at the sweat running down his face with the back of his hand, and wished he'd brought a water canteen. He also wished he'd followed regulations for once and waited for a backup team, but there hadn't been time. They had to get to the vampire while he still slept. And besides, Councillor Trask's daughter was still missing. Which was why finding the vampire had suddenly become such a high priority. As long as he'd kept to the poorer sections of the city, and preyed only on those who wouldn't be missed, no one paid much attention to him. But once he snatched a Councillor's daughter out of her own bedroom, in full view of her screaming mother . . . Hawk worried his lower lip between his teeth. She should still be alive. Vampires were supposed to take two to three days to drain a victim completely, and she couldn't become one of the undead until she'd died and risen again. At least, that was what the legends said. Hawk sniffed. He didn't put much trust in legends.

'We should have stopped off and picked up some garlic,' he said suddenly. 'That's supposed to be a protection, isn't it?'

'Garlic?' said Fisher. 'At this time of the year? You know how much that stuff costs in the markets? It has to come clear across the country, and the merchants charge accordingly.'

'All right, it was just a thought. I suppose hawthorn is out as well.'

'Definitely.'

'I assume you have at least brought the stake with you? In fact, you'd better have the stake, because I'm bloody well not going in there without one.'

'Relax, love. I've got it right here.' Fisher pulled a thick wooden stake from the top of her boot. It was over a foot long, and had been roughly sharpened to a point. It looked brutally efficient. 'As I understand it, it's quite simple,' said Fisher briskly. 'I hammer this through the vampire's heart, and then you cut off his head. We burn the two parts of the body separately, scatter the ashes, and that's that.'

'Oh, sure,' said Hawk. 'Just like that.' He paused a moment, looking at the closed door before him. 'Did you ever meet Trask, or his daughter?'

'I saw Trask at the briefing yesterday,' said Fisher, slipping the stake back into her boot. 'He looked pretty broken up. You know them?'

'I met his daughter a few months back. Just briefly. I was bodyguarding Councillor DeGeorge at the time. Trask's daughter had just turned sixteen, and she looked so . . . bright, and happy.'

Fisher put her hand on his arm. 'We'll get her back, Hawk. We'll get her back.'

'Yeah,' said Hawk. 'Sure.'

He hammered on the door again with his fist. *Do it by the*

book . . . The sound echoed on the quiet, and then died quickly away. There was no response from the house, or from any of its neighbours. Hawk glanced up and down the empty street. It could always be a trap of some kind . . . No. His instincts would have been screaming at him by now. After four years in the city Guard, he had good instincts. Without them, you didn't last four years.

'All right,' he said finally. 'We go in. But watch your back on this one, lass. We take it one room at a time, by the book, and keep our eyes open. Right?'

'Right,' said Fisher. 'But we should be safe enough as long as the sun's up. The vampire can't leave his coffin till it's dark.'

'Yeah, but he might not be alone in there. Apparently most vampires have a human servant to watch over them while they sleep. A kind of Judas Goat, a protector who also helps to lure victims to his master.'

'You've been reading up on this, haven't you?' said Fisher.

'Damn right,' said Hawk. 'Ever since the first rumours. I wasn't going to be caught unprepared, like I was on that werewolf case last year.'

He tried the door handle. It turned jerkily in his hand, and the door swung slowly open as he applied a little pressure. The hinges squealed protestingly, and Hawk jumped despite himself. He pushed the door wide open and stared into the dark and empty hall. Nothing moved in the gloom, and the shadows stared silently back. Fisher moved softly in beside Hawk, her hand resting on the pommel of her sword.

'Strange the door wasn't locked,' said Hawk. 'Unless we were expected.'

'Let's get on with it,' said Fisher quietly. 'I'm starting to get a very bad feeling about this.'

They stepped forward into the hall and then closed the front door behind them, leaving it just a little ajar. Never know when you might need a quick exit. Hawk and Fisher stood together in the gloom, waiting for their eyes to adjust. Hawk had a stub of candle in his pocket, but he didn't want to use it unless he had to. All it took was a sudden gust of wind at the wrong moment and the light would be gone, leaving him blind and helpless in the dark. Better to let his sight adjust while he had the chance. He heard Fisher stir uneasily beside him, and he smiled slightly. He knew how she felt. Patiently standing and waiting just wasn't in their nature; they always felt better when they were doing something. Anything. Hawk glared about him into the gloom. There could be someone hiding in the shadows, watching them, and they'd never know it until it was too late. Something could already be moving silently towards them, with reaching hands and bared fangs . . . He felt his shoulders growing stiff and tense, and made himself breathe deeply and slowly. It didn't matter what was out there; he had his axe and he had Fisher at his side. Nothing else mattered. His eyesight slowly grew used to the gloom, and the narrow hall gradually formed itself out of the shadows. It was completely empty. Hawk relaxed a little.

'You all right?' he whispered to Fisher.

'Yeah, fine,' she said quietly. 'Let's go.'

The hall ended in a bare wooden stairway that led up to the next floor. Two doors led off from the hall, one to each side. Hawk drew his axe, and hefted it in one hand. The heavy weight of it was reassuring. He glanced at Fisher, and smiled as he saw the sword in her hand. He caught her eye, and gestured for her to take the right-hand door while he took the left. She nodded, and padded quietly over to the right.

Hawk listened carefully at his door, but everything was quiet. He turned the handle, eased the door open an inch, and then kicked it in. He leapt into the room and glared quickly about him, his axe poised and ready. The room was empty. There was no furniture, and all the walls were bare.

A little light filtered past the closed shutters, taking the edge off the gloom. The woodwork was flecked with mould, and everywhere was thick with dust. There was no sign to show the room had ever been lived in. The floorboards creaked loudly under Hawk's weight as he walked slowly forward. There was a strong smell of dust and rotten wood, but underneath that there was a faint but definite smell of corruption, as though something long dead lay buried close at hand. Hawk sniffed at the air, but couldn't decide if the smell was really there or if he was just imagining it. He moved quickly round the room, tapping the walls and listening to the echo, but there was no trace of any hidden panel or passageway. Hawk stood in the middle of the room, looking around him to check he hadn't missed anything, and then went back into the hall.

Fisher was waiting for him. He shook his head, and Fisher shrugged disappointedly. Hawk smiled slightly. He already knew Fisher hadn't found anything; if she had, he'd have heard the sound of battle. Fisher wasn't known for her diplomacy. Hawk started towards the stairs, and Fisher moved quickly in beside him.

The bare wooden steps creaked and groaned beneath their feet, and Hawk scowled. If there was someone here, watching over the vampire, they had to know there was someone else in the house. You couldn't put your foot down anywhere without some creaking board giving away your position. He hurried up the rest of the stairs and out onto the landing. He felt a little less vulnerable on the landing; there was more room to move, if it came to a fight. The floor was thick with dust and rat droppings, and the bare wooden walls were dull and scarred. Two doors led off from the landing, to their right. It was just as gloomy as the ground-floor hall, and Hawk thought fleetingly of his candle before deciding against it. If the sound hadn't given them away, a light certainly would. He moved over to stand before the first door, and listened carefully. He couldn't hear anything. Hawk smiled slightly. If this house did turn out to be empty, he was going to feel bloody ridiculous. He looked at Fisher, and gestured for her to guard his back. She nodded quickly. Hawk tried the door handle, and it turned easily in his grasp. He pushed the door slightly ajar, took a deep breath, and kicked the door in.

He darted forward into the room, axe at the ready, and again there was no one there. Without looking around, Hawk knew that Fisher was looking at him knowingly.

I said this was a wild goose chase, Hawk . . .

He didn't look back. He wouldn't give her the satisfaction. He glared about him, taking in the darkened room. A sparse light seeped past the closed shutters to show him a wardrobe to his left and a bed to his right. A large wooden chest stood at the foot of the bare bed. Hawk eyed the chest suspiciously. It looked to be a good four feet long and three feet wide; quite large enough to hold a body. Hawk frowned. Like it or not, he was going to need some light to check the room out properly. He peered about him, and his gaze fell on an old oil lamp lying on the floor by the bed. He bent down, picked the lamp up and shook it gently. He could feel oil sloshing back and forth in the base of the lamp. Hawk worried his lower lip between his teeth. The house might appear deserted, but somebody had to have been here recently . . . He took out flint and steel and lit the lamp. The sudden golden glow made the room seem smaller and less threatening.

Hawk moved over to the chest and crouched down before it. There didn't seem to be any lock or bolts. He glanced at Fisher, who took a firm hold on the wooden stake in her left hand and nodded for him to try the lid. He clutched his axe tightly, and then threw the lid open. Hawk let out his breath in a slow sigh of relief, and he and Fisher relaxed a little as they took in the pile of old bed linen that filled the chest. The cloth was flecked with a rather nasty-looking mould, and had obviously been left in the chest for ages, but Hawk rummaged gingerly through it anyway, just in case there might be something hidden under it. There wasn't. Hawk wiped his hand thoroughly on his trousers.

All this taking it slow and easy was getting on his nerves. He suddenly wanted very badly just to run amok and tear the place apart until he found the missing girl, but he knew he couldn't do that. Firstly, if there was no one here the house's owners would sue his arse in the courts, and secondly, if there was a vampire here he was bound to be well hidden, and nothing less than a careful, methodical search was going to find him.

One room at a time, one thing at a time, by the book. Follow the procedures. And he and Fisher might just get out of this alive yet.

He moved over to the bed and got down on his hands and knees to look underneath it. A big hairy spider darted out of the shadows towards him, and he fell backwards with a startled yelp. The spider quickly disappeared back into the shadows. Hawk quickly regained his balance and shot a dirty look at Fisher, who was trying hard not to laugh and only just making it. Hawk growled something under his breath, picked up the lamp from the floor and swept it back and forth before him. There was nothing under the bed but dust.

Not in the chest, and not under the bed. That only left the wardrobe, though it seemed a bit obvious. Hawk clambered to his feet, put the lamp on the chest, and moved over to stand before the wardrobe. It was a big piece of furniture, almost seven feet tall and four feet wide. *Wonder how they got it up the stairs?* thought Hawk absently. He took a firm hold on the door handle, gestured for Fisher to stand ready, and then jerked open the door. Inside the wardrobe a teenage girl was hanking naked from a butcher's hook. Her eyes were wide and staring, and she'd been dead for some time. Two jagged puncture wounds showed clearly on her throat, bright red against the white skin. The steel tip of the butcher's hook protruded from her right shoulder, just above the collarbone. No blood had run from the wound, suggesting she was already dead when the hook went into her. Hawk swallowed hard and reached forward to gently touch the dead girl's hand. The flesh was icy cold.

'Damn,' he said quietly. 'Oh, damn.'

'It's her, isn't it?' said Fisher. 'Councillor Trask's daughter.'

'Yes,' said Hawk. 'It's her.'

'The vampire must have been thirsty. Or maybe just greedy. I doubt there's a drop of blood left in her body.'

'Look at her,' said Hawk harshly. 'Sixteen years old, and left to hang in darkness like a side of beef. She was so pretty, so alive . . . She didn't deserve to die like this. No one deserves to die like this.'

'Easy,' said Fisher softly. 'Take it easy, love. We'll get the bastard that did this. Now let's get the girl down.'

'What?' Hawk looked at Fisher confusedly.

'We have to get her down, Hawk,' said Fisher. 'She died from a vampire's bite. If we leave her, she'll rise again as one of the undead. We can spare her that, at least.'

Hawk nodded slowly. 'Yes. Of course.'

Somehow, between them, they got the body off the hook and out of the wardrobe. They laid the dead girl out on the bed, and Hawk tried to close the staring eyes. They wouldn't stay shut, and in the end Fisher put two coins on the eyes to hold the lids down.

'I don't even know her name,' said Hawk. 'I only knew her as Trask's daughter.'

The scream caught him off guard, and he'd only just started to turn round when a heavy weight slammed into him from behind. He and his attacker fell sprawling on the floor, and the axe flew out of Hawk's hand. He slammed his elbow back into his attacker's ribs and pulled himself free. He scrambled away and went after his axe. The attacker lurched to his feet, and Fisher stepped forward to run him through with her sword. The man dodged aside at the last moment and grabbed Fisher's extended arm. She groaned aloud as his fingers crushed her arm, grinding the muscles against the bone. Her sword fell from her numbed fingers. She clawed at his hand, and couldn't move it. He was strong, impossibly strong, and she couldn't tear herself free . . .

He flung her away from him. She slammed against the far wall and slid dazedly to the floor. Hawk started forward, axe in hand, and then stopped dead as he finally saw who his attacker was.

'Trask . . .' Hawk gaped at the nondescript, middle-aged man standing grinning before him. The Councillor was little more than medium height and painfully thin, but his eyes burned in his gaunt face.

'She was your daughter, you bastard!' said Hawk. 'Your own daughter . . .'

'She will live forever,' said Trask, his voice horribly calm and reasonable. 'So will I. My master has promised me this. My daughter was afraid at first; she didn't understand. But she will. We will never grow old and ugly and die and lie forever in the cold earth. We will be strong and powerful and everyone will fear us. All I have to do is protect the master from fools like you.'

He darted forward, and Hawk met him with his axe. He swung it double-handed with all his strength, and the wide metal blade punched clean through Trask's ribs. The Councillor screamed, as much with rage as with pain, and staggered back against the bed. Hawk pulled his axe free and got ready to hit him again if necessary. Trask looked down at his ribs, and saw the blood that flowed from the gaping wound in his side. He dipped his fingers into the blood, lifted them to his mouth and licked them clean. Hawk lifted his axe and Trask went for his throat. Hawk fought for breath as Trask's bony fingers closed around his throat and tightened. He tried to swing his axe, but he couldn't use it at such close quarters. He dropped it, and grabbed Trask's wrists, but the Councillor was too strong. Hawk's gaze began to dim. He could hear his blood pounding in his ears.

Fisher stepped in beside them and cut at Trask's right arm with her sword. The gleaming blade sliced through the muscle, and the arm went limp. Hawk gathered the last of his strength and pushed Trask away from him. Trask lashed out at Fisher with his undamaged arm. She ducked under the blow and ran her sword through his heart with a single thrust. Trask stood very still, looking down at the gleaming steel blade protruding from his chest. Fisher jerked it out, and Trask collapsed, as though only the sword had been holding him up. He lay on his back on the floor, blood pooling around his body, and glared silently up at Hawk and Fisher. And then the light went out of his eyes, and his breathing stopped.

Hawk leaned back against the wall and felt gingerly at his bruised throat. Fisher stirred Trask's body with her boot, and when he didn't react, knelt down beside him and felt cautiously for a pulse. There wasn't one. Fisher nodded, satisfied, and got to her feet again.

'He's gone, Hawk. The bastard's dead.'

'Good,' said Hawk, and frowned at how rough his voice sounded. He wouldn't have minded, but it felt even worse than it sounded. 'You all right, lass?'

'I've felt worse. Could Trask be the vampire, do you think?'

'No,' said Hawk. 'He hasn't got the teeth for it. Besides, we saw him at the briefing yesterday morning, remember?'

'Yeah, right. Trask was just the Judas Goat. But I think we'd better stake him anyway. Just to be sure.'

'Let's see to the girl first.'

'Sure.'

Hawk pounded the stake into her heart. It was hard work. He let Fisher stake Trask, while he cut off the girl's head as cleanly as he could. There was no blood, but that somehow made it worse. Cutting off Trask's head was no problem at all. When it was finished, Hawk and Fisher left the room and shut the door quietly behind them. Hawk had thought the air would smell fresher on the landing, but it didn't. He held up the oil lamp he'd brought from the room, and studied the next door in its flickering light.

'He has to be in there somewhere,' said Fisher quietly.

Hawk nodded slowly. He looked at her, and then frowned as he saw she was holding a wooden stake in her left hand. 'How many of those did you bring?'

'Three,' said Fisher calmly. 'I used two on Trask and his daughter. If there's more than one vampire here, we're in big trouble.'

Hawk smiled in spite of himself. 'You always did have a gift for understatement.'

He opened the door a crack, stepped back a pace and then kicked the door in. It flew back to slam against the inner wall, and the sound was very loud on the quiet. The echoes took a long time to die away. Hawk stepped cautiously into the room, his axe in one hand and the lamp in the other. The room was empty, save for a heavy metal bed pushed up against the far wall. Fisher moved slowly round the room, tapping the walls and looking for hidden panels. Hawk stood in the middle of the room, and glared about him. *He's here somewhere. He has to be here somewhere.* He moved over to the bed, and looked underneath it. Nothing but dust and shadows. He straightened up and looked at Fisher. She shook her head and looked uneasily about her. Hawk scowled and looked back at the bed. And then he smiled slowly as an idea came to him.

'Isobel, give me a hand with this.'

Between them they got the bed away from the wall, and Hawk studied the wall panelling carefully in the light from his lamp. He smiled grimly as he made out the lines of a hidden panel, fitted his axe blade into one of the cracks, and applied a slow pressure. The wood creaked and groaned loudly, and then a whole section of the wall swung open on a concealed hinge. Behind the panel was a hidden compartment, and in that compartment lay a huge coffin. Hawk felt his mouth go dry, just looking at it. The coffin was seven feet long and three feet wide, built from a dark red wood Hawk didn't recognise. Glyphs and runes had been carved into the sides and lid. He didn't recognise them either. Hawk looked at Fisher, standing close beside him. Her face was very pale.

'Come on,' he said quietly. 'Let's get it out of there.'

The coffin was even heavier than it looked. They had to drag it into the room, inch by inch. It smelled bad. It smelled of blood and death and decay, and Hawk had to keep turning his head away in search of fresher air. He and Fisher finally got the coffin out of the hidden compartment and into the room, then stepped back to take a look at it.

'Big, isn't it?' said Fisher softly.

'Yeah,' said Hawk. 'Look, as soon as I get the lid open, you get that stake into him. As soon as the stake's home, I'll cut off the head. I'm not taking any chances with this one.'

'Got it,' said Fisher. 'We've been on some dirty jobs in the past, Hawk, but this has got to be the dirtiest.'

'Remember the girl,' said Hawk. 'Now, let's do it.'

They bent over the coffin and the lid flew open, knocking them both backwards. The vampire sat up in its coffin and grinned at them with pointed teeth. Hawk's hand tightened round the haft of his axe till his fingers ached. He'd thought he knew what a vampire would look like, but he'd been wrong. The creature before him might once have been a man, but it wasn't anymore. It looked like what it was: something that had died and been buried, and then dug its way up out of the grave. Its face was sunken and wrinkled, and there was a bluish tinge to the dead white skin. The eyes were a dirty yellow, without pupil or retina, as though the eyeballs had rotted in their sockets. A few wisps of long white hair frayed away from the bony skull. The hands were horribly thin, the fingers little more than claws. But the real horror lay in subtler things. The vampire's black robes were rotting and falling apart. Graveyard lichens and moss grew here and there on the dead skin. Its chest didn't move, because it no longer needed to breathe. And it smelled like rotting meat that had been left to hang too long.

It rose up from its coffin in a single smooth movement and looked at Hawk and Fisher with its empty yellow eyes. Hawk looked away despite himself, and his gaze fell on the shuttered window. No light showed around the shutters' edges. *We left it too late! The sun's gone down* . . . The vampire stepped elegantly out of its coffin. Its bare feet made no sound on the wooden floor.

Fisher wrinkled her nose at the smell. 'Dirty stinking bastard. Lying down or standing up, it makes no difference. Let's do it, Hawk.'

Hawk nodded slowly, and then sprang forward, swinging his axe double-handed at the vampire's neck. The creature put up a spindly arm to block the blow, and the axe bounced off, vibrating as though it had struck an iron bar. Hawk's hands went numb from the impact, and it was all he could do to hang onto the axe. Fisher thrust at the vampire with her stake, using it like a dagger. The vampire avoided the blow easily, and knocked Fisher sprawling with a single backhanded blow. She lay where she had fallen, her head swimming madly. There was an inhuman power in the creature's slender frame. Fisher clutched desperately at the wooden stake, and struggled weakly to get her feet under her. The vampire looked down at her and chuckled suddenly – a low, filthy sound.

Hawk swung his axe at it again. The vampire raised its head and caught the heavy blade in mid-swing, wrenching the weapon from Hawk's hand. It threw the axe away, and reached for Hawk with its bony hands. He darted back out of range and looked desperately about him for another weapon. The vampire laughed again, and bent over Fisher. It grabbed her by the shoulder, and she moaned aloud as the clawlike fingers sank into her flesh. Blood ran down her arm in a steady stream. She tried to break free, and couldn't. The vampire drew her slowly closer, grinning widely to show her its long pointed teeth. Fisher tried again to stab the vampire with the stake. It grabbed her wrist and squeezed hard. The feeling went out of her fingers and she dropped the stake. It rolled away and disappeared into the shadows.

Hawk watched helplessly. He'd found his axe again, but he didn't dare attack the vampire. Cold steel was no use against it. He needed a wooden stake . . . He glared wildly about him, and his gaze fell on the coffin. A vampire must always return to its coffin before break of day . . . Hawk grinned savagely as the answer came to him. He stepped forward, lifted his axe, and brought it swinging down onto the side of the coffin. The heavy wood split and splintered under the blow. Hawk jerked the blade free and struck again. The side sagged inwards, and splinters flew on the air. The vampire threw Fisher aside and darted forward. Hawk dropped his axe, grabbed the heaviest splinter from the coffin and buried it in the vampire's chest as the creature reached for him. For a moment they stood facing each other, the yellow eyes and grinning mouth only inches away from Hawk's face, and then the vampire suddenly collapsed and fell limply to the floor. It made surprised mewling sounds, and clutched at the thick wooden splinter protruding from its chest. Hawk threw himself down beside the vampire, snatched up his axe, and used the flat of the blade to hammer the splinter into the vampire's heart. It screamed and tore at him with its clawed hands, but he didn't care. He hit the wooden splinter again and again and again, driving it deep into the vampire's chest, and with every blow he struck he saw the dead girl's face as she hung from the butcher's hook. After a while he realised that the vampire had stopped struggling, and that Fisher was kneeling beside him.

'It's all right, Hawk. It's over.'

He looked down at the vampire. The dirty yellow eyes stared sightlessly at the ceiling, and the clawed hands lay still at its sides. He raised his axe one last time, and cut savagely at the creature's neck. The steel blade sliced clean through and sank into the wooden floor beneath. The vampire seemed to collapse and fall in upon itself, and in a few seconds there was nothing left but dust. Hawk sighed slowly, pulled his axe out of the floor, and then sat back on his haunches. Some of the tension began to drain out of him. He looked wearily at Fisher, still kneeling beside him.

'You all right, lass?'

'I'll live.'

Hawk smiled slightly. 'Well, we got the vampire. Not exactly according to the book, but what the hell. You can't have everything.'

He and Fisher rose painfully to their feet and leaned on each other a while until they felt strong enough to make their way back down the stairs. They left Trask and his daughter where they were. Burning the bodies could wait. Let the backup unit earn its pay for a change. Hawk and Fisher slowly made their way through the empty house and out into Chandler Lane. It was still hot and muggy, and the air stank of smoke and tannin, but after the house and what they'd found in it, the lane looked pretty good to them.

'You know,' said Hawk reflectively, 'there has to be an easier way to make a living.'

2

Friends, Enemies and Politicians

At the house of the sorcerer called Gaunt, the party was just beginning. It was an old house, situated in one of the better parts of the city. The party was being held in the parlour, a comfortably large room that took up half the ground floor. The walls were lined with tall slender panels of beechwood, richly worked with carvings and motifs, and the ceiling boasted a single huge mural by one of Haven's most famous painters. But even without all that, Gaunt's parlour would have been impressive enough simply for its collection of priceless antique furniture. Chairs and tables and sideboards of an elegant simplicity mingled with the baroque styles of decades past. It was a tribute to the sorcerer's taste that the contrasting styles mixed so compatibly.

His parties were renowned throughout Haven; all the best people, wonderful food, and plenty of wine. Invitations were much coveted among the city Quality, but only rarely received. Since taking over the old DeFerrier house some four years earlier, the sorcerer Gaunt had shot up the social ladder with a speed that other newcomers could only envy. Not that Gaunt himself was in any way a snob. At his select affairs the elite of politics and business and society mixed freely, whatever their calling. But this evening the party was a strictly private affair, for a few friends. Councillor William Blackstone was celebrating his first year in office.

Blackstone was a large, heavyset man in his mid forties. Always well-groomed, polite and disarmingly easygoing, he had a politician's smile and a fanatic's heart. Blackstone was a reformer, and he had no time for compromise. He'd done more to clean up the city of Haven in his one year as Councillor than the rest of the Council put together. This made him very popular in the lower city, and earned him the undying enmity of the rich and powerful who made their living out of Haven's dark side. Unfortunately for those with a vested interest in other people's misery, Blackstone was himself quite wealthy, and not in the least averse to putting his money where his mouth was. At the end of his first year in office, the odds on his surviving a second year were being quoted as roughly four thousand to one. When Blackstone heard this he laughed, and bet a thousand in gold on himself.

His wife stood at his side as he talked animatedly with the sorcerer Gaunt about his next crusade, against the child prostitution rackets. Katherine Blackstone was a short, good-looking brunette in her mid thirties, and only slightly less feared than her husband. In her day she'd been one of the finest actresses ever to tread the boards in Haven, and though she'd put all that behind her on marrying Blackstone, she still possessed a mastery of words that left her enemies red-faced and floundering. Katherine had always had a gift for the barbed bon mot and the delicately judged put-down. She was also not averse to a little discreet character assassination when necessary.

Gaunt himself looked to be in his mid thirties, but was reputed to be much older. Tall, broad-shouldered but elegantly slim, he dressed always in sorcerer's black. The dark robes contrasted strongly with his pale, aquiline features. His voice was rich and commanding, and his pale grey eyes missed nothing. He shaved his head, but indulged himself with a pencil-thin moustache. He'd arrived in Haven from no-one-knew-where some four years ago, and immediately made a name for himself by single-handedly cleaning up the infamous Devil's Hook area.

Devil's Hook was a square mile of slums and alleyways

backing onto the main docks, a breeding ground of poverty and despair. Men, women, and children worked appalling hours for meagre wages, and prices in the Hook were carefully controlled to keep the people permanently in debt. Those who spoke out against the conditions were openly intimidated and murdered. The city Guard avoided the Hook rather than risk a war with the gangs who ran it. And then the sorcerer Gaunt came to Haven. He walked into the Hook, unarmed, to see for himself what conditions were like. He walked out again some two hours later. Not long after, the Guard were called in to start the long business of carting away the dead bodies. Every member of every gang was dead. None of them had died easily.

The Hook held a celebration that lasted for over a week.

Certain businessmen tried to send new people into the Hook to start the various businesses up again, but Gaunt simply visited each man in turn and pointed out that any attempts to run sweatshops would be taken by him as a personal insult. Conditions within the Hook began to improve almost overnight.

Gaunt poured himself more wine, and savoured the bouquet.

'Darling, I don't know how you can drink that stuff,' said Katherine Blackstone. 'Hillsdown has some excellent orchards, but their grapes aren't worth the treading.'

'I have no palate for wines,' Gaunt admitted calmly. 'But there's always been something about the Northern vintages that appeals to me. They're not particularly subtle, but there's no mistaking their power. If this wine was any stronger, it would leap out of the bottle and mug you. Would you care to try some, William?'

'Perhaps just a little,' said Blackstone, grinning. 'I had hoped it would get a little cooler once the sun went down, but I'm damned if I can tell the difference. Looks like it's going to be another long, dry summer.' He gulped thirstily

at the wine the sorcerer poured him, and nodded appreciatively.

Katherine tapped him gently on the arm. 'You be careful
with that stuff. You know you've no head for wine.'

Blackstone nodded ruefully. 'A grave drawback in a
politician's life. Still, it has its bright side. Because I spend
most of the evening with a glass of water in my hand, I'm
still there listening when other people are getting flustered
and careless.'

'That's right,' said Katherine sweetly. 'Sometimes I'm
surprised you don't go around taking notes.'

'I have an excellent memory,' said Blackstone.

'When it suits you,' said Katherine.

'Now, now,' said Gaunt quickly. 'No quarrelling.'

'Don't be silly, dear,' said Katherine. 'We enjoy it.'

The three of them chuckled quietly together.

'So, William,' said Gaunt. 'How's your new bill going? Is
the debate finally finished?'

'Looks that way,' said Blackstone. 'With a bit of luck, the
bill should be made law by the end of the month. And not
before time. Haven depends on its docks for most of its
livelihood, and yet some of the owners have let them fall
into a terrible state. Once my bill becomes law, those
owners will be compelled to do something about renovat-
ing them, instead of just torching the older buildings for the
insurance.'

'Of course, the Council will help them out with grants
for some of the work,' said Katherine. 'Just to sweeten the
pot. '

'One of your better ideas, that,' said Blackstone.

'I'll be interested to see how it works out,' said Gaunt.
'Though I have a feeling it won't be that simple.'

'Nothing ever is,' said Blackstone.

'How's your latest project going, Gaunt?' asked Katherine. 'Or aren't we allowed to ask?'

Gaunt shrugged. 'It's no secret. I'm afraid I'm still not

having much success. Truthspells are difficult things to put together. All the current versions produce nothing but the literal truth. They don't allow for nuances, half-truths and evasions. And then of course there's subjective truth and objective truth . . .'

'Spare us, darling,' protested Katherine, laughing. 'You'd think I'd know enough by now not to enquire into a sorcerer's secrets. Magic must be the only thing in the world more complicated than politics.'

'You obviously haven't had to spend half an evening listening to an old soldier talking about military tactics,' said Blackstone dryly. 'And speaking of which, aren't the Hightowers here yet? You did say they'd be coming.'

'They'll be here,' said Gaunt.

'Good,' said Blackstone. 'I want a word with Lord Hightower. He's supposed to be backing me on my next bill, but I haven't seen the man in almost a month. It wouldn't surprise me if he'd started getting cold feet.'

'I shouldn't think so,' said Gaunt. 'Roderik's all right, when you get to know him. These old military types can be a bit of a bore when it comes to refighting all their old battles, but their word is their bond. If he's said he'll support you, he will. Count on it.'

'It's not his support I need so much as his money,' said Blackstone dryly. 'Politicians can't live on applause alone, you know. The kind of campaigns I run are expensive. They need a constant flow of gold to keep them going, and even my resources aren't unlimited. Right now, Hightower's gold would come in very handy.'

'Mercenary,' said Katherine affectionately.

At the other end of the huge parlour, Graham Dorimant and the witch called Visage were helping themselves to the fruit cordial in the silver punch bowl. As a refreshing fruit drink the cordial was something of a letdown, there being too much emphasis on the various powerful wines involved and not nearly enough on the fruit, but Dorimant was well known for drinking anything, provided he was thirsty enough. And the current heat wave had left him feeling very thirsty.

Graham Dorimant was medium height, late thirties, and somewhat overweight. He smiled frequently, and his dark eyes held an impartial warmth. He'd been Blackstone's political adviser for almost three years, and he was very good at his job. He had an encyclopaedic knowledge of Haven's electoral system, and he knew where the bodies were buried. Sometimes literally. He was on first-name terms with most of the Council, and quite a few of their staffs. He knew who could be persuaded, who could be browbeaten, and who could be bought. He knew when to talk and when to push, but most important of all, he had no political interests himself. Ideologies left him cold. He didn't give a damn one way or the other. He aided Blackstone simply because he admired the man. Dorimant himself was lazy, amoral, and uninterested in anything outside Haven, but he nevertheless found much to admire in a man who was none of these things and yet attacked life with a zest Dorimant could only envy. Though he rarely admitted it to himself, Dorimant had found more fun and excitement in his time with Blackstone than at any other time in his life.

He drank thirstily at his fruit cordial, and smiled winningly at the witch Visage. Dorimant fancied himself a ladies' man and aspired to an elegance he was too lazy to fully bring off. He wore nothing but the finest and most fashionable clothes, but lacked the self-conscious élan of the true dandy. Basically, he had too much of a sense of humour to be able to take fashion seriously. His only real vanity was his hair. Although he'd just entered his late thirties, his hair was still jet black. There just wasn't as much of it as there used to be.

The witch Visage smiled back at Dorimant and sipped daintily at her drink. She was in her early twenties, with a great mass of wavy red hair that tumbled freely about her shoulders. Her skin was very pale, and her broad open face was dominated by her striking green eyes. There was a subtle wildness about her, like an animal from the Forest that had only recently been tamed. Men sensed the wildness and were attracted to it, but even the most insensitive knew instinctively that her constant slight smile hid very sharp teeth. Visage was tall for a woman, almost five foot nine, but painfully thin. She made Dorimant feel that he wanted to take her out to a restaurant and see that she had at least one good meal before he had his wicked way with her. Such a paternal, protective feeling was new to Dorimant, and he pushed it firmly to one side.

'Well, my dear,' he said briskly, 'how is our revered master? Your magics still keeping him safe and sound?'

'Of course,' said Visage shyly, her voice as ever low and demure. 'As long as I am with him, no magic can harm him. And you, sir, does your advice protect his interests as well as I protect his health?'

'I try,' smiled Dorimant. 'Of course, a man as honest as William is bound to make enemies. He's too open and honest for his own good. If he would only agree to turn a blind eye now and again . . .'

'He would not be the man he is, and neither of us would be interested in serving him. Am I not right?'

'As always, my dear,' said Dorimant. 'Would you care for some more cordial?'

'Thank you, I think I will. It is very close in here. Are you not having any more?'

'Perhaps later. I fear all this fruit is terribly fattening, and I must watch my waistline.'

'That shouldn't be too difficult,' said Visage sweetly. 'There's enough of it.'

Dorimant looked at her reproachfully.

Hawk and Fisher stood together before Gaunt's front door,

waiting for someone to answer the bell. The sorcerer's house was a fair-sized two-storey building, standing in its own grounds, situated near the Eastern boundary of the city. A high wall surrounded the grounds, the old stonework mostly buried under a thick blanket of ivy. The grounds had been turned into a single massive garden, where strange herbs and unusual flowers grew in ornate patterns that were subtly disturbing to the eye. The night air was thick with the rich scent of a hundred mingled perfumes. Light from the full moon shimmered brightly on the single gravelled path. The house itself had no particular character. It stood simply and squarely where it had stood for hundreds of years, and though the stonework was discoloured by wind and rain and the passing of years, its very simplicity suggested a strength that would maintain the house for years to come.

The front door was large and solid, and Hawk eyed the bell pull dubiously, wondering if he should try it again in case it hadn't worked the first time. He tugged impatiently at his high collar and shifted his weight from foot to foot. Both he and Fisher were wearing the formal Guards' uniform of navy blue and gold, topped with their best black cloaks. The heavy clothes were stiff, uncomfortable, and very hot. Hawk and Fisher had protested loudly before they set out, but to no avail. Guards had to look their best when mixing with High Society. To do otherwise would reflect badly on the Guards. Hawk and Fisher had given in. Eventually.

'Leave your collar alone,' said Fisher. 'You're not doing it any good.'

'I hate formal clothes,' growled Hawk. 'Why did we have to draw this damned duty? I thought that after staking a vampire we'd have been entitled to a little time off at least, but no; just time for a quick healing spell, and off we go again.'

Fisher chuckled dryly. 'Nothing succeeds like success.

We solved the vampire case where everyone else had failed, so naturally we get handed the next most difficult case, bodyguarding Blackstone.'

Hawk shook his head dolefully. 'The only really honest Councillor in the city. No wonder so many people want him dead.'

'You ever meet him?' asked Fisher.

'Shook his hand once, at an election rally.'

'Did you vote for him?'

'Well, the other guy was handing out money.'

Fisher laughed. 'An honest Guard; you stayed bought.'

Hawk smiled. 'Like hell. I took their money, voted for Blackstone anyway, and defied them to do anything about it. It didn't exactly make their day.' He grinned broadly, remembering.

'I admire Blackstone's courage,' said Fisher, 'if not his good sense. Standing up against all the vested interests in this city takes real guts. We could do a lot more in our job if half our superiors weren't openly corrupt.'

Hawk grunted, and pulled at his collar again. 'What do you know about this sorcerer, Gaunt?'

'Not much. Fairly powerful, as sorcerers go, but he's not flashy about it. Likes to throw parties, but otherwise keeps himself to himself. Not married, and doesn't chase women. Or men, for that matter. No one knows where he came from originally, but rumour has it he was once sorcerer to the King. Then he left the Court under something of a cloud, and came and settled here in Haven. Made a name for himself in the Hook. You remember that?'

'Yeah,' said Hawk. 'I was part of the team that had to go in there and clean up the mess. We were still carrying out the bodies a week later.'

'That's right,' said Fisher. 'I was still working on the Shattered Bullion case.' She looked at Hawk thoughtfully. 'You never told me about this before. Was it bad? I heard stories . . .'

'It was bad,' said Hawk. 'There were no survivors among the gangs – no wounded, no dying; only the dead. We still don't know what killed them, but it wasn't very neat. Most of the bodies had been ripped apart. There's no doubt the gangs were evil. They did some terrible things. But what happened to them was worse.'

'And this is the man whose party we're attending as bodyguards,' said Fisher, grimacing. 'Great. Just great.'

She broke off as the front door swung suddenly open. A bright, cheerful light filled the hall beyond and spilled out into the night. Hawk and Fisher blinked uncertainly as their eyes adjusted to the glare, and then they bowed politely to the man standing before them. Gaunt took in their Guards' cloaks, and inclined his head slightly in return.

'William's bodyguards. Do come in; I've been expecting you.'

He stepped back a pace and waited patiently as they made their way past him into the hall. He shut the door carefully and turned back to extend a slender, well-manicured hand. Hawk shook it firmly, and then gritted his teeth as Gaunt all but crushed his fingers in a powerful grip. He hated people who did that. Somehow he kept his polite smile in place, and then surreptitiously flexed his fingers as Gaunt turned to Fisher. The sorcerer took Fisher's hand and raised it to his lips. Hawk frowned slightly. He wasn't too keen on people who did that, either. Fisher smiled politely at the sorcerer. He wasn't quite what she'd expected. After Hawk's tale of what he'd found in the Hook, she'd been expecting someone more . . . impressive. With his mild grey eyes and pleasant smile, Gaunt just didn't look the part.

The sorcerer looked at the two Guards thoughtfully. 'Captain Hawk and Captain Fisher,' he said, after a moment. 'I've heard of you.'

'Nothing good, I hope,' said Fisher, and Gaunt chuckled. 'You did an excellent job of taking care of the Chandler Lane vampire. Most impressive.'

Hawk raised an eyebrow. 'News travels fast in Haven.'

Gaunt smiled. 'I have my sources.'

'Yeah,' said Hawk. 'I'll just bet you do.'

'If you'll follow me,' said the sorcerer politely. 'Councillor Blackstone is already here, with some of my other guests.'

He led the way down the hall to a heavy oaken door on the right. He pushed it open, and then stood back to usher the two Guards into the parlour. The guests looked briefly at Hawk and Fisher, took in their black cloaks, and went back to their conversations. Hawk looked casually about him, getting the feel of the place. Two huge windows were blocked off by closed wooden shutters, despite the heat. There was only the one door, leading into the hall. Hawk relaxed a little. If push came to shove, it shouldn't be too difficult to defend the parlour against an attack. Assuming anyone was suicidal enough to take on the sorcerer Gaunt in his own home.

Gaunt went over to Blackstone and spoke quietly to him. Blackstone glanced at Hawk and Fisher, excused himself to the witch Visage, and walked back with Gaunt to meet them. He shook them both by the hand; the usual quick, firm handshake of the seasoned politician.

'Glad you're both here,' he said briskly. 'I'm sure I'll feel a lot safer with you two at my side. It's only for the next few days, until my bill has become law. After that, the danger will be over.'

'Really?' said Fisher. 'The way I hear it, you've got more enemies in Haven than the Chancellor on tax day.'

Blackstone laughed. 'Well, the immediate danger, anyway. If I'd wanted a safe occupation, I wouldn't have entered politics.'

'Well then, Councillor,' said Hawk briskly, 'what would you like us to do?'

'For tonight, just mingle with the guests and enjoy yourselves,' said Blackstone pleasantly. 'I'm in no danger here, not in Gaunt's house. Even my enemies know better than to risk his anger.'

'You are always safe here, William,' said Gaunt quietly. 'This house is protected against any and all intrusions.'

'And now, if you'll excuse us,' said Blackstone, flashing a quick smile at Hawk and Fisher, 'Gaunt and I have some business to discuss. Do help yourself to a drink and something to eat.'

The politician and the sorcerer moved away, talking animatedly. Hawk and Fisher looked at each other.

'Free booze,' said Fisher. 'This may not be such a bad assignment after all.'

'Yeah,' said Hawk.

They made their way over to the punch bowl and helped themselves to the fruit cordial. Hawk wrinkled his nose at the taste, but drank it anyway. The room was hot, he was thirsty, and besides, it was free. Various canapés had been laid out beside the punch bowl, arranged in interesting patterns in the mistaken belief that this would make the food appear more appetising. Hawk didn't even recognise half of it, but he tried one anyway, just to show himself willing.

'Not bad,' he said indistinctly.

'I'm glad you think so,' said Katherine Blackstone. 'Gaunt prides himself on his culinary skills.'

Hawk chewed and swallowed quickly to empty his mouth as the Councillor's wife looked him and Fisher over. She seemed friendly enough, in a condescending way. Katherine's gaze lingered on Hawk more than Fisher, and he wondered if he'd imagined the sudden glitter in her eyes. The way she was acting, he half expected her to lean forward and pin a rosette on him.

'So you're the best the Guard could supply,' said Katherine finally. 'I do hope you're as fearsome as your reputation suggests.'

'We try,' said Hawk.

Katherine looked thoughtfully at his face. 'The scars are certainly impressive, darling. What happened to your eye?'

'I lost it in a card game.'

Katherine gave him a startled look, and then dissolved into giggles. It made her look much younger. 'My dear, I think you won that one on points. Do help yourself to the spiced lamb; it's really quite delicious. I believe there's even some asparagus, though where Gaunt managed to get it at this time of the year is beyond me. Knowing a sorcerer does have its advantages, I suppose.'

There was a pause, while they all busied themselves with the food. Fisher smiled suddenly as she bit into a piece of cold garlic sausage.

'We could have used some of this earlier today.'

'What?' said Katherine. 'Oh, the garlic. Gaunt was just telling us about the vampire before you arrived. Horrible creatures. Did you really kill it by driving a wooden stake through its heart?'

'Eventually,' said Hawk.

'Such a pity about Trask,' said Katherine. 'I mean, he wasn't much of a Councillor, but he did a good enough job, and at least you knew where you were with him. And his was a marginal seat, you know. Now there'll have to be another election, and I hate to think who we might get in his place. Better the devil you know, and all that.'

Hawk and Fisher nodded politely and said nothing. They hadn't told anyone about Trask being the vampire's Judas Goat. They just passed him off as another victim, along with his daughter. It was true enough, in a way. And besides, his widow was going to have a hard enough time as it was. Katherine Blackstone chattered on for a while, talking lightly about this and that, and then fluttered away to talk to Graham Dorimant. Hawk looked at Fisher.

'Well?' he said dryly. 'What did you make of that?'

'Beats me,' said Fisher. 'Katherine Blackstone, coming

on like an empty-headed socialite? That's not the woman I've heard so much about.'

'Maybe it's a test of some kind. Checking us out to see if we're smart enough to see through the act.'

Fisher scowled dubiously. 'Could be, I suppose.'

'Actually, it's a little more complicated than that,' said the witch Visage.

Hawk and Fisher turned quickly to find her standing beside them. Hawk's hand dropped to his axe. He hadn't heard her approaching . . . Visage saw the movement, and smiled slightly.

'I'm not your enemy, Captain Hawk. In fact, I'm glad you're here. I've had a premonition about William.'

Hawk and Fisher looked quickly at each other, and then back at the slender redhead before them.

'A premonition,' said Hawk slowly. 'You think he's in danger?'

'Yes. I'm Visage. I'm a witch. It's my job to protect William from magical threats. He should be safe enough here in Gaunt's house. I've never seen so many defensive spells. The place is crawling with them. And yet . . . there's a feeling in the air. It worries me. I've given William some extra protection, but still . . .'

'Have you sensed anything in particular?' asked Fisher quietly.

Visage shook her head, frowning. 'Nothing definite. Somebody here, or close by, is planning a death; and the victim is either William or someone connected with him. That's all I can get.'

'Have you told Blackstone?' asked Hawk.

'Of course. He isn't taking the threat seriously enough.'

'Somebody here or close by,' said Fisher. 'Maybe we should check the grounds.'

'I suggested that to Gaunt,' said Visage. 'He said no one could get into the grounds or the house without his knowing.' She looked at Hawk steadily. 'Unless you do something to stop it, someone is going to die in this house. Tonight.'

She turned suddenly and walked away. Hawk and Fisher watched her go.

'Great start to the party,' said Hawk.

'Isn't it,' said Fisher.

'Did you notice,' said Hawk thoughtfully, 'that she never did get around to explaining why Katherine Blackstone was acting out of character?'

'Yeah,' said Fisher. 'Interesting, that.'

They looked at each other a moment, shrugged, and helped themselves to more of the fruit cordial.

'Who the hell would be desperate enough to attack Blackstone in Gaunt's house?' said Hawk. 'All right, Gaunt isn't the most powerful sorcerer I've ever met, but I'd put him right up there in the top ten. I certainly wouldn't cross him without a damn good reason.'

'Right,' said Fisher. 'If nothing else, our potential murderer must be pretty damn confident. Or crazy. Or both.'

'Or he knows something we don't.' Hawk scowled grimly. 'Think we should say something to Blackstone?'

'Not yet,' said Fisher. 'What could we tell him that he doesn't already know? Besides, like you said, who could get to him here?'

'There's no place so well-defended that someone determined enough can't find a way in,' said Hawk firmly. 'After all, it might not be a direct attack. It could be something that's been planned in advance.'

Fisher nodded slowly. 'A prearranged spell, or curse. Or maybe they poisoned the food.'

'Or the drink,' said Hawk.

They looked at their empty glasses.

'Unlikely,' said Fisher. 'The witch said someone was planning *a* death tonight, not several. And anyway, Gaunt would surely be able to detect the presence of anything poisonous. Same for any spells.'

'I suppose so,' said Hawk. 'All right, poison is out. But a direct attack seems even more unlikely. In order to get to Blackstone, an assassin would have to get past all of Gaunt's defences, and then fight his way past us. There are assassins that good in the Low Kingdoms, but I don't really think Blackstone's important enough to warrant their attentions. No, I think a magical attack of some kind has to be the most likely.'

'But according to the witch, this house is covered with defensive spells.'

'Yeah.' Hawk shook his head disgustedly. 'Nothing's ever simple, is it? You know, Isobel, just once I think I'd like to work on a case that was simple and straightforward. Just for a change.'

'So what are we going to do?' asked Fisher.

'Stay close to Blackstone, and watch everyone else very closely.'

'Sounds like an excellent idea.' said Dorimant.

Hawk and Fisher looked him over coldly, and Dorimant didn't miss the way their hands fell naturally to the weapons at their sides. He felt a sudden chill run down his spine. As a political adviser, Dorimant had mixed with some hard people in his time, but one look into Hawk's cold eye was enough to convince him that everything he'd heard about Hawk and Fisher was true. These people were dangerous. He smiled at them calmly, and hoped they'd put the sweat on his brow down to the heat.

'Allow me to introduce myself. Graham Dorimant, William's political adviser.'

Hawk nodded politely. 'I'm . . .'

'Oh, I know who you two are,' said Dorimant quickly. 'Everyone in Haven's heard of Hawk and Fisher.'

'Fame at last,' said Fisher dryly.

Dorimant chuckled. 'Honest Guards are as rare as honest politicians. That's why I particularly asked for you as William's bodyguards.'

'The witch says that Blackstone is in danger,' said Fisher bluntly. 'She thinks that someone's going to try and kill him tonight.'

Dorimant frowned. 'I wouldn't take Visage too seriously, Captain Fisher. She's good enough at her job, but she sees threats in every shadow.'

'But Blackstone does have enemies,' said Hawk.

'Oh, certainly. What politician doesn't? And William's policies aren't exactly aimed at making him popular with the vested interests who make this city the cesspool it is. But when all is said and done, he's safe here. Gaunt was telling me about some of his defences earlier, and I can assure you that nothing and nobody gets into this house unless Gaunt says so. Believe me, William has absolutely nothing to worry about tonight.'

'Unless one of his guests turns out to be an assassin,' said Fisher.

Dorimant looked at her sharply. 'Captain Fisher, everyone at this party is a friend of William's, and has been for years. Not one of them has anything to gain by his death. The only people at this party that I can't personally vouch for are you and Captain Hawk. And your reputations suggest you lack the taste for assassination work.'

'Yeah,' said Hawk. 'The pay's good, but the working conditions are lousy.'

Fisher nodded solemnly. Dorimant looked from one to the other, and then smiled reluctantly.

'Captain Hawk, Captain Fisher, right now William's under a lot of pressure. His political opponents are doing their best to sabotage his new bill, and there have been a few death threats. Usual anonymous rubbish. I thought having you two around for the next few days might make him feel a little more secure. All you have to do is stick with him, and don't let anyone within arm's reach of him unless I vouch for them. All right?'

'Sure,' said Hawk. 'I've done bodyguarding work before.'

'Good,' said Dorimant. 'You do know you'll be staying the night here, along with the rest of us?'

'Yeah,' said Fisher. 'We didn't have time to pack a bag, but no doubt Gaunt can provide us with what we need.'

'Of course,' said Dorimant. 'I'll have a word with him.'

The doorbell rang, and Gaunt went into the hall to answer it. Hawk frowned slightly.

'Why does a great sorcerer like Gaunt answer his own door? Doesn't he have any servants?'

Dorimant smiled. 'Gaunt doesn't trust servants. Afraid they might be after his secrets, I suppose. Industrial espionage is rife among magicians.'

'Secrets,' said Fisher. 'What do you know about Gaunt, sir Dorimant?'

'Not much. He's a private man. William knows him better than I do. There are rumours he used to be sorcerer to the King, until they had a falling out. The rumours don't say what they might have argued about. Gaunt's a quiet sort, usually. Don't think I've ever known him to raise his voice in anger. On the other hand, you know what he did in the Hook . . .'

'Yeah.' Fisher scowled, her hand idly caressing the pommel of her sword. 'I don't trust sorcerers.'

'Not many people do,' said Dorimant dryly. 'But Gaunt is no threat to William. They've been friends for years.'

He broke off as Gaunt came back into the parlour, accompanied by a tall, wiry man in his late twenties. He had a shock of long dark hair and a thick curly beard, so that most of his face was hidden from casual view. He smiled easily, but the smile didn't reach his eyes. He was dressed in the latest fashion, and wore it well. Considering that the latest fashion included tightly cut trousers and a padded jerkin with a chin-high collar, this was no mean achievement. It would have been easy to dismiss him as a dandy, if it hadn't been for the sword that hung at his left hip, in a well-worn scabbard. Blackstone and his wife went over to greet the newcomer.

'Now there's a man you can distrust,' said Dorimant quietly. 'Edward Bowman. William's right-hand man. A brilliant politician with a first-class mind. Watch him. The man's a rat.'

Hawk frowned, and started to ask him more, but Dorimant was already walking away, heading back to the witch Visage. Hawk looked back at Bowman. Gaunt and Blackstone were deep in conversation, leaving Katherine chatting with Bowman. Hawk's eye narrowed as he watched them. There was nothing specific he could put his finger on, but there was something about the way Katherine and Bowman were talking together . . . They were *too* friendly. They smiled too much, their concentration was too intense, and they touched each other politely but too often.

'Yeah,' said Fisher. 'They're certainly glad to see each other, aren't they?'

'Probably just good friends,' said Hawk.

'Sure. Sure.'

The doorbell sounded again, and Gaunt disappeared into the hall. Blackstone moved over to join Bowman and Katherine. Hawk watched closely, but couldn't see any obvious signs of tension between them. They all smiled a little too brightly and too often, but then, they were politicians . . . Hawk sighed, and looked away.

'I assume the bell means more guests,' he said tiredly. 'That's all we need; more suspects to watch.'

'You worry too much,' said Fisher, pouring herself more of the fruit cordial. 'Look, all we've got to do is keep the man alive for the next three days until his bill becomes law. After that, the pressure will be off, and he won't need us anymore. Surely we can keep him out of trouble for three days.'

Hawk shrugged, unconvinced. 'I don't like coming onto a case unprepared. We don't know enough about what's going on here, and we certainly don't know enough about the people involved. Katherine Blackstone is acting out of character. Visage knows why, but won't tell us. Instead, she tells us that Councillor Blackstone is in danger, in one of the best defended houses in the city. Blackstone's political adviser warns us about Blackstone's right-hand man, who turns out to be very friendly with the Councillor's wife. I've got a bad feeling about this, Isobel.'

'You're always getting bad feelings.'

'And I'm usually right.'

Fisher chuckled affectionately. 'We've had a long hard day, my love. It's just the tiredness talking, that's all. Blackstone is perfectly safe here. We're just window dressing. Now, have a drink, and relax a little. Okay?'

'Okay.' Hawk smiled fondly at Fisher. 'You were always the sensible one. What would I do without you, lass?'

'Beats the hell out of me,' said Fisher, smiling. 'Now, relax. Everything's going to be fine.'

Gaunt came back into the parlour, and Hawk's heart sank. He knew the middle-aged couple with the sorcerer only too well. Lord and Lady Hightower were a prominent part of Haven's High Society. They moved in all the right circles, and knew all the right people. In a very real sense, they were part of the moneyed and influential elite who controlled Haven. They were also, surprisingly, two of Blackstone's strongest supporters.

Lord Roderik Hightower was a stocky, medium-height man in his early fifties. His short-cropped hair was iron grey, and his piercing dark eyes stared unyieldingly from a harsh, weatherbeaten face. Only a few years earlier, he'd been the Chief Commander of the Low Kingdoms' army, and a legend in his own lifetime. He always led his men into battle, and he was always the last to retreat. His grasp of strategy was second to none, and he had guts of solid steel. A soldier's soldier. He was still solidly muscled, but signs of wear were finally beginning to show. He was getting slower, and old wounds gnawed at him when it rained. He'd retired from the army rather than accept the desk job they offered him, and had immediately looked for a new challenge with which to occupy himself. He finally settled on politics, and took on the campaign to clean up Haven with the same determination and gusto he'd shown in his army days.

Hawk knew him from a year or so back. There had been a series of werewolf murders on the lower Northside, and Hawk had been one of the investigating Guards. It had been a complicated, messy case. Hawk had finally identified the shapechanger and destroyed it, but not before three more men had been killed. One of them was Hightower's only son. Hawk's superiors had stood by him, but Hightower still blamed him for his son's death.

Great, thought Hawk. *Just what I needed. More complications.*

He looked curiously at Hightower's wife, the Lady Elaine. A very well-preserved early fifties, she wore the latest fashion with style and dignity. Her dress was long and flowing, despite the muggy weather, and studded with semiprecious stones. She fanned herself constantly with an intricately painted paper fan, but otherwise seemed unaffected by the heat. She had a long mane of pure white hair and showed it off to advantage. Her face had a strong bone structure, and she was still stunningly good-looking, despite her years. All in all, she looked splendid, and she knew it. She held her husband's arm protectively, and looked around Gaunt's parlour with such poise that she seemed to be suggesting that simply by entering such a room she was most definitely slumming.

Hawk felt an almost overwhelming urge to sneak up behind her and kick her in the bustle.

Fisher leaned closer to Hawk. 'Hightower . . .' she said softly. 'Wasn't he the one who . . . ?'

'Yeah,' said Hawk.

'Maybe he's forgotten by now.'

'I doubt it.'

Hightower looked across the room, saw Hawk and Fisher, and stiffened slightly. He spoke quietly to his wife, who looked at the two Guards as though they'd just crawled out from under a rock. She reluctantly let go of her husband's arm and moved away to greet Blackstone. Lord Hightower glared at Hawk for a long moment, and then walked slowly across the length of the room to confront him. Hawk and Fisher bowed politely. Hightower didn't bow in return. He waited for Hawk to straighten up, and then studied him coldly.

'So. You're William's bodyguards.'

'That's right, my Lord,' said Hawk.

'I should have had you drummed out of the Guard when I had the chance.'

'You tried hard enough, my Lord,' said Hawk calmly. 'Luckily my superiors knew the facts of the matter. Your son's death was a tragic accident.'

'He'd still be alive if you'd done your job properly!'

'Perhaps. I did my best, my Lord.'

Hightower sniffed, and looked disparagingly at Fisher. 'This is your woman, is it?'

'This is my partner and my wife,' said Hawk. 'Captain Fisher.'

'And if you raise your voice to my husband again,' said Fisher calmly, 'I'll knock you flat on your arse, right here and now.'

Hightower flushed angrily, and started to splutter a reply. And then his voice died away as he looked into Fisher's steady eyes and saw that she meant it. Hightower had a lifetime's experience of fighting men, and knew without a shadow of a doubt that Fisher would kill him if she thought he was a threat to her husband. He recalled some of the things he'd heard about Hawk and Fisher, and suddenly they didn't seem quite so impossible after all. He sniffed again, turned his back on the two Guards, and walked back to his wife with as much dignity as he could muster.

'How to make friends and influence people,' said Hawk.

'To hell with him,' said Fisher. 'Anyone who wants to take you on has to go through me first.'

Hawk smiled at her fondly. 'I knew there had to be some reason why I put up with you.' His smile faded away. 'I liked Hightower's son. He hadn't been in the Guard long, but he meant well, and he tried so hard. He was just in the wrong place at the wrong time, and he died because of it.'

'What happened on that werewolf case?' said Fisher. 'That's another one you never told me much about.'

'Not much to tell. The case started badly and went downhill fast. We didn't have much to go on, and what little we thought we knew about werewolves turned out to be mostly untrue. According to legend, the werewolf in human shape is excessively hairy, has two fingers the same length, and has a pentacle on his palm. Rubbish, all of it. Also according to the legend, the man takes on his wolf shape when the full moon rises, and only turns back again when the moon goes down. Our shapechanger could turn from man to wolf and back again whenever he felt like it, as long as the full moon was up. That made finding him rather difficult. We got him eventually. Ordinary-looking guy. You could walk right past him in the street and never notice him. I killed him with a silver sword. He lay on the ground with the blood running out of him, and cried, as though he couldn't understand why any of this was happening to him. He hadn't wanted to kill anyone; the werewolf curse made him do it. He hadn't wanted to die either, and at the end he cried like a small child that's been punished and doesn't know why.'

Fisher put an arm across his shoulders and hugged him.

'How very touching,' said an amused voice. Hawk and Fisher looked round to see Edward Bowman standing to their right, smiling sardonically. Fisher moved unhurriedly away from Hawk. Bowman put out his hand, and Hawk shook it warily. Like Blackstone, Bowman had a politician's quick and impersonal handshake. He shook Fisher's hand too.

'Enjoying the party?' he asked, smiling impartially at Hawk and Fisher.

'It has its ups and downs,' said Hawk dryly.

'Ah yes,' said Bowman. 'I saw you and Hightower. Unfortunate business about his son. You'd do well to be wary of Hightower, Captain Hawk. The Lord Roderik is well known for his ability to hold a grudge.'

'What's his connection with Blackstone?' asked Fisher. 'I'd have thought a man like Hightower, old army and High Society, would be conservative by nature, rather than a reformer.'

Bowman smiled knowingly. 'Normally you'd be right; and thereby hangs a tale. Up until a few years ago, Lord Roderik was a devoted advocate of the status quo. Change could only be for the worse, and those who actually lobbied for reforms were nothing but malcontents and traitors. And then the King summoned Lord Hightower to Court, and told him it had been decided by the Assembly that he was too old to lead the army anymore, and he would have to step down to make way for a younger man. According to my spies at Court, Hightower just stood there and looked at the King like he couldn't believe his ears. Apparently he hadn't thought the mandatory retirement from the field at fifty would apply to someone as important as him. The King was very polite about it, even offered Hightower a position as his personal military adviser, but Hightower wouldn't have any of it. If he couldn't be a real soldier, he'd resign his commission. I don't think he really believed they'd go that far. Until they did.

'He was never the same after that. Thirty years of his life given to the army, and he didn't even get a pension, because he resigned. Not that he needed a pension, of course, but it was the principle of the thing. He came back here, to his home and his family, but couldn't seem to settle down. Tried to offer his advice and expertise to the Council, but they didn't want to know. I think he joined up with Blackstone originally just to spite them. Told you he carried grudges. Then he discovered Reform, and he's been unbearable ever since. There's no one more fanatical than a convert to a Cause. Still, there's no denying he's been very useful to us. His name opens quite a few doors in Haven.'

'It should,' said Hawk. 'His family owns a fair chunk of it. And his wife's family is one of the oldest in the city.' He looked thoughtfully at Bowman. 'How did you get involved with Blackstone?'

Bowman shrugged. 'I liked his style. He was one of the few politicians I met who actually seemed interested in doing something to improve the lives of the people who live in this rat hole of a city. I've been in politics all my life; my father was a Councillor till the day he died, but I hadn't really been getting anywhere. It's not enough in politics to have a good mind and good intentions; you have to have a good personal image as well. I've never had much talent for being popular, but William has. I knew he was going places from the first day I met him. But, at that time, he didn't have any experience. He threw away chances, because he didn't even know they were there. So, we decided to work together. I provided the experience, he provided the style. It hasn't worked out too badly. We get on well together, and we get things done.'

'And he gets all the power, and all the credit,' said Fisher.

'I'm not ambitious,' said Bowman. 'And there's more to life than credit.'

'Indeed there is,' said Katherine Blackstone. She moved in to stand beside Bowman, and Hawk and Fisher didn't miss the way they stood together.

'Tell me,' said Katherine, sipping daintily at her drink, 'where did you and your wife come from originally, Captain Hawk? I'm afraid I can't quite place your accent.'

'We're from the North,' said Hawk vaguely. 'Up around Hillsdown.'

'Hillsdown,' said Katherine thoughtfully. 'That's a monarchy, isn't it?'

'More or less,' said Fisher.

'The Low Kingdoms must seem rather strange to you,' said Bowman. 'I don't suppose democracy has worked its way up North yet.'

'Not yet,' said Hawk. 'The world's a big place, and change travels slowly. When I discovered the Low Kingdoms were in fact governed by an elected Assembly, presided over by a constitutional monarch with only limited powers, it was as though my whole world had been tipped upside down. How could he be King if he didn't rule? But the idea; the idea that every man and woman should have a say in how the country should be run: that was staggering. There's no denying the system does have its drawbacks, and I've seen most of them right here in Haven, but it has its attractions too.'

'It's the way of the future,' said Bowman.

'You might just be right,' said Hawk.

The doorbell rang, and Gaunt went off to answer it. Bowman and Katherine chatted a while longer about nothing in particular, and then moved away to talk quietly with each other. Fisher looked after them thoughtfully.

'I don't trust Bowman; he smiles too much.'

Hawk shrugged. 'That's his job; he's a politician, remember? But did you see the way Katherine's face lit up every time Bowman looked at her?'

'Yeah,' said Fisher, grinning. 'There's definitely something going on there.'

'Scandalmonger,' said Hawk.

'Not at all,' said Fisher. 'I'm just romantic, that's all.'

Gaunt came back into the parlour with a tall, muscular man in his late forties. Hawk took one look at the new arrival and nearly spilled his drink. Standing beside Gaunt was Adam Stalker, possibly the most renowned hero ever to come out of the Low Kingdoms. In his time he'd fought every monster you could think of, and then some. He'd single-handedly toppled the evil Baron Cade from his mountain fortress, and freed hundreds of prisoners from the foul dungeons under Cade's Keep. He'd been the confidant of kings and the champion of the oppressed. He'd served in a dozen armies, in this cause and that, bringing aid and succour to those who had none. His feats of daring and heroism had spread across the known world, and were the subject of countless songs and stories. Adam Stalker: demonslayer and hero.

He stood a head and shoulders taller than anyone else in the room, and was almost twice as wide as some of them. His shoulder-length black hair was shot with grey now, but he was still an impressive and powerful figure. His clothes were simple but elegantly cut. He looked around the room like a soldier gazing across a battlefield, nodding at the familiar faces, and then his cold blue eyes fell on Hawk and Fisher. He strode quickly over to them, crushed Hawk's hand in his, and clapped him on the back. Hawk staggered under the blow.

'I heard about your run-in with the Chandler Lane vampire,' Stalker said gruffly. 'You did a good job, Captain Hawk. A damned good job.'

'Thanks,' said Hawk, just a little breathlessly. 'My partner helped.'

'Of course.' Stalker nodded briefly to Fisher. 'Well done, my dear.' He looked back at Hawk. 'I've heard good things about you, Hawk. This city has much to thank you for.'

'Yeah,' said Fisher. 'We're thinking of putting in for a raise.'

'Thank you, sir warrior,' said Hawk quickly. 'We do our best, but I'm sure we've a long way to go before we become as renowned as Adam Stalker.'

Stalker smiled and waved a hand dismissively. 'Minstrels exaggerate. I take it you're here as William's bodyguards. You shouldn't have any trouble, not with me and Gaunt to look after him. Still, I can always use a backup. I'll talk to you again later; I want to hear all about this vampire killing. I once stumbled across a whole nest of the things, up in the Broken Crag range. Nasty business.'

He nodded briskly, and strode off to speak to Blackstone. Hawk and Fisher watched him go.

'Big, isn't he?' said Hawk.

'I'll say,' said Fisher. 'He must be close on seven feet tall. And did you see the size of those muscles?'

'Yeah.' Hawk looked at her narrowly. 'You were a bit short with him, weren't you?'

'He was a bit short with me. He's obviously one of those men who think women should stay at home while the men go out to be heroes. You ever met him before, Hawk?'

'No. Heard most of the songs, though. If only half of them are true, he's a remarkable man. I wasn't sure I believed some of the stories, but now I've met him . . . I don't know. He's certainly impressive.'

'Right.' Fisher sipped thoughtfully at her drink. 'A very dangerous man, if crossed.'

Hawk looked at her sharply. 'Oh, come on. Stalker as an assassin? That's ridiculous. What reason could a great hero like Stalker possibly have for taking on a small-time politician like Blackstone? We're talking about a man who's supposed to have toppled kings in his time.'

Fisher shrugged. 'I don't know. He just strikes me as a little too good to be true, that's all.'

'You're just jealous because he congratulated me, and not you.'

Fisher laughed, and emptied her glass. 'Maybe.'

'How many of those have you had?' asked Hawk suddenly.

'Two or three. I'm thirsty.'

'Then ask for a glass of water. This is no time to be getting legless. Hightower would just love to find some reason to drop us in it.'

'Spoilsport.' Fisher put down her empty glass and looked about her. The party seemed to be livening up. The chatter of raised voices filled the parlour, along with a certain amount of self-satisfied laughter. Every hand held a wine-glass, and the first few bottles were already empty.

Hawk moved away to talk to Blackstone about the security arrangements, and Fisher was left on her own. She looked disinterestedly around her. Society gatherings didn't appeal to her much. Private jokes, malicious gossip, and sugary wines were no substitute for good food and ale in the company of friends. Not that she was particularly fond of that kind of gathering, either. *I guess I'm just basically antisocial*, thought Fisher sardonically. She shrugged and smiled, and then stood up a little straighter as Edward Bowman came over to stand before her. She bowed politely, and he nodded briefly in return.

'Captain Fisher. All alone?'

'For the moment.'

'Now that is unacceptable; a good-looking woman like yourself should never want for company.'

Fisher raised a mental eyebrow. Her face was striking rather than pretty, and she knew it. *He's after something . . .*

'I'm not very fond of company,' she said carefully.

'Don't much care for crowds myself,' said Bowman, smiling engagingly. 'Why don't we go somewhere more private, just the two of us?'

'I don't think Gaunt would like that. We are his guests. And after all, I'm here to do a job.'

'Gaunt won't say anything.' Bowman leaned closer, his

voice dropping to a murmur. 'No one will say anything. I'm an important man, my dear.'

Fisher looked him straight in the eye. 'You don't believe in wasting time, do you?'

Bowman shrugged. 'Life is short. Why are we still talking? There are so many other, more pleasurable things we could be doing.'

'I don't think so,' said Fisher calmly.

'What?' Bowman looked at her sharply. 'I don't think you understand, my dear. No one turns me down. No one.'

Fisher smiled coldly. 'Want to bet?'

Bowman scowled, all the amiability gone from his face as though it had never been there. 'You forget your place, Captain. I have friends among your superior officers. All I have to do is drop a word in the right quarter . . .'

'You'd really do that?'

'Believe it, Captain. I can ruin your career, have you thrown in jail . . . You'd be surprised what can happen to you. Unless, of course . . .'

He reached out a hand towards her, and then stopped suddenly and looked down. Fisher had a dagger in her left hand, the point pressed against his stomach. Bowman stood very still.

'You threaten me again,' said Fisher quietly, 'and I'll cut you one you'll carry for the rest of your days. And be grateful my husband hasn't noticed anything. He'd kill you on the spot, and damn the consequences. Now go away, and stay away. Understand?'

Bowman nodded jerkily, and Fisher made the dagger disappear. Bowman turned and walked away. Fisher leaned back against the buffet table and shook her head resignedly.

I think I preferred the party when it was boring . . .

Gaunt stood alone by the doorway, keeping a careful eye on the time. The first course would be ready soon, and he didn't want it to be overdone. The first course set the mood for the meal to come. He looked around at his guests, and then winced slightly as he saw Stalker making his way determinedly towards him. Gaunt sighed, and bowed politely to Stalker. The giant warrior inclined his head briefly in response.

'I'd like a word with you, sir sorcerer.'

'Of course, Adam. What can I do for you?'

'Sell me this house.'

Gaunt shook his head firmly. 'Adam, I've told you before: I'm not interested in selling. This house suits me very well, and I've spent a great deal of time investing both it and the grounds with my own magical protections. Moving now would be not only expensive and highly inconvenient, it would also mean at least six months' hard work removing those spells before anyone else could live here.'

'The money needn't be a problem,' said Stalker. 'I'm a rich man these days. You can name your price, sorcerer.'

'It's not a question of money, Adam. This house suits me. I'm quite happy here and I don't want to move. Now I hate to be ungracious about this, but there's really no point in your continuing to pester me about selling. Your gold doesn't tempt me in the least; I already have all I need. I don't see why this house is so important to you, Adam. There are others just like it scattered all over the city. Why are you so obsessed with mine?'

'Personal reasons,' said Stalker shortly. 'If you should happen to change your mind, perhaps you would give me first refusal.'

'Of course, Adam. Now, while you're here, I'd like a word with you.'

'Yes?'

'What's happened between you and William? Have you quarrelled?'

'No.' Stalker looked steadily at Gaunt. 'Why do you ask?'

'Oh, come on, Adam; I'm not blind. I don't think the pair of you have exchanged two words you didn't have to in the

[56]

last few weeks. I thought perhaps you'd had a falling-out, or something.'

Stalker shook his head. 'Not really. I'm here, aren't I? It was just a difference of opinion over what our next project should be. It'll work itself out. And now, if you'll excuse me . . .'

He nodded stiffly to Gaunt, and walked away. The sorcerer watched him go, his face carefully impassive. Something was wrong; he could feel it. Stalker might talk calmly enough, but the man was definitely on edge. Still, it wasn't likely he'd make any trouble. Not here, not at William's party. Gaunt frowned. Just the same, perhaps he'd better have a word with Bowman; see if he knew anything. If something had happened to upset Stalker, he'd make a dangerous enemy.

Lord and Lady Hightower stood together, a little apart from the rest of the guests. Lord Roderik looked out over the gathering, his eyes vague and far away. Lady Elaine put a gentle hand on his arm.

'You look pale, my dear. Are you feeling all right?'

'I'm fine. Really.'

'You don't look it.'

'It's the heat, that's all. I hate being trapped in the city during the summer. Damn place is like an oven, and there's never a breath of fresh air. I'll be all right, Elaine. Don't fuss.'

Lady Elaine hesitated. 'I saw you talking to the Guards. That is him, isn't it?'

'Yes. He let our boy die.'

'No, Rod. It wasn't that man Hawk's fault, and you know it. You can't go on blaming him for what happened. Do you blame yourself for every soldier under your command who died in battle because you didn't predict everything that could go wrong? Of course you don't.'

'This wasn't a soldier. This was our son.'

'Yes, Rod. I know.'

'I was so proud of him, Elaine. He wasn't going to waste his life fighting other people's battles; he was going to make something of his life. I was so proud of him . . .'

'I miss him as much as you, my dear. But he's gone now, and we have to get on with our lives. And you've more important things to do than waste your time feuding with a Captain of the city Guard.'

Lord Roderik sighed, and looked at her properly for the first time. For a moment it seemed he was going to say something, and then he changed his mind. He looked down at her hand on his arm, and put his hand on top of hers. 'You're right, my dear. As usual. Just keep that man out of my sight. I don't want to have to talk to Captain Hawk again.'

Stalker picked up one of the canapés and studied it dubiously. The small piece of meat rolled in pasta looked even smaller in his huge hand. He sniffed at it gingerly, shrugged, and ate it anyway. When you're out in the wilds for days on end you can't ever be sure where your next meal's coming from. So you eat what you can, when you can, or risk going hungry. Old habits die hard. Stalker looked about him, and his gaze fell on Graham Dorimant, talking with the witch Visage. Stalker's lip curled. Dorimant. Political adviser. Probably never drew a sword in anger in his life. All mouth and no muscle. He had his uses, but . . . Stalker shook his head resignedly. These were the kinds of people he was going to have to deal with, now that he'd entered the political arena. Stalker smiled suddenly. He'd thought life in the wilds was tough, until he'd entered politics. These people would eat you alive, given half a chance.

And politics was going to have to be his life, from now on. He was getting too old for heroics. He didn't feel old, but he had to face the fact that he just wasn't as strong or as fast as he once was. Better to quit now, while he was still ahead. He hadn't lasted this long by being stupid. Besides, politics had its own rewards and excitements. The pursuit of power . . . Long ago, when he was young and foolish, a princess of a far-off land had offered to marry him, and make him king, but he'd turned her down. He hadn't wanted to be tied down. Things were different now. He had money, and he had prestige, so what was there left to reach for, except power? The last great game, the last challenge. Stalker frowned suddenly. Everything had been going fine. He and William had been an unbeatable team, until . . . Damn the man. If only he hadn't proved so stubborn . . . Still, there wouldn't be any more arguments after tonight. After tonight, he'd be free to go his own way, and to hell with William Blackstone.

Stalker looked over at the young witch Visage, and smiled slightly. Not bad-looking. Not bad at all. Not quite to his usual taste, but there was a quiet innocence in her demure mouth and downcast eyes that appealed to him. *It's your lucky night, my girl.* He moved over to join her and Dorimant. They both bowed politely to him, but Stalker didn't miss the barely suppressed anger in Dorimant's eyes.

'Good evening, sir warrior,' said Dorimant smoothly. 'You honour us with your presence.'

'Good to see you again,' said Stalker. 'Keeping busy, are you? Still digging up secrets and hauling skeletons out of cupboards?'

'We all do what we're best at,' said Dorimant.

'And how are you, my dear?' said Stalker to Visage. 'You're looking very lovely.'

'Thank you,' said Visage quietly. She glanced at him briefly and then lowered her eyes again.

'Not drinking?' said Stalker, seeing her hands were empty. 'Let me get you some wine.'

'Thank you, no,' said Visage quickly. 'I don't care for wine. It interferes with my concentration.'

'But that's why we drink it, my child,' said Stalker,

grinning. 'Still, the alcohol in wine needn't always be a problem. Watch this.'

He poured himself a large glass of white wine from a handy decanter, and then held up the glass before him. He said half a dozen words in a quick, rasping whisper, and the wine stirred briefly in the glass, as though disturbed by an unseen presence. It quickly settled itself, and the wine looked no different than it had before.

'Try it now,' said Stalker, handing the glass to Visage. 'All the taste of wine, but no alcohol.'

Visage sipped the wine tentatively.

'Good trick,' said Hawk.

Stalker looked quickly round. He hadn't heard the Guard approach. *Getting old*, he thought sourly. *And careless*. He bowed politely to Hawk.

'A simple transformation spell,' he said calmly. 'The wine doesn't change its basic nature, of course; that would be beyond my simple abilities. The alcohol is still there; it just can't affect you anymore. It's a handy trick to know, on occasion. There are times when a man's survival can rest on his ability to keep a clear head.'

'I can imagine,' said Hawk. 'But I always thought you distrusted magic, sir warrior. That seems to be the one thing all the songs about you agree on.'

'Oh, them.' Stalker shrugged dismissively. 'I never wrote any of them. When you get right down to it, magic's a tool, like any other; just a little more complicated than most. It's not that I distrust magic; I just don't trust those who rely on it too much. Sorcery isn't like a sword or a pike; magic can let you down. And besides, I don't trust the deals some people make to gain their knowledge and power.'

He looked at Gaunt on the far side of the room, and his eyes were very cold. Hawk looked thoughtfully at Stalker. Dorimant and Visage looked at each other.

'Thank you for the wine, sir warrior,' said Visage. 'It's

really very nice. But now, if you'll excuse us, Graham and I need to discuss some business with the Hightowers.'

'And I must return to my partner,' said Hawk.

They bowed politely, and then moved quickly away, leaving Stalker standing alone, staring after Visage. *You rotten little bitch*, he thought finally. *Ah, well, she wasn't really my type anyway*.

The sorcerer Gaunt raised his voice above the babble of conversation, and called for everyone's attention. The noise quickly died away as they all turned to face him.

'My friends, dinner will soon be ready. If you would like to go up to your rooms and change, I will be serving the first course in thirty minutes.'

The guests moved unhurriedly out of the parlour and into the hall, talking cheerfully among themselves. Gaunt disappeared after them, presumably to check on how the first course was coming along. Hawk and Fisher were left alone in the great parlour.

'Change for dinner?' said Hawk.

'Of course,' said Fisher. 'We're among the Quality now.'

'Makes a change,' said Hawk dryly, and they both laughed.

'I'm getting rid of this cloak,' said Fisher. 'I don't care if we are representing the Guard; it's too damned hot to wear a cloak.'

She took it off and draped it carelessly over the nearest chair. Hawk grinned, and did the same. They looked wistfully at the great table at the rear of the parlour, covered with a pristine white tablecloth and gleaming plates and cutlery. There was even a massive candelabrum in the middle of the table, with all the candles already lit.

'That looks nice,' said Hawk.

'Very nice,' said Fisher. 'I wonder if we're invited to dinner.'

'I doubt it,' said Hawk. 'We probably get scraps and leftovers in the kitchen, afterwards. Unless Blackstone decides he wants a food taster, and I think Gaunt would probably take that as an insult to his culinary arts.'

'Ah, well,' said Fisher. 'At least now we can sit down for a while. My feet are killing me.'

'Right,' said Hawk. 'It's been a long day . . .'

They drew up chairs by the empty fireplace, dropped into them, and stretched out their legs. The chairs were almost indecently comfortable and supportive. Hawk and Fisher sat in silence a while, almost dozing. The unrelenting muggy heat weighed down on them, making sleep seem very tempting. The minutes passed pleasantly and Hawk stretched lazily. And then Katherine Blackstone came hurrying into the parlour, and Hawk sat up with a jolt as he saw the worry in her face.

'I'm sorry to trouble you,' said Katherine hesitantly.

'Not at all,' said Hawk. 'That's what we're here for.'

'It's my husband,' said Katherine. 'He went into our room to get changed while I paid a visit to the bathroom. When I came back, the door to our room was locked from the inside. I knocked and called, but there was no answer. I'm afraid he may have been taken ill or something.'

Hawk and Fisher looked quickly at each other, and got to their feet.

'I think we'd better take a look,' said Hawk. 'Just in case. If you'd show us the way, please . . .'

Katherine Blackstone nodded quickly, and led them out of the parlour and into the hall. Hawk's hand rested on the axe at his side. He had a bad feeling about this. Katherine hurried down the hall and up the stairs at the far end, grabbing at the banister as though to pull herself along faster. Hawk and Fisher had to push themselves to keep up with her. Katherine reached the top of the stairs first, and ran down the landing to the third door on the left. She hammered on the door and rattled the doorknob, then looked worriedly at Hawk.

'It's still locked, Captain. William! William, can you hear

me?' There was no reply. Katherine stepped back and looked desperately at Hawk. 'Use your axe. Smash the lock. I'll take the responsibility.'

Hawk frowned as he drew his axe. 'Perhaps we should talk to Gaunt first . . .'

'I'm not waiting! William could be ill in there. Break the door down now. That's an order, Captain!'

Hawk nodded, and took a good grip on his axe. 'Stand back, then, and give me some room.'

'What the hell is going on here?' said Gaunt, from the top of the stairs. 'Captain, put down your axe.'

Hawk looked steadily at the sorcerer. 'Councillor Blackstone doesn't answer our calls, and his door is locked from the inside. Do you have a spare key?'

Gaunt came forward to join him. 'No,' he said slowly, 'I've never needed any spares.' He looked at the closed door, and his mouth tightened. 'William could be hurt. Smash the lock.'

Hawk nodded, and swung his axe at the brass lock, using all his strength. The blade sank deep into the wood, and the keen edge bit into the brass. The heavy door shook violently in its frame, but didn't open. Hawk jerked the blade free, and struck again. The axe sheared clean through the lock. Hawk smiled slightly as he pulled the blade free. It was a good axe. He kicked the door open, and he and Fisher hurried into the room, with Katherine and Gaunt close behind.

William Blackstone lay on his back on the floor, staring sightlessly at the ceiling. A knife hilt protruded from his chest, and his shirtfront was red with blood.

3

Questions and Answers

Katherine Blackstone pushed past Hawk and Fisher, and ran forward to kneel beside her husband. Her hand went briefly to his chest, and then to his face. She looked back at Hawk, and her face was blank and confused.

'He's dead. He's really dead. Who . . . ? Who . . . ?'

She suddenly started to cry, great rasping sobs that shook her whole body. Fisher moved forward and knelt beside her for a moment before putting an arm round her shoulders and helping her to her feet. She led Katherine away from the body and made her sit down on the bed. Katherine accepted this docilely. Tears rolled down her face, but she made no attempt to wipe them away. Shock. Hawk had seen it before. He looked at Gaunt, standing beside him in the doorway. The sorcerer looked shaken and confused, unable to take in what had happened.

'Gaunt,' said Hawk quietly, 'you're her friend; get her out of here. Fisher and I have to examine the body.'

'Of course,' said Gaunt. 'I'm sorry, I . . . of course.'

'And, Gaunt . . .'

'Yes?'

'Take her downstairs, get somebody to sit with her, and then set up an isolation spell. I don't want anyone or anything getting in or out of this house.'

'Yes. I understand.'

Gaunt went over to Katherine and spoke softly to her. Katherine shook her head dazedly, but got to her feet as Gaunt went on talking to her, his voice low and calm and persuasive. They left the room together, and Hawk shut the door behind them. Hawk and Fisher looked at the dead body, and then at each other.

'Some bodyguards we turned out to be,' said Hawk.

Fisher nodded disgustedly. 'This is going to be a real mess, Hawk. Blackstone was the best thing to happen to this city in years. What's going to happen with him gone?'

'If we don't find out who killed him, and quickly, there'll be riots in the streets,' said Hawk grimly. 'Damn. I liked him, Isobel. He trusted us to keep him safe, and we let him down.'

'Come on,' said Fisher. 'We've got work to do. I'll check the room, you check the body.'

Hawk nodded, and knelt down beside Blackstone. He looked the body over from head to toe, careful not to touch anything. Blackstone's face was calm and relaxed, the eyes open and staring at the ceiling. His hands were empty. One leg had buckled under him as he fell back, and was trapped beneath the other. The knife had been driven into his heart with such strength that the crosspiece of the knife was flush with Blackstone's chest. Hawk looked at the weapon closely, but it seemed a perfectly ordinary knife. There were no other wounds on the body, or any sign that Blackstone had tried to defend himself. The shirt around the knife was soaked with blood. Hawk frowned. With a wound like that, you'd expect a lot more blood . . .

'Look at this,' said Fisher.

Hawk looked up sharply.

Fisher was crouched down beside the bed, staring at a wineglass lying on its side on the thick rug. There was a little red wine left in the glass, and a few drops had spilled out onto the rug. The crimson stains looked disturbingly like blood. Fisher dipped a finger into the wine in the glass, and then lifted it to her mouth.

'Don't,' said Hawk. 'It could be poisoned.'

Fisher sniffed at her finger. 'Smells okay.'

'Leave it anyway, until we've had a chance to check it.'

'Come on, Hawk. Why poison Blackstone and then stab him through the heart?'

'All right, I'll admit it's highly unlikely. But you never know. Wipe your fingers off thoroughly, okay?'

'Okay.' Fisher wiped her finger on the bedspread, and then moved over to crouch down beside Hawk. She stared glumly at the body, and shook her head slowly. 'Well. How do you see it happening?'

Hawk frowned. 'The door was locked from the inside, and Blackstone had the only key. At least, I assume he had it. I'll check in a minute to make sure. Anyway, I think we're fairly safe in assuming it wasn't suicide. First, he had everything to live for. Second, there had been threats on his life. And third, he'd have a hell of a hard job stabbing himself like that. Apart from anything else, the angle's all wrong. No, suicide is definitely out.'

'Right,' said Fisher. 'So, somebody got in here, stabbed Blackstone, and then left, leaving the door locked from the inside. Tricky. Could Blackstone have locked the door himself, after he was stabbed?'

'No,' said Hawk. 'With a wound like that, he must have died instantly.'

'Yeah,' said Fisher. 'All right. Who could have killed Blackstone? It had to be one of the guests. A stranger would have one hell of a hard time getting into Gaunt's house, and even if he had, Blackstone would have taken one look at him and yelled the place down. And since he was stabbed in the chest, he must have seen his attacker.'

'Right,' said Hawk. 'So, if Blackstone saw whoever it was, and didn't cry out, that can only mean he knew his attacker, and didn't consider him a threat until it was too late.'

'Nasty,' said Fisher.

'Very,' said Hawk. 'I'd better make sure Gaunt's set up the isolation spell. I don't want any of our guests disappearing before I have a chance to question them. You stay with the body. No one is to touch anything, right?'

'Right.'

Hawk straightened up and stretched slowly. 'You know, Isobel, this is going to be a complicated case. I can feel it in my bones.'

He left Blackstone's room and went out onto the landing, pulling the door shut behind him. The guests were crowded together on the landing, waiting for him. Lord Hightower stepped forward to block Hawk's way.

'You. Guard! What's going on?'

'My Lord . . .'

'Why have you smashed down William's door?' demanded Bowman. 'Gaunt took Katherine away in tears, but he wouldn't tell us anything. Just said we weren't to go in the room. What's happened?'

'William Blackstone has been murdered,' said Hawk tightly.

The guests stared silently back at him, all of them apparently shocked and stunned.

'I have instructed the sorcerer Gaunt to seal off the house,' said Hawk. 'Have any of you seen or heard anything suspicious? Anything at all?' There was a general shaking of heads, which was pretty much what Hawk had expected. He sighed quietly. 'I have to talk to the sorcerer. My partner is guarding the body. I must ask you all not to enter Councillor Blackstone's room for any reason, until the investigation into his death is over. I suggest you all go downstairs and wait in the parlour, and I'll fill you in on the details of what's happened as soon as I can.'

He turned quickly away before they could start asking questions, and hurried down the stairs to find Gaunt.

Fisher moved slowly around Blackstone's room, looking for anything out of the ordinary. She'd tried all the obvious things, like looking in the wardrobe and under the bed, but so far the only clue to be found was the wineglass. Fisher scowled. The trouble with searching for clues was that half the time you didn't know what you were looking for until you found it. And even then, you couldn't be sure. She stood still in the middle of the room and looked about her. The colour scheme was a little garish for her taste, but there was no denying that all the furniture and fittings were of the best possible quality. Nothing seemed to have been moved, or in any way disturbed. Everything was as it should be. Fisher glanced down at Blackstone's body, and scowled thoughtfully. The killer had to be one of the guests, but they were all supposed to be friends of the dead man. One of them must have a motive. Find the motive, and you find the killer . . . Fisher sat down on the edge of the bed and methodically worked her way through the list of suspects again.

Katherine Blackstone had looked to be very fond of Edward Bowman. Perhaps she'd grown tired of being married to a man ten years older than herself, and had decided to get rid of him so that she could take up with a younger man.

Lord Hightower claimed to have joined with Blackstone because of the way he'd been treated by the city Council, but that could have been just a cover, a way of getting close to Blackstone. And Lord Roderik was a military man; he'd know how to kill quickly and silently. But then again, why should he want to? Blackstone just wasn't that important, outside of Haven.

And then there was the death wound itself. It must have taken quite a bit of strength to ram the knife all the way home. A great deal of strength . . . or desperation.

Fisher shook her head. There was no point in making guesses at this stage. She didn't have enough evidence to go on yet. The door creaked loudly as it swung suddenly open, and Fisher leapt to her feet, sword in hand, as Lord Hightower entered the room.

'That's far enough, my Lord.'

Hightower glared at her coldly. 'Watch your manners, girl. I'm here to take a look at the body.'

'I'm afraid I can't allow that, my Lord.'

'You'll do as you're damn well told. I still have my rank as General . . .'

'And that doesn't count a damn with me,' said Fisher politely. 'As the only Guards present, Hawk and I have taken charge of the investigation. And at the scene of the crime, we are answerable only to our superior officers. That's city law, Lord Hightower. Now I'm afraid I must insist that you leave. I can't risk you accidentally destroying any evidence.'

Hightower started forward, and then stopped dead as Fisher raised her sword. He took in her calm, professional stance, and the old scars that scored her muscular forearm. The sword point didn't waver, and neither did her narrowed eyes. Hightower stared at her coldly, and stepped back a pace.

'You'll regret this, Guard,' he said softly. 'I'll see to that.'

He turned and left, slamming the door shut behind him. Fisher lowered her sword. Some days you just shouldn't get out of bed.

Downstairs, Hawk stood in the middle of the hall and looked around him, but there was no sign of Gaunt. Katherine Blackstone was sitting alone in the parlour. She had a glass of wine in her hand, but she wasn't drinking it. She just sat in a chair by the empty fireplace, staring at nothing. A door opened behind Hawk and he spun round, axe in hand, to see Gaunt stepping into the hall from the room opposite the parlour.

'Where the hell have you been?' said Hawk quietly, not wanting to disturb Katherine.

'Just checking my defences,' said Gaunt. 'I can assure you that apart from those I invited, no one has got in or out of this house, before or since the murder. I'm now ready to set up the isolation spell. Are you sure you want to do this,

Captain? Once the spell is established, this house and everyone in it will be sealed off from the outside world until dawn. That's a good seven hours.'

'Do it,' said Hawk. 'I know; these are important people, and they're not going to like being held here against their will, but I can't risk letting the killer escape. In the meantime, I really don't think we should leave Katherine on her own. I thought I told you to find someone to sit with her?'

'There wasn't time,' said Gaunt. 'I thought it was more important to check my defences, in case the assassin was still here. Believe me, Katherine will be perfectly all right on her own for a few minutes. I've given her a specific of my own devising; it should help to stave off the shock.'

Hawk frowned. 'It won't knock her out, will it? I'm going to have to ask her some questions in a while.'

'No, it's only a mild sedative. Now, if you've finished with me for the moment, I think I'd better set up the isolation spell.' The sorcerer's mouth twisted angrily. 'I still can't really believe that one of my guests murdered William . . . but I suppose I must.'

Gaunt strode down the hall to stand before the closed front door. He stood motionless for a long moment, and then said a single word aloud. The sound of it echoed loudly on the air, and Hawk clutched tightly at the shaft of his axe as Gaunt's hands began to glow with an eerie blue light. The atmosphere in the hall grew tense and brittle, and Hawk could feel a pressure building on the air. Gaunt threw up his arms in the stance of summoning, and his hands glowed so brightly it hurt to look at them. His mouth moved soundlessly, his eyes squeezed shut as he concentrated. Hawk winced as a juddering vibration ran suddenly through his bones, chattering his teeth. And then the sorcerer spoke a single Word of Power, and a deafening roar filled the whole house. Hawk staggered as the floor shook beneath his feet and then grew still. The sound was suddenly gone. Hawk got his balance back and looked around him. Everything seemed to be normal again. The sorcerer walked back to join him. Hawk glanced quickly at Gaunt's hands, but they were no longer glowing.

'The spell is set,' said Gaunt. 'It cannot be broken. So if there is a murderer in my house, we're trapped in here with him until first light. I do hope you know what you're doing, Captain Hawk.'

'There is a murderer,' said Hawk calmly, 'and I'll get him. Now let's go back upstairs. I want you to take another look at Blackstone's body.'

Gaunt nodded briefly, and Hawk sheathed his axe and led the way back down the hall to the stairs. The guests had all assembled in the parlour, but Hawk didn't stop to talk to them. They could wait a while. He and Gaunt made their way up the stairs and onto the landing. Gaunt stopped before the door to Blackstone's room and looked hard at Hawk. He took in the scarred wood and shattered lock, and shrugged. Gaunt sighed audibly, and looked away. Hawk pushed open the door and walked in, followed by Gaunt.

Fisher looked up sharply, and then put away her sword as she saw who it was. Hawk raised an eyebrow.

'Any problems while I was gone?'

'Not really,' said Fisher, 'I had to throw Lord Hightower out. He wanted to examine the body.'

'You threw him out?' said Gaunt.

'Of course,' said Hawk. 'We're in charge at the scene of a crime. Always. That's Haven's law. On such occasions, anyone refusing to obey a Guard's lawful orders, or failing to answer his questions, is liable to a heavy fine or a stay in prison.'

'That sounded suspiciously like a threat,' said Gaunt.

'Just trying to clarify the situation, sir sorcerer,' said Hawk.

Gaunt nodded stiffly. 'Of course. I'm sorry, I'm a little

over-sensitive at the moment; I'm rather upset. I suppose we all are. William's death is a great loss to us all.'

'Not to everyone, it isn't,' said Fisher. 'Somebody must have stood to gain by it. All we have to do is work out why, and then we should have our murderer. That's the theory, anyway.'

'I see,' said Gaunt.

Hawk frowned slightly. He'd been watching the sorcerer closely, and Gaunt's perpetual calmness was beginning to get on his nerves. The sorcerer might claim to be upset over his friend's death, but if he was, he was doing a damn good job of hiding it. In fact, if William had been the close friend that Gaunt claimed him to be, the sorcerer was being suspiciously cool and collected. Then again, sorcerers weren't exactly famous for behaving normally. If they were normal, they wouldn't have become sorcerers in the first place.

'Well,' said Gaunt, 'I'm here. What do you want of me, Captain Hawk?'

'I'm not really sure,' said Hawk. 'I don't know that much about sorcery. Is there anything your magic can do to help us detect or re-create the events leading up to William's murder?'

Gaunt frowned slightly. 'I'm afraid not. My magic isn't really suited to such work. You see, all sorcerers specialise in their own particular area of interest. Some deal with transformational magic, others with weather control, constructs and homunculi, spirits of the air and of the deep . . . We all start out with the same basic grounding in the four elements, but after that . . . the High Magic takes many forms.'

'What is your specialisation?' asked Fisher patiently.

'Alchemy,' said Gaunt. 'Medicines, and the like.'

'And poisons?' said Hawk.

'On occasion.' Gaunt looked at Hawk sharply. 'Did you have any reason for such a question?'

'Possibly.' Hawk indicated the wineglass lying on the rug beside the bed. 'It seems likely Blackstone was drinking from that glass just before he was attacked. Can you tell whether or not the wine had been poisoned?'

'I'll need a sample to test before I can be sure,' said Gaunt. 'But I can tell you straightaway whether the wine contained anything harmful. That's a simple spell.'

He stretched out his left hand towards the wineglass and muttered something under his breath. A cold breeze seemed to blow suddenly through the room, and then was gone. Gaunt shook his head, and lowered his arm. 'It's perfectly harmless.' He knelt down beside the glass, dipped his finger into the remaining dregs, and then sucked his finger clean. 'One of my better wines. I'll run some checks in my laboratory, just to be sure there isn't anything else in it, like a mild soporific, but I'm sure my spell would have detected even that. May I take the glass?'

'I'm afraid not,' said Hawk. 'That has to stay where it is for the moment. We may need it for evidence later on. But you're welcome to take a sample of the wine itself; just don't disturb the glass.'

Gaunt hesitated. 'Captain Hawk, there's something else . . . something unusual in this room.'

'Where?' said Hawk quickly.

'I don't know, but it's definitely something magical.' Gaunt frowned, and looked at Blackstone's body. 'Of course. William was carrying a protective charm.'

Hawk looked at Fisher. 'Have you searched the body?'

'Not yet. I was waiting for you to get back.'

'All right; let's take a look.'

Hawk knelt down beside Blackstone's body, took a deep breath to steady himself, and started with the jerkin pockets. He found two handkerchiefs, one badly in need of a wash, and a handful of loose change. He dumped both the handkerchiefs and the money beside the body, then tried the trouser pockets. Some more loose change, and a half dozen visiting cards. Hawk dumped them with his other finds. He thought a moment, and then carefully undid Blackstone's high collar. He nodded slowly as the stiff cloth fell away to reveal a silver chain around the dead man's neck. Using only his fingertips, Hawk pulled gently at the chain until the amulet it held came out from under the dead man's shirt. It was a bone amulet, with a series of tiny runes etched deep into the bone. It was spotted with the dead man's blood. Hawk held it up so that Gaunt could see it.

'Do you know what this is, sir sorcerer?'

'Yes. It's an amulet of protection. The witch Visage made it for William. I tested it for her myself a few days ago, to make sure it would work. It was designed to protect the wearer against magical attacks. Any spell aimed at William would have ceased to work in his vicinity. A very useful defence.'

'So curses and the like would have had no effect on him?' said Fisher slowly.

'Not as long as he wore the amulet,' said Gaunt. 'Anything of a magical nature would cease to be magical once it came anywhere near William. It would become magical again once it had moved beyond the amulet's sphere of influence, of course.'

'Of course,' said Hawk. He dropped the amulet onto Blackstone's chest. 'How big a sphere of influence would such an amulet have?'

'No more than a few inches. It's not a very powerful amulet, but then, it doesn't need to be.'

'So whatever else happens,' said Fisher, 'we can safely assume that Councillor Blackstone wasn't killed by magic?'

'I don't see how he could have been,' said Gaunt.

'Thank you, sir sorcerer,' said Hawk. 'You've been very helpful. Perhaps you would now be so kind as to join your guests in the parlour. My partner and I will join you shortly.'

'Very well,' said Gaunt. He looked from Hawk to Fisher,

and then settled on Hawk, his dark eyes steady and disconcertingly cold. 'William was my friend. I don't think I've ever known a man I admired more. I'll do everything I can to help you find the man who killed him. I give you my word on it.'

He nodded abruptly to them both, turned quickly on his heel, and left. Hawk sat down on the bed and stared moodily at the dead man. Fisher leaned lazily against the wall.

'A very pretty exit speech,' she said calmly.

'Very,' said Hawk. 'I hope he doesn't turn out to be the murderer. Trying to arrest a sorcerer as powerful as he's supposed to be might prove rather difficult. Not to mention extremely dangerous. On the other hand, if he isn't our killer, we'd better find the man responsible before Gaunt does. At least with us he'd live to stand trial.'

'Yeah.' Fisher leaned her head back against the wall and frowned thoughtfully at the ceiling. 'Do we assume that Gaunt is right, and Blackstone wasn't killed by magic?'

'It's a simple choice,' said Hawk. 'Either the amulet is what Gaunt said it is, or it isn't. If it is, Blackstone couldn't have been killed by magic. But if Gaunt was lying . . .'

'Unlikely. He must have known we'd check with Visage.'

'Unless they're working together.'

'I hate conspiracies,' said Fisher.

'Yeah,' said Hawk. 'And I hate it when there's magic involved; it complicates the hell out of a case.'

'Have you found the key yet?' said Fisher suddenly, looking vaguely about her.

'Damn. Knew I forgot something.' Hawk scowled down at the dead man. 'It wasn't in his pockets.' He got to his feet and looked around him.

He and Fisher moved back and forth around the room, but couldn't see anything that even looked like a key. Finally they both got down on their hands and knees and started combing through the thick rugs with their fingers.

'Here!' said Fisher. She clambered awkwardly to her feet, holding up a key she'd found by the door. 'It must have been left in the keyhole, and fell out when you smashed the lock.'

'Assuming that is the right key,' said Hawk, getting to his feet.

'Oh, come on, Hawk! What are the odds on there happening to be another key lying on the floor right by the door?'

Hawk smiled and shrugged. 'Sorry, lass. that's the trouble with cases like this; you start doubting everything. We'll show Gaunt the key, and he can tell us for sure.'

'Why don't we just try it in the lock?'

'Because after what I did to that lock with my axe, no key would work it.'

Fisher glanced at the smashed lock, and nodded reluctantly. 'I see what you mean. We'll ask Gaunt.' She slipped the key into her trouser pocket.

'All right,' said Hawk, 'let's try and re-create what happened here. Blackstone was stabbed with a knife. The door was locked from the inside. So how did the killer get in and out?'

'Teleport?' said Fisher.

Hawk frowned. 'It's possible, I suppose, but a spell like that takes a lot of power and a hell of a lot of expertise. And the only person here who fits that description is . . .'

'Gaunt,' said Fisher.

'Visage wouldn't have the power,' said Hawk. 'Would she?'

'So far, this case has been nothing but questions with no trustworthy answers,' said Fisher disgustedly. 'This case is going to be a challenge. I hate challenges. We were better off with the vampire. At least we knew where we were with him.'

'Come on,' said Hawk. 'Let's go down and face the crowd

in the parlour. Maybe we can get some answers out of them.'

'We might,' said Fisher. 'But I doubt it.'

They left the room, and Hawk pulled the door shut behind him. It wouldn't stay closed. Hawk looked at the splintered wood and the shattered lock, and wasn't surprised.

'You always were efficient,' said Fisher, smiling. 'But if we can't lock the door, how are we going to keep people out?'

'Beats me,' said Hawk. 'Ask them nicely? There's not a lot in the room in the way of real evidence, as far as I can tell . . . And any attempt to interfere with the scene of the crime would be a pretty good indication of guilt. So let's just leave the door open and see what happens.'

'I love it when you're devious,' said Fisher.

They chuckled quietly together, and made their way down the stairs and into the parlour. Hawk and Fisher paused a moment in the doorway, taking in the waiting suspects. The sorcerer Gaunt stood at the rear of the room by the main table. His face was calm, but his eyes were dark and brooding. Katherine Blackstone was still sitting in her chair by the empty fireplace. Her eyes were red and puffy from crying, and she had a tired, defeated look. Bowman stood beside her. His face was calm and controlled, as always. The Lord and Lady Hightower stood together by the buffet table. Their backs were straight and their heads erect, and they stood protectively close to each other. Hawk looked at the Lady Elaine's hands. They were held tightly together, the knuckles white from the pressure, as though to stop them trembling. Anger? Or fear? Not far away, Dorimant was helping himself to another glass of the fruit cordial. His normally ruddy face was pale and strained, and his hands were unsteady. The witch Visage stood beside him. She looked lost and frightened and very young. As Hawk watched, Dorimant put his arm around the witch's shoulders. Visage leaned against him gratefully, as though all the strength had gone out of her. Adam Stalker stood alone in the middle of the room. He glared impatiently at Hawk and Fisher as they stood in the doorway.

'Well?' he said finally. 'What's happened? And why have we been kept waiting all this time?'

'Councillor Blackstone is dead,' said Hawk quietly. He waited a moment, but no one said anything. Hawk walked forward into the parlour with Fisher at his side, and Stalker reluctantly gave way to allow them to take up the centre position. Hawk looked slowly about him, to be sure he had everyone's attention, and then continued. 'William Blackstone was stabbed to death, in his room. So far, we have no clues as to the identity of the killer. At my request, the sorcerer Gaunt has sealed off the house with an isolation spell. No one can get in or out.'

The guests stirred uneasily, but still nobody said anything. For a moment, Hawk thought Hightower might. His face had lost all its colour, and his hands had clenched into fists. But the moment passed, and Hightower remained silent. Hawk took a deep breath, and continued.

'Now, as Guards, my partner and I are required to question you each in turn, to help build up a picture of what was happening at the time of the killing. In the meantime, of course, no one is to go near the body.'

'Wait a minute,' said Bowman. 'Question us? Are you saying you think one of us is the killer?'

'Ridiculous!' snapped Hightower. 'And I'm damned if I'm answering any questions from a jumped-up Guard!'

'Refusal to assist us in our enquiries is in itself a crime,' said Fisher calmly. 'I'm sure you all know the penalties for obstructing the Guard in the performance of their duty.'

'You wouldn't dare . . .' said Hightower.

'Wouldn't I?' said Hawk. He locked eyes with Hightower, and Hightower was the first to look away. Stalker stepped forward.

'I've had experience with murders before, Captain. If I can help in any way, you have only to ask.'

'Thank you, sir Stalker,' said Hawk politely. 'I'll bear that in mind.' He turned to Gaunt. 'Sir sorcerer, is there a room my partner and I can use to talk privately with your guests?'

'Of course, Captain. There's my library; it's just across the hall.'

The library proved to be a small, cosy room directly opposite the parlour. Gaunt ushered Hawk and Fisher in, and lit two of the library's oil lamps with a wave of his hand. All four of the walls were lined with bookshelves, each packed with books of various shapes and sizes. The books were stacked neatly, though apparently according to size and shape as much as contents. There were two comfortable-looking chairs by the empty fireplace, and two other doors, one to the left and one to the right.

'Where do they lead?' said Hawk, indicating the doors.

'The door to your right leads to the kitchen,' said Gaunt. 'The door to your left leads to my private laboratory. That door is locked and shielded at all times.'

'Fine,' said Hawk. 'This room should do nicely. I think we'll make a start with you, sir Gaunt, if it's convenient.'

'Of course,' said Gaunt. 'But we'll need another chair.' He gestured sharply, and the library door swung open. A chair came sliding out of the parlour. It crossed the hall and entered the library, and the door swung shut behind it. Gaunt carefully positioned the chair before the empty fireplace and sat down. Hawk and Fisher pulled up the other two chairs, and sat facing him.

'That was very impressive,' said Hawk.

'Not really,' said Gaunt. 'Well, what do we do now? I've never been involved in a murder investigation before. What kind of things do you need to ask me?'

'Nothing too difficult,' said Hawk. 'To start with, do you recognise this key?' He nodded to Fisher, who dug the key out of her pocket and handed it to Gaunt. The sorcerer looked at the key, and then turned it over in his hand a few times.

'It looks like one of mine. Is it the key to William's room?'

'That's what we want to know.'

Gaunt shrugged. 'All the keys look the same to me. Since I live on my own most of the time, I don't have much use for the upstairs rooms. Usually I keep all my keys on one ring, in the right order so that I can tell them apart. And now they've all been split up . . . Still, it shouldn't be too difficult to work out which key it is. Where did you find it?'

'In Blackstone's room,' said Fisher. 'On the floor, not far from the door.'

Gaunt looked at Hawk. 'Then why ask me if this is William's key?'

'Because in a case like this we need to be very sure of our facts,' said Hawk. 'You can never tell what's going to turn out to be significant. Please let me know when you're sure that's Blacktone's key. Now, sir Gaunt, what did you do earlier this evening, after your guests had gone upstairs to change?'

'I went into the kitchen,' said Gaunt. 'The meal was almost ready. All I had to do was pour the soup into the bowls, and baste the meat one last time. I did that, and then I thought I'd better check that the table was ready. I walked out into the hall, and that was when I sensed the murder.'

Fisher leaned forward in her chair. 'You *sensed* the murder?'

'Oh, yes,' said Gaunt. 'I didn't know what it was at the time. I just felt a disturbance in the house, as though something terrible had happened. I ran upstairs to check that my guests were all right, and that's when I found you preparing to cut down my door with an axe. You know the rest.'

'Yes,' said Hawk thoughtfully. 'Tell me, sir Gaunt, could

anyone use a teleport spell in this house without you knowing?'

'A teleport? Certainly not. Such spells take a great deal of power and skill to bring off correctly. One small mistake in the arrival coordinates, and you'd have a very nasty accident. I can see what you're getting at, Captain Hawk, but there's no way the assassin could have teleported into William's room and out again. I have wards set up all over the house to prevent just such a thing. I have my enemies too, you know. Even I couldn't teleport in this house, without first dismantling the wards.'

'I see,' said Hawk. 'Perhaps we should discuss Councillor Blackstone's enemies. It's common knowledge he was unpopular in some quarters, but can you suggest any names? Especially anyone who would profit by his death.'

'There's no one in particular,' said Gaunt, frowning. 'There are any number of people in Haven who'll breathe easier, knowing that William is dead, but I can't think of anyone insane enough to murder William in my house. They must have known that I would take this as a personal insult.'

'I see your point,' said Hawk dryly.

'There is one thing,' said Gaunt, and then he hesitated. Hawk waited patiently. Gaunt looked at him steadily. 'I really don't know if this is at all relevant. I feel rather foolish even mentioning it, but . . . William had an argument recently, with Adam Stalker. I don't know what it was about, but it must have been serious. They've hardly spoken to each other for weeks.'

'You did the right thing in telling us,' said Hawk. 'I shouldn't think it means anything, but we'll check it out, just in case. I think that's all for the moment, sir Gaunt. You can rejoin the others in the parlour now. And tell the witch Visage we'd like to see her next.'

'Of course,' said Gaunt. 'I'll send her in.' He got to his feet and crossed to the door. It swung open before him, and then he hesitated in the doorway and looked back at Hawk. 'What should I do about dinner?'

'Serve it if you like,' said Fisher. 'But I think you'll find most people have lost their appetite.'

Gaunt nodded, and left. The door swung shut behind him. Hawk looked at Fisher.

'How am I doing?'

'Not bad,' said Fisher. 'Just the right mix of authority and politeness. Do you believe him about the anti-teleport wards?'

'Makes sense to me,' said Hawk. 'Every sorcerer has enemies. And again, it's something we can check with Visage. If there are such wards in the house, she should be able to detect them.'

'Good point. Now, what about the keys? Gaunt said there were no duplicates, but he could be lying. If he did have a duplicate, he could easily have let himself in, killed Blacktone, and left again, locking the door after him.'

'No,' said Hawk firmly. 'I don't buy that. It's too obvious.'

'So what? Look, there's already one hole in his story. He said that during the time of the murder he left the parlour with the guests and went into the kitchen. He poured out the soup and basted the meat, and then had his premonition about Blackstone's death. It doesn't add up, Hawk. Between everyone leaving the parlour and us breaking the door down, there had to have been at least fifteen to twenty minutes. I remember looking at the clock in the parlour. Now, it doesn't take that long to pour out some soup and baste a joint of meat. So what else was he doing?'

'Another good point,' said Hawk. 'But I still can't see Gaunt as the murderer. If he'd wanted to kill Blackstone, surely he would have found a more subtle way than to stab the man under his own roof. Remember the Hook? Two hundred and forty-seven dead, and nothing to connect any of them with Gaunt. The forensic magicians couldn't find a single shred of evidence against him, and it wasn't for want of trying. I think he injured their pride.'

'All right, I see what you mean.' Fisher stirred uneasily in her chair. 'But it could just be misdirection, so that we wouldn't suspect him. Remember how Gaunt used his magic to move that chair without touching it? Perhaps he could use a knife the same way. Or open a lock, just as he opened and shut that door, just by looking at it. If by some chance we find proof that Gaunt is the murderer, we'd better watch ourselves. If we start getting too close to the truth, he might decide to do someting subtle about us.'

'Great,' said Hawk. 'Just great. This case is getting more fun by the minute.'

There was a hesitant knock at the door, and then the witch Visage came in. She shut the door quietly behind her and looked uncertainly from Hawk to Fisher. Hawk nodded at the empty chair, and Visage sank into it. Her face was still deathly pale, and she kept her eyes modestly downcast. Fisher looked at Hawk, who nodded slightly.

'We need to ask you some questions,' said Fisher.

'Yes,' said Visage. Her voice was little more than a whisper.

'Where were you when Blackstone was killed?' said Fisher bluntly.

'In my room, I suppose. I don't know exactly when William died.'

'Gaunt said he sensed the killing,' said Hawk. 'Are you saying you didn't feel anything?'

'Yes,' said Visage. She raised her head and met his gaze for the first time. 'Gaunt is much more powerful than I'll ever be. He's a sorcerer.'

'All right, so you were in your room,' said Fisher. 'Did anyone see you there?'

'No. I was alone.'

'So you can't prove you were in your room.'

'No.'

'Earlier this evening you said you knew why Katherine Blackstone was acting strangely,' said Hawk. 'But you didn't get around to telling us then. Tell us now.'

'Why don't you ask Bowman?' said Visage.

Hawk and Fisher glanced quickly at each other.

'Why Bowman?' said Hawk.

Visage smiled slightly. Her green eyes were very cold. 'You must have seen him and Katherine together. They're not exactly subtle about it.'

'They do seem very friendly,' said Fisher.

'They've been lovers for at least six months,' said Visage flatly. 'That's why she's always laughing and smiling. She's found another fool.'

'Did Blackstone know?' asked Hawk.

'I don't think so. William could be very good at not seeing things he didn't want to.'

Hawk frowned thoughtfully. 'How long have you been working for Blackstone?'

'Four, five years. Since his first campaign in the Heights area. I protected him from magical threats. He's always had enemies. Good men always do.'

'You gave him the amulet he wore?'

'Yes. As long as he wore it, no magic could harm him.'

'You mentioned enemies,' said Fisher. 'Can you give us any names?'

Visage shook her head firmly. 'William wasn't killed by an assassin. The only people in this house are Gaunt, his guests, and you. There is no one else. I'd have known.'

'Are you sure?' said Hawk.

'Yes. At least . . .' Visage frowned slightly. 'There is a part of this house that is closed to me. I can't see into it.'

'Where?' said Fisher, leaning forward.

Visage looked at the left-hand door. 'Gaunt's laboratory. It's surrounded by a very powerful shield. He's always been very jealous of his secrets.'

'Could someone be hiding in there?' asked Hawk.

Visage shook her head. 'No one could have left that room without my knowing about it.'

'Then why mention the room?' said Fisher.

'Because it disturbs me,' said Visage.

For a while no one said anything. Visage's words seemed to hang on the air. Hawk cleared his throat.

'Gaunt said this house was warded against teleport spells. Is that true?'

Visage nodded soberly. 'Of course. It was one of the first things I checked for when I entered the house. It's not unusual; all sorcerers have such protections. Why are you wasting time with all these questions? Edward Bowman killed William. Isn't it obvious? Bowman wanted Katherine, and they both knew William would never agree to a divorce. It would have destroyed his political career.'

'That's an interesting theory,' said Hawk, 'but we can't arrest a man without some kind of proof. For the time being, everyone is equally suspect.'

'Including me?'

'Yes.'

'I could never have harmed William,' said Visage flatly.

Hawk studied her thoughtfully. 'Earlier on, I saw Gaunt bring a chair into this room by magic. He just looked at it, and it moved. Could he have manipulated a knife in the same way?'

'Through a locked door, you mean?' Visage shook her head. 'That kind of magic is simple enough, but it needs eye contact with the object to be moved.'

'All right,' said Hawk, 'could he have used that magic to pick the lock?'

'No. There are wards in this house to prevent such tamperings.'

'Of course,' said Hawk. 'There would be. Damn.'

'I think that's all, for the moment,' said Fisher. 'Please wait in the parlour, and ask Bowman to come in next.'

Visage sat where she was, and looked hotly at Hawk

and Fisher. 'You're not going to do anything, are you? Bowman's too important. He has influence. I'm warning you: I won't let him get away with this. I'll kill him first!'

She jumped to her feet and hurried out of the library, slamming the door behind her. Fisher raised an eyebrow.

'If she's prepared to kill one man, she might have killed another.'

'Right,' said Hawk. 'There's a fire burning under that cool and quiet surface. She was obviously very fond of Blackstone . . . Maybe she was having an affair with him. It went sour – perhaps she wanted him to divorce his wife and marry her and he refused – so she killed him for revenge. Or maybe she wanted an affair and he didn't, so she killed him out of injured pride.'

'That's reaching a bit, isn't it?' said Fisher.

Hawk shrugged. 'This early in the game, how can we tell?'

'No,' said Fisher. 'It still doesn't feel right. If there were hard feelings between Blackstone and Visage, he'd hardly have kept her on as his bodyguard, would he? I mean, that's what her job amounted to. And anyway, Visage is a witch; if she wanted to kill someone, she wouldn't need a knife to do it . . . Unless she was trying to be misleading . . .'

'I think we've had this conversation before,' said Hawk dryly.

The door opened, and Bowman came in. He smiled briefly, and sat down in the empty chair without waiting to be asked. Hawk frowned slightly. For a man whose friend and employer had just been murdered, Bowman looked very composed. But then, he always did.

'You were Blackstone's right-hand man,' said Fisher.

'That's right,' said Bowman pleasantly.

'Would you mind telling us where you were at the time of the murder?'

'I was in my room. Changing for dinner.'

'Can anyone verify that?' asked Hawk. Bowman looked at him steadily.

'No.'

'So you don't really have an alibi?'

Bowman smiled. 'Do I need one?'

'How long have you known William Blackstone?' asked Fisher.

'Seven, eight years.'

'How long have you known Katherine Blackstone?' asked Hawk.

'About the same,' said Bowman.

Hawk and Fisher looked at him silently, but his pleasant smile didn't waver. The silence dragged on.

'Who do you think killed Blackstone?' said Hawk finally.

'He had a great many enemies,' said Bowman.

'Are you aware of the penalties for refusing to cooperate with the Guard during an investigation?' asked Fisher.

'Of course,' said Bowman. 'I am doing my best to cooperate, Captain Fisher. I've answered every question you've asked me.'

'All right,' said Hawk. 'That's all for now. Wait in the parlour with the others, and send in Dorimant.'

Bowman nodded briefly to them both, rose unhurriedly to his feet and left the library, closing the door quietly behind him.

'Politicians,' said Hawk disgustedly. 'Getting answers to questions is like pulling teeth. The trouble is, technically he's in the right. He did answer all our questions; we just didn't know the right questions to ask him. We can't come flat out and accuse him of bedding his employer's wife. Firstly, he'd deny it anyway, and secondly, if by some chance we were wrong, he'd have us thrown out of the Guard.'

'Yeah,' said Fisher. 'But there's no doubt in my mind. You saw them together – the way they were reacting to each other. It's as clear as the nose on his face. I can't believe Blackstone didn't know. Or at least suspect . . .'

Hawk shrugged. 'You heard Visage; perhaps he chose not to know. He couldn't risk a divorce, and Bowman was useful to him . . .'

'Only as long as Bowman was discreet about it, and in my experience, he's not very subtle when it comes to approaching women.'

Hawk looked at her sharply. 'Oh, yes? Do I take it he approached you somewhen this evening?'

'Yes. I took care of it. I explained that I wasn't interested, and he went away.'

'Just like that?'

'Pretty much. Oh, I explained that you'd kill him slowly and painfully, and I did have my knife pressed against his gut, but . . .'

'Yeah,' said Hawk, grinning. 'You've always been . . . persuasive, Isobel.'

'Thank you. To get back to the subject. If Bowman had been indiscreet about his affair with Katherine, and Blackstone got to hear of it . . .'

'No man likes to believe the woman he loves doesn't love him anymore,' said Hawk. 'Older man, younger woman; it's an old story. But even if Katherine and Bowman were having an affair, it doesn't mean they committed the murder. It's not proof.'

'No, but it is a motive. And Katherine was the one who came and told us that something must have happened to her husband . . .'

There was a knock on the door, and Dorimant came in. He hesitated in the doorway a moment, as though unsure of his reception, and then stepped quickly into the library and shut the door behind him. Hawk nodded curtly at the empty chair, and Dorimant came forward and sank into it. His face was pale and drawn, and his movements were clumsy, as though some of the strength had gone out of him. But when he finally raised his head to look at Hawk, his mouth was firm and his eyes didn't waver.

'Did you have much luck with Bowman?' he asked quietly.

'Some,' said Hawk.

Dorimant smiled harshly. 'I'd lay good odds he's already told you one lie. You asked him where he was at the time of the murder, and he said alone in his room. Right? I thought so. He wasn't alone. I saw Katherine go into his room, just after we all came upstairs to change. I was just leaving the bathroom. She didn't see me.'

'Thank you for telling us,' said Fisher. 'We'll bear it in mind. Now, sir Dorimant, where were you at the time of the murder?'

'In my room.'

'Alone?'

'No. Visage was with me.'

Hawk raised an eyebrow. 'Now, that's strange,' he said slowly. 'She told us she was in her room, alone. Why should she lie to us about that?'

'She wants to protect me,' said Dorimant, looking at his hands. 'I'm currently separated from my wife, but not yet divorced. The separation is far from amicable, and my dear wife would just love to find some scandal she could use as ammunition against me.'

'So why are you telling us?' said Fisher.

'To prove I've nothing to hide.'

'You were Blackstone's political adviser,' said Hawk. 'I've heard a lot about Blackstone's enemies, but so far nobody seems ready to actually name them. How about you?'

Dorimant shrugged. 'It's no secret, Captain Hawk. There's Geoffrey Tobias; he used to represent the Heights in Council before William took his seat away from him at the last election. Then there's the DeWitt brothers; they stand to lose a lot of money if William's bill becomes law.

They own property down in the docks. It's in a foul state, and they've neither the money nor the inclination to make the repairs the bill will require. There's Hugh Carnell, the leading conservative on the Council; old and mean and hates change in general and William's changes in particular. I could go on, but why bother? You said yourself earlier on that no one could have got into the house to kill William. The murderer has to be one of us.'

'That's true,' said Hawk. 'But someone here could be in the pay of one of those enemies.'

'It's possible, I suppose,' said Dorimant. He didn't sound too convinced.

'Let's talk about Katherine and Bowman,' said Fisher. 'Do you think they're capable of murder?'

'We're all capable of murder,' said Dorimant. 'Providing we're pushed hard enough by something we want, or fear. Edward Bowman has had years of being second-in-command to William, and he's always been ambitious. And he knew Katherine would never leave William. She liked the money and the prestige too much, and in her own way, she was always fond of William. Even though she was cheating on him.'

'Let us suppose for a moment,' said Hawk, 'that Bowman did kill Blackstone. Would Katherine have supported him in that, or would he have to do it on his own, and hope she never found out he was responsible?'

'I don't know.' Dorimant shrugged angrily. 'I'm not a mind reader. People can do strange things when they're in love.'

'What about the other guests?' said Fisher. 'Is there anyone else in this house with a motive to kill Blackstone?'

'I don't know about motives,' said Dorimant slowly. 'I know William had quarrelled recently with Adam Stalker.'

'Really?' said Hawk. 'That's interesting. What did they quarrel about?'

'I don't know. I don't think anybody knows. Neither of them would talk about it. But it must have been pretty serious. William was very angry about it; I could tell.'

'Anything else you can tell us?' said Fisher.

'Not really. We all admired William; we all believed in him. And most of us liked him.'

'How did you feel about him?' said Fisher.

Dorimant looked at her steadily. 'William Blackstone was the bravest and finest man I ever met.'

'Thank you,' said Hawk. 'That will be all for the moment. Please wait in the parlour with the others, and send in Katherine Blackstone.'

Dorimant nodded and got to his feet. He left without looking back.

'He seemed very eager to lay the blame on Bowman,' said Hawk slowly. 'Almost too eager.'

'Yeah,' said Fisher. 'I don't know about you, Hawk, but my head hurts. The more people we see, the more complicated and impossible this case gets. We've got more suspects than we can shake a stick at, and we still haven't got a clue as to how the murder was committed!'

'Stay with it, lass,' said Hawk, smiling in spite of himself. 'After all, we've both had experience with Court intrigues in the past, and if we can handle that, we can certainly handle this. Let's face it. Compared to some courtiers we've known, these people are amateurs. Now, how do you feel about Dorimant? He seemed sincere enough.'

'Yeah,' said Fisher. 'But we've only his word that Visage was with him at the time of the murder. He could be lying.'

'It's possible. But then again, it's not the kind of thing you'd expect him to admit if it wasn't true.'

'Right.' Fisher frowned thoughtfully. 'And if Dorimant and Visage are having an affair, that takes away Visage's motivation, doesn't it? I mean, she couldn't be having an affair with Dorimant *and* Blackstone. Could she?'

'It does seem rather unlikely,' said Hawk, 'but we don't know that Visage and Dorimant were having an affair. All right, they were both in his room, but Dorimant never actually said why. Perhaps they had some other reason for being there . . .'

Fisher groaned. 'My head's starting to hurt again . . .'

The door opened and Katherine Blackstone came in. She looked pale but composed. She shut the door carefully behind her and glanced quickly round the library, as though searching for some hidden listener. She looked steadily at Hawk and Fisher, and then sank gracefully into the chair before them.

'Well?' she said harshly. 'Who killed my husband?'

'We're still working on it,' said Hawk politely. 'Detective work is a slow process, but we usually get there in the end. There are a few questions we need to ask you.'

'All right. Go ahead.'

'Let's start with the events leading up to the murder. You and your husband went upstairs to change for dinner. He went into the bedroom and you went to the bathroom. You came back, and found the door to your room locked. You called to your husband, but couldn't get any reply. You became worried, and went downstairs to fetch Fisher and myself. We went back with you, broke the door in, and found your husband dead. Is that correct?'

'Yes. That's what happened.'

'Is there anything missing from that account?'

'No.'

'Did anyone see you, or talk to you, on the landing?'

'No.'

'It has been suggested,' said Fisher carefully, 'that you visited Edward Bowman in his room.'

'That's a lie,' said Katherine flatly. 'I suppose you've also been told that we're having an affair? I thought so. William's enemies have been trying to use that slander against him for years. Who said it this time? Graham? No, he's too loyal to William. Visage. I'll bet it was that simpering bitch Visage. She always had eyes for William, but he hardly even knew she existed. Edward and I have been friends for a long time, but never more than that. I loved my husband, and no one else. And now he's dead, all his enemies will come crawling out of their holes to try and blacken his reputation with the same old lies, in the hope they can destroy what he achieved!'

'Who do you think killed him?' asked Fisher.

'I don't know.' Katherine suddenly seemed very tired, as though all the defiance had gone out of her along with her angry words. She sat slumped in her chair, her eyes vague and far away. 'I can't think straight anymore. William had any number of enemies.'

'Had he quarrelled with anyone recently?' asked Fisher.

Katherine shrugged. 'Not that I know of. I know he wasn't too pleased with Adam about something, but it couldn't have been that important. William never said anything about it to me.'

'Who actually invited Stalker to this party?' asked Fisher.

'I did,' said Katherine. 'William didn't bother himself with minor matters like that. But he knew Adam would be here. If we hadn't invited him, it would have been a frightful snub.'

'Thank you,' said Hawk. 'I think that's all for now. Please wait with the others in the parlour, and ask Lord High-tower to come in.'

'Is that it?' said Katherine. 'Is that all you wanted to ask me?'

'For the moment,' said Fisher. 'There might be a few more questions later.'

Katherine Blackstone nodded slowly, and got up out of her chair. 'Find my husband's killer,' she said softly. 'I don't care how you do it, but find him.' She left the library without looking back.

Hawk scowled unhappily. 'If she is lying, she's a very good liar.'

'From what I've heard, she was the finest actress in all Haven,' said Fisher. 'In her day. She might be a little rusty after so long away from the stage, but a few lies with a straight face shouldn't be beyond her abilities.'

'But what if she is telling the truth?' said Hawk. 'Dorimant could have his own reasons for lying.'

'Yes,' said Fisher. 'He could. But one of the unpleasant truths of murder is that when a man or woman meets a violent end, the wife or the husband is usually the most likely suspect. Katherine could have good reasons for wanting her husband dead. Blackstone might have overlooked his wife's infidelity in the past rather than risk damaging his political career with a scandal, but if the affair got too blatant he'd have to divorce her, or lose all respect. You heard what Dorimant said. Katherine was fond of her husband, but she loved the money and prestige of being a Councillor's wife. As his widow, she could have the money and the prestige, and her lover as well.'

'Right,' said Hawk. 'And there's a few holes in her story, as well. According to her, she went upstairs, went to the bathroom, came back and found the door locked, and then came down to us. And as you said, between her going up and coming down again there had to be a gap of about twenty minutes. That's a long time in the bathroom . . . And – if she did bang on the locked door and call out to her husband – how is it that no one else heard her? No one else has mentioned hearing her call out. You'd have thought someone would come out to see what was happening . . .'

'Yeah,' said Fisher. 'Mind you, if you're looking for another front-runner, the one thing that practically everyone agrees on is that Blackstone had a big row with Adam Stalker not long ago.'

'Now that is pushing it,' said Hawk. 'Adam Stalker . . . ?'

The library door suddenly flew open, and Lord and Lady Hightower strode in. Lord Roderik slammed the door shut, and he and his wife stood together facing Hawk and Fisher. Their expressions were openly defiant.

'I asked to see you alone, my Lord,' said Hawk.

'I don't give a damn what you asked for,' said Hightower. 'There's nothing you could possibly have to say to me that can't be said in front of my wife.'

'Very well,' said Hawk. 'Where were you at the time of the murder, my Lord?'

'In my room. With my wife.'

'Is that right, my Lady?' asked Fisher.

'Of course,' said the Lady Elaine, disdainfully.

'Thank you,' said Hawk. 'That will be all for the moment, my Lord and Lady.'

Hightower looked startled for a moment, and then his face was hard and unyielding again. 'I demand to know why I was prevented from examining the body. What are you trying to hide from us?'

'I said that will be all, my Lord,' said Hawk politely. 'You may rejoin the others in the parlour. And ask Adam Stalker to come in, if you please.'

Hightower glared at him. Hawk met his gaze calmly, and after a moment Hightower turned away. He took his wife by the arm, opened the door for her and led her out. He slammed the door shut behind him, and the sound echoed loudly in the small room. Fisher looked at Hawk.

'That's all? What about all the other questions we should have asked them?'

'What was the point?' said Hawk. 'They've got each other as an alibi, and Hightower isn't going to volunteer any information to the likes of us. Whatever we ask, he'll just say it's none of our business. If he has anything to say, he'll save it for our superiors tomorrow. He wants us to fail, lass. That way he can prove to himself that his son's death was my fault after all.'

'He'd actually risk his friend's murderer getting away?'

'He knows there'll be a full forensic team in here

tomorrow, once the isolation spell is down and we can file our report. He'll talk to them if he's got anything to say, which I doubt.'

Fisher frowned. 'The law is on our side. We could compel him to talk.'

'I don't think so. Hightower's an important man in this city. He may no longer be Chief Commander, but he still has influential friends. No, Isobel, anything we learn about Hightower will have to come from other people. He wouldn't give us the time of day if we held a sword to his throat.'

Fisher shrugged unhappily. 'I suppose you're right. The Lady Elaine might not be such a tough nut, though. I'll see if I can get her on her own, later. I might get some information out of her, woman to woman.'

'Worth a try,' said Hawk. 'But don't raise your hopes too high.'

The door swung open, and Stalker stood framed in the doorway. He held the pose a moment, and then entered the library, ducking his head slightly to avoid banging it on the doorframe. He sat down facing Hawk and Fisher, and the chair creaked loudly under his weight. Even sitting down, Stalker was still a head taller than Hawk or Fisher.

'All right,' said Stalker grimly. 'You've talked to everyone else and heard their stories. Who killed William?'

'It's too early to say, yet,' said Hawk.

'You must have learned something!'

'Yes,' said Hawk. 'Most of it contradictory. Where were you at the time of the murder, sir Stalker?'

'In my room. Alone. I don't have any witnesses, or an alibi. But I didn't kill William.'

'Is there any reason why we should think you did?' asked Fisher.

Stalker smiled briefly. 'Someone must have told you by now that William and I hadn't been getting on too well of late.'

'There was some talk that the two of you had argued about something,' said Hawk.

'We'd decided to go our separate ways,' said Stalker. 'William was always too slow, too cautious, for me. I wanted to get out there and do things, change things. William and I were always arguing, right from the start. We both wanted the same things, more or less, but we could never agree on the best way to achieve them. Looking back, it's a wonder we stayed together as long as we did. Anyway, I finally decided to go off on my own, and see what my reputation could do for me at the next election. I think I'll make a pretty good Councillor, myself. Haven could do a lot worse. It often has, in the past. But that's all there was to our quarrel – just a parting of the ways. I had nothing against the man; I admired him, always have. Straightest man I ever met.'

'So who do you think killed Councillor Blackstone?' said Fisher.

Stalker looked at her pityingly. 'Isn't it obvious? William died alone, in a room locked from the inside. Sorcery. Has to be.'

'Gaunt doesn't think so,' said Hawk.

Stalker shrugged. 'I wouldn't trust him further than I could throw him. Never trust a sorcerer.'

'How long had you known Blackstone?' asked Fisher.

Stalker stirred restlessly in his chair and glanced irritably at Fisher. 'Not long. Two years, maybe.'

'Apart from the sorcerer,' said Hawk, 'can you think of anyone with a reason for wanting Blackstone dead?'

Stalker smiled sourly. 'I suppose you've heard about Katherine and Edward?'

'Yes,' said Fisher. 'Is it true?'

'I don't know. Maybe. Women are fickle creatures. No offence intended.'

'What about political enemies?' said Hawk quickly.

'He had his share. No one in particular, though.'

'I see,' said Hawk. 'Thank you, sir Stalker. That will be all for now. If you'd care to wait with the others in the parlour, my partner and I will join you in a while. By the way, I gave orders that no one was to go near the body. Perhaps you could remind the others, and make it clear to them that I meant it . . .'

'Of course,' said Stalker. 'Glad to be of help, Captain Hawk.' He nodded briefly to Fisher, got up and left the library. Hawk and Fisher sat in silence a while, staring at nothing and thinking furiously.

'You know,' said Fisher, 'I think things were less complicated before we started asking questions.'

Hawk laughed briefly. 'You could be right, lass. Let's try and sort out the wheat from the chaff. What actual suspects have we got? It seems to me that Katherine Blackstone heads the list, with Bowman a close second. Either separately or together, they had good reason to want Blackstone dead. Assuming they were having an affair. Unfortunately, we don't have any real evidence that they were. Gossip isn't evidence.'

'Dorimant said he saw Katherine going into Bowman's room,' said Fisher. 'But Dorimant could have his own reasons for lying. Which leaves us right back where we started. So, who else can we point the finger at? I think Gaunt has to be a suspect, if only because at the moment he's the only one who could have committed the murder.'

'On the other hand,' said Hawk, 'he couldn't have used sorcery to get into the room without Visage knowing.'

'She did say she was nowhere near as powerful as Gaunt.'

'True. And just maybe they were working together.'

'No, Hawk, I still don't buy that. You saw the witch when she was talking about Blackstone; she all but worshipped the ground he trod on.'

Hawk frowned. 'That kind of worship can be dangerous. If something happened to disillusion her, and that worship turned sour . . .'

'Yeah,' said Fisher reluctantly. 'You're right, Hawk. Visage has to be a suspect.'

'Ah, hell,' said Hawk tiredly. 'Until we've got something definite to go on, they're all suspects.'

'Including Stalker?'

'I don't know, lass. Adam Stalker is a hero and a legend . . . but like Dorimant said, we're all capable of murder if we're pushed hard enough. And Stalker was definitely jumpy all the time we were talking to him.'

'So we count him as a suspect?'

'Yes,' said Hawk. 'He's killed often enough in the past, with good reason. Maybe this time he found a bad reason.' He sighed wearily, and stretched out his legs before him. 'I think we've done all we can, for the moment. Gaunt's isolation spell won't wear off until first light, so we're all stuck here for the night anyway. Let's call it a day, and yell for some help in the morning. A forensic magician should get us some answers, even if he has to set up a truthspell to do it.'

'Gaunt could set up a truthspell,' said Fisher thoughtfully.

'Yeah, I suppose he could, but we don't have the authority to order everyone to submit to it, and somehow I don't see them volunteering. There are some powerful people out there, Isobel. We're going to need some pretty solid backing before we can start pushing them around.'

'Right,' said Fisher. 'Come on, let's get out of here. The sooner we face our jovial bunch of suspects, the sooner we can pack them all off to bed, and then maybe we can get a little peace and quiet.'

Hawk nodded tiredly, and he and Fisher got to their feet. Fisher started towards the door, and then stopped as she realised Hawk wasn't with her. He was standing still in the middle of the room, head cocked to one side, listening.

'What is it?' said Fisher.

'I'm not sure,' said Hawk slowly. 'I thought I heard

something. Something . . . strange.' He looked about him, frowning, and then his gaze fell on the closed door to his left.

'Forget it, Hawk,' said Fisher quickly. 'That's Gaunt's laboratory. It's private, and it's locked.'

'Yeah,' said Hawk. 'And Visage said she found it . . . disturbing.'

He moved quietly over to the door and pressed his ear against the wood. Fisher glanced quickly about her, and then moved over to stand beside him.

'Can you hear anything?' she asked quietly.

'No.'

'What did you think you heard?'

'I'm not sure.' Hawk straightened up and stepped back from the door. He frowned, and looked thoughtfully at the door handle. 'It sounded like a growl, or something . . .' He tried the handle cautiously. It turned easily in his grasp, but the door wouldn't open. He let go of the handle.

'Hawk,' said Fisher slowly, 'there's something strange about that door . . . I'm getting a very bad feeling about it. Come away.'

'Nothing to worry about, lass. The door's locked.'

'I don't care. Come away.'

Hawk nodded stiffly. He could feel the hackles rising on the back of his neck. Whatever it was he'd heard, it was gone, but still he knew, with absolute certainty, that there was something awful on the other side of the laboratory door. Something that was listening, and waiting for him to open the door . . . He stepped back a pace and the feeling was gone. He swallowed dryly, and looked away.

'I suppose you're bound to come across a few strange things in a sorcerer's house,' he said slowly. 'Let's get out of here.'

'Right,' said Fisher.

Hawk moved over to the main door, pulled it open and walked quickly out into the hall. Fisher stayed close behind him all the way, her hand on the pommel of her sword. Once out in the hall, they both felt a little ridiculous. Hawk shook himself quickly and pulled the library door shut. When he had a moment, he'd better have a word with Gaunt about his laboratory . . . He glanced at Fisher, and she nodded quickly. Hawk smiled wryly, and then walked confidently forward into the parlour, with Fisher at his side. The sorcerer and his guests looked at the Guards with a thinly disguised mixture of politeness and hostility.

'Thank you for your patience,' said Hawk. 'This part of the investigation is at an end. Everything else will have to wait until we can bring in the experts tomorrow morning.'

Bowman stepped forward a pace. 'Gaunt tells us we can't leave the house till morning, because of the isolation spell. Did you order him to cast that spell?'

'Yes,' said Hawk. 'I couldn't take the risk of the killer getting away, and I had no other means of ensuring that he couldn't leave the house.'

'But that means we're all stuck here!'

'That's right,' said Hawk. 'I suggest you retire to your rooms and get what sleep you can.'

'Are you saying,' said Hightower slowly, 'that because of you we have to spend the night here, when one of us may be a killer?'

'You can always lock your door,' said Fisher.

'That didn't save William,' said Dorimant.

'All right,' said Hawk sharply. 'That's enough. It's not a happy situation, I know, but there's nothing we can do about it. If you've got any complaints, you can take them up with my superiors in the morning. In the meantime, I don't think any of us are in any real danger as long as we act sensibly. I suggest you all go to your rooms and stay there. Fisher and I will be here in the parlour all night, on guard. If anyone feels at all worried, they have only to call out and we'll be there in the time it takes to run up the stairs. If anyone starts moving about, we'll know. So I suggest that once you're in your room, you stay there.'

'What if I want to go to the bathroom?' asked Bowman.

'Use the pot under your bed,' said Fisher.

There was a slight pause as the guests looked at each other uncertainly. Then Katherine made for the door and the group broke apart. There was a muttering of good nights, and one by one the guests left the parlour and made their way up the stairs to their rooms. Hawk signalled for Gaunt to stay behind, and the sorcerer did so. When everyone else had gone, Hawk and Fisher looked steadily at the sorcerer.

'What have you got in your laboratory, sir Gaunt?' said Hawk bluntly.

'Odds and ends. Chemicals and the like. Why?'

Hawk scowled uncertainly. 'I felt something . . . something strange . . .'

'Oh, of course,' said Gaunt, smiling slightly. 'I should have warned you. The door has an avoidance spell on it, as a precaution. If you get too close to it, the spell makes you feel so uncomfortable and worried that you daren't try to force open the door. Simple, but effective.'

'Ah, I see,' said Hawk, trying not to sound too relieved. 'Well, sir sorcerer, I think that's all. Fisher and I will spend the night here in the parlour. One of us will always be on watch.'

'That sounds very reassuring,' said Gaunt. 'I'll be sleeping in my laboratory tonight. If you need me for any reason, just call. I'll hear you. Well, I'll see you both in the morning. Good night, Captain Hawk, Captain Fisher.'

He bowed politely, and left the parlour. Hawk and Fisher looked round the empty room.

'We never did get our dinner,' said Fisher.

'Yeah,' said Hawk. 'It's a tough life in the Guard.'

'Toss you for the first watch?'

'Your coin or mine?'

'How well you know me,' said Fisher, grinning.

4

Secrets

Edward Bowman sat back in the chair by his bed and looked round the room Gaunt had given him. It was a comfortable enough room, all told, but the colour scheme was a dark, disturbing shade of mauve. It looked like the room had died. Bowman wondered vaguely why the sorcerer should have chosen such an unrelentingly repulsive décor. The man usually showed such excellent taste. On the other hand, Gaunt hardly ever used these rooms. Maybe he'd inherited the décor from the old days, when the house still belonged to the DeFerrier family. Now that was a definite possibility. The DeFerriers had always been . . . strange. Bowman looked again at the clock on the mantelpiece. The clock had a loud aggressive tick, but its hands seemed to crawl round the dial. Bowman stirred impatiently in his chair. He'd wait another three quarters of an hour, to be sure everyone was asleep, and then, finally, he could go and see Katherine.

He frowned thoughtfully. Katherine had taken the death of her husband pretty badly. He'd known she was still fond of William, even though their marriage had fallen apart, but he'd still been surprised at how upset she'd been . . . He wondered if she'd have taken the news of his death as badly. Bowman shook his head irritably. He hadn't been jealous of William when he was alive, and he wasn't going to start now the man was dead. Katherine was his, just as she'd always been his. He'd go and see her in a while, and hold her in his arms, and everything would be fine again.

Another three quarters of an hour . . . He'd have to be careful, though, or Hawk and Fisher might hear him. And that might prove rather embarrassing.

Hawk and Fisher . . . Bowman's mouth tightened. They were going to be a nuisance; he could tell. Damn their impertinence! Of all the Guards Dorimant could have chosen as William's bodyguards, he had to pick those two – the only really honest Guards in the city. Anyone else would have had enough sense to ask a few polite questions, and then step aside and let their superiors take over – men who understood the political considerations. But not these two. They didn't seem to care how much dirt they stirred up, or who got hurt in the process. All right, finding William's killer was important, but the cause for which William had stood was more important. A scandal now could set Reform back a dozen years.

Bowman scowled thoughtfully. Maybe he shouldn't have tried to chat up Captain Fisher after all. It had seemed like a good idea at the time. It would draw attention away from him and Katherine, and besides, he'd always had a thing about tall blondes . . . But now he was a murder suspect, and one of the investigating officers had a grudge against him. Great. Just what he needed.

His scowl deepened as he tried to think which ranking officers in the Guard owed him a favour or two. There had to be someone; there was always *someone*. He finally shook his head and gave up. It was late and he was tired; he couldn't even think straight anymore. Besides, pulling strings was the last resort. It might not even come to that. As long as he and Katherine kept their mouths shut and brazened it out, no one could prove anything. Let people think what they liked; without proof they wouldn't dare say anything.

Bowman looked at the clock again. He'd better not stay long with Katherine tonight. He'd have to get some sleep if he was to get any work done tomorrow. And there was a hell of a lot to be done. With William dead, Reform could lose the whole Heights area if someone didn't step into the breach pretty damned quick. Tobias had never made any bones about wanting his old seat on the Council back, and with William's last bill still hanging in the balance . . . There were a great many pressure groups with an interest in that bill, and together they could make or break the man who took over from William. Bowman shook his head angrily. Whatever else happened, Tobias had to be kept out of the Council. All on his own that scheming hypocritical crook could undo everything Reform had achieved so far. Someone would have to stand against him at the next election. And who better than William Blackstone's loyal and faithful right-hand man?

But he couldn't just stand up and announce his candidacy. That would look bad, so soon after William's death. No, he'd need someone else, to suggest him. Someone like Katherine, perhaps. Only that might look bad, too . . . He smiled, and shook his head. There had to be a way. There was always a way, if you looked hard enough.

He leaned back in his chair, and carefully didn't look at the clock again. He could be patient, when he had to. He'd learned a lot about patience during his long years as William's right-hand man. Bowman frowned thoughtfully. It was going to feel strange, working without William. They'd been partners for so long . . . but now, finally, he had his own chance to be the front-runner, and that felt very good. It was a shame about William's death, but then, life goes on . . . He thought about Katherine, waiting for him to come to her, and smiled.

Life goes on.

Adam Stalker slowly pulled off his shirt and dropped it on the chair by his bed. He was tired, and his back ached unmercifully. He sat on the edge of the bed, and felt it give perceptibly under his weight. Damn thing was too soft for his liking. He preferred a hard support for his back. The room was hot and muggy with the shutters closed, but he knew better than to try and open them. Gaunt would have fixed them not to open. The sorcerer worried about assassins. Stalker stretched slowly and looked down at himself. His frame was still muscular, his stomach still flat and hard, but the scars depressed him. The thin white lines sprawled across his chest and gut, digging pale furrows in his tan, crossing and recrossing, and finally spilling down his arms. There were more on his back. Stalker hated them. Each and every one was a constant reminder of how close he'd come to dying. Each scar was a wound that might have killed him if he'd been a little slower or a little less lucky. Stalker hated reminders of his own mortality.

He looked round the room Gaunt had given him. Not bad. The dull red colour scheme looked grim and disturbing in the light from the single candle, but he didn't mind. He'd known worse in his time, in his travels. He lay back on his bed and stretched out, without bothering to remove his trousers or his boots. It wouldn't be the first time he'd slept in his clothes; he'd done it often enough in the past, out in the wilds. And he was tired. Very tired. It had been a long hard day . . . He stared drowsily at the ceiling, letting his mind drift where it would. Hawk and Fisher . . . the Guards. A good team. They worked well together, and from what he'd heard, they'd done a good job on the Chandler Lane vampire. He sighed wistfully. Staking vampires . . . that was real work for a man. Not like all this standing around at political meetings he'd had to get used to. Politics . . . He'd rather face a vampire than another committee. Maybe he should take a break for a while; get out of the city and back into the open lands, into the wilder areas where he belonged.

Stalker frowned, and grimaced resignedly. No, that was a younger man talking. Those days were over for him. Sleeping in the rough would play hell with his back, even in this weather. Besides, he had a real chance of taking

William's place as the official Reform candidate at the next election, if he played his cards right. It shouldn't be too difficult. With his name and reputation, the opposition wouldn't stand a chance. Stalker yawned widely, and wriggled himself into a more comfortable position. If he was going to take over William's place, he'd better start talking to the right people. Not too soon; that would look bad. But leave it too late, and other people might get in ahead of him. He'd start with Katherine . . . She'd need some support in the next few months. Though she'd probably be getting enough of that from Bowman. Stalker's lip curled. William should have done something about that, not let it go dragging on. A man looks after what's his, no matter what. William should have been tougher with her, knocked some sense into her, made it clear who wore the trousers. Stalker sighed. He'd been tempted to do something about Bowman himself, but he never had. Never interfere in other people's domestic problems. He'd learned that the hard way.

Still, Katherine was going to need him a damn sight more than she would Bowman, for the time being at least. Things were liable to get a bit rough, once the various factions in the Council learned of William's death. And you could bet there'd be factions jostling for position within the Reform cause, as well. Katherine was going to need a bodyguard. Stalker smiled sourly. Bowman might fancy himself a duellist, but he'd be damn-all use in a back-alley brawl. And Visage might be good at fending off magic, but she'd be no use at all when it came to stopping a dagger thrown from a crowd. No, Katherine was going to need him for a while yet. And he could make good use of her . . .

Unless she decided to go into politics herself. Stalker scowled. She just might; women didn't seem to know their place anymore. That Captain Fisher might look and talk tough, but she'd probably fold in a minute when the going got really hard. Women always did.

Stalker stirred restlessly. The room was swelteringly hot, and he thought seriously about trying to open the shutters. He finally decided against it. Knowing Gaunt, even if he could get the shutters open, he'd probably set off an alarm or something. The whole house was crawling with sorcery. Stalker sneered silently. Magic . . . He never did trust sorcerers. A man should make his way in the world, with courage and a sword, not by hiding away in stuffy rooms, poring over old books and making nasty smells with chemicals. All of Gaunt's so-called power hadn't been enough to protect William.

Stalker sighed. If only he and William hadn't quarrelled . . . so many things might have been different.

If only . . . the most futile phrase in the language. Stalker looked up at the ceiling, mostly hidden in the gloom. It had been a long time since he'd last slept under this roof, in this room. Must be all of thirty years, and more. He wondered if Gaunt knew this had once been his bedroom, when he was a boy. Probably not. Just one of life's little ironies no doubt. There was no one left now who knew that Adam Stalker had been born a DeFerrier, and that this house had once been his home. Until he ran away, sickened at what his family had become. They were all dead now: parents, brothers, sisters, aunts and uncles. All gone. The DeFerriers were no more, and Adam Stalker was happy with the name he had made for himself.

He closed his eyes and breathed deeply. Get some sleep. There was a lot to be done, come the morning.

Graham Dorimant paced up and down in his room, and wondered what to do for the best. William was dead, and the Guards were no nearer finding his killer. And all too soon that slimy little creep Bowman would be angling for William's seat in Council. The man was barely cold, and already the vultures were gathering. All right, somebody had to take his place, but it didn't have to be Bowman. And it wouldn't be, as long as Dorimant had any say in the matter.

He stopped pacing, and frowned thoughtfully. There was no guarantee it would be any of his business. He'd worked for William, and William was dead. Katherine might well decide she had no more use for him, and bring in her own advisers. Dorimant bit his lip uncertainly. Losing the job wasn't in itself a problem; even after his divorce he should have more than enough money left to last him out. But to give up the excitement of politics, to go back to the empty-headed social whirl of endless parties at fashionable places, the childish fads and games and intrigues . . .

Maybe Lord Hightower could offer him some kind of position; the old man wanted to get more deeply involved in politics, and he'd need an adviser he could trust . . . Yes. That might be it. Lord Roderik wasn't anything like the man William had been, but he was honest and sincere, and that was rare enough these days. He'd have a word with Hightower in the morning. Assuming William's killer didn't strike again, and murder everyone in their beds. Dorimant glanced nervously at his door. It was securely locked and bolted, with a chair jammed up against it for good measure. He was safe enough. The two Guards were just downstairs, keeping watch. After the Chandler Lane business a simple assassin shouldn't give them too much trouble.

He frowned uncertainly. Maybe he should have told them about Visage, and what she'd seen. He'd wanted to, but she had begged him not to. Now both he and she were in the position of having lied to the Guard. If they ever found out . . . He remembered Hawk's cold, scarred face, and shivered suddenly. He didn't care, he told himself defiantly. He'd done the right thing. Visage had come to him for help, and he had given it. Nothing else mattered.

He hadn't realised before just how important Visage was to him.

He sighed, and sank into the chair by the bed. He knew he ought to go to bed and get some rest, but he wasn't sleepy. It was hard for him to believe that William was really gone. He'd admired the man for so long, and been his friend for such a short time . . . And now, here he was helping to conceal evidence that might help find William's killer.

I'm sorry, William. But I think I love her, and I can't risk her being hurt.

Lord and Lady Hightower got ready for bed in silence. Lord Roderik sat in the chair by the bed and watched his wife brush her hair before the dressing table mirror. When fully unbound, her long white hair hung halfway down her back. Roderik had always liked to watch her brush her hair, a simple intimate moment she shared with no one but him. He wondered wistfully when her hair had turned white. He couldn't remember. When they were first married her hair had been a beautiful shade of honey yellow, but that had been long ago, when he was still a Captain. With something like shock, Roderik realised that that had been almost thirty years ago. Thirty years . . . Where had the time gone?

Elaine looked into the mirror and caught him watching her. She smiled, but he looked quickly away. She put down her brush, and turned around to face him. She was wearing the white silk nightdress he'd bought her for her last birthday. She looked very lovely, and very defenceless.

Don't ask me, Elaine. Please. I can't tell you. I can't tell anyone . . .

'What is it, Rod?' she said quietly. 'Something's been bothering you for months now. Why won't you tell me about it?'

'Nothing to tell,' said Roderik gruffly.

'Bull,' said his wife. 'I haven't known you all these years without being able to tell when something's gnawing at you. Is it Paul? I thought you were finally getting over his death. You should never have gone off on those stupid campaigns, the werewolf hunts. I should never have let you go.'

'They helped . . .'

'Did they? Every time some fool jumped at his own shadow and shouted "werewolf!" you went racing off to track it down. And how many did you find, out of all those dozens of hunts? One. Just one. That was why the King made you resign, wasn't it? Not just because you'd reached the retirement age, but because you were never there when he needed you!'

'Don't,' whispered Roderik, squeezing his eyes shut. Elaine rose quickly out of her chair and hurried over to kneel beside him. She put a hand on his arm, and he reached blindly across to squeeze it tightly.

'It's all right, my dear,' said Elaine softly. 'I'm not angry with you, I'm just worried. Worried about you. You've been so . . . different lately.'

'Different?' Roderik opened his eyes and looked at her uncertainly. 'How do you mean, different?'

'Oh, I don't know; moody, irritable, easily upset. I'm not blind, you know. And there've been other things . . .'

'Elaine . . .'

'Once a month, you go off on your own. You don't come back for days on end, and when you do, you won't tell me where you've been or what you've been doing.'

'I have my reasons,' said Roderik gruffly.

'Yes,' said Elaine, 'I think you do. You mustn't feel badly about it, Rod. When a man gets to your age I know that sometimes they, well, start to feel insecure about . . . themselves. I just want you to know that I don't mind, as long as you come home to me.'

'You don't mind?' said Roderik slowly. 'Elaine, what are you talking about?'

'I don't mind that you have another woman,' said Elaine steadily. 'You shouldn't look so astonished, my dear. It wasn't that difficult to work out. You have a mistress. It really doesn't matter.'

Roderik stood up, took his wife by the shoulders and made her stand up, facing him. He tried to say something, and couldn't. He took her in his arms and held her tightly. 'Elaine, my dear, my love. I promise you I don't have another woman. You're the only woman I ever wanted, the only woman I've ever loved. I promise you; there's never been anyone in my life but you, and there never will be.'

'Then where have you been going all these months?'

Roderik sighed, and held her away from him so that he could look at her. 'I can't tell you, Elaine. Just believe me when I say I don't go because I want to, I go because I have to. It's important.'

'You mean it's . . . political?'

'In a way. I can't talk about it, Elaine. I can't.'

'Very well, my dear.' Elaine leaned forward and kissed him on the cheek. 'Tell me about it when you can. Now let's go to bed. It's been a long day.'

'I think I'll sit up for a while. I'm not sleepy. You go to bed. I won't be long.'

Elaine nodded, and turned away to pull back the sheet. She didn't see the tears that glistened in Roderik's eyes for a moment. When she looked at him again, having first settled herself comfortably in bed, he was sitting on the chair, staring at nothing.

'Rod . . .'

'Yes?'

'Who do you think killed William?'

'I don't know. I can't even see how he was killed, never mind who or why.'

'Are we in any danger?'

'I shouldn't think so. Gaunt is on guard now; nothing will get by him. And there's always the two Guards downstairs. They're proficient enough at the simple things, I suppose.

There's nothing for you to worry about, my dear. Go to sleep.'

'Yes, Rod. Blow out the lamp when you come to bed.'

'Elaine . . .'

'Yes?'

'I love you. Whatever happens, never doubt that I love you.'

The witch Visage lay in her bed and stared at the ceiling. She didn't really like the bed. It was very comfortable, but it was too big. She felt lost in it. She stirred restlessly under the single thin sheet covering her. She felt hot and clammy, but she didn't like to throw back the sheet, not in a stranger's house. She'd feel naked and defenceless. Not that she was in any danger. She'd locked the door and set the wards. No one and nothing could get to her now. She was safe.

But only for the moment. She'd worked for William Blackstone all her adult life, and she didn't know what would become of her now that he was dead. William had always been much more than an employer to her; he had been her god. He was wise and just, and he fought the forces of evil in Haven. He always knew what to do, and he was always right, and if he hardly ever noticed the quiet young witch at his side, well, that was only to be expected. He always had so many important things on his mind.

Graham Dorimant had noticed her. He was always kind to her, and said nice things, and noticed when she wore a new dress. Perhaps he would look after her and take care of her. It was a nice thought.

Visage thought of the two Guards who'd questioned her, and frowned. They'd been polite enough, she supposed, but they hadn't really liked her. She could tell. She could always tell. And Hawk, the one with the scars and the single cold eye . . . He frightened her. She didn't like to be frightened. Visage pouted unhappily in the darkness. She'd told the

Guards about Katherine and Edward, but they hadn't believed her. Not really. But all they had to do was start digging, and they'd find out the truth. And then everyone would see what had really been going on.

If the truth was ever allowed to come out. Visage scowled. There were a great many people who wouldn't want the truth to get out. After all, it might taint William's memory. Well, she didn't want that, but she couldn't let Katherine and Edward get away with it. She couldn't let that happen. She wouldn't let that happen. They had murdered her William, and they would pay for it, one way or another. Her hand went to the bone amulet that hung on a silver chain around her neck. She might be only a witch, but she had power of her own, and she would use it if she had to. If there was no other way to get justice for William.

Visage sighed tiredly. Poor William. She would miss him very much. She'd followed him for so many years . . . and now she would have to find someone else to follow. Someone else to tell her what to do. She'd talk to Graham about it in the morning. He liked her. She could tell.

The sorcerer Gaunt lay on his bed, in his laboratory. The air was deliciously cool and fresh, the summer heat kept at bay by his spells. The room was brightly lit by half a dozen oil lamps. For many reasons, some of them practical, Gaunt felt uneasy about sleeping in the dark. He lay on his back and looked slowly round the familiar, crowded room, taking in the plain wooden benches and their alchemical equipment, the shelves of ingredients, all neatly stacked in their proper order . . . Gaunt felt at home in the laboratory, in a way he never did anywhere else in the house. He didn't really like the house much, if truth be told, but he needed it. He needed the security and the privacy it gave him, even if he did tend to rattle around in it like a single seed in a pod. There were times when he was tempted to give in to Stalker and sell him the damn house, but he never did. He couldn't.

He put forth his mind and tested the wards in and around the house, like a spider testing the many strands of its web. Everything was peaceful, everything as it should be. All was quiet. Gaunt frowned slightly. It worried him that he still had no idea how William had died. It worried him even more that the killer had to be one of his guests. There was no way an assassin could have got past his defences without him knowing. And yet he'd known these people for years, known and trusted them . . . It just didn't seem possible.

Gaunt sighed tiredly. Everyone had their secrets, their own hidden darkness. He of all people should know that.

'Darling . . .'

The voice was soft, husky, alluring. Gaunt swallowed dryly. Just the sound of her voice sent little thrills of pleasure through him, but he wouldn't look at her. He wouldn't.

'Why don't you call to me, darling? All you have to do is call, and I'll come to you. You'd like that, wouldn't you?'

He didn't answer. He was a sorcerer, and he was in control.

'Always the same. You want me, but you won't admit it. You desire me, but you fight against it. I can't think why. If you don't want me, why did you summon me?'

'Because I was weak!' snapped Gaunt. 'Because I was a fool.'

'Because you were human,' purred the voice. 'Is that such a terrible thing to be? You are powerful, my sweet, very powerful, but you still have human needs and weaknesses. It's no shame to give in to them.'

'Shame?' said Gaunt. 'What would you know about shame?'

'Nothing. Nothing at all.' The voice laughed softly, and Gaunt shivered at the sound of it. 'Look at me, darling. Look at me.'

Gaunt looked at the pentacle marked out on the floor on the far side of the laboratory. The blue chalk lines glowed faintly with their own eerie light. Inside the pentacle sat the succubus. She looked at Gaunt with jet black eyes, and smiled mockingly. She was naked, and heart-stoppingly beautiful. The succubus was five feet tall, with a disturbingly voluptuous figure and a rawboned sensual face. The lamplight glowed golden on her perfect skin. Two small horns rose up from her forehead, almost hidden among the great mane of jet black hair. She stretched languidly, still smiling, and Gaunt groaned softly as the old familiar longing began again, just as he'd known it would.

'Yes,' said the succubus. 'I am beautiful, aren't I? And I'm yours, any time you want me. All you have to do is call me, darling, and I'll come to you. All you have to do is call to me . . .'

'Come to me,' said Gaunt. 'Come to me, damn you!'

The succubus laughed happily and rose to her feet in a single lithe movement. She stepped out of the pentacle, the blue chalk lines flaring up briefly as she crossed them, and strode unhurriedly over to the sorcerer's bed. She pulled back the single sheet and sank down beside him.

'Damn me, my darling? No. You're the one who's damned, sorcerer. And isn't it lovely?'

Gaunt took her in his arms, and the old sweet madness took him once again.

Katherine Blackstone sat in the chair by the bed and looked listlessly round the spare room that Gaunt had opened up for her. The air was close and dusty, and the bed hadn't been aired, but she didn't care. At least it was a fair distance away from the room where her husband had died; the room where the body still lay . . .

The *body*. Not her husband, or her late husband, just the body. William was gone, and what was left behind didn't even have to be addressed by name.

Katherine looked at the bed beside her, and looked away. Sleep might help, but she couldn't seem to summon the energy to get up, get undressed, and go to bed. And anyway, if she waited long enough she was sure Edward would come to her. She'd thought he'd be here by now, but he was probably just being sensible. It wouldn't do for them to be caught together tonight, of all nights. He'd be here soon. Maybe then she'd know what to do, what to say, for the best. For the moment, all she wanted to do was sit where she was and do nothing. She'd been married less than seven years, and here she was a widow. Widow . . . There was a harsh finality to the word; that's all there is, there isn't going to be any more. It's over. Katherine's thoughts drifted back and forth, moving round the subject of her husband's death but unable to settle on it. It was impossible to think of the great William Blackstone being dead. He'd been such an important man; meant so much to so many people. Katherine wanted to cry. She might feel better if she could only cry. But all she had inside of her was tiredness.

How could he have done it? How could he have left her in this mess? How could William have killed himself?

The Guards thought it was murder. So did everyone else. Only she knew it was really suicide. The Guards were already looking for signs of guilt, for something they could use as a motive. She'd known they were bound to bring up Edward Bowman, so she'd met that attack as she always had, by throwing it back in their faces as a lie and defying them to prove otherwise. *It has been suggested to us* . . . Oh, yes, she'd just bet it had. That little bitch Visage wouldn't have waited long to start spreading the poison.

She and Edward would have to be very careful in the future. For a while, at least.

Hawk and Fisher sat stretched out in their comfortable chairs, facing the hall. They'd put out all the lamps save two, and the parlour was gloomy enough to be restful on the eyes while still leaving enough light to see by. The house was quiet, the air hot and stuffy. Hawk yawned widely.

'Don't,' said Fisher. 'You'll set me off.'

'Sorry,' said Hawk. 'I can't sleep. Too much on my mind.'

'All right, then; you stand watch and I'll get some sleep.'

'Suits me,' said Hawk. 'I shouldn't think we'll have any more trouble tonight.'

'You could be right,' said Fisher, settling herself comfortably in her chair and wishing vaguely that she had a pillow. 'Whoever killed Blackstone, it didn't have the look of a spur-of-the-moment decision. A lot of careful planning had to have gone into it. What we have to worry about now is whether the killer had a specific grudge against Blackstone, or if he's just the first in a series of victims.'

'You know,' said Hawk, 'we can't even be sure that Blackstone was the intended victim. Maybe he just saw someone in the wrong place at the wrong time, and had to die because he was a witness. The killer might still be waiting for his chance at the real victim.'

'Don't,' said Fisher piteously. 'Isn't the case complicated enough as it is?'

'Sorry,' said Hawk. 'Just thinking . . .'

'Have you had any more ideas on who the killer might be?'

'Nothing new. Bowman and Katherine Blackstone have to be the most obvious choices; they had the most to gain. But I keep coming back to *how* the murder was committed. There's something about that locked room that worries me. I can't quite figure out what it is, but something keeps nagging at me . . . Ah, well, no doubt it'll come to me eventually.'

'My head's starting to ache again,' said Fisher. 'I'm no good at problems. Never have been. You know, Hawk, what gets me is the casual way it was done. I mean, one minute we're all standing around in here, knocking back the fruit cordial and chatting away nineteen to the dozen, and the next minute everyone goes off to change and Blackstone is killed. If the killer was one of the people in this room, he must have cast-iron nerves.'

'Right,' said Hawk.

They sat together a while, listening to the quiet. The house creaked and groaned around them, settling itself as old houses will. The air was still and hot and heavy. Hawk dropped one hand onto the shaft of his axe, where it stood leaning against the side of his chair. There were too many things about this case he didn't like, too many things that didn't add up. And he had a strong feeling that the night still had a few more surprises up its sleeve.

Time passed, and silence spread through the old house. Everyone was either asleep or sitting quietly in their rooms, waiting for the morning. The hall and the landing were empty, and the shadows lay undisturbed. A door eased slightly open, and Edward Bowman looked out onto the landing. A single oil lamp glowed dully halfway down the right-hand wall, shedding a soft orange light over the landing. There was no one else about, and Bowman relaxed a little. Not that it mattered if anyone did see him. He could always claim he was going to the bathroom, but why complicate matters? Besides, he didn't want to do anything that might draw the attention of the Guards. He stepped out onto the landing and closed his bedroom door quietly behind him. He waited a moment, listening, and then padded down the landing to Katherine's room. He tried the door handle, but the door was locked. He looked quickly up and down the landing, and tapped quietly on the door. The sound seemed very loud on the silence. There was a long pause, and then he heard a key turning in the lock. The door eased open, and Bowman darted into the room. The door shut quietly behind him.

Katherine clung desperately to Bowman, holding him

so tightly he could hardly breathe. She burrowed her face into his neck, as though trying to hide from the events of the day. He murmured soothingly to her, and after a while she quietened and relaxed her grip a little. He smiled slightly.

'Glad to see me, Kath?'

She lifted her face to his and kissed him hungrily. 'I was so afraid you wouldn't come to me tonight. I need you, Edward. I need you now more than ever.'

'It's all right, Kath. I'm here now.'

'But if we're caught together . . .'

'We won't be,' said Edward quickly. 'Not as long as we're careful.'

Katherine finally let go of him, and sat down on the edge of the bed. '*Careful*. I hate that word. We're always having to be careful, having to think twice about everything we do, everything we say. How much longer, Edward? How much longer before we can be together openly? I want you, my love; I want you with me always, in my arms, in my bed!'

'We won't have to keep up the pretence much longer,' said Edward. 'Just for a while, till things have quietened down. All we have to do is be patient for a little while . . .'

'I'm sick of being patient!'

Edward gestured sharply at the wall. Katherine nodded reluctantly, and lowered her voice before speaking again. It wouldn't do to be overheard, and there was no telling how thin the walls were.

'Edward, did the Guards say anything to you about who they think killed William?'

'Not really, but they'd be fools if they didn't see us as the main suspects. There's always been some gossip about us, and we both stood to gain by his death. We could have killed him . . .'

'In a way, perhaps we did.'

'What?' Edward looked at her sharply. 'Katherine, you didn't . . .'

'William committed suicide,' said Katherine. 'I . . . told him about us.'

'You did what?'

'I had to! I couldn't go on like this, living a lie. I told him I was still fond of him, and always would be, but that I loved you and wanted to marry you. I said I'd do it any way he wanted, any way that would protect his political career, but that whatever happened I was determined on a divorce. To begin with he refused to listen, and then . . . then he told me he loved me, and would never give me up. I said I'd walk out on him if I had to, and he said that if I did, he would kill himself.'

'Dear God . . .' breathed Bowman. 'And you think William . . .'

'Yes,' said Katherine. 'I think he killed himself. I think he died because of us.'

'Have you told anyone else about this?'

'Of course not! But that's not all, Edward, I . . .'

She broke off suddenly and looked at the door. Out on the landing someone was walking past the door. Katherine rose quickly to her feet and held Edward's arm. They both stood very still, listening. The sound came again – soft, hesitant footsteps that died quickly away as they retreated down the landing. Bowman frowned. There was something strange about the footsteps . . . Katherine started to say something, and Bowman hushed her with a finger to his lips. They listened carefully for a while, but the footsteps seemed to be gone.

'Did anyone see you come in here?' said Katherine quietly.

'I don't think so,' said Bowman. 'I was very careful. It could have been one of the Guards, just doing the rounds to make sure everything's secure. It could have been someone going to the bathroom. Whoever it was, they're gone now. I'd better get back to my room.'

'Edward . . .'

'I can't stay, Kath. Not tonight, not here. It's too much of a risk. I'll see you again, in the morning.'

'Yes. In the morning.' Katherine kissed him goodbye, and then moved away to ease the door open a crack. The landing was completely deserted. Katherine opened the door wide, and Bowman slipped silently out onto the landing. She shut the door quietly behind him, and Bowman waited a moment while his eyes adjusted to the dimmer light. He started along the landing towards his own room, and then stopped as he heard a faint scuffing sound behind him. He spun round, but there was no one there. The landing stretched away before him, open and empty, until it disappeared in the shadows at the top of the stairs. And then the smell came to him – a sharp, musky smell that raised the hackles on the back of his neck. Bowman reached into the top of his boot and drew out a long slender dagger. The cool metal hilt felt good in his hand. He was in danger; he could feel it. Bowman smiled grimly. If all this was supposed to frighten him, his enemy was in for an unpleasant surprise. He'd never backed away from a duel in his life, and he'd never lost one. He wondered if this was William's killer after all. He hoped so; he would enjoy avenging William's death. He might not always have liked the man, but he'd always admired him. Bowman stepped forward, dagger in hand, and something awful came flying out of the shadows at the top of the stairs. Bowman had time to scream once, and then there was only the pain and the blood, and the snarls of his attacker.

Hawk sat bolt upright in his chair as a scream rang out on the landing and then was cut suddenly short. He jumped to his feet, grabbed his axe and ran out of the parlour, followed closely by Fisher with her sword in her hand. They ran down the hall and pounded up the stairs together. The first scream had been a man's scream, but now a woman was screaming, on and on. Hawk drove himself harder, taking the stairs two at a time. He burst out onto the landing and skidded to a halt as he looked around him for a target.

Edward Bowman lay twisted on the floor, his eyes wide and staring. His clothes were splashed with blood, and more had soaked into the carpet around him. His throat had been torn out. Katherine Blackstone stood over the body, screaming and screaming, her hands pressed to her face in horror. Fisher took her by the shoulders and turned her gently away from the body. Katherine resisted at first, and then all the strength went out of her. She stopped screaming and stood in silence, her hands at her sides, staring blindly at the wall as tears ran unheeded down her cheeks. The other guests were spilling out of their doors in various stages of undress, all of them demanding to know what had happened. Hawk knelt beside the body. There was a dagger on the carpet, not far from Bowman's hand, but there was no blood on the blade. The attack must have happened so quickly that Bowman never even had a chance to defend himself. Hawk looked closely at Bowman's throat, and swore softly. The killer hadn't been as neat with Bowman as he had with Blackstone. Hawk sat back on his haunches and scowled thoughtfully at the body.

There were footsteps on the stairs behind him. He straightened up quickly and turned, axe in hand, to find Gaunt almost on top of him. He was wearing only a dressing gown, and looked flushed and out of breath.

'What is it?' he rasped, staring past Hawk. 'What's happened?'

'Bowman's dead,' said Hawk. 'Murdered.' He looked quickly around to see if anyone was missing, but all the guests were there, kept at a respectable distance from the body by Fisher's levelled sword. Dorimant was the nearest, with the witch Visage at his side. Their faces were white with shock. Lord and Lady Hightower stood in their doorway, halfway down the landing, both in their nightclothes. Lord Roderik was holding his wife protectively close to him. Stalker stood in the middle of the landing, his face set and grim, wearing only his trousers and boots but holding a sword in his hand. Hawk looked carefully at the sword, but there was no blood on the blade. He looked again at Stalker, taking in the dozens of old scars that crisscrossed the huge muscular frame, and then looked away, wincing mentally.

'All right,' said Hawk harshly. 'Everyone downstairs. I can't work with all of you cluttering up the place. Stay in a group, and don't go off on your own for any reason. Don't argue, just move! You can wait in the parlour. You'll be all right; there's safety in numbers. Gaunt, you stay behind a minute.'

Hawk waited impatiently as the guests filed past him, keeping well clear of the body. Lord and Lady Hightower helped Katherine down the stairs. Her tears had stopped, but her face was blank and empty from shock. Hawk stopped Stalker as he passed.

'I'll have to take your sword, sir Stalker.'

Stalker looked at Hawk steadily, and his eyes were very cold. Fisher stepped forward, and lifted her blade a fraction. Stalker looked at her, and smiled slightly. He turned back to Hawk and handed him his sword, hilt first.

'Of course, Captain Hawk. There are tests you'll want to run.'

'Thank you, sir warrior,' said Hawk, sliding the sword through his belt. 'The sword will be returned to you as soon as possible.'

'That's all right,' said Stalker. 'I have others.'

He followed the other guests down the stairs and into the parlour. Hawk and Fisher looked at each other, and relaxed a little.

'For a minute there,' said Hawk, 'I wondered . . .'

'Yeah,' said Fisher. 'So did I.'

Hawk turned to Gaunt, who was kneeling by the body.

'Careful, sir sorcerer. We don't want to destroy any evidence, do we?'

Gaunt nodded, and rose to his feet. 'His throat's been torn out. There's no telling what the murder weapon was; the wound's a mess.'

'That can wait for the moment,' said Hawk. 'Is your isolation spell still holding?'

'Yes. I'd have known immediately if it had been breached. There can't be any more doubt; the killer has to be one of us.'

'All right,' said Hawk. 'Go on down and wait with the others. And you'd better take a look at Katherine Blackstone. She's in shock. And coming so soon after the last shock to her system . . .'

'Of course,' said Gaunt. He nodded quickly to Hawk and Fisher, then made his way back down the stairs. Hawk and Fisher looked thoughtfully at the body.

'We can't afford to wait till the experts get here in the morning,' said Fisher. 'We've got to find the killer ourselves.'

'Right,' said Hawk. 'If we don't, there might not be anybody left come the morning.'

5

Blood in the Night

'Well, first things first,' said Hawk. 'Let's check the body.'

He and Fisher put away their weapons, knelt down beside Bowman, and studied the dead man carefully. Bowman's throat had been torn apart. Hawk frowned grimly as he examined the wounds.

'This wasn't done with a sword,' he said slowly. 'The edges of the wounds are ragged and uneven. It could have been a knife with a jagged edge . . . See how it's ripped through the skin? What a mess. If I didn't know better, I'd swear Bowman had been attacked by some kind of animal.'

'Right,' said Fisher. 'Take a look at his chest and arms.'

There were long bloody rents in Bowman's shirtfront. Similar cuts showed on both his forearms, as though he'd held them up to try and protect his throat.

'Strange, that,' said Hawk, indicating the torn and bloody arms. 'If he had time to raise his arms, he should have had time to use his dagger. But there isn't a drop of blood on the blade.'

'Maybe he dropped it in the struggle,' said Fisher. 'It must have all happened pretty fast. Bowman never stood a chance. Poor bastard.' She sank back on her haunches and stared unhappily at the body. 'You know, Hawk, I wouldn't feel so bad if I hadn't disliked Bowman so much. There were times when I could quite happily have run the arrogant bastard through myself. I was so sure he was the murderer . . .'

'I know what you mean,' said Hawk. 'I'd almost

convinced myself he was the killer. It all made sense. He had both the motive and the opportunity . . . and I didn't like him either.' He shook his head tiredly. 'Well, we can't apologise to him now, lass. But maybe we can bring his killer to justice. So, with Bowman gone, who's the main suspect now?'

Fisher rubbed her jaw thoughtfully. 'Katherine? She was first on the scene at both the murders.'

'I don't think so,' said Hawk. 'A knife in the chest is one thing, but this . . . Whatever actually made these wounds, there must have been a hell of a lot of strength behind it to have done so much damage in so short a time. A starving wolf couldn't have done a better job on his throat. And remember, Katherine was standing right over the body when we found them, and there wasn't a trace of blood on her clothing.'

'Very observant,' said Fisher approvingly. 'Whoever killed Bowman had to have got blood all over him. Did you see . . . ?'

'No,' said Hawk. 'I checked them all carefully as they filed past me, and no one had any blood on their clothes. The killer must have had time to change.'

'Damn,' said Fisher. 'It would have simplified things.'

'There's nothing simple about this case,' said Hawk dourly. 'We'd better check all the rooms, just in case there's some bloodstained clothing to be found, but I'm betting we won't find a damned thing. Our killer's too clever for that.'

'What about Stalker's sword?' said Fisher suddenly.

'All right,' said Hawk. 'What about it?'

Fisher gave him a hard look. 'You said you wanted to run some tests on it. What did you have in mind?'

'Nothing, really,' said Hawk. 'I just didn't want him looming over me with a sword in his hand. Remember, at the time all he had on were his trousers and boots. Where was his shirt? It occurred to me that he might have had to take it off because he'd got blood on it.'

'I see,' said Fisher. 'You know, Hawk, we've been on some messy cases before, but this has got to be one of the messiest. Nothing makes sense. I mean, I can understand someone wanting Blackstone dead; he had more enemies than most of us make in a lifetime. But why Bowman? And why rip him apart like this?'

'Beats me,' said Hawk. He got to his feet, and then bent down again to retrieve Bowman's dagger. He studied it a moment, and then tucked it into the top of his boot. Fisher got to her feet and looked about her. Hawk didn't miss that her hand was resting on the pommel of her sword. He looked down at Bowman's body. 'Maybe . . .'

'Yeah?'

'Maybe he was just in the wrong place at the wrong time. He came out onto the landing, maybe to use the bathroom, and saw something or someone he shouldn't have. So the killer hit him then and there, on the spot. No time to be subtle or clever; just do the job.'

Fisher thought about it. 'That doesn't explain the savagery of the attack. Or the nature of the wounds. I don't know about the throat, but those cuts on his chest and arms look a hell of a lot like claw marks to me.'

'So what does that mean? He was killed by an animal?'

'Not necessarily. Remember the Valley killer a couple of years back? Everyone thought it was a bear, and it turned out to be a man using a stuffed bear paw strapped to a club.'

'Yeah,' said Hawk. 'I remember that case. But why should the killer use something weird like that, when a knife was good enough for Blackstone? Unless . . .'

'Unless what?' said Fisher as Hawk hesitated.

'Unless this is a different killer,' said Hawk slowly. 'Remember, Visage swore she'd kill Bowman in revenge for his murdering Blackstone . . .'

'Two killers under one roof?' said Fisher incredulously. 'Oh, come on, Hawk! It's hardly likely, is it? I know what the witch said, but that was just anger and grief talking. I mean, you saw her. Can you honestly see a timid, mousy little thing like her tearing into a man like this?'

'No, I suppose not.' Hawk scowled suddenly. 'Mind you, I have seen something like this before . . .'

'Really? Where?'

'In the Hook,' said Hawk grimly. He looked at the body, and shook his head angrily. 'This case gets more complicated all the time. Come on, let's check the bedrooms. Maybe we'll get lucky.'

'That'll be a change,' said Fisher.

They started with the first door on the left at the top of the stairs, the spare room that Gaunt had opened up for Katherine after her husband's death. The room looked dusty and empty. The single oil lamp was still burning, and the bed obviously hadn't been slept in. The sheets hadn't even been turned back.

'Odd, that,' said Hawk, looking at the bed. 'She'd had a terrible shock, and Gaunt had given her a sedative, but she didn't go to bed. She should have been out on her feet, but she hadn't even changed into her nightclothes.'

'Maybe she was waiting for someone,' said Fisher. 'Bowman, for example.'

'Yeah,' said Hawk. 'That would explain what he was doing out on the landing . . . Okay, let's take a look around.'

'Apart from bloodstained clothing, what are we looking for?'

'Anything, everything. We'll know it when we see it.'

'That's a great help, Hawk.'

'You're welcome.'

They searched the room slowly and methodically. It didn't take long. The wardrobe was empty, and so were most of the drawers in the dressing table. There wasn't anywhere else to hide anything. Hawk looked under the bed, just on general principles, but all he found were a few piles of fluff and an ancient chamber pot with a crack in it. He straightened up and looked vaguely about him, hoping for inspiration. Fisher was leaning over the dressing table.

'Found something, lass?'

'I'm not sure. Maybe. Come and take a look.'

Hawk moved over to join her. Fisher had found a small wooden box pushed to the back of one of the dressing table's drawers. The wood had been nicely stained and polished, but there was nothing special about it. Hawk looked at Fisher enquiringly. She grinned, and flipped open the lid. A tangled mess of rings, earrings, and necklaces glistened brightly in the lamplight. There were gold and silver, emeralds and rubies and diamonds, all mixed carelessly together.

Hawk picked out a ring and inspected it closely. 'Good quality,' he said approvingly. He dropped the ring back into the jewel box, and studied the collection thoughtfully. 'That little lot is probably worth more than both our annual salaries put together. And she didn't even bother to lock the case.'

'Which means,' said Fisher steadily, 'that either she's very careless or she's got a lot more like that at home.'

'Wouldn't surprise me,' said Hawk. 'So, what's your point?'

'Think about it, Hawk. Suppose Katherine and Bowman got together and decided to kill Blackstone, for the reasons we've already established. Then Katherine decides that while she still wants the prestige and the money, she doesn't need Bowman anymore. He comes to her room, they argue, there's a fight, and she kills him.'

'With what?' said Hawk. 'Where's the murder weapon? She was standing right over the body when we got there, so she couldn't have had much time to hide anything. And even though she was fully dressed, there wasn't a spot of blood on her. And anyway, we've got the same problem with her as we had with Visage. How could she possibly have caused wounds like those? Even if she had such a weapon, she's not exactly muscular, is she?'

'You'd be surprised what people can do, when they're angry enough,' said Fisher darkly.

'Yeah, maybe. Let's try the next room.'

The next room proved to be the bathroom. Hawk and Fisher stared open-mouthed at the gleaming tilework and the huge porcelain tub. It was at least six feet long and almost three feet wide. Beyond the tub was a delicate porcelain washstand with its own mirror, and a wonderfully crafted wooden commode.

'Now that's what I call luxury,' said Fisher, bending over the bath and running her fingers lovingly over the smooth finish. 'No more copper tub in front of the fire for me, Hawk. I want one of these.'

'You have got to be joking,' said Hawk. 'Do you have any idea how much something like that costs? Besides, from what I've heard, those things aren't really healthy.'

'Not healthy? How can a bath be not healthy?'

'Well, think of all the steam and water in such an enclosed space. You could end up with rheumatism.'

'Oh, but think of the luxury,' said Fisher wistfully. 'Feel how smooth this is, Hawk. And imagine being able to stretch out in one of these, up to your chin in hot water, soaking for as long as you wanted . . .' She looked at him sideways. 'There might even be room for both of us . . .'

'I'll order one tomorrow,' said Hawk. 'But you can ask for the raise we'll need in order to pay for it.'

They chuckled quietly together, and then set about searching the bathroom. It didn't take long; there was nowhere to hide anything.

'I don't know,' said Hawk finally. 'Could something have been stuffed down the commode, do you think?'

'I wouldn't have thought so,' said Fisher. 'If it was blocked, it would probably have flooded over by now. Of course, there's only one way to be sure . . .'

'If you think I'm sticking my hand down that thing, you're crazy,' said Hawk. 'It was just an idea, anyway . . . Come on, let's try the next room.'

'That's where we left Blackstone.'

'We'd better take a quick look, just to be sure.'

'What about Bowman?' said Fisher suddenly.

Hawk looked at her. 'What about him?'

'Well, we can't just leave him lying out there on the landing, can we? I thought maybe we could put him in with Blackstone. At least he'd be out of the way there.'

'Makes sense,' said Hawk. 'All right, let's move him.'

They left the bathroom, and went back to where Bowman lay huddled on the landing. He looked smaller somehow, now that he was dead. Hawk took his shoulders while Fisher took the legs, and between them they got him off the floor. The carpet clung to Bowman's back for a moment, stuck there by the drying blood, and then he came free.

'He's heavier than he looks,' said Fisher, panting a little as she backed away towards Blackstone's door.

'You should worry,' said Hawk. 'You've got the lighter end, if anything. And he's staring at me.'

Fisher backed into the closed door and kicked it open. She and Hawk then manoeuvred Bowman's body through the doorway and dropped him unceremoniously on the floor next to Blackstone. They waited a moment while they got their breath back, and then looked about them. Hawk took in the uneven trail of blood Bowman's body had left behind on the landing carpet. He winced slightly. Gaunt wasn't going to be pleased.

Tough, thought Hawk. *I've got my own problems.*

'Doesn't look like anything's been moved,' said Fisher.

'Yeah, but we'd better check anyway,' said Hawk. 'It shouldn't take long.'

They checked the wardrobe and the dressing-table drawers and under the bed, and drew a blank every time. No trace of a murder weapon, or any bloodstained clothing.

'It was worth a try,' said Hawk as he and Fisher stepped out onto the landing again.

'Yeah,' said Fisher, pulling the door to behind her. 'We're not doing very well, though, are we?'

'Not very,' said Hawk. 'But then, this isn't really our normal line of business. Locked-room murder mysteries are usually reserved for the experts. But . . .'

'Yeah,' said Fisher. '*But*. We have to cope because we're all there is. Who does the next room belong to?'

'Bowman,' said Hawk.

The room was clean and tidy, and the bed hadn't been slept in. Bowman's sword was still in its scabbard, hanging from the bedpost. Hawk drew the sword, checked the blade was clean, and then tried the balance. He nodded slowly. It was a good blade, long and thin and light.

'Duelling sword,' said Fisher. 'Apparently Bowman had something of a reputation as a duellist.'

'Didn't help him at the end,' said Hawk. 'In fact, come to think of it, why wasn't he wearing his sword? After all, he was trapped in a strange house with a murderer on the loose . . .'

'Yeah, but you don't wear a sword on a lover's tryst, do you?'

'If that was where he was going.'

'Seems likely. Doesn't it?'

Hawk shrugged. 'I suppose so.' He sheathed Bowman's sword and dropped it onto the bed. He and Fisher moved quickly round the room, checking in all the usual places, and once again ended up with nothing to show for their pains.

'This is a waste of time,' said Fisher. 'We're never going to find anything.'

'Probably not, but we have to check. How would it seem if we missed some important piece of evidence, just because we couldn't be bothered to look for it?'

'Yeah, I know. Where next?'

'Across the hall,' said Hawk. 'Stalker's room.'

Fisher looked at him uncomfortably. 'Are you serious about this, Hawk? I mean, can we really treat *Adam Stalker* as a suspect? He's a hero, a genuine hero. One of the greatest men this city ever produced. They were making up songs and legends about his exploits when I was still a child.'

'I don't trust songs or legends,' said Hawk. 'We check his room.'

'Why? Just because he wasn't wearing a shirt?'

'Partly. And also because he was one of the last people to arrive on the scene.'

Stalker's room looked lived in. His clothes lay scattered across the floor, as though he'd just dropped them wherever he happened to have taken them off. A broadsword in a battered leather scabbard lay across the foot of the bed. Hawk picked it up, and grunted in surprise at the weight of it. He drew the sword out, with some difficulty, and checked the blade. It was clean. Hawk took a firm grip on the hilt and hefted the sword awkwardly.

'How he swings this, even with both hands, is beyond me,' he said finally.

'It probably helps if you're built like a brick outhouse,' said Fisher.

'Probably.' Hawk slipped the sword back into its scabbard and dropped it onto the bed. He took a long look at the rumpled bed with its thrown-back sheets, and smiled sourly. 'At least someone got some sleep tonight.'

'The joys of an undisturbed conscience,' said Fisher, rummaging through the dressing-table drawers.

'Found anything?' said Hawk.

'No. You?'

'No. I'm beginning to think I wouldn't recognise a clue if it walked up to me and pissed up my leg.'

They checked all the usual places; no murder weapon, no bloodstained clothes.

'Let's try the next room,' said Hawk. 'That's Dorimant's, isn't it?'

'Yeah.'

The room was neat and tidy, and the bed hadn't been slept in. They looked everywhere and found nothing.

'I could do this in my sleep,' said Fisher disgustedly. 'And if I was just a little more tired, I would.'

'Only two more rooms, and we can call it a day,' said Hawk.

'You mean a night.'

'Whatever. The next room is the Hightowers'.'

'Good. Let's make a mess.'

Hawk chuckled. 'You're getting vindictive, you.'

'What do you mean, getting?'

The Hightowers' room was neat and tidy, and the bed had been slept in. Hawk and Fisher turned the place upside down, and didn't find anything. They conscientiously cleared up the mess they'd made, and moved on to the last room, feeling pleasantly virtuous. They felt even better when the usual search turned up a small wooden casket tucked under Visage's pillow. Hawk removed the casket carefully and placed it in the middle of the rumpled bed. It was about a foot square, and four inches deep, made from a dark yellow wood neither of them recognised. The lid was carved with enigmatic runes and glyphs that spilled over the edges and down the sides. Hawk reached out to open it, and Fisher grabbed his arm.

'I wouldn't. If that is a witch's casket, it could be booby-trapped with all kinds of spells.'

Hawk nodded soberly. Fisher drew a dagger from the top of her boot, and cautiously slipped the tip of the blade into the narrow crack between the casket and its lid. She took a deep breath, flipped the lid open, and stepped quickly back. Nothing happened. Hawk and Fisher moved forward to look inside the casket. There were half a dozen bone amulets, two locks of dark hair, each tied with a green ribbon, and a few bundles of what appeared to be dried herbs. Fisher picked up one of the bundles and sniffed at it gingerly. It smelled a little like new-mown hay. Fisher dropped it back into the casket.

'You recognise any of this?' she asked quietly.

Hawk nodded slowly. 'Those amulets are similar to the one Blackstone was wearing. I think we could be on to something here, Isobel. What if these are real protective amulets, and the one Blackstone was wearing was a fake? That way, everyone would think Blackstone was protected against magic, when actually he wasn't.'

'If he could be attacked by magic,' said Fisher patiently, 'why bother to stab him? Besides, we know the amulet was magical. Gaunt detected it, remember?'

'Oh. Yeah. Damn.'

He closed the casket, and put it back under the pillow again. He and Fisher took one last look round the room, and then went back out onto the landing, shutting the door behind them. They stood together a while, thinking.

'Well,' said Hawk, 'that was pretty much a waste of time.'

'I told you that,' said Fisher.

'It just doesn't make sense,' said Hawk doggedly. 'How could someone kill two men in a matter of hours, and then disappear without a trace?'

'Beats me,' said Fisher. 'Maybe there's an old secret passage, or something.'

They looked at each other sharply.

'Now that is an idea,' said Hawk. 'A secret passage would explain a lot of things . . . I think we'd better have a word with Gaunt.'

'Worth a try,' said Fisher, 'but if he knew of any, he'd have told us by now. Unless he's the murderer, in which case he'd only lie anyway.'

'This is true,' said Hawk. 'Let's check Blackstone's room anyway, just for the hell of it.'

Fisher groaned wearily, and followed him down the hall

and back into Blackstone's room. They moved slowly round the walls, tapping every foot or so and listening for a hollow sound. They didn't find one. They tried the floor, in case there was a trapdoor, and even had a good look at the ceiling, but to no avail. They stood together by the door and glared about them. Hawk shook his head irritably.

'If there is a secret passage here, it must be bloody well hidden.'

'Secret passages usually are,' said Fisher dryly. 'If they weren't, they wouldn't be secret, would they?'

'You're so sharp you'll cut yourself one of these days,' said Hawk. He took one last look round the room, and then frowned suddenly. 'Wait a minute . . . Something's wrong.'

Fisher looked round the room, but couldn't see anything out of place. 'What do you mean, wrong?'

'I don't know. Something here isn't quite the way I remember it.' He glared about him, trying to work out what had changed. And then he looked down at Blackstone's body, and the answer came to him. 'The wineglass! It's gone!'

He got down on his knees beside Blackstone's body. The wine stain on the carpet was still there, but the glass Blackstone had been drinking from was gone. Hawk peered under the bed in case the glass had rolled away, but there was no sign of it.

'Was it there the first time we checked this room?' asked Fisher.

'I don't know. I didn't look. Did you see it?'

'No. I didn't look either. I wouldn't have noticed it was gone now if you hadn't spotted it.'

Hawk straightened up slowly. 'Well, at least that tells us something.'

'Like what?' said Fisher.

'It tells us the wineglass was important,' said Hawk. 'If it wasn't, why bother to remove it? In some way, that wine-glass must have played an important part in Blackstone's death.'

'The wine wasn't poisoned,' said Fisher. 'Gaunt told us that.'

'Yeah,' said Hawk. 'He also said he was going to take a sample of the wine so that he could run some tests on it. We'd better check that he did.'

'If he didn't, we're in bother.'

'Right.' Hawk scowled fiercely. 'Why should the wine be important? I'm missing something, Isobel, I can feel it. It's important, and I'm missing it.'

Fisher waited patiently as Hawk concentrated, trying to grasp the elusive thought, but in the end he just shook his head.

'No. Whatever it is, I can't see it. Not yet, anyway. Let's go downstairs. I want to check the lower rooms as well, before I talk to Gaunt about the wine sample.'

'And if he didn't take one?'

'Burn that bridge when we come to it.' Hawk looked down at the two bodies lying side by side on the floor. 'I've got a bad feeling about this, Isobel. I don't think our murderer is finished with us yet.'

Hawk thought furiously as he and Fisher made their way down the stairs and into the hall. He'd gone about as far as he could on his own. If he was going to get any further, he had to have more information from Gaunt and his guests, and that meant more cooperation on their part. Some would cooperate, some might, and some wouldn't. In theory, he could order them to do anything and they were legally obliged to obey him, but in reality he had to be very careful about what orders he gave. Most of his suspects were important people in Haven. They had a great deal of clout, if they chose to use it. Hawk worried his lower lip between his teeth. If and when he felt able to accuse someone, he'd better have overwhelming evidence to back him up. Nothing else would do.

Unfortunately, evidence was in very short supply at the moment. All he had were endless theories, none of which seemed to lead anywhere. He couldn't be sure of anything anymore. He stopped suddenly at the foot of the stairs, and looked down the hall at the closed front door. Fisher stopped beside him and looked at him curiously.

'Hawk, what is it?'

'I just had an intriguing thought,' said Hawk. 'We've been assuming that no one could get in or out of this house because of the isolation spell. Right?'

'Right.'

'How do we know there is an isolation spell?'

'Gaunt said so. And besides, we felt the effects when he cast it.'

Hawk shook his head. 'Gaunt has said a lot of things. We felt a spell being cast, all right, but how do we know it was an isolation spell? Could have been anything. You go into the parlour and talk to Gaunt a minute. Keep him occupied. I'm going to open that front door and see if we really are isolated from the outside world.'

Fisher nodded reluctantly. 'All right. But you be careful, Hawk.'

Hawk grinned, and set off down the hall as Fisher went into the parlour. The hall was large and gloomy, and the shadows seemed very dark. His footsteps echoed loudly on the quiet. He finally came to a halt before the closed front door, and looked it over carefully. It looked normal enough. He reached out his left hand and gently pressed his fingers to the wood. It felt strangely cold to the touch, and seemed almost to pulse under his fingertips. Hawk snatched his hand away and rubbed his fingers together. They were still cold. Hawk braced himself, and took a firm hold of the door handle. It seemed to stir in his hand, and he tightened his grip. He turned the handle all the way round, and then eased the door open a crack. The hall was suddenly very cold. Hawk opened the door a little wider and looked out. And outside the door there was nothing; nothing at all.

Hawk clung desperately to the door. It was like standing on a narrow ledge and looking out over a bottomless drop. No matter where he looked there was only the dark, as though the house were falling on and on into an endless night. A cold wind blew from nowhere, searing his bare face and hands. Hawk swallowed sickly, and with a great effort tore his eyes away from the dark. He stepped back, and slammed the door shut. He moved quickly away from the door and leaned against the nearest wall while he got his breath back. His hands and face were numb from the cold, but feeling quickly returned as the summer heat inside the house drove the cold out of him. He smiled slightly. If nothing else, he had established that the house was very definitely isolated from the outside world. He wondered how Fisher was getting on.

When Fisher had entered the parlour, the assembled guests met her with a frosty silence. They were sitting together in a group, having apparently discovered that there was comfort as well as safety in numbers. They made an ill-assorted group, with some fully dressed and some still in their nightclothes. Katherine Blackstone was once again sitting by the empty fireplace. She'd regained some of her composure, but her face was still very pale and her eyes were red and swollen. She held a handkerchief in one hand as though she'd forgotten it was there. Stalker sat beside her, drinking thirstily from a newly filled glass of wine. Lord and Lady Hightower sat together, staring into the empty fireplace, both lost in their own thoughts. Visage had pulled her chair up next to Dorimants', and she leaned tiredly against him, his arm round her shoulders. The young witch looked frightened and confused, while Dorimant looked stubbornly protective. Gaunt was sitting nearest the door, and stood up as Fisher entered.

'Well, Captain Fisher, what have you found?'

'Nothing particularly helpful, sir sorcerer. Judging from the extent of his wounds, it seems likely Edward Bowman was attacked by a madman or an animal. Or by someone who wanted it to look like an animal attack.'

Gaunt raised an eyebrow. 'Why should anyone want to do that?'

'Beats me,' said Fisher. 'Nothing in this case seems to make sense.'

'Some things never do, girl,' said Stalker. 'You learn that as you get older.'

Fisher looked at him sharply. There had been something in his voice, something . . . bitter. Stalker finished off the last of his wine and stared moodily into the empty glass. Fisher turned back to Gaunt.

'Earlier on this evening, Hawk asked you to run some tests on the wine Blackstone was drinking just before his death,' she said quietly. 'Did you take a sample to test?'

'I'm afraid not,' said Gaunt. 'I was going to do it first thing in the morning.'

'Damn.'

'Is there a problem, Captain Fisher?'

'You could say that. Someone has removed the wineglass from Blackstone's room.'

'You should have put a guard on the door,' said Lord Hightower suddenly. His voice was flat and harsh.

'We could have, my Lord,' said Fisher. 'But we thought it more important to protect all of you against further attacks.'

'You failed at that too,' said Hightower. 'I'll have your heads for this incompetence, both of you!'

Fisher started to answer him, and then stopped as Gaunt's head suddenly snapped round to stare at the hall.

'Someone's trying to open the front door!'

'It's all right, sir Gaunt,' said Fisher quickly. 'It's only Hawk. He's just checking that the house is properly secure.'

Gaunt relaxed a little, and stared sardonically at Fisher. 'You mean he's checking the isolation spell. What's the matter, Captain? Don't you trust me anymore?'

'We don't trust anyone,' said Fisher carefully. 'That's our job, sir sorcerer.'

Gaunt nodded curtly. 'Of course, Captain. I understand.'

'Then you'll also understand why we have to search all the rooms on the ground floor.'

Gaunt frowned. 'You've already seen them once.'

'Not all of them, sir sorcerer. We haven't seen the kitchen, or your laboratory.'

'My laboratory is strictly private,' said Gaunt. 'No one uses it but me. There's really no need for you to check it; you felt the avoidance spell yourself. It's impossible for anyone to enter the laboratory apart from myself.'

'We'll still have to check it,' said Fisher.

'I can't allow that,' said Gaunt flatly.

'I'm afraid I must insist.'

'No.'

'Then we'll have to arrest you,' said Fisher.

'On what charge?'

'We'll think of something.'

Gaunt smiled coldly. 'Do you really think you have the power to arrest me?' he said softly.

'We can give it a damn good try,' said Hawk.

Everyone looked round to see Hawk standing in the parlour doorway, axe in hand. Gaunt started to raise his left hand, and then stopped as Fisher drew her sword in a single swift movement that set the tip of her blade against his ribs. Gaunt stood very still. The guests watched in a fascinated silence. Hawk took a firm grip on his axe. The tension in the parlour stretched almost to breaking point. And then Gaunt took a deep breath and let it out, and some of the strength seemed to go out of him with it.

'I could kill you both,' he said quietly, 'but what would be the point? They'd only send somebody else. And much as it pains me to admit it, you're the best chance I've got of finding William's killer. I will show you my laboratory. But if either of you ever draws steel on me again, I'll strike you down where you stand. Is that clear?'

'I hear you,' said Hawk. 'Now let's take a look at this laboratory of yours. Fisher, you come with us. Everyone else, stay here. We won't be long.'

'One moment,' said Stalker, rising unhurriedly to his feet. 'You still have my sword, Captain Hawk. I'm afraid I must ask you to return it. With the murderer still loose in the house, somebody has to be able to protect these people.'

Hawk nodded reluctantly, drew Stalker's sword from his belt, and stepped forward to hold it out to Stalker hilt first. Although it was nowhere near as heavy as Stalker's broadsword, the weight of the sword was still almost too much for Hawk to support one-handed. Stalker took the sword from him as though it were a child's toy. Hawk bowed politely, and turned to Gaunt.

'Shall we go, sir sorcerer?'

Gaunt led the way out of the parlour, across the hall, and into the library in tight-lipped silence. Hawk and Fisher followed close behind. Neither of them had put away their weapons. Gaunt opened the door into the kitchen and waved Hawk and Fisher through. They had a quick look round, but it looked like any other well-stocked kitchen, though surprisingly tidy for a man living on his own. They went back into the library, and found Gaunt standing before the laboratory door.

'Your partner asked me about the wine sample,' said Gaunt, not looking around. 'I'm afraid I didn't take one. But I can assure you the wine was perfectly harmless. My magic would have told me if it was poisonous. I even tasted some myself, remember?'

'That's not really the point,' said Hawk patiently. 'The wineglass must have been important in some way, or it wouldn't have been taken. Did Fisher ask you about the secret passages?'

'No,' said Gaunt. 'I can see what you're suggesting, Captain, but there are no secret passages or hidden doors in this house. If there were, my magic would have found them.'

'I see,' said Hawk. 'Well, then, I think that's all we have to talk about, sir sorcerer. Now, why don't you take off the avoidance spell and open that door?'

'I can't,' said Gaunt quietly. 'There is no avoidance spell.'

Hawk and Fisher looked at each other, and then at the sorcerer.

'Then what the hell was it we felt?' asked Hawk.

Gaunt turned round and looked at them. He held his head high but his eyes were full of a quiet desperation. 'She is my Lady,' he said simply. 'No one knows she's here. No one but me, and now you. If either of you ever talk about her to anyone else, I'll kill you. You'll understand why when you see her.'

He turned back to the door and took a key from a hidden inner pocket. Hawk and Fisher looked at each other and shrugged. Gaunt unlocked the door, pushed it open, and walked forward into his laboratory. Hawk and Fisher followed him in, and then stopped just inside the doorway. Hawk clutched at his axe, and Fisher lifted her sword. The succubus smiled at them sweetly.

She reclined lazily in the pentacle, her feet just brushing the edge of the blue chalk lines. Hawk swallowed dryly. He'd never seen anyone so beautiful. He wanted her, he had to have her; he'd kill anyone who tried to stop him. He stepped forward, and Fisher grabbed his arm. He tried to pull free, and when he couldn't he spun furiously on Fisher and lifted his axe to split her skull. Their eyes met, and he hesitated. Reality came flooding back, and he slowly lowered his axe, horrified at what he'd almost done. He looked at the succubus again, and felt the same insane desire stir within him. He fought it down ruthlessly, and wouldn't look away until he was sure the beautiful creature no longer had any hold over him. He looked at Gaunt, standing beside him with his head bowed.

'You fool,' said Hawk softly. 'You bloody fool.'

'Yes,' said Gaunt. 'Oh, yes.'

The succubus laughed sweetly. 'Visitors. It's not often I'm allowed visitors.'

Fisher stirred uncomfortably. 'Is that what I think it is?'

'Yes,' said Hawk grimly. 'That's a succubus. A female demon, the embodiment of sexual attraction.'

Fisher looked at the creature in the pentacle, and shuddered. She felt a strange attraction burning deep within her, and her skin crawled. She shook her head sharply, and the feeling slowly died away. Fisher glared coldly at Gaunt. 'No wonder you didn't want us in here. Your friends in the parlour would disown you in a moment at the merest hint that you kept a succubus under your roof. When did you summon her out of the dark?'

'A long time ago,' said Gaunt. 'Please. She's no danger to anyone. She can't leave the pentacle except at my bidding, and she can't leave the house at all. My wards see to that.'

'You let her out once, though, didn't you?' said Hawk. 'You let her loose in the Hook, and she killed at your command.'

'Yes,' said Gaunt. 'But that was the only time. She was under my control . . .'

'I was there,' said Hawk harshly. 'I saw what she did to those men. It took weeks to get the stench of the blood off the streets. She's too dangerous, Gaunt. It would only take one slip on your part, and she'd be loose. With her power, she could destroy all Haven in a single night. You have to dismiss her, Gaunt. You have to send her back into the darkness.'

'I can't,' said Gaunt miserably. 'Do you think I haven't tried? To begin with I couldn't because she was the source of my power. Without her, I was just another alchemist, with only a smattering of the High Magic. And then . . . I grew to need her. She's like a drug I have to have. Women don't mean anything to me anymore; they can't compare with her. I have to have her. I can't give her up. I won't. If you try to make me, I'll kill you.'

His voice was uneven and feverish, and there was a fey look in his eyes. Fisher lifted her sword a little.

'Don't,' said Hawk quickly. Fisher looked at him, and Hawk smiled grimly. 'Unfortunately, if Gaunt dies his hold over the demon is gone, and she would be free of all restraints. For the time being at least, we have to keep him alive.'

'Am I really so terrible?' asked the succubus. Her voice was slow and deep and soft as bitter honey. 'I am love and joy and pleasure . . .'

'And you'd kill us all if it weren't for that pentacle,' said Hawk. 'I've met demons before. You kill to live, and live to kill. You know nothing but destruction.' He met her gaze unflinchingly with his one remaining eye, and the succubus looked away first.

'You're strong,' said the succubus. 'Such a pity. Still, I think I'll enjoy killing you, when the time comes. After all, Gaunt can't deny me anything. Can you, darling?'

'These death threats are starting to get on my nerves,' said Fisher. 'The next person to threaten Hawk or me is going to regret it, because I will personally chop them into chutney. You remember, demon: a sword blade doesn't care how powerful you are.'

The succubus just smiled at her.

'Please,' said Gaunt. 'There's no need for any of this. As you can see, there's nowhere here an assassin could be hiding. You must leave. Now.'

Hawk looked around him, refusing to be hurried. The laboratory was jammed with solid wooden benches, half-buried under various alchemical equipment, and all four walls were lined with simple wooden shelves bearing stoppered glass bottles in various sizes. Fisher moved over to examine some of the bottles. One large specimen contained a severed monkey's head. Fisher leaned forward to get a closer look, and the head opened its eyes and smiled at her. She stepped back, startled. The monkey's head winked at her slyly, and then closed its eyes again.

'Hawk,' said Fisher, 'let's get the hell out of here.'

Hawk nodded, and he and Fisher backed slowly out of the laboratory and into the library. Neither of them felt entirely safe in turning their backs on the succubus. Gaunt backed out after them. The succubus blew him a kiss, and chuckled richly. Gaunt slammed the door shut on her, and locked it. When he turned round to face Hawk and Fisher, they saw a sheen of sweat on his face. He squared his shoulders and did his best to meet their accusing eyes.

'I know I have to get rid of her,' he said quietly. 'Perhaps when this is over . . .'

'Yes,' said Hawk. 'Perhaps. We'll talk more about this later. In the meantime, I want you to do something for me.'

'If I can,' said Gaunt. 'What is it?'

'I want you to set up a truthspell.'

The sorcerer frowned. 'Are you sure that's wise, Captain?'

'You can do it, can't you?'

'Of course I can do it,' snapped Gaunt. 'It's not exactly a complicated spell; in fact, it's something of an interest of mine. But the spell only lasts for a limited time, and if you're not very careful about the questions you ask, the answers you get will be worthless. There are all kinds of truth, Captain Hawk. And I should point out that some of the people here aren't going to take kindly to the idea of being questioned under a truthspell . . .'

'I'll deal with that,' said Hawk. 'All you have to do is set up the spell. I take full responsibility.'

'Very well,' said Gaunt. 'Where do you want the spell cast?'

'In the parlour,' said Hawk. 'Why don't you go on in and break the news to them? They might take it better, coming from you. Fisher and I will join you in a minute.'

Gaunt bowed politely and left the library. Hawk waited until the door was closed, and then sank tiredly into the nearest chair. Fisher pulled up another chair and sat down beside him.

'A succubus . . .' said Hawk slowly. 'I'd heard about such things, but I never thought I'd actually meet one.'

'Right,' said Fisher. 'I feel like I want to take a bath, just from being in the same room with her. All right, she was beautiful, but she made my skin creep every time she looked at me.'

'Yeah,' said Hawk.

They sat in silence a while, thinking.

'Hawk, do you really think Gaunt let the succubus loose in the Hook?'

'It seems likely.'

'The bodies you found there; you said they'd been ripped apart. Like Bowman?'

Hawk frowned. 'Not really; the Hook was much worse. But I see your point, Isobel. The succubus has to be a suspect, either as the murderer or the murder weapon. Gaunt can let her out of that pentacle any time he likes. At the time of the first murder Gaunt said he was in the kitchen, but he could easily have slipped out long enough to release the succubus. All he had to do was go via the library, and we'd never have seen him. The succubus's powers are probably limited in the house by the sorcerer's wards, but she could still have killed Blackstone and Bowman while Gaunt remained in plain view, giving him a perfect alibi.'

'Except he wasn't in plain view during either of the murders,' said Fisher. 'Besides, could something like a succubus prowl around the house without Visage detecting it?'

'I don't know,' said Hawk. 'She sensed there was something nasty in the laboratory, even though the demon was shielded by the pentacle. But then again, she's not in the same class as Gaunt . . .'

'A succubus,' said Fisher. 'Just what we needed. Another suspect with magical powers.'

Hawk laughed. 'It's not that bad, lass. If the succubus had intended to kill someone, I really can't see her stabbing them neatly through the heart and then scurrying back later to steal their wineglass. It doesn't make sense.'

'When has this case ever made sense?'

'You might just have a point there,' said Hawk. 'Come on, let's get back to the parlour. Maybe the truthspell will help to sort things out.'

'We're going to have some trouble there,' said Fisher. 'They're really not going to be happy about the truth-spell.'

'I don't give a rat's arse,' said Hawk. 'One way or the other, I'm going to get some answers out of them, and to hell with the consequences.'

Fisher looked at him fondly. 'What the hell; we're still young. We can get other jobs. Let's do it.'

They left the library and went into the parlour. The guests were arguing furiously with Gaunt. Hawk raised his voice and called for everyone's attention. There was a sudden hush as everyone turned to stare at him. He looked about him, taking in the silent, hostile faces, and knew that Gaunt hadn't been able to persuade them. Not that he'd expected it for one minute.

'Just in case there's any doubt among you,' he said steadily, 'Edward Bowman is dead. From the nature of his wounds, it's clear it was a frenzied and vicious attack. This second murder means that I have no choice but to proceed with the official investigation now, rather than wait for my superiors in the morning. I have therefore instructed the sorcerer Gaunt to set up a truthspell.'

Instead of the babble of outrage he'd expected, Hawk found himself facing a stubborn, unyielding silence. They'd all clearly decided they weren't going to cooperate. *That's the trouble with politics*, thought Hawk sourly. *Everyone's got something to hide.*

'I'm sorry,' he said firmly, 'but I have to insist.'

'You can insist all you like,' said Lord Hightower flatly. 'I won't answer any of your damned questions.'

'The law is quite clear, my Lord . . .'

'To hell with the law and to hell with you.'

Hawk sighed quietly. 'In that case, my Lord, we'll just have to do it the hard way. I will instruct the sorcerer Gaunt to prepare a truth drug. I will then knock you down, and Fisher will kneel on your chest while I feed you the drug.'

Hightower's jaw dropped. 'You wouldn't dare!'

'Oh, yes he would,' said Fisher, moving forward to stand beside Hawk. 'And so would I. One way or another, my Lord, you will answer our questions, just like everyone else. I'd advise you to settle for the truthspell. It's so much more dignified.'

Hightower looked at Hawk and Fisher, and saw that they meant it. For a moment he considered defying them anyway, but the moment passed. He held his wife's hand tightly. There were ways round a truthspell. To start with, it couldn't compel him to talk.

Hawk took Hightower's silence for assent and looked round to see if there were any further objections. Lady Hightower was glaring daggers at him, and Stalker was frowning thoughtfully, but nobody had anything to say.

Gaunt stepped forward. 'Everything is ready, Captain Hawk. We can begin whenever you wish.'

'I'm not too clear on what a truthspell entails,' said Dorimant hesitantly. 'How does it work?'

'It's really very simple,' said Gaunt. 'Once the spell is cast, no one in this room will be able to tell a lie for a period of about twenty to twenty-five minutes. The duration of the spell is limited by the number of people involved. You can of course refuse to speak, or even evade the question, but that in itself tells us something. For as long as the spell lasts, nothing can be said but the absolute truth.'

'If we're going to do some serious talking, how about a little wine to wet our whistles before we start?' said Stalker. He held up the bottle of white wine he'd been using to fill his own glass.

'Hold it,' said Hawk. 'I'm not too keen on wine at the moment. Gaunt, can you check it hasn't been tampered with?'

'Of course,' said Gaunt. He gestured lightly with his left hand, and the wine seemed to stir briefly in the bottle. 'It's perfectly sound, Captain. Not one of my better vintages, but . . .'

Stalker shrugged. 'With your taste in wine, it's hard to tell. Now, who's for a drink?'

It seemed everybody was. Gaunt passed round the glasses, and Stalker poured the wine. People began to relax a little. Stalker left Hawk to last, and gestured with his head that he wanted to speak privately with him. They moved away a few feet.

'Just a thought,' said Stalker quietly, 'about the locked room. You staked a vampire earlier today, right?'

'Right,' said Hawk. 'What's that got to do with anything?'

'Think about it,' said Stalker. 'Vampires are shape-shifters, remember? They can turn themselves into bats, or even into mist.'

Hawk nodded slowly. 'Right . . . A locked door wouldn't stop a vampire, not once it had been invited into the house. It could turn to mist and seep through the cracks round the door! No, wait a minute; it doesn't work.'

'Why not?'

'The undead don't usually need to stab their victims with a knife. And besides, vampires don't eat or drink; they can't. But everyone here was invited to dinner, and I've seen everybody with a glass in their hand at one stage or another. No, it's a nice idea, but there are too many ways a vampire would have given himself away by now. Thanks anyway, sir Stalker.'

'You're welcome. It was just a thought.' Stalker moved back to rejoin the others.

'If everyone would care to take a seat,' said Gaunt, 'we can begin.'

Hawk and Fisher and the guests pulled up chairs in a rough semicircle facing the sorcerer. He waited patiently till they were settled, and then made a sweeping motion with his left hand. Time seemed to slow and stop. Gaunt spoke a single word of Power and there was a sudden jolt as the whole room shook. There was a vague tension in the air, and then everything snapped back to normal. Hawk frowned. He didn't feel any different.

'Who's going to ask the questions?' said Gaunt.

'I will,' said Hawk. 'I suppose we'd better start with a test. My partner is . . .' He tried to say the word *short*, and found he couldn't. His mouth simply wouldn't form the word. 'Tall,' he said finally. 'Your spell seems to be working quite efficiently, sir sorcerer.'

Gaunt nodded calmly. Fisher gave Hawk a hard look, and he smiled awkwardly. He looked quickly round the assembled guests, and braced himself. *All right; in at the deep end.*

'Sir Gaunt, let's start with you.'

'Very well.'

'You are a sorcerer.'

'Yes.'

'Did you kill Blackstone and Bowman?'

'No.'

'Did you bring about their deaths indirectly, by use of your magic?'

'No.'

'You have an acquaintance, who helped you in the Hook. Is that person in any way associated with the murders?'

'That is . . . highly unlikely.'

He didn't say it was impossible, thought Hawk. *Let's push this a little further.*

'You were once sorcerer to the King,' he said carefully.

'Yes.'

'You quarrelled with him.'

'Yes.'

'Was it about your acquaintance?'

'In a way.'

'What happened? Why did you leave the court and come here, to Haven?'

Gaunt hesitated, and then sighed jerkily. 'The King wanted her for himself, and I wouldn't give her up. I couldn't. So I came here, to . . . work things out on my own.'

'Wait a minute,' said Lord Hightower. 'Who are you two talking about? What's this woman got to do with anything?'

'Apparently nothing,' said Hawk. 'Please relax, my Lord; we'll get to you in good time. That's all for the moment, sir sorcerer. Now then, sir Dorimant . . .'

'I didn't kill them,' said Dorimant quickly.

'I have to ask the question,' said Hawk politely. 'Otherwise your answer won't mean anything. Did you kill Blackstone and Bowman?'

'No. No, I didn't.'

Hawk looked at him narrowly. Dorimant was sitting awkwardly in his chair. His smile was weak and his eyes were evasive. *He's hiding something*, thought Hawk. *I wonder what?*

'You said earlier that Visage was with you at the time of the first murder,' he said slowly. 'Was that true?'

'Yes,' said Dorimant, though he didn't look too happy about admitting it.

'Why was she with you?' said Hawk.

Dorimant looked at Visage, who bit her lip and then nodded unhappily. Dorimant looked back at Hawk. 'She was the first one to find William's body,' he said reluctantly. 'She'd gone to his room to talk to him, and found him lying dead on the floor. She came to me for help.'

Everyone sat up straight in their chairs. Hawk felt a sudden rush of excitement as he finally put two and two together. He looked at Visage.

'The room wasn't locked when you found him? You just walked right in?'

'Yes,' said Visage. 'It wasn't locked.'

'Of course,' said Hawk happily. 'That's it! That's what I've been missing all along!'

Fisher looked at him dubiously. 'What are you going on about, Hawk?'

Hawk grinned. 'I've finally worked out how the murder took place in a room locked from the inside. Simple: the door was never locked to begin with!'

'Of course the door was locked,' said Fisher. 'You had to break it down with your axe! I was there, remember?'

'How did you know the door was locked?' said Hawk. 'Did you try to open it?'

'Well, no . . .'

'Exactly. Neither did I. Katherine came down and told us the door was locked. We went back with her, but she was careful to get to the door first. She rattled the door handle convincingly, told us again that it wouldn't open, and ordered me to break the door down. Afterwards, the lock was such a mess we couldn't tell it hadn't been locked. And that's why we found the key on the floor, and not in the lock.'

Everyone looked at Katherine, who stared at the floor with her head bowed.

'Is this true?' asked Gaunt.

Katherine nodded tiredly. 'Yes. I lied about the door being locked. But I didn't kill William.'

'If you didn't, then who did?' said Stalker.

'No one,' said Katherine, looking up for the first time. 'He committed suicide.'

'*What*?' said Fisher. 'You have got to be joking!'

Everyone started talking at once. Hawk yelled for quiet, and went on yelling till he got it. The voices died away to a rebellious silence as Hawk glared impartially about him.

'Let's take this from the beginning,' he said grimly. 'Visage, you found Blackstone's body. Tell us what happened.'

Visage glanced briefly at Dorimant for support, and then began her story in a low whisper.

'I wanted to talk to William. There was something about Gaunt's house that made me feel uneasy, and I wanted to be sure he was wearing his amulet of protection.'

'The one you designed for him,' said Hawk.

'Yes. Stalker gave me the idea. He'd seen something like it in his travels.'

Hawk looked at Stalker, who nodded. 'That's right, Captain. They're very common in the East, and with all the recent threats I thought the amulet might be a good idea. I explained the theory to Visage, and she made the amulet for William.'

'All right,' said Hawk. 'Go on, Visage.'

'I went to William's room and knocked on the door. There was no answer, but the door was ajar, so I pushed it open. William was lying on the floor. I ran over to him and checked his breathing, but he was already dead.'

'Did you touch the knife?' asked Fisher.

'There wasn't any knife,' said Visage flatly. 'When I found William, there wasn't a mark on him. I saw the wineglass by his hand, and I assumed one of his enemies had poisoned him. I didn't know what to do. I know I should have gone to you, Captain Hawk, but I was afraid to. I was the one who'd found him, and I thought I'd be blamed . . . I panicked, that's all. I ran back to Graham's room and told him what I'd found. He was kind to me. He said that we'd go and tell you together, and say that we'd both found the body. We were just getting ready to go downstairs when we heard you breaking down William's door. And then . . . well, we heard about the knife and the locked door, and we didn't know what to think. Graham never doubted me, but . . . In the end, we decided to say nothing. I was afraid you wouldn't believe me, and I didn't want Graham to get into trouble by supporting me.'

Hawk waited a moment, but Visage said nothing more. He looked at Dorimant. 'Is this true? You conspired to conceal evidence in a murder case? Even though the victim was your friend?'

'I had to,' said Dorimant. 'You and your partner have a reputation for violence. I had to protect Visage. William would have understood.'

'Let me just check that I've got this straight,' said Fisher. 'Visage found Blackstone's body before Katherine did. Only then, the door wasn't locked and there was no knife wound. Katherine finds the body later, brings us up to see it, but fools us into thinking the door is locked when it isn't, and never was. And when we find the body, there's a knife in Blackstone's chest.' Fisher looked at Katherine. 'I think you've got some explaining to do.'

Katherine Blackstone looked at the glass of wine in her hand. She hadn't drunk any. 'Captain Hawk was right about the locked door,' she said finally. 'But I had to do it. When we first left the parlour and went upstairs to change for dinner, I went to visit Edward Bowman in his room. We were lovers. When I returned to my own room, I pushed the door open to find my husband lying dead on the floor, a half-empty wineglass lying by his hand. Like Visage, I thought immediately of poison, but I knew it wasn't murder. It was suicide. A few days ago I finally confessed to William about my love for Edward. I was going to divorce my husband, in order to marry Edward. William threatened to kill himself if I left him.' She looked pleadingly at Hawk and Fisher. 'Don't you understand? I *couldn't* let his death be suicide! The scandal would have destroyed his reputation, and everything he'd achieved. People believed in William; he was Reform. The truth about me and William and Edward would have been bound to come out, and William's enemies would have used the scandal to undo everything he'd achieved. My life would have been ruined, and Edward's political career would have been at an end. I had to protect my husband's reputation, for all our sakes. So I took William's knife from his boot and thrust it into his chest, to make it look like a murder. As a martyr, William could still serve the party he founded. Particularly, if no murderer was ever found. And how could the killer be found, when there never was any murder?'

There was a long pause. Hightower stirred restlessly.

'That is possibly the most ludicrous story I have ever heard,' he said finally.

'But true,' said Gaunt. 'Every word of it. The truthspell is still in force.'

'So William killed himself,' said Dorimant.

'I don't think so,' said Hawk. 'I can see how it would have looked that way to you, Katherine, but I still believe your husband was murdered. You see, the wineglass has mysteriously disappeared from Blackstone's room.'

'The wine wasn't poisoned,' said Gaunt. 'I checked. I even tasted it myself.'

'It still has to be significant,' said Hawk stubbornly, 'or it wouldn't have been taken. But we can come back to that later. Katherine, is there anything else about your husband's death that you haven't told us? Anything else that you've concealed from us?'

'No. There's nothing else. I didn't kill my husband, and I didn't kill Edward.'

Hawk thought a moment, and then turned to look at Visage. 'Did you kill Blackstone and Bowman?'

'No,' said the witch quietly. 'William was already dead when I found him. And I don't know anything about what happened to Edward. Although . . .'

'Yes?' said Hawk.

Visage frowned. 'There was a funny smell on the landing . . .'

Hawk waited, but she said nothing more. He turned to face Lord Hightower. 'My Lord . . .'

'I object to this whole proceeding.'

'Just answer the questions, my Lord. Did you kill Blackstone and Bowman?'

'No,' said Lord Roderik. 'I did not.'

Hawk looked at him thoughtfully. He couldn't think of any more specific questions to ask the Lord Hightower, and he had a strong feeling that what answers he did get would be as unhelpful as Hightower could make them. Hawk sighed silently. He could tell Lord Hightower was edgy about something – it was plain in his face and his manner – but there was nothing he could do about it for the moment. If he did put the pressure on, and found nothing to justify his actions . . . Hawk turned to the Lady Hightower.

'My Lady, did you kill Blackstone and Bowman?'

'No.'

Hawk looked at her for a moment, but her level eyes and the tight line of her mouth made it clear that he wasn't going to get anywhere with her either. Hawk scowled. The truthspell had seemed like such a good idea at the time . . . He turned to Stalker.

'Sir Stalker, did you kill Blackstone and Bowman?'

'No.'

Hawk sat back in his chair and frowned thoughtfully. He'd asked everybody outright, and each had denied being

[158]

the murderer. That was impossible. One of them had to be the killer, so one of them must be lying. But since the truthspell was still in force, they couldn't be lying . . . He thought hard. He was missing something again; he could feel it.

'Sir Stalker . . .'

'Yes, Captain Hawk.'

'Whoever the killer is, he must have extensive knowledge of this house, to be able to move about it as freely as he has. Gaunt told me earlier that you had been very insistent in your attempts to buy this house. Perhaps you could tell me why this house is so important to you.'

Stalker hesitated. 'I can assure you my reasons have nothing to do with killing Blackstone and Bowman.'

'Please answer the question, sir Stalker.'

'This used to be my home,' said Stalker quietly. 'I was born here.'

Everyone gaped at him. Dorimant got his breath back first.

'You mean you're actually a DeFerrier? I thought they were all dead!'

'They are,' said Stalker. 'I'm the last, now. And I prefer to use the name I made for myself. I ran away from home when I was fourteen. My family had become . . . corrupt, and I couldn't stand it any longer. But this house is still my home, and I want it.'

Hawk thought furiously. He and Fisher had only lived in Haven a few years, but he'd heard of the DeFerriers. Everybody had. They were an arrogant and evil family, sexually perverse and heavily involved with black magics of the foulest kind. It took a long time to prove anything against them; they were after all an old, established family, with friends in high places. But then children began to disappear. The Guard finally forced their way into the DeFerrier house, and what they found there shocked even the hardest Guards . . . Three DeFerriers were hanged for murder, and two more were torn to pieces in the streets while trying to escape. The others had all died in prison, one way or another. And this was the family that had produced the legendary Adam Stalker, hero and avenger of evil . . .

'Is that all?' asked Stalker. 'I really don't have anything else I wish to say.'

'Yes,' said Hawk, snapping alert again. 'I think I'm finished now. I don't have any more questions.'

'You may not have,' said Lord Hightower, 'but I do.' He looked about him. 'There are two people here who haven't been questioned under the truthspell. Don't any of you find it suspicious that these murders only began after Hawk and Fisher entered this house?'

'Oh, come on,' said Fisher.

'Wait just a minute,' said Dorimant. 'We all know William had enemies. What better way to get to him than by the very Guards who were supposed to be defending him? Who'd ever suspect them?'

'That's ridiculous!' said Hawk.

'Is it?' said Visage. 'We've all had to answer under the truthspell. Why shouldn't you?'

'Very well,' said Fisher. 'I didn't kill Blackstone and Bowman. Hawk, did you kill them?'

'No,' said Hawk. 'I didn't.'

There was a long silence.

'Well, that was a waste of a good truthspell,' said Stalker.

'Right,' said Dorimant. 'We're no nearer finding the murderer than when we started.'

'It wasn't a complete waste,' said Hawk. 'At least now we know how Blackstone died.'

'And we know the murderer isn't one of us,' said Visage.

'There's no one else in this house,' said Gaunt. 'There can't be. One of us has to be the killer.'

'You heard the answers,' said Hawk. 'Everyone here denied being the murderer.'

Gaunt frowned unhappily. 'Maybe you didn't word the questions correctly.'

'Grabbing at straws,' growled Lord Hightower.

'If the murderer isn't one of us, then he must be hiding somewhere in the house,' said Dorimant. 'It's the only explanation!'

'There's no one else here!' snapped Fisher. 'Hawk and I have been through every room, and there isn't a hiding place we haven't checked. There's no one here but us.'

'Exactly,' said Gaunt. 'My wards are up and secure. No one could have got in without my knowing about it, and they certainly couldn't have moved about the house without setting off a dozen security spells. There can't be anyone else here!'

'All right then, maybe the truthspell was defective!' said Hawk. 'That's the only other answer I can see!'

'I am not in the habit of casting defective spells,' said Gaunt coldly. 'My truthspell was effective, while it lasted.'

Fisher looked at him quickly. 'While it lasted? You mean it's over? I thought we had twenty-five minutes.'

Gaunt shrugged. 'The more people involved, the greater the strain on the spell. It's over now.'

'Can you cast another?' asked Dorimant.

'Certainly,' said Gaunt. 'But not for another twenty-four hours.'

'Great,' said Hawk. 'Just great.'

'All right,' said Stalker. 'What do we do now?'

'There is one place we didn't check as thoroughly as the others,' said Fisher suddenly. 'The kitchen.'

Hawk shrugged. 'You saw for yourself; there wasn't anywhere to hide.'

'I think we ought to check it anyway. Just to be sure.'

Hawk looked at Gaunt, who shrugged. Hawk sighed and got to his feet. 'All right, Fisher, let's take another look.' She nodded, and got to her feet. Hawk glared round at the guests. 'Everyone else, stay here; that's an order. I don't want anyone leaving this room till we get back. Come on, Fisher.'

They left the parlour and went out into the hall, closing the door behind them. Gaunt and his guests sat in silence, lost in their own thoughts. After a while, Visage stirred uncomfortably in her chair, then rose suddenly to her feet.

'I really think we should stay here,' said Gaunt. 'It would be safer.'

'I have to go to the bathroom,' said Visage quietly, her cheeks crimson. 'And no, I can't wait.'

'I don't think you should go off on your own,' said Dorimant.

'Quite right,' said Lord Hightower. He turned to his wife. 'Why don't you and I go up with her? Just to keep her company, so to speak?'

'Of course,' said Lady Elaine. 'You don't mind, do you, dear?'

Visage smiled, and shook her head. 'I think I'd feel a lot safer, knowing I wasn't on my own.'

'Don't be too long,' said Gaunt. 'We don't want to upset Captain Hawk, do we?'

Lord Hightower snorted loudly, but said nothing. He and his wife got to their feet and followed Visage out of the parlour. Dorimant stirred uncertainly in his chair. He would have liked to go with her too, to be sure she was safe, but the poor girl wouldn't want a crowd following her to the toilet. Besides, the Hightowers would look after her. Dorimant sank back in his chair and tried to think about something else. He felt a little better, now that Hawk and Fisher knew about the evidence he'd been concealing. Even if it didn't seem to have helped much. He glanced surreptitiously at Katherine. How could she have done it? To kneel beside her dead husband, and drive his own dagger into his chest . . . Dorimant shuddered.

'The wineglass worries me,' he said finally. 'If the wine wasn't poisoned . . .'

'It wasn't,' said Gaunt flatly. 'I tasted some myself.'

'The wine . . .' said Katherine suddenly. Everyone looked at her. Katherine looked into the empty fireplace, frowning. 'William didn't drink much, even at private parties. It was a rule of his. He'd already told me he'd had enough for one evening . . . but he had a fresh glass of wine in his hand when he went upstairs to change. So who gave him that glass . . . ?'

'I don't remember,' said Dorimant. 'I wasn't really watching.' He looked at the others, and they all shook their heads.

'I'm sure I saw who it was,' said Katherine, frowning. 'But I can't remember . . . I can't . . .'

'Take it easy,' said Stalker. 'It'll come to you, if you don't try and force it.'

'It's probably not that important anyway,' said Dorimant.

Hawk and Fisher checked the kitchen thoroughly from top to bottom, and found nothing and no one. There were no hidden passages, no hiding places, and nothing that looked even remotely suspicious. Not that they'd expected to find anything. Hawk and Fisher had just needed an excuse to go off on their own so that they could talk in private. They leaned back against the sink and looked gloomily about them.

'Hightower was right,' said Fisher. 'Much as I hate to admit it. The truthspell didn't get us anywhere. The new angle on Blackstone's death is all very interesting, but we're still no nearer finding his killer.'

'Maybe,' said Hawk, 'and maybe not. I wouldn't know a clue if I fell over it, but I know a guilty face when I see one. Hightower's hiding something. He was jumpy as hell when he first discovered we were all stuck here for the night, and he was almost in a panic at the thought of a truthspell. There was something he didn't want to talk about . . .'

'You didn't ask him many questions,' said Fisher.

[163]

'He wouldn't have answered them if I had.'

'We could have leaned on him.'

Hawk smiled. 'Do you honestly think we could make Lord Roderik Hightower say one damned thing he didn't want to?'

Fisher smiled reluctantly. 'I see your point. Besides, there's no actual evidence that whatever's worrying him has anything to do with the murders. Old soldiers and politicians always have something to hide. After all, you asked him if he killed Blackstone and Bowman, and he said *no*. Didn't even hesitate.'

Hawk scowled, thinking. 'How do we know Gaunt actually cast a truthspell? Maybe . . . No. No, it worked all right; I tested it myself.'

'Maybe he only cast it on you,' said Fisher.

'Maybe. And maybe we're both getting paranoid.'

'There is that.'

'Let's get back to the parlour,' said Hawk. 'I don't like leaving them alone too long. I'll hit them with some more questions; try and break someone's story. Hightower's hiding something. I'd stake my career on it.'

'We are,' said Fisher dryly. 'We are.'

Visage waited alone on the landing, not far from the bathroom door. The Lady Elaine was taking her turn in the bathroom, while Lord Roderik had gone back to his room to change into more suitable clothes. The landing was still lit by only the one lamp, and the shadows seemed very dark. Visage glanced nervously about her. She wished the Lord and Lady would hurry up.

She shivered suddenly, and wrapped her arms around her. The house was still full of the sweltering summer heat, but Visage kept finding cold spots. She bit her lip and frowned unhappily. She didn't like Gaunt's house. She hadn't liked it from the moment she first crossed the threshold, but now she knew why. The DeFerriers might be dead and gone, but their house still held dark memories locked into its stone and timber. It was hard to think of a man like Stalker being a DeFerrier, but she didn't doubt it for a minute. Despite all the songs and legends, and even though he was always studiously polite to her, she'd never warmed to him. Visage had never known what William saw in him. She'd never liked Stalker. He had cold eyes.

She looked along the landing to what had been William's door. Poor William. He'd had such hopes, such dreams . . . And poor Edward had died right there on the landing, at the top of the stairs. She looked at the ragged bloodstains on the carpet, and then looked away. She felt sorry for Edward, now he was gone. She shouldn't have said those awful things about him. They were all true, but she shouldn't have said them.

She heard footsteps behind her and turned, smiling, expecting to see Lord Roderik. Her smile faltered.

'I'm sorry,' said the low, growling voice, 'but you could tell them what I am. I can't allow that. I'm so sorry, Visage.'

Visage started to back away, and stammered out the first few words of a defensive spell, but there wasn't enough time. Something awful surged out of the shadows towards her, and blood flew on the still, hot air.

Hawk and Fisher pounded up the stairs to the landing, cold steel in their hands. The screams they'd heard had already stopped, and Hawk had a sick feeling that he was going to be too late again.

Not another one. Please, not another one.

He stopped suddenly at the top of the steps, and Fisher bumped into him from behind. The witch Visage lay face down in the middle of the landing. Hawk moved cautiously forward, Fisher at his side. They looked quickly about them, but there was no sign of the attacker. Hawk knelt down beside Visage while Fisher stood guard. There was blood all around the witch's body. Hawk took a handful of her hair and gently lifted her head. Visage's eyes were wide and staring. Her throat had been torn out. Hawk lowered her face back onto the bloody carpet.

'And that's three,' he said tiredly. 'We've lost another one.'

'You should be getting used to that by now,' said Lord Hightower.

Hawk and Fisher straightened up quickly to find Hightower watching them from the door to his room. Hawk opened his mouth to say something, and then stopped as he heard a faint creaking sound behind him. He and Fisher spun round, weapons at the ready, to find Lady Elaine watching from the bathroom door. Her face was pale and shocked. She moved slowly forward to stand with her husband, her eyes never leaving Visage's body.

'What the hell were you all doing up here?' yelled Hawk, lowering his axe. 'I told you to stay in the bloody parlour!'

'The witch had to go to the bathroom,' said Hightower stiffly. 'We came with her to protect her.'

'Didn't do a very good job,' said Fisher. 'Did you?'

'Where were you when Visage died?' said Hawk.

'I was in the bathroom,' said Lady Elaine.

'I was in my room, changing,' said Lord Roderik.

Hawk stared at them incredulously. 'You left her out here on her own?'

'It was only for a moment,' said Hightower.

There were footsteps behind them, and then Dorimant came forward to kneel beside Visage's body. He reached out a hand to touch her face, and his fingers came back flecked with blood.

'She was so frightened,' he said softly. 'I told her there was nothing to worry about. I told her I'd look after her, and she trusted me.'

Hawk looked past Dorimant. Gaunt and Stalker were standing together at the top of the stairs. Hawk glared about him.

'Where the hell were you all? What took you so long to get here?'

Nobody said anything. They looked away rather than meet his gaze, but Hawk had already seen the answer in their faces. No one had wanted to be first on the scene, for fear of being accused.

You and your partner have a reputation for violence . . .

'Did any of you see anything?' asked Hawk. 'Did anyone hear anything?'

'Only her screams,' said Stalker. 'I knew we shouldn't have let her go, but we all thought she'd be safe with the Hightowers.'

'You left her alone,' said Dorimant. He raised his head slowly and looked at Lord Hightower. 'She was afraid, and you went off and left her alone in the dark. You bastard.'

He threw himself at Hightower, and they fell heavily to the floor. Dorimant flailed away wildly with his fists, and then got his hands round Hightower's throat. Lord Roderik choked and gagged, tearing at Dorimant's hands. Hawk started forward, and then Hightower braced himself and flung Dorimant away. He flew backwards, and slammed up against the opposite wall. Hawk and Fisher got to him before he could go after Hightower again.

'That's enough!' said Hawk sharply. 'I know how you feel, but that's enough.'

Dorimant started to cry. His whole body shook from the force of the racking sobs. Fisher patted him on the shoulder, but he didn't even feel it. Hawk shook his head slowly.

What a mess . . .

Hightower got to his feet, with his wife's help, and fingered his throat gingerly. 'Well?' he said loudly. 'Aren't you going to arrest him? He assaulted me. I have witnesses.'

'Shut your face,' said Hawk. 'He only beat me to it by a couple of seconds.' He turned his back on Hightower, and then looked about him. 'Wait a minute; where's Katherine?'

Everyone looked around, but she was nowhere to be seen.

Gaunt frowned. 'She was with us in the parlour when we heard the screams. I thought she was right behind us.'

Hawk's breath caught in his throat. He turned and ran back down the stairs, Fisher close behind him. He charged down the hall, kicked open the parlour door, and then skidded to a halt just inside the door. Katherine Blackstone was sitting in her chair by the empty fireplace, just as he'd last seen her. Only now there was a knife sunk deep into her chest, the hilt protruding between her breasts. The front of her dress was soaked with blood. Her head was sunk forward, and her staring eyes saw nothing, nothing at all.

6

Killer's Rage

Hawk glared furiously about him, but there was no trace of any attacker. Fisher moved forward and bent over Katherine. She checked briefly for a pulse, and then looked back at Hawk and shook her head. Hawk cursed softly. There was a clatter of feet outside in the hall, and Hawk turned quickly to face the door.

'That's close enough!' he said tightly. 'Stand where you are.'

Gaunt and his guests stumbled to a halt as they took in the gleaming steel axe held at the ready in Hawk's hand.

'What is it?' said Gaunt. 'What's happened?'

'Katherine Blackstone is dead,' said Hawk. 'Murdered. I want all of you to come into the parlour slowly and in single file, keeping your hands where I can see them.'

'Who the hell do you think you're talking to . . . ?' began the Lady Elaine.

'Shut up and move,' said Hawk.

Lady Elaine took in his cold, determined face and did as she was told. The others followed her into the parlour, giving Hawk and his axe as wide a berth as possible. Hawk backed slowly away as they filed into the parlour. There was a horrified murmur as they saw Katherine's body.

'She can't have been killed,' said Hightower faintly. 'It's just not possible.'

'Is that right?' said Fisher. 'I suppose she committed suicide too?'

'But how could the killer have got down from the landing

without anyone seeing him?' said Gaunt. 'No one passed us on the stairs, and there's no other way down. Katherine was perfectly all right when we went running out of the parlour to investigate Visage's screams.'

'Nevertheless,' said Hawk, 'she's still dead.'

'Maybe she did commit suicide,' said Stalker suddenly. 'Her husband and her lover had both been killed . . .'

'No,' said Dorimant flatly. 'Katherine wasn't like that. She was a fighter; always had been. Once she got over the shock of Edward's death, all she could think of was revenge. She'd already started working on how William could have been killed . . .' He broke off, and looked a little confused. He put a hand to his forehead and swayed slightly on his feet. 'Do you think I could sit down, Captain Hawk? I feel a little . . . upset.'

'All right,' said Hawk. 'Everybody find a chair and sit down, but keep your hands in plain sight. Sir Stalker, lay your sword down on the floor by your feet, and don't touch it again until I tell you to.'

Stalker studied him carefully a moment, and then nodded and followed Hawk's instructions. Fisher watched unblinkingly until Stalker was sitting in his chair with his sword at his feet, and only then lowered her sword. Stalker didn't even look in her direction. Soon everyone except Hawk and Fisher had found themselves a chair. The two Guards stood on either side of Katherine Blackstone.

'All right,' said Hawk. 'Let me see if I've got this straight. Lord and Lady Hightower were up on the landing with Visage. Stalker, Gaunt, Dorimant, and Katherine were all down here in the parlour. The Lady Elaine went into the bathroom, Lord Hightower went into his bedroom, and Visage was left alone on the landing. Shortly afterwards, she was attacked and killed. Fisher and I heard her screams just as we were leaving the kitchen. We ran up the stairs to find Visage already dead, and her attacker gone. Lord and Lady Hightower came out onto the landing to see what had happened, and those in the parlour came running out into the hall. While they were leaving the parlour, or shortly afterward, Katherine was stabbed to death.'

'We must have missed something,' said Fisher. 'Put like that, the two murders couldn't have happened. It just wasn't possible.'

'It has to be possible!' Hawk hefted his axe angrily. 'I don't believe this. Four people have been murdered, in a house full of witnesses, and nobody sees anything!'

He glared round at Gaunt and his guests, and then turned disgustedly away to look at Katherine. He frowned slightly. He'd thought at first that she might have been stabbed somewhere else and then brought back and dumped in her chair, but while the front of her dress was soaked with blood, there were no bloodstains to be seen anywhere else. So, the killer must have struck no more than a few seconds after the others had left the parlour . . . Hawk scowled. It was possible. Everyone had been so intent on what was happening on the landing that they wouldn't have noticed someone sneaking into the parlour. But how the hell had the killer got down from the landing to the hall? Hawk shook his head and leaned over Katherine to get a closer look at the dagger that had killed her. The hilt jutted obscenely from between her breasts. Hawk noted that the blow had been struck with professional skill: just under the sternum and straight into the heart. The hilt itself was a standard metal grip wrapped in leather, with nothing to distinguish it from a thousand others just like it. Hawk straightened up and turned reluctantly back to the sorcerer and his guests.

'Some of you must have seen something, even if you don't recognise it. Have any of you seen or heard anything out of the ordinary, no matter how silly or trivial it may sound?'

There was a long silence as they all looked at each other, and then Stalker stirred thoughtfully.

'It could be nothing,' he said slowly, 'but up on the landing I could have sworn I smelt something.'

'You smelt something?' said Hawk. 'What did it smell like?'

'I don't know. It was a musky, animal smell.'

Fisher nodded slowly. 'Visage said she smelt something earlier on, just after Bowman's death. She wasn't sure what it was.'

'I'm not sure either,' said Stalker. 'But it was definitely some kind of animal . . .'

'Like a wolf?' said Hawk suddenly.

Stalker looked at him, and nodded grimly. 'Yes . . . like a wolf.'

'This is ridiculous,' said Gaunt. 'There are no wolves in Haven. And anyway, how could a wolf have got into my house, past all my wards and defences?'

'Quite simply,' said Hawk. 'You invited him in.'

'Oh, my God,' said Lady Elaine. 'A werewolf . . .'

'Yes,' said Hawk. 'A shapeshifter. It all makes sense now, if you think about it. What kind of murderer kills sometimes with a knife and sometimes like a wild animal? A man who is sometimes a wolf. A werewolf.'

'And there's a full moon tonight,' said Fisher.

'You've had some experience in tracking down werewolves, haven't you?' said Dorimant.

'Experience,' said Hightower bitterly. 'Oh, yes, Hawk knows all about werewolves, don't you, Captain? How many this time, Captain? How many more of us are going to die because of your incompetence?' His wife put a gentle hand on his arm, and he subsided reluctantly, still glaring at Hawk.

'I don't understand,' said Gaunt. 'Are you seriously suggesting that one of us is a werewolf?'

'Yes,' said Hawk flatly. 'It's the only answer that fits.'

They all looked at each other, as though expecting to see telltale fur and fangs and claws.

Dorimant looked at Gaunt. 'Can't your magic tell you which one of us is the werewolf?'

Gaunt stirred uncomfortably. 'Not really. There are such spells, but they're rather out of my field.'

'There are other means of detecting a werewolf,' said Hawk.

'Oh, of course,' said Gaunt quickly. 'Wolfsbane, for example. A lycanthrope should react very strongly to wolfsbane.'

'I was thinking more of silver,' said Hawk. 'Do you have any silver weapons in the house, sir sorcerer?'

'There's a silver dagger somewhere in my laboratory,' said Gaunt. 'At least, there used to be. I haven't used it in a long time.'

'All right,' said Hawk patiently. 'Go and look for it. No, wait a minute. I don't want anyone going off on their own. Fisher and I will come with you.'

'No,' said Lord Hightower flatly. 'I don't trust you, Hawk. You were involved with a werewolf before. How do we know you didn't get bitten and become infected with the werewolf curse?'

'That's crazy!' said Fisher angrily. 'Hawk's no werewolf!'

'Take it easy,' said Hawk quickly. 'Lord Hightower is right. Until we can prove otherwise, no one is above suspicion. Absolutely no one.'

Hightower stiffened slightly. 'Are you suggesting . . . ?'

'Why not?' said Hawk. 'Anyone can become a werewolf.'

'How dare you?' said Hightower softly, furiously. 'You of all people should remember what good cause I have to hate shapeshifters.'

For a moment, nobody said anything.

'Why don't you come with me, Rod,' said Gaunt quietly. 'I'm sure I'll feel a lot safer with an old soldier like you along to watch my back.'

'Of course,' said Hightower gruffly. 'You come along too, Elaine. You'll be safer with us.'

Lady Elaine nodded, and she and her husband followed Gaunt out of the parlour and into the hall. The door closed quietly behind them.

'A werewolf,' said Dorimant slowly. 'I never really believed in such creatures.'

'I wasn't sure I believed in vampires,' said Fisher. 'Until I met one.'

'Werewolves are magical creatures,' said Stalker. 'And there's only one of us left with magical abilities. Interesting, that, isn't it?'

Hawk looked at him. 'Are you suggesting that Gaunt . . . ?'

'Why not?' said Stalker. 'I never did trust sorcerers. You heard how those people died in the Hook, didn't you?'

Hawk and Fisher looked at each other thoughtfully. Fisher raised an eyebrow, and Hawk shrugged slightly. He knew she was thinking of the succubus. Hawk tried to consider the point dispassionately. He'd assumed the succubus had been responsible for the deaths in the Hook, but they could just as easily have been the result of a werewolf on a killing spree. And Gaunt was an alchemist; he'd know about poisons. They only had his word that Blackstone's wine hadn't been poisoned. In fact, if the sorcerer was a werewolf he could probably have tasted poisoned wine and not taken any harm from it. And perhaps most important of all, Gaunt had been one of the last people in the parlour with Katherine . . .

Hawk scowled. It all made a kind of sense. He glanced at the closed parlour door and wondered if he should go after them. No, better not. Not yet, anyway. Hightower could look after himself, and it wasn't as if there was any real proof against Gaunt . . . Hawk sat back in his chair and silently cursed his indecision. He was a Guard, and he couldn't make a move without some kind of proof.

Lord and Lady Hightower waited impatiently in the library

while Gaunt searched his laboratory for the silver dagger. Gaunt had politely but firmly refused to let them enter the laboratory with him. Lady Elaine understood. All men liked to have one room they could think of as their own; a private den they could retreat to when the world got a little too hard to cope with. Lady Elaine watched her husband pacing up and down, and wished she could say something to calm him. She'd never seen him so worried before. It was the werewolf, of course. Ever since Paul's death, Roderik had been obsessed with finding the creatures, and making them pay in blood. Despite his endless hunts he'd never found but one, and that one escaped, after killing three of his men. Now he finally had a chance to come face to face with a werewolf, and the odds were it was going to be one of his friends. No wonder he was torn . . .

Elaine sighed quietly. She was starting to feel some of the pressure herself. The unending heat was getting to her, and she jumped at every sudden noise. She was tired and her muscles ached, but she couldn't relax, even for a minute. It wasn't just the deaths. They were upsetting, of course, but it was the horrid feeling of helplessness that was most disturbing. No matter what anyone said or did, no matter what theories they came up with, people kept dying. No wonder her head ached unmercifully and Roderik's temper kept shortening by the minute. Elaine sighed again, a little louder this time, and sat down in one of the chairs. She tried to look calm and relaxed, in the hope that Roderik would follow her example, but he didn't.

Elaine hoped they'd got it right this time, and that the killer really was a werewolf. Roderik needed so badly to kill a werewolf. Perhaps when he saw the creature lying dead and broken at his feet he'd be able to forget about Paul's death and start thinking about his own life again. Perhaps . . .

Roderik suddenly stopped pacing, and stood very still. His shoulders were hunched and his head was bowed, and

Elaine could see a faint sheen of sweat on his face. His hands were clenched into fists.

'Why doesn't he hurry up?' muttered Roderik. 'What's taking him so long?'

'It's only been a few minutes, my dear,' said Elaine. 'Give the man time.'

'It's hot,' said Roderik. He didn't look at her, and didn't even seem to have heard her. 'So damned hot. And close. I can't stand it. The rooms are all too small . . .'

'Rod?'

'I've got to get out of here. I've got to get out of this place.'

Elaine rose to her feet and moved quickly over to take his arm. Roderik looked at her frowningly, as though he knew her face but couldn't quite place it. And then recognition moved slowly in his eyes, and he reached across to gently pat her hand on his arm.

'I'm sorry, my dear. It's the heat, and the waiting. I hate being cooped up in here, in this house.'

'It's only until the morning, dear. Then the spell will be gone and we can leave.'

'I don't think I can wait that long,' said Roderik. He looked at her for a long moment, his eyes tender but strangely distant. 'Elaine, my dear, whatever happens, I love you. Never doubt it.'

'And I love you, Rod. But don't talk anymore. It's just the heat upsetting you.'

'No,' said Roderik. 'It's not just the heat.'

His face twisted suddenly and his eyes squeezed shut. He bent sharply forward, and wrapped his arms around himself. Elaine grabbed him by the shoulders to stop him falling.

'Rod? What is it? Do you have a pain?'

He pushed her away from him, and she staggered back a step. Hightower swayed from side to side, bent almost double. 'Get out of here! Get away from me! Please!'

'Rod! What's the matter?'

'It hurts . . . it hurts, Elaine! The moonlight's in my mind! Run, Elaine, run!'

'No! I can't leave you like this, Rod . . .'

And then he turned his shaggy head and looked at her. Elaine's eyes widened and her throat went dry. He growled, deep in his throat. The air was heavy with the smell of musk and hair. Elaine turned to run. The werewolf caught her long before she got to the door.

In the parlour, Stalker poured himself another glass of wine, and looked thoughtfully at the clock on the mantelpiece.

'They're taking their time, aren't they? How long does it take to find one dagger and some herbs in a jar?'

Hawk nodded slowly. 'Not this long. We'll give them a few more minutes, but if they're not back then, I think we'd better go and take a look for ourselves.'

Stalker nodded and sipped at his wine. Fisher continued to pace up and down before the closed parlour door. Hawk smiled slightly. Fisher never had cared much for waiting. Dorimant was sitting slumped in a chair, as far away from Katherine as he could get. His hands were clasped tightly together in his lap, and every now and again he would look quickly at the tablecloth covering Katherine's body, and then look away. Hawk frowned. Dorimant wasn't holding together too well, but you couldn't really blame him. The tension and the uncertainty were getting to everyone, and the night seemed to be never-ending. It was only to be expected that someone would start to crack. Hawk looked at the clock on the mantelpiece and chewed worriedly at his lower lip. Gaunt was taking too long.

'All right,' he said sharply. 'That's it. Let's go and find out what the hell's happening. Everyone stick together. No one is to go off on their own, no matter what.'

Stalker reached for his sword before getting to his feet.

Hawk started to say something and then decided against it. If the others had been attacked, he was going to need Stalker's expertise with a sword to back him up. Hawk headed for the door, and Fisher opened it for him. He smiled slightly as he saw she'd already drawn her sword. He drew his axe and stepped cautiously out into the hall. The library door stood slightly ajar, and the hall was empty. Hawk crossed over to the library, the others close behind him. He pushed the library door open. Lady Elaine Hightower lay in a crumpled heap on the floor. Her throat had been torn out. There was no sign of Gaunt or Roderik.

Hawk moved cautiously forward into the library, glaring about him. Fisher moved silently at his side, the lamplight shining golden on her sword blade. Stalker and Dorimant moved quickly in behind them. Hawk moved over to the laboratory door, and felt his hackles rise as he realised the door was standing slightly ajar. Gaunt would never have left that door open, for any reason . . . A wolf's howl sounded suddenly from inside the laboratory, followed by the sound of breaking glass and rending wood. Hawk ran forward, kicked the door open, and burst into the laboratory.

The werewolf threw himself at the succubus's throat, and they fell sprawling to the floor, snarling and clawing. They slammed up against a wooden bench and overturned it. Alchemical equipment fell to the floor and shattered. Hawk looked quickly at the pentacle on the far side of the room. Its blue chalk lines were smudged and broken. Gaunt lay unmoving on the floor, not far away. Hawk hurried over to crouch beside him, keeping a careful eye on the werewolf and the succubus as they raged back and forth across the laboratory. Fisher and Stalker stood together in the doorway, swords in hand, guarding the only exit. Dorimant watched wide-eyed from behind them.

The succubus tore at the werewolf with her clawed hands. Long rents appeared in the werewolf's sides, only to close again in a matter of seconds. The succubus's eyes blazed with a sudden golden light and flames roared up around the werewolf. But the sorcerous fire couldn't consume him. He threw himself at her again, and his fangs and claws left bloody furrows on her perfect skin. The succubus's head snapped forward, and she sank her teeth into the werewolf's throat. He howled with rage and pain, and flung her away. They quickly regained their balance and circled each other warily.

Fisher lifted her sword and started forward from the doorway, but Hawk waved her back. Cold steel was no defence against a werewolf, let alone an enraged succubus. Gaunt stirred slowly beside him, and Hawk took the sorcerer by the shoulder and turned him over. He had a few nasty cuts and bruises but otherwise looked unharmed. Hawk shook him roughly, and the sorcerer groaned and tried to sit up.

The succubus screamed, and Hawk turned just in time to see the werewolf rip out her throat with one savage twist of his jaws. Horribly, the succubus didn't die. She stood where she was, backed up against the laboratory wall, and blood ran down her chest in a steady stream. The werewolf hit her again, and blood flew on the air, but still she didn't die. And then Gaunt said a single Word of Power, and she slumped forward and fell lifeless to the floor. The werewolf sniffed warily at the unmoving body, and then turned to snarl at Fisher and Stalker, still blocking the only door.

'I had to do it,' said Gaunt. 'She was bound to me. She couldn't die until I let her go. I couldn't bear to lose her, but I couldn't let her suffer . . .' Tears ran down his face, but he didn't seem to notice them.

Hawk grabbed him by the arm and dragged him to his feet. 'The silver dagger,' he hissed. 'Did you find the silver dagger?'

Gaunt shook his head dazedly. 'No . . . not yet.'

'You have to find it!' said Hawk. 'We'll try and keep the beast occupied.'

'Yes,' said Gaunt. 'The dagger. I'll kill the creature.' His eyes suddenly focused, and he was back in control of himself again. He looked hard at the werewolf, crouched beside the dead succubus. 'Who is that? Who wore the mark of the beast?'

'Hightower,' said Hawk. 'Lord Roderik Hightower. I recognise what's left of his clothes.'

Gaunt nodded slowly and moved away to start searching through the drawers of a nearby table. The werewolf turned his shaggy head to watch Gaunt, but made no move to attack him. The werewolf's fur was matted with drying blood, and his claws and teeth had a crimson sheen.

'How?' said Dorimant shakily. 'How can Roderik be the werewolf? He hates the creatures; one of them killed his son . . .'

'Exactly,' said Hawk. 'He hated them so much he spent all his time leading expeditions to track them down and kill them. In the end, it became an obsession with him. That's why the army made him resign. As I understand it, he only found one werewolf, but it seems one was enough. The creature must have bitten him.'

'And whoever feels a werewolf's bite, shall become a wolf when the moon is bright,' said Fisher. 'The poor bastard.'

'Ironic,' said Stalker. He hefted his sword, and the werewolf snarled soundlessly at him.

'But why did Roderik want to kill all those people?' said Dorimant. 'They were his friends.'

'Werewolves kill because they have to,' said Hawk. 'When the moon is full, the killing rage fills their mind until there's nothing left but wolf. God knows how Hightower managed to hide it this long. Maybe he just went off and locked himself up somewhere safe until the full moon was past and his madness was over.'

'And then we trapped him here,' said Fisher. 'With a fresh supply of victims, and no way out . . .'

'It's not your fault,' said Stalker. 'You couldn't have

known. In the meantime, it's up to us to stop him, before he kills again.'

'Stop him?' said Hawk. 'There's only one thing that will stop a werewolf, and Gaunt isn't even sure he's got one. The best we can hope to do is slow the beast down.'

'Let me talk to him,' said Stalker. 'I've known Roderik on and off for more than twenty years. Maybe he'll listen to me.'

He lowered his sword and stepped forward. The werewolf crouched before him, watching him unblinkingly. The beast stood on two legs like a man, wrapped in the tatters of a man's clothing, but his stance wasn't in any way human. His body was long and wiry and covered with thick bristly hair. The hands were elongated paws, with long curved claws. The narrow tapering muzzle was full of teeth, and blood dripped from the grinning jaws. The werewolf's eyes were a startling blue, but there was nothing human in their unwavering gaze. He growled once, hungrily, and Stalker stopped where he was.

'Why didn't you come to me?' said Stalker quietly. 'I would have helped you, Rod. I'd have found someone who could take the curse away from you.'

The werewolf rose slowly out of his crouch and padded forward. His hands flexed eagerly.

'He can't hear you,' said Hawk. 'There's nothing left now but the beast.'

The werewolf sprang forward, and Stalker met him with his sword. The long steel blade cut into the werewolf's chest and out again, and didn't even slow him down. He knocked Stalker to the ground and dashed the sword from his hand. Stalker grabbed the werewolf by the throat with both hands, and fought to keep the grinning jaws away from his throat. The werewolf's quick panting breath slapped against his face, thick with the stench of fresh blood and rotting meat. Fisher stepped forward and thrust her sword through the werewolf's ribs. The beast howled with pain and fury. Fisher pulled back her sword for another thrust, and then cursed as the wound healed itself in seconds. Hawk moved in and swung his axe double-handed. The heavy blade sank deep into the werewolf's shoulder, smashing the collarbone. The werewolf tried to pull away, but Stalker held on grimly, digging his fingers into the beast's throat. Fisher cut at the werewolf again and again. The beast sank his claws into Stalker's chest. Hawk pulled out his axe for another blow, and the werewolf broke Stalker's hold and jumped back out of range. A jagged wound showed clearly in the beast's shoulder, but it didn't bleed. There was a series of faint popping sounds as the broken bones reknit themselves, and then the wound closed and was gone.

We're not going to stop him, thought Hawk slowly. *There's not a damn thing we can do to stop him . . .*

The werewolf lowered his shaggy head and sprang forward. Hawk and Fisher braced themselves, weapons at the ready. Stalker looked to where he'd dropped his sword, but it was too far away. The werewolf went for his throat. Stalker ducked under the werewolf's leap and gutted the beast with a dagger he snatched from his boot at the last moment. The werewolf crashed heavily to the floor, screaming in an almost human voice. He lay helpless for a moment as the wound healed, and Stalker dropped his dagger, leant over the beast, and taking a firm hold at neck and tail, lifted the werewolf over his head. The beast kicked and struggled but couldn't break free. Stalker held it there, his muscles creaking and groaning under the strain. Sweat ran down his face with the effort, but he wouldn't let the beast go. As long as the werewolf couldn't reach anyone, he was harmless. Pain ran jaggedly through Stalker's arms and chest from the weight of the beast, but he wouldn't give in. He wouldn't give in. Hawk and Fisher watched in awe. This was the Stalker they'd heard about, the legendary hero who'd never known defeat.

And then Gaunt stepped forward, a silver dagger gleaming in his hand. Stalker slammed the werewolf to the floor with the last of his strength. The impact stunned the werewolf for a moment, and Gaunt plunged the silver dagger into the beast's chest, just under the breastbone. Gaunt and Stalker stepped quickly back as the werewolf writhed and twisted on the laboratory floor. He scrabbled forward a few feet, and then suddenly coughed blood. It was a quiet, almost apologetic sound. The werewolf lay still and closed his eyes. The wolf shape stirred and shifted. The fur and fangs and claws slowly disappeared, and bones creaked softly as their shape changed. When it was over, Lord Roderik Hightower lay still on the floor, curled around the silver dagger embedded in his heart. Gaunt knelt down beside him.

'Why didn't you tell us, Rod?' he said quietly. 'We were your friends; we'd have found some way to help you.'

Hightower opened his eyes and looked at the sorcerer. He smiled slightly, and there was blood on his lips. 'I liked being a wolf. I felt young again. Is Elaine dead?'

'Yes,' said Gaunt. 'You killed her.'

'My poor Elaine. I never could tell her . . .'

'You should have told us, Rod.'

Hightower raised an eyebrow tiredly. 'You should have told us about your succubus, but you didn't. We all have our secrets, Gaunt. Some of them are just easier to live with than others.'

Gaunt nodded slowly. 'Why did you kill William, Rod?'

Hightower laughed soundlessly. 'I didn't,' he said quietly. And then he died.

Gaunt slowly straightened up and looked at the others. 'I don't understand,' he said slowly. 'Why should he lie about it? He knew he was dying.'

'He didn't lie,' said Hawk. Everyone looked at him sharply, and he smiled grimly. 'All along I've been saying this case didn't make sense, and I was right. The evidence didn't tie together because there wasn't just one murderer. There were two.'

7

A Hidden Evil

The parlour seemed somehow larger, now there were so few people left to sit in it. The chair with Katherine's body had been pushed to the rear of the room. The still, sheeted figure sat slumped in its chair like a sleeping ghost. The two Guards and their suspects sat in a rough semicircle around the empty fireplace. They sat in silence, looking at each other with tired, suspicious eyes. Hawk and Fisher sat side by side. Hawk was scowling thoughtfully, while Fisher glared at everyone impartially, her sword resting across her knees. Dorimant sat on the edge of his chair, mopping at his face with a handkerchief. The heat was worse if anything, and the parlour was almost unbearably close and stuffy. Gaunt sat stiffly in his chair, staring at nothing. He hadn't said a word since they left the laboratory. Stalker handed him a glass of wine, and the sorcerer looked at it dully. Stalker had to coax him into taking the first sip, but after that Gaunt carried on drinking mechanically, until the glass was empty. Stalker noted Hawk's disapproving frown and leant forward conspiratorially.

'Don't worry,' he said quietly. 'The wine contains a strong sedative. Let him sleep off the shock; it's the best thing for him.'

Hawk nodded slowly. 'You must be very skilled at sleight of hand, sir Stalker; I didn't see you drop anything into his wine.'

Stalker grinned. 'I didn't. It's a variation on my transformation trick with the alcohol, only this time I used the spell to change some of the wine into a sedative. Simple, but effective.'

Hawk nodded thoughtfully, and Stalker sank back in his chair. He glanced at the clock on the mantelpiece, and then looked sharply at Hawk.

'Your time's nearly up, Captain. In just under half an hour it will be dawn, and the isolation spell will collapse. If Hightower was telling the truth, you don't have much time left to find your second killer.'

'I don't need any more time,' said Hawk calmly. 'I know who the second murderer is.'

Everyone looked at him sharply, including Fisher. 'Are you sure, Hawk?' she said carefully. 'We can't afford to be wrong.'

'I'm sure,' said Hawk. 'Everything's finally fallen into place. I'd pretty much worked out the who and why a while back, but I still couldn't work out how it had been done . . . and without that, I couldn't make an accusation.'

'But now you've got it?' said Fisher.

'Yeah,' said Hawk. He looked unhurriedly around him, letting the tension build. Stalker was watching him interestedly, his hand resting on the sword at his side. Dorimant was perched right on the edge of his chair, leaning eagerly forward. Gaunt watched quietly, sitting slumped in his chair, his eyes already drooping from the sedative Stalker had given him. Fisher was glaring at him impatiently, and Hawk decided he'd better make a start.

'Let me recap a little to begin with,' said Hawk slowly. 'This has been a complicated case, made even more so because right from the word *go* there were two killers, working separately, with completely unconnected motives. That's why the truthspell didn't work. I asked everyone if they killed Blackstone *and* Bowman. And of course each killer could truthfully say no; they'd only killed one man, not both.

'The first killer was of course Lord Roderik Hightower.

Under the influence of the full moon, his killer's rage drove him to become a wolf and kill Edward Bowman. The choice of victim was pure chance. If Hightower hadn't found Bowman on the landing, he would undoubtedly have found someone else to attack. He killed his second victim, the witch Visage, while his wife was out of sight in the bathroom and Visage was left alone on the landing. I think he probably killed her deliberately. She'd smelt something strange on the landing after Bowman's murder, and given time she might have been able to identify what it was. So Hightower killed her, while he had the chance. By the time he killed his wife, the Lady Elaine, the werewolf in him was too strong to be denied. The killing rage must have been overpowering. It's a wonder he was able to fight it off and stay human as long as he did.

'But while all this was going on, another killer was moving among us, the man who killed William Blackstone and his wife, Katherine. Again, the case was made more complicated by outside factors. To begin with, we were distracted by the door having been apparently locked from the inside. Once Katherine admitted her part in that deception, and in the stabbing of the dead body to mislead us as to the cause of death, the situation grew a little clearer. The wineglass in Blackstone's room intrigued me. The wine had to have been poisoned, but Gaunt swore that it was harmless. He even tasted some of it himself, to prove it. But then someone secretly removed the wineglass from Blackstone's room, proving that the wine had in some way contributed to Blackstone's death. If it hadn't, why go to all the trouble and risk of removing it?'

'So William definitely was poisoned?' said Dorimant.

'In a way,' said Hawk. 'The poison killed him, but he really died by magic.'

'That's impossible!' snapped Gaunt. He struggled to sit up straighter, and glared at Hawk. 'William was still wearing the amulet Visage made for him. It was a good amulet; I tested it myself. As long as he was wearing it, magic wouldn't work in his vicinity.'

'Exactly,' said Hawk. 'And that's why he died.'

Gaunt looked at him confusedly, and some of the fire went out of his eyes as the sedative took hold of him again. Hawk looked quickly around at the other listeners. Dorimant was leaning so far forward it was a wonder he hadn't fallen off his chair. Stalker was frowning thoughtfully. And Fisher was looking as though she'd brain him if he didn't get on with his story.

'It was a very clever scheme,' said Hawk. 'Since there was no trace of poison, if it hadn't been for Katherine's interference, we'd probably have put Blackstone's death down to natural causes. So, how did he die? It all comes down to the amulet and the glass of wine. The killer took a glass of poison and worked a transformation spell on it, so that it became a glass of perfectly normal wine. He then gave the glass to Blackstone. However, once Blackstone raised the glass to his lips, the amulet cancelled out the transformation magic, and the wine reverted to its original and deadly state. Blackstone must have died shortly after entering his bedroom. He fell to the floor, dropping the wineglass. It rolled away from the body, passed beyond the amulet's influence, and the poison became wine again. Which is why Gaunt was able to taste it quite safely. Later on, the killer went back to the room and removed the wineglass. He knew a thorough examination would reveal the wine's true nature. If everything had gone according to plan, and Blackstone's death had been accepted as a heart attack, he would probably have switched the original glass for another, containing normal wine, but as things were he was no doubt pressed for time.'

'Ingenious,' said Gaunt, blinking owlishly.

'Yes, but is it practical?' said Dorimant. 'Would it have worked?'

'Oh, yes,' said Gaunt. 'It would have worked. And that's

why Katherine had to die! Just before Visage's death, Katherine was trying to remember who had given William that last glass of wine. She was sure she'd seen who it was, but she couldn't quite remember. She had to die, because the killer was afraid she might identify him.'

'Right,' said Hawk. 'So, we've established how William Blackstone died. Now we come to the suspects. Gaunt, Dorimant, Stalker. Three suspects; but only one of you had the means and the opportunity and the motive.

'Gaunt could have worked the transformation spell on the wine. He knew about the amulet, and he is both a sorcerer and an alchemist. But he also had a succubus, with all the power and abilities that granted him. If he'd wanted Blackstone dead, there were any number of ways he could have managed it, without any danger of it being traced back to him. He certainly wouldn't have committed a murder in his own house; an investigation might have discovered his succubus, and he couldn't risk that.

'Dorimant . . . I did wonder about you for a while. You were obviously very attached to the witch Visage, and jealousy can be a powerful motive. If you thought Blackstone was all that stood between you and her . . . but you know nothing about magic. You didn't even know how a truthspell worked.'

Hawk turned slowly to Stalker. 'It had to be you, Stalker. You worked your transformation trick on the wine once too often. Taking the alcohol out of wine was one thing. I might have overlooked that, but changing the wine to a sedative for Gaunt was a mistake. Once I'd seen that, a lot of things suddenly fell into place. I wondered why Blackstone had taken that last glass of wine, when he'd already said he wasn't going to drink any more because he had no head for wine. He took that final glass because you told him you'd worked your trick on it to take out the alcohol. Also, when Visage was killed on the landing, you were one of the last people to leave the parlour, which meant you had plenty of time to kill Katherine, while everyone else's attention was distracted.

'It was the lack of motive that threw me for a long time, until I discovered you were a DeFerrier. Blackstone's next main cause would have been a drive against child prostitution, and those who supported it. Fisher and I were working on just such a case before we were called away to go after the Chandler Lane vampire. The word was that we were called off because we were getting too close to one of the main patrons, an influential and very respectable man with a taste for abusing children. The DeFerriers had a thing about children, didn't they? We'll never know exactly how many children were tortured and killed in their black magic rituals. You were the patron, Stalker. You were the one who had us called off. And that's why you had to kill Blackstone. During his investigation, he'd discovered your obsession with child prostitutes, and he was going to turn you over to the Guard, as soon as he had some concrete evidence to use against you. And he'd have found it, eventually. Oh, you argued with him, promised him anything and everything, but Blackstone was an honest man. You couldn't buy him, and you couldn't intimidate him, so you killed him. You couldn't have let him tell the world what you really are. It would have destroyed your reputation and your legend, and that's all you've got left to live on.

'You must have put a lot of planning into Blackstone's death, Stalker. After all, you were the one who first told Visage how to make the protective amulet. Ironic, isn't it? By wearing that amulet, he was unknowingly collaborating in his own murder. If it hadn't been for Katherine, you might well have got away with it, and your dirty little secret would have been safe. Adam Stalker, I hereby place you under arrest for the murder of William and Katherine Blackstone.'

For a long moment nobody said anything, and then Stalker chuckled quietly. 'I said you were good, didn't I?

You worked it all out, from beginning to end. If it hadn't been for that bitch Katherine . . . I forgot how tough she was. She always could think on her feet, and she was one hell of an actress. If it hadn't been for her muddying the waters, you wouldn't have suspected a thing. But it doesn't matter. I'm not going to stand trial.'

Hawk threw himself sideways out of his chair as Stalker suddenly lunged forward, sword in hand. Hawk hit the floor rolling as the sword slammed into the back of the chair where he'd been sitting. He was quickly back on his feet again, axe in hand. Fisher was also on her feet, sword at the ready. Gaunt and Dorimant watched, shocked, as Stalker retrieved his sword, kicked aside his chair, and backed quickly away.

'You've got good reflexes, Hawk,' said Stalker. 'But you still don't stand a chance against me. The only one who could have stopped me is Gaunt, and my sedative's taken care of him. In a few minutes the isolation spell will collapse, and I'll be on my way. The Guard will find nothing but a house full of bodies, and I'll be long gone. This will be just another unsolved mystery. Haven's full of them.'

'You're not going anywhere,' said Fisher, lifting her sword slightly.

'You think you're going to stop me, girl?'

'Why not? I've dealt with worse than you in my time.'

Stalker smiled contemptuously and stepped forward, his long sword shining brightly as it cut through the air towards her. Fisher braced herself and parried the blow, grunting at the effort it cost her. The sword was heavy, and Stalker was every bit as strong as they said he was. She cut at his unprotected leg, and he parried the blow easily. Hawk moved in to join her, swinging his axe. Stalker picked up a chair with his free hand and threw it at Hawk. One of the chair legs struck him a glancing blow to the head and he fell to the floor, stunned. Fisher threw herself at Stalker, and he stepped forward to meet her. He quickly took the advantage, and Fisher was forced to retreat round the room, blocking his sword with hers as she searched and waited for an opening in his defence that never came. She was good with a blade, but he was better.

Sparks sputtered and died on the still air, and the parlour was full of the ring of steel on steel. Hawk got to his feet and shook his head to clear it. Stalker scowled briefly. He couldn't fight them both, and he knew it. He turned suddenly and cut viciously at Dorimant, who shrank back in his chair, unharmed. Fisher threw herself forward to block the blow, and Stalker spun round at the last moment and kicked her solidly under the left knee. Fisher collapsed as her leg betrayed her, groaning with agony. Stalker drew back his sword to finish her, and then Hawk was upon him, swinging his axe double-handed, and Stalker had to retreat.

Stalker and Hawk stood toe to toe, their blades a flashing blur in the lamplight. Sword and axe rose and fell, cut and parry and riposte, with no quarter asked or given. The pace was too fast for the fight to last long. Stalker tried every dirty trick and foul move he knew, but none of them worked against Hawk. In the end he felt himself beginning to slow, and grew desperate. He used the same trick once too often, and Hawk stepped inside his guard and knocked the sword from his hand. Stalker staggered back, nursing his numbed hand. He leaned against the wall, breathing hard.

'I said you were good, Hawk. Ten years ago you wouldn't have touched me . . . but that was ten years ago.' He waited a moment while his breathing slowed and steadied. 'It's not really my fault, you know. You can't imagine what it was like, growing up in this house, seeing the things my family did . . . What chance did I have? They were vile, all of them, and they tried to corrupt me, too. I couldn't stop them; I was only a child. So I ran away. And I became a hero, to help others, because there was no one to help me when I needed it. But still I was tainted, full of the corruption they'd taught me. I fought it; I fought it for years. But it was too strong, and I was too weak . . . I even tried to buy this house, so I could burn it to the ground and break its hold on me. But Gaunt wouldn't sell. It wasn't my fault. None of it was my fault! I didn't choose to be . . . what I am.'

'I saw what you did to that girl in the brothel over the Nag's Head,' said Hawk. 'I would have killed myself before I did such a thing.'

Stalker nodded slowly. 'I was never that brave. Till now. I told you I wouldn't stand trial.'

He drew a dagger from his boot, turned it quickly in his hand, and thrust it deep into his heart. He fell to his knees, looked triumphantly at Hawk, and then fell forward and lay still. Hawk moved cautiously forward and stirred the body with his boot. There was no response. He knelt down and tried for a pulse. There wasn't one. Adam Stalker was dead.

'It's over,' said Dorimant. 'It's finally over.'

'Yes,' said Hawk, getting tiredly to his feet. 'I think it is.' He looked at Fisher. 'Are you all right, lass?'

'I'll live,' said Fisher dryly, flexing her aching leg.

'He was one of the best,' said Dorimant, staring sadly at Stalker's body. 'I never liked him, but I always admired him. He was one of the greatest heroes ever to come out of the Low Kingdoms. He really did do most of the things the legends say he did.'

'Yes,' said Hawk. 'I know. And that's why we're going to say Hightower was responsible for all the deaths. No one really blames a werewolf. Haven needs legends like Stalker more than it needs the truth.'

Dorimant nodded slowly. 'I suppose you're right. A man's past should be buried with the man.'

There was a sudden lurch as the house seemed to drop an inch. A subtle tension on the air was suddenly gone.

'The isolation spell,' said Fisher. 'It's finished. Let's get the hell out of this place.'

They all looked at Gaunt, sleeping peacefully in his chair.

'You go on,' said Dorimant. 'I'll stick around till he wakes up. Someone's got to brief him on the story we're going to tell. Besides . . .' Dorimant looked levelly at Hawk and Fisher. 'I promised Visage I'd look after her. I don't want to leave her here, in the company of strangers.'

'All right,' said Hawk. 'We won't be long. What will you do now, Dorimant, now that Blackstone is dead . . . ?'

'I'll think of something,' said Dorimant. 'If nothing else, I'll be able to dine out on this story for months.'

They laughed, and then Hawk and Fisher made their goodbyes and left. They walked unhurriedly down the hall to the closed front door. Hawk hesitated a moment, and then pulled the door open. A cool breeze swept in, dispelling the heat of the long night. The sun had come up, and there were rain clouds in the early morning skies, and a hint of moisture on the air. Hawk and Fisher stood together a while, quietly enjoying the cool of the breeze.

'It was partly the heat,' said Fisher finally. 'It brings out the worst in people.'

'Yeah,' said Hawk. 'But only if the evil is there to be brought out. Come on, lass, let's go.'

They shut the door behind them, and walked out of the grounds and down the steep hill that led back into the shadowed heart of the city. Even in the early morning light, Haven is a dark city.

Devil
take the
Hindmost

1

The Hollow Men

Every city has its favourite blood sports. Some cities prefer the traditional cruelties of bearbaiting or cockfights, while others indulge their baser appetites with gladiators and arenas. The city port of Haven gets its thrills from the dirtiest, bloodiest sport of all: politics.

It was election time in Haven, and the shutters were going up all over town. It was a time for banners and parades, speeches, and festivities, and the occasional, good old-fashioned riot. The streets were packed with excited crowds, pickpockets and cutpurses were having the time of their lives, and the taverns were making money hand over fist. Work in the city slowed to a standstill as everyone got caught up in election fever. Everyone except the Guards, who were working double shifts in an increasingly vain attempt to keep Haven from turning into a war zone.

It was autumn in Haven, and the weather was at its most civilised. The days were comfortably warm, and the nights delightfully cool. There was a constant breeze from off the ocean, and it rained just often enough to make people grateful for the times when it didn't. Just the kind of weather to make a man dissatisfied with his lot, and determined to get out and enjoy the weather while it lasted. Which meant there were even more people out on the streets than was usual for an election. The smart money was betting on a complete breakdown of law and order by mid-afternoon. Luckily the city only allowed twenty-four hours for electioneering. Anything more than that was begging for trouble. Not to mention civil war.

Hawk and Fisher, husband and wife and Captains in the city Guard, strolled unhurriedly down Market Street, and the bustling crowds parted quickly before them. Patience tended to be in short supply and tempers flared quickly around election time, but no one in Haven, drunk or sober, was stupid enough to upset Hawk and Fisher. There were quicker and less painful ways to commit suicide.

Hawk was tall and dark, but no longer handsome. A series of old scars ran down the right side of his face, pale against the tanned skin, and a black silk patch covered his right eye. He wore a simple white cotton shirt and trousers, and the traditional black cloak of the Guards. Normally he didn't bother with the cloak. It got in the way during fights. But with so many strangers come to town for the election, the cloak served as a badge of authority, so he wore it all the time now, with little grace and even less style. Hawk always looked a little on the scruffy side, and his boots in particular were old and battered, but a keen eye might have noticed that they had once been of very superior quality and workmanship. There were many rumours about Hawk's background, usually to do with whether or not his parents had been married, but no one knew anything for sure. The man's past was a mystery, and he liked it that way.

On the whole, he didn't look like much. He was lean and wiry rather than muscular, and beginning to build a stomach. He wore his dark hair at shoulder length, in defiance of fashion, swept back from his forehead and tied with a silver clasp. He had only just turned thirty, but already there were thick streaks of grey in his hair. At first glance he looked like just another bravo, past his prime and going to seed. But few people stopped at the first glance. There was something about Hawk, something in the scarred face and single cold eye that gave even the drunkest hardcase pause for thought. On his right hip Hawk carried a short-handled axe instead of a sword. He was very good with an axe. He'd had plenty of practice, down the years.

Isobel Fisher walked at Hawk's side, echoing his pace and stance with the naturalness of long companionship. She was tall, easily six feet in height, and her long blond hair fell to her waist in a single thick plait, weighted at the tip with a polished steel ball. She was in her mid to late twenties, and handsome rather than beautiful. There was a rawboned harshness to her face that contrasted strongly with her deep blue eyes and generous mouth. Somewhere in her past something had scoured all the human weaknesses out of her, and it showed. Like Hawk, she wore a cotton shirt and trousers, and the regulation black cloak. The shirt was half unbuttoned to show a generous amount of bosom, and her shirt sleeves were rolled up above her elbows, revealing arms corded with muscle and lined with old scars. Her boots were battered and scuffed and looked as though they hadn't been cleaned in years. Fisher wore a sword on her left hip, and her hand rested comfortably on the pommel.

Hawk and Fisher were known throughout Haven. Firstly, they were honest, which was in itself enough to mark them as unusual amongst Haven's overworked and underpaid Guards. And secondly, they kept the peace; whatever it took. Hawk and Fisher brought in the bad guys, dead or alive. Mostly dead.

People tended to be very law-abiding while Hawk and Fisher were around.

They made their way unhurriedly down Market Street, enjoying the early morning warmth, and keeping an eye on the street traders. The election crowds meant good pickings for the fast-food sellers, souvenir stalls, and back-alley conjurers with their cheap charms and amulets. Stalls lined the streets from one end to the other without a gap, varying from tatty affairs of wood and canvas to established family concerns with padded silk and beaded awnings. The clamour of the merchants was deafening, and the more tawdry the goods, the louder and more extravagant were the claims made on their behalf.

There were drink stands everywhere, competing with the taverns by offering cheap spirits with the traditional sign: DRUNK FOR A PENNY; DEAD DRUNK FOR TUPPENCE. There was beer as well, for the less adventurously minded. That came free, courtesy of the Conservatives. On the whole, they preferred the electorate to be well the worse for drink on polling day. That way, they were either grateful enough to vote Conservative in the hope of more free booze, or too drunk to raise any real opposition. And since the populace was also usually too drunk to riot, the Guards liked it that way too.

Everywhere Hawk and Fisher looked there were more traders' stalls, crowding the streets and spilling into the alleyways. There were flags and fireworks and masks and all kinds of novelties for sale, every one of them guaranteed to be worth a damn sight less than what you paid for it. If you wanted more upmarket souvenirs, like delicate china and glassware tastefully engraved with designs and slogans from the election, then you had to go uptown to find them. The Northside might have been upmarket once, but if so, it was so long ago that no one could remember when. These days the Northside was the hardest, poorest, and most dangerous area in Haven. Which was why Hawk and Fisher got the job of patrolling it. Partly because they were the best, and everyone knew it, but mainly because they'd made just as many enemies inside the Guard as out. It was possible to be too honest, in Haven.

Hawk looked wistfully at a stall offering spiced sausage meat on wooden skewers. It looked quite appetising, if you ignored the flies. Fisher noticed his interest, and pulled him firmly away.

'No, Hawk; we don't know what kind of meat went into those sausages. You can't afford to spend the rest of the day squatting in the jakes with your trousers round your ankles.'

Hawk laughed. 'You're probably right, Isobel. It doesn't matter; if I remember correctly, there's a tavern down here on the right that does an excellent lobster dinner for two.'

'It's too early for dinner.'

'All right; we'll have a lobster lunch, then.'

'You're eating too many snacks these days,' said Fisher sternly. 'It's a wonder you can still do up your sword belt.'

'Everyone's entitled to a hobby,' said Hawk.

They walked on in silence for a while, just looking around them, seeing what there was to be seen. People in the crowds waved and smiled, or ostentatiously ignored them. Hawk and Fisher gave them all the same polite nod, and walked on. They couldn't trust the smiles, and the rest didn't matter. Hawk's attention began to drift away. He'd been in Haven for five years now, and some days it seemed like fifty. He missed his homeland. He felt it most of all at autumn. Back in the Forest Kingdom, the leaves would be turning bronze and gold, and the whole sight and sound and smell of the Forest would be changing as the great trees prepared for winter. Hawk sighed quietly and turned his attention once again to the grimy stone houses and filthy cobbled streets of Haven. For better or worse, he was a city boy now.

Explosions shook the air ahead, and Hawk's hand went to his axe before he realised it was just more fireworks. The Haven electors were great ones for fireworks; the louder and more extravagant the better. Bright splashes of magically augmented colours burst across the sky, staining the clouds contrasting shades until they looked like a rather messy artist's pallet. There were several attempts at sign-writing in the sky, but they all got entangled with each other, producing only broken lines of gibberish. The various factions quickly grew bored, and began using the fireworks as ammunition against each other. There were shouts and yells and the occasional scream, but luckily the fireworks weren't powerful enough to do any real damage.

Hawk and Fisher just looked the other way and let them get on with it. It kept the crowds amused.

Sudden movement up ahead caught Hawk's eye, and he increased his pace slightly. The crowd at the end of the street had turned away from the fireworks to watch something more interesting. Already there were cheers and catcalls.

'Sounds like trouble,' said Hawk resignedly, drawing his axe.

'It does, doesn't it?' said Fisher, drawing her sword. 'Let's go and make a nuisance of ourselves.'

They pressed forward, and the crowd parted unwillingly before them, giving ground only because of the naked steel in the Guards' hands. Hawk frowned as he saw what had drawn the crowd's attention. At the intersection of two streets two rival gangs of posterers were fighting each other with fists, clubs, and anything else they could get their hands on. The crowd cheered both sides impartially, and hurried to lay bets on the outcome.

Since most of the electorate was barely literate, the main political parties couldn't rely on pamphlets or interviews in Haven's newspapers to get their message across. Instead, they trusted to open-air gatherings, broadsheet singers, and lots of posters. The posters tended to be simple affairs, bearing slogans or insults in very large type. COUNCILLOR HARDCASTLE DOES IT WITH TRADESMEN was a popular one at the moment, though whether that was a slogan or an insult was open to interpretation.

Posters could appear anywhere: on walls, shopfronts, or slow-moving passersby. A gang of posterers moving at full speed could slap posters up all over Haven in under two hours. Assuming the paste held out. And also assuming no one got in their way. Unfortunately, most gangs of posterers spent half their time tearing down or defacing posters put up by rival gangs. So when two gangs met, as was bound to happen on occasion, political rivalry tended to express itself through spirited exchanges and open mayhem, to the delight of whatever onlookers happened to be around at the time. Haven liked its politics simple and direct, and preferably brutal.

Hawk and Fisher stood at the front of the crowd and watched interestedly as the fight spilled back and forth across the cobbles. It was fairly amateurish, as fights went, with more pushing and shoving than actual fisticuffs. Hawk was minded to just wander off and let them get on with it. They weren't causing anyone else any trouble, and the crowd was too busy placing bets to get involved themselves. Besides, a good punch-up helped to take some of the pressure off. But then he saw knives gleaming in some of the posterers' hands, and he sighed regretfully. Knives changed everything.

He stepped forward into the fight, grabbed the nearest posterer with a knife, and slammed him face first against the nearest wall. There was an echoing meaty thud, and the posterer slid unconscious to the ground. His erstwhile opponent rounded on Hawk, knife at the ready. Fisher knocked him cold with a single punch. Several of the fallen posterers' friends started forward, only to stop dead as they took in Hawk's nasty grin and the gleaming axe in his hand. Some turned to run, only to find Fisher had already moved to block their way, sword in hand. The few remaining fights quickly broke up as they realised something was wrong. The watching crowds began booing and catcalling at the Guards. Hawk glared at them, and they shut up. Hawk turned his attention back to the posterers.

'You know the rules,' he said flatly. 'No knives. Now, turn out your pockets, the lot of you. Come on, get on with it, or I'll have Fisher do it for you.'

There was a sudden rush to see who could empty their pockets the quickest. A largish pile of knives, knuckle-dusters, and blackjacks formed on the cobbles. There were also a fair number of good-luck charms and trinkets, and one shrunken head on a string. Hawk looked at the posterers disgustedly.

'If you can't be trusted to play nicely, you won't be allowed to play at all. Understand? Now, get the hell out of here before I arrest the lot of you for loitering. One group goes North, the other goes South. And if I get any more trouble from any of you today, I'll send you home to your families in chutney jars. Now, move it!'

The posterers vanished, taking their wounded with them. Only a few crumpled posters scattered across the street remained to show they'd ever been there. Hawk kicked the pile of weapons into the gutter, and they disappeared down a storm drain. He and Fisher took turns glaring at the crowd until it broke up, and then they put away their weapons and continued their patrol.

'That was a nice punch of yours, Isobel.'

'My strength is as the strength of ten, because my heart is pure.'

'And because you wear a knuckle-duster under your glove.'

Fisher shrugged. 'On the whole, I thought we handled that very diplomatically.'

Hawk raised an eyebrow. 'Diplomatically?'

'Of course. We didn't kill anyone, did we?'

Hawk smiled sourly. Fisher sniffed. 'Look, Hawk, if we hadn't stepped in when we did, the odds were that fight would have developed into a full-blown riot. And how many would we have had to kill to stop a riot in its tracks?' Fisher shook her head. 'We've already had five riots since they announced the date of the election, and that was less than two days ago. Hawk, this city is going to the dogs.'

'How can you tell?' said Hawk, and Fisher snorted with laughter. Hawk smiled too, but there wasn't much humour in it. 'I don't think that bunch had it in them to riot. It was taking them all their time to work up to a disturbance of the peace. We didn't *have* to come down on them so hard.'

'Yes, we did.' Fisher gave Hawk a puzzled look. 'This is Haven, remember? The most violent and uncivilised city in the Low Kingdoms. The only way we can hope to keep the lid on things here is by being harder than everyone else.'

'I'm not sure I believe that anymore.'

They walked a while in silence.

'This is to do with the Blackstone case, isn't it?' said Fisher eventually.

'Yeah. That witch Visage might be alive today if she and Dorimant had talked to us in time. But they didn't trust us. They kept their mouths shut because they were afraid of our reputation. Afraid of what we might do to them. We've spent too long in this city, Isobel. I don't like what it's done to us.'

Fisher took his arm in hers. 'It's not really that much different here than anywhere else, love. They're just more open about it in Haven.'

Hawk sighed slowly. 'Maybe you're right. If we had arrested those posterers, I don't know where we could have put them. The gaols are crammed full to bursting as it is.'

'And there's still more than half a day to go before they vote.' Fisher shook her head slowly. 'I don't know why they don't just have a civil war and be done with it.'

Hawk smiled. 'About forty years ago they did. The Reformers won that one, and the result was universal suffrage throughout the Low Kingdoms. These days, the lead-up to the elections acts as a safety valve. People are allowed to go a little crazy for a while. They get to let off some steam, and the city avoids the buildup of pressures that lead to civil wars. After the voting's over, the winners declare a general amnesty, everyone goes back to work, and things get back to normal again.'

'Crazy,' said Fisher. 'Absolutely bloody crazy.'

Hawk grinned. 'That's Haven for you.'

They walked on in companionable silence, pausing now and then to intimidate some would-be pickpocket, or caution a drunk who was getting too loud. The crowds bustled around them, singing and laughing and generally making the most of their semiofficial holiday. The air was full of the smell of spiced food and wine and burning catherine wheels. A band came marching down the street towards them, waving brightly coloured banners and singing loudly the praises of Conservatism. Hawk and Fisher stood back to let them go by. A burly man wearing chain mail approached them, carrying a bludgeon in one hand and a collecting tin in the other. He took one look at their faces, thought better of it, and hurried after the parade. The crowd, meantime, showed its traditional appreciation of free speech by pelting the singers with rotten fruit and horse droppings. Hawk watched the banner holders disappear down the street with fixed smiles and gritted teeth, and wondered where the Conservatives had found enough idiots and would-be suicides to enter the Northside in the first place.

Nice banners, though.

'I'll be glad when this election nonsense is over,' said Fisher as they started on their way again. 'I haven't worked this hard in years. I don't think I've ever seen so many drunks and fights and street-corner rabble-rousers in my life. Or so many rigged games of chance, for that matter.'

'Anyone in this city stupid enough to play Find the Lady with a perfect stranger deserves everything that happens to him,' said Hawk unfeelingly. 'And when you get right down to it, things aren't that bad, actually. You're bound to get some fights during an election, but there's hardly anyone here wearing a sword or a knife. You know, Isobel, I'm almost enjoying myself. It's all so *fascinating*. I'd heard all the stories about past elections, but I never really believed them till now. This is democracy in action. The people deciding their own future.'

Fisher sniffed disdainfully. 'It'll all end in tears. The

people can vote till they're blue in the face, but at the end of the day the same old faces will still be in power, and things will go on just as they always have done. Nothing ever really changes, Hawk. You should know that.'

'It's different here,' said Hawk stubbornly. 'The Reform Cause has never been stronger. There's a real chance they could end up dominating the Haven Council this time, if they can just swing a few marginal Seats.'

Fisher looked at him. 'You've been studying up on this, haven't you?'

'Of course; it's important.'

'No, it isn't. Not to us. Come tomorrow, the same thieves and pimps and loan sharks will still be doing business as usual in the Northside, no matter who wins your precious election. There'll still be sweatshops and protection rackets and back-alley murders. This is Haven's dumping ground, where the lowest of the low end up because they can't sink any further. Let the Council have its election. They'll still need us to clean up the mess afterwards.'

Hawk looked at her. 'You sound tired, lass.'

Fisher shrugged quickly. 'It's just been a bad day, that's all.'

'Isobel . . .'

'Forget it, Hawk.' Fisher shot him a sudden smile. 'At least we'll never want for work, while the Northside still stands.'

Hawk and Fisher turned down Martyrs' Alley, and made their way out onto the Harbourside Promenade. The market stalls quickly disappeared, replaced by elegant shop-fronts with porticoed doors and fancy scrollwork round the windows, and an altogether better class of customers. The Promenade had been 'discovered' by the Quality, and its fortunes had prospered accordingly. Of late it had become quite the done thing for the minor aristocracy to take the air on the Promenade, and enjoy a little fashionable slumming. There were goods for sale on the edge of the Northside to tempt even the most jaded palates, and it did no harm to a gentleman's reputation to be able to drop the odd roguish hint of secret dealings and watch the ladies blush prettily at the breath of scandal. Not that a gentleman ever went into the Northside alone, of course. Each member of the Quality had his own retinue of bodyguards, and they were always careful to be safely out of the Northside before dark.

But during the daylight hours the Promenade was an acknowledged meeting place for the more adventurous members of the Quality, and as such it attracted all kinds of well-dressed parasites and hangers-on. Scandalmongers did a busy trade in all the latest gossip, and confidence tricksters strolled elegantly down the Promenade, eyeing the Quality in much the same way as a cruising shark might observe a passing shoal of minnows. Hawk and Fisher knew most of them by sight, but made no move to interfere. If people were foolish enough to throw away good money on wild-sounding schemes, that was their business, and nothing to do with the Guards. Hawk and Fisher were just there to keep an eye on things, and see that no one stepped out of line.

For their part, the Quality ignored Hawk and Fisher. Guards were supposed to know their place, and Hawk and Fisher were notorious throughout Haven for not having the faintest idea of what their place was. In the past, members of the Quality who'd tried to put them in their place had been openly laughed at and, on occasion, severely manhandled. Which was perhaps yet another reason Hawk and Fisher had spent the past five years patrolling the worst section of Haven.

The sun shone brightly over the Promenade, and the Quality blossomed under its warmth like so many eccentrically coloured flowers. Youngsters wearing party colours hawked the latest editions of the Haven newspapers, carrying yet more details of candidates' backgrounds, foul-ups, and rumoured sexual preferences. A boys' brigade of pipes and drums made its way along the Promenade, following a gorgeously coloured Conservative banner. The Conservatives believed in starting them young. Hawk stopped for a while to enjoy the music, but Fisher soon grew bored, so they moved off again. They left the bustling Promenade behind them, and made their way through the elegant houses and well-guarded establishments of Cheape Side, where the lower merchant classes held sway. They'd been attracted to the edge of the Northside by cheap property prices, and were slowly making their mark on the area.

The streets were reasonably clean, and the passersby were soberly dressed. The houses stood back from the street itself, protected by high stone walls and iron railings. And a fair sprinkling of armed guards, of course. The real Northside wasn't that far away. This was usually a quiet, even reserved area, but not even the merchant classes were immune to election fever. Everywhere you looked there were posters and broadsheet singers, and street-corner orators explaining how to cure all Haven's ills without raising property taxes.

Hawk and Fisher stopped suddenly as the sound of a gong resonated loudly in their heads. The sound died quickly away, to be replaced by the dry, acid voice of the Guard communications sorcerer:

Captains Hawk and Fisher, you are to report immediately to Reform candidate James Adamant, at his campaign headquarters in Market Faire. You have been assigned to protect him and his staff for the duration of the election.

A map showing the headquarters' location burned briefly in their minds, and then it and the disembodied voice were gone. Hawk shook his head gingerly. 'I wish he wouldn't use that bloody gong; it goes right through me.'

'They could do without the sorcerer entirely, as far as I'm

concerned,' said Fisher feelingly. 'I don't like the idea of magic-users having access to my mind.'

'It's just part of the job, lass.'

'What was wrong with the old system of runners with messages?'

Hawk grinned. 'We got too good at avoiding them.'

Fisher had to smile. They made their way unhurriedly through Cheape Side and on into the maze of interconnecting alleyways popularly referred to as The Shambles. It was one of the oldest parts of the city, constantly due for renovation but somehow always overlooked when the budget came round. It had a certain faded charm, if you could ignore the cripples and beggars who lined the filthy streets. The Shambles was no poorer than anywhere else in the Northside, but it was perhaps more open about it. Shadowy figures disappeared silently into inconspicuous doorways as Hawk and Fisher approached.

'Adamant,' said Fisher thoughtfully. 'I know that name.'

'You ought to,' said Hawk. 'A rising young star of the Reform Cause, by all accounts. He's contesting the High Steppes district, against a hardline Conservative Councillor. He might just take it. Councillor Hardcastle isn't what you'd call popular.'

Fisher sniffed, unimpressed. 'If Adamant's so important, how did he end up with us as his bodyguards?'

Hawk grunted unhappily. The last time he and Fisher had worked as bodyguards, everything had gone wrong. Councillor Blackstone had been murdered, despite their protection, and so had six other people. Important people. Hawk and Fisher had caught the killer eventually, but that hadn't been enough to save their reputation. They'd been in the doghouse with their superiors ever since. Not that Hawk or Fisher gave a damn. They blamed themselves more than their superiors ever could. They'd liked Blackstone.

'Well,' said Fisher finally, 'you've always said you wanted

a chance to study an election close-up, to see how it worked. It looks like you've got your chance after all.'

'Yeah,' said Hawk. 'Wait till you see Adamant in action, Isobel; he'll make a believer out of you.'

'It'll all end in tears,' said Fisher.

They were halfway down Lower Bridge Street, not far from the High Steppes boundary, when Hawk suddenly noticed how quiet it had become. It took him a while to realise, being lost in his thoughts of actually working with a Reform candidate, so the quiet hit him all the harder when it finally caught his attention. At first everything looked normal. The usual stalls lined the street, and the crowds bustled back and forth, like any other day. But the sound of the crowd barely rose above a murmur. The stall-holders stood quietly in their places, waiting patiently for customers to come to them, instead of following their usual practice of shouting and haranguing until the air itself echoed from the noise. The crowd made its way from stall to stall with bowed heads and down-cast eyes. No one exclaimed at the prices, or browbeat the stall-holders, or tried to bargain for a lower price. And strangest and most unsettling of all, no one stopped to speak to anyone else. They just went from stall to stall, speaking only when they had to, in the lowest of voices, as though they were just going through the motions. Hawk slowed to a halt, and Fisher stopped beside him.

'Yeah,' said Fisher. 'I noticed it too. What the hell's going on here? I've been to livelier funerals.'

Hawk grunted, his hand resting uneasily on the axe at his side. The more he studied the scene before him, the more unnerving it became. There were no street-corner orators, no broadsheet singers, and the few banners and posters in evidence flapped forlornly in the drifting breeze, ignored by the crowd. There should have been street-conjurers and knife grinders and itinerant tinkers, and all the other human flotsam and jetsam that street markets attract. But there was only the crowd, quiet and passive, moving unhurriedly between the stalls. Hawk looked up and down the narrow street, and all around him the empty windows stared back like so many blank idiot eyes.

'Something's happened here,' said Fisher. 'Something bad.'

'It can't be that bad,' said Hawk. 'We'd have heard something. News travels fast in Haven; bad news fastest of all.'

Fisher shrugged. 'Something still feels wrong. Very wrong.'

Hawk nodded slowly in agreement. They started down the street again, cloaks thrown back over their shoulders to leave their sword-arms free. The crowd made way before them, their heads averted so as not to meet the Guards' eyes. Their movements were slow and listless, and strangely synchronised, as though everyone on the street was moving in step with each other. The hackles began to stir on Hawk's neck. He glared about him, and then felt a sudden rush of relief as he spotted a familiar face.

Long Tom was a permanent fixture of Lower Bridge Street. Other stalls might come and go, but his was always there, selling the finest knives any man could wish for. He'd sell you anything from a kitchen knife to matched duelling daggers, but he specialised in military knives, in all their variations. Long Tom had lost both his legs in the army, and stomped around on a pair of sturdy wooden legs that added a good ten inches to his previous height. Hawk had gone to great pains to cultivate him. Long Tom always knew what was happening.

Hawk approached the stall with a friendly greeting on his lips, but the words died away unspoken as Long Tom raised his head to meet Hawk's gaze. For a moment Hawk thought a stranger had taken over the stall. The moment passed, and he quickly recognised the size and shape of the face before him, but still something was horribly wrong.

Long Tom's eyes had always been a calm and peaceful blue; now they were dark and piercing. His mouth was turned down in a bitter, unfamiliar smile. He even held himself differently, as though his weight and figure had changed drastically overnight. They were small differences, and a stranger might not have noticed them, but Hawk wasn't fooled. He nodded casually to Long Tom, and moved off without saying anything.

'What was that all about?' said Fisher.

'Didn't you notice anything different about him?' said Hawk, looking unobtrusively about.

Fisher frowned. 'He looked a bit off, but so what? Maybe he's had a lousy day too.'

'It's more than that,' said Hawk. 'Look around you. Look at their faces.'

The two Guards moved slowly through the quiet crowd, and Fisher felt a strange sense of unreality steal over her as she saw what Hawk meant. Everywhere she looked she saw strange eyes in familiar faces. Everyone had the same dark, piercing eyes, the same bitter smile. They even moved to the same rhythm, as though listening to the same silent song. It was like a childhood nightmare, where everyday friends and faces become suddenly cold, menacing strangers. Hawk reached surreptitiously inside his shirt and grasped the bone amulet that hung on a silver cord round his neck. It was a simple charm; standard issue for Guards during an election. It detected the presence of magic, and could lead you to whoever was responsible. Its range was limited, but it was never wrong. Hawk closed his hand around the carved bone, and it vibrated fiercely like a struck gong. He swore silently and took his hand away. He knew now why all the crowd shared the same dark eyes.

'They're possessed,' he said softly. 'All of them.'

'Oh, great,' said Fisher. 'You any good at exorcisms?'

'I was never any good at Latin.'

'Terrific.'

They'd kept their voices low, little more than murmurs, but already the crowd seemed to sense that something was wrong. Heads began to turn in the Guards' direction, and people began to drift towards them. Long Tom moved out from behind his stall, a knife in each hand. Hawk and Fisher began to back away, only to discover there were as many people behind them as in front. Fisher drew her sword, but Hawk put a hand on her arm.

'We can't use our weapons, Isobel. These people are innocent; just victims of the spell.'

'All right; so what do we do?'

'I don't know! I'm thinking!'

'Then think quickly. They're getting closer.'

'Look, it can't be a demon, or something escaped from the Street of Gods. Our amulets would have alerted us long before this if something that powerful was loose. No, this has to be some out-of-town sorcerer, brought in to stack the vote in this district.'

'I think we're in trouble, Hawk. They've blocked off both ends of this street.'

'We can't fight them, Isobel.'

'The hell we can't.'

The crowd closed in around them. The same dark eyes blazed in every face, and every hand held a weapon of some kind. Hawk reluctantly drew his axe, his mind working furiously. The sorcerer had to be somewhere close at hand, to be controlling so many people. He grabbed at his amulet with his free hand. The carved piece of bone burned with an uncomfortable heat. He spun round in a circle, and the amulet burned more fiercely for a moment. Hawk grinned. The amulet had been designed to track down sorcerers, as well as react to their spells. All he had to do was follow where it led him. He spun quickly back and forth to get a fix on the right direction, and then he charged into the crowd, knocking men and women out of the way with the flat of his axe. Fisher hurried after him.

The crowd fought back, lashing out with knives and cudgels and broken glass. Hawk parried most of the blows, but couldn't stop them all. He hissed with pain as a knife grated raggedly across his ribs, but fought down the impulse to strike back. Everywhere he looked he saw the same twisted smile, the same dark and angry eyes. The possessed washed against Hawk and Fisher like waves breaking on a stubborn rock, a never-ending tide of hollow men and women, fuelled by an alien anger. Knives and cudgels rose and fell, and blood flew on the quiet morning air.

Hawk careered down the street, the amulet burning painfully hot in his hand, and then ducked suddenly into a side alley. Fisher followed him in, and pulled over a stack of barrels so that they fell and blocked the alley mouth. The Guards leaned together against a cold brick wall, gasping for breath. Hawk wiped sweat and blood from his face with a shaking hand. He glanced across at Fisher, and winced at the cuts and bruises she'd acquired in their short run down the street.

'I hope you're still thinking,' said Fisher, her voice calm and steady. 'Those barrels won't hold them back for long.'

'The sorcerer's here somewhere,' said Hawk. 'Has to be. The amulet's practically burning a hole in my hand.'

There was a rasping clatter at the end of the alley as the hollow men pulled aside the fallen barrels. Light gleamed on knives and broken glass. Hawk glared quickly about him. There was a door to his right, set flush with the brickwork so that he almost missed it. He tried the handle, but it wouldn't budge. He shot a glance at Fisher.

'I'm going in. Hold them here as long as you can.'

'Sure, Hawk; I may have to kill some of them.'

'Do what you have to,' said Hawk. 'Just hold the door. Whatever it takes.'

Fisher moved forward to block the alleyway, and Hawk swung his axe at the door. The blade bit deeply into the rotten wood, and Hawk had to use all his strength to pull the blade free. He could hear the scuff of moving feet behind him, and the muffled thud of steel cutting into flesh, but he didn't look round. He swung his axe again and again, taking out his anger and frustration on the stubborn door. Finally it collapsed inward, and he forced his way past the splintered edges into the dark hallway beyond. A little light spilled in through the broken door, but it quickly faded away into an impenetrable gloom.

Hawk moved quickly away from the door. The light made him an easy target. He crouched down on his haunches in the dark, and waited impatiently for his eyes to adjust to the gloom. He could still hear sounds of a struggle in the alleyway outside, and his hands closed tightly around the shaft of his axe. He tried to concentrate on the hall itself, and strained his ears for any sound in his vicinity, but there was only the dark and the quiet. Hawk had never liked the dark. His hands were sweaty, and he wiped them one at a time on his trousers. The hall and a long flight of stairs slowly formed themselves out of the shadows before him. Hawk moved forward, one foot at a time, alert for any sign of a trap. Nothing moved in the shadows, and the stairway grew gradually closer.

He'd just reached the foot of the stairs when he heard footsteps on the landing above. Hawk froze in his tracks as four armed men started down the stairs towards him. He lifted his axe threateningly, but there was no reaction from any of them. He couldn't make out their faces in the dim light, but he had no doubt they all shared the same dark eyes and smile. Hawk hesitated a moment, torn by indecision. They were innocent men, all of them. Victims of the sorcerer's will. But he couldn't let them stop him. He licked his dry lips once, and went forward to meet them.

The first man cut viciously at Hawk's throat with his sword. Hawk ducked under the blow, and slammed his axe into the man's gut. The force of the blow threw the man back against the banisters. Hawk jerked his axe free, and blood and entrails fell out of the hideous wound it left. The possessed man ignored the wound and swung his sword again. Hawk parried the blow and brought his axe across in a quick vicious arc that sank deep into the man's throat, nearly tearing his head from his shoulders. He fell backwards, still trying to swing his sword, and Hawk pushed quickly past him to face the other three men, who were already advancing down the stairs towards him.

There was a flurry of steel on steel, and blood flew on the air. For all their unnatural stubbornness, the hollow men weren't very good fighters. Hawk parried most of the blows, and his axe cut and tore at them without mercy. But still they pressed forward, blood streaming from hideous wounds, unfeeling and unstoppable. Even the broken figure on the stairs behind him tried to grab at his ankles to pull him down. Hawk swung his axe with both hands, already bleeding from a dozen minor wounds. The sheer force of his attack opened up a space for a moment, and he threw himself forward. He burst through the hollow men, and ran up the stairs onto the landing. He paused for a moment to get his bearings. Above the sound of his own harsh breathing he could hear the hollow men coming after him. Light showed round the edges of a closed door at the end of the hallway. Hawk ran towards it, the hollow men close behind.

He hit the door without slowing, and it burst open. Strange lights blazed and flared within the room, and Hawk flinched as the sudden glare hurt his eye. A crudely drawn pentagram covered the bare wooden floor, the blue chalk lines flaring with a fierce, brilliant light. Inside the pentagram sat a tall spindly man wrapped in a shabby grey cloak. He looked round, startled at Hawk's sudden entrance, and in his face Hawk saw the familiar dark eyes and a mouth turned down in a bitter smile. Hawk moved purposefully forward. The amulet round his neck burned fiercely hot.

The sorcerer gestured with one hand, and the lines of the pentagram blazed suddenly brighter. Hawk slammed into a wall he couldn't see, and staggered backwards, off balance. An arm curled round his throat from behind and cut off his air. Hawk bent sharply forward at the waist, and threw the hollow man over his shoulder. He crashed into the invisible barrier and slid to the ground, momentarily stunned. Hawk heard more footsteps outside on the landing. He swore briefly, and beat at the barrier with his fist, to no avail. He cut at it with his axe, and the great steel blade passed through, unaffected. Hawk grinned savagely. Cold iron. The oldest defence against magic, and still the best. He lifted his axe, and threw it at the sorcerer.

The axe cut through the barrier as though it wasn't there. The sorcerer threw himself frantically to one side, and the axe just missed him, but one of his hands inadvertently crossed one of the lines of his pentagram. The brilliant blue light snapped out in a moment. There was the sound of falling bodies in the doorway behind Hawk, and the hollow man at his feet stopped struggling to rise. He lay still, in a widening pool of his own blood. The sorcerer scrambled to his feet. Hawk drew a knife from his boot and started forward. The sorcerer turned and ran towards a full-length mirror propped against the far wall.

Hawk felt a sudden prickling of unease, and ran after him. The sorcerer threw himself at the mirror and vanished into it. Hawk skidded to a halt, and stood before the mirror, staring at his own scowling reflection. He reached out a hand and hesitantly touched the mirror with his fingertips. The glass was cold and unyielding to his touch. He turned away and recovered his axe, and then smashed the mirror to pieces. Just to be sure.

Out in the alley, Fisher was sitting on one of the barrels, polishing her sword. There was blood on her face and on her clothes, some of it hers. She looked up tiredly as Hawk emerged from the house, but still managed a small smile for him. There were bodies scattered the length of the alley. Hawk sighed, and looked away.

'Seventeen,' said Fisher. 'I counted them.'

'What happened to the others?'

'They snapped out of it when you killed the sorcerer, and made a break for it.' She saw the look on his face, and frowned. 'Not dead?'

'Unfortunately, no. He got away.'

Fisher looked down the alley. 'Then, this was all for nothing.'

'Come on, lass; it's not that bad.' He sat down on the barrel beside her, and she leaned wearily against him. He put an arm round her shoulders. 'All right, he got away. But once we've spread the word, he won't be able to try this scam again for years.'

'What was the point of it, anyway?'

'Simple enough. He possesses a whole bunch of people, as many as he can control. A first-class sorcerer could easily manage a thousand or more, as long as they didn't have to do much. When polling starts, they all troop off and vote for whoever was paying the sorcerer. Afterwards, the sorcerer would kill them all, so they couldn't talk out of turn. The mastermind is elected, becomes a Councillor, and there's no one left to say it was anything but fair and aboveboard. Don't take this so badly, Isobel. We may have killed a few people here today, but we've saved a hell of a sight more.'

'Yeah,' said Fisher. 'Sure.'

'Come on,' said Hawk. 'We've just got time for a quick healing spell before we have to meet Adamant.'

They got to their feet and started down the alley. The flies were already settling on the bodies.

2

A Gathering of Forces

High Steppes wasn't the worst area in Haven. That dubious honour went to the Devil's Hook: a square mile of festering slums and alleyways bordering on the docks. The Hook was held together by abject poverty on the one hand, and greed and exploitation on the other. Some said it was the place plague rats went to die, because they felt at home there. Those who lived in the High Steppes thought about the Hook a lot. It comforted them to know there was at least one place in Haven where the people were worse off than themselves.

There was a time when the High Steppes had been a fairly respectable area, but that was a long time ago. The only reminders of that time were a few weathered statues, a public baths closed down for health reasons, and some of the fancier street names. The old family mansions had long since been converted into separate rooms and apartments, and the long, terraced streets were falling apart from a general lack of care and repair. Predators walked the streets day and night, in all their many guises. A few minor merchant houses had moved into the fringes, attracted by the relatively cheap property prices, but so far their efforts to improve the area had met with little success. As with so many other things in Haven, there were too many vested interests who liked things the way they were. Politically, the Steppes had always been neutral. Not to mention disinterested. The Conservatives won the elections because they paid out the most in bribes, and because it was dangerous to vote against them.

James Adamant might just be the one to change all that.

He'd been born into a minor aristocratic line, and seen it collapse as a child when the money ran out. The Adamants eventually made it all back through trade, only to find themselves snubbed by the Quality, because they'd lowered themselves to become merchants. Adamant's father died young. Some said as the result of a weak heart; some said through shame. All of this, plus first-hand experience of what it was really like to be poor, had given James Adamant a series of insights not common to those of his standing. On coming of age he discovered politics and, more particularly, Reform. They'd done well by each other.

Now he was standing for the High Steppes Seat: his first election as a candidate. He had no intention of losing.

James Adamant was a tall, powerful man in his late twenties. He dressed well, but not flamboyantly, and favoured sober colours. His dark hair was long enough to be fashionable but short enough that it didn't get in his eyes. Most of the time it looked as though it could use a good combing, even after it had just had one. He had strong patrician features, and a wide easy smile that made him a lot of friends. You had to know him some time before you could see past the smile to recognise the cool, steady gaze and the stubborn chin. He was a romantic and an idealist, despite being a politician, but deep within him he kept a carefully cultivated streak of ruthlessness. It had stood him well in the past, and no doubt would do so again in the future. Adamant valued his dreams too much to risk losing them through weakness or compromise.

His political adviser, Stefan Medley, was his opposite in practically every way there was. Medley was average height and weight, with bland, forgettable features saved by bright red hair and piercing green eyes that missed nothing. He burned with nervous energy from morning till night, and even standing still he looked as though he were about to leap on an enemy and rip his throat out. He was several years older than Adamant, and had seen a great deal more of political life. Perhaps too much. He'd spent all his adult life in politics, for one master or another. He'd never stood as a candidate, and never wanted to. He was strictly a backstage man. He worked in politics because he was good at it; no other reason. He had no Cause, no dreams, and no illusions. He'd fought elections on both sides of the political fence, and as a result was respected by both sides and trusted by neither.

And then he met Adamant, and discovered he believed in the man, even if he didn't believe in his Cause. They became friends, and eventually allies, each finding in the other what they lacked in themselves. Working together, they'd proved unstoppable. Which was why Reform had given them the toughest Seat to fight. Adamant trusted Medley, in spite of his past. Medley trusted Adamant because of it. Everyone needs something to believe in. Particularly if they don't believe in themselves.

Adamant sat at his desk in his study, and Medley sat opposite him, perched on the edge of a straight-back chair. The study was a large, comfortable room with well-polished furniture and well-padded chairs. Superbly crafted portraits and tapestries added a touch of colour to the dark-panelled walls. Thick rugs covered the floor, from a variety of beasts, few of them from the Low Kingdoms. There were wine and brandy decanters on the sideboard, and a selection of cold food on silver platters. Adamant liked his comforts. Probably because he'd had to do without so many as a child. He looked at the bank draft before him – the latest of a long line – sighed quietly, and signed it. He didn't like paying out money for bribes.

He shuffled the money orders together and handed them to Medley, who tucked them into his wallet without looking at them.

'Anything else you need, Stefan?' said Adamant,

stretching slowly. 'If not, I'm going to take a break. I've done nothing but deal with paperwork all morning.'

'I think we've covered everything,' said Medley. 'You really should develop a more positive attitude to paperwork, James. It's attention to details that wins elections.'

'Perhaps. But I'll still feel better when we're out on the streets campaigning. You do your best work with paper; I do my best with people. And besides, all the time I'm sitting here I can't escape the feeling that Hardcastle is hard at work setting up traps and pitfalls for us to fall into.'

'I've told you before, James; let me worry about things like that. You're fully protected; Mortice and I have seen to that.'

Adamant nodded thoughtfully, not really listening. 'How long have we got before my people start arriving?'

'About an hour.'

'Perhaps I should polish my speech some more.'

'You leave that speech alone. It doesn't need polishing. We've already rewritten it within an inch of its life, and rehearsed the damn thing till it's coming out of our ears. Just say the words, wave your arms around in the right places, and flash the big smile every second line. The speech will do the rest for you. It's a good speech, James; one of our best. It'll do the job.'

Adamant laced his fingers together, and stared at them pensively for a long moment before turning his gaze to Medley. 'I'm still concerned about the amount of money we're spending on bribes and . . . gratuities, Stefan. I can't believe it's really necessary. Hardcastle is an animal and a thug, and everyone knows it. No one in their right mind would vote for him.'

'It's not that simple, James. Hardcastle's always been very good at maintaining the status quo, and that's what Conservatism is all about. They're very pleased with him. And most Conservatives will vote the way their superiors tell them to, no matter whose name is on the ticket. Hardcastle's also very strong on law and order, and violently opposed to the Trade Guilds, both of which have made him a lot of friends in the merchant classes. And there are always those who prefer the devil they know to the devil they don't. That still leaves a hell of a lot of people unaccounted for, but if we're going to persuade them to vote for us, we've got to be able to operate freely. Which means greasing the right palms.'

'But seven and a half thousand ducats! I could raise a small army for not much more.'

'You might have to, if I didn't approach the right people. There are sorcerers to be paid off, so they won't interfere. There are Guard officers to sweeten, to ensure we get the protection we're entitled to. Then there's donations to the Street of Gods, to the Trade Guilds; do I really need to go on? I know what I'm doing, James. You worry about the ideals, and leave the politics to me.'

Adamant fixed him with a steady gaze. 'If something's being done in my name, I want to know about it. All about it. For example, hiring mercenaries for protection. Apparently we have thirty-seven men working for us. Is that really the best we can do? At the last election, Hardcastle had over four hundred mercenaries working for him.'

'Yeah, well; mercenaries are rather scarce on the ground this year. It seems there's a major war shaping up in the Northern countries. And wars pay better than politicians. Most of those who stayed behind had long-term contracts with the Conservatives. We were lucky to get thirty-seven men.'

Adamant gave Medley a hard look. 'I have a strong feeling I already know the answer to this – but why weren't these thirty-seven men already signed up?'

Medley shrugged unhappily. 'Nobody else would take them . . .'

Adamant sighed, and pushed his chair back from the

desk. 'That's wonderful. Just wonderful. What else can go wrong?'

Medley tugged at his collar. 'Is it me, or is it getting warm in here?'

Adamant started to reply, and then stopped as his adviser suddenly stared right past him. Adamant spun round, and found that the great study window was completely steamed over, the glass panes running with condensation. As he watched, the lines of condensation traced a ragged face in the steam, with staring eyes and a crooked smile. A thick, choking voice eased through their minds like a worm through wet mud.

I know your names, and they have been written in blood on cooling flesh. I will break your bones and drink your blood, and I will see the life run out of you.

The voice fell silent. The eye patches slowly widened, destroying the face, and the air was suddenly cool again.

Adamant turned his back on it. 'Nasty,' he said curtly. 'I thought Mortice's wards were supposed to protect us from things like that?'

'It was just an illusion,' said Medley quickly. 'Very low power. Probably sneaked in round the edges. Believe me, nothing dangerous can get to us here. They're just trying to shake us up.'

'And doing a bloody good job of it, from the looks on your faces,' said Dannielle Adamant, sweeping into the study. Adamant got to his feet and greeted his wife warmly. Medley nodded politely, and looked away. Adamant took his wife's hands in his.

'Hello, Danny; I didn't expect you back for ages.'

'I had to give up on the shops, dear. The streets are simply impossible, even with those nice men you provided to make a way for me. Oh, by the way; one of them is sulking, just because he dropped a few parcels and I was rude to him. I didn't know bodyguards were so sensitive. Anyway, the crowds got too much to bear, so I came home early. The

Steppes must be bursting at the seams. I've never seen so many people out in daylight before.'

'I know you don't like the area,' said Adamant. 'But it's politically necessary for us to live in the area I intend to represent.'

'Oh, I quite understand, dear. Really.'

She sank into the most comfortable chair, and nodded pleasantly to Medley. Away from Adamant, they didn't really get on. It was hardly surprising, considering the only thing they had in common was James Adamant.

Dannielle came form a long-established Society family, and until she met Adamant, she'd never even thought about politics. She voted Conservative because Daddy always had. Adamant had opened her eyes to a great many injustices, but like Medley she was more interested in the man than his politics. Still, her strong competitive streak made her just as enthusiastic a campaigner as her husband. Even though most of her family were no longer talking to her.

Dannielle was just twenty-one years old, with a neat figure, a straight back, and a long neck that made her look taller. She was dressed in the very latest fashion and wore it with style, though she had strong reservations about the bustle. She looked very lovely in ankle-length midnight-blue, and she knew it. She particularly liked the way it set off her powdered white shoulders and short curly black hair.

Her face was well-known throughout Haven, having been immortalised by several major portrait painters. She had a delicate, heart-shaped face, with high cheekbones and dark eyes you could drown in. When she smiled, you knew it was for you, and you alone. James Adamant thought she was the most beautiful woman he'd ever seen, and he wasn't alone in that. The younger aristocracy had marked Dannielle as their own from the moment she entered High Society. After she married Adamant several young blades from among the Quality declared a vendetta against him for stealing her away from them. They tended to be rather quiet about it after Adamant killed three of them in duels.

'So,' said Dannielle, smiling brightly, 'How are things going, darling? Are you and Stefan finished talking business?'

'For the moment,' said Adamant, sinking back into his chair. 'I haven't had much time for you lately, have I, my dear? I'm sorry, Danny, but it's been a madhouse round here these last few weeks. Still, there's a good hour or so before the big speech. Better get some rest while you can, love. After the speech we have to go out into the streets to shake hands and kiss babies. Or possibly vice versa.'

'That can wait,' said Dannielle. 'Right now, your friend Mortice wants a word with you.'

Adamant looked at Medley. 'Have you ever noticed that whenever Mortice does something aggravating, he's always *my* friend?'

Medley nodded solemnly.

Market Faire had a bad reputation, even for the Northside, which took some doing. You could buy anything at the Faire, if you had the price; anything from a curse to a killing. You could place a bet or buy a rare drug, choose a partner for the evening or arrange an unfortunate fire for a bothersome competitor. Judges lived in the Faire, and high-ranking members of the Guard, along with criminals and necromancers and anarchists. The Faire was a meeting ground; a place to make deals. Hawk couldn't help wondering if that was why Adamant had chosen to place his campaign headquarters in Market Faire.

He and Fisher made their way unhurriedly down the main street, and the crowds made way before them. The two Guards nodded politely to familiar faces, but their hands never moved far from their weapons. Market Faire was an old, rather shabby area, for all its brightly painted façade. The stone walls were weathered and discoloured, there were cracks in the pavements, and from the smell of it the drains had backed up again. Still, all things were relative. At least the Faire had drains. Bravos swaggered through the bustling crowds, thumbs tucked into their sword belts, eyes alert for anything they could take as an insult. None of them were stupid enough to lock stares with Hawk and Fisher.

Adamant's house was planted square in the middle of the main street, tucked away behind high stone walls and tall iron gates. There were jagged spikes on the gates and broken glass on top of the walls. Two armed men in full chain mail stood guard before the gates. The younger of the two stepped forward to block Hawk and Fisher's way as they approached the gates. Hawk smiled at him easily.

'Captains Hawk and Fisher, city Guard, to see James Adamant. We're expected.'

The young guard didn't smile back. 'Anyone can claim to be a Guard Captain. You got any identification?'

'You're new in town, aren't you?' said Fisher.

Hawk lifted his left hand, to show the Captain's silver torc at his wrist. 'The man's just doing his job, Isobel.'

'Things have been a little unsettled around here recently,' said the older of the two guards. 'I know you, Captain Hawk, Captain Fisher. I'm glad you're here. Adamant's going to need some real protection before this election's over.'

The younger guard sniffed loudly. Hawk looked at him. 'Anything the matter?'

The young guard looked insolently at him. 'You're a lot older than I thought you'd be. Are you really as good as they say?'

Fisher's sword leapt into her hand, and a split second later the point of her sword was hovering directly before the young guard's left eyeball. 'No,' she said calmly. 'We're better.'

She stepped back and sheathed her sword in a single fluid

movement. The young guard swallowed loudly. The older guard smiled, unlocked the heavy gates, and pushed them open. Hawk nodded politely, and he and Fisher entered the grounds of Adamant's house.

'Show-off,' said Hawk quietly. Fisher grinned.

The gates swung shut behind them with a dull, emphatic thud. The house at the end of the gravel pathway was a traditional two-storey mansion, with gable windows and a front porch large enough to shelter a small army. Anywhere else in the Steppes, a place like this would have had a whole family living in each room. Ivy sprawled across most of the front wall, its thickness suggesting that it alone was holding the aged brickwork together. There were four squat chimney pots at one end of the roof, all of them smoking. Hawk looked unhappily around him as he and Fisher made their way through the grounds towards the house. The wide grass lawns were faded and withered, and there were no flowers. The air smelled rank and oppressive. The single tree was dark and twisted, its branches bare. It looked as though it had been poisoned and then struck by lightning.

'This,' said Fisher positively, 'is a dump. Are you sure this is the right place?'

'Unfortunately, yes.' Hawk sniffed the air cautiously. 'Nothing's grown here for years. Still, not everyone likes gardening.'

They walked the rest of the way in silence. Hawk strained his ears for some sound apart from their own boots on the gravel drive, but the grounds were unnaturally quiet. By the time they got to the massive front door, Hawk had managed to thoroughly unsettle himself. At the very least there should have been the bustling sounds of the heavy crowds outside, the everyday clamour of a city at work and at play. Instead, Adamant's house and grounds stood stark and still in their own little pool of silence.

There was a large and blocky brass knocker on the door, shaped like a lion's head with a brass ring in its jaws. Hawk knocked twice, raising loud echoes, and then quickly let go of the brass ring. He had an uneasy feeling the lion's head was looking at him.

'Yeah,' said Fisher quietly. 'I feel it too. This place gives me the creeps, Hawk.'

'We've seen worse. Anyway, you can't judge a man by where he happens to be living. Even if he has got a graveyard for a garden.'

They fell silent as the massive door swung silently open on its counterweights. The man standing in the doorway was tall, broad-shouldered, and dressed immaculately in the slightly out-of-date formal wear that identified him immediately as a butler. He looked to be in his early fifties, with a supercilious expression, a bald head, and ridiculous tufts of white hair above his ears. He held himself very correctly, and his gaze said that he had seen it all before, and hadn't been impressed then, either. He bowed very politely to Hawk, and, after a moment's hesitation, to Fisher.

'Good morning, sir and madam. I am Villiers, Master Adamant's butler. If you'll follow me, Master Adamant is expecting you.'

He stepped back a careful two paces, and then stood at attention while Hawk and Fisher entered. He closed the door quietly, and Hawk and Fisher seized the opportunity for a quick look around the hall. It was comfortably spacious without seeming overbearing, and the wood-panelled walls glowed warmly in the lamplight. Hawk approved of the lamps. Too many halls were oversized and underlit, as though there was something fashionable about eyestrain. He realised Villiers was standing politely at his side, and turned unhurriedly to face him.

'Villiers, you're standing on my shadow. I don't normally like people like that close to me.'

'I'm sorry, sir. I was just wondering if you and your . . . partner would care to remove your cloaks. It is customary.'

'I don't think so,' said Hawk. 'Maybe later.'

Villiers bowed slightly, his impassive face somehow managing to convey that of course they knew best, even when they were wrong. He led the way down the hall, without looking to see if they were following, and ushered them into a large, comfortably appointed library. All four walls were lined with bookshelves, and leather-bound book spines gleamed dully from every direction. There was one comfortable chair by the fireplace, which Fisher immediately appropriated, stretching her legs out before her. Villiers cleared his throat politely.

'If you would be so kind as to wait here, I will inform Master Adamant of your arrival.'

He bowed again, to just the right degree, and left the library, closing the door quietly but firmly behind him.

'I never did like butlers,' said Fisher. 'They're always such terrible snobs. Worse than their employers, usually.' She looked at the empty fireplace, and shivered. 'Is it just me, or is it freezing cold in here?'

'Probably just feels that way, coming in from the warmth outside. These big places hold the cold.'

Fisher nodded, looking absently around her. 'Do you suppose he's really read all these books?'

'Shouldn't think so,' said Hawk. 'Probably bought them by the yard. Having your own library is quite fashionable, at the moment.'

'Why?'

'Don't ask me. I've never understood fashion.'

Fisher looked at him sharply. There had been something in his voice . . . 'This isn't what you'd expected, is it?'

'No,' said Hawk. 'It isn't. James Adamant is supposed to be a man of the people, representing the poor and the downtrodden. This kind of lifestyle is the very thing he's always campaigned against. A big house, a butler, books he's never read. Dammit, he can't even be bothered to look after the place properly.'

'Don't blame me,' said Adamant. 'I didn't choose this monstrosity.'

Hawk turned round quickly, and Fisher rose elegantly to her feet as James Adamant entered the library, followed by Dannielle and Medley.

'I'm sorry to have kept you waiting,' said Adamant. 'Captains Hawk and Fisher, may I present my wife, Dannielle, and my adviser, Stefan Medley.'

There was a quick flurry of bows and handshakes. Dannielle extended a hand for Hawk to kiss. He shot a quick glance at Fisher, and shook the hand instead.

'I think we'd all be much more comfortable in my study,' said Adamant easily. 'This way.'

He led them back down the hall and ushered them into the study, chatting amiably all the way. 'My superiors insisted we take on this draught-ridden folly as Reform Headquarters, and in a moment of weakness, I agreed. It's quite unsuitable, of course, but the current thinking is that we have to put on as good a show as the Conservatives or the voters won't take us seriously. Personally, I think it's that kind of half-baked nonsense that's undermined Reform's credibility with the electorate these past few years. But since I'm only a very junior candidate, I don't get much say in these matters.'

Medley brought in some more chairs, and Dannielle bustled around making sure that everyone was comfortably seated and had a brimming glass of wine in their hand.

'How do you feel about this place?' Hawk asked her politely.

'Ghastly old heap. Smells of damp, and half the time the toilets don't work properly.'

'Your garden's not up to much, either,' said Fisher. Hawk winced.

Dannielle and Adamant shared a look, their faces suddenly grim.

'We have enemies, Captain Fisher,' said Adamant evenly.

'Enemies not averse to using sorcery, when they can get away with it. Three days ago we had a splendid garden. Fine lawns, well-tended flower beds, and a magnificent old apple tree. And now it's all gone. Nothing will grow there. It's not safe even to walk far from the path. There are things moving in the dead earth. I think they come out at night, sometimes. No one's ever seen them, but come the morning there are scratches on the door and shutters that weren't there the night before.'

There was a cold silence for a moment.

'It's illegal for political candidates to use sorcery in any form,' said Hawk finally. 'Directly or indirectly. If you can prove Hardcastle was responsible . . .'

'There's no proof,' said Dannielle. 'He's too clever for that.'

There was another silence.

'You made good time in getting here,' said Medley brightly. 'I only put in my request for you this morning.'

Hawk looked at him. 'You asked for us specifically?'

'Well, yes. James has many enemies. I wanted the best people I could get as his bodyguards. You and your partner have an excellent reputation, Captain Hawk.'

'That isn't always enough,' said Fisher. 'The last time we got involved with guarding a politician, the man died.'

'We know about Councillor Blackstone,' said Medley. 'It wasn't your fault he died; you'd done everything you reasonably could to protect him. And you found his murderer, long after any other Guards would have given up.'

Hawk looked at Adamant. 'Are you happy with this arrangement, sir Adamant? It's not too late for you to find somebody else.'

'I trust my adviser,' said Adamant. 'When it comes to picking the right people for the job, his judgement is impeccable. Stefan knows about such things. Now then, if you and your partner are going to be spending some time with us, I'd better bring you up to date on what's happening in the election. What kind of things do you need to know, Captain Hawk?'

'Everything,' said Hawk flatly. 'Who your enemies are, what kind of opposition you'll be facing. Anything that might give us an edge.'

Dannielle got to her feet. 'If you're going to get all technical, I think I'll go and see how dinner's coming along.'

'Now, Danny, you promised you wouldn't bother the cook anymore,' said Adamant. 'You know she hates people looking over her shoulder.'

'For what we're paying her, she can put up with a little criticism,' said Dannielle calmly. She smiled graciously at Hawk and Fisher, and left the room, closing the door quietly behind her.

'Now then,' said Adamant, leaning comfortably back in his chair. 'When you get right down to it, there are only two main parties: Conservative and Reform. But there's also a handful of fringe parties, and a few well-supported independents, just to complicate things. There's Free Trade, the Brotherhood of Steel, No Tax on Liquor (also known as the Who's for a Party Party), and various pressure groups, such as the Trade Guilds and some of the better organised militant religions.'

'The Conservatives are the main threat,' said Medley. 'They've got the most money. Free Trade is mainly a merchants' party. They make a lot of speeches, but they're short on popular support. Mostly they end up throwing their weight behind the Conservatives. No Tax on Liquor is the Lord Sinclair's personal party. He funds it and runs it, practically single-handed. There are always people willing to go along with him, if only for the free booze he dishes out. He's harmless, apart from this one bee in his bonnet. The Trade Guilds mean well, but they're too disorganised to mount any real threat to the Conservatives, and they know it. Usually they end up working hand-in-hand with Reform. That's where a lot of our funding comes from.'

'What about the Brotherhood of Steel?' said Fisher. 'I always thought they were more mystical than political.'

'The two are pretty much the same in Haven,' said Adamant. 'Power and religion have always gone hand-in-hand here. Luckily most of the Beings on the Street of Gods are more interested in feuding with each other than getting involved in the day-to-day politics of running Haven. The Beings have always been great ones for feuds. But, over the past few years the Brotherhood of Steel has changed its ways. They're nowhere near as insular as they used to be; they're much better organised, and just lately a militant branch has started flexing its political muscle. They've even got a candidate standing in this election. He won't win; they're not that strong yet. But they could be a deciding factor in who does win.'

Hawk frowned. 'Who would they be most likely to side with?'

'Good question,' said Medley. 'I can think of any number of political fixers who'd pay good money for the answer. I don't know, Captain Hawk. Ordinarily I'd have said the Conservatives, but the Brotherhood's mystical bent confuses the hell out of me. I don't trust fanatics. There's no telling which way they'll jump when the pressure's on.'

'All right,' said Hawk. 'Now that we're clear on that . . .'

'Speak for yourself,' muttered Fisher.

'. . . perhaps you could explain exactly what's at stake in this election. A lot of people have been saying Reform could end up dominating the Council, even if the Conservatives still hold most of the Seats. I don't get that.'

'It's really very simple,' said Adamant, and Hawk's heart sank. Whenever people said that, it always meant things were about to become very, very complicated. Adamant steepled his fingers, and studied them thoughtfully. 'There are twenty-one Seats on the Council, representing the various districts of Haven. After the last election, Reform held four Seats, the Conservatives held eleven, and there were six unaffiliated Seats. Which meant in practice that the Conservatives ran the Council to suit themselves. But this time there are at least three Seats that could go either way. All Reform has to do is win one extra Seat, and together with the six independents we could take control of the Council away from the Conservatives. Which is why this particular election is all set for some of the dirtiest and most vicious political infighting Haven has ever seen.'

'Great,' said Fisher. 'Just what the people need. Another excuse to go crazy, riot in the streets, and set fire to things. How long is this madness going to go on for?'

'Not long,' said Medley, smiling. 'After the result has been announced this evening, there will be general fighting and dancing in the streets, followed by the traditional fireworks display and the paying off of old scores by the victorious party. After that, Haven will go deathly quiet, as everyone disappears to bind their wounds, get some sleep, and nurse their hangovers. Not necessarily in that order. Everything clear now?'

'Almost,' said Hawk. 'What are we doing here?'

Adamant looked at Medley, and then back at Hawk. 'I understood you'd been told. You and your partner are here to act as my bodyguards until the election is over.'

'You don't need us for that,' said Hawk flatly. 'You've got armed men at your gates, and probably quite a few more scattered around the house. And if you'd still felt the need for a professional bodyguard, there are any number of agencies in Haven that could have provided you with one. But you asked for us, specifically, despite our record. Why us, Adamant? What can we do for you that your own men can't?'

Adamant leaned back in his chair, and some of his strength seemed to go out of him for a moment, only to return again as he lifted his eyes and met Hawk's gaze squarely. 'Two main reasons, Captain Hawk. Firstly, there have been death threats made against me and my wife. Quite nasty threats. Normally I wouldn't worry too much. Elections always bring out the cranks. But I have reason to believe that these threats may be genuine. There have been three separate attempts on my life already, all of them quite professional. Stefan tells me there are whispers that the attacks were sanctioned by Councillor Hardcastle himself.

'Secondly, it seems I have a traitor among my people. Someone has been leaking information, important information, about my comings and goings, and my security arrangements. That person has also been embezzling money from my campaign funds. According to Stefan's investigations, it's been going on for some months; small amounts at first, but growing larger all the time. What evidence we have been able to piece together suggests the traitor has to be someone fairly close to me; my friends, my servants, my fellow campaign workers. Someone I trusted has betrayed me. I want you two to act as my bodyguard, and identify the traitor.'

Out in the hall, a woman screamed. Hawk and Fisher surged to their feet, reaching for their weapons. The scream came again, and was suddenly cut short.

'Danny!' Adamant jumped up from his chair and ran for the door. Hawk got there first, and yanked the door open. Out in the hall it was raining blood. Thick crimson gobbets materialised near the ceiling and poured down with unrelenting ferocity. The walls ran with blood, and the rugs were already soaked. The stench was sickening.

Dannielle had been caught halfway up the stairs. She was drenched in blood. Her dress was ruined, and thick rivulets of gore ran out of her matted hair and down her face. She ran down the stairs to Adamant, and he held her in his arms, glaring about him through the pouring blood. Hawk and Fisher stood back to back in the middle of the hall, weapons at the ready, but there was only the blood, streaming down around them, thick and heavy. Medley flailed about him with his arms, as though trying to swat the falling drops of blood like flies.

'Get your wife out of here!' Hawk yelled to Adamant. 'This is sorcerer's work!'

Adamant started to hurry Dannielle towards the front door, and then stopped short as a dark shape began to materialise between them and the door. The falling blood ran together, drop joining with drop, to form the beginnings of a body. In the space of a few moments it grew arms and legs and a hunched misshapen body. It stood something like a man, but the proportions were all wrong. It had huge teeth and claws, and swirling dark clots of blood where its eyes should have been. It moved slowly towards its prey, its body heaving and swelling with every movement.

Hawk stepped forward and cut at it with his axe. The heavy steel blade sliced through the creature's neck and out again without slowing, sending a wave of blood splashing against the wall. The creature stood its ground, unaffected. It was only blood, nothing more. Its substance ran away onto the floor, but more blood continued falling from the ceiling to replenish it.

Hawk and Fisher both cut at the figure, and it laughed silently at them. It lashed out at Hawk with a dripping arm. Hawk braced himself and met the blow with his axe, but even so, the impact sent him staggering backwards. The creature had weight and substance, when it chose to. It started towards Hawk, ignoring Fisher's attempts to draw its attention to her. It struck at Hawk again, and he ducked under the blow at the last moment. Its claws dug ragged furrows in the wall panelling. Hawk scuttled away from the creature, snarling curses at the thing as it turned to follow him.

'Right,' he said breathlessly, 'That's it. We're no match for this kind of magic. Adamant, get your people together and then herd them out the back door. We'll try and buy you some time. Most sendings can't travel far from where they materialise. Maybe we can outrun the bloody thing.'

Adamant nodded quickly, and urged his wife down the hall away from the creature. The rain of blood suddenly increased, pouring down even more thickly than before. Through the crimson haze, Hawk could just make out a second shape beginning to form between them and the other exit. Hawk wiped blood from his face, and took a firmer grip on his axe.

He heard Fisher's warning scream behind him, and had just started to turn when the first blood-creature swept over him like a wave and all the world went red. As the creature enveloped him, he staggered back a pace, scrabbling frantically at the blood that covered his face, cutting off his air. Fisher was quickly at his side, trying to wipe the blood away from his nose and mouth, but it resisted her efforts and clung to his face like taffy. Hawk fell forward onto his hands and knees, shaking his head frantically as his lungs screamed for air. He caught a glimpse of Adamant hovering before him, and gestured weakly for him to make a run for the front door while he had the chance. Adamant hesitated; then lifting his head, he raised his voice in a carrying shout:

'Mortice! Help us!'

A blast of freezing air suddenly swept through the hall, a bitter icy wind that froze the falling blood into shimmering scarlet crystals. The creature enveloping Hawk cracked apart around him and fell away in hundreds of crimson slivers. He stayed hunched on his knees for a moment, gratefully drawing the icy air into his lungs, then rose slowly to his feet and looked around him. The bloody rain had stopped, and the hall was covered in a sheen of crimson ice. Fisher was standing nearby, beating scarlet ice from her cloak. Adamant, Medley, and Dannielle looked shocked but otherwise unhurt. Beyond them stood the second blood-creature, caught half-formed by the icy wind. It stood, crouching and incomplete, like an insane sculpture carved from blood-stained ice. Hawk walked over to it and hit it once with his axe. It fell apart and littered the hall floor with jagged shards of crimson ice. Hawk kicked a few of them around, just to be sure, and then turned to face Adamant.

'All right, sir Adamant; I think there are a few questions that need answering. Like, what was all that about, and who or what is Mortice?'

Adamant sighed quietly. 'Yes. I was hoping you wouldn't have to know about him, but . . . I think you had better meet him.'

'May I suggest we get out of these clothes first?' said Dannielle. 'I'm soaked and half-frozen, and this dress is ruined.'

'She has a point,' said Fisher. 'I look like I've been skinny-dipping in an abattoir.'

'I'm sure we can find you and your partner some fresh clothes,' said Dannielle. 'Come with me, Captain Fisher, and I'll see what I can dig out for you. James, you look after Captain Hawk.'

Fisher and Dannielle disappeared up the stairs together. Hawk looked at Adamant. 'All right, first a change of clothes, but then I want to meet Mortice. No more delays; is that clear?'

'Of course, Captain,' said Adamant. 'But . . . do try and make allowances for Mortice's temper. He's been dead for some five months now, and it hasn't done a thing for his disposition.'

Hawk walked up to the full-length mirror, and studied himself for some time. It didn't help. He still looked like a poor relation down on his luck. He and Adamant were roughly the same height, but Adamant had a much larger frame. As a result, the clothes Adamant had lent Hawk hung around him like he'd shrunk in the wash overnight. It wasn't even a particularly fetching outfit. Grey tights, salmon-pink knickerbockers, and a frilly white shirt; whatever the current fashion was, Hawk was pretty damn sure this wasn't it. The frilly shirt in particular worried him. The last time he'd seen a shirt this frilly a barmaid had been wearing it. And no matter what Adamant said, he was damned if he was going to wear that bloody silly three-cornered hat.

He looked at himself in the mirror one last time, and sighed deeply. He'd worn worse, in his time. At least he still had his Guardsman's cloak. He picked it up off the bed and put it on, pulling the heavy cloak around him so that it hid the clothes beneath. Luckily all Guards' cloaks came with a built-in spell that kept them clean and immaculate no matter what indignities they were subjected to. It was part of the Guard's image, and along with the occasional healing spell, was one of the few good perks of the job.

He ought really to be rejoining the others, but it wouldn't do them any harm to wait a while. He had several things he wanted to think through, while he had the chance. He looked around Adamant's spare bedchamber. It was clean, tidy, and very comfortably appointed. The bed itself was a huge four-poster, with hanging curtains. Very elegant, and even more expensive. What was a champion of Reform doing, living like a king? All right; no one expected him to live like a pauper just to make a point, but this ostentatious display of wealth worried Hawk. According to Adamant, the house had been provided by Reform higher-ups. So where were they getting the money from? Who funded the Reform Cause? The Trade Guilds, obviously, and donations from the faithful. Wealthy patrons like Adamant. But that wouldn't be enough to pay for houses like this. Hawk frowned. This wasn't really any of his business. He was just here to protect Adamant from harm.

Not that he was doing such a great job so far. The blood-creatures had caught him off guard. If Mortice hadn't saved their hides with his sorcery, the election would have been over before it had even begun. More mysteries. Mortice had to be a sorcerer of some kind. And Adamant had to know that associating with a sorcerer was grounds for disqualification. So why was he willing to let Hawk and Fisher meet him? And what was that crack about him being dead for five months? What was he? A ghost? Hawk sighed. He'd only been on the case an hour and already he had more questions than he could shake a stick at. This was going to be just like the Blackstone case all over again, he could tell. He settled his axe comfortably on his right hip, and made his way out onto the landing and down the stairs.

The hall was sparkling clean, with no trace of blood or ice. Mortice again, presumably. Fisher was waiting for him at the foot of the stairs, wrapped in her Guard's cloak. One look at the thunderclouds in her face was enough to tell Hawk that she'd been no luckier in her choice of new clothes than he. He went down to join her, looked ostentatiously round to make sure they were alone, and then whispered, 'I'll show you mine if you'll show me yours.'

Fisher snorted a quick laugh, and smiled in spite of herself. 'You first.'

Hawk opened his cloak with a flourish and stood posed in the traditional flasher's stance. Fisher shook her head. 'Hawk, you look like a Charcoal Street ponce. And it's still not as bad as mine.'

She opened her cloak, and Hawk had to bite his lip to keep from laughing. Apparently they hadn't been able to find any of Dannielle's clothing that would fit Fisher, and had compromised by lending her men's clothing. Very old and very battered men's clothing. The shirt and trousers had probably started out white, but had degenerated over the years into an uneven grey. The cuffs were frayed, there were patches of different colours on the elbows and knees, and there were several important buttons missing.

'Apparently they originally belonged to the gardener,' said Fisher through gritted teeth. 'We can't go out looking like this, Hawk; people will laugh themselves to death.'

'Then we'll just have to keep our cloaks shut and save what's underneath as a weapon of last resort,' said Hawk solemnly.

'Ah, Captain Hawk,' said Medley, poking his head out of the study door. 'I thought I heard voices. Everything all right?'

'Fine,' said Hawk. 'Just fine.'

Medley stepped out into the corridor, followed by Adamant and Dannielle. They were all in fresh clothes and looked very smart.

'If you're quite ready, could we please get a move on?' said Medley. 'Mortice knows we're coming, and he hates to be kept waiting. The last time he got impatient, he called down a plague of frogs. It took us hours to get those nasty little creatures out of the house.'

'If he's your friend,' said Fisher dryly, 'your enemies must really be something.'

'They are,' said Adamant. 'If you'd care to follow me . . .'

He led them down the hall and through a series of corridors that opened eventually onto a simple stone-walled laundry room. There were tables and towels and a freshly scrubbed stone floor. Hawk looked expectantly around him, and wondered if he was supposed to make a comment of some sort. As he hesitated, Medley moved over to the middle of the floor and bent down. He took hold of a large steel ring set into the floor, and for the first time Hawk spotted the outlines of a trapdoor. Fisher looked at Adamant.

'You keep your sorcerer in the cellar?'

'He chose it,' said Medley. 'He finds the dark a comfort.'

Hawk looked at Adamant. 'You said Mortice was dead. Perhaps you'd care to explain that.'

Adamant gestured for Medley to move away from the

trapdoor, and he did. Adamant frowned unhappily. When he spoke, his voice was low and even, and he chose his words with care. 'Mortice is my oldest friend. We've faced many troubles together. I trust him implicitly. He's a first-class sorcerer; one of the most powerful in the city. He died just over five months ago. I even went to his funeral.'

'But if he's dead,' said Fisher, 'what have you got in your cellar?'

'A lich,' said Medley. 'A dead body, animated by a sorcerer's will. We don't know exactly what happened, but Mortice was defending us from a sorcerous attack when something went wrong. Terribly wrong. The spell killed him, but somehow Mortice managed to trap his spirit within his dead body. In a sense he's both living and dead now. Unfortunately his body is still slowly decaying, despite everything he can do to prevent it. The pain and rot of corruption are always with him. It makes him rather . . . short-tempered.'

'He's haunting his own body,' said Adamant. 'Trapped in a prison of decaying flesh, because he wouldn't leave me unprotected.'

'His name was Masque, but he calls himself Mortice, these days,' said Dannielle, a faint *moue* of distaste pulling at her mouth. 'Igor Mortice. It's a joke. Sort of.'

Hawk and Fisher looked at each other. 'All right,' said Hawk. 'Let's go meet the corpse.'

'I can see you and he are going to get on like a house on fire,' said Medley.

He reached down and took a firm hold of the steel ring set into the trapdoor. He braced himself and pulled steadily. The trapdoor swung open on whispering hinges, and a rush of freezing air billowed out into the laundry room. Hawk shivered suddenly, gooseflesh rising on his arms. Adamant lit a lamp, and then started down the narrow wooden stairway that led into the darkness of the cellar.

Dannielle lifted her dress up around her knees and followed him down. Hawk and Fisher looked at each other. Hawk shrugged uneasily, and followed Dannielle, his hand resting on the axe at his side. Fisher followed him, and Medley brought up the rear, slamming the trapdoor shut behind him.

It was very dark and bitterly cold in the cellar. Hawk wrapped his cloak tightly around him, his breathing steaming on the still air. The stairs seemed to go a long way down before they finally came to an end. Adamant's lamp revealed a large square box of a room, packed from wall to bare wall with great slabs of ice. A layer of glistening frost covered everything, and a faint pearly haze softened the lamplight. In the middle of the room, in a small space surrounded by ice, sat a small mummified form wrapped in a white cloak, slumped and motionless on a bare wooden chair. There was no way of approaching it, so Hawk studied the still figure as best he could from a distance. The flesh had sunk clean down to the bone, so that the face was little more than a leathery mask, and the bare hands little more than bony claws. The eyes were sunken pits, with tightly closed eyelids. The rest of the body was hidden behind the cloak, for which Hawk was grateful.

'I take it the ice is here to preserve the body,' he said finally, his voice hushed.

'It slows the process,' said Adamant. 'But that's all.'

Fisher's mouth twisted in a grimace. 'Seems to me it'd be kinder to just let the poor bastard go.'

'You don't understand,' said Medley. 'He *can't* die. Because of what he did, his spirit is tied to his body for as long as it exists. No matter what condition the body is in, or how little remains of it.'

'He did it for me,' said Adamant. 'Because I needed him.' His voice broke off roughly. Dannielle put a comforting hand on his arm.

Hawk shivered, not entirely from the cold. 'Are you sure he's still . . . in there? Can he hear us?'

The mummified body stirred on its chair. The sunken eyelids crawled open, revealing eyes yellow as urine. 'I may be dead, Captain Hawk, but I'm not deaf.' His voice was low and harsh, but surprisingly firm. His eyes fixed on Hawk and Fisher, and his sunken mouth moved in something that might have been meant as a smile. 'Hawk and Fisher. The only honest Guards in Haven. I've heard a lot about you.'

'Nothing good, I hope,' said Fisher.

The dead man chuckled dryly, a faint whisper of sound on the quiet. 'James, I think you'll find you're in excellent hands with these two. They have a formidable reputation.'

'Apart from the Blackstone affair,' said Dannielle.

'Everyone has their off days,' said Hawk evenly. 'You can trust us to keep you from harm, sir Adamant. Anyone who wants to get to you has to get past us first.'

'And there's damn few who've ever done that,' said Fisher.

'You weren't doing so well against the blood-creatures,' said Dannielle. 'If Mortice hadn't intervened, we'd have all been killed.'

'Hush, Danny,' said Adamant. 'Any man can be brought down by sorcery. That's why we have Mortice, to take care of things like that. Is there anything you need while we're here, Mortice? You know we can't stand this cold for long.'

'I don't need anything anymore, James. But you need to take more care. It would appear Councillor Hardcastle is more worried about your chances in the election than he's willing to admit in public. He's hired a first-class sorcerer, and turned him loose on you. The blood-creatures were just one of a dozen sendings he's called up out of the darkness. I managed to keep out the others, but there's a limit to what my wards can do. I don't recognise my adversary's style, but he's good. Very good. If I were alive, I might even be worried about him.'

Adamant frowned. 'Hardcastle must know he's forbidden to use sorcery during an election.'

'So are we, for that matter,' said Medley.

'That's different,' said Dannielle quickly, darting a quick glance at Hawk and Fisher. 'Mortice just uses his magic to protect us.'

'The Council isn't interested in that kind of distinction,' said Mortice. 'Technically, my very presence in your house is illegal. Not that I ever let technicalities get in my way. But the Council's always had ants in its pants about magic-users. Right, Captain Hawk?'

'Right,' said Hawk. 'That's what comes of living so near the Street of Gods.'

'Tough,' said Mortice. 'All the candidates have some kind of sorcery backing them up. If they didn't, they wouldn't stand a chance. Magic is like bribery and corruption; everyone knows about it and everyone turns a blind eye. I don't know why I should sound so disgusted about it. This is Haven, after all.'

'Being dead doesn't seem to have dulled your faculties at all,' said Hawk.

Mortice's mouth twitched. 'I find being dead unclutters the mind wonderfully.'

'Where do you stand when it comes to sorcery, Captain Hawk?' said Dannielle sharply. 'Are you going to turn us in, and get James disqualified from the election?'

Hawk shrugged. 'My orders are to keep James Adamant alive. As far as I'm concerned, that has overall priority. I'll put up with anything that'll make my job easier.'

'Well, if that's settled, we really should be going,' said Adamant. 'We've a lot to do and not much time to do it in.'

'Do you really have to go, James?' said Mortice. 'Can't you just stay and talk for a while?'

'I'm sorry,' said Adamant. 'Everything's piling up right now. I'll come down and see you again, as soon as I can. And I'll keep searching for someone who can help with your condition, no matter how long it takes. There must be someone, somewhere.'

'Yes,' said Mortice. 'I'm sure there is. Don't worry about Hardcastle's sorcerer, James. He may have caught me by surprise once, but I'm ready for him now. Nothing can harm you as long as I am here. I promise you that, my friend.'

His eyes slowly closed, and once again to all appearances he became nothing more than a mummified corpse, without any trace of life. Dannielle shivered quickly, and tugged at Adamant's arm.

'Let's get out of here, James. I'm not dressed for this kind of weather.'

'Of course, my dear.'

He nodded to Medley, who led the way out of the cellar and back into the laundry room. After the bitter cold of the cellar, the pleasant autumn day seemed uncomfortably warm. There was frost in their hair and eyebrows, and they all mopped at their faces as it began to melt. Adamant let the trapdoor fall shut, and blew out his lamp. Hawk looked at him.

'Is that it? Aren't you going to bolt it, or something? If Hardcastle is as ruthless and determined as you've made him out to be, what's to stop him sending assassins here to destroy Mortice's body?'

Medley laughed shortly. 'Anyone stupid enough to go down there wouldn't be coming back out again. Mortice's temper wasn't very good when he was alive, and since he died he's developed a very nasty sense of humour.'

Adamant's study seemed reassuringly normal after the freezing cold and darkness of Mortice's cellar. Hawk picked out the most comfortable-looking chair, turned it so he wouldn't have to sit with his back to the door, and sank down into it. Adamant started to say something and then thought better of it. He gestured for the others to take a seat, and busied himself with the wine decanters. Dannielle made as though to sit next to Hawk, and then quickly chose another chair when Fisher glared at her. Medley sat down beside Dannielle, who ignored him. Hawk leaned back in his chair and stretched out his legs. First rule of the Guard: if you get a chance to sit down, take it. Guards spend a lot of time on their feet, and it tends to colour their thinking.

The last of the cellar chill began to seep out of Hawk's bones, and he sighed quietly. Adamant poured him a drink from one of the more expensive-looking decanters. Hawk sipped it, and made appreciative noises. It seemed a good vintage, though Fisher always insisted he had no palate for such things. Just as well, on a Guard's wages. He put down his glass, and waited patiently for Adamant to finish pouring wine for the others. There were things that needed to be said.

'Sir Adamant, just how reliable is Mortice?'

Adamant finished putting the decanter away before answering. 'Before he died – very. Now – I don't know. After everything he's been through it's a wonder he's still coherent, never mind sane. The experience would have broken a lesser man. It still might. As it is, his life now consists mainly of pain and despair. He has no hope and no future, and he knows it. His friendship with me is his last link with normality.'

'What about his magic?' said Fisher. 'Is he still as powerful as he used to be?'

'He seems to be.' Adamant emptied his glass and poured himself another drink. His hand was perfectly steady. 'In his day, Mortice was a very powerful sorcerer. He says he's as strong now as he ever was, but there's no denying his mind does tend to wander on occasion. No doubt that's how those blood-creatures got in. If he ever cracks and gives in to all that pain and madness, I think we could all be in very great trouble.'

'You must realise this changes things,' said Hawk. 'I can't overlook something like this. Mortice could end up as a threat to the whole city.'

'Yes,' said Adamant. 'He could. That's why I'm telling you all this. I didn't have to. Originally, I'd hoped you wouldn't have to know about him at all. That's why he took so long to deal with those blood-creatures. I'd instructed him not to give away his presence unless he absolutely had to. It wasn't until I met him just now, and saw him through your eyes, that I realised how much he's changed since his death. He used to be such a powerful man.'

'But as things stand we're in no danger,' said Medley quickly. 'You saw for yourself how calm and rational he is. Look; you'll be right here with us all through the election. You can keep a close watch on him. If he shows any sign that his control's slipping, then you can report him. It's not as if he was that dangerous. There's no doubt he's a very powerful individual, but he couldn't hope to stand against the combined might of all the Guard's sorcerers. I mean those people take on rogue Beings from the Street of Gods. And Mortice isn't exactly the High Warlock, now is he? In the meantime, we need him. Adamant won't survive the election without Mortice's support.'

Hawk looked at Fisher, who nodded slightly. 'All right,' he said finally. 'We'll see how it goes. But once the election is over . . .'

'Then we can talk about it again,' said Adamant.

'And if he turns dangerous?' said Fisher.

'Then you do what you have to,' said Adamant. 'I know my responsibilities, Captain.'

An uncomfortable silence fell across the room. Dannielle cleared her throat, and everyone looked at her. 'This isn't the first time you've worked with a magic-user, is it,

Captain Hawk? I seem to remember the sorcerer Gaunt was involved in the Blackstone case, wasn't he?'

'Only marginally,' said Hawk. 'I never knew him very well. He left Haven shortly afterwards.'

'Damn shame, that,' said Medley. 'His loss was a great blow to the Reform Cause. Gaunt and Mortice were the only sorcerers of any note ever to ally themselves openly with the Reformers.'

'You're better off without them,' said Hawk flatly. 'You can't trust magic, or the people who use it.'

Dannielle raised a painted eyebrow. 'You sound as though you've had some bad experiences with sorcery, Captain Hawk.'

'Hawk has a long memory,' said Fisher. 'And he bears grudges.'

'How about you, Captain Fisher?' said Adamant.

Fisher grinned. 'I don't get mad. I get even.'

'Right,' said Hawk.

'We haven't discussed your politics yet,' said Adamant slowly. 'What beliefs do you follow, if any? In my experience, Guards tend to be uninterested in politics, apart from the usual favours and payoffs. Most of the time they just support the status quo.'

'That's our job,' said Hawk. 'We don't make the laws, we just enforce them. Even the ones we don't agree with. Not all the Guards in Haven are crooked. You've got to expect some bribery and corruption, that's how Haven works, but on the whole the Guard takes its job seriously. We have to; if we didn't, the Council would replace us with someone who did. Too much corruption is bad for business, and the Quality doesn't like its peace disturbed.'

'But what do you believe in?' said Medley. 'You, and Captain Fisher?'

Hawk shrugged. 'My wife is basically disinterested in politics. Right, Isobel?'

'Right,' said Fisher, holding out her empty glass to

Adamant for a refill. 'Only thing more corrupt than a politician is a week-old corpse after the blowflies have been at it. No offence, sir Adamant.'

'None taken,' said Adamant.

'As for me . . .' Hawk pursed his lips thoughtfully. 'Isobel and I come from the far North. We were both raised under absolute monarchies. Things were different there. It's taken us both some time to adjust to the changes democracy has made in Haven and the Low Kingdoms. I don't think we'll ever get used to the idea of a constitutional monarch.

'On the whole, it seems to me that the same kind of people end up on top no matter what system you have, but at least in a democracy there's room for change. Which is why I tend to favour Reform. The Conservatives don't want any change because for the most part they're rich and privileged, and they want to stay that way. The poor and the commoners should know their place.' Hawk grinned. 'I've never known my place.'

'But as far as this election is concerned, we're strictly neutral,' said Fisher. 'It's our job to protect you, and we'll do that to the best of our ability. No one will bother you while we're around. Not openly, anyway. But don't waste time preaching to us. That's not what we're here for.'

'Of course,' said Medley. 'We quite understand. Still, you're being put to a great deal of trouble on our account. You'll become targets, just by being associated with us. Under the circumstances, perhaps you would allow James and myself to show our appreciation by providing you with a little extra money, for expenses and the like. Shall we say five hundred ducats? Each?'

He reached inside his coat for his wallet, and then froze as he took in Hawk's face. Silence fell across the room. Medley looked from Hawk to Fisher and back again, and a sudden chill went through him. A subtle change had come over the two Guards. There was a cold anger and violence in their faces; a violence barely held in check. For the first time, Medley realised how the two Guards had earned their grim reputation, and he believed every word of it. He wanted to look to Adamant for support, but he couldn't tear his gaze away from the Guards.

'Are you offering us a bribe?' said Fisher softly.

'Not necessarily,' said Medley, trying to smile. The joke fell flat. Medley could feel sweat beading on his forehead.

'Get your hand away from that wallet,' said Hawk, 'or we'll do something unpleasant with it. You don't want to know what.'

'We don't take bribes,' said Fisher. 'Ever. People trust us because they know we can't be bought. By anyone.'

'My adviser meant no offence,' said Adamant quickly. 'He's just not used to dealing with honest people.'

'Politics does that to you,' said Dannielle.

'And you have to admit, you are rather . . . unusual, as Haven goes,' said Adamant.

'As Haven goes, we're bloody unique,' said Fisher.

Hawk grinned. 'You got that right.'

Medley pulled at his coat to straighten it, though it didn't need straightening, and looked at the ornate brass-bound clock on the mantelpiece. 'We're running late, James. The faithful will be arriving soon for your big speech.'

'Of course, Stefan.' Adamant got to his feet, and smiled at Hawk and Fisher. 'Come along, bodyguards. You should find this interesting.'

'You got that right,' said Dannielle.

Hawk leaned morosely against the landing wall and wished halfheartedly for a riot. Adamant's followers filled the ballroom below, all of them cheerful and excited and buoyantly good-natured. They listened politely to Adamant's stewards, and went where they were told without a murmur. Hawk couldn't believe it. Usually in Haven you tracked down a political meeting by following the trail of broken bottles and mutilated corpses. Adamant's followers were enthusiastic as all hell, particularly about him, but seemed uninterested in the traditional pastimes of cursing the enemy and planning his destruction. They actually seemed more interested in discussing the issues. Hawk shook his head slowly. As if elections in Haven had anything to do with issues. He'd bet good money that Hardcastle's people weren't wasting time discussing the issues. More likely they were busy planning death and bloodshed and general mayhem, and where best to make a start. Hawk glanced across at Fisher. She looked just as bored as he did. Hawk looked back at the crowd. Maybe someone would faint in the crush. Anything for a little excitement. Hawk had reached the stage where he would have welcomed an outbreak of plague, to relieve the tedium.

He looked hopefully at Adamant, but he seemed in no hurry to make his entrance. He sat quietly in his chair halfway down the landing, well out of sight of his followers. Thick velvet drapes had been hung the length of the landing, blocking off the view, just so that Adamant could make a dramatic entrance at the top of the stairs. He seemed cool and perfectly relaxed, hands laced together in his lap, his eyes vague and far away. Medley, on the other hand, was stalking back and forth like a cat with piles, unable to settle anywhere for a moment. He was clutching a thick sheaf of papers, and shuffling them back and forth like the cards in a losing hand. He kept up a muttered running monologue of comment and advice concerning Adamant's speech, even though it was obvious no one was listening to him. Dannielle glared at him irritably from time to time, but seemed mostly interested in studying her appearance in the full-length mirror on the wall.

Down below, the crowd was getting noisy. They'd been patient a long time, and some of them looked a little tired of being good-natured about it. Hawk moved a little to one side so that he could see the mirror opposite him more clearly. It was the last in a series of mirrors, all cleverly arranged so that he could see down into the ballroom without being seen himself. One of Medley's better ideas.

It wasn't a very big ballroom, as mansion ballrooms went, but the packed crowd made it seem larger. Massed lamps and candles supplied a blaze of light, though the air was starting to get a little thick. Portraits of stern-faced ancestors from the original owner's family lined the walls, all of them looking highly respectable. Hawk's mouth twitched. If they'd still been alive, they'd have probably had coronaries at what their house was being used for. Adamant's supporters filled the ballroom from one end to the other, latecomers pushed tight against the closed doors, while the front of the crowd spilled over onto the first few steps of the stairs to the second storey. They seemed to blend together into a mass of shiny faces and eager eyes. A handful of stewards stopped them from getting any further up the stairs. A few more moved slowly through the crowd, keeping an eye out for unfamiliar faces and paid saboteurs. They looked very alone and very vulnerable in the crowd. Everyone there was supposed to be Adamant's friend, but Hawk didn't trust any crowd that large. They'd been well-behaved so far, but Hawk had seen enough crowds in his time to know that they could turn ugly in a moment. Should things get out of hand, there was precious little Adamant's men would be able to do to restrain such a mob. They weren't even wearing swords. Hawk sniffed. It took more to handle a crowd than good intentions.

Hawk looked round as Adamant stirred in his chair, but the candidate was just shifting his weight more comfortably. He still looked cool and calm and utterly at ease. He could have been waiting for his second cup of tea at breakfast, instead of his first real test of popularity and support. At first, Hawk had thought it was all just a pose, a mask to hide his nervousness behind, but there was none of the over-stillness that betrayed inner tension. He shot a glance at Fisher, who nodded slightly to show she'd noticed it too. Adamant might be new to politics, but it seemed he already knew the first rule: politicians inspire fervour, but they don't fall prey to it themselves. Or, to put it another way, Adamant was professional enough to be a coldhearted son of a bitch when he had to be. A point worth remembering.

Medley, on the other hand, looked as though he might explode at any moment. His face was covered with a sheen of sweat and his hands were shaking. His hair was a mess, and he ran his fingers through it like a comb when he thought no one was looking. He kept glancing at the crowd's image in the mirror as they grew increasingly noisy, and his running monologue became even more urgent as he ran through a list of things Adamant absolutely had to remember once he got out there in front of the crowd.

Medley began to repeat himself, and Dannielle shot him another dark look before going back to fussing over her appearance. Her dress was stylish, her makeup immaculate, but she couldn't seem to assure herself of that without constant checking. Hawk smiled. Everyone had their own way of dealing with nerves. For the most part, Hawk dealt with them by keeping busy. He studied the scene in the mirror again, and stirred uneasily. The crowd was definitely getting restive. Some of them had started chanting Adamant's name. The thin line of stewards at the foot of the stairs looked thinner than ever.

Hawk smiled briefly. It was one thing to wish for a little action to relieve the boredom, but quite another when it came to actually having to deal with it.

Medley made one comment too many, and Dannielle snapped at him. They locked gazes for a moment, and then Dannielle turned to Adamant for support. He smiled at both of them, and got up out of his chair. He traded a few quiet, reassuring words with each, taking just long enough for some of his calm to rub off on them. Down in the ballroom, the crowd was chanting *We want Adamant!* more or less in unison. He smiled at Hawk and Fisher.

'There's an art to this, you know. The longer we make them wait, the greater their response will be when I finally appear. Of course, let it go on too long, and they'll riot. It's all in the timing.' He strode purposefully out onto the top of the stairs, and the crowd went mad.

They cheered and stamped and waved their banners, releasing their pent-up emotions in a single great roar of love and acclaim. The sound rose and rose, beating against the walls and echoing back from the ceiling. Adamant smiled and waved, and Dannielle and Medley moved out onto the top of the stairs to join him. The cheers grew even wilder, if that was possible. Dannielle smiled graciously at the crowd. Medley nodded briskly, his face grave and impassive.

Back in the hidden part of the landing, Hawk's gaze darted across the viewing mirror, checking the crowd for trouble spots. Letting this much raw emotion loose in a confined space was a calculated risk; all it needed was one unfortunate incident and the whole thing could turn very nasty. The trick, according to Medley, was to concentrate all the emotion on Adamant, through a combination of speeches and theatrics, and then turn the people loose on the city while they were still boiling over with enthusiasm. A good trick, if you can pull it off. Adamant probably could. He was good with words. The right words at the right time can topple thrones and build empires. Or bring on rebellions and civil wars, and dead men lying in burning fields.

Fisher stirred uneasily at Hawk's side, picking up some of his tension, and he made himself relax a little. Nothing was going to happen. Adamant and Medley had everything planned, right down to the last detail. Hardcastle's people wouldn't interfere here. They might not know about

Mortice himself, but they had to know some magic-user was looking out for Adamant. Hawk gnawed at his lower lip, and looked across at Adamant. He was still smiling and waving, milking the moment for all it was worth. Dannielle stood serenely at his side, doing her best to be openly supportive without drawing any attention away from her husband. Medley looked uncomfortable in the spotlight, but no one expected him to be charismatic. It was enough that he was there, openly allied with Adamant.

Hawk looked back at the crowd in the mirror, which still showed no signs of cooling down. They all had flags or banners or placards, and they all wore the blue ribbon of the Reform Cause. They were a mixture of types and classes, with no obvious connections. There were a large number of poorly dressed, hard-worn characters whose reasons for supporting Reform seemed clear. But there were others whose clothes and bearing marked them clearly as tradesmen and merchants, and there were even some members of the Quality. Usually the only place you'd find such a combination gathered peacefully together was in the city morgue or the debtors' prison. And yet here they were, standing happily shoulder to shoulder, united in friendship and purpose by the man they trusted and cheered for. Politics made for strange bedfellows. Adamant lifted his hands suddenly, and the crowd's cheering died quickly away, replaced by an expectant hush.

Hawk watched closely from the shadows of the landing. There was something different about Adamant now. Something powerful. He seemed to have grown suddenly in stature and authority, as though the crowd's belief in him had made him the hero they needed him to be. The man Hawk had met earlier had been pleasant enough, even charming. But this new Adamant had a power and charisma that set him ablaze like a beacon in the night. His presence filled the ballroom. For the first time, Hawk understood why Hardcastle was afraid of this man.

The room was totally silent now. All eyes were fixed on Adamant. There was a hungry, determined feel to the silence that Hawk didn't like. It occurred to him that the relationship between Adamant and his followers wasn't just a one-way street. These people worshipped him, they might even die for him, but in a way they owned him too. They defined what he was and what he might be.

Adamant's speech lasted the better part of an hour, and the crowd lapped it up. He talked about the dark side of Haven, the sweatshops and the work gangs, the company shops that made sure their employees stayed poor, and the company bullies who dealt with anyone who dared speak out. He talked about rotten food and foul drinking water, about houses with holes in the roof and rats in the walls – and the crowd reacted with shock and outrage, as though they'd never known such things existed. Adamant made them see their world with fresh eyes, and see how bad it really was.

He told them about the powerful and privileged men who cared nothing for the poor because they were born into the wrong class and therefore were nothing more than animals, to be used and discarded as their betters saw fit. He told them of the titled men and women who gorged themselves on six-course meals in gorgeous banquet halls, while the children of the poor died in the streets from hunger and exposure – and the raw hatred from the crowd was a palpable presence in the ballroom.

And then he told them things didn't have to be that way anymore.

He told them of the Cause. Of Reform, and how the evils of Haven would finally be done away with, not by violence and revolution, but by slow, continued change. By people working together, instead of against each other, regardless of class or wealth or position. It wasn't going to be easy. There were those in Haven who would fight and die rather than see the system change. Reform would be a long fight and a hard fight, but in the end Reform would win, because working together the people were stronger by far than the privileged individuals who sought to keep them in their place, in the gutter. Adamant smiled proudly down at the men and women before him. *Let others call us trouble-makers and anarchists*, he said quietly. *We will show the people of Haven it isn't true. We are just men and women who have had enough, and will see justice done. Whatever it takes.*

They can't kill us all.

Adamant finally stopped speaking, and for a moment there was silence. And then the crowd roared its agreement in a single, determined voice. Adamant had taken a crowd of individuals and forged them into an army, and they knew it. All they needed now was an enemy to fight, and they'd find that soon enough out on the streets. Hawk watched the crowd in the mirror, impressed but deeply disturbed. Raising violent emotions like these was dangerous for everyone involved. If Hardcastle could raise similar feelings in his followers, there would be blood and death in the streets when the two sides met.

Adamant raised his hands again, and the crowd grew still. He paused a moment, as though searching for just the right words, and then talked to them slowly and calmly about how they should deal with the enemy. Violence was Hardcastle's way, not theirs. Let the voters see who needed to resort to violence first, and then they'd see who spoke the truth, and who dared not let it be heard. Adamant looked out over his people. It was inevitable that people were going to be hurt in the hours ahead, maybe even killed. But whatever happened, they were only ever to defend themselves, and then only as much as was needed. It was easy to fall into the trap of hatred and revenge, but that was the enemy's way, not theirs. Reform fought to change, not destroy.

He paused again, to let the thought sink in, and then suddenly raised his voice in happiness and good cheer. He filled the audience's hearts with hope and resolve, wished them all good fortune, bowed once, and then strode unhurriedly off into the shadows of the landing, followed by Dannielle and Medley. His audience cheered him till their hearts were raw, and then filed slowly out of the ballroom, laughing and chattering excitedly about the day ahead. Back in the concealing shadows of the landing, Adamant sank wearily into his chair and let his breath out in a long, slow sigh of relief.

'I think that went rather well,' he said finally. He put out a hand to Dannielle, and she took it firmly in both of hers.

'It should have,' said Medley. 'We spent long enough rehearsing it.'

'Oh, never mind him,' said Dannielle, glaring at Medley. 'You were wonderful, darling! Listen to them, James; they're still cheering you!'

'It's a hard life being a politician,' said Adamant solemnly. 'All this power and adulation . . . How will I ever stand the pressure?'

Medley snorted. 'Wait till we get out on the streets, James. That's when the real work starts. They do things differently out there.'

Half an hour later the faithful had all departed, but Adamant and company were back in the study again. Adamant had visitors. Garrett Walpole and Lucien Sykes were businessmen, so successful that even Hawk and Fisher had heard of them. Their families were as old as Haven, and if their money hadn't come from trade, they could both have been leading members of the Quality. As it was, the lowest member of High Society wouldn't have deigned to so much as sneer in their direction. Tradesmen used the back door, no matter how wealthy they were. Which was at least partly why Walpole and Sykes had come visiting. Not that they would ever have admitted it, of course. They shook hands formally with Adamant, and nodded generally around them as Adamant made the introductions.

'Your adviser can stay,' said Sykes briskly, 'but the others will have to leave. Our business here is confidential, Adamant.'

Hawk smiled, and shook his head. 'We're bodyguards. We stay with sir Adamant.'

Walpole looked at Hawk and Fisher amusedly. 'Call off your dogs, will you, James? Perhaps your wife could take them to the kitchens for a cup of tea, or something, until our business is finished.'

'Don't care much for tea,' said Fisher. 'We stay.'

'You'll do as you're damned well told!' snapped Sykes. 'Now, get out, and don't come back till we call you. Adamant, tell them.'

Hawk smiled slowly, and Sykes paled suddenly as his breath caught in his throat. Without moving a muscle, a change had come over Hawk. He suddenly looked . . . dangerous. The scarred face was cold and impassive, and Sykes couldn't help noticing how Hawk's hand rested on his axe at his side. The room suddenly seemed very small, with nowhere to turn.

'We're bodyguards,' said Hawk softly. 'We stay.'

'Gentlemen, please!' said Adamant quickly. 'There's no need for any unpleasantness. We're all friends here. Hawk, Fisher, these gentlemen are my guests. I would be obliged if you would show them every courtesy while they're in my house.'

'Of course,' said Hawk. His tone was impeccably polite, but the gaze from his single dark eye was still disturbingly cold. Sykes looked at Fisher, but if anything her smile was even more disturbing.

'There's no cause for alarm, my friends,' said Adamant. 'My bodyguards fully understand our need for confidentiality. You have my word that nothing discussed here will go beyond the walls of this room.'

Walpole looked at Sykes, who nodded grudgingly. Hawk smiled. Fisher leaned against the mantelpiece and folded her arms.

'But your wife will still have to leave,' said Sykes stubbornly. 'This is not women's business.'

Dannielle flushed angrily, and looked to Adamant for support, but he was already nodding slowly. 'Very well, Lucien, if you insist. Danny, if you wouldn't mind . . .'

Dannielle shot him a quick look of betrayal, and then gathered her composure sufficiently to smile graciously round the room before leaving. She didn't slam the door behind her, but it felt as though she had. Adamant gestured for Walpole and Sykes to be seated, and waited patiently for them to settle themselves comfortably before pouring them wine from the most delicately fashioned decanter. Hawk and Fisher held out their glasses for a refill. Adamant handed them the decanter, and pulled up a chair opposite his visitors. The two Guards remained standing. Hawk studied the two businessmen surreptitiously over his wineglass. He didn't move in their circle, but he knew them both by reputation. Guards made it their business to know the movers and shakers of Haven's community by sight. You could avoid a lot of embarrassment that way.

Garrett Walpole was a bluff military type in his late fifties. He'd spent twenty years in the Low Kingdoms army before retiring to take over the family business, and it showed. He still wore his hair in a regulation military cut, and his back was straight as a sword blade. He wore sober clothes of a conservative cut, and sat back in his chair as though he owned the place.

Lucien Sykes was an overweight, ruddy-faced man in his late forties. He wore the latest fashion with more determination than style, and looked more than a little uneasy in present company. Sykes was big in the import-export business, which was why he'd come to Adamant. The Dockworkers Guild was in the second week of its strike, and nothing was moving in or out of the docks. The Conservative-backed DeWitt brothers were trying to break the strike with blackleg zombie workers, but so far that hadn't worked out too well. Zombies needed a lot of supervision, and weren't what you'd call efficient workers. As it was, the Dock-workers Guild had more reason than usual to be mad at the Conservatives, and had lined up firmly behind the Reformers. So if Sykes wanted to get his ships in or out of the docks any time soon, he was going to need help from the right people. Reform people.

Hawk grinned. He might be new to politics, but he knew a few things.

'Well,' said Adamant finally, after everyone had sipped their drinks and the silence had dragged on uncomfortably long, 'what exactly can I do for you, my friends? Normally I'd be only too happy to sit and chat for a while, but I have an election to fight, and very little time to do it in. If you'll just tell me what you want, I'll be happy to tell you what it will cost you.'

Walpole raised a sardonic eyebrow. 'Plain speaking may be a virtue, James, but if I were you I'd keep it to myself. There's no room for it in politics or business.'

'You should know,' said Medley, and Walpole laughed briefly.

'James, I can't say I'm hopeful of your chances, because I'm not. High Steppes has been a safe Conservative Seat for more than thirty years. All right, Hardcastle is a bit of a rotter, but people will vote for the devil they're familiar with rather than a Cause they don't know.'

'Even though the devil has bled them dry for years, and the Cause will fight on their behalf?' Adamant smiled. 'Or perhaps you don't believe in Reform?'

'My dear chap, it hasn't a hope.' Walpole took a cigar out of his pocket, looked at it wistfully, and put it away again. 'Only allowed one a day,' he explained. 'Doctor's orders. I'd get another doctor, but he's the wife's brother. James,

Reform is a nice idea, but that's all. These fashions come and go, but they never last long. Too many vested interests concerned for it to get anywhere.'

'Is that why you came here?' said Medley. 'To tell us we can't win?'

Walpole laughed briefly. 'Not at all. You asked me for money, James, and I'm here to give it to you. Who knows? You might win after all, and it wouldn't do me any harm to have you owe me a favour. Besides, I've been a friend of your family most of my life. Fought beside your father in the Broken Ridges campaign. He was a good sort. I'm more than comfortably well-off these days, and I can afford to throw away a few thousand ducats.' He took a banker's draft from his pocket and handed it to Medley. 'Put it to good use, James, and let me know if you need some more. And after this nonsense is over, do come and see me. I'm sure I can put some business your way. Now I really must be going. Things to do, you know. Good luck in the election.'

He didn't say *You're going to need it*. His tone said it for him.

He rose unhurriedly to his feet, and stretched unobtrusively as Adamant got up and rang for the butler. Medley tucked the banker's draft safely away in his wallet before rising to his feet. The butler came in, Walpole shook hands all around, and then the butler escorted him out. The room was suddenly very quiet. Adamant and Medley sat down again and turned their attention to Lucien Sykes. He glanced quickly at the two Guards, scowled unhappily, and then leant forward to face Adamant, his tone hushed and conspiratorial.

'You know my position. I have to get my ships in and out of the docks soon, or I stand to lose every penny I've got. You know I've donated money to the Cause in the past. I've been one of your main backers. Now I need your help. I need your word that the first thing you'll do as a Councillor is to put pressure on those bastards in the Dock-workers Guild to call off their strike. For a while, at least.'

'I'm afraid I can't do that,' said Adamant. 'But I could put some pressure on the DeWitt brothers to be more reasonable. After all, they caused the strike, by refusing to spend the money needed to make the docks safe to work in.'

Sykes's scowl deepened. 'That won't do any good. I've already talked to Marcus and David DeWitt. They don't give a damn for anyone but themselves. It's become a matter of principle to them, not to give in to their workers. If they want to dig their own financial grave, that's up to them, but I'm damned if I'm going to let them drag me down with them.'

'You could always go to Hardcastle,' said Medley.

'I tried,' said Sykes. 'He wouldn't see me. Three thousand ducats, Adamant. That's my offer. I've got the bank draft right here.'

'I'll talk to the Guild and put what pressure I can on the DeWitts,' said Adamant. 'That's all I can promise you. If that's not good enough, then we'll have to do without your money.'

Sykes took a folded bank draft out of his coat pocket, hefted it in his hand, and then tossed it onto the desk. 'I'll see you again, Adamant – if you win the election.'

He pulled his coat around him, glared briefly at Hawk and Fisher, and left the study. The door swung shut behind him. Hawk turned slightly to look at Adamant.

'Is it normally this blatant? I mean, when you get right down to it, those two were giving you bribes in return for future favours. Reform's always campaigned against that kind of corruption in the past.'

'Fighting an election costs money,' said Medley. 'Lots of it. James couldn't hope to pay all the bills on his own, and the Cause can't do much to help. What money they have has to be spread around among the poorer candidates. All they could give us was this house. So, we take funds where we can find them. You can bet Hardcastle isn't bothered by any such niceties. If his supporters don't make big enough donations, all he has to do is threaten to raise property taxes. And it's not as if we promised to do anything against our principles. In the end, all politics is based on people doing favours for each other. That's what keeps the system going. It may not be a very pretty system, but then, that's one of the things we're fighting to change.'

The door flew open, and Dannielle swept in. She glared at them all impartially, and then sank into her favourite chair. 'I feel like I ought to open all the windows and set up incense sticks, just to get the smell of politics out of this room.'

'Sorry, Danny,' said Adamant. 'But they really wouldn't have talked freely with you there, and we needed the money they were offering.'

Dannielle sniffed. 'Let's change the subject.'

'Let's,' said Medley. 'Is there anything more you need to know before we start campaigning, Captain Hawk, Captain Fisher?'

'Yes,' said Hawk. 'I need more information on the other candidates. Hardcastle, for example. I gather he's unpopular, even among his own people.'

'The man's a brute,' said Adamant. 'He runs the High Steppes like his own private Barony. Even levies his own separate tax, though it's not called that, of course. It's an insurance policy. And people who don't or can't keep up their payments find their luck's suddenly changed for the worse. It starts with beatings, moves on to fires, and ends with murder. And no one says anything. Even the Guard looks the other way.'

Hawk smiled coldly. 'We're the Guard here now. Tell me about Hardcastle himself.'

'He's a thug and a bully, and his word is worthless,' said Medley unemotionally. 'He takes bribes from everyone, and then welshes on the deal, as often as not. He's been very successful in business, and it's rumoured he knows where some very important bodies are buried. He has his own little army of men-at-arms and hired bullies. Anyone who tries to speak out against him gets their legs broken as a warning. I don't think he has any friends, but he has acquaintances in high places.'

'Anything else?' said Fisher.

'He's married,' said Dannielle. 'But I've never met her.'

'Not many have,' said Medley. 'She doesn't go out much. From what I hear, it was an arranged marriage, for business reasons. They've been married seven years now. No children.'

'An army of men-at-arms,' said Hawk thoughtfully. 'You mean mercenaries?'

'That's right,' said Medley. 'It's hard to get an accurate figure, but he's got at least three hundred armed men under his personal command. Probably more.'

'And this is the man you're standing against?' said Fisher. 'You must be crazy. You're going to need your own private army just to walk the streets in safety.'

'What do I need an army for?' said Adamant. 'I've got you and Captain Hawk, haven't I? Relax, Captain Fisher. We have our own mercenaries. Not as many as Hardcastle, but enough. They'll keep the worst elements off our backs. We'll just have to play the rest by ear.'

'Terrific,' said Fisher.

'Tell me about the other candidates,' said Hawk.

Adamant looked at Medley, who frowned thoughtfully before speaking. 'Well, first, there's Lord Arthur Sinclair. Youngish chap, inherited the title a few years back under rather dubious circumstances, but that's nothing new in Haven. Plays politics for the fun of it as much as anything. Likes all the attention, and the chance to stand up in public and make a fool of himself. He's standing as an independent, because nobody else would have him, and he wants to see an end to all forms of tax on alcohol. He has some backing, mostly from the beer, wine, and spirits industry, and he's wealthy enough to buy himself a few votes, but the only way he'll get elected is if all the other candidates drop dead. And even then there'd have to be a recount.'

'He means well,' said Adamant, 'but he's no danger to anyone except himself. He drinks like a fish, from what I've heard.'

'Then there's Megan O'Brien,' said Medley, having waited patiently for Adamant to finish. 'He's a spice merchant, also independent, standing for Free Trade. Given that a great deal of Haven's income comes from the very taxes O'Brien wants stopped, I don't think much of his chances. He'll be lucky to get through the election without being assassinated.

'And, of course, there's General Longarm. Once a part of the Low Kingdoms army, now part of a militant movement within the Brotherhood of Steel. He's been officially disowned by the Brotherhood, though whether that means anything is open to question. The Brotherhood's always been devious. He's campaigning as an independent, on the Law and Order ticket. Believes every lawbreaker should be beheaded, on the spot, and wants compulsory military service introduced for every male over fourteen. He's crazier than a brewery-yard rat, and about as charismatic. His Brotherhood connections might get him a few votes, but otherwise he's harmless.'

'I wouldn't count him out completely,' said Adamant. 'Brotherhood militants took The Downs away from the Conservatives at the last election. I think it would be wise to keep a good weather eye on General Longarm.'

'Any more candidates?' said Fisher, helping herself to more wine from the nearest decanter.

'Just one,' said Medley. 'A mystery candidate. A sorcerer, called the Grey Veil. No one's seen or heard anything about him, but his name's on the official list. Magicians aren't actually banned from standing in the election, but the rules against using magic are so strictly enforced, most magic-users don't bother. They say they're unfairly discriminated against, and they may well be right. Mortice says he's never even heard of the Grey Veil, so he can't be that powerful.'

Hawk frowned. 'We had a run-in with a sorcerer, earlier today. It might have been him.'

'Doesn't make any difference,' said Fisher. 'We ran him off. If he was the Grey Veil, I think we can safely assume he's no longer standing. Running, maybe, but not standing. The report we filed will see to that.'

'Let me get this straight,' said Hawk. 'Apart from us, there's Hardcastle and his mercenaries, militant Brothers of Steel, and a handful of independents with whatever bullies and bravos they can afford. Adamant, this isn't just an election, it's an armed conflict. I've known battles that were safer than this sounds like it's going to be.'

'Now you're getting the hang of it,' said Dannielle.

'I think that's covered everything,' said Adamant. 'Now, would anyone like a quick snack before we leave? I doubt we'll have time to stop to eat once we've started.'

Hawk looked hopefully at Fisher, but she shook her head firmly. 'Apparently we're fine,' said Hawk. 'Thanks anyway.'

'It's no trouble,' said Dannielle. 'It'll only take a minute to send word to the kitchen staff and the food taster.'

Hawk looked at her. 'Food taster?'

'People are always trying to poison me,' said Adamant, shrugging. 'Reform has a lot of enemies in Haven, and particularly in the High Steppes. Mortice sees to it that none of the attempts get past the kitchens, so the food taster's really only there as a backup. Even so, you wouldn't believe what he's costing me in danger money.'

'I don't think we'll bother with the snack,' said Hawk. Fisher gave the wine at the bottom of her glass a hard look.

'You stick with us, Hawk,' said Medley, grinning. 'And

we'll give you a solid grounding on politics in Haven. There's a lot more to it than meets the eye.'

'So I'm finding out,' said Hawk.

3

Wolves in the Fold

Brimstone Hall stood aloof and alone in the middle of its grounds, surrounded by a high stone wall emblazoned with protective runes. Armed men watched from behind the massive iron gates, and guard dogs patrolled the wide-open grounds. Rumour had it the dogs had been fed human meat just long enough to give them a taste for it. There used to be apple trees in the grounds. Hardcastle had them torn up by the roots; they offered shelter to potential assassins.

Cameron Hardcastle was a very careful man. He trusted nothing and no one, with good cause. He had destroyed many men in his time, one way or another, and helped to ruin many more. It was said he had more enemies than any other man in Haven. Hardcastle believed it, and took pride in the fact. In a city of harsh and ruthless men, he had made himself a legend. Constant death threats were a small price to pay.

The Hall itself was a crumbling stone monstrosity held together by ancient spells and never-ending repair work. It was stiflingly hot in the summer and impossible to heat in the winter, but it had been home to the Hardcastles for years past counting, and Cameron would not give it up. Hardcastles never gave up anything that was theirs. They were supposed to have been instrumental in the founding of Haven, which might have been why so many of them had been convinced they should be running it.

Cameron Hardcastle began his career in the Low Kingdoms army. It was expected of him, his class, and his family, and he hated every minute of it. He left the army after only seven years, retiring in haste before he could be court-martialled. It was said the charges would have been extreme cruelty, but no one took that seriously. Extreme cruelty was usually what got you ahead in the Low Kingdoms army. The men fought so well because they were more afraid of their officers than they were of the enemy.

More importantly, there were rumours of blood sacrifice behind locked doors in the officers' mess, but no one talked about that. It wasn't considered healthy.

Hardcastle himself was an average-height, stocky man, with a barrel chest and heavily muscled upper arms. He was good-looking in a rough, scowling way, with a shock of dark hair and an unevenly trimmed moustache. He was in his mid forties, and looked it, but you only had to meet him for a few moments to feel the strength and power that radiated from him. Whatever else people said about him – and there was a lot of talk, most of it unpleasant – they all admitted the man had presence. When he entered a crowded room, the room fell silent.

He had a loud, booming laugh, though his sense of humour wasn't very pleasant. Most people went to the theatre for their entertainment; Hardcastle's idea of a good time was a visit to the public hangings. He enjoyed bear-baiting, prizefights, and kept a half-dozen dogs to go ratting with. On a good day he'd nail the rats' tails to the back door to show his tally.

He was Conservative because his family always had been, and because it suited his business interests to be so. The Hardcastles were of aristocratic stock, and no one was allowed to forget it. Of late, most of their money came from rents and banking, but no one was foolish enough to treat Hardcastle as a merchant or a businessman. Even as a joke. It wouldn't have been healthy. When he thought about politics at all, which wasn't often, Hardcastle believed in everyone knowing their place, and keeping to it. He thought universal suffrage was a ghastly mistake, and one he fully intended to rectify at the first opportunity. Reform was nothing more than a disease in the body politic, to be rooted out and destroyed. Starting with James bloody Adamant.

Hardcastle sat in his favourite wing chair, staring out the great bow window in his study and scowling furiously. Adamant was going to be a problem. The man had a great deal of popular support, more than any previous Reform candidate, and taking care of him was going to be difficult and expensive. Hardcastle hated spending money he didn't have to. Fortunately, there were other alternatives. He turned his gaze away from the window, and looked across at his sorcerer, Wulf.

The sorcerer was a tall, broad-shouldered man, with a fine noble head that was just a little too large for his body. Thick auburn hair fell to his shoulders in a mass of curls and knots. His face was long and narrow, and heavy-boned. His eyes were dark and thoughtful. He dressed always in sorcerer's black, complete with cape and cowl, and looked the part to perfection.

Wulf was a newcomer to Haven, and as yet hadn't shown much evidence of his power, but no one doubted he had it. A few weeks back he'd been attacked by four street thugs. It took the city Guard almost a week to find a horse and cart sturdy enough to carry the four stone statues away. They ended up on the Street of Gods. Tourists burn incense sticks before them, but the statues are still silently screaming.

Sitting quietly in a chair in the corner, with head bowed and hands clasped neatly in her lap, was Jillian Hardcastle, Cameron's wife. She was barely into her mid twenties, but she looked twenty years older. She had been pretty once, in an unremarkable way, but life with Hardcastle had worn her away until there was no character left in her face; only a shape, and features that faded from memory the moment she was out of sight. She dressed in rich and fashionable clothes because her husband expected it of her, but she still looked like what she was: a poor little country mouse who'd been brought into the city and had every spark of individuality beaten out of her. Those who spent time in Hardcastle's company had learned not to comment on the occasional bruises and black eyes that marked Jillian's face, or the mornings she spent lying in bed, resting.

They'd been married seven years. It was an arranged marriage. Hardcastle arranged it.

He glared at Wulf for a long moment, and when he finally spoke his voice was deceptively calm and even. 'You told me your magics could break through any barrier Adamant could buy. So why is he still alive?'

Wulf shrugged easily. 'He must have found himself a new sorcerer. I'm surprised anyone would work with him after what I did to his last magic-user, but then, that's Haven for you. There's always someone, if the money's right. It won't make any difference in the long run. It may take a little time to find just the right opening, but I doubt this magic-user will be any more difficult to dispose of than the last one.'

'More delays,' said Hardcastle. 'I don't like delays, sorcerer. I don't like excuses, either. I want James Adamant dead and out of the way before the people vote. I don't care what it costs, or what you have to do; I want him dead. Understand, sorcerer?'

'Of course, Cameron. I assure you, there's no need to worry. I'll take care of everything. I trust the rest of your campaign is running smoothly?'

'So far,' said Hardcastle grudgingly. 'The posterers have been out since dawn, and my mercenaries have been dealing with Adamant's men quite successfully, in spite of the interfering Guard. If Adamant is foolish enough to try and hold any street gatherings, my men will see they don't last long. Commoners don't have the guts to stand and fight.

Spill some blood on the cobbles, and they'll scatter fast enough.'

'Quite right, Cameron. There's nothing at all to worry about. We've thought of everything, planned for every eventuality. Nothing can go wrong.'

'Don't take me for a fool, sorcerer. Something can always go wrong. Adamant's no fool, either; he wouldn't still be investing so much time and money in his campaign if he didn't think he had a bloody good chance of beating me. He knows something, Wulf. Something we don't. I can feel it in my bones.'

'Whatever you say, Cameron. I'll make further enquiries. In the meantime, I have someone waiting to meet you.'

'I hadn't forgotten,' said Hardcastle. 'Your chief of mercenaries. The one you've been so mysterious about. Very well; who is it?'

Wulf braced himself. 'Roxanne.'

Hardcastle sat up straight in his chair. 'Roxanne? You brought that woman into my house? Get her out of here now!'

'It's perfectly all right, Cameron,' said Wulf quickly. 'I brought two of my best men to keep an eye on her. I think you'll find her reputation is a little exaggerated. She's the best sword-for-hire I've ever come across. Unbeatable with a blade in her hand, and a master strategist. She works well on her own, or in charge of troops. She's done an excellent job for us so far, with remarkably few fatalities. She's a genuine phenomenon.'

'She's also crazy!'

'There is that, yes. But it doesn't get in the way of her work.'

Hardcastle slowly settled back into his chair, but his scowl remained. 'All right, I'll see her. Where is she?'

'In the library.'

Hardcastle sniffed. 'At least there's not much there she can damage. Jillian, go and get her.'

His wife nodded silently, got to her feet and left the study, being careful to ease the door shut behind her so that it wouldn't slam.

Hardcastle turned away from the bow window, and stared at the portrait of his father, hanging on the wall opposite. A dark and gloomy picture of a dark and gloomy man. Gideon Hardcastle hadn't been much of a father, and Cameron had shed no tears at his funeral, but he had been a Councillor in Haven for thirty-four years. Cameron Hardcastle was determined to do better. Being a Councillor was just the beginning. He had plans. He was going to make the name Hardcastle respected and feared throughout the Low Kingdoms.

Whatever it took.

Roxanne prowled restlessly back and forth in Hardcastle's library, her boots sinking soundlessly into the thick pile carpet. The two mercenaries set to guard her watched nervously from the other side of the room. Roxanne smiled at them now and again, just to keep them on their toes. She was tall, six foot three even without her boots, with a lithe, muscular body. She wore a shirt and trousers of bright lime-yellow, topped with a battered leather jacket. She looked like a vicious canary. She wore a long sword on her left hip, in a well-worn scabbard.

At first sight she was not unattractive. She was young, in her early twenties, with a sharp-boned face, blazing dark eyes, and a mass of curly black hair held in place with a leather headband. But there was something about Roxanne, something in her unwavering gaze and disturbing smile that made even the most experienced mercenary uneasy. Besides, everyone knew her reputation.

Roxanne first made a name for herself when she was fifteen, fighting as a sword-for-hire in the Silk Trail vendettas. The rest of her company were wiped out in an ambush, and she had to fight her way back alone through the enemy lines. She killed seventeen men and women that night, and had the ears to prove it. The people who saw her stride back into camp that night, laughing and singing, covered in other people's blood and wearing a necklace of human ears, swore they'd never seen anything more frightening in their lives.

She went through a dozen mercenary companies in less than three years, and despite her swordsmanship they were always glad to see her go. She was brave and loyal, as long as she was paid regularly, and always the first to lead an attack, but there was no getting away from the fact that Roxanne was stark staring crazy. When there wasn't an enemy to fight she'd pick quarrels among her own people, just to get a little action. She was even worse when she got drunk. People who knew her learned to recognise the signs early, and head for the nearest exit. Roxanne had a nasty temper and a somewhat strange sense of humour. Her idea of a good night out tended to involve knife fights, terrorising the locals, and burning down inns that expected her to pay her bar bills.

Not that she limited her arson to inns. Quite often she'd set fire to a tent or two in her own camp, for reasons that made sense only to her. Roxanne liked a good fire. She also liked betting everything she had on one roll of the dice, and then refusing to pay up if she lost. She worshipped a god no one had ever heard of, had an entirely unhealthy regard for the truth, and picked fights with nuns. She said they offended her sense of the rightness of things. If Roxanne had a sense of the rightness of things, it was news to everyone who'd ever met her.

Everyone agreed that Roxanne would go far, and the sooner the better.

She ended up in Haven after a disagreement with a Captain of the Guard over the prices in a Jaspertown company store. When someone explained to her that she'd just killed the local Mayor's son, she decided it might be time to start looking for new employment. So she threw the Captain's head through the Mayor's front window, set fire to a post office as a distraction, and headed for Haven as fast as her stolen horse could carry her.

Roxanne roamed about Hardcastle's library, picking things up and putting them down again. She'd never seen so many resolutely ugly pieces of ornamental china in her life. And there wasn't a damn thing worth stealing. She broke a few ornaments on general principles, and because they made such a pleasant sound as they smashed against the wall. The two mercenaries stirred uneasily, but said nothing. Ostensibly they were there to keep her out of trouble and make sure she didn't set fire to anything, but Roxanne knew they wouldn't do anything unless they absolutely had to. They were scared of her. Most people were, particularly when she smiled. Roxanne smiled widely at the two mercenaries. They both paled visibly, and she turned away, satisfied. She started to pace up and down again, tapping her fingertips on her sword belt. She never could stay still for long. She had too much energy in her.

She looked round quickly as the library door swung open, and then took her hand away from her sword as a pale, colourless woman came in. At first Roxanne thought she must be a servant, but a quick glance at the quality of her clothes suggested she had to be very upper-class, even if she didn't act like it. She ignored the two mercenaries and addressed herself to Roxanne, without raising her eyes from the floor.

'My husband will see you now,' she said quietly, her voice entirely free of inflection. 'Please follow me and I'll take you to him.'

The two mercenaries looked at each other, and one of them cleared his throat diffidently. 'Pardon me, ma'am, but we're supposed to stay with her.'

Jillian Hardcastle glanced at him briefly, and then looked

back at the floor. 'My husband wants to see Roxanne. He didn't mention you.'

The mercenary frowned uncertainly. 'I don't really think we should . . .'

'You stay put,' said Roxanne flatly. 'Don't touch the booze and don't break anything. Got it?'

'Got it,' said the mercenary. 'We'll stay right here.' The other mercenary nodded quickly.

Roxanne followed Jillian Hardcastle out of the library and into the hall. It was a large hall, wide and echoing, and Roxanne did her best to look unimpressed. She quickly realised she needn't bother, as Jillian kept her gaze firmly on the ground at all times. Roxanne stared at her thoughtfully. This beaten-down little mouse was Hardcastle's wife? Perhaps the rumours about him were true after all.

Jillian opened the study door, and gestured politely for Roxanne to go in first. She did so, swaggering in with her thumbs tucked into her sword belt. Hardcastle and Wulf got to their feet. Hardcastle studied her narrowly. Roxanne smiled at them both, and didn't miss the little *moue* of unease that crossed their faces. She knew the effect her smile had on people. That was why she used it. She glanced quickly round the study. Not bad. Quite luxurious in its way. She did her best to look as though she'd seen better, in her time.

'Welcome to my house, Roxanne,' said Hardcastle heavily. 'Wulf tells me you've done good work for me. As a reward, I have a special assignment for you. You'll be working mostly alone, but there's an extra five hundred ducats in it for you.'

'Sounds good,' said Roxanne. 'What's the catch?'

Hardcastle frowned. Out of the corner of her eye, Roxanne saw Jillian wince momentarily, and then her face was blank and empty again. Roxanne dropped insolently into the most comfortable-looking chair and draped one leg over the padded arm. Hardcastle looked at her for a moment, and then drew up a chair opposite her. Wulf and Jillian remained standing. Hardcastle met Roxanne's gaze for a moment, and then looked away, despite himself.

'James Adamant is standing against me in the election,' he said finally. 'I want him stopped. Hurt him, kill him, I don't care. Spend as much as you need, use whatever tactics you like. If there's any repercussions I'll get you out of Haven in plenty of time.'

'The catch,' said Roxanne.

'Adamant has two Captains of the city Guard as body-guards,' said Hardcastle steadily. 'They're called Hawk and Fisher.'

Roxanne smiled. 'I've heard of them. They're supposed to be good. Very good.' She laughed happily. It was an unpleasant, disturbing sound. 'Hardcastle, I'd almost do this for free, just for the chance to go up against those two.'

'They're not the target,' said Hardcastle sharply. 'If you have a grudge against them, you deal with it on your own time.'

'Of course,' said Roxanne.

'Even apart from them. Adamant's going to be hard to reach. He has his own mercenaries, and a new magic-user. I understand you have a special contact of your own among his people, so I'll leave the details to you. But it has to be done soon.' He picked up his wineglass. 'Jillian, get me some wine.'

She moved quickly forward, took the glass from his hand, and went over to the row of decanters on the nearby table.

'Do I get any support on this?' said Roxanne, 'Or am I working entirely on my own?'

'Use whatever people you need, but make sure there are no direct links to me. Officially, you're just another of my mercenaries.'

Jillian brought him a glass of wine. Hardcastle looked at it without touching it. 'Jillian, what is this?'

'Your wine, Cameron.'

'What kind of wine?'

'Red wine.'

'And what kind of wine do I normally drink when I have guests?'

'White wine.'

'So why have you brought me red?'

Jillian's mouth began to tremble slightly, though her face remained blank. 'I don't know.'

'It's because you're stupid, isn't it?'

'Yes, Cameron.'

'Go and get me some white wine.'

Jillian went back to the decanters. Hardcastle looked at Roxanne, who was studying him thoughtfully. 'Have you got something to say, mercenary?'

'She's your wife.'

'Yes. She is.'

Jillian came back with a glass of white wine. Hardcastle took it, and put it down on the desk without tasting it. 'I'll talk with you about this later, Jillian.'

She nodded, and stood silently beside his chair. Her hands were clasped so tightly together that the knuckles showed white.

'It's time you spoke to your people, Cameron,' said Wulf softly. 'We need them out on the streets as quickly as possible, and you need to speak to them before they go.'

Hardcastle nodded ungraciously and got to his feet. He looked at Roxanne. 'You'd better come too. You might learn something.'

'Wouldn't miss it for the world,' said Roxanne.

The main hall at Brimstone Hall was uncomfortably large. Two chandeliers of massed candles spread a great pool of light down the middle of the hall, and oil lamps lined the walls. Even so, dark shadows pressed close around the borders of the light. Silence lay heavily across the hall, and the slightest sound seemed to echo on forever. Armed men stood at intervals along the walls, staring blankly straight ahead, somehow all the more menacing for their complete lack of movement. A wide set of stairs led up to a gallery overlooking the hall. Hardcastle stood at ease on the gallery, smiling faintly at some pleasant thought of things to come. Jillian stood at his side – quiet, pliant, head bowed, and eyes far away, as though trying to pretend she wasn't really there at all.

Roxanne stood back a way, hidden in the shadows of the gallery. Wulf sat on a chair beside her, legs casually crossed, hands folded neatly in his lap. He might have been waiting for a late dessert, or a promised glass of wine, but there was something unsettling in the air of anticipation that hung about him, something . . . unhealthy. Roxanne kept a careful watch on him from the corner of her eye. She didn't trust sorcerers. Not that she trusted anyone, when you got right down to it, but in her experience magic-users were a particularly treacherous breed.

Hardcastle finally nodded to the two armed mercenaries at the end of the hall, and they pulled back the bolts and swung open the heavy main doors. The crowd of Conservative supporters came surging in, herded by polite but firm stewards. There were flags and banners and a steady hum of anticipation, but it had to be said that the crowd didn't exactly look enthusiastic to be there. Roxanne couldn't help but wonder whether the armed guards were there to keep people out, or keep them in. The main doors slammed shut behind the last of the crowd. Hardcastle looked out over his supporters, and cleared his throat loudly. The hall fell silent.

Afterwards, Roxanne was never really clear what the speech had been about. It was an excellent speech, no doubt of that, but she couldn't seem to sort out what exactly had been so enthralling about it. She only knew that the moment Hardcastle began to speak he became magnetic. She couldn't tear her eyes away from him, and she strained to hear every word. The crowd below were besotted with him, cheering and applauding and waving their banners frantically every time he paused. Even the stewards and mercenaries seemed fascinated by him. The speech finally came to an end, amid rapturous applause. Hardcastle looked out over the ecstatic crowd, smiling slightly, and then gestured for silence. The cheers gradually died away.

'My friends, there is one among you who has proved himself worthy of my special attention. Joshua Steele, step forward.'

There was a pause, and then a young man dressed in the gaudy finery of the minor Quality made his way through the crowd to stand at the foot of the stairs. Even from the back of the gallery Roxanne could tell he was scared. His hands had clenched into fists at his sides, and his face was deathly pale. Hardcastle's smile widened a little.

'Steele, I set you a task. Nothing too difficult. All you had to do was use your contacts to find out whether James Adamant was still magically protected. You told me he wasn't. That's not true, is it, Steele?'

The young man licked his lips quickly, and shifted his weight from one foot to the other. 'I did everything I could, Councillor. Honestly! His old sorcerer, Masque, is dead, and Adamant hasn't made any move to replace him. My informants were very precise.'

Hardcastle shook his head sadly. 'You lied to me, Steele. You betrayed me.'

Steele suddenly turned and ran, pushing his way through the crowd. Hardcastle looked back at Wulf, and nodded quickly. The sorcerer frowned, concentrating. Steele screamed shrilly, and the crowd drew back from him in horror as he fell writhing to the floor. Blood spurted from his nose and ears, and then from his eyes. He clawed at his face, and then at his stomach as bloody spots appeared on his tunic. Small fanged mouths burst out of his flesh all over his body, as hundreds of bloodworms chewed their way out of him. One of them ruptured the carotid artery in his neck and blood flew out, soaking the nearest members of the crowd. They moaned in revulsion, but couldn't tear their eyes away. Steele kicked and struggled feebly for a few moments longer, and then let out his breath in a long, ragged sigh. His body continued to twitch and jerk as the bloodworms ate their way out. Some of the crowd stamped on the horrid things as they left the body, but it quickly became clear the worms were already dying. They couldn't survive for long once they'd left their host.

Roxanne looked thoughtfully at Hardcastle's back, and then at the sorcerer Wulf. There was a lesson here worth remembering. If she ever fell out with Hardcastle, she'd better make sure the sorcerer was dead first. She looked back at the crowd. They were silent and shocked, sullen now. Their holiday mood had been ruined. Hardcastle raised his voice to get their attention, and began to speak again.

And once more his marvellous oratory worked its magic. In a matter of moments, the crowd was won over again, and soon they were stamping and cheering and shouting his name, just as they had before. They seemed to have forgotten all about the dead man in their midst. Hardcastle filled their hearts and minds with good cheer, and sent them out into the streets to campaign on his behalf. The crowd filed out of the hall, laughing and chattering animatedly among themselves. Soon the hall was empty, apart from the stewards and the mercenaries. Hardcastle looked down at the body lying alone in the middle of the floor.

'Have someone clean up the mess,' he said coldly, and then turned and left the gallery, followed by Wulf and Jillian. Roxanne looked at the torn and blood-soaked body down below.

Hardcastle strode into his study and poured himself a large drink. The speech had gone down well, and that little bastard Steele had got what was coming to him. Maybe there was some justice in the world after all. He was just lowering himself into his favourite chair when the commotion began. Someone was shouting in the corridor, and there was the sound of running feet and general panic. Hardcastle rose quickly from his chair, and his gaze went immediately to the family long-sword hanging on the wall over the fireplace. It had been a good few years since he'd last drawn that in anger, but he'd had a strong feeling he'd need the blade sooner or later during this campaign. And with Wulf's war on Adamant's house finally beginning to warm up, it was only to be expected that Adamant would resort in kind. Hardcastle snorted angrily as he put down his glass and pulled the long-sword from its sheath. So much for Adamant's puerile insistence on playing by the rules. There was only one rule in politics, and that was to win.

It felt good to have a sword in his hands again. He'd spent too long in smoke-filled rooms, arguing with fools for money and support that should have been his by right. The commotion in the hall was growing louder. Hardcastle nodded grimly. Let them come. Let them all come. He'd show them he was a force to be reckoned with. He shot a quick glance at Jillian, who was standing uncertainly by the door, one hand raised to her mouth. Useless damned mouse of a wife. He'd tried to knock some backbone into her, and little good it had done him. He gestured curtly for her to get away from the door, and she fled to the nearest chair and stood behind it. The sorcerer Wulf stayed by the door, making hurried gestures with his hands and muttering under his breath.

'Well?' said Hardcastle impatiently, 'What's out there? Are we under attack?'

'Not by magic, Cameron. My wards are still holding. The attack must be on the physical plane. Mercenaries, perhaps.' He stopped suddenly, and sniffed at the air. 'Can you smell smoke?'

They looked at each other as the same thought struck them both at the same time. They didn't need to say her name. Hardcastle hurried out into the hall, sword in hand, followed by Wulf. Roxanne had her back to the wall and her sword at the ready as she faced off against two of Hardcastle's mercenaries. She was grinning broadly. The mercenaries looked scared but determined. A little further down the hall, a huge wall tapestry was going up in flames. Several servants were trying to put it out with pans of water.

Hardcastle's face purpled dangerously. 'Roxanne! What's the meaning of this?'

'Just having a little fun,' said Roxanne easily. 'I was doing all right till these two spoilsports interfered. I'll be with you in a minute, as soon as I've dealt with them.'

'Roxanne,' said Wulf quickly, before Hardcastle could say something unwise, 'please put away your sword. These men belong to your employer, Councillor Hardcastle. They are under his protection.'

Roxanne sniffed ungraciously, and sheathed her sword. The mercenaries put away their swords, looking more than a little relieved. Wulf gestured for them to leave, and they did so quickly, before he could change his mind. Wulf looked at Roxanne reproachfully.

'When you signed the contract to work for Councillor Hardcastle, there was a specific clause stating that you wouldn't start any fires except those we asked you to.'

Roxanne shrugged. 'You know I can't read.'

'I read it aloud to you.'

'It was an ugly tapestry anyway.'

'That's as may be. But as long as you work for the Councillor you will abide by your contract. Or are you saying your word is worthless?'

Roxanne glared at him. Wulf's stomach lurched, but he stood his ground. He knew any number of spells that would stop her in her tracks, but he had a sneaking suspicion she'd still survive long enough to kill him, no matter what he did to her. Confronting her this early was a definite risk, but it had to be done. Either her word was binding or it wasn't. And if it wasn't, then she was too dangerous a weapon to be used. He'd have to let her go, and hope he could kill her safely from a distance.

Roxanne scowled suddenly, and leaned against the wall with her arms folded. 'All right, no more fires. You people have no sense of fun.'

'Of course not,' said Wulf. 'We're in politics.'

'If you've quite finished,' said Hardcastle acidly, 'perhaps you'd care to accompany me back to my study. I'm expecting some very important guests, and I want both of you present. If you can spare the time.'

'Of course,' said Roxanne cheerfully. 'You're the boss.'

Hardcastle gave her a hard look, and then led the way back to his study. The DeWitt brothers were already there, waiting for him. Hardcastle silently promised his butler a slow and painful death for not warning him, and then smiled courteously at the DeWitts and walked forward to shake hands with them. At the last moment he realised he was still holding his sword, and handed it quickly to Wulf to replace on the wall. At least Jillian had had the sense to get the DeWitts a glass of wine. Perhaps the situation could still be saved.

Marcus and David DeWitt were both in their late forties, and on first impression looked much the same: tall, slender, elegant, and arrogant. Dark hair and eyes made their faces appear pale and washed out, giving their impassive features the look of a mummer's mask. There was a quiet, under-stated menace in their unwavering self-possession, as though nothing in the world would dare disturb them. They'd left their swords at the front door, along with their bodyguards, as a sign of trust, but Hardcastle wasn't fool enough to believe them unarmed. The DeWitts had many enemies and took no chances. Even with a supposed ally.

Between them, Marcus and David DeWitt ran a third of

the docks in Haven, on the age-old principle of the minimum investment for the maximum gain. Their docks were notorious for being the worst maintained and the most dangerous work areas in Haven. If the DeWitts gave a damn, they hid it remarkably well. Life was cheap in Haven, and labour even cheaper. And the DeWitts' charges were attractively low, so they never wanted for traffic. But now the dock strike was crippling them, despite the zombie scab labour. The dead men were cheap enough to run and never got tired, but they weren't very bright and needed constant supervision. They were also easy targets for dock-worker guerrilla units armed with salt and fire.

A Conservative-backed Council would support the De-Witts against the Dock-workers Guild, even if it came down to open violence and intimidation. Reform would back the Guild. So the DeWitts were making the rounds before the election, buying themselves Councillors. Unfortunately for them, they needed Hardcastle more than he needed them. So if they wanted his support, they were going to have to pay through the nose for it.

Wulf leaned back in his chair and quietly studied the DeWitt brothers. They were an unpleasant pair, by all accounts, but he'd worked with worse in his time. Like Hardcastle, for example. A brute and a bully and not nearly as clever as he thought he was. Wulf had done a great many unpleasant things himself, down the years; his style of magic demanded it. But he did them in a businesslike way, because they were necessary. Hardcastle did unpleasant things because he enjoyed it. He was one of those people who can only prove how important they are by showing how unimportant everyone else is. Wulf frowned slightly. Such men are dangerous – to themselves, and those around them.

But for the moment, he was a man with power, a rising star; a man on the way up. Wulf could go far, riding the coattails of such a man. And when Hardcastle's star began to wane, Wulf would move on. He had ambitions of his own. Hardcastle was just a means to an end.

'Twenty thousand ducats,' said Marcus DeWitt in his cold, flat voice. He took a folded bank draft from his coat pocket and laid it carefully on the table before him. 'I trust that will be sufficient?'

'For the moment,' said Hardcastle. He gestured easily to Wulf, who leaned forward and picked up the bank draft.

'James Adamant has a hell of a lot of followers out on the streets,' said David DeWitt, opening a small silver snuff box and taking out a pinch of white powder. He sniffed delicately, and then sighed slowly as the dust hit his system. He smiled, and looked steadily at Hardcastle. 'Just how do you intend to deal with this very popular Reformer, sir Hardcastle?'

'The traditional way,' said Hardcastle. 'Money, and force of arms. The carrot and the stick. It never fails, providing it's applied properly. My people are already out on the streets.'

'Adamant has money,' said Marcus. 'He also has Hawk and Fisher.'

'They're not infallible,' said Hardcastle. 'They couldn't keep Blackstone from being killed.'

'They caught his killer,' said David DeWitt. 'And made sure he didn't live to stand trial.'

'There's no need to worry,' said Wulf. 'We have our own wild card. Gentlemen, may I present the legendary Roxanne.'

She smiled at the DeWitt brothers, and they both flinched a little.

'Ah, yes,' said Marcus. 'I thought I smelt something burning as we came in.'

'I always thought she'd be taller,' said David. 'Taller, and covered with fresh blood.'

Wulf smiled. 'She's everything the legends say she is, and more.'

Marcus DeWitt frowned. 'Does Adamant know she's working for you?'

'No,' said Hardcastle. 'Not yet. We're saving that for a surprise.'

The sorcerer known as the Grey Veil huddled in a corner of the deserted church, shivering with the cold. He'd been there for several hours, gathering together what was left of his magic. He couldn't believe how fast everything had fallen apart. One moment he had been a force to be reckoned with, a sorcerer with hundreds of lesser minds under his command; and then suddenly his control was broken by an interfering Guard, and he'd had to run for his life like a thief in the night. His slaves were free again, and he was a wanted man with a price on his head.

It had all seemed so simple in the beginning. Enter the election as a candidate, and then possess enough people to raise an army of voters. Once on the Council, all kinds of powerful men would have been vulnerable to his possession. A simple plan; so simple it seemed foolproof. He should have known something would go wrong. Something always went wrong. Veil hugged his knees to his chest and rocked back and forth on his haunches. He had no idea how the Guards had found him out. It didn't really matter. He'd staked everything he had on one roll of the dice and had nothing left with which to start again. He'd be lucky to get out of Haven alive.

He pulled his thin cloak tightly about him. He should have known it would come to this. All his life everything he'd turned his hand to had failed him. He'd been born into a debt-ridden family, which, as time went on, only slid further and further into poverty. He was put to work as soon as he was able, at the age of seven. He spent his childhood in the sweatshops of the Devil's Hook, and in his adolescence moved restlessly from one lousy job to another, searching always for the one lucky break that would change his life. Whatever money he made went on plans and schemes and desperate gambles, but none of them ever came to anything. Even the girl he loved went to another man.

And then he met the old man, who found in Veil a gift for magic. He worked himself to exhaustion to pay for the old man's lessons in sorcery, and when that wasn't enough he stole what he needed from his friends. When he was powerful enough he killed the old man, and took his grimoires and objects of power. He became the Grey Veil, and swore an oath on his own blood that whatever happened, whatever he had to do, he would never be poor again.

Veil smiled bitterly. He should have known better. A loser was still a loser, no matter what fancy new name he took. He breathed heavily on his hands, trying to coax some warmth into his numb fingers. It was very cold in the Temple of the Abomination.

There were many abandoned churches on the Street of Gods. A Being's power would wane, or its followers prove fickle, or perhaps simply the fashion would change, and overnight a church whose walls had once rung to the sound of hymns of adoration and the dropping of coins into offertory bowls would find itself suddenly deserted and abandoned. Eventually another congregation would take over the building, worshipping another god, and business would go on as usual. But some abandoned churches were left strictly alone, for fear of what might linger in the silence.

The Temple of the Abomination had stood empty and alone for centuries; a simple, square stone building on the lower end of the Street of Gods. It wasn't very large, and from the outside it looked more like a downmarket mausoleum than a church. It had no windows, and only the one door. It wasn't locked or bolted. The Temple of the Abomination had a bad reputation, even for the Street of

Gods. People who went in tended not to come out again. Veil didn't give a damn. He needed a place to hide where no one else would think to look. Nothing else mattered.

It slowly occurred to him that the church didn't seem as dark as it had been. When he'd first crept inside the church, he'd pulled the door shut behind him, closing out the light. The pitch darkness had been a comfort to him then, an endless night that would hide him from prying eyes. But now he could clearly make out the interior of the church, such as it was. There wasn't much to see, just plain stone walls and a broken stone altar set roughly in the centre of the room. Veil frowned. Where the hell was the light coming from?

Curiosity finally stirred him from his hiding place in the corner, and he rose slowly to his feet. He moved forward, wincing as his stiff joints creaked protestingly. The small sounds seemed very loud on the quiet. Outside on the Street of Gods the clamour of a hundred priests filled the air from dawn to dusk, augmented by the hymns and howls of the faithful, but not a whisper of that turmoil passed through the thick stone walls.

Veil peered about him, but there seemed no obvious source to the dim blue light that filled the church. He glanced down at his feet to see which way his shadow was pointing, and his heart missed a beat. He didn't have a shadow. A cold hand clutched at his heart, and for a moment his breath caught in his throat. There had to be a shadow; there were other shadows all around him. Some of them were moving. Veil stumbled back a step and looked quickly about him, but there was nothing and no one in the church with him, and the quiet remained unbroken. He took a deep breath and made himself hold it for a long moment before letting go. This was no time to be letting his imagination get the better of him. The light was nothing to worry about. There were bound to be stray vestiges of magic in a place like this.

He made himself walk over to the stone altar. It didn't look like much, up close. Just a great slab of stone, roughly the shape and size of an average coffin. He winced mentally at the comparison, and walked slowly round the altar. It was cracked from end to end, and someone had cut runes of power into the stone with a chisel. Veil's lips moved slowly as he worked out the meaning. The runes were part of a restraining spell, meant to hold something in the stone.

Veil frowned. All he knew about the Temple of the Abomination was what everybody knew. Hundreds of years ago, when the city was still young, a cult of death and worse than death had flourished on the Street of Gods, until the other Beings had joined together to destroy the Abomination and all its worshippers. It all happened so long ago that no one even remembered what the Abomination was anymore. On an impulse, Veil placed his hands on the altar and called up his magic, trying to draw out whatever impressions still remained in the stone.

Power rushed through him like a tidal wave, awful and magnificent, blinding and deafening him with its intensity. He staggered drunkenly back and forth as strange thoughts and feelings swept through him, none of them his own. Memories of priests and carriers swept through him and were gone, blazing up and disappearing like so many candles snuffed by an unforgiving darkness. There were too many to count, but all of them had served the Abomination, and it had granted them power over the earth and everything that moved upon it.

Veil slowly lifted his head and looked about him. The church was lit as bright as day. He could feel the power surging within him, impatient to be released. He would use that power to gather followers, and bring them to what moved within him. And the thing that men had once called the Abomination would thrive and grow strong again.

That was not its true name, of course. Veil knew what the

Abomination really was. He'd known it all his life. He laughed aloud, and the horrid sound echoed on and on in the silence.

4

Various Kinds of Truth

Hawk and Fisher lounged around Adamant's study, waiting impatiently for him to make an appearance. They were due to go out campaigning in the streets soon, but Adamant had promised them a chance to talk with everyone first. Hawk and Fisher still thought of themselves primarily as bodyguards, but there was still the problem of a possible traitor and embezzler somewhere in Adamant's inner circle. Hawk was determined to get to the bottom of that. He didn't like traitors.

Fisher helped herself to a large drink from one of the decanters, and looked enquiringly at Hawk. He shook his head. 'You shouldn't either, Isobel. We're going to need clear heads to get through today.'

Fisher shrugged, and poured half the drink back into the decanter. 'Where the hell is Adamant, anyway? He promised us at least an hour for these interviews.'

'We'll manage,' said Hawk. 'Maybe we should start with someone else. Adamant's got a lot on his mind right now.'

'You like him, don't you?' said Fisher.

'Yes. He reminds me a lot of Blackstone. Bright, compassionate, and committed to his Cause. I'm not going to lose him as well, Isobel.'

'Don't get carried away,' said Fisher. 'Remember, as Guards we're strictly neutral. We don't take sides. We're protecting the man, not his Cause. If you want to get enthusiastic about Reform, do it on your own time.'

'Oh, come on, Isobel. Doesn't Adamant stir your blood

even a little? Think of the things he could do once he gets elected.'

'If he gets elected.'

The door opened, and they quickly fell silent. Adamant nodded briskly to the two Guards, and pretended not to notice the drink in Fisher's hand. 'Sorry I'm late, but Medley keeps coming up with problems he insists only I can deal with. Now, what can I do for you?'

'We need more detail on the death threats, the information leaks, and the embezzlement,' said Hawk. 'Let's start with the death threats.'

Adamant sat on the edge of his desk, and frowned thoughtfully. 'I didn't pay them much attention at first. There are always threats and crank letters. Reform has many enemies. But then the threats became specific. They said my garden would die, and it did. More magical attacks followed, including the one that killed Mortice. The last communication said I would die if I didn't resign. Blunt as that.

'There's not much I can tell you about the embezzling. My accountants stumbled across it quite by accident. Medley has the details. They've agreed to keep quiet about it until we can find the traitor, but they won't stay silent for long. They work for the Cause, not me personally.'

'The information leaks,' prompted Fisher.

'After the embezzlement I started checking through my records, and I found that what I'd thought of as nothing more than a run of really bad luck was actually something more than that. Something more sinister. Someone had been tipping off the Conservatives about my plans and movements. Crowds were dispersed before I could address them, potential allies were intimidated, and meetings were disrupted by planted thugs. Not everyone has access to that kind of information in advance. It has to be someone close to me.'

'Assuming we identify the traitor,' said Hawk slowly, 'what if it turns out to be someone very close to you?'

'You let the law take its course,' said Adamant flatly.

'Even if it's a friend?'

'Especially if it's a friend.'

In the cellar, in the darkness, the sorcerer Mortice sat alone amid blocks of ice and felt his body decay. The pain howled within him, awful and never-ending, gnawing away at his courage and his sanity. At first the concentration needed to maintain Adamant's defences had helped to protect him from the pain and the horror of his situation, but it wasn't enough anymore. Through all the endless hours of the day and night there was nothing for him to do but sit and think and feel.

He had gone through anger and acceptance and horror, and now existed from minute to minute in quiet desperation. He had long ago given up on hope. He would have gladly gone mad, if he hadn't needed to keep control to protect Adamant. He still might. More and more his thoughts tended to wander and fray at the edges.

No one had been to see him for a long time. He could understand that. It was cold in the cellar, and they all had things to do, important things. But time passed slowly in the dark, and no one had been to see him in a very long time. And Adamant, his good friend James Adamant, came least of all.

Mortice sat alone in the cold, in the dark, in the pain, going slowly insane and knowing there was nothing he could do to stop it.

Medley came breezing into the study with a sheaf of papers in his hand, and then stopped dead as he saw Hawk and Fisher.

'Oh, damn! You wanted to see me, didn't you? Sorry, but James has been running me off my feet this morning. What can I do for you?'

'To start with, tell us about the embezzlement,' said Hawk. 'Exactly how much money has gone missing?'

'A fair amount,' said Medley, sitting casually on the edge of Adamant's desk. 'About three thousand ducats in all, spread over a period of three months. Small amounts at first, but growing steadily larger.'

'Who has access to the money?' said Fisher.

Medley frowned. 'That's the problem; quite a few people. James and myself, of course; Dannielle, the butler Villiers and half a dozen other servants, and of course several Reform people who worked on the campaign with us.'

'We'll need a list of names,' said Hawk.

'I'll see you get it.'

'How was the money taken?' said Fisher.

'I'm not actually sure,' said Medley. 'The accountants were the first to notice something was wrong. Do you want to take a look at the books?'

Hawk and Fisher looked at each other. 'Maybe later,' said Hawk. 'Tell me about Adamant. How has he responded to the death threats?'

'Fairly coolly. They're not the first he's had, and they won't be the last. It's a part of politics in Haven. The magic attacks worry him, of course; Mortice isn't as reliable as he once was.'

'Then why doesn't he hire a new sorcerer?' said Fisher.

'Mortice is James's friend. And he lost his life defending James from attack. James can't just abandon him. And besides, when he's in form, Mortice is still one of the most powerful sorcerers in Haven.'

They sat in silence for a while, each looking expectantly at the other.

'If there's nothing else . . .' said Medley.

'You're in charge of Adamant's affairs,' said Hawk. 'Who do you think has been leaking information?'

'I don't know,' said Medley. 'It has to be someone with a

grudge against James, but I'm damned if I know who. James is one of the fairest and most honourable men I know. The only enemies he has are political ones. Now if you'll excuse me . . . '

He dropped his papers on the desk, nodded briskly to the Guards to indicate the interview was over, and left the study. Hawk let him go. He leafed through the papers on the desk, but they told him nothing.

'For a political adviser, he's either extremely tactful or not very bright,' said Fisher. 'I can think of several possible enemies among Adamant's own people. Mortice, to start with. He saves Adamant's life, and ends up a rotting corpse for his trouble. And then there's his wife, Dannielle. She wouldn't be the first woman to be mad at her husband because he was more interested in his work than he was in her. And finally, what about Medley himself? He's in charge of the day-to-day running of the campaign; who has a better chance to embezzle money without it being missed?'

'Wait a minute,' said Hawk. 'Mortice and Dannielle I'll go along with, but Medley? What's his motive?'

'As I understand it, he worked both sides of the political fence before he came to work for Adamant. He could still be on the Conservative payroll as an undercover agent.'

Hawk scowled unhappily. 'This is going to be another tricky one. If we point the finger at the wrong person, or even the right person but without enough proof, we could end up in a hell of a lot of trouble.'

'You got that right,' said Fisher.

Up in the Adamants' bedroom, Dannielle sat elegantly on the edge of the bed and watched critically as James held a shirt up against himself for her approval. It didn't look any better than the first two, but she supposed she'd better agree to this one or he'd get annoyed with her. She wouldn't have minded if he just got red in the face and shouted at her, but James tended more to looking terribly hurt and put upon, and being icily polite. When he wasn't sulking. Dannielle sometimes found herself picking fights with the servants just to have someone she could yell at. At least some of them would yell back at her. She realised James was still waiting patiently, and she quickly smiled and nodded her approval of the shirt. He smiled, and put it on.

Dannielle bit her lip. Better to say it now, while he was in a good mood. 'James, what do you think of Hawk and Fisher?'

'They seem competent enough. And surprisingly intelligent, for Guards.'

'But do you think they'll be good at their job? As bodyguards?'

'Oh, certainly.'

'Then we don't need to rely on Mortice so much anymore, do we?' James looked at her sharply, and she hurried on before he could say anything. 'You've got to do something about Mortice, James. We can't go on as we are. We need real magical protection. It was different when we had no one else we could trust, but now we've got Hawk and Fisher . . .'

'Mortice is one of the most powerful sorcerers in Haven,' said Adamant flatly.

'He used to be; now he's just a corpse with delusions of grandeur. His mind's going, James. Those blood-creatures weren't the first things to get past his wards, were they?'

'He's my friend,' said Adamant quietly. 'He gave his life for me. I can't just turn my back on him.'

'When was the last time you went to see him, before today?'

Adamant came and sat down on the bed beside her. He suddenly looked very tired. 'I can't bear to see him anymore, Danny. Just looking at him makes me feel sick and angry and guilty. If he'd just died, I could mourn for him and let him go. But he isn't dead or alive . . . Just being in the cellar with him makes my skin crawl. The sorcerer

Masque was my friend, not that thing rotting in the darkness! But he was my friend, and if it wasn't for him I would have died. Oh, Danny, I don't know what to feel anymore!'

Dannielle put her arms around him and rocked him back and forth. 'I know, love. I know.'

Dannielle came into the study only a few minutes after Hawk sent for her. She smiled brightly at the two Guards, and sank gracefully into her favourite chair.

'I do hope this won't take long. James is almost ready to go.'

'We just need to get a few things clear,' said Hawk easily. 'Nothing too difficult. How involved are you with the day-to-day running of Adamant's campaign?'

'Not very. Stefan handles all that. I've no head for organising things, so I let the two men get on with it. My job is to stand conspicuously at James's side and smile at anyone who looks like they might vote for him. I'm rather good at that.'

'What about the financial side?' said Fisher.

'I'm afraid I'm not very good with figures, either. It's all I can do to handle the household accounts. Once I went a few hundred ducats over budget and James was positively rude to me. Stefan handles all the money to do with the campaign. That's part of his job.'

'Let's talk about the gossip,' said Hawk.

Dannielle looked at him guilelessly. 'What gossip?'

'Come on,' said Fisher. 'There's always gossip, and you're in the best position to know about it. Servants will talk to you where they wouldn't talk to Adamant or Medley. Or us.'

Dannielle thought for a moment, and then shrugged. 'Very well, but I can't vouch for how authentic any of this is. Stefan's been a bit . . . distracted recently. Apparently he's got a new girlfriend he's very fond of, but he's trying to keep it quiet because James wouldn't approve of her. It seems she's minor Quality, from a very Conservative family with strong connections to Hardcastle. You can imagine what the broadsheet singers would make of that, if it ever got out.'

'How long has this been going on?' said Hawk.

'I'm not sure. About a month. I think.'

'After the problems with the embezzlement began?'

'Oh, well after. Besides, Stefan would never betray James. He's far too *professional*.'

Hawk caught the emphasis, and raised an eyebrow. 'I thought that was why Adamant hired him?'

'There's such a thing as being too professional. Stefan lives, eats, and breathes his work. His word is never broken, and he defends his reputation the way some women defend their honour. What's more, he works all the hours God sends, and expects James to do the same. It's all I can do to get the pair of them to eat regularly. I'll be glad when this bloody campaign is over and we can all get back to normal.'

'Is there anything else you can tell us?' said Hawk. 'Has anything unusual happened recently?'

'You mean apart from my garden disappearing overnight and a rain of blood in my hall?'

Hawk nodded glumly. 'I take your point.'

Dannielle got to her feet. 'Well, it was very nice talking to you both, but if you'll excuse me, James is waiting.'

She swept out, without waiting for permission to leave. Hawk waited until the door had closed behind her, and then looked at Fisher. 'So, Medley has a Conservative lover. That could be significant. Perhaps there's some kind of blackmail involved.'

'Maybe; but the embezzlement started months before he met her.'

'We can't be sure of that. He could have been seeing her for months before the servants got to hear of it.'

Fisher scowled. 'This is going to be another complicated case, isn't it?'

Stefan Medley sat alone in the library, staring at a wall of books and not seeing them. He should have told Hawk and Fisher about his lady love, but he hadn't. He couldn't. They wouldn't have understood.

Love was a new experience for Medley. The only passion he'd ever known before was for his work. Medley had long ago come to the conclusion that whatever women wanted in a man, he didn't have it. He wasn't much to look at, he had few social graces and even less money, and his chosen career wasn't exactly glamorous. He didn't want much out of life; he just wanted someone to care for him who didn't have to, someone to give him a reason for living. He just wanted what everyone else had and took for granted, and he'd never known.

Now he'd found someone, or she'd found him, and he wouldn't give her up. He couldn't. She was all he had. Except for James's friendship. Medley beat softly on the arm of his chair with his fist. James had believed in him, made him his right-hand man and his friend, trusted him above all others. And now here he was, selfishly keeping a secret that could destroy James's campaign if word ever got out.

But he had to do it. James would never understand. Of all the women he could have fallen in love with, it had to be *her* . . . except, of course, he'd had no choice in the matter. It had just . . . happened. Medley had always thought that falling in love, when it finally happened, would be gentle and romantic. In fact, it was more like being mugged. Overnight, his whole life had changed.

Medley sat quietly while his mind worked frantically, turning desperately this way and that, searching for a way out of the trap he'd built for himself. There was no way out. Sooner or later he was going to have to choose between his friend and his love, and he didn't know what would happen then. He couldn't give up either of them. They were the two sides of his nature. And they were tearing him apart.

'More and more, this reminds me of the Blackstone case,' said Fisher. 'Something nasty's going to happen. We can all feel it in the air, and there's nothing we can do about it.'

'At least then we had a handful of suspects to choose among,' said Hawk. 'Now we're stuck with two: the man's wife and his best friend. And the only skeleton in the cupboard we've been able to find is that Medley *might* be seeing a Conservative girlfriend on the quiet. Hardly a burning motive for murder and betrayal, is it?'

'Don't look at me,' said Fisher. 'You're the brains in this partnership; I just take care of the rough stuff. Conspiracies make my head hurt.'

'Right.' Hawk scowled. 'There's still the butler, Villiers. Maybe he knows something. Servants always know things.'

Fisher smiled sourly. 'Whether he's prepared to talk to us about it is a different matter. If you ask me, Villiers is one of the old school – faithful unto death and beyond, if necessary. We'll be lucky to get the time of day out of him.'

Hawk looked at her. 'That's great. Think positively, why don't you?'

They both fell silent as the door swung open and Villiers came in. He bowed politely to the two Guards, shut the door firmly behind him, and then stood to attention, waiting to hear what was required of him. His poker-straight back and patient, dour expression gave him a solid dignity that was only partly undermined by the fluffy white tufts of hair that blossomed above his ears, in contrast to his resolutely bald head. He had dressed with exquisite care, and wouldn't have looked out of place in a Lord's mansion.

So what was he doing, working for a champion of the common people?

'Take a seat,' said Hawk.

Villiers shook his head slightly but definitely. 'I'd rather not, sir.'

'Why not?' said Fisher.

'It's not my place,' said Villiers, 'ma'am.' He added the last word just a little too late.

'How long have you been James Adamant's butler?' said Hawk quickly.

'Nine years, sir. Before that I was butler to his father. The Villiers family has served the Adamant family for three generations.'

'Even during the bad times, when they lost everything?'

'Every family knows disappointments from time to time.'

'How do you feel about Adamant's politics?' said Fisher.

'It's not my place to say, ma'am. My duty is to Master Adamant, and the Villiers have always known their duty.'

'How do you get on with Mrs Adamant?' said Hawk.

'An excellent young lady, from a fine background. A strong support to Master Adamant. Her health has been a little delicate of late, but she had never allowed that to interfere with her duties to her husband and the household. Mrs Adamant is a very determined young lady.'

'What's wrong with her health?' said Fisher.

'I really couldn't say, ma'am.'

'How do you feel about Stefan Medley?' said Hawk.

'Master Medley seems quite competent in his work, sir.'

'How about his private life?'

Villiers drew himself up slightly. 'None of my business, sir,' he said firmly. 'I do not hold with gossip, and I do not encourage it below stairs.'

'Thank you, Villiers,' said Hawk. 'That will be all.'

'Thank you, sir.' Villiers bowed formally to Hawk, nodded politely to Fisher, and left, closing the door softly behind him.

'I never met a butler yet who wouldn't be improved by a swift kick up the behind,' said Hawk.

'Right,' said Fisher. 'Snobs, the lot of them. Even if he

did know anything, he wouldn't tell the likes of us. It wouldn't be proper.'

'Maybe there's nothing to tell,' said Hawk. 'Maybe there is no traitor, and this is all part of an elaborate smear job by the Conservatives to rattle Adamant and undermine his confidence.'

Fisher groaned. 'My head hurts.'

'Stick with it,' said Hawk. 'The answer's here somewhere, if we just dig deep enough. Those blood-creatures were real enough. I'm damned if I'll let Adamant die the way Blackstone did. I'll keep Adamant alive, even if I have to kill all his enemies personally.'

'Now you're talking,' said Fisher.

All the day's talk and planning hadn't prepared Hawk and Fisher for the reality of life on the campaign trail. Adamant set out while the day was still young, taking with him Medley and Dannielle, Hawk and Fisher, and a small army of followers, mercenaries, and speech-writers. Hawk felt a little insulted by the presence of the mercenaries; it seemed to imply that Adamant felt Hawk and Fisher weren't enough to ensure his safety. But once Adamant and his party ventured into the streets, the crowds quickly grew so thick and so vociferous that only the mercenaries kept him from being mobbed. Hawk and Fisher contented themselves with walking on either side of Adamant and glaring at anyone who got too close.

The morning passed in a blur of streets and crowds and speeches. Adamant went from hall to hall, from meeting place to open gatherings, delivering endless speeches, raising the crowds to fever pitch and leaving them with a burning intent to vote Reform, which would hopefully last until polling time later that evening. Adamant's followers spread coins around to anyone with enough wit to stick out an empty palm, and the free booze flowed like water. The speech-writers busied themselves with constant rewrites to suit specific areas, often thrusting hastily scrawled extra lines into Adamant's hands only moments before he was due to make his speech. Somehow he always managed to learn them in time and deliver the lines as though he'd only just thought of them. Hawk was impressed. And yet for all the carefully crafted speeches and crowd-handling, the one thing that stood out whenever Adamant spoke was his sincerity, and the crowds recognised it. He believed in his Cause, and he made the crowds believe.

Down on Eel Street they found a landlord dictating how his tenants should vote, on pain of eviction. Adamant did a half-hour speech on the evils of oppression and the virtues of the secret ballot, and Fisher punched the landlord in the mouth. Not far away, in Baker Street, Hardcastle had planted a sorcerously altered double of Adamant to make damaging claims and speeches. Unfortunately for him, he grew too enamoured of the sound of his own voice and didn't get out of the area fast enough. Adamant's mercenaries took care of the double's protectors, and Hawk and Fisher caught up with him before he managed a dozen yards. Adamant made a blockbuster speech on the need to outlaw dirty tricks in politics, and Hawk and Fisher took turns ducking the double in a horse-trough until he admitted who hired him.

A bunch of rather shabbily dressed men began following Adamant and his people from location to location. They shouted impertinent questions and generally made a nuisance of themselves, but Adamant let them get away with it. Hawk and Fisher began to grow a little annoyed with them. Medley spotted the danger signs.

'They're reporters,' he said quickly. 'Please don't break them.'

'We don't hit everyone we don't like,' said Fisher.

'Of course not,' said Medley. 'It just seems that way. Look, we need the press on our side. The two main papers may be written by and for the Quality and the upper middle classes, but they have votes too, and they have a lot of influence over how other people vote. Luckily for us, Hardcastle's always hated the press and never made any bones about it. So, anything that makes us look good is going to get reported, and that's another nail in Hardcastle's coffin. Besides, a lot of the reporters out there are freelancers, making notes for broadsheets. We definitely don't want to upset them.'

Adamant finished his speech, about the opening of a small free Hospital for the Poor and Needy, and the crowd applauded loudly. Adamant then formally declared the hospital open, cut a length of ribbon that served no purpose Hawk could make out, and got cheered again. Hawk decided he'd never understand politics. A large and muscular heckler pushed his way to the front of the crowd, accompanied by two mercenaries in full chain mail. He started insulting Adamant, loudly and obscenely. The crowd stirred unhappily but did nothing, intimidated by the two mercenaries. Adamant's mercenaries were hesitant about going into the crowd themselves, for fear of starting a panic. Hawk and Fisher looked at each other, and drew their weapons. The fight lasted less than a minute, and the heckler was left on his own, looking a lot less imposing, and staring unhappily at Fisher's sword-point hovering before his eyes.

'If I were you,' said Hawk, 'I'd leave now. Otherwise, Fisher will show you her party trick. And we haven't really got the time to clean up the blood afterwards.'

The heckler looked at the two dead men at his feet, swallowed hard, and disappeared back into the crowd. They let him go, being more interested in putting questions to Adamant while they had the chance. Most of their questions concerned sewers, or the lack of them, but on the whole the crowd was good-natured. Seeing one of Hardcastle's men put to flight had put them almost into a party mood. Adamant answered their questions clearly and concisely, with just enough wit to keep the crowd amused without dampening the fire he was trying to build in them.

Hawk leaned against a nearby wall and surveyed the scene before him. Everything seemed quiet. The crowd was friendly, and there was no sign of any more of Hardcastle's men. Hawk nodded, satisfied, and seized the chance for a short rest. The campaign trail so far had been hard and tiring, and there was still a lot of territory to cover. He looked round to see how the others were taking the strain.

Fisher looked calm and collected, but then, it took a lot to get to Fisher. Adamant was in his element and had never looked better. Dannielle, on the other hand, had found an overturned crate to sit on. Her face was pale and drawn, her shoulders were slumped with tiredness, and her hands were shaking. Hawk frowned. Villiers had said she was ill . . . He decided to keep an eye on her. If she didn't find her second wind soon, he'd have Fisher escort her home. The last thing Adamant needed was something else to worry about. Dannielle would be safe enough with Fisher, and maybe a couple of mercenaries, just to be on the safe side. He looked round for Medley, to tell him what he intended, and felt a sudden chill as he realised there was no sign of him. He turned quickly to Fisher, who smiled briefly.

'Don't panic; he's just popped into the inn across the road for a swift drink. He'll be back before we have to move on. You're getting old, Hawk, missing things like that.'

'Right,' said Hawk. 'This election is putting years on me.'

The inn wasn't much to look at, even by High Steppes standards. Inside, the lights were dim enough to keep everything vague and indistinct. Most of the patrons preferred it that way, but then, they weren't much to look at either. It was that kind of neighbourhood. Medley didn't give a damn. This was where he'd first met his lady love, and it would always be a special place to him. He nodded to the indifferent bartender behind the stained wooden bar, and moved quickly on to the private booths at the back of the inn. She was there, waiting for him, just as she'd promised. As always, just the sight of her was enough to make his heart beat faster. He sat down beside her, and his hands reached out and found hers. They sat staring into each other's eyes for a long moment, and it seemed to Medley that he'd never been so happy.

'I can't stay long,' he said finally. 'Now, what's so important that I had to come here today? You know I'm always glad to see you, but with Adamant's people just outside . . .'

She smiled, and squeezed his hands. 'I know, I'm sorry. But I had to see you. I didn't know when I'd be able to get away again. How's your campaign going?'

'Fine, fine. Look, I can't stay long, or they'll come looking for me. And we can't afford to be seen even talking together.'

'I know. They wouldn't understand. They'd stop us from seeing each other.'

'I wouldn't let them,' said Medley. 'There's nothing in the world I value more than you.'

'You say the nicest things.'

'I love you.'

'I love you too, Stefan,' said Roxanne.

Cameron Hardcastle strode steadily and purposefully through the High Steppes, and the people lined the streets to watch him pass. Armed mercenaries surrounded him at all times, making sure the crowds kept a respectful distance. There was scattered applause from the onlookers, but little cheering. The bunting he'd ordered put up hung limply on the still air, and although his people had handed out Conservative flags and banners by the dozen well in advance, he could only see a few being waved. If it hadn't been for his followers singing campaign songs as they marched, the streets would have been embarrassingly quiet. Hardcastle smiled tightly. That would change soon enough. It always did, once he started to speak.

Jillian hurried quietly along beside him, eyes downcast as always. Hardcastle would just as happily have left her behind, but that was politically unacceptable. A strong marriage and a stable family were central tenets of Conservative thinking, so he had to show off his own wife in public. It was expected of him. She wouldn't disgrace him. She wouldn't dare.

The sorcerer Wulf walked a few paces behind them, disguised as one of the mercenaries. He couldn't afford to be recognised in public as Hardcastle's sorcerer. Firstly, it would have upset the crowds. They tended to distrust magic, and everyone associated with it. Usually with good reason. Secondly, his support was illegal. And thirdly, he would have made too tempting a target. A great many people would have liked a chance at him. But he couldn't let Hardcastle walk the streets unprotected, for the same reason. Even more people would have liked to see Councillor Hardcastle dead. So the great sorcerer Wulf tramped the streets of Haven in Hardcastle's shadow, sweating profusely under a mercenary's chain mail. Besides, he had to be there. Hardcastle couldn't make his speeches without him.

Hardcastle himself was in a surprisingly good mood. His speeches had all gone down very well and, according to first reports, his mercenaries were winning practically every encounter with Adamant's. He reached the platform his people had prepared for him, and climbed the steps onto the stage. Jillian came and stood silently at his side, smiling blankly at the crowd. The campaign song came to an end, and the crowd cheered him, one eye warily watching the mercenaries. Hardcastle lifted his hands for quiet, and silence fell quickly across the packed street. He began to speak, and the crowd's attention became fixed and rapt. A wave of euphoria and commitment swept over them, and soon they were stamping and shouting, and cheering at the end of every sentence. By the end of the speech the crowd was his, to a man. He could have ordered them naked and unarmed into battle, and they would have gone. Hardcastle smiled out over the cheering crowd, relishing the power he had over them.

There was a slight disturbance to one side, as someone pushed their way through the crowd towards him. Hardcastle tensed, and then relaxed a little as he recognised Roxanne. He gestured quickly for her to join him on the platform.

'I was beginning to wonder where you were,' he said quietly, still smiling at the crowd.

'Just taking care of business,' said Roxanne.

'I suppose I might as well make use of you while you're here.' Hardcastle nodded graciously to her, as though he'd been expecting her, and then held up his hands for quiet again. The crowd was silent in a moment. 'My friends, may I present to you the latest addition to our ranks, the renowned warrior, Roxanne! I'm sure you all know her fine reputation!'

He paused for a cheer that didn't come. The crowd stirred uneasily. 'Oh, great,' said an anonymous voice. 'Someone send for the fire brigade now, while there's still time.'

One of the mercenaries moved in quickly to shut him up with a mailed fist to the kidneys, but the damage had been done. The mood of the crowd had been broken. Most of the people there had heard of Roxanne, and while they were undoubtedly impressed, they were also extremely worried. If not downright scared. Her reputation had preceded her. She looked out over the crowd with a raised eyebrow, but had enough sense not to smile. Wulf glared surreptitiously about him, testing the feel of the crowd, and didn't like what he found. The euphoria of a moment before had vanished, as though it had never been. Wulf shrugged.

There would be other times. He moved in close beside the platform and looked up at Hardcastle.

'I think we should be leaving now, Cameron. And in the future it might be wise to keep Roxanne in the background.'

Hardcastle nodded curtly. He turned to give the order to leave, and at that moment the crowd went mad. Suddenly everyone was screaming and shouting and kicking out in all directions, and then scattering as fast as their legs would carry them. Hardcastle stared blankly about him, angry and confused, and then he saw the rats moving among the crowd. Hundreds of rats, in all shapes and sizes, many still sleek and shining with slime from the sewers. They scurried this way and that, mad with rage, sinking fangs and claws into anything that came within range. Hardcastle's hands clenched into fists and his face reddened. There was only one way so many rats could have appeared in one place at one time, and that was by magic. A sorcerer must have teleported them into the crowd. Adamant's sorcerer . . .

Wulf fought his way back to the platform. 'We have to get out of here, Cameron! There's too many of them! There's nothing I can do!'

Hardcastle nodded stiffly, and signalled for his mercenaries to open a path through the chaos. A blazing anger pulled at his self-control as he descended from the platform, followed by Jillian and Roxanne. One way or another, Adamant would pay for this insult . . . whatever it cost.

Hardcastle arrived at his next meeting place to find a crowd already gathered, listening to someone else address them. He brought his people to a halt and gestured to one of his mercenary officers.

'I thought you said you'd cleared the Reformers out of this area.'

'I did, sir. I can't understand it; my people were most thorough. I left men here with strict instructions not to allow any other speakers. If you'll excuse me, sir, I'll go and see what's happening.'

He gestured quickly to half a dozen of his men. They drew their swords and followed him into the crowd. Wulf stirred suddenly at Hardcastle's side.

'There's trouble here, Cameron. Bad trouble.'

Hardcastle smiled grimly. 'My people will take care of it.'

'I don't think so,' said Wulf. 'Not this time. There's a power here, and I don't like it. It's old magic; Wild Magic.'

Hardcastle frowned impatiently and turned to glare at him. 'What the hell are you talking about, Wulf?'

The sorcerer was staring at the man addressing the crowd, and Hardcastle reluctantly followed his gaze. The man was tall and slender, wrapped in a shabby grey cloak that had seen better days. He was too far away for Hardcastle to hear what he was saying, but there was no denying the impact his words had on the crowd. They couldn't take their eyes off him. And yet there was none of the shouting and clapping that Hardcastle's own speeches always elicited. The crowd was almost eerily silent, utterly engrossed with the speaker. Hardcastle suddenly realised the mercenaries he'd sent into the crowd hadn't come back. He looked quickly about him, but there was no sign of them anywhere. There was a faint whisper of steel on leather as Roxanne drew her sword from its scabbard.

'They've been gone too long,' she said quietly. 'Want me to go look for them?'

'Not on your own,' said Hardcastle. 'Jillian, you stay here with my people. Wulf, you and Roxanne follow me. We're going to take a closer look at this . . . phenomenon.'

He gestured to two of his mercenaries, and they opened up a path through the crowd for him. More mercenaries spread out through the crowd, flanking Hardcastle and his party as they moved. No one in the crowd paid them any attention, their gaze fixed on the slight grey figure on the platform. *My platform*, thought Hardcastle resentfully. There was still no sign of any of the missing mercenaries.

'I am the Lord of the Gulfs,' said the Grey Veil, his eyes wide and unblinking, his face full of a cold and awful wonder. 'He has given me power, power beyond imagining, and he will do the same for you. Only come to him and serve him, and he will make you masters among men. He is ancient and magnificent, older than mankind itself, and his time has come round again.'

Hardcastle frowned, and looked about him. The grey figure was saying nothing new, and on the Street of Gods no one would have given him a second glance. So why was everyone so rapt? Why weren't there any hecklers in the crowd? He muttered instructions to the nearest mercenary, who nodded and moved quickly through the crowd, passing the instructions on to the other mercenaries. Soon the silence was broken by jeers and insults and catcalls, and the crowd began to stir.

The Grey Veil turned slowly to face the jeers, and some of the mercenaries' voices faltered. The Veil stopped speaking, and raised his hands above his head. The day suddenly grew dark. Hardcastle looked up and saw the sky was full of angry, swollen clouds, cutting off the daylight and spreading a chill across the crowd. He frowned uncertainly. He would have sworn the sky had been clear only moments before. He looked back at the grey figure, just in time to flinch as lightning cracked down to strike the upraised hands. An eerie blue glow crackled around the Grey Veil's hands, and then the lightning leapt out into the crowd, striking down each and every one of Hardcastle's men who'd raised their voices in mockery. The crowd screamed and shrank back as the mercenaries burst into flames and fell dying to the ground. The smell of burnt flesh filled the air, but somehow the crowd still held their ground instead of scattering, bound together by the Grey Veil's will. He slowly lowered his hands, and the sky began to clear.

The Veil smiled at Hardcastle, and fixed him with his disturbingly direct gaze. 'What else would you have me do? Shall I call down the rain or call up a hurricane? Shall I fill your lungs with water, or cause your blood to boil in your veins? Or shall I heal the sick and raise the dead? I can do all those things, and more. The Lord of the Gulfs has given me power beyond your petty dreams.'

'Want me to kill him?' said Roxanne.

'You wouldn't get within ten feet of him,' snapped Wulf. 'Cameron, let me deal with him.'

'Do it,' said Hardcastle. 'Destroy him. No one murders my men and gets away with it.'

'I wouldn't stand any more of a chance than Roxanne,' said Wulf. 'I told you: he has the Wild Magic in him.'

'So what do we do?' said Hardcastle.

'If we're lucky, we make a deal.'

Wulf made his way through the silent crowd and approached the platform. He and the Grey Veil spoke together for some time, and then Wulf bowed to him and made his way back to Hardcastle and Roxanne. His face was carefully impassive, but there was no hiding its pallor, or the beads of sweat on his forehead.

'Well?' said Hardcastle.

'He's agreed to meet us privately,' said Wulf. 'I think we can do business.'

'Who the hell is he? And what's this Lord of the Gulfs nonsense? I've never heard of him.'

'You wouldn't,' said Wulf. 'It's a very old name. You probably know him better as the Abomination.'

Hardcastle looked at him sharply. 'The Abomination was destroyed. Every schoolchild knows that. Its Temple on the Street of Gods has been abandoned for centuries.'

'Apparently he's back. Not as powerful as he once was, or he wouldn't need to make deals with us.'

Hardcastle nodded, back on familiar ground. 'All right; what does he want?'

'That's what we're going to discuss.' Wulf looked sharply at Hardcastle. 'Cameron, we've got to get him on our side. Whatever it takes. With his power, he could hand us the election on a plate.'

'What if the price is too high?' said Roxanne.

'No price is too high,' said Hardcastle.

Harlequin and Other Beings

Dressed in chequered black and white, with a white, clown's face and a domino mask, Harlequin dances on the Street of Gods. No one has ever seen his eyes, and he casts no shadow. He dances with a splendid ease, graceful and magnificent, pirouetting elegantly to a music only he can hear. And he never stops.

Morning, noon, and night, Harlequin dances on the Street of Gods.

Everyone needs something to believe in. Something to make them feel safe and secure and cared for. They need it so badly they'll give up anything and everything, just for the promise of it. They'll pay in gold and obedience and suffering, or anything else that has a market value. Which is why religion is such big business in Haven.

Right in the centre of the city, square in the middle of the high-rent district, lies the Street of Gods. Dozens of different churches and temples stand side by side and ostentatiously ignore each other. Then there are the smaller, more intimate meeting houses, for adherents of the lesser known or more controversial beliefs, who for the most part deal strictly in cash. And then there are the street preachers. No one knows where they come from or where they go, but every day they turn up by the hundreds to line the Street of Gods and spread the Word to anyone who'll listen.

There's never any trouble in the Street of Gods. Firstly,

the Beings wouldn't like it, and secondly, it's bad for business. The people of Haven firmly believe in the right of everyone to make a profit.

Or prophet.

Hawk and Fisher looked curiously about them as they accompanied Adamant down the Street of Gods. It wasn't a part of Haven they knew much about, but they knew enough to be wary. Anything could happen on the Street of Gods. Not for the first time, Hawk wondered if they'd done the right thing in leaving the mercenaries behind, but Adamant had insisted. He'd left his followers behind as well. Apart from his bodyguards, only Medley and Dannielle remained with him now.

We're here to ask a favour, said Adamant. *That means we come as supplicants, not as heads of a private army.*

Besides, said Medley, *we're here to make deals. We don't need witnesses.*

The Street itself was a mess. The assorted temples and churches varied widely in size and shape and style of architecture. Fashions from one century stood side by side with modes and follies from another. Street preachers filled the air with the clamour of their cries, and everywhere there was the din of bells and cymbals and animal horns, and the sound of massed voices raised in praise or supplication. The Street itself stretched away into the distance for as far as Hawk could see, and his hackles stirred as he realised the Street of Gods was a hell of a lot larger than the official maps made it out to be. He pointed this out to Medley, who just shrugged.

'The Street is as long as it has to be to fit everything in. With so many magics and sorceries and Beings of Power jammed together, it's no wonder things get a little strange here from time to time.'

'You got that right,' said Fisher, watching interestedly as a street preacher thrust metal skewers through his flesh. He showed no sign of pain, and no blood ran from the wounds.

Another preacher poured oil over his body, and set himself on fire. He waited until he'd burned out, and then did it again.

'Ignore them,' said Adamant. 'They're just exhibitionists. It takes more than spectacle to impress anyone here.' He looked expectantly at Medley. 'What's the latest news, Stefan?'

Medley gathered together a handful of notes and papers, presented to him by messengers reporting on the day's progress. 'So far, not too bad. Hardcastle's mercenaries are wiping the streets with ours whenever the two sides meet, but they can't be everywhere at once. All the main polls show us running neck and neck with Hardcastle, which is actually pretty good this early in the campaign. We could even improve as the day goes on. Wait until the drink wears off and they've spent all their bribe money; then we'll see how many Conservative voters stay bought . . .

'Mortice has been keeping busy. Apparently he's broken up several Conservative meetings by teleporting rats into the crowd. His sense of humour's got very basic since he died.

'As for the other candidates: General Longarm has been making some very powerful speeches. He seems to be building quite a following among the city men-at-arms. Megan O'Brien isn't getting anywhere. Even his fellow traders don't believe he can win. And Lord Arthur Sinclair was last seen hosting one hell of a party at the Crippled Cougar Inn, and getting smashed out of his skull. No surprises there.'

They walked on a while in silence. In the Street of Gods the time of day fluctuated from place to place, so that they walked sometimes in daylight and sometimes in moonlight. Once it snowed briefly and rained frogs, and the stars in the sky outshone the sun. Gargoyles wept blood, and statues stirred on their pedestals. Once, Hawk looked down a side alley and saw a skeleton, held together by copper wire, beating its skull against a stone wall over and over again, and for a time a flock of burning birds followed Adamant's party down the Street, singing shrilly in a language Hawk didn't recognise. Adamant looked always straight ahead, ignoring everything outside of his path, and after a while Hawk and Fisher learned to do the same.

'How many Gods are there here?' said Fisher finally.

'No one knows,' said Medley. 'The number's changing all the time. There's something here for everyone.'

'Who do you believe in?' said Hawk to Adamant.

Adamant shrugged. 'I was raised orthodox Brotherhood of Steel. I suppose I'm still a believer. It appeals to my pragmatic nature, and unlike most religions they're not always bothering me for donations.'

'Right,' said Medley. 'You pay your tithes once a year, show up at meetings once a month, and they pretty much leave you alone. But it's a good church to belong to; you can make very useful contacts through the Brotherhood.'

'Tell me about the Brotherhood,' said Hawk. 'Isobel and I haven't had much contact with them here, and they're not very well-known in the Northlands where we were raised.'

'They're pretty straightforward,' said Adamant. 'Part militaristic, part mystical, based upon a belief in the fighting man. It started out as a warrior's religion, but it's broadened its appeal since then. They revere cold steel in all its forms as a weapon, and teach that all men can be equal once they've trained to be fighting men. It's a particularly practical-minded religion.'

'Right,' said Medley. 'And if we can get their support, every man-at-arms in the High Steppes will vote for us.'

'I would have thought they'd be more interested in Hardcastle,' said Fisher.

'Normally, yes,' said Adamant. 'But luckily for us, Hardcastle has not only not paid his tithes in years, he also had the effrontery to levy a special tax on the Brotherhood in his territory. And on top of that, just recently the

Brotherhood's been split down the middle by an argument over how involved they should get in local politics. The new militant sect already has one Seat on the Council: The Downs. Their candidate in the Steppes is General Longarm. We're going to see the High Commander of the orthodox sect, and see if we can stir up some support for us, as part of their struggle against the militants.'

'Great,' said Fisher. 'Just what this campaign needed. More complications.'

Adamant looked at Hawk. 'How about you, Captain? What do you believe in?'

'Hard cash, cold beer, and an axe with a good edge.' Hawk walked on in silence for a while, and then continued. 'I was raised as a Christian, but that was a long time ago.'

'A Christian?' Dannielle raised a painted eyebrow. 'Takes all sorts to make a world, I suppose.'

'Who exactly are we here to see?' said Fisher, changing the subject.

'There are only a few Beings who will talk to us,' said Adamant. 'Most of them won't interfere in Haven's civil affairs.'

'Why not?' said Hawk.

'Because if one got involved, they all would, and it wouldn't be long before we had a God War on our hands. No one wants that, least of all the Beings. They've got a good racket here, and no one wants to rock the boat. But there are a few Beings who've developed a taste for a little discreet and indirect meddling. The trick is to get to them before Hardcastle does. I think we'll start with the Speaking Stone.'

The Speaking Stone turned out to be a huge jagged boulder of granite, battered and weather-beaten beyond all shape or meaning. Plainly robed acolytes guarded it with drawn swords all the time Adamant and his party were there. After all the things he'd seen so far on the Street of Gods, Hawk was very disappointed in the Stone. He tried hard to feel some holy atmosphere or mystical aura, but the Stone looked like just another lump of rock to him. Adamant spoke with the Stone for some time, but if it had anything to say for itself, Hawk didn't hear it. Adamant seemed neither pleased nor displeased, but if he had got anything out of his visit, he kept it to himself.

The Madonna of the Martyrs had a bad reputation. Her church was tucked away in a quiet little backwater of the Street of Gods. There were no signs to proclaim what it was; the people who needed to would always find their way there. There was a constant stream of supplicants to the Madonna's doors: the lost and the lonely, the beaten and the betrayed. They came to the Madonna with heavy hearts, and she gave them what they asked for: an end to all pain. After they died, they rose again in her service, for as long as she required them.

Some called her a God, some a Devil. There isn't always that much difference on the Street of Gods.

The Madonna herself turned out to be a plain, pleasant woman dressed in gaudily coloured robes. She had a tray of sickly looking boiled sweets at her side and sucked one noisily all the time they were there. She didn't offer them round, and Hawk, for one, was grateful. Dead men and women shuffled through her chamber on unknown errands. Their faces were colourless and slack, but once or twice Hawk thought he caught a quick glimpse of something damned and suffering in their eyes. He kept his hand near his axe, and his eye on the nearest exit.

Adamant and the Madonna made a deal. In return for her withdrawing her support for the DeWitt brothers, Adamant would allow the Madonna access to the High Steppes hospitals. It wasn't quite as cold as it sounded. The Madonna was bound by her nature only to take the willing, and every hospital has some who would welcome death as a release from pain. Even so . . . Hawk studied Adamant thoughtfully. He'd always suspected the politician had a ruthless streak. He caught Medley's eye on the way out, but the adviser just shrugged.

La Belle Dame du Rocher, the Beautiful Lady of the Rocks, refused to see them. So did the Soror Marium, the Sister of the Sea. They were both old patrons of Haven, and Adamant was clearly disappointed. He left an offering for each of them anyway, just in case.

The Hanged Man was polite but noncommittal, the Carrion In Tears asked too high a price, and the Crawling Violet's answer made no sense at all. And so it went down the Street of Gods. Even those few Beings who would allow Adamant to approach them were usually uninterested in his problems. They had their own affairs and vendettas to pursue. Adamant remained calm and polite throughout it all, and Hawk kept his hand near his axe. The various Beings were disturbing enough, but their followers gave him the creeps. They all had the same flat, unwavering stare of the fanatic.

And finally, when they had been everywhere else, Adamant brought his party to the Brotherhood of Steel. Their Headquarters looked less like a church, and more like an upmarket barracks. The carved wood and stonework was only a few hundred years out of date, which made the place look almost modern compared to most of the Street of Gods. Armed guards patrolled the front of the building, but fell back respectfully once they recognised Adamant. Hawk looked at him sharply.

'You're not just a casual visitor here, are you?'

'I've had dealings with the Brotherhood before,' said Adamant. 'Every politician has.'

A scarred man-at-arms in brightly shining chain mail led them through a series of open corridors to an impressively large library, where he left them. Fisher grabbed the most comfortable chair and sank into it, stretching out her long legs with a satisfied sigh. Hawk was tempted to do the same.

His feet were killing him. But every instinct he had was telling him to keep alert. Every man he'd seen in the Headquarters had been wearing a sword, and looked like he knew how to use it. If by some chance Hardcastle had already been here and struck a deal with the Brotherhood, getting out of the Headquarters might prove a lot more difficult than getting in. He sat on the arm of Fisher's chair and fixed Adamant with a steady glare.

'All right, sir Adamant. Who are we waiting to see?'

'Jeremiah Rukker. He's the Commander here. Not a bad sort; we can talk with him.'

'How does he feel about Reform?'

'Couldn't care less, one way or the other. Officially, the Brotherhood is above politics. Actually, they'll work with anyone, if it's kept under the table and the price is right. And the Brotherhood strikes a very hard bargain.'

'Fill me in on the Brotherhood,' said Fisher. 'Just how much influence do they really have in Haven?'

'More than you'd think,' said Medley. 'Essentially, any man who can wield a sword or an axe can apply for membership in the Brotherhood. Once admitted, they can learn skills and tactics preserved over hundreds of years and become part of a mystical fellowship that owes loyalty to nothing save itself. A Brother of Steel will defy any law, ruler, or religion – if the Brotherhood requires it.'

'And there are Brothers everywhere,' said Adamant. 'In the Council, in the Guard, and in all the political parties.'

Hawk frowned. 'How can you be sure of that?'

'This is Haven, remember? Nothing stays secret here for long.' Adamant looked at Hawk steadily. 'According to my sources, the Brotherhood has spread throughout the Low Kingdoms; even among the King's advisers. So far, they've managed to avoid a purge of declaring themselves totally impartial when it comes to politics, but the new militants may change all that.'

'So why have we come here?' said Hawk. 'Why should

the orthodox Brotherhood want to make a deal with Reform?' And then he paused, and his face cleared suddenly. 'Of course: the most important thing for them is to see that the militants lose this election. In the Steppes, that means backing either Hardcastle or you, and they know they can't trust Hardcastle. I think I'm getting the hang of politics.'

'There's more to politics than just being cynical,' said a deep, resonant voice behind him. Hawk spun round, one hand dropping to his axe. A tall, impressively muscled man in his mid forties stood smiling in the library doorway. He paused a moment to make sure they'd all got a good look at him, and then he strode forward into the room. His polished chain mail gleamed brightly in the lamplight, and a long sword hilt peered over his left shoulder. The sword on his back reached almost to the floor. He had jet-black hair, sharp classical features that were a little too perfect to be handsome, and a broad smile that wasn't reflected in his eyes. All in all, he looked more like a politician than Adamant did. Hawk decided that if he had to shake hands, he'd better count his fingers afterwards. He nodded warily to the newcomer, who smiled briefly in his direction before bowing formally to Adamant.

'Jeremiah Rukker, at your service once again, sir Adamant. It's always good to see you here. Won't you introduce me to your companions?'

'Of course, Commander. This is my wife, Dannielle. You know my adviser. The two Guards are Captain Hawk and Captain Fisher. Perhaps you've heard of them.'

'Yes,' said Rukker. 'I've heard of them.'

Hawk raised an eyebrow at the ice in Rukker's voice. 'Do we have a problem, Commander?'

'We don't,' said Rukker carefully. 'Your reputation as a warrior precedes you. But your woman also claims the rights of a warrior, and this is unacceptable.'

Fisher rose lithely to her feet and stood next to Hawk, one hand resting idly on her sword hilt. Rukker drew himself up to his full height, and fixed her with a cold stare.

'Women do not use weapons,' he said flatly. 'They are not suited to it. They know nothing of the glory of steel.'

'Nice-looking sword you've got there,' said Fisher easily. 'Want to go a few rounds?'

'Isobel . . .' said Hawk quickly.

'Don't worry; I won't damage him too much. Just take some of the wind out of his sails. Come on, Rukker, what do you say? Best out of five, and I'll give you two points to start with. Just to make the match even.'

Adamant glared at her, and then at Hawk. 'Captain, if you wouldn't mind . . .'

'Don't look at me,' said Hawk. 'She goes her own way. Always has. Besides, if Rukker's stupid enough to take her on, he deserves everything that happens to him. If I were you, I'd send for a doctor. And a mop.'

Rukker stared haughtily at Fisher. The effect was rather spoiled because he had to look up slightly to do it. 'A Brother of Steel does not fight with women,' he said coldly. 'It is not seemly.'

'Yeah,' said Fisher. 'Sure.'

She turned away and sat down in the chair again. Rukker ignored her and inclined his head courteously to Hawk.

'I understand you worked with the legendary Adam Stalker on your last case, Captain Hawk. He was a great man. His death is a loss to us all.'

'There's no doubt he'll be missed,' said Hawk. 'Was he a Brother of Steel?'

'Of course. All the great heroes are. You might care to make application yourself, some day. Your skills and reputation would make you a valued member.'

'Thanks,' said Hawk. 'But I'm not really the joining type.'

'Don't dismiss us so casually, Captain. We have much to

offer.' Rukker fixed Hawk with a burning gaze, and his voice became earnest and compelling. 'The Brotherhood is dedicated to the glory of Steel. It is the symbol that holds mankind together, that enables him to impose order on a savage and uncaring universe. Steel gives us mastery over the world and ourselves. In learning to control our bodies and our weapons, we learn to control our minds and our destinies.

'Think of what we could teach you, Captain. Every move, every trick and skill of fighting there has ever been is to be found here somewhere, in our libraries and instructors. Our fighters are unbeatable, our warriors suitable to advise Kings. We are the future; we decide the way the world will turn.'

'Thanks,' said Hawk. 'But I have enough problems dealing with the present. Besides, Isobel and I are a team. We work together. Always.'

'And that's why you'll never be anything more than a city Guard,' said Rukker. 'A pity. You could have gone far, Hawk; if it hadn't been for your woman.'

Hawk smiled suddenly. 'Commander, I'm giving you a lot of slack, because I'm here as Adamant's guest. But if you insult my wife one more time, I will hurt you severely. Even worse, I might let Isobel do it. Now, be a good fellow and get on with your business with Adamant.'

Rukker flushed pinkly, and his hand rose to the sword hilt at his shoulder. Hawk and Fisher were both on their feet facing him, weapons drawn and at the ready, before Rukker's hand could close around the hilt. Adamant moved quickly forward to stand between them.

'That's enough! Hawk, Fisher, put your weapons away. That's an order. I do apologise, Commander. We've had a very trying day, and I feel all our nerves are somewhat on edge.'

Rukker nodded stiffly and took his hand away from his sword. Bright spots of colour burned on his cheekbones, but when he spoke his voice was perfectly steady. 'Of course, James, I quite understand. Let's get down to business, shall we? What exactly can I do for you?'

'Hardcastle's mercenaries are grinding my campaign into the ground,' said Adamant. 'My people are holding their own for the moment, but they can't last long without armed support. I need your support, Jeremiah; I need your men.'

Rukker pursed his lips thoughtfully. 'The Brotherhood doesn't take sides, James; you know that. We're above politics. We have to be.'

'The militants feel differently.'

'They're fools. We're only allowed free rein as long as we support all sides equally. We're not strong enough yet to stand as a political force in our own right. We survive because we're useful, but the powers that be would crush us in a moment if they thought we were dangerous. No, James. We've worked together in the past when we found ourselves walking the same path, but we can't afford to be openly allied with your Cause.'

'You can't afford not to,' said Adamant. 'According to all the reports, General Longarm and his militants are doing very well at the moment. They haven't got enough support to win on their own, but if they were to ally themselves with Hardcastle, they'd make an unbeatable team. And Hardcastle's just rattled enough by their successes and mine to agree to such an alliance.'

'You make a good argument, James. But not good enough. Longarm's certainly ambitious, but he's not stupid enough to trust promises from Hardcastle.'

'Who said anything about trust? For the moment they need each other, but all kinds of things could happen once the election is safely over. After all, Hardcastle maintains his position through armed force. Forces that in the future would be exclusively controlled by General Longarm . . . But you're missing the point, Jeremiah. The point is, can you afford to bet that Longarm won't make an alliance with Hardcastle?'

'No,' said Rukker. 'I can't. All right, James. I'll have to consult with the High Commander, but I'm pretty sure he'll say yes. We can't allow Longarm to win this election. You'll have your men in a few hours. And we should be able to call off most of Hardcastle's mercenaries. A large proportion of them belong to the Brotherhood. You've got your support, James. But you'd better make damned sure I don't have reason to regret it.'

Out on the Street of Gods, three different clocks were striking fifteen, although it was still barely midday. Given some of the Street's earlier excesses, Hawk felt only a mild relief that nothing worse was happening. He looked carefully about him, and then stopped as a commotion broke out further down the Street. Fisher noticed his reaction, and her hand dropped to her sword.

'Trouble, Hawk?'

'Could be. Take a look.'

Halfway down, on the other side of the Street, a very tall woman dressed in bright yellow and battered leathers was beating up half a dozen nuns from the Convent of the Bright Lady. The nuns were armed with wooden staves and lengths of steel chain, but the tall woman was wiping the floor with them, using only her bare hands.

'Who the hell is that?' said Hawk.

'That is Roxanne,' said Medley. 'I'm surprised you haven't heard of her.' He winced as Roxanne lifted a nun bodily into the air and slammed her face-first into the nearest wall.

'So that's Roxanne,' said Hawk. 'I always thought she'd be taller.'

'There's a good price on her head,' said Fisher.

'With her reputation as a fighter, there'd have to be. I'm not tackling her without being paid extra.'

'She's probably overrated. No one's that good.'

'Bets?' said Hawk, as Roxanne head-butted one nun and punched out another.

'All right,' said Fisher. 'Who goes first?'

'Toss you for it.'

Fisher fumbled for a coin.

'Wait a minute,' said Dannielle. 'Look.'

Hawk and Fisher looked back just in time to see two new figures dragging Roxanne away from her latest victims, just as she was about to start putting the boot in. She shrugged them off easily, but made no move to attack them. Hawk whistled softly as he realised one of them was Councillor Hardcastle. The other man, dressed in ill-fitting chain mail, was the sorcerer Wulf. Hawk studied him thoughtfully. He'd heard about Wulf.

'Now, that is interesting,' said Adamant. 'I didn't know Roxanne was working for Hardcastle.'

'She won't be much longer,' said Hawk. 'She's about to be arrested.'

'I'd rather you didn't,' said Medley quickly. 'We don't want to draw attention to ourselves. Officially, we were never here. Our agreement with the Brotherhood will last only as long as we can keep it quiet. In fact, we'd better get out of here now, before Hardcastle spots us. Right, James?'

'I'm afraid so,' said Adamant. 'If it's a question of the bounty money, Captain Hawk . . .'

'It isn't,' said Hawk shortly. 'She's wanted on a dozen warrants, most of them for murder and arson. But she can wait. Protecting you has top priority until I receive fresh orders. Let's go.'

Fisher nodded reluctantly, and the party moved quickly off down the Street of Gods, keeping to the shadows.

'It's probably just as well,' said Medley. 'Roxanne's supposed to be unbeatable with a sword.'

Fisher sniffed. 'I could take her.'

'I'm sure you could,' said Adamant. 'After the election.'

'Well, at least now we've got something to look forward to,' said Hawk.

Roxanne liked the Street of Gods. Its constantly shifting realities appealed to her own mercurial nature. She almost felt at home. Of course, not everyone felt the same. The Street had terrorised Jillian to the point that not even Hardcastle's threats could make her accompany them. He'd had to send her home, along with all his followers and mercenaries. The Grey Veil had insisted on that. Apparently his God didn't like large audiences when it came to hard bargaining. Roxanne kept a close watch on Veil. She didn't trust him any further than she could spit into the wind.

Veil led them past churches and temples decorated with imps and gargoyles and demons. None of them looked particularly healthy places. Veil passed them all by, and Roxanne pouted disappointedly. Finally, they came to the Temple of the Abomination, and Veil smiled sardonically as he took in their reactions. It wasn't much to look at, just a plain stone building with no windows, the stonework scarred and pitted by long years of neglect, but something about it put Roxanne's teeth on edge.

Veil gestured for his guests to enter. Hardcastle and Wulf looked at the rough wooden door hanging slightly ajar, and then looked at Roxanne. She grinned broadly, drew her sword, and moved forward to kick the door open. At the last moment, the door swung open before her. Roxanne stopped and waited a moment, but there was no one there. The gloom beyond the door was still and quiet. She looked back at Veil. He was watching her mockingly with his disquieting eyes. Roxanne turned her back on him and swaggered into the Temple of the Abomination.

A dim crimson glow filled the huge stone hall, radiating in some obscure fashion from a broken stone altar. The hall stretched away into the distance, and the ceiling towered impossibly high above her. She moved slowly forward, her sword held out before her. There was a sluggish movement of shadows, but nothing came out of the gloom to challenge her. Roxanne curled her lip disappointedly. Faint scuffing sounds behind her spun her round, but it was only Veil, leading Hardcastle and Wulf into the Temple. Roxanne went back to join them.

Hardcastle looked briefly about him, and did his best to look unimpressed. 'All right,' he growled finally. 'We're here. Now tell me why I've come all this way to a deserted Temple when I could be talking with Beings of real Power.'

'Gently, Cameron,' murmured Wulf. 'You don't know what you're dealing with here.'

'And you do?' said Veil.

'I think so, yes,' said Wulf. 'You're one of the Transient Beings, aren't you?'

Veil laughed delightedly. It wasn't a healthy sound. The echoes seemed to go on forever in the great hall.

'What the hell's a Transient Being?' said Roxanne.

'An abstraction given shape and form,' said Wulf. 'A concept clothed in flesh and blood and bone. They have Power beyond reason, for their birth lies in the Wild Magic, and once summoned into the world of men they cannot easily be dismissed.'

Roxanne frowned at the slender figure wrapped in grey before her. 'You mean he's a God?'

Veil laughed, but when he spoke his voice was subtly different, as though something else spoke through him. 'The Lord of the Gulfs has been asleep for centuries, and it will be some time before he can physically manifest himself in this world again. For now, he needs a host to walk in the world of men.'

Hardcastle scowled unhappily. 'What kind of Being are you?'

The light around them grew subtly darker, like sunset fading into night. Here and there in the gloom, pale sparks of light appeared, growing quickly into transparent human shapes. Soon there were hundreds of ghosts glowing palely in the great hall, drifting endlessly back and forth as though in search of something they could no longer remember. All of them were hideously shrivelled and emaciated, reduced by some awful hunger to nothing more than flesh-covered skeletons with distended bellies and wide, agonised eyes. More and more appeared until they filled the hall from end to end, and then without warning they turned upon each other, tearing ravenously at their ghostly flesh with frenzied hands and teeth. They ate each other with desperate haste, screaming silently at the horror of what they did, but the broken bones and ripped flesh brought no end to their hunger.

'I have had many names but only one nature,' said the Being through Veil's voice. 'Call me Hunger. Call me Famine.'

The ghosts were suddenly gone, and the gloom in the Temple of the Abomination was still and quiet once again.

'The Lord of the Gulfs has more power than you could ever dream of,' said Veil. 'They drive me out again and again, but I always come back. Serve me, and my power is yours.'

'Serve you?' said Wulf. 'How?'

'Bring me followers. The more who worship me, the greater my power will become. They will feed me with their devotion, and my influence will spread across the land, as it did before. My host must be protected. I cannot be destroyed by the living or the dead – that gift was given to me at my creation – but my host is always . . . vulnerable.'

'Can you destroy my enemies?' said Hardcastle.

'Of course.'

'Then you've got a deal; whatever you are.'

'Excellent,' said the Lord of the Gulfs. 'But this host has done all it can. It had enough power to raise me, but not enough to sustain me. As a sign of good faith, you must provide me with a new host.'

'Take me,' said Wulf. 'Let me share your power. I have enough sorcery to contain you until we can find you a new host.'

Veil looked at him, and then smiled suddenly. 'Very well, sorcerer. If that's what you want.'

Hardcastle frowned at Wulf. 'Are you sure you know what you're doing?'

'Of course I'm sure,' muttered Wulf. 'Don't rock the boat.'

The Grey Veil grinned widely, the smile spreading and spreading until the mouth cracked and broke, splitting the cheeks and opening up the face to show the bones and muscle beneath. The face sloughed off like a mask, and the muscles turned to dust and fell away. The eyes sank back into the sockets and disappeared, leaving only a grinning skull. Dust fell out of the grey robe in streams, and then it crumpled and fell limply to the floor. The jaw fell away from the skull in one silent laugh, and then they too were gone and there was only dust and an empty grey robe. A wind rose up out of nowhere and blew the dust away.

Wulf put an unsteady hand to his mouth and shook his head slightly. His eyes were glazed, as though he was listening to a faint voice very far away. Hardcastle looked at Roxanne, and then back at Wulf.

'I'm all right, Cameron,' said Wulf quietly. He lowered his hand slowly and smiled at Hardcastle. 'He really wasn't very bright, for a God. He hasn't been awake long, and he wasn't nearly as strong as he thought he was. I've got him, held securely within my wards, and all his power is mine, Adamant doesn't know it yet, but the election is yours, Cameron. No other sorcerer can stand against me now. Let's go.'

The wooden door swung open, and Hardcastle and Wulf went back out into the Street of Gods. Roxanne looked round the deserted hall one last time and then followed them out. She put away her sword, and wondered if there'd be time to stop for dinner any time soon.

6

Truth and Consequences

The afternoon dragged slowly on towards evening as Adamant led his party through the bustling streets of the High Steppes, making speeches, addressing gatherings, and generally beating the drum for Reform. The crowds were thicker than ever as even those who'd been working spilled out onto the streets to make the most of the unofficial holiday. Street traders sold out their wares, closed their stalls, and joined the celebrations. Conjurers and mummers provided traditional entertainments, innkeepers ran low on stock and began hauling dusty bottles from off the back shelves, and fireworks spattered the darkening sky.

Adamant finally took a break from the crowds, who were more interested in partying than politics, and led his people into the more upmarket sections of the Steppes. He was looking for personal endorsements and promises of funds. What he got were kind words, good wishes, and vague promises. When anybody could be bothered to speak to him. Adamant declined to be disheartened, and pressed on with unfailing enthusiasm.

And along the way two new members joined his party and walked along with him: Laurence Bearclaw and Joshua Kincaid.

Bearclaw was a big man in his late forties, with broad shoulders, and a barrel chest that was slipping slowly towards his belt. He first won fame by killing a bear with nothing but a knife, and he still wore the animal's claws on a chain around his neck to prove it. His shoulder-length hair was still jet-black because he dyed it regularly. He'd served in a hundred different campaigns as a freelance mercenary, and he'd come away with credit and scalps from all of them. He didn't really give much of a damn for Reform, but he liked Adamant, and the idea of supporting the underdog appealed to him.

Kincaid was an average-height man in his mid forties, with a shock of butter-yellow hair and icy blue eyes. He was muscular in a lean kind of way, didn't smile much, and was even more dangerous than he looked. He'd made his reputation by fighting in the infamous Bloody Ridges campaign alongside the legendary Adam Stalker. He was famous throughout Haven, and moderately well-known outside it. There were several broadsheets and songs telling of his heroic deeds, all of them written by Kincaid under an assumed name. Like his friend and sometime fighting companion Bearclaw, Kincaid wasn't what you'd call political. But it had been too long since his last campaign, and he was bored sitting around waiting for a call to action that never came. He hated just sitting around; it made him feel old. If nothing else, working with Adamant was bound to supply enough material for a new broadsheet.

The afternoon wore on, and took its toll from all of them. Adamant seemed as full of bounce and vinegar as ever, but some of his party were beginning to wilt under the strain. Dannielle in particular seemed to be having an increasingly hard time keeping up with him. She'd disappear now and again for a quick sit-down and a rest, and return later revitalised and full of bounce. But it never lasted. Dark bruises began to appear under her eyes. Medley was becoming increasingly distracted as he tried to keep up with the growing number of reports on how the campaign was going. Hawk and Fisher stayed close by Adamant and kept their eyes open for trouble. As Guards, they were used to spending long hours on their feet, but the pace was getting to them too. Things nearly came to a head when

Adamant visited the few members of the Quality who lived on the edges of the Steppes, in a last-ditch gamble for funding and support. Mostly they got the door slammed in their faces; the rest of the time they were invited in, only to be subtly sneered at or not-so-subtly threatened. This did not go down well with Fisher. She tended to take it personally when she got looked down on. In fact, she tended to get very annoyed and hit people. After one unfortunate incident, Adamant decided it would be better if she waited outside thereafter.

But finally even Adamant had to admit they'd done all they could. Evening was falling, and the voting would begin soon. He looked out over the milling crowds for a long moment, his eyes far away, and then he smiled and shook his head and took his people home.

Back in Adamant's study, Hawk and Fisher sank immediately into the nearest chairs, put their feet up on his desk, and watched interestedly as Adamant bustled around checking reports and planning future strategy. Medley did his best to listen and pay attention, but he was beginning to look decidedly wilted round the edges. Dannielle had already disappeared upstairs for a little lie-down. Hawk for one did not blame her. He could quite happily have spent the next few months just sitting in his chair doing nothing. He smiled slightly. He'd always suspected he was officer material.

Bearclaw and Kincaid had gone in search of the kitchens to do a little restorative foraging. The butler Villiers came and went bearing messages and reports for Adamant, with a haughty expression that suggested he considered himself above such things. Hawk and Fisher helped themselves to the wine. Medley finally shuffled the reports into some kind of order, and Adamant settled down behind his desk to listen. He glared at Hawk and Fisher until they took their boots off his desk, and then looked expectantly at Medley.

'First the good news,' said Medley. 'The Brotherhood of Steel is out on the streets in force. Together with our people, they're knocking the hell out of Hardcastle's mercenaries. Also, street crimes have dropped sixty per cent.

'Megan O'Brien, the spice trader, has pulled out of the election. He's given his money and support to Hardcastle, in return for future favours. No surprises there.

'Lord Arthur Sinclair, standing on the No Tax On Liquor platform, was last seen passed out cold in the middle of a riotous party that covered an entire block. The Guard have roped off the area and set up barricades. Anyway, Sinclair is officially out of the running, or will be as soon as anyone can wake him up long enough to tell him.

'The mystery candidate known as the Grey Veil has disappeared. No one's seen hide nor hair of him since midday. He's probably retired quietly to save face.

'Now we come to the bad news. Hardcastle has been campaigning just as hard as we have, if not more so. His speeches have all gone down very well, and his people are handing out booze and money like they're going out of fashion. He's made the rounds of some very influential people, and gained a lot of support. The Quality may not like him much, but they're scared to death of James Adamant. It also appears that Hardcastle has picked up some very powerful support from something on the Street of Gods. Mortice isn't sure who or what is behind it, but just recently Hardcastle's sorcerer Wulf has been using all kinds of powerful magics he didn't have access to before. He's still not strong enough to break through Mortice's wards, but Mortice can't break through Wulf's either. So, as far as magic goes we have a stalemate. For the moment.

'The rest of the bad news concerns General Longarm.' Medley paused for a moment to gulp thirstily at a glass of wine before continuing. 'Longarm and his militants are doing surprisingly well. There's no doubt his armed supporters have been practising subtle and not-so-subtle intimidation, but there does seem to be some real grass-roots support for Longarm. People are responding well to his theme of political strength through military strength. He's also sworn to accept any man with a sword into the militant branch of the Brotherhood, once he's elected. A lot of people want that. Being a Brother of Steel opens a lot of doors, and not just in Haven.'

Medley checked his papers to make sure he'd covered everything, and then dropped them on the desk before Adamant. Adamant frowned thoughtfully.

'What do we know about General Longarm, Stefan?'

'Solid, professional soldier; not very imaginative. Had a reasonably good record with the Low Kingdoms army, before he retired and moved here. Came to politics late in life, which is probably why he takes it so seriously. Speaks well in public, as long as he sticks to a prepared text. This offer of guaranteed entry into the militant Brotherhood sounds a lot like desperation tactics. Might be worth sounding out other militants to find out whether it's a genuine offer or just something Longarm came up with off his own bat.'

Adamant looked at Hawk and Fisher. 'The militants already have one Seat on the Council: The Downs. Have you heard anything about that district since the militants took over?'

'It's not really our district,' said Hawk slowly. 'But I have heard a few things. Ever since Councillor Weaver came to power in The Downs, street crime has dropped by more than half throughout the area. That's been very popular. On the other hand, it seems clear that militant Brothers have been working as unofficial Guards in The Downs, and that hasn't been at all popular. There's no doubt they've been cracking down on street violence, but they've also been pushing their beliefs very strongly, and anyone who dares speak out against that gets very short shrift. I'm not just talking about bloody noses either; apparently the militants can turn quite nasty if they're crossed. I haven't any hard figures on how the election's going there, but I wouldn't be at all surprised if Weaver lost his Seat.'

'Thank you, Captain,' said Adamant. 'There may be something there I can use. Campaign rhetoric is always better for having some basis in truth.'

The door flew open and Dannielle swept in, looking much refreshed. She smiled brightly at Hawk and Fisher, still slumped in their chairs.

'What's this; still tired? I don't know what the Guard's coming to these days. James, darling, will you please come with me and talk to the cook? I've been trying to get her to agree to the menu we decided on for tonight's banquet, but she keeps going all mulish on me.'

'Of course, Danny,' said Adamant tolerantly. He nodded to Medley and the two Guards, and allowed his chattering wife to drag him out from behind his desk and out into the hall. Hawk looked at Fisher.

'I don't know where she gets her energy from, but I could sure use some of it.'

Hardcastle and his people trudged determinedly round the High Steppes, making speeches, shaking hands, and generally waving the flag. The crowds had been drinking most of the day and were starting to get a little rowdy, but Roxanne and the mercenaries kept them in line. And the speeches were still going down very well. As long as Hardcastle kept talking the crowds would listen, rapt and enthusiastic. Hardcastle was glad something was still going right; the news from the rest of the Steppes was almost universally bad. Somehow Adamant had put together an army of fighting men and turned them loose, and they were wiping the streets with Hardcastle's mercenaries. He'd lost nearly every advantage he'd gained, and areas that should have been safely under his thumb were now singing Reform songs and throwing stones at his people.

Hardcastle fought to hold onto his temper. He couldn't afford to let himself be distracted. He still had to make the rounds and talk to the people who mattered; people of standing and influence. Adamant might crawl to the commoners for their grubby little votes, but it was the Quality and the merchant houses who really ran Haven. That was where the real power lay. When they spoke, people listened – if they knew what was good for them. And so Hardcastle went from house to house, knocking on doors and glaring at servants, only to find himself fobbed off with vague promises and excuses as often as not. Apparently they were disturbed by the rising violence in the streets. Hardcastle fumed quietly to himself. These were the same people who'd bleated the loudest to the Council at the advances Reform had been making.

The afternoon darkened towards evening, and Hardcastle headed for the last address on the list. His last friend, and his last hope.

He stood before Tobias' door, and waited impatiently for an answer to the bell pull. It was taking a long time. Roxanne was idly trimming a fingernail with a nasty-looking dagger, and Wulf was staring off into the distance, lost in his dreams of power. Hardcastle looked at his followers and mercenaries, standing clumped together and muttering rebelliously under their breath, and he gestured irritably for them to disperse across the street. He wouldn't put it past Adamant to launch a sneak attack, if he thought he could get away with it. It was what Hardcastle would have done. Besides, he didn't need an army to visit a friend. Assuming the friend would talk to him.

Geoffrey Tobias had a reputation for being tight with money, and his house reflected it. Tobias was one of the six richest men in Haven, but his house was a cheap and nasty two up, two down, in one of the more subdued areas of the Steppes. The walls hadn't been painted in years, and wooden shutters covered the windows, locked tight even though it was still light. Tobias believed there were always thieves and cut-throats waiting for a chance at his money. Hardcastle shrugged. The man was probably right. A miser living on his own and apparently unprotected was an obvious target. Not that he was unprotected, of course. Hardcastle had no doubt the nasty little house was absolutely crawling with defensive spells.

Tobias had always been careful with money, but since he'd lost his Seat on the Council he'd given all his attention to his financial dealings. The man who had once been one of the real firebrands of the Conservative Cause had become a bitter and secretive recluse. He wouldn't see anyone he didn't absolutely have to, and even then strictly only by appointment. But he'd see Hardcastle. Hardcastle was a friend, and more importantly, he had something Tobias wanted. The offer of a Seat on the Council . . .

In return for a sizeable contribution to campaign funds, of course.

The door finally opened a crack, and Tobias glared out at them. He recognised Hardcastle with a scowl and opened the door a little wider. He was a grey, shabby man with pale skin and stringy grey hair that hung listlessly around his shoulders. His clothes were filthy and years out of style, and you had to look hard to see that under the dirt and wrinkles they had once been of exquisite style and cut. His face was all sharp planes and angles, with a down-turned mouth, and his eyes were cold and knowing. Tobias looked at Hardcastle for a long time and then sniffed loudly.

'Hello, Cameron. I should have known you'd come scratching at my door, with the election so close. Are all these people with you?'

'Yes, Geoffrey,' said Hardcastle patiently. 'I vouch for them.'

Tobias sniffed again. 'They stay out here, all of them. I won't have them in my house.'

He stepped back to allow Hardcastle to enter, and then slammed the door shut behind him. The narrow hall was gloomy and oppressive and smelled of damp. There was cracked plaster on the walls, and the floor was nothing but bare boards. Tobias led Hardcastle down to the end of the hall, pushed open a door and gestured for him to enter. He did so, and found himself in a comfortable, brightly lit room. The walls were covered with highly polished wood panels, and there was a deep pile carpet on the floor. A huge padded armchair stood by the fireplace, next to a delicate wooden table covered with papers and set with an elegant silver tea service. Tobias grunted with amusement at Hardcastle's surprise.

'I may be eccentric, Cameron, but I'm not crazy. I haven't much use for show or vanity anymore, but I still like my comforts.'

He sank carefully into the armchair, and gestured for Hardcastle to pull up the only other chair opposite him. They sat looking at each other for a moment.

'Been a while, Geoffrey.'

'Two years, at least,' said Tobias. 'I've kept busy, with one thing and another.'

'So I hear. They tell me you've doubled your fortune since you left the Council.'

'Leave? I didn't *leave* anything, and you damned well know it! I was forced out of my Seat, by that little snot Blackstone and his whining Reformers. He promised them the earth and the moon, and they believed it. Little good it did them. Their precious Blackstone is dead, and his successor couldn't make money if his life depended on it. Just wait till the Heights is hurting for money and can't balance its budget, and see how fast they scream for me to come back and save them!'

His voice had been rising steadily, and by the end he was

practically shouting. He stopped as his breath caught in his throat, and he coughed hard for several moments.

'You should take better care of yourself,' said Hardcastle. 'You've let yourself go.'

'That's one way of putting it, I suppose.' There were flecks of blood around Tobias' mouth. He patted his lips with a folded handkerchief, looked indifferently at the crimson stains on the cloth, and put it away. 'What do you want here, Cameron? I've no influence anymore.'

'That could change,' said Hardcastle. 'With a little persuasion I think I can get you official Conservative backing in the next election for the Heights. Full support; right across the board. Of course, a large contribution to Conservative funds would help to sway things in the future. That's how the world works.'

'Oh, I know all about how the world works, Cameron.' Tobias chuckled briefly. 'Sorry to disappoint you, but I don't really care about the Heights anymore. I still get mad about how they treated me, but I wouldn't go back if they got down on their knees and begged. Being a Councillor always meant more to my poor Maria than it ever did to me. I still miss her, you know . . .' Hardcastle looked non-plussed for a moment, and Tobias chuckled again. 'Not used to being caught out, are you, Cameron? You've been surrounded by advisers for too long. You can't trust advisers. They just tell you what they think you want to hear.'

'I need them,' said Hardcastle. 'I can't do everything myself. And my friends haven't always been there when I needed them.'

'You never needed me,' said Tobias quietly. 'You never really needed anyone. And I had my own problems.'

'Why didn't you tell me you were ill? I would have come to you long before this.'

'I go my own way, Cameron. Always have, always will. I don't lean on anyone. Don't worry; you can have your contribution. Tell my lawyers how much you need, and I'll see it gets to you. Buy some more mercenaries. Buy whatever it takes to crush those Reform scum into the dirt. Make them pay for what they did to me.'

'I'll do that, Geoffrey, I promise you. Is there anything else I can do for you?'

'Yes. Leave me in peace. Goodbye, Cameron. Don't slam the door on your way out.'

In Brimstone Hall Jillian Hardcastle sat on her bed, her back pressed against the headboard, hugging her knees to her. Her husband had finally returned. She could hear him moving about downstairs, talking to people. His people; none of them were hers. She had no friends, no one came to visit her, and she wasn't even allowed a servant of her own. All she had was her husband, the great Cameron Hardcastle.

She looked at her bare arms, and the bruises stood out plainly even under the extra layer of makeup. She'd have to put on some long gloves before she went downstairs. Her back still ached, but it was bearable now. At least there hadn't been any blood in her urine this time.

She often thought about leaving, but she had no one to go to. And wherever she went, Cameron would be sure to find her. He had people everywhere. She sometimes thought about killing herself, but she could never find the courage. Hardcastle had beaten all the courage out of her.

She heard footsteps outside on the landing, and fear rushed through her like icy water, freezing her in place. It was Cameron, come to look for her. She knew it. She stared fixedly at the closed bedroom door, barely breathing, her stomach churning with tension. The footsteps approached the door, and then went on past it, continuing on down the hall. It wasn't Cameron. Just one of the servants.

She ought to go down and welcome Cameron home. He expected it of her. If she didn't go downstairs, he would come looking for her, and then he would be angry. But she couldn't go down to meet him. Not yet. She'd go downstairs in a minute, and greet him in the polite monotone he'd taught her. She would go down. In a minute. Or two.

Hardcastle sank into his favourite chair, looked round his warm, comfortable study, and sighed gratefully. It had been a long hard day, and he wasn't as young as he used to be. He started to order Jillian to fetch him a drink, and then scowled as he realised she wasn't there. She ought to have been there. It was her place to be at his side, to carry out his wishes. He'd have to have another little talk with her, later on.

He got to his feet, ignoring his protesting back, and poured himself a large drink. He rather thought he'd earned it. There was a polite knock on the door. He grunted acknowledgement, and Wulf and Roxanne came in. He dropped back into his chair, noting sourly that neither of them looked particularly tired. Roxanne leaned against the fireplace with her arms folded, waiting patiently for new orders. Hardcastle made a mental note that she wasn't to be offered a guest room for the night. They'd probably wake up in the early hours to find the whole damned Hall going up in flames. Wulf was standing to attention before him, waiting to report on the day's activities. Let him wait. Do him good to be reminded of his place. Hardcastle sipped unhurriedly at his wine and then nodded to the sorcerer to begin.

Most of the reports were pretty straightforward. All the minor candidates had dropped out. That simplified things; he wouldn't have to have them crushed or killed, after all. General Longarm was still making a nuisance of himself, but he was nothing more than a retired soldier with delusions of grandeur. And with all the mercenaries currently battling on the streets, soldiers weren't particularly popular right now.

Adamant was still a problem. The Brotherhood of Steel had declared in his favour, and were actually out on the streets sticking their noses into things that didn't concern them. Hardcastle scowled. He'd better send word to the right people, and have them called off.

Wulf droned on, showing off as usual on how professional he was, and Hardcastle waited impatiently. He had a question he wanted to ask, but he didn't interrupt. He didn't want the sorcerer to be able to hide behind the excuse of any other business. Wulf eventually ground to a halt, and Hardcastle looked at him steadily.

'You said you had power now, Wulf. Real power. Power enough to break through Adamant's wards and destroy him and his new sorcerer. So why are they still alive?'

Wulf met Hardcastle's gaze unflinchingly. 'It will take time before I can use my power safely. For the moment I'm still concentrating on the wards that hold the Abomination safely within me. We were lucky to find him while he was still relatively weak after his awakening. If he was to escape now, he would be very angry with us. He'd destroy us, the whole of Haven, and probably most of the Low Kingdoms. We're talking about one of the Transient Beings, Cameron, not some low-level demon. We can't risk something like that getting loose.'

'So what am I supposed to do about Adamant?'

'Nothing, for the moment. Let's wait and see how the polling goes. There's still plenty of time to intervene directly, if it should prove necessary.'

Hardcastle glared at him. 'That's not good enough, sorcerer.' He looked across at Roxanne. 'According to my sources, Longarm is planning an attack on Adamant tonight. I want you to use your inside contact to get into Adamant's house. Stay hidden and wait for the attack, and then take advantage of the confusion to make sure Adamant dies. You'd better kill your contact as well. Is that clear?'

'Of course,' said Roxanne. 'Sounds like fun.' She smiled

at Hardcastle, and he had to look away. Few people could meet Roxanne's smile without flinching. Even when she was on their side.

The banquet at Adamant's mansion was a noisy affair. There were so many guests that even the main dining hall was barely sufficient to hold them all. The single great table had all but disappeared under huge servings of food and wines, and there wasn't a spare place left for anyone. The huge candelabra and dozens of wall lamps filled the hall with a blaze of light, and the guests filled the air with a roar of chatter. It was a victory celebration, in every way that mattered. No one had any doubts as to the election's outcome. This night would be Reform's night. They could tell. They could feel it on the air and in the streets.

Adamant sat in the seat of honour, of course, with Dannielle on one side and Medley on the other. Dannielle was busy feeding Adamant by hand with something covered in a sticky sauce, half of which seemed to be ending up on his face, to their mutual amusement. Medley was busy sampling several wines to see which was the tastiest. The two warriors, Bearclaw and Kincaid, sat side by side discussing old battles, and using the table cutlery to mark troop positions. The rest of the guests were Adamant's followers and party faithfuls, being rewarded for their services to Adamant's campaign. Servants came and went, bringing yet more courses and side dishes. Adamant's food taster sat quietly to one side, nibbling at a light salad, having given up trying to keep up with everyone else. A dozen or so dogs wandered round the hall, enjoying all the noise and attention, and feeding on bones and scraps thrown to them by indulgent guests.

Hawk and Fisher were there too, but they weren't part of the banquet. They were on duty. They'd get their dinner later, in the kitchens. If they were lucky. Reform only went so far, after all. Hawk was fatalistic about such things and, if anything, preferred to have his attention free to watch for threats, but Fisher was simmering with barely repressed bile. Hawk kept a watchful eye on her. She tended to take such things personally. At the moment she was scowling dubiously at a chicken leg she'd snatched from under the nose of a resentful hound. The animal was about to challenge her for it, but one glare from Fisher was enough to change his mind.

'You're not really going to eat that, are you?' said Hawk.

'Damn right I am,' said Fisher. 'I'm hungry.' She gnawed industriously at the leg for a while, and then gestured with it at the banquet table. 'Look at them all, stuffing their faces. There's not one of them who's worked half as hard as we have today. I hope they all get wind.'

'Don't take it so hard,' said Hawk. 'I'm sure Adamant would have invited us to table if he could, but it would do his image no good at all, and he knows it. The Cause is great for political reform, but it's got a long way to go before it can start meddling with the social structure.'

'I'd like to meddle with his structure,' muttered Fisher. 'Preferably with a large mallet.'

'It's not as if we've been singled out,' said Hawk reasonably. 'Adamant's got a good twenty to thirty mercenaries and men-at-arms scattered round this house standing guard, and none of them were invited either.'

'We're different,' said Fisher.

'Maybe,' said Hawk. 'Hello! Where's Medley going?'

Hawk and Fisher watched interestedly as Medley made his excuses to Adamant, and left the table. He seemed to be in something of a hurry, and by the time he got to the main door he was practically running.

'The fish must be off,' said Hawk.

Fisher looked at him fondly. 'You have no romance in your soul, Hawk. Now he's no longer needed here, he's probably off to see his mysterious girlfriend. I wonder if we'll get to meet her?'

'I doubt it. Hello! Now Dannielle's leaving as well.'

Hawk and Fisher watched again as Dannielle made her excuses to Adamant and left the table.

'Maybe the fish *is* off,' said Fisher.

'I don't know,' said Hawk thoughtfully. 'She's been up and down all day. Maybe her illness is catching up with her.'

'Or she's gone after Medley to try and sneak a look at his girlfriend.'

'Either that, or someone's slipped poison in their food . . .'

They looked at each other.

'No,' said Hawk finally. 'They haven't eaten anything the others haven't, and anyway, Mortice is keeping a close watch on the banquet.'

Fisher shrugged. 'No doubt we'll find out what's happening eventually. We usually do.'

'That was before we got involved in politics.'

'True.'

They watched everyone else eating for a while. Hawk's stomach rumbled.

'Something's wrong,' said Fisher suddenly.

Hawk looked at her. 'How do you mean?'

'We're supposed to get regular security updates from Adamant's people, but no one's been by here in almost half an hour.'

'That's right,' said Hawk. He frowned, and bit his lip thoughtfully. 'You wander over and take up a position by Adamant. I'll take a quick look out the door and see if anyone's about. It's always possible Adamant's people are just getting slack now the worst is over, but . . .'

'Yeah,' said Fisher. 'But.'

She headed casually in Adamant's direction, while Hawk made unhurriedly for the main door. No point in upsetting the guests if they didn't have to. The banquet hall was set right in the centre of the mansion and had just the two doors. The far door led straight to the kitchens; a servants' route. Hawk had checked it out earlier. It was too narrow and twisting to move an attack force through. The main door led out onto a wide corridor that ran pretty much the length of the house, with only a couple of bends. Hawk scowled. He didn't like the direction his thoughts were taking. Any attack force would have to get past all of Adamant's men and Mortice's protective wards. He'd have been bound to hear something. Unless the attack force was very, very good. Hawk stopped before the main door and listened. He couldn't hear a thing over the racket the dinner guests were making. Why the hell had Medley and Dannielle chosen this particular time to disappear? He reached out a hand to the doorknob, and then stopped as the doorknob began to turn slowly on its own. Hawk backed away.

The door flew open and a dozen cloaked and masked men burst in. Hawk yelled a warning to Fisher, and drew his axe. The guests at table screamed and yelled and struggled to get to their feet. Fisher moved to stand between Adamant and his attackers, sword at the ready. Bearclaw and Kincaid rose to their feet and looked around for weapons. Neither of them had worn swords to table. That would have been an insult to Adamant. Bearclaw seized a heavy silver candlestick and hefted it professionally. Kincaid broke a bottle against the wall with practised ease.

The attackers came spilling round Hawk like rushing water past a rock. He stood his ground and cut down two men with his axe. Bearclaw came charging forward, deftly avoided a vicious sword stroke, and clubbed the man to the ground. He quickly stepped over the fallen body to tackle another intruder, and Kincaid came forward to guard his back with the broken bottle. Two swordsmen thought he'd be an easy target. Kincaid smiled easily, cut one man's throat, and blinded the other, his hand moving too quickly to be seen. He threw aside the bottle and snatched up a dead man's sword. Blood flew on the air as he moved swiftly among the scattering enemy, his sword darting back and forth in textbook cuts and parries.

Three men got past Hawk and the two warriors, and made straight for Adamant. Fisher met them with her sword. The first man went down almost immediately, clutching at the wide rip in his gut. The second forced Fisher back step by step with a whirlwind attack of cuts and thrusts. The third man closed in on Adamant. Fisher tried desperately to finish her man so that she could get back to protect Adamant, but her opponent was too good to be that easily dismissed. Fisher cut and parried and then faked a stumble. The masked man thought he saw his chance and moved in, and Fisher ran him through. She jerked her sword free and turned quickly round just in time to see Adamant throw a bowl of soup into the third man's face, blinding him. The intruder clawed at his eyes, and Adamant kicked him in the groin. As the man sank to his knees, Adamant took away his sword and looked around for another victim.

Hawk cut down two more men, the wide head of his axe punching through hidden chain mail as though it wasn't there. Bearclaw and Kincaid fought back to back, and the last two intruders went down in a flurry of blood and steel. A sudden silence fell across the dining hall, broken only by the gradually slowing breathing of the fighting men and mutters of shock and amazement from the guests. Bearclaw bound up a nasty-looking gash in his shoulder with a dubious-looking handkerchief taken from his sleeve.

'I must be getting old, Joshua,' he said easily. 'Was a time they'd never have got near me.'

Kincaid nodded solemnly. 'Well, it must be said the candlestick never was your preferred weapon. Grab one of their swords and we'll go and see if there are any more of these bastards in the house.'

The guests stirred uneasily at that, and Adamant moved quickly forward to address them. 'It's all right, my friends, the worst is over. Please stay where you are while I have my people search the house and make it secure.' He moved quickly over to Bearclaw and Kincaid and kept his voice low as he spoke to them. 'Joshua, Laurence, find out what's happened to my men-at-arms, and report back here when the house is fully secure again. And remember, Danny and Stefan went off on their own just before the attack; make sure they're all right.'

The two warriors nodded silently and left the hall, sword in hand. Hawk wanted to go with them, but knew he couldn't. His priority had to be Adamant's safety. He went over to Fisher, and made sure she was all right. They looked around at the mayhem they'd helped to cause, and shared a grin. Adamant approached them and nodded his thanks.

'It may not look like it,' he said quietly, 'but this is still something of a disaster. A whole lot of nasty questions come to mind, starting with how the hell they got in. Mortice's wards are supposed to keep out anyone I haven't personally vouched for. And why the hell didn't Medley's intelligence people warn him there was a raid in the offing?'

'No problem,' said Hawk. 'We handled it. Any idea who they were?'

'Not really,' said Adamant. 'A last-chance assault by Hardcastle's people, presumably. Let's take a look.'

They moved quickly among the bodies, pulling off masks and studying faces. Hawk and Fisher didn't recognise anyone, but Adamant remained kneeling beside the body of a grey-haired man with a harsh, scarred face that hadn't relaxed at all in death. Hawk and Fisher moved over to join him.

'General Longarm himself,' said Adamant. 'He always did take his politics too personally.'

'Let's keep looking,' said Fisher. 'Maybe we'll get really lucky and find Hardcastle's here as well.'

Adamant smiled in spite of himself, and then looked round quickly as the main door opened and Kincaid came in. He walked straight over to Adamant, who rose to his feet.

'We have something of a problem, James,' he said quietly. 'Not with the house; that's secure. It seems there were fifty of the intruders originally. Your people took care of the others before they got this far. No one heard anything because of the noise of the banquet. We've got quite a few casualties, and even more dead. These people were professionals.'

'Militant Brothers of Steel,' said Hawk.

Kincaid nodded, but didn't look all that impressed. 'Well, they're dead militants now.'

'So what's the problem?' said Fisher.

'I think you'd better come and see for yourself, James.' Kincaid couldn't seem to meet Adamant's eyes. 'It's Dannielle.'

Adamant's face lost all its colour, as though someone had just punched him in the gut. 'How badly is she hurt?'

'I really think you'd better see for yourself James.'

'You're not going anywhere without us,' said Hawk quickly.

Adamant nodded impatiently. 'Let's go.'

Kincaid led the way out into the main corridor. There were bodies and blood everywhere. Preoccupied as he was, Adamant still had room in him to be sickened at the sight of so many men who had died on his behalf. He stepped carefully over the bodies, nodding here and there at a familiar face, and then he stopped and knelt by one man. It was the butler, Villiers. He'd taken a dozen wounds before he died, and a broken sword was still clutched in his hand.

'He never believed in Reform,' said Adamant. 'But he stayed with me anyway, because I was family. He never left us, even during the bad days. He protected me as a child. And all it got him was a bad death, in a house where he should have been safe.' He got to his feet, and nodded for Kincaid to carry on. They walked on down the corridor.

When Adamant spoke again his voice was perfectly steady. 'You haven't said anything about Stefan. Is he all right?'

'Oh, he's fine,' said Kincaid. 'Locked himself in your study with his girlfriend. I don't think he knows anything's happened. Just shouted at me to go away when I knocked on the door.'

Adamant nodded, not really listening, and Kincaid led the way up the stairs to the next floor. His face was fixed and drawn. *She must be dead*, thought Hawk. *Anything else, he would have said*. They moved along the hallway to Adamant's bedroom. Bearclaw was waiting outside the door. There was pity in his face as he looked at Adamant. Pity, and something else Hawk couldn't read. Bearclaw opened the bedroom door, and everyone drew back a few steps to let Adamant go in first.

In the bedroom, Dannielle was sitting on the bed. Her face was flushed, and she wouldn't look Adamant in the eye. Kincaid picked up a small silver snuff box from the dressing table and handed it to Adamant. He looked at it blankly for a moment and then opened it. Inside was a small amount of grey-white powder.

'Cocaine,' said Bearclaw. 'We found her helping herself when we were searching this floor.'

'Oh, great,' said Fisher. 'That's going to look really good when it gets out.'

'It's not going to get out,' said Adamant. 'Not until after the election.' He looked at Dannielle, and his mouth tightened. 'How could you, Danny? How could you do this to me?'

'Oh, that's typical, James. Never mind why I'm taking drugs; all you care about is your precious reputation.' Dannielle glared at him sullenly, her voice shrill and bitter. 'I've been sniffing dust ever since you started campaigning for the Steppes. The best part of three months, and it's taken you till now to notice. It's all your fault, anyway. You never had time for me anymore; all you thought and dreamed about was your bloody campaign. I tried to go along, to be a part of it for your sake, but you never even noticed I was there.

'We aren't all as strong as you, James. You've been full of energy right from the beginning, inspired by your Cause, running full tilt from one thing to the next, with the rest of us straggling along behind you, trying to keep up. I just couldn't anymore. I was tired all the time, and lonely and depressed. So I started sniffing dust now and again, just to give me a boost, make me feel human, and keep me going. Only the campaign just ground on and on, and I got more and more tired, and there were always more and more things that needed doing for your bloody Cause. And I needed more and more dust just to feel normal and get me through the day. I even had to embezzle from you to pay for the dust.'

'Why didn't you tell me?' said Adamant. He realised he was still holding the snuff box, and put it down on the dressing table. He wiped his fingers unconsciously on his sleeve, as though they were dirty.

'When did I ever get a chance to talk to you?' said Dannielle. 'We haven't had a moment to ourselves in months.'

Adamant started to say something heated in reply, and then stopped himself. When he spoke again his voice was low and cold and very controlled. 'Perhaps you're right, Danny. I don't know. We'll talk about it later. In the meantime, I have to think about how best to keep this quiet. A lot of people are counting on me to win this election, and I won't let them down. If news of this gets out, I'll be ruined. I've made a lot of enemies in my stand against the drug trade, and they'd use a scandal like this to destroy me. Who else knows, apart from us? Who was your supplier?'

Dannielle smiled almost triumphantly. 'Lucien Sykes.'

'What?'

'Drugs come in through the docks, and he takes his share.

Where do you suppose all the money came from that he's been donating to your campaign?'

Adamant turned away and closed his eyes for a moment. Nobody said anything. Adamant turned to Hawk and Fisher. 'How much of this do you need to report?'

'Not all of it,' said Hawk. 'Keeping quiet about your wife comes under the general heading of protecting you. But Sykes is a different matter. We can't ignore someone in his position. But he can wait until after the election tonight.'

'Thank you,' said Adamant. 'That's all I can ask. Danny, pull yourself together, and then come down and help with my guests. People have been hurt.'

'Do I get to keep my dust?'

'Do you need it?'

'Yes.'

'Then keep it.'

Adamant turned and left the room, and the others followed him out.

'I'm going to have to put out some kind of statement about the attack,' said Adamant as they went back downstairs. 'To reassure my followers that I'm all right. Rumours spread like wildfire in Haven, particularly when it's bad news. I'd better talk to Stefan. He's probably still in my study with his lady friend.' He smiled briefly. 'I did promise no one would barge in on them while they were there, but I'm sure he won't mind, under the circumstances.'

He led the way back to his study, and knocked briskly on the door. 'Stefan, it's James. I need to see you. Something's come up.' He waited a moment, but there was no reply. Adamant smiled slightly, produced a key, and unlocked the door. He knocked again, and pushed the door open. Medley and Roxanne were sitting together. For a moment nobody moved as the two sides stared at each other, and then Roxanne grabbed her sword belt and drew her sword.

'Get out of here, Stefan! They'll kill us both!'

She started towards Adamant, sword at the ready, and then stopped as Hawk and Fisher moved quickly forward to protect him. Medley got to his feet, but stood where he was, staring at Adamant's horrified face. Roxanne grabbed a burning brand from the fire and set it to a hanging tapestry. Flames ran up the wall. She grabbed Medley's arm and urged him towards the other door. Hawk and Fisher went after them as Bearclaw and Kincaid tried to beat out the fire before it could spread. Adamant just stood where he was, watching.

Roxanne backed away from Hawk and Fisher one step at a time, her sword sweeping back and forth before her, keeping the Guards at bay. She was grinning broadly, and her eyes were full of death. She glanced back over her shoulder just long enough to be sure that Medley was safely through the door. Then after a moment's hesitation, she turned and ran after him. Hawk and Fisher plunged after her, but she slammed the door in their faces and turned the key on the other side. Hawk lifted his axe to break down the door, and then lowered it again. His job was to protect Adamant, not to chase after traitors. Medley and Roxanne would keep for another day. He put away his axe, and after a moment Fisher sheathed her sword. Kincaid and Bearclaw had torn down the burning tapestry, and were stamping out the flames. Adamant was still standing in the doorway, staring at nothing. Hawk glanced at Fisher, who shrugged uncertainly. He moved tentatively towards Adamant, and the politician's eyes came back into focus. He had to swallow two or three times before he could speak.

'My wife is taking drugs supplied by one of my main backers. My guests have been attacked in my own dining hall, and most of my men-at-arms are dead. And now it turns out my closest friend has been a traitor all along. I never knew politics could cost so much.' For a moment he couldn't get his breath, and Hawk thought Adamant might cry, but the moment passed and some of his strength came back to him. His face hardened, and when he spoke again his voice was strained but steady.

'Not a word of this to anyone. We can't afford for my supporters to know how badly we've been betrayed. It will all come out after the election, but by then it won't matter, whatever the result. So, we'll go back to the dining hall, reassure my guests, and keep our mouths shut about all this.

'But win or lose, Stefan Medley is a dead man.'

Medley followed Roxanne through the packed streets, dazed and unquestioning. It was all like some horrible nightmare he couldn't wake up from. One moment he'd been cherishing a snatched moment with Roxanne, and the next he was running for his life. He didn't know where he was running to; Roxanne had taken over as soon as they left the house. He couldn't seem to concentrate on anything; all he could see was Adamant's face, and the look of betrayal in his eyes. Roxanne led him through increasingly narrow and squalid streets until finally they came to the Sheep's Head Inn, a quiet backwater tavern they'd used before for their few assignations.

The bartender showed no interest in seeing them again, but then he never did. That was one of the reasons why they'd chosen the place. Roxanne collected the key and led the way up the back stairs to their usual room, and for the first time they were able to sit down and look at each other.

'All in all, it's been an interesting day,' said Roxanne. 'Pity I didn't have time to kill Hawk and Fisher, but there'll be other times.'

'Is that all you've got to say?' said Medley. 'My life is ruined, my reputation isn't worth spit anymore, and all you can think about is fighting a couple of Guards? We've got to get out of Haven, Roxanne. James won't move against us while the election's still running, but once that's over he'll send every man he's got after us. His pride won't let him do anything else. And you can bet he won't have given them orders to bring us back alive.'

'We can go to Hardcastle,' said Roxanne. 'He'll protect us. If only to spite Adamant.'

'No,' said Medley. 'Not Hardcastle. I've hurt him too badly in the past. He has scores to settle with me. Look, Roxanne, this is our chance to get away from all this and start over.'

'But I don't want to leave,' said Roxanne. 'I don't run from anyone. Besides, I like working for Hardcastle. The pay's good, and the work is interesting. I'm staying.'

Medley looked at her for a long moment. 'Why are you doing this to me, Roxanne?'

'Doing what?'

'I love you, Roxanne, but I can't go to Hardcastle. If you love me, you won't ask me to.'

Roxanne looked down at the floor, and then back at him again. 'Sorry, Stefan, but I told you: I work for Hardcastle. You were just another job. Hardcastle's sorcerer set me on you, as a way of getting to Adamant. You told me all kinds of useful things without realising it. You were fun, but now the masks are off and the game's over. You lost. I'm sorry to rush you, Stefan, but I have to be going now.'

She got to her feet, and Medley stood up to face her. 'So it was all nothing but lies; all the things you said to me. I betrayed my best friend and dragged my honour through the mud, all for you; and now you're telling me it was all for nothing? I can't believe that, Roxanne. I won't believe that.'

She shrugged. 'Don't take it so personally. It's just business. No hard feelings?'

Medley sat down again, as though all the strength had gone out of his legs. 'No; no hard feelings, Roxanne.'

She smiled at him briefly, and left, closing the door

quietly behind her. Medley stared at the closed door, listening to the sound of her footsteps disappearing down the stairs.

7

Desperate Choices

All the clocks in Haven struck eight in the evening, and the polls finally opened. Brightly coloured election booths appeared on the designated street corners, in the time it took for the bells to toll the hour. Magically created and maintained by the Council's circle of sorcerers, they were as near to being corruption-proof as anything in Haven could be. Once a vote had been registered and placed in the metal box, nothing but the most powerful sorceries could get at it again. There were fingerprint checks to make sure everyone was who they claimed to be, and to keep out simulacra and homunculi. Haven's voters were a devious lot when it came to corruption and cheating.

The inns and the brothels were still going strong, though the free booze had run out long ago. Some of the day-long revellers were busy sleeping it off on tavern floors and tables, uncaring that they were missing the very chance to vote that they'd been celebrating. Bets were still being made, at widely varying odds, and rumour and speculation ran rife. People thronged the streets, dressed in their best. An election was an Occasion, a chance to see and be seen. Pickpockets and cutpurses had never had it so good. Ballad singers stood at every street corner, singing the latest broadsheets about the two main candidates, interspersed now and then with requested old favourites. There were jugglers and conjurers and stilt-walkers, and of course any number of street preachers making the most of the occasion, always on the lookout for a crowd and anyone who looked like they might stand still long enough to be preached at.

The voting began, as Haven made its choice.

Roxanne leaned back in her chair and stretched her legs languorously as Hardcastle poured her a glass of his best wine. He was smiling broadly, and positively radiating good cheer. It didn't suit him. Wulf and Jillian stood quietly in the background.

'You've done well, Roxanne,' said Hardcastle, pouring himself a large drink. 'Without Medley to help him, Adamant's organisation will fall apart at the seams, and he'll lose every advantage he's gained. All it needs now is a few more pushes in the right places, and everything he's built will collapse around him. It's a pity you didn't get a chance to kill him, but it's just as well. I've changed my mind. I don't want him dead just yet. I want him to suffer first.

'It's not enough to kill Adamant. Not anymore. I want to beat him first. I want to humiliate the man; rub his nose in the fact that all his whining Reformers are no match for a Conservative. I don't just want him dead; I want him broken.'

Roxanne shrugged noncommittally and sipped at her wine. She'd taken advantage of the speech to study Jillian Hardcastle and the sorcerer Wulf. Both of them looked rather the worse for wear. Jillian had a bruised and swollen mouth, and was holding herself awkwardly, as though favouring a hidden pain. Wulf looked tired and drawn. There were dark bruises of fatigue under his eyes, and his gaze was more than a little wild. He seemed preoccupied, as though listening to a voice only he could hear. Roxanne realised Hardcastle had stopped talking, and quickly turned her attention back to him.

'All right,' she said equably. 'What do we do now?'

'We need to isolate Adamant even further,' said

Hardcastle. 'We've taken away his adviser. Who does that leave him to lean on? The two Guards, Hawk and Fisher. They've been acting all along like Adamant's paid men, for all their vaunted impartiality. With them out of the way, Adamant should crumble and fall apart nicely.'

Roxanne nodded. 'I can take either of them on their own, but killing both of them would be tricky.' She smiled suddenly. 'Fun, though.'

'I don't want them killed,' said Hardcastle flatly. 'I want them kidnapped. They have interfered in my life far too often, and they're going to pay the price. They'll beg for death before I'm finished with them.'

'I can't guarantee to take both of them alive,' said Roxanne. 'One perhaps, but not both.'

'I thought you might say that,' said Hardcastle, 'So I've arranged some help for you.' He tugged at the bell pull by his desk. There was a short, uncomfortable pause, and then the study door opened and Pike and Da Silva came in. Roxanne studied them warily from her chair.

Pike was tall and muscular, in his mid twenties, with a clear open face and a nasty smile. He moved well, and carried his chain mail as though it were weightless. He was a familiar type; throw a stick in a gladiators' training school and you'd hit a dozen just like him. Da Silva was short and stocky, with a broad chest and a wrestler's overdeveloped arm muscles. He was a few years older than Pike, and looked it. His face was heavy and bony, and would have looked brutish even without the perpetual scowl that tugged at his features. As well as a sword, he carried a four-foot-long headbreaker of solid oak weighted with lead at both ends.

Independently they were proficient-enough mercenaries, but working together as a team they'd built a reputation for death and mayhem that almost rivalled Roxanne's. She glared at them both, and then switched her glare to Hardcastle.

'Why do you need them? You've got me.'

'I want Hawk and Fisher taken alive,' said Hardcastle. 'The only way to do that without major casualties to my side is to make sure we have the advantage of overwhelming numbers. Pike and Da Silva command a troop of fifty mercenaries. You will lead them against Adamant's people. Wulf will supply magical protection. Is that clear?'

Roxanne shrugged. 'You're the boss, Hardcastle. What do we do after we've taken Hawk and Fisher?'

'I've set aside a place for them. Pike and Da Silva have the details. Adamant and his people should be hitting the streets in about half an hour. Follow them, pick your spot, and do the job. No excuses on this one; I want them alive. I have plans for Hawk and Fisher.'

James Adamant led his people out into the High Steppes, determined to make as many speeches as he could while the polls were still open. None of his people said anything, but it was clear to everyone that Adamant needed to reassure himself of his popularity after so many things having gone wrong. So with tired limbs and weary hearts they followed him out onto the streets one last time. Adamant strode ahead, out in front for all to see, with Dannielle at his side. Hawk and Fisher followed close behind. Adamant's supporters had dispersed and gone home after the debacle of the victory banquet, so only half a dozen mercenaries accompanied Adamant on his last excursion into the Steppes, with Bearclaw and Kincaid bringing up the rear. It was a far cry from the cheerful, confident host that had followed him on his first outing, but a lot had happened since then.

Adamant hurried from street to street at a pace his retinue was hard pressed to match, as though he was trying to leave his most recent memories behind and be again the confident, unworried politician he had been at the start of the day. Hawk and Fisher stretched their legs and kept up with him. They walked with weapons drawn, just in case Hardcastle tried for a last-minute assassination. Hawk kept a careful watch on Dannielle. He'd wanted to leave her behind, but she'd insisted on going with them. Trouble was, she was right. Her presence was a vote winner, and her absence would have raised questions Adamant couldn't afford to answer. She'd thrown the last of her dust on the fire before she left. Adamant had just nodded stiffly, and turned away. They were walking arm in arm and smiling at the crowds, but they hadn't exchanged five words since they left the house.

Hawk sighed quietly to himself. As if he didn't have enough things to worry about. Medley had disappeared, along with the notorious Roxanne, but it was too early to tell just how much information he'd betrayed to Hardcastle. Worst of all was the damage he'd done to Adamant's confidence. Adamant had trusted Stefan Medley implicitly, and allowed him to shape and plan his whole campaign. Now Medley was gone, and Adamant didn't know who or what he could rely on anymore.

On top of all that he'd found he couldn't rely on Mortice anymore either. Longarm and his men shouldn't have been able to break into his house at all, but the dead man's mind had been wandering again, and his wards had slipped. He'd promised it wouldn't happen again, and Adamant had pretended to believe him, but neither of them were fooled.

Adamant made another speech on yet another street corner, and as always a crowd gathered to listen. Even now, after all that had happened, Adamant could still sway a crowd with his voice. Perhaps because he still believed in his Cause, even if he was no longer sure of himself. The speech started off well enough. The crowd was responsive and enthusiastic, and cheered in all the right places. Bearclaw and Kincaid moved unobtrusively among them, making sure no one got out of hand. Hawk and Fisher leaned wearily against a wall, feeling unneeded. And then the crowd's cheers turned to screams as fifty mercenaries came pouring out of a side street with swords in their hands.

They cut their way through the scattering crowd, uncaring who they hurt. Bearclaw and Kincaid drew their swords and fought side by side as the tide of mercenaries hit them. Bearclaw swung his great sword two-handed, cutting down his attackers like a scythe slicing through overripe wheat. Kincaid leapt and danced, his blade cutting and thrusting in swift steel blurs. But there were only two of them, and the vast body of mercenaries swept past them without even slowing. The two warriors were quickly surrounded, and moved to stand back to back, still fighting. Adamant's mercenaries tried to make a stand, but there were only six of them and they were quickly overrun. Hawk and Fisher moved quickly forward and put themselves between Adamant and Dannielle and their attackers. They waited grimly, weapons at the ready.

The first mercenary to reach them went for Fisher, mistakenly supposing her to be the easier target. She parried his blow easily, cut his throat on the backswing, and was back on guard before the next mercenary could reach her. Hawk roared a Northern war cry and swung his axe in short, vicious arcs, scattering the mercenaries around him as one by one they fell before his unwavering attack. Soon the street was a boiling cauldron of milling men and flashing steel, and blood flew on the air. Adamant had drawn his sword and was keeping his attackers at bay, but he had trained as a duellist, not a street fighter, and it was all he could do to hold his ground. Dannielle cowered behind him, clutching a dagger he'd given her, hoping she'd find the strength to use it when the time came.

Hawk and Fisher fought side by side, and the mercenaries fell before them, unable to match their skill or their fury. Bearclaw and Kincaid fought alone, separated by the mercenaries, bleeding from a dozen wounds but refusing to fall. Dead men lay piled about them. And then Roxanne appeared out of nowhere, laughing aloud as her sword flashed out to slice through the meat of Kincaid's leg. His mouth gaped soundlessly as his leg crumpled beneath him, unable to bear his weight. He fell to one knee, still trying to swing his sword. Roxanne swept past him, grinning fiercely, heading for Hawk and Fisher. Pike and Da Silva came after her. Pike's sword lashed out to deflect a blow from Bearclaw, and Da Silva's heavy wooden staff swept across to slam into Bearclaw's side. Ribs broke under the impact. Bearclaw coughed blood, and fell forward onto his hands and knees. The mercenaries closed in around Bearclaw and Kincaid, and their swords rose and fell in steady butchery.

Roxanne burst through the milling crowd of fighters and threw herself at Fisher. Fisher tried to hold her ground and couldn't, forced back by the sudden strength and speed of the attack. Hawk tried to reach her, but Pike and Da Silva were quickly upon him, Pike engaging his axe while Da Silva circled patiently with his headbreaker, trying for a clear shot.

Roxanne thrust and parried, laughing breathlessly, and step by step Fisher was driven back, until her back was pressed up against a wall and there was nowhere else to go. Fisher was good with a sword, but Roxanne was an expert, inhumanly strong, and she never seemed to get tired.

For a moment, desperation gave Fisher new strength and she was able to beat aside Roxanne's attack long enough to cut through the mercenary's leathers and open a long, shallow wound along her ribs. Roxanne didn't even flinch, and her return attack drove Fisher back against the wall. Fisher's moment passed, and her strength faded away, replaced by the day's weariness. She struggled frantically to fend off Roxanne's sword, and then a mercenary stepped in from her blind side and clubbed her down with the hilt of his sword. Fisher dropped to one knee, still clinging to her sword. Blood spilled down her face from a torn scalp. Roxanne and the other mercenary hit her again with their sword hilts, and she fell blindly forward onto the bloody cobbles and lay still. Roxanne kicked her in the head.

Hawk saw Fisher fall, and screamed in fury that he couldn't get to her. He swung his axe savagely at Pike, and the mercenary was forced to retreat. The heavy axe blade smashed through Pike's defences and knocked him to the ground. Hawk stepped in for the kill, and Da Silva's headbreaker swung round in a tight arc, slamming into Hawk's side, knocking the breath out of him. Hawk staggered backwards, favouring his injured side, and snarled soundlessly at his opponents, daring them to come after him.

Adamant swept his sword back and forth, keeping the mercenaries at bay. For some reason they seemed more interested in keeping him occupied than in trying to kill him. Whatever the reason, it hadn't prevented them from whittling away at him like a carpenter with a block of wood. Blood ran freely from a dozen wounds, staining his fine clothes. Dannielle screamed behind him, and he spun round to see her struggling with a grinning mercenary. Adamant ran him through and turned quickly back to face his opponents. Their attitude changed immediately with the death of their companion, and for the first time they began to press their attack in earnest. Swords seemed to come at him from everywhere at once, and Adamant realised sickly that he couldn't keep off such an attack for more than a few moments. One of the mercenaries beat aside his sword and lunged forward. Dannielle screamed and threw herself in the blade's way. It plunged into her side. She grabbed the blade with both hands as she crumpled to the ground. Adamant screamed hoarsely, and ran the mercenary through. Two men stepped forward to take his place, their faces grim and determined. Adamant lifted his head and screamed at the dark sky above.

'Damn you, Mortice! You promised you'd protect her! Help us!'

The mercenaries froze in their attack, looked briefly startled, and then vomited blood explosively. They fell to the ground, kicking and shaking helplessly as blood poured from their mouths. Adamant looked round dazedly as one by one the attacking mercenaries dropped, coughing up their life's blood in harsh, painful spasms. In a matter of moments, Hawk and Adamant were the only ones left standing, surrounded by the dead and the dying. Adamant turned his back on them and knelt beside Dannielle, lying at his feet, curled around the bloody wound in her side. He took her hand, and she clutched it tightly. Her breathing was quick and ragged, and her face was covered with sweat.

'Screwed up again, didn't I?' she said breathlessly.

'Be quiet,' said Adamant gently. 'We've got to get you to a doctor.'

Dannielle shook her head. 'Bit late for that, James. I'm sorry.'

'What for?'

'Everything.'

'You've nothing to be sorry for, Danny. Nothing at all. Now, shut up and save your strength.'

Dannielle gasped suddenly and clutched at her side. Adamant's heart missed a beat before he realised she was smiling in amazement.

'My side; it doesn't hurt anymore. What's happening, James?'

Just doing my job, said Mortice's voice quietly in their minds. *The wound is healed. But you'd better get back to the house as fast as you can. You're right on the edge of my limits. I don't know how much longer I can protect you . . .*

His voice faded away and was gone. Adamant helped Dannielle to her feet and looked around him. Hawk was checking quickly through the bodies.

'Where's Bearclaw and Kincaid?' said Adamant hoarsely.

'Dead,' said Hawk.

'And Captain Fisher?'

'Taken. Roxanne and her two friends must have had their own magical protection.'

Adamant rubbed tiredly at his aching head. 'I'm sorry. So many dead, and all because of me.'

Hawk turned and glared at him. 'Stop talking nonsense. There's only one man responsible for all this, and that's Hardcastle. And Isobel isn't dead. She was alive when they took her. Now I'm going to get her back. Can you and Dannielle get home safely without me?'

'I think so. Mortice is back looking after us.'

'Right. Go home and stay there until the result comes in. I'm going to find Isobel, and then I'm going to pay Hardcastle a visit. This has gone beyond politics now.

'This is personal.'

Stefan Medley sat on the grimy bed in the dimly lit room, staring at nothing. He'd been sitting there ever since Roxanne left. He'd tried to work out what he was going to do next, but he couldn't seem to concentrate on anything. In the space of a few moments his whole world had collapsed, and he was left alone in a filthy little tavern he wouldn't have been seen dead in by daylight.

It hadn't seemed so bad when he was there with Roxanne. They only had eyes for each other, then. Now he could see how cheap and shabby it really was. Just like him. He rubbed tiredly at his aching temples, and tried to think. He wasn't safe as long as he stayed in Haven. Adamant would have no choice but to believe he'd defected to the other side. And Adamant was a first-class duellist. Even assuming Adamant wouldn't kill a man who'd once been his friend, there were certainly many in the Reform Cause with ready swords and no love for traitors.

Traitor. It was a harsh word, but the only one that fitted.

Hardcastle would be after him too, as soon as Roxanne revealed he wasn't going to defect. He'd insulted

Hardcastle too many times, frustrated his plans too often. And Hardcastle was well-known as a man who bore grudges.

Medley frowned. With so many hands turned against him the odds were he wouldn't be able to get out of Haven at all. And when he got right down to it, Medley wasn't sure he wanted to leave Haven anyway. It was a cesspool of a city, no doubt of that, but Haven was his home and always had been. Everyone he knew, everything he cared for, was in Haven.

But all that was gone, now. He'd thrown it all away, all for the love of a woman who didn't love him. His friends would disown him, his career was over, his future . . . Medley sighed quietly, and lowered his head into his hands. He would have liked to cry, but he was too numb for tears.

There hadn't been many women in his life. There had always been girls, part of the social whirl, but they never seemed to have time for a quiet young man whose only interest was politics, and the wrong kind of politics, at that. The bright young things, with their games and laughter and simple happy souls, went to other men, and Medley went on alone. There were a few women who saw him as a potential business partner. Marriage was still the best way to acquire wealth and social standing in Haven, and Medley's family had always been comfortably well-off. There were times when he was so lonely he was tempted to say yes, to one or other of the deals his family made for him, but somehow he never did. He had his pride. He couldn't give that up. It was all he had.

Roxanne had been different. No empty-headed, powdered and perfumed flower of the lesser aristocracy. None of the quiet calculation of a woman looking for a husband as an investment. Roxanne was bright and wild and funny and free, and just being with her had made him feel alive in a way he'd never known before. He could talk to her, tell her things he'd never told anyone else. He'd never been so happy as in the few precious moments he'd shared with her.

Looking back, he supposed he'd been a fool. He should have known a living legend like her couldn't really have seen anything in a nobody like him. Roxanne was beautiful and famous. She could have had anyone she wanted. Another hero or legend, like herself. Someone who mattered. Not just another minor politician, in a city full of them. How could he ever have believed that she cared for him?

No one had ever cared for him before. Not really. Not in the way of a man with a woman. He hadn't realised how bleak and lonely his life had been, until she was there to share it with him. She'd made him feel alive, for the first time in a long time.

And now she was gone, and he was alone again.

Alone. He'd never realised how final that word sounded. It seemed to echo on in his mind, as he saw his future spread out before him. His career was over. No one would ever trust him again, now that he'd betrayed his friend and colleague in the middle of an election. His friends would spurn him, and he'd gone against his family's wishes too often in the past to hope for any support from them.

There was no hope for him now. Hope was for men with a future before them.

But there was still one thing he could do. One last thing that might win him some rest, some peace. And perhaps then his friends would realise how much he regretted the harm he'd done them.

Medley drew the knife from his boot. It was a short knife, barely six inches long, but it had a good blade and a sharp edge. It would do the job. He sat on the edge of the bed for a long time, staring at the knife. He thought about what he was going to do very carefully. It was the last important thing he would ever do, and he didn't want to make a mess of it. He put the knife down beside him on the bed, and rolled up his sleeves. The flesh of his arms seemed very pale, and very vulnerable. He stared at his arms for a while. The long blue veins and the sprinkling of hairs fascinated him, as though he'd never seen them before. He picked up the knife and automatically stropped the blade against his trouser-leg to clean it. He realised what he was doing, and smiled. As if that mattered now.

He held the knife against his left wrist, and then had to stop, because his hands were shaking too much. He was breathing in great heaving gasps, and goose flesh had sprung up on his arms. He concentrated, summoning his courage, and his hands grew steady again. The blade shone dully in the lamplight. He pressed the knife into his flesh, and the skin parted easily under the blade. Blood welled up, and he bit his lip at the sharp pain. He gritted his teeth, and pulled the knife across his wrist. The pain was awful, and he groaned aloud. He could feel the tendons popping as they pulled apart under the blade. Blood spurted out into the air. He quickly grabbed the knife in his left hand, before the feeling could leave his fingers, and slashed at the veins in his right wrist. His aim wavered, and he had to cut twice more before he was sure he'd done a good enough job.

The knife slipped out of his fingers and fell to the floor. He was crying now. Tears and snot ran down his face as he struggled for breath amidst his tears. The blood pumped out surprisingly quickly, and he began to feel faint and dizzy. He lay back on the bed, squeezing his eyes shut against the horrid pain that burned all the way up his arms to his elbows. He hadn't thought it would hurt so much. He held his mouth firmly closed, despite the sobs that shook him. He couldn't afford to make any noise. Someone might hear him, and come to help.

He began to feel sick. He couldn't stop crying. This wasn't how he'd thought it would be. But he wasn't surprised; not really. He should have known he wouldn't even be allowed to leave his life with a little dignity. He could see his fingers flexing spasmodically, but he couldn't feel them any longer. The blood was still coming. It soaked the bedding around his arms. So much blood.

He looked up at the ceiling, and then closed his eyes, for the last time.

I loved you, Roxanne, I really loved you.

The darkness closed in around him.

8

Rescues

Roxanne was furious, and the mercenaries were keeping their distance. Pike and Da Silva had disappeared the moment they reached Hardcastle's safe house, ostensibly to lock Fisher safely away, but actually to get out of Roxanne's reach until she calmed down a little and took her hand away from her sword belt. The twenty mercenaries Hardcastle had detailed to guard the safe house weren't as quick-thinking, which meant they ended up taking the brunt of Roxanne's displeasure. They stayed as far away from her as they could, nodded or shook their heads whenever it seemed indicated; mostly they just tried to fade into the woodwork. Roxanne paced back and forth, growling and muttering to herself. She'd never felt so angry, and what made it worse was that she wasn't all that sure what she was so angry about.

Part of it came from losing so many men to Adamant's sorcerer. If she hadn't insisted on full magical protection from Wulf for herself and Pike and Da Silva, she and they would have died along with her men. Roxanne hated losing men. She took it personally.

Some of her anger came from not having taken Hawk as well as Fisher. She'd vowed to take them both, and she hated to fail at things she set her word to. Legends can't afford to fail; if they do, they stop being legends.

But most of her anger came from how they'd taken Fisher. She'd been looking forward to crossing swords with the legendary Captain Fisher ever since she came to Haven, and in the end somebody had struck the Guard down from behind while she wasn't looking. That was no way to beat a legend. Winning that way made Roxanne feel cheap; like just another paid killer. And on top of all that, she hadn't even been allowed to kill Fisher cleanly. Hardcastle had specifically ordered that Fisher was to be kept alive for interrogation. Roxanne sniffed. She knew a euphemism for torture when she heard it.

She glared about her as she paced, and the mercenaries avoided her gaze. The safe house was a dump; a decaying firetrap in the middle of a row of low-rent tenements. Somehow that was typical of Hardcastle and his operations. Cheap and nasty. All in all, the whole operation had left a bad taste in Roxanne's mouth. She was a warrior, and this kind of dirty political fighting didn't sit well with her. She'd killed and tortured before, and delighted in the blood, but that was in the heat of battle, where courage and steel decided men's fates, not dirty little schemes and back-room politics. If anyone had ever accused Roxanne of being honourable, she'd have laughed in their faces, but this . . . this whole mess just stank to high heaven.

She wondered fleetingly what Medley would have thought of all this, and then pushed the thought firmly to one side.

She stopped pacing about, and took several deep breaths. It calmed her a little, and she took her hand away from her sword. The mercenaries began to breathe a little more easily, and stopped judging the distances to possible exits. Pike and Da Silva chose that moment to reappear. Roxanne glared at them.

'Well?' she said icily.

'Sleeping like a baby,' said Pike. 'But we've tied her hand and foot, just in case.'

Roxanne nodded. 'I'll take a quick look at her, and then I'd better report back to Hardcastle. He'll need to know what's happened. You two stay here.'

Pike and Da Silva nodded quickly, and watched in silence as Roxanne disappeared into the adjoining room where they'd dumped Fisher. They waited until the door had swung shut behind her, and then looked at each other.

'She's getting out of control,' said Da Silva quietly.

'If I didn't know better, I'd swear she was developing scruples,' said Pike. 'Still, Hardcastle knew there was a risk in using Roxanne for political work. Everyone knows Roxanne's crazy. It doesn't matter on a battlefield, but we can't have her running wild in Haven. She knows too much.'

'So she's expendable?'

'Everyone's expendable in politics. Especially her. That's official, from Hardcastle.'

'Which of us gets to kill her?'

Pike grinned. 'I wasn't thinking of fighting a duel with her. I was thinking more along the lines of dosing her wine with a fast-acting poison, waiting until she'd collapsed, and then cutting her head off. There's a good price for her head in the Low Kingdoms.'

'Sounds good to me,' said Da Silva.

Roxanne stood just inside the doorway of the adjoining room, listening. She'd always had good hearing. It had kept her alive on battlefields more than once. She'd known Pike and Da Silva were up to something, but the casualness with which they discussed her death made her blood boil. The orders had to have come from Hardcastle; they wouldn't have dared make such a decision themselves. Hardcastle had sold her out to a couple of back-alley assassins. She wanted to just charge out into the next room, draw her sword, and cut them both down, but even she wasn't crazy enough to take on twenty-two armed men in a confined space. She hadn't made her reputation as a warrior by being stupid. She had to get out of there and think things over.

She threw the door open, stalked back into the main room, and pretended not to notice the sudden silence. 'I'm going to see Hardcastle. Keep a close eye on Fisher, but don't damage her any further. Hardcastle's going to want that privilege for himself.'

She nodded briskly to Pike and Da Silva, and headed for the door before they could come up with some excuse to stop her. Her back crawled in anticipation of an attack, her ears straining for any hint of steel being drawn from a scabbard, but nothing happened. She stepped out into the street, and slammed the door behind her, almost disappointed. She moved quickly off down the street to lose herself in the crowds.

She still wasn't sure what she was going to do next. She was damned if she'd go on working for Hardcastle, but she couldn't just walk out on him either. Deserting ship in midcontract would ruin her name. Most of the time Roxanne didn't give a rat's arse what anyone thought of her, but her professional name was a different matter. If word got round she couldn't be trusted to complete her commissions, no one would hire her.

Most people were too frightened to approach her as it was.

But she couldn't let Hardcastle get away with threatening her, either. That would do her reputation even more damage. She scowled as she strode along, and people all around her hurried to get out of her way. All this thinking made her head hurt. She needed someone she could talk to, someone she could trust. But she'd never trusted anyone . . . except Stefan Medley.

The thought surprised her, as did the warmth of feeling that went through her at the thought of seeing him again. Stefan had been a good sort, for a politician. He understood things like honesty and honour. She'd go and see him. He was probably still mad at her, but they'd work something out. She headed back to the tavern where she'd left him. Someone there would be able to tell her where he'd gone.

*

The tavern was full of customers. Smoke hung heavily on the air, and the crowd round the bar were singing a Reform anthem, cheerfully if not too accurately. Roxanne made her way to the bar, elbowing people out of her way. She yelled for the bartender, but he was busy taking orders and pretended he hadn't heard her. Roxanne leaned across the bar, grabbed him by the shirtfront, and pulled his face close to hers. The bartender started to object, realised who she was, and went very pale.

'Stefan Medley,' said Roxanne quietly, dangerously. 'The man I came here with. Where did he go after he left here?'

'He didn't go anywhere,' said the bartender. 'He's still in his room.'

Roxanne frowned, dropped the bartender and turned away. What the hell was Stefan doing, hanging around here? He must know the Reformers would already be hot on his trail, and it wouldn't take them long to find out about this place. Medley had always been very careful about their assignations here, but Roxanne had deliberately left clues all over the place. That had been part of her job, then. She shook her head. The sooner she talked to Stefan and got the hell out of here, the better. She hurried up the stairs behind the bar, taking the steps two at a time. Everything would be all right once she'd talked to Stefan. He'd know what to do. He always did.

The door to their room was locked. Roxanne looked quickly around, knocked twice and waited impatiently. There was no sound from inside the room. She knocked again, and called his name quietly. There was no answer. Roxanne frowned. He must be there; the door was still locked. Was he sulking? That wasn't like Stefan. Maybe he was asleep. She knocked again, and called his name as loudly as she dared, but there was no reply. Roxanne began to get a bad feeling about the room. Something was wrong. Maybe the Reformers had already caught up with him . . .

She drew her sword, and kicked at the door savagely with the heel of her boot. The door shuddered, but held. Roxanne cursed it briefly and tried again. The crude lock broke, and the door swung inwards. The room beyond was dark and quiet. Roxanne moved quickly into the room and darted to one side so that she wouldn't be caught silhouetted against the light from the open door. She stood poised in the gloom, sword at the ready, but it only took her a few moments to realise there were no ambushers in the room. She put away her sword and lit one of the lamps.

Light filled the room, and for a moment all Roxanne could see was the blood. It covered the bedclothes, and had spilled down the sides to form pools on the floor. Some of it had already dried. Roxanne moved forward quietly and felt for a pulse on Medley's neck. It was still there, slow and feeble, but his skin was deathly cold. At first she thought the Reformers had got to him, and then she looked at his arms and saw the ugly black wounds at his wrists. Her breath caught in her throat as she realised what he'd done, and why. She turned and ran from the room.

She hurried back down the stairs and into the bar, fought her way through the crowd, and grabbed the bartender again. 'I need a healer! Now!'

'There's a Northern witch on the first floor. Calls herself Vienna. She knows a few things. She's all there is, unless you want me to send out for someone . . .'

'No! You don't talk to anyone about this. You do, and I'll gut you. Which room is she in?'

'Room Nine. Just round the corner from the stairs. You can't miss it.'

Roxanne dropped the bartender, and ran back up the stairs. It didn't take her long to find Room Nine, but it seemed like ages. She hammered on the door with her fist until it opened a crack, and a suspicious eye looked out at her.

'Who is it? What do you want?'

'I need a healer.'

'I don't do abortions.'

Roxanne kicked the door in, grabbed a handful of the woman's gown, and slammed her up against the wall. She struggled feebly, her feet kicking helplessly several inches above the floor. She started to call out for help, and Roxanne thrust her face up close to the witch's. The witch went very quiet and stopped struggling.

'A friend of mine is hurt,' said Roxanne. 'Dying. Save his life or I'll kill you slowly. Now move it!'

She put Vienna down and hauled her up the stairs to the next floor and Medley's room. Vienna took one look at the blood and started to leave, then stopped as she met Roxanne's gaze. The witch was a tiny frail little thing, in a shabby green dress, and at any other time Roxanne might have felt guilty about bullying her, but this was different. All she could think of was Stefan, dying alone in a dirty tavern room, because of her. She gestured curtly at Medley, and Vienna turned back and examined his wrists.

'Nasty,' said the witch quietly. 'But you're in luck, warrior. He didn't make a very good job of it. He cut across the veins instead of lengthwise. The blood's been able to clot and close off the wounds. He's lost a lot of blood, though . . .'

'Can you save him?' said Roxanne.

'I think so. A simple healing spell on the wrists, and another to speed up production of new blood . . .' She started reciting a series of technicalities that Roxanne didn't understand, but she just let the witch babble on, unable to concentrate on anything but the great wave of relief surging through her. He wasn't going to die. He wasn't going to die because of her. She nodded harshly to Vienna, and the witch began her magic. The rites were simple and rather unpleasant, but very effective. The torn flesh at the wrists closed together and fused, and faint tinges of colour began to seep back into Medley's face. His breathing became steadier and deeper.

'That's all I can do,' said Vienna finally. 'Let him rest for a couple of days, and he'll be as good as new. Keeping him alive is your problem. Those cuts on his wrists were deep. He meant business.'

'Yes,' said Roxanne. 'I know.' She untied the purse from her belt and tossed it to Vienna, without checking to see how much was in it. 'Not a word to anyone,' said Roxanne, still looking at Medley. The witch nodded, and left quickly before Roxanne could change her mind.

Roxanne sat on the edge of the bed beside Medley, ignoring the blood that soaked into her trousers. He looked drawn and tired, as though he'd been through a long fever. She let her hand rest on his forehead for a moment. The flesh felt cool and dry.

'What am I going to say to you, Stefan?' she said quietly. 'I never thought you'd do anything like this. You were just a job to me, but . . . I liked you, Stefan. Why did you have to do this?'

'Why not?' said Medley hoarsely. He licked his lips and swallowed dryly. Roxanne poured him a glass of water from the pitcher on the table, and held the glass to his mouth while he drank. He managed a few swallows, and she put the glass down. Medley lifted his arms and looked at the healed wounds on his wrists. He smiled sourly, and let his arms fall back onto the bed. 'You shouldn't have bothered, Roxanne. I'll only have to do it again.'

'Don't you dare,' said Roxanne. 'I can't go through all this again. My nerves won't stand it. Why did you do it, Stefan?'

'It's not enough just to live,' said Medley. 'You have to have something to live for. Something, or someone. For a while I had politics, and when I grew tired of that, I found Adamant. He needed me, made me feel important and valued; made me his friend. But even at its best I was

[386]

just living someone else's life, following someone else's lead.

'And then I met you, and you gave my life meaning. I was so happy with you. You were all the things that had been missing from my life. You made me feel that I mattered, that I was someone in my own right, not just someone else's shadow. And then you told me it was all a lie, and walked out of my life forever. I can't go back to being what I was, Roxanne. I'd rather die than do that. I love you, and if what we had was just a lie, then I prefer that lie to reality. Even if I have to die to keep it.'

'No one ever felt that way for me before,' said Roxanne slowly. 'I'm going to have to think about that. But I promise you this, Stefan; I'll stay with you for as long as you need me. I'm not sure why, but you're important to me, too.'

Medley looked at her for a long moment. 'If this is . . . just another game you're playing, a way to get more information out of me, I don't mind. Just tell me what you want to know, and I'll tell you. But don't pretend you care for me if you don't. Please. I can't go through that again.'

'Forget all that,' said Roxanne. 'Hardcastle can go stuff himself. Things will be different from now on.'

'I love you,' said Medley. 'How do you feel about me?'

'Damned if I know,' said Roxanne.

Hawk was tired, and his arm and back muscles ached from too much use and too little rest. During the past hour he'd been through half the dives in the Steppes, looking for a lead on Fisher. No one knew anything, no matter how forcefully he put the question. Eventually he came to the reluctant belief that they were telling the truth. And that only left one place to look. Brimstone Hall. Hardcastle's home.

He stood outside the great iron gates, and stared past the two nervous men-at-arms on duty. The old Hall looked quiet and almost deserted, with lights showing at only a few windows. Somewhere in there he'd find what he was looking for; someone or something that would put him on the right trail.

The two men-at-arms looked at each other uncertainly, but said nothing. They recognised Hawk, and knew what he was capable of. They hadn't missed the fresh blood dripping from the axe in his right hand. Hawk ignored them, concentrating on the Hall. Hardcastle and his people would be out on the streets now, so the chances were good he'd only have to face a skeleton staff. Maybe he'd get really lucky and find Isobel locked away in some cellar here. He remembered the way she'd looked as she'd been dragged away, bloody and unconscious, and the slow cold rage began to build in him again. He shifted his gaze to the two men-at-arms, and they stirred uneasily.

'Open the gates,' said Hawk.

'Hardcastle isn't here,' said one of the men. 'Everyone's out.'

'Somebody will talk to me.'

'Not to you, Captain Hawk. We have our orders. You're not to be allowed entrance under any circumstances. As far as you're concerned, everyone's out and always will be.'

'Open the gates,' said Hawk.

'Get lost,' said the other. 'You've no business here.'

Hawk hit him low, well below the belt. He doubled up and fell writhing to the ground. The other man-at-arms backed quickly away. Hawk pushed the gates open, stepped over the man on the ground, and entered the grounds of Brimstone Hall. The man-at-arms left standing took one look at Hawk's face and turned and ran for the Hall. Hawk went after him at a steady walk. No point in hurrying. No one was going anywhere.

He heard the approach of soft, padding feet, and looked round to see three huge dogs charging silently towards him. Hawk studied them carefully. Hardcastle's dogs were supposed to be man-killers and man-eaters, but they looked ordinary enough to Hawk. He took a bag of powder from his belt, opened it, held his breath, and threw the powder into the air right in front of the dogs. The dogs skidded to a halt, sniffed suspiciously at the air, and then sat down suddenly with big sloppy grins on their faces. Hawk waited a moment to be sure the dust had done its job, then walked cautiously past them. Two of the dogs ignored him completely, and the third rolled over on its back so that Hawk could rub its belly. Hawk smiled slightly, careful not to breathe till he was well past the dogs. He'd known the second bag of dust he'd found in Dannielle's room would come in handy.

He headed for the Hall. Everything seemed quiet. He'd almost reached the main door when it suddenly swung open before him, and five men-at-arms in full chain mail spilled out to block his path. Hawk smiled at them, and held his bloody axe so they could see it clearly.

'Where is she?' he said softly. 'Where's Hardcastle keeping my wife?'

'I don't know what the hell you're talking about,' said the foremost man-at-arms. 'I'm Brond. I speak for Hardcastle in his absence, and he doesn't want to speak to you. You'd better leave now. You're already in a lot of trouble.'

'Last chance,' said Hawk. 'Where's my wife?'

'Wouldn't you like to know,' said Brond. He half-turned away and addressed the other men. 'Throw him out. Don't be gentle about it. Show the man what happens when he messes with his betters.'

Hawk slammed his axe into Brond's side. The heavy steel head punched clean through Brond's chain mail, and buried itself in his rib cage. Brond stood and stared at it for a moment, unable to believe what had happened, then fell to his knees, blood starting from his mouth. Hawk jerked his axe free, and the four remaining men-at-arms jumped him. The first to reach Hawk went down screaming in a flurry of blood and guts as Hawk's axe opened him up across the belly.

The other three tried to surround Hawk, but his axe swept back and forth, keeping them at arm's length. They surged around him, darting in and jumping back, like dogs trying to bring down a bear. Hawk smiled at them coldly, calculating the odds. The men-at-arms were good, but he was better. He could take them. It was only a matter of time. And then four more men-at-arms came running out of the main door, and Hawk knew he was in trouble. With Fisher to watch his back, he'd have taken them on without a second thought, but fighting on his own the odds were murder. Nevertheless he was damned if he'd back down. Fisher needed him. Besides, he'd faced worse odds in his time. He took a firm hold on his axe and threw himself at his nearest opponent.

And then suddenly there was another figure, fighting at his side; tall and lithe and very deadly. Two men-at-arms fell to the newcomer's blade in as many seconds. Hawk cut down a third, and suddenly the men-at-arms scattered and ran for their lives. Hawk slowly lowered his axe, and turned to face Roxanne. For a long moment they stood looking at each other, and then Roxanne lowered her sword.

'All right,' said Hawk. 'What's going on?'

'We've come to help,' said Medley, approaching the two of them cautiously. 'We know where your wife is. We can take you right to her.'

'Why the hell should I trust you?' said Hawk. 'You both work for Hardcastle.'

'Not anymore,' said Roxanne. 'He broke his contract with me.'

'And I never worked for him,' said Medley flatly.

'Besides,' said Roxanne, 'Without our help you haven't a hope of finding and rescuing your wife.'

Hawk smiled slightly. 'That's a good reason.'

He hesitated, and then put away his axe. Roxanne sheathed her sword, and the three of them walked back through the grounds to the main gates. They had to go slowly so that Medley could keep up with them. Hawk looked at him more closely.

'You don't look too good, Medley. Are you sure you're up to this?'

'He's been ill,' said Roxanne quickly. 'He's fine now.'

Hawk looked at them both, and then let the matter drop. There was obviously a story there, but it could wait. 'How did you find me?' he asked finally.

Medley smiled. 'You seem to have spent the last hour or so cutting a path right through the seedier half of the High Steppes. All we had to do was follow the path of blood and bodies.'

'You haven't said what you expect to get out of this,' said Hawk.

'The dropping of any and all charges against us,' said Medley. 'A clean slate.'

'All right,' said Hawk. 'You help me rescue Isobel, and I'll come through for you. But if I even suspect you're trying to set me up, I'll kill you both. Deal?'

'How could we refuse?' said Medley.

'Deal,' said Roxanne.

Pike had been stuck in the safe house for over an hour, and the ale had run out. He couldn't send out for more because they weren't supposed to draw attention to themselves. He leaned his chair back against the wall and looked thoughtfully at the locked door that stood between him and Captain Isobel Fisher. The beautiful, arrogant Captain. Not so arrogant now, though. Pike smiled at the thought, and let his hand drop to the key ring at his belt. Hardcastle's orders had been quite specific about delivering her alive, but no one had said anything about intact . . .

Pike looked around him. Six of his men were playing dice and arguing about the side bets. Two more were doing running repairs on their chain mail. The rest were scattered around the house, acting as lookouts. All in all, the house was thoroughly secure, and no one would miss him if he took a little break. He called quietly to Da Silva, and the mercenary left the dice game and came over to join him.

'This had better be good, Pike; I was winning.'

'You can cheat at dice any time. I've got a more pleasurable game in mind.'

Da Silva looked at the locked door, and frowned. 'Wondered how long it would take for you to get the itch for her. Forget it, Pike. That's Captain Fisher in there. We can't afford to take any chances with her.'

'Come on,' said Pike. 'She's just a woman. We can handle her between us. Are you game?'

'I'm game if you are.' Da Silva smiled suddenly. 'Who gets first shot?'

'Toss you for it.'

'My coin or yours?'

'Mine.'

Pike took a silver mark from his purse, and handed it to Da Silva, who examined both sides carefully before returning it. Pike flipped the coin and caught it deftly before slapping it flat on his arm. Da Silva called *heads*, and then swore when Pike revealed the coin. Pike grinned and put it away. Da Silva glanced at the other mercenaries.

'What about the others?' he said quietly.

'What about them?' said Pike. 'Let them find their own women.'

Da Silva looked at the locked door and licked his lips thoughtfully. 'We're going to have to be very careful with her, Pike. If we give her a chance, she'll cut our throats with our own knives.'

'So we won't give her a chance. Will you stop worrying? First, she's already had a hell of a beating. That should have taken some of the starch out of her. And secondly, I tied her up hand and foot while she was unconscious, remember? She's in no position to give us any trouble. So, I untie her feet, and then you hold her steady while I give her a good time. Afterwards, we swop over. Right?'

'Right.' Da Silva grinned broadly. 'You always did know how to show your friends a good time, Pike.'

They walked purposefully towards the locked door. A few of the other mercenaries looked in their direction, but nobody said anything. Pike unlocked the door, and took a lamp off the wall. He grinned once at Da Silva, and then the two of them went in to see Captain Fisher.

The room had no windows or other light, and Fisher screwed up her eyes at the sudden glare. She'd been awake from some time, but alone in the dark she had no way of telling how much time had passed. Her head ached fiercely, and she knew she was lucky not to have a concussion. There were cramps in her arms from being tied behind her, and her hands were numb because the ropes at her wrists were too tight. Her ankles were hobbled and there was no sign of her sword. All in all, she'd been in better condition.

She struggled to sit upright, and looked at the two men standing by the door. They closed it carefully behind them, and from the way they looked at her, she had a good idea of what they had in mind. A sudden horror gripped her, and she had to grit her teeth to stop her mouth from trembling. She'd faced death before, been hurt so many times she'd lost count of the scars, but this was different. She'd thought about rape, she supposed every woman had, but she'd never really thought it would happen to her. Not to her, not to Captain of the Guard Fisher; the warrior. She was too strong, too good with a sword, too determined to protect herself for anything like that to happen to her. Only now her sword was gone, the strength had been knocked out of her, and determination on its own wasn't enough to protect her . . . She bit down firmly, on her growing panic. She had to keep her wits about her, and watch for a chance to thwart them. If all else failed, there was always revenge.

Pike put the lamp into a niche high up on the wall. He

could feel Fisher watching him. He moved unhurriedly towards her. Her eyes were steady, but just a bit too wide. He grinned, knelt down beside her, and put one hand on her thigh. In spite of herself, Fisher shrank away from his touch.

'No need to worry, Captain,' said Pike, giving her thigh a little squeeze, just hard enough to let her feel the strength in his hand. 'My friend and I won't hurt you, as long as you behave yourself. No. You just be nice and cooperative and show us a nice time, and you don't have to get hurt at all. Of course, if you're determined to be unpleasant about it, my friend Da Silva here knows some real nasty tricks with a skinning knife. Isn't that right, Da Silva?'

'Right.' Da Silva laughed as Fisher's eyes darted to him and then away again.

'I'm a Captain of the Guard,' said Fisher. 'If anything happens to me, you'll be in real trouble.'

'That's out there,' said Pike. 'Things like that don't matter in here. In here, there's just you and us.'

'My husband will track me down. You've heard of Hawk, haven't you?'

'Sure,' said Pike. 'We're waiting for him. He's good, but so are we. And there are a lot more of us than there is of him.'

Fisher thought frantically. There was the sound of truth and confidence in his voice, and that frightened her more than anything. They didn't just want her, they wanted Hawk as well.

'All right,' she said finally, her voice not quite as steady as she would have liked. 'I won't fight you. Just . . . don't hurt me. Why not untie me? I could be more . . . cooperative then.'

Pike's hand lashed out, slapping her viciously across the face. Her head rang from the force of the blow. She could feel blood running down her chin from her crushed mouth. She gritted her teeth against the pain and the dizziness.

She'd been hurt worse in her time, but this kind of cold and casual violence was new to her, and all the more intimidating because of her utter helplessness.

'That's for thinking we're stupid,' said Pike. 'If I untie your hands, I'm a dead man. You're not going to get that chance, Captain.'

He drew a knife from his boot, and Fisher tensed, but he only used it to cut the ropes binding her ankles together. Da Silva moved quickly in to hold her ankles while Pike put away his knife. Fisher's heart speeded up, and her breathing became ragged and uneven. Pike put a hand on her breast and pushed her so that she fell onto her back. He began to undo his trousers. Fisher struggled to sit upright again, as though that could somehow put off the inevitable. Pike laughed. He leaned forward and grabbed her hair, tilting her head back. He held her head steady as he put his face down to kiss her.

Fisher sank her teeth into his lower lip. Her teeth met, and she jerked her head back, taking most of Pike's lip with her. Blood ran from his mouth, and for a moment the pain and shock held him rigid. Fisher spat out the lip and snapped her head forward in a savage butt to Pike's face. There was the flat, definitive sound of his nose breaking, and he fell backwards against Da Silva, sending him sprawling. Fisher scrambled to her feet while Da Silva pushed Pike aside and struggled up onto his knees. Fisher stepped forward and kicked Da Silva squarely in the groin, putting all her weight behind it. Da Silva's breath caught in his throat before he could scream, and he fell forward onto the floor, clutching at the awful pain between his legs. Pike was rolling back and forth on the floor with both his hands at his face, unable to think straight for the pain. Fisher kicked him solidly in the head until he stopped moving.

She heard movement behind her, and turned quickly to find Da Silva was back on his feet again. He was crouched around his pain, but he had a knife in his hand, and his eyes were cold and angry. Fisher backed away, and Da Silva went after her. He feinted at her with his knife, but she saw it for what it was, stepped quickly inside his reach while he was off balance, and kicked him in the knee. Da Silva fell forward as his leg collapsed under him, and Fisher's knee came up and caught him squarely on the chin. Da Silva's head snapped back, and he fell limply to the floor and lay still.

Fisher leaned back against the cold stone wall, shaking violently. Her head ached so badly she could barely think, but she knew she couldn't stop and rest. If the other mercenaries had heard anything of the fight, they might decide to see what was happening. And she was in no condition to take on anyone else. She took a deep breath and held it, and some of her shakes went away. She got down on her knees and groped around on the floor until she found the knife Da Silva had dropped. All she had to do now was cut the bonds at her wrists, which were knotted in the middle of her back where she couldn't see them, then work out a plan that would get her out of here without having to take on however many other mercenaries were waiting in the next room. Fisher smiled sourly, and concentrated on cutting the ropes and not her arms. One thing at a time.

The narrow street was almost completely dark, with only a single street lamp shedding pale golden light across the decaying, stunted houses. The parties and parades had passed them by, and nothing disturbed the street's sullen quiet. In the shadows, Hawk and Roxanne drew their weapons, while Medley kept a careful watch on the safe house. The shutters were all closed and there was no sign of any life. Hawk studied the house for some time, and scowled unhappily.

'Are you sure this is the right place? Where the hell are the lookouts?'

'There are spy-holes and concealed viewing slits all over the house,' said Roxanne quietly. 'Hardcastle's used this place before. There's at least twenty armed men inside that house, just waiting for you to try and rescue Captain Fisher.'

'Maybe we should send to Adamant for reinforcements,' said Medley.

'There isn't time,' snapped Hawk. 'Every minute Isobel's in there, she's in danger. I want her out *now*.'

'All right,' said Medley. 'What's the plan?'

Roxanne smiled, a familiar darkness in her eyes. 'Who needs a plan? We just storm the front door, cut down the guards, and kill anyone who gets between us and freeing Captain Fisher.'

Hawk and Medley exchanged a glance. Roxanne had many qualities as a warrior, but subtlety wasn't one of them.

'We can't risk a straightforward assault,' said Hawk carefully. 'They might just kill Isobel at the first sign of a rescue attempt. We need some kind of diversion, something to distract attention.'

'I could set fire to something,' said Roxanne.

'I'd rather you didn't,' said Medley quickly. 'This whole street's a firetrap. Start a blaze here and we'll lose half the Steppes.'

'I've got a better idea,' said Hawk. 'Since they're going to see us approaching anyway, let's show them something they won't find threatening. We just walk up to the door with me unarmed, and Roxanne's sword at my back. Medley can carry my axe. They'll think you've captured me. Once inside, we study the situation and choose our moment. With any luck they'll want to lock me up with Fisher. So, we wait until they unlock the right door, then Medley passes me my axe and we kill everything that moves. Any questions?'

Roxanne looked at Hawk. 'You're ready to trust me with a sword at your back?'

'Sure,' said Hawk. 'Because if you try anything, I'll take the sword away from you and make you eat it.'

Roxanne looked at Medley. 'He just might.'

'Let's make a start,' said Medley. 'Before I get a rush of brains to the head and realise just how dangerous this is.'

Fisher shook the last of the rope bindings from her wrists and flapped her hands hard to try and get the blood moving again. There were angry red cuts on her arms and wrists from where the knife had cut her as well as the ropes, but she ignored them. Feeling began to come back into her hands, and she winced as pins and needles moved in her fingers. She padded silently over to the closed door and listened carefully. So far, no one seemed to have missed Pike and Da Silva, but she didn't know how long that would last. She went back to Pike and drew his sword from its scabbard. It was a good blade.

She looked at the two men lying bloody and unconscious on the floor. They would have raped her, abused her, and then handed her over to Hardcastle for a slow, painful death. Assuming she got out of this mess alive, she could have them both sent to the mines for the rest of their lives. No one messes with a Guard and gets away with it. But there was always the chance Hardcastle would buy the judge and Pike and Da Silva would go free. She couldn't allow that to happen. As long as they were free, she would never feel safe again.

She knelt beside Pike and put the edge of his sword against his throat. She could do it. No one would ever know. She knelt there for a long time, and then she took the sword away from his throat and stood up. She couldn't kill a helpless man in cold blood. Not even him. She was a Guard, and a Guard enforces the law; she doesn't take revenge.

She turned her back on Pike and Da Silva, moved over to the door and eased it open an inch. She didn't know how many mercenaries were out there, but from the muttered talk it sounded like quite a few. Her best bet would be to throw open the door and then make a mad dash for the main door. She might make it. If she was lucky. She eased the door open a little further, and then froze as there was a sudden pounding on the front door.

Hawk looked calmly about him, as though he couldn't feel the point of Roxanne's sword digging into his back. It occurred to him that if he'd misjudged the situation, he was in a whole lot of trouble. There were twelve mercenaries in the room, some carrying weapons, some not. According to Roxanne, there were more mercenaries on the next floor up. So, assume twenty men, all told. Ten to one odds. Hawk smiled. He'd faced worse in his time. One of the mercenaries walked over to him. Tall, muscular, chain mail. Wore a sword in a battered scabbard and looked like he knew how to use it. Regular issue mercenary. He nodded briefly to Roxanne, and looked Hawk up and down.

'So this is the famous Captain Hawk. Do come in, Captain. Don't stand on ceremony.' He laughed softly. 'You know, Captain, Hardcastle's just dying to see you. As for you, you're just dying.'

'Where's my wife?' said Hawk.

The mercenary backhanded Hawk across the face. He saw it coming, but still couldn't ride much of the blow. His head rang, and he swayed unsteadily on his feet for a moment.

'You speak when you're spoken to, Captain. I can see we're going to have to teach you some manners before we let you meet Councillor Hardcastle. But don't worry about your wife. We haven't forgotten her. Even as we speak, she's being entertained by two of our men. I'm sure they're giving her a real good time.'

He laughed, and Hawk kneed him in the groin. The mercenary bent forward around his pain, almost as though bowing to Hawk, and Hawk rabbit-punched him on the way to the floor. The other mercenaries jumped to their feet and grabbed for their weapons.

Hawk snatched his axe from Medley, yelled for Roxanne to guard his back, and started toward the first mercenary without looking to see if Roxanne was there. Hawk swung his axe up and then buried it almost to the hilt in the shoulder of the first mercenary, shearing through the chain mail. The force of the blow drove the mercenary to his knees. Hawk put his boot against the man's chest and pulled the blade free. Blood flew on the air as Hawk turned to face his next opponent. There was the clash of steel on steel as Roxanne struck down a second mercenary, and Hawk allowed himself a small smile of relief.

And then the door on the other side of the room burst open, and Fisher charged out, sword in hand. Hawk's smile widened. All this time he'd been worried about her, and here she was safe and sound. He should have known. She seemed a little startled to see Roxanne guarding his back, but she quickly set about carving a path through the mercenaries to reach him.

Hawk swung his axe double-handed, and blood splashed across the filthy floor. The heavy steel blade easily deflected the lighter swords, and punched through chain mail as though it wasn't there. Fisher fought at his side, her sword a steel blur as she cut and parried and thrust. Roxanne laughed and danced and cut her way through her fellow mercenaries with a deadly glee. Medley stayed out of the way. He knew his limitations.

A bearded mercenary duelled Hawk to a halt, his heavy long-sword almost a match for Hawk's axe. They locked blades, and stood face to face for a moment. Muscles bunched across the mercenary's shoulder, and Hawk quickly realised he couldn't hold the man back for long. So he spat in his eye. The mercenary jerked back his head instinctively and lost his balance. Hawk swept the sword aside and slammed the axe into the man's chest.

Fisher stood toe to toe with a tall, slender mercenary, trading blow for blow. She knew she daren't keep that up for long. He was bigger than her, and she was still weakened from what she'd been through. She locked eyes with him, stepped forward and brought her heel down hard on the instep of his right foot. She could feel bones crush and break in his foot. The sudden pain sucked the colour from his face and the strength from his arms. Fisher beat aside his blade and cut his throat on the backswing. The mercenary dropped his sword and clutched at his throat with both hands, as though he could somehow hold the ghastly wound together. He was already sinking to his knees as Fisher turned to face her next opponent.

Roxanne swung her sword in wide, vicious arcs, and the mercenaries fell back before her. Her eyes were wide with uncomplicated delight, and she laughed breathlessly as her blade cut through their flesh. She was doing what she did best, what she was born to do. She moved among her former companions with neither mercy nor compassion, and none of them could stand against her. She killed them with professionalism and style, and the blood sang in her head.

Suddenly the mercenaries broke and ran, even though they still outnumbered their attackers. Pike and Da Silva might have been able to rally them, but without their leaders the mercenaries hadn't the nerve to face three living legends.

Hawk looked round the suddenly empty room, and lowered his axe. He was almost disappointed the fight was over so soon. He had a lot of pent-up anger to work off. He turned, smiling, to Fisher, and his anger turned suddenly cold and merciless as he saw what they'd done to her. Her mouth was bruised and swollen, and blood from a nasty cut on her scalp had spilled down one side of her face. He took her in his arms and held her tightly, and she hugged him back as if she would never let him go. Finally Medley coughed politely, and Hawk and Fisher broke apart. Fisher looked at Medley, and then at Roxanne.

'They're on our side,' said Hawk. 'Don't ask; it gets complicated.'

Fisher shrugged. 'That's politicians and mercenaries for you. Let's hope Adamant's the forgiving kind. There are two more mercenaries in the other room, out cold. We're taking them with us; I'll be pressing charges.'

Hawk caught some of the undertones in her voice. 'Are you all right, lass?'

'Sure,' said Fisher. 'I'm fine now.'

9

Winners and Losers

The election was almost over, and Hardcastle was hosting a victory party in his ballroom. The faithful had come by the hundreds to share his hospitality and celebrate another Conservative victory in the Steppes. Hardcastle looked out over the milling crowd and smiled graciously at his favourites. People came to congratulate him, and politely remind him of all their labours on his behalf. Hardcastle had a smile and a nod for all of them, but his mind was elsewhere. The voting had to be nearly over by now, but so far he'd heard nothing about how the voting was going. None of his people had reported back, and Wulf had locked himself away in his room. Of course, he was bound to win. He always did. But the complete lack of news worried him.

There was no word on Hawk and Fisher, though they should have been captured or dead by now. There was no word at all from Pike or Da Silva. And Roxanne had disappeared. No one had seen or heard from her for hours. Hardcastle scowled. Something was wrong. He could feel it in his bones. But there was still one source of information open to him. He gestured to one of his servants and curtly ordered the man to fetch the sorcerer Wulf. The servant hesitated, but one look at Hardcastle's face convinced him there was no point in protesting. He bowed quickly and left the ballroom.

Hardcastle looked around him, and his scowl deepened. The party seemed as loud and cheerful as ever, but somehow the mood didn't feel right. The laughter was too loud, the smiles too forced, and here and there, there were pockets of quiet, almost furtive talk. The musicians were playing sprightly music, but no one was dancing. Hardcastle frowned. He had to give them some positive news soon or their nerves would crack. Everywhere he looked he seemed to see worried faces with wide, desperate eyes. His guests looked more and more like wild animals gathered together, sensing a storm in the air.

Wulf entered the ballroom, and a sudden silence spread quickly across the guests. The musicians stopped playing. Wulf walked slowly forward, and the crowd drew back from him so that he walked alone. He wore his long black sorcerer's cloak wrapped tightly about his slender frame. The cowl had been pulled forward to hide his face. He came to a halt before Hardcastle, and the cowled head bowed slightly. A sudden chill swept through Hardcastle like an awful premonition, and he fought to keep it out of his face. He smiled at Wulf, and gestured for the musicians to begin playing again. They did so, and the party chatter slowly resumed.

Hardcastle glanced at his wife, standing silently beside him, as always. She was staring at the floor, her face calm and impassive. Hardcastle told her to move back a few paces, and she did so without looking up. Hardcastle fixed his gaze on Wulf. There were things he had to discuss with the sorcerer, and he didn't want any witnesses. Not even Jillian.

'All right, Wulf; what's going on? You've been cowering in your room ever since we got back from the Street of Gods. What's the matter with you?'

'It's the Being,' said Wulf, his voice low and toneless. 'The Abomination. The Lord of the Gulfs. I didn't understand. I couldn't understand what it was, what it meant . . .'

'Pull yourself together, man,' snapped Hardcastle. 'I need information. I need to know what's happening in the city. What are the results? What's Adamant up to? Why haven't I heard from my people? Dammit, use your magic and tell me what's happening!'

'I daren't. He's too strong. I can feel him growing.'

Hardcastle looked sharply at Wulf. 'You told me you could control him. You told me that hosting that thing would make you so powerful no one could stand against us.'

'You don't understand,' said Wulf. 'The Lord of the Gulfs isn't some demon or elemental, to be bent to my will by my magic. The Abomination is one of the Transient Beings; an aspect of reality given shape and form by man's perception. A single concept given flesh and blood and bone. It isn't real, as we understand the term. There are things that live outside the world, in the spaces between spaces, and they hunger for strange and awful things. I thought I could control it while it was still weak and confused from its long sleep, but it's so powerful . . . I can feel it in my mind, clawing at the wards I built to hold it. It's going to get out, Cameron . . .'

'We can talk about this later,' said Hardcastle. 'Now get a hold of yourself. You're supposed to be a top rank sorcerer; act like one! I must have information, Wulf. I need to know what's happening out there on the streets. Use your magic to locate my people, and tell me what's happening in the election. That's an order!'

For a long moment Wulf just stood there, head bowed, and Hardcastle began to think the sorcerer was going to defy him. But finally Wulf nodded slightly and began to speak, his voice barely loud enough to be heard over the nervous chatter of the guests.

'The mercenaries you sent after Captain Hawk and Fisher are either dead or scattered. Their leaders, Pike and Da Silva, are under arrest. They have agreed to give evidence against you in return for lesser sentences. The voting is almost over. Adamant is winning.'

Hardcastle stood very still. At first there was only disbelief and shock, but both gradually gave way to a cold and vicious anger. How dare they? How dare they turn against him and elect Adamant? They'd forgotten who was really in charge of the High Steppes, but he'd remind them. He'd teach the Reformers a lesson they'd never forget. He glared at Wulf, his voice slow and steady and very deadly.

'You are my man, Wulf; bound to me by vows sealed in blood.'

'Yes, Cameron. I am yours to command.'

'Then use this great power of yours. Go to Adamant's house and kill him. Kill him, and every other person there.'

'That . . . may not be wise, Cameron. You need me here. Without my magic to augment and magnify your presence, you won't be able to control your followers with your speeches anymore.'

'I was making speeches long before I had your magic to back me up. I can deal with my people. They'll do as they're told, as always. You have your orders, Wulf. Kill Adamant, and everyone with him. Obey me.'

'Cameron . . . please. The Abomination . . .'

'*Obey me!*'

Wulf put back his head and screamed. The horrible piercing sound silenced the crowd in a moment. His cowl fell back, revealing what was left of his face. All the flesh was gone, devoured by some hideous internal hunger. There was only a grinning skull, barely covered by skin stretched tight across the bone like splitting parchment. His eyes were gone, the sockets raw and bloody. He rose up into the air, still screaming, his body twitching with awkward, ungainly movements that suggested the form inside the black robe was no longer entirely human.

He disappeared, and there was a small clap of thunder as air rushed in to fill the space where he had been. Someone in the crowd laughed uneasily, and slowly the babble of voices began again, as though if they could speak loud enough, they wouldn't have to think about what they had just seen. Hardcastle smiled. With Adamant and all his people dead there would have to be another election in the Steppes, but no one would dare stand against him. People would talk, but no one would be able to prove anything. He would be Councillor again. And then he'd make the scum in the streets pay for daring to defy him.

Medley hesitated outside the door to Adamant's study. He glanced at Roxanne, who nodded encouragingly. Hawk and Fisher stood back a few paces, keeping a tactful distance. Medley was glad of their company, but if he was going to make his peace with Adamant, he had to do it on his own. He knocked on the door, and a familiar voice told him to enter. Opening the door and walking in was one of the hardest things Medley had ever done.

Adamant was sitting behind his desk, with Dannielle standing beside him. They both looked tired, and there were lines in their faces Medley had never seen before. Adamant gestured for Medley to sit down on the chair facing the desk. Roxanne leaned against the doorframe, her thumbs tucked into her sword belt, her eyes bright and watchful. Hawk and Fisher stayed in the doorway. Silence filled the room, an almost palpable presence filled with words no one wanted to say but that couldn't be ignored.

Finally Hawk coughed politely, and everyone looked at him. 'With your permission, sir Adamant, Isobel and I will take a look around the house and make sure everything's secure.'

'Of course, Captain. I'll call you if I need you.'

Adamant's voice was as calm as ever, but his gaze never left Medley. Hawk and Fisher left the study, shutting the door quietly behind them.

'The house seems very quiet,' said Medley finally. 'What happened to the victory party?'

'I cancelled it,' said Adamant. 'It didn't seem right, with so many people dead.'

Medley winced. 'I should have known about Longarm's

attack. My intelligence people provided enough hints. But I was too engrossed with Roxanne, and I didn't put the pieces together in time. I'm sorry, James. How many of our men-at-arms were hurt?'

'Twenty-seven dead, fourteen wounded. Luckily none of the guests got hurt.' He looked at Roxanne. 'So, this is your mysterious girlfriend.'

'Yes,' said Medley. 'Isn't she splendid?'

Adamant's mouth quirked. 'I suppose that's one way of describing her. The last time I saw her, she was cutting down my people and showing them no quarter.'

Roxanne met his gaze calmly. 'That's my job. I'm good at it.'

'You killed Bearclaw and Kincaid. They were good men.'

'They would have killed me, given the chance. That's how they play politics in this city. You know that.'

'Yes,' said Adamant. 'Murder and betrayal have always been popular in Haven.'

'For what it's worth, Stefan didn't betray you. Pumping him for information was part of my job, and he was so besotted with me he never even noticed. He told me all kinds of useful things without realising, and I passed them on to Hardcastle.'

'Does he know you're here?' said Dannielle.

'No. I don't work for him anymore.'

'Why not?'

'He broke our contract.'

Dannielle looked from Roxanne to Medley and back again. 'Is that the only reason? What about you and Stefan?'

Roxanne shrugged. 'I don't know. We're just taking things one day at a time and seeing what happens.'

Adamant leaned forward and fixed Medley with his gaze. 'What are you doing here, Stefan? What do you want from me? Forgiveness? Your old job back?'

'Damned if I know,' said Medley. 'I'm sorry you were hurt, and I'm sorry people died, but I never meant for any of that to happen. I loved Roxanne, and nothing else seemed to matter.'

'How do you feel about her now?' said Dannielle. 'Knowing what she is. What she's done. Do you forgive her?'

'Of course,' said Medley. 'I love her, in spite of everything. Can't you understand that?'

Adamant looked at Dannielle, and put out a hand to hold hers. 'Yes,' he said finally. 'I understand.'

Hawk and Fisher prowled restlessly through the empty house. The rooms felt strange and deserted, and the quiet had a texture of its own. They went from room to room, but there was no sign of any life. Adamant's people were either dead or evacuated, and the guests had long gone home. Nothing remained to mark Longarm's assault save for a few patches of dried blood here and there, and the contents of the downstairs library.

Hawk found them, quite by accident. He pushed open the library door on his way back down the hall, and stopped dead in his tracks at the sight of the bodies. There were twenty-seven of them altogether. Hawk counted them twice, to make sure. All of Adamant's men who'd died at the hands of the militants. They'd been stacked together like bundles of kindling, face to face, arms and legs neatly arranged. Hawk felt strangely angry at the sight. These men had died for Adamant; they deserved a more dignified rest than this.

They'll get one, said Mortice's voice in his head. *But things have been rather rushed here of late. I did the best I could.*

Hawk looked at Fisher, and saw that she'd heard it too. 'So you're still here, sorcerer.'

Of course. Where else would I be?

'What happened to the bodies of the people who did this? Longarm and his militants?'

I disposed of them.

Hawk decided not to press the question any further. He didn't think he really wanted to know.

Get back to Adamant, said Mortice suddenly. *He's going to need you.*

Hawk and Fisher looked at each other. 'Why?' said Fisher. 'What's happening?'

Something's coming.

'What? What's coming?'

Something's coming.

Hawk drew his axe and Fisher drew her sword, and they ran back into the entry hall. They could see the study door standing open. Everything seemed quiet. Hawk yelled Mortice's name, but he didn't answer. Adamant came out of the study, his face grim.

'You heard him too?'

'Yeah,' said Hawk. 'I think we'd better get out of here, Adamant. I've got a bad feeling about this.'

Adamant nodded quickly, and gestured for Dannielle to come and join him. She did so, and Medley and Roxanne followed her out into the hall. Roxanne had her sword in her hand. She was smiling. Hawk looked away.

It's here.

Hawk moved quickly over to the front door, pulled it open, and looked out. In the last of the evening light, he could see a man in sorcerer's black walking through the grounds, heading for the house. As he passed, the things that lived in the ground writhed to the surface and died, the grass withered away, and the earth turned to sand and blew away. The sorcerer's power hung heavily on the evening air, like the tension before an approaching storm. Hawk eased the door shut, and turned to face the others.

'We're in trouble. Wulf's here, and he doesn't look friendly. Mortice, can you handle him? Mortice? Mortice!' There was no reply. Hawk cursed briefly. 'That's it. We're getting out of here now. Isobel, take them out the back way. I'll follow as soon as I can.'

'Why aren't you coming?' said Fisher.

'Someone's got to slow him down. Now, get moving. We haven't much time.'

'I can't leave you,' said Fisher.

'You have to. Our job is to keep Adamant alive, no matter what. We lost the last man we guarded. I won't let that happen again.'

Fisher nodded, and led the others back down the hall. Hawk turned to the front door and slammed home the heavy bolts. He considered pushing furniture up against it as a barricade, but he had a strong feeling it wouldn't make any difference.

'Mortice? If you're listening, sorcerer, I can use all the help I can get.'

There was a sharp cracking sound, and Hawk looked back at the door. It had split from top to bottom. As Hawk watched, the wood decayed and fell apart. The rotting fragments fell away from the rusting hinges, and there, in the open doorway, stood what remained of the sorcerer Wulf. Its face was little more than bone now, its grinning teeth yellowed with age. But still it moved and breathed and lived, and something else lived within it. Something hungry. Hawk gripped his axe tightly and backed away from the motionless figure. And then he heard raised voices and sounds of struggle behind him, and realised the others hadn't got very far. He risked a quick glance back over his shoulder, and his heart missed a beat as he saw the dead men filing out of the library.

Fisher had only just reached the end of the hall when the library door flew open and the first of the dead men lurched into the hall. It was one of Adamant's men-at-arms. No blood ran from the gaping wounds in the corpse, and its face was dull and empty. But its eyes saw, and it carried a sword in its hand. Another lich came out of the door after it, and another. Fisher and Roxanne stood between the dead men and the others, swords at the ready, backing slowly away to give themselves room to fight. And still the dead men came filing out of the library with weapons in their hands.

Roxanne stepped forward and brought her long sword across in a sharp vicious arc that cut clean through the first lich's neck. The head fell to the floor and rolled away, the mouth working soundlessly. The headless corpse moved relentlessly forward, sweeping its sword back and forth. Roxanne sidestepped and cut at the body, and it swayed under the force of the blow, but would not fall. Its sword arced out deceptively quickly, and Roxanne had to retreat a step. Fisher moved in beside her and cut at the lich's leg. It staggered and fell to one knee, but didn't release its hold on its sword. And then the rest of the liches were upon them, and there was nothing but flying steel and the growing army of the walking dead.

Hawk raised his axe to strike at the sorcerer, and an invisible force tore the axe from his hand. It spun clattering down the hall, and Hawk ran after it. He knew when he was outclassed. He snatched up his axe and waded into one of the liches from behind, severing its spine. It fell to the floor, and tried to crawl forward. Hawk jumped across it and moved among the dead with his axe, and they fell back from the sheer force of his attack. Medley seized the moment to move in beside Roxanne, his sword at the ready.

'You've got to get Adamant out of here,' he said quickly. 'He's the important one. The Guards and I can hold these things off long enough to give you a good start.'

'But what about you?' said Roxanne.

'I don't matter.'

'You matter to me,' said Roxanne, and kept on fighting.

Adamant had drawn his sword and Dannielle had her dagger, but even with their help, the little group was still driven back down the hall towards the waiting sorcerer. The dead men wouldn't stop, no matter how badly they were injured. They just kept pressing forward, swinging their swords, even if they had to crawl and drag themselves along the floor to do it. Adamant swung his sword in short, efficient arcs, even though he knew the faces that clustered before him. They had been his men, sworn to his service. Some of them had even been friends. They died because they sided with him, and now he had to kill them again.

Get ready, said Mortice suddenly in Hawk's mind. *I'm going to use my magic to cancel out Wulf's. When I give you the word, kill him. You'll have to be quick. He's become very powerful; I can't hold him more than a moment or two. If I wasn't already dead, I think I might be frightened. I never thought to see the Abomination rise again. Now, Hawk; do it now!*

Hawk drew back his arm and threw the axe with all his strength. It flew down the hall and buried itself in Wulf's skull. The sorcerer staggered back a pace under the impact, and then fell to one knee. His head slowly bowed, as though the weight of the axe was dragging it down. The liches froze in their tracks, and then slumped to the floor and didn't move again. Wulf fell forward and lay still.

Hawk hesitated a moment, unable to believe it was all over, and then walked forward to stand over the fallen sorcerer. He put his boot on the skull, reached down, and pulled the axe free. One look at the jagged wound was enough to convince him that the sorcerer was dead. No one could have survived a wound like that.

And then the body began to twitch. Hawk backed quickly away. Wulf's body shook and trembled and convulsed, the limp arms and legs flapping wildly. The black robe stretched and tore and the dead sorcerer's body split apart like some monstrous chrysalis. And out of the broken body blossomed the Abomination, drawing substance from the dead sorcerer to form a new body that was closer to its own nature. It filled the hall, its bony head brushing the ceiling. Its face was all mouth and teeth, and its muscles glistened wetly around its misshapen bones. Its twisted arms ended in foot-long claws. It stood like a man, but there was nothing human in it.

It was Hungry.

Free, said an awful voice. *Free* . . .

'I think we're in trouble,' said Hawk.

'You might just be right,' said Fisher. 'Everyone start backing away. Maybe we can outrun the bastard.'

'Stuff that,' said Roxanne. 'I'm going to kill it.'

The Abomination surged forward, covering the space between them with impossible speed. The small group stood together and braced themselves to meet it. It burst among them with horrid strength, shrugging off their blows and scattering the group like so many skittles. The Abomination had got out, and there was nothing they could do to stop it.

In the laundry room, the trapdoor suddenly blew open, shattering its hinges and flinging the pieces aside. Down in the darkness of the cellar something stirred, and then slowly, one step at a time, the dead man came up the stairs and out into the light. Mortice was little more than a shrivelled husk by now, but his power was upon him, rippling the air around him like a heat haze. He moved purposefully towards the door, his cold body steaming in the warmth of the laundry room.

Hawk and Fisher fought side by side, keeping the Abomination at bay with the sheer energy of their attack. Their blades struck the Being again and again, but did it no harm, the steel ringing harmlessly from its hide as though it were armoured. Roxanne threw herself at the Abomination again and again, howling with fury and frustration. Adamant and Medley protected Dannielle as best they could, but all of them knew the Being was only toying with them. Soon it would grow tired of its game and let its hunger run free, and then all the steel in the world wouldn't be enough to save them. They fought on anyway. There was nothing else to do.

The Abomination spun round suddenly, ignoring its attackers to stare down the hall. Mortice grinned back at it, his skin cracking like brittle parchment. The Lord of the Gulfs cocked its awful head to one side, and a voice burned in all their minds like a red-hot iron sinking into flesh.

You cannot save them. I am free. I walk the world again. Neither the living nor the dead can stop me. This was promised me at my creation.

'I'm neither living nor dead,' said Mortice. 'I'm both. Goodbye, James.'

He spoke a Word of Power, and an unnatural fire roared up around him, consuming him. The Abomination screamed and turned to flee. Mortice gestured sharply with one burning arm, and a fireball shot down the hall to engulf the Being. It fell to the floor, tearing at its own flesh as it strove to put out the flames. Mortice strode unsteadily down the hall, already half-consumed by the flames, and embraced the Being in his burning arms. There was a blinding flash of light and a fading scream, and then they were both gone, and the hall was still and quiet once again.

Hawk and Fisher looked at each other and put away their weapons. Adamant and Medley did the same. Roxanne padded down the hall, glaring about her, and only then reluctantly put away her sword. Adamant looked sombrely at the wide scorch mark on the floor that was all that remained to show where Mortice and the Abomination had been destroyed.

'Rest easy, my friend,' he said quietly. 'Maybe now you'll find some peace.'

There was a polite cough from behind them, and they all spun round, weapons once more at the ready. The Council messenger standing in the open doorway looked at the levelled blades and swallowed hard. 'I could always come back later . . .'

'I'm sorry,' said Adamant, lowering his sword. 'We've had a rather trying day. What can I do for you?'

'I bear greetings and salutations from the Council,' said the messenger, looking a little happier now that he was back on familiar ground. 'The election's over. You won. Congratulations. Can I go now?'

Adamant smiled and nodded, and the messenger disappeared at speed. Adamant turned and looked at the others.

'I always thought it would mean more. I've paid a high price in friends and lives for this moment, and now I'm not even sure it's worth it.'

'Of course it's worth it,' said Medley. 'You didn't fight this election for yourself; you fought it for the poor and the scared and the helpless, who couldn't fight for themselves. They believed in you. Are you going to let them down?'

Adamant shook his head slowly. 'No. You're right, Stefan. The battle's over, but the war goes on.'

Hawk and Fisher looked at each other. 'I wonder if Hardcastle got a message too?' said Hawk.

Fisher grinned. 'If he did, I hope the messenger's quick on his feet.'

At Brimstone Hall, the silence was deafening. The messenger had delivered the election results written down on a scroll, thus ensuring he had time to get away before the storm broke. Hardcastle looked disbelievingly at the parchment in his hands. He didn't need to read it out. His expression was enough. People put down their plates and glasses, and one by one they began to leave.

Hardcastle snapped out of his daze, stepped forward and began to speak in a loud, carrying voice. He would win them back. He always had. But this time the crowd reacted to his usual mixture of boasts and threats with sullen glances and open anger. Someone shouted an insult. Somebody else threw something. In moments the crowd became an angry mob, pushing and shoving. Fights broke out.

Hardcastle was forgotten in the flurry of old grudges and recriminations. He stopped speaking and looked around him with something like horror. They weren't listening. He had lost the election, and as far as the Conservatives were concerned, that meant he wasn't anybody anymore.

He never heard the quiet scuff of steel on leather as Jillian drew the knife from its hidden sheath. The first he knew of it was when she plunged it into his back, again and again and again.

10

Making Deals

Adamant was throwing another victory party, and everyone who was anyone was there. He hadn't really felt like it, but his superiors had insisted. With Reform now holding the High Steppes, the Council was under Reform control for the first time in its history. As long as they were careful not to upset the independents.

The party filled the main dining hall, and spilled over into adjoining rooms. There was a huge buffet, and a dozen different kinds of highly alcoholic punch. The noise was deafening. All the movers and shakers from both the Reform and Conservative Causes had come to meet the new Councillor, and jockey for position. The Brotherhood of Steel had provided a small army of men-at-arms to ensure the party's security, for which Hawk and Fisher were grateful. It meant they could finally relax and get some serious drinking done. It had been a long day.

Adamant and Dannielle stood together, arm in arm, smiling at everyone. They seemed thoroughly reconciled, though whether that was just for public consumption was of course open to question. Personally, Hawk thought they'd make it. He hadn't missed the way Dannielle shielded Adamant with her own body when Roxanne led the attack against him. If it hadn't been for Mortice's magic she'd have died out there on the streets, and both of them knew it. Hawk smiled to himself. They'd make it.

Speaking of Roxanne . . . Hawk let his gaze wander across the crowd and there she was, towering over everyone, with an arm draped comfortably across Medley's shoulders. Everyone was giving her plenty of room, but she seemed to be behaving herself. Officially, Hawk was supposed to arrest her on sight, but he wasn't in the mood. Both she and Medley were leaving Haven first thing the next morning, and he'd settle for that. If his superiors didn't like it, they could go after her themselves. He'd send flowers to their funerals.

He looked at Fisher, standing beside him lost in her own thoughts, and smiled fondly. 'Well, Isobel, what do you think of democracy in action, now that you've seen it up close?'

Fisher shrugged. 'Looked much like any other form of politics to me: corruption and scandal and a sprinkling of honest men. I know what you want me to say, Hawk; you want me to get all excited because Reform won this one. But take a look around you; the big men from both sides are already getting together and making deals.'

'Yes, Isobel, but the difference here is in what the Reformers are making deals about. The deals they make are for other people's benefit, not their own.'

Fisher laughed, and put her arm through his. 'Maybe. In the meantime, let's count our blessings. Adamant is still alive; so are we, and Haven got through the election without civil war breaking out.'

'Yeah,' said Hawk. 'Not a bad day's work, all told.'

They laughed and drank wine together, while all around them the chatter of guests filled the hall, deciding the future.

The
God
Killer

Prologue

They come and they go.

There are Beings on the Street of Gods. More and less than human, they inspire worship and adoration, fear and awe, and dreams of endless power. No one knows who or what the Beings are. They existed before men built the Street of Gods, and will exist long after the Street is nothing more than rubble and memories. Some say the Beings are distillations of specific realities; abstract concepts given shape and form by human fears or wishes, or simply by the times themselves. Others claim they are simply supernatural creatures, intrusions from other planes of existence. No one knows. They are real and unreal, both and neither. They are Beings of Power, and the Street of Gods is theirs and theirs alone.

They come and they go.

1

Killer on the Loose

Winter had come early to the city port of Haven, ushered in on blustering winds full of sleet and snow and bitter cold. Thick blankets of snow lay heavily across the roofs and city walls, and hoarfrost pearled the brickwork. Down in the street, the first of the day's pedestrian traffic struggled through the muddy slush, slipping and sliding and cursing each other through numb lips. The cold wind cut through the thickest furs, and frostbite gnawed savagely at exposed flesh. Winter had come to Haven, and honed its cutting edge on the slow-moving and the infirm.

It was early in the morning, the sun little more than a bloody promise on the starless night. The street lamps glowed bravely against the dark, islands of amber light in an endless gloom. Ruddy lanterns hung from horses and carts, bobbing like live coals on the night. And trudging through the cold and dark came Hawk and Fisher, husband and wife and Captains in the city Guard. Somewhere up ahead in the narrow streets and alleyways of the Northside lay a dead man. It wasn't clear yet why he was dead. Apparently the investigating Constables were still trying to find some of the pieces.

Murder was nothing new in the Northside. Every city has a dark and cruel side to its nature, and Haven was no different. Haven was a dark city, the rotten apple of the Low Kingdoms, but murder and corruption flourished openly in the Northside, fuelled by greed and hate and bitter need. People died there every day for reasons of passion, desperation, or business. Nevertheless, this latest in a line of bloody murders had shocked even the hardened Northsiders. So the Guard sent in Hawk and Fisher. There wasn't much that could shock them.

Hawk was tall, dark, but no longer handsome. A series of old scars ran down the right side of his face, and a black silk patch covered his right eye. He wore a long furred jacket and trousers and a heavy black Guardsman's cloak. He didn't look like much. He was lean and wiry rather than muscular, and he was beginning to build a stomach. He wore his long dark hair swept back from his forehead and tied with a silver clasp at the nape. He had only just turned thirty, but already there were streaks of grey in his hair. It would have been easy to dismiss Hawk as just another bravo, perhaps a little past his prime and going to seed, but there was something about Hawk; something hard and unyielding and almost sinister. People walked quietly around him, and were careful to keep their voices calm and reasonable. On his right hip Hawk carried a short-handled axe instead of a sword. He was very good with an axe. He'd had lots of practice in his five years as a Guard.

Isobel Fisher walked at Hawk's side, echoing his pace and stance with the naturalness of long companionship. She was tall, easily six feet in height, lithely muscular, and her long blond hair fell to her waist in a single thick plait, weighted at the tip with a polished steel ball. She was in her mid to late twenties, and handsome rather than beautiful. There was a rawboned harshness to her face which contrasted strongly with her deep blue eyes and generous mouth. Somewhere in the past, something had scoured all the human weaknesses out of her, and it showed. Like Hawk, she wore the Guard's standard uniform for winter, with a sword at her left hip. Her hand rested comfortably on the pommel.

A thin mist hung about the street, though the weather wizards had been trying to clear it for hours. The cold seeped relentlessly into Hawk's bones as he strode along, and he stamped his boots hard into the slush to try and keep some warmth in his feet. His hands were curled into fists inside his gloves, but it didn't seem to be helping much. Hawk hated the cold, hated the way it leached all the warmth and life out of him. And in particular, he hated being out in the cold and the dark at such an ungodly hour of the morning. But this shift paid the best, and he and Fisher needed the money, so . . . Hawk shrugged irritably, trying to get his cloak to fall more comfortably about him. He hated wearing a cloak; it always got in the way during fights. But braving the winter cold without a cloak was about as sensible as skinny-dipping in an alligator pool; you tended to lose important parts of your anatomy. So Hawk wore his cloak, and moaned about it a lot. He shrugged his shoulders again, and tugged surreptitiously at the cloak's hem.

'Leave that cloak alone,' said Fisher, without looking at him. 'It looks fine.'

Hawk sniffed. 'It doesn't feel right. The day's supposed to get warmer, anyway. If the mists clear up, I think I might drop the cloak off somewhere and pick it up at the end of the shift.'

'You'll do no such thing. You know you get colds and flus easily, and I'm not nursing you through another one of those. A couple of degrees of fever and you think you're dying.'

Hawk stared straight ahead, pretending he hadn't heard that. 'Where is this body we're supposed to look at, anyway?'

'Silver Street. Just down here, on the left. It sounded fairly gruesome. Do you suppose it'll look like the others?'

'I hope so,' said Hawk. 'I'd hate to think there was more than one homicidal maniac running around on our patch.'

Fisher nodded glumly. 'I hate maniacs. They don't play

by the rules. Trying to figure out their motives is enough to drive you crazy.'

Hawk smiled slightly, but the smile didn't last long. If this corpse was as bad as the others he'd seen, it wasn't going to be a pretty sight. A Guard Constable had found the first body down by the Devil's Hook, hanging from a lamppost on a rope made from its own intestines. The second body had been found scattered the length of Hawthorne Alley. The killer had got inventive with the third victim, on Lower Eel Street. The hands had been nailed to a wall. The head was found floating in a water butt. There was no trace of the body's genitals.

Hawk and Fisher turned into Silver Street, and found a crowd already gathered despite the early hour. Nothing like a good murder to bring out a crowd. Hawk wondered briefly what the hell all these people were doing out on the streets at such an unearthly hour, but he knew better than to ask. They'd only lie. The Northside never slept. There was always somebody ready to make a deal, and someone else ready to cheat him.

Hawk and Fisher pushed their way through the crowd. Some of the sightseers reacted angrily at being jostled out of the way, but quickly fell silent as they recognised the two Guards. Everyone in the Northside knew Hawk and Fisher. Hawk paused briefly at the thick line of blue chalk dust the Guard Doctor had laid down to keep the crowd back, and then he took a deep breath and walked quickly over it. The silver torc at his wrist, his badge of office, protected him from the ward's magic, but the blue line always made him nervous. He'd once made the mistake of crossing the line on a day he'd absent-mindedly left his torc at home, and the agonising muscle cramps had lasted the best part of an hour. Which was why the crowd had pushed right up to the edge of the line but made no move to cross it. Thus ensuring that the scene of the crime remained intact and the Guard Doctor had room to work.

A Guard Constable was standing by, at a respectful distance from the body. His dark red cloak and tunic looked almost garish against the winter snow. He nodded affably to Hawk and Fisher. The Doctor was squatting in the blood-stained snow beside the body, but rose to his feet to nod briefly to the two Captains. He was a short, delicate man with pale face and eyes and large, clever hands. His official cloak was too large for him and looked like a hand-me-down, but he had the standard look of calm assurance that all doctors seem to be issued along with their diplomas.

'I'm glad you're here, Captain Hawk, Captain Fisher. I'm Dr Jaeger. I haven't had much time with the body yet, but I can tell you this much: the killer didn't use a weapon. He did all this with his bare hands.'

Hawk looked at the body, and had to fight to keep his face impassive. The arms had been torn out of their sockets. The torso had been ripped open from throat to groin and the internal organs pulled out and strewn across the bloody snow. The legs had been broken repeatedly. Jagged splinters of bone pierced the tattered skin. There was no sign of the head.

'Hell's teeth.' Hawk tried to imagine how much sheer strength was needed to destroy a body so completely, and a disturbing thought came to him. 'Doctor, is there any chance this could have been a nonhuman assailant? Were-wolf, vampire, ghoul?'

Jaeger shook his head firmly. 'There's no evidence of blood drainage; you can see for yourself how much there is around the body. There's no tooth or claw marks to indicate a shapeshifter. And apart from the missing head, everything's here somewhere. No evidence of feasting. No, Captain, the odds are this is your standard homicidal maniac, with a very nasty disposition.'

'Great,' said Fisher. 'Just great. How long before the forensic sorcerer gets here?'

Jaeger shrugged. 'Your guess is as good as mine. He's

been contacted, but you know how he hates to be dragged from his nice warm bed at this hour of the morning.'

'All right,' said Hawk. 'We can't wait; the trail will get cold. We'd better use your magic to get things started, Doctor. How much can you do?'

'Not a lot,' Jaeger admitted. 'When he finally gets here, the forensic sorcerer might be able to re-create the entire killing and show us exactly what happened. The best I can give you is a glimpse of the killer's face.'

'That's more than we've got from the last three killings,' said Hawk.

'We were lucky with this one,' said Jaeger. 'Death couldn't have taken place more than half an hour ago. The chances of scrying the face are very good.'

'Wait a minute,' said Fisher. 'I thought you needed the head for that, so you could see the killer's face in the victim's eyes?'

Jaeger smiled condescendingly. 'Medical sorcery has progressed far beyond those old superstitions, Captain Fisher.' He knelt down beside the body again, grimacing as the bloody slush stained his clothes, and bent over the torso. The fingers of his left hand moved slowly in a complex pattern, and he muttered something short and guttural under his breath. Blood gushed suddenly from the neck of the torso, spilling out in a steady stream to form a wide pool. Jaeger gestured abruptly, and the blood stopped flowing. Ripples spread slowly across the pool, as though disturbed by something under the surface. Hawk and Fisher watched, fascinated, as a face slowly formed in the blood. The features were harsh, brooding, and quite distinct. Hawk and Fisher bent forward and studied the face thoroughly, committing it to memory. The image suddenly disappeared, and the blood was only blood again. Hawk and Fisher straightened up, and Jaeger got to his feet again. Hawk nodded appreciatively to him.

'Anything else you can do for us?'

'Not really. From the pattern of the bloodstains, I don't think the victim had time to struggle much. Which suggests that most if not all the mutilations took place after death.'

'Cause of death?' said Fisher.

Jaeger shrugged. 'Take your pick. Any one of those injuries would have been enough to kill him.'

Hawk gestured for the Guard Constable to come over and join them. He was a dark, heavy-set man in his mid forties, with a twenty-year star on his uniform. He had the calm, resigned look of the seasoned Guard who'd seen it all before and hadn't been impressed then, either. He glanced briefly at the body as he came to stand beside it, but nothing showed in his face.

'Constable Roberts at your service, Captain Hawk, Captain Fisher.'

'Who found the body?' said Hawk.

'Couple of kids coming back from a party. Merchant families. Took a shortcut through the Northside on a dare, and found a bit more than they bargained for. They're in the house opposite with my partner, having a cup of tea. It's good for shock, tea.'

'They see anything, apart from the body?'

'Apparently not, Captain.'

'We'd better have a word with them, anyway. See if you can move that crowd along. The forensic sorcerer should be here soon, and he hates working in front of an audience.'

The Constable nodded, and Hawk and Fisher headed for the house he'd indicated, stepping around the bloodstains where they could.

'You know,' said Fisher quietly, 'it's times like this I seriously think about getting out of this job. You think you've seen every nasty sight and spectacle the Northside can throw at you, and then something like this happens. How can one human being do that to another?'

Hawk felt like shrugging, but didn't. It had been a serious

question. 'Drugs. Passion. Possession. Maybe just plain crazy. There are all sorts in the Northside, on their way up or on their way down. If a man's got any darkness in his soul, the Northside will bring it out. Don't take it so personally, Isobel. We've seen worse. Just concentrate on finding the clues that will help us nail the bastard.'

The young couple who'd found the body were still in the house where they'd been left, too shocked and disorientated even to think about making a fuss about leaving. They were clearly merchant-class by their dress, lower-middle by the look of them, and looked distinctly out of place in the dim smoky kitchen, being fussed over by a motherly washer-woman. Another Guard Constable was sitting comfortably by the fire, keeping an eye on them. He wore a ten-year star, but looked like he'd spent most of those years indoors. He nodded pleasantly to Hawk and Fisher, but made no move to get up. The merchant boy looked to be in his late teens, the girl a year or two younger. Hawk drew up a chair opposite them, and concentrated his questions on the boy. The girl was half asleep in her chair, worn out by shock and emotional exhaustion.

'I'm Captain Hawk, of the city Guard. This is my partner, Captain Fisher. What's your name, lad?'

'Fairfax, sir. Calvin Fairfax.'

'All right, Calvin, tell us about finding the body.'

Fairfax swallowed once, and nodded stiffly. 'We were walking down Wool Street, Belinda and I, when we heard something. Footsteps, like someone running away. Then Belinda saw spots of blood on the ground, leading into the next street. She didn't want to get involved, but I thought we should at least take a look, in case someone was injured and needed help. We walked a little way down the street . . . and that's when we saw the body.'

'Did you see anyone else in Silver Street?' said Fisher.

'No. There was no one else there. Belinda screamed, but no one came to help. A few people looked out their windows at us, but they didn't want to get involved. Finally the Guard Constables heard her, and came to see what was happening.'

Fisher nodded understandingly. 'What time was this?'

'About three o'clock. I heard the tower bell sound the hour not long before. The Constables took over once they saw the body. We've been waiting here ever since. Can we go now, please? We're very late. Our parents will be worried.'

'In a while,' said Hawk. 'The forensic sorcerer will want to see you, when he finally gets here, but after that you're free to go. You'll have to make a statement for the Coroner's Court, but you can do that any time. And in future, stay out of the Northside. This isn't a safe place to be walking about, especially early in the morning.'

'Don't worry,' said Fairfax earnestly, 'I never want to see this place again for the rest of my life. We wouldn't have come this way anyway if Luther hadn't dared us to walk past the Bode house.'

Hawk's ears pricked up. The Bode house. The name rang a faint but very definite bell. 'What's so special about the Bode house?'

Fairfax shrugged. 'It's supposed to be haunted. People have seen things, heard things. We thought it would be a lark.' His mouth twisted sourly. 'We thought it would be fun . . .'

Hawk talked reassuringly with him for a while, and then he and Fisher left the house and walked back down Silver Street. The cold morning air seemed even harsher after the comfortable warmth of the kitchen.

'Bode house . . .' Hawk frowned thoughtfully. 'I know that name from somewhere.'

'You should do,' said Fisher. 'It's been mentioned in our briefings for the past three nights. There are some indications the place may be haunted. Neighbours have complained of strange lights and sounds, and no one's seen the occupant for days. Since Bode is an alchemist and a sorcerer, no one's taking it too seriously yet, but there's no doubt it's got the neighbours rattled.'

'Beats me how you can take in all that stuff,' said Hawk. 'It's all I can do to keep my eyes open at the beginning of the shift. I don't really wake up till I've been on the streets an hour.'

'Don't think I haven't noticed,' said Fisher.

'Where is this Bode house?'

'Just down the street and round the corner.'

Hawk stopped and looked at her. 'Coincidence?'

'Could be.'

'I don't believe in coincidence. I think we'd better take a look, just to be sure.'

'Might be a good idea to have a word with Constable Roberts first,' said Fisher. 'This is his particular territory; he might know something useful.'

Hawk looked at her approvingly. 'You're on the ball today, lass.'

Fisher grinned. 'One of us has to be.'

As it turned out, Constable Roberts wasn't much help.

'Can't tell you anything definite about the house, Captains. I've heard a few things, but there are always rumours with a sorcerer's house. Bode's a quiet enough fellow; lives alone and keeps himself to himself. No one's seen him for a while, but that's not unusual. He often goes off on journeys. Since no one's been actually hurt or threatened, I've just let the place be. Bode wouldn't thank me for sticking my nose into his business, and I'm not getting a sorcerer mad at me for no good reason.'

Hawk's mouth tightened, and for a moment he almost said something, but in the end he let it go. Looking out for Number One was standard practice in Haven, even amongst the Guard. Especially amongst the Guard. 'Fair enough, Constable. I think we'll take a look anyway. You stay here until the forensic sorcerer arrives. And keep your eyes open. The killer could still be around here some-where.'

He got exact directions from Roberts, and then he and Fisher pushed their way through the thinning crowd and set off down the street. It wasn't far. The sorcerer's house was set on the end of a row of fairly well-preserved tenements. Not too impressive, but not bad for the area. The window shutters were all firmly closed, and there was no sign of any light. Hawk tried to feel any uneasy atmosphere that might be hanging about the place, but either there wasn't one or he was so cold by now he couldn't feel it. He took off his right glove and slipped his hand inside his shirt. Hanging around his neck on a silver chain was a carved bone amulet. Standard issue for all Guards, the amulet could detect the presence of magic anywhere nearby. He held the amulet firmly in his hand, but the small piece of bone was still and quiet. As far as it was concerned, there was no magic at all in the vicinity. Which was unusual, to say the least. A sorcerer's house should be crawling with defensive spells. He took his hand away and quickly pulled his glove back on, flexing his numbed fingers to drive out the cold.

'Have you got the suppressor stone?' he asked quietly.

'I thought you'd get round to that,' said Fisher. 'You've been dying to try the thing out, haven't you?'

Hawk shrugged innocently. The suppressor stone was the latest bright idea from the Council's circle of sorcerers. They weren't standard issue yet, but a number of Guards had volunteered to try them out. Working the streets of Haven, a Guard needed every helpful device he could get his hands on. Theoretically, the suppressor stone was capable of cancelling out all magic within its area of influence. In practice, the range was very limited; it misfired as often as it worked, and they still weren't sure about side effects. Hawk couldn't wait to try it out. He loved new gadgets.

Which was why Fisher carried the stone.

'Great big overgrown kid,' she muttered under her breath.

Hawk smiled, walked up to the front door and studied it warily. It looked ordinary enough. There was a fancy brass door-knocker, but Hawk didn't try it. Probably booby-trapped. Sorcerers were a suspicious lot. He knelt down suddenly as something caught his eye. Someone had used the iron boot-scraper recently. There was mud and slush and a few traces of blood. Hawk smiled, and straightened up. Sooner or later, they always made a mistake. You just had to be sharp enough to spot it. He looked at Fisher, and she nodded to show she'd seen it too. They both drew their weapons. Hawk hammered on the door twice with the butt of his axe. The loud, flat sound echoed on the quiet. There was no response.

'All right,' said Hawk. 'When in doubt, be direct.' He lifted his axe to strike at the door, but Fisher stopped him.

'Hold it, Hawk. We could be wrong. If by some chance the sorcerer has come home, and is just a slow answerer, he's not going to look too kindly on us if we break his door down. And if that isn't him in there, why warn him we're coming? I've got a better way.'

She reached into a hidden pocket and pulled out a set of lock-picks. She bent over the door lock, fiddled expertly for a few seconds, and then pushed the door quietly ajar. Hawk looked impressed.

'You've been practising.'

Fisher grinned. 'Never know when it might come in handy.'

Hawk pushed the door open, revealing a dark, empty hall. He and Fisher stood where they were, weapons at the ready, studying the hallway.

'There's bound to be some kind of security spell, to keep strangers out,' said Fisher. 'That's standard with all magic-users.'

'So we'll use the stone,' said Hawk. 'That's what it's for.'

'Not so fast. If I was a sorcerer, I'd put a rider on my security spell, designed to go off if anybody messed with it.'

Hawk frowned thoughtfully. 'According to the Constable, Bode's a fairly low-level sorcerer. Something like that would need more sophisticated magic.'

'Try the amulet again.'

Hawk held the carved bone firmly in his hand, but it was still quiescent. As far as it was concerned, there wasn't any magic in the area. Hawk shook his head impatiently. 'We're wasting time. We're going in there. Now.'

'Fair enough.'

'After you.'

'My hero.'

They walked slowly into the dim hallway, side by side. They paused just inside the doorway, but nothing happened. Hawk found a lamp in a niche on the wall, and lit it. The pale golden glow revealed a long narrow hallway, open but not particularly inviting. The walls were bare, the floorboards dull and unpolished. There was a door to their right, closed, and a stairway straight ahead at the end of the hall. Fisher moved silently over to the door, listened a moment, and then eased it open. Hawk braced himself, axe at the ready. Fisher pushed the door open with the toe of her boot and stepped quickly into the room, sword held out before her. Hawk moved quickly forward, holding up the lamp to light the room. There was no one there. Everything looked perfectly normal. Furniture, carpet, paintings and tapestries on the walls. Nothing expensive, but comfortable. The two Guards went back into the hall, shutting the door quietly behind them. They headed for the stairs.

'Something's wrong here,' said Hawk softly. 'According to the amulet there's still no sign of any magic, but this house should be saturated with it. At the very least, there should be defensive spells all over the place. Industrial espionage is rife among magic-users. There's always someone trying to steal your secrets.'

They made their way up the stairs, the steps occasionally creaking under their weight. The sounds seemed very loud on the quiet. The lamplight bobbed around them, unable to make much impression on the darkness. The landing at the top of the stairs led off onto a narrow hallway. There were three doors, all firmly closed. Hawk and Fisher stood together, listening, but there was only the quiet, and the sound of their own breathing. Hawk sniffed the air.

'Can you smell something, Isobel?'

'Yeah . . . something. Can't tell what it is, or where it's coming from, though.'

The nearest door suddenly flew open, slamming back against the passageway wall with a deafening crash. Hawk and Fisher moved quickly to stand on guard, weapons at the ready. At first Hawk thought the figure before them was some kind of beast, and it took him a moment to realise it was a man wrapped in furs. He was barely average height, but bulging with muscles, overdeveloped almost beyond reason. His furs were dark and greasy, covered with filth and dried blood. There was blood on his face and hands. He was grinning widely, his cheeks stretched near to distortion. Even so, Hawk had no trouble recognising the face Dr Jaeger had shown him in the pool of blood. The killer was carrying something in his right hand, and Hawk darted a glance at it. It was a severed head, held by the hair. Hawk concentrated on the killer's face. The unnatural smile didn't falter and the eyes were fixed and wild. His bearing was savage and menacing, but he made no move to attack them. Drugs? Possession? Crazy? Hawk took a firm hold on his axe. He remembered what the killer had done to the body in Silver Street with his bare hands.

'We're Captains in the city Guard,' he said evenly. 'You're under arrest.'

'You can't stop me,' said the killer, his voice breathy and excited. 'I'm the Dark Man.'

He swung the severed head viciously at Hawk, and he

stepped aside automatically. The head crashed into the wall and rebounded, leaving a bloody smudge behind it. Fisher stepped forward, her sword held out before her. The Dark Man slapped the blade aside with the flat of his hand and swung the severed head at her. She ducked, and the Dark Man darted back into the room he'd come from. Hawk and Fisher charged in after him, but the room was empty. Fisher swore briefly.

'How the hell did he manage that? He was only out of our sight for a second or two.'

'Place is probably full of sliding panels and secret passageways,' said Hawk. 'He could be anywhere in the house by now.'

'Or out of it.'

'No, I don't think so. We've seen his face. He has to silence us, and he knows it. He'll be back. In the meantime, let's take a look round these rooms. Maybe we'll find a clue, or something to explain what's going on.'

'Optimist,' said Fisher.

The room they were in was a small, cosy bedchamber. The bedclothes had been pulled back, but the bed was empty. The bedclothes felt cold and faintly damp to the touch. There was a light covering of dust over all the furniture. Hawk and Fisher poked around for a few minutes, but there was nothing significant to be found. They went back out into the hallway, keeping their weapons at the ready.

The next room turned out to be some kind of laboratory. There were glass instruments and tubing, earthenware bowls, and stacked phials of chemicals. The room looked neat and undisturbed, but once again there was a layer of dust over everything. At the back of the room there was a simple desk with two locked drawers. Fisher opened them. Inside there was nothing but a handful of papers, covered with complex equations that made no sense to either of them. Hawk put them back, and then paused and sniffed the air. The smell seemed somewhat stronger, and he had an uncomfortable suspicion he knew what it was.

The third and last room was a study. Small, compact, and tidy. Bookshelves covered one wall, packed with leather-bound volumes of varying sizes. There was a broad, functional desk, its top covered with scattered papers. The smell of death and decay was very strong. Posed limply in the chair by the desk was a dead man dressed in sorcerer's black. He'd been dead for some time. His head was bowed forward, his chin resting on his chest.

'Well, at least now we know what happened to the sorcerer Bode,' said Fisher. 'And why there's no magic in this place. His protective spells must have collapsed when he died.'

'I don't think so,' said Hawk. 'Protective spells don't work like that.'

'They couldn't have been very good spells. They didn't keep the killer out.'

'Yes,' said Hawk. 'Interesting, that.'

'So, how did he die?'

'Good question,' said Hawk. 'There's no obvious wound.' He put the lamp down on the desk, gingerly took hold of the sorcerer's hair, and tilted the head back. When he saw Bode's face he almost let it drop forward again. The sorcerer had the same face at the Dark Man.

'That's not possible,' said Fisher. 'It can't be him. This man's been dead for days.'

Hawk nodded, and let the head fall forward again. 'So what did we just fight? A ghost?' He started to wipe his fingers on his cape, and then stopped as he realised what he'd just said. They looked at each other for a moment.

'This house is supposed to be haunted,' said Fisher.

'Ghosts don't usually try to bash your brains out with a severed head,' said Hawk firmly. 'Not unless it's their own. And they're not usually built like weightlifters, either.' He looked back at the body as a thought struck him. 'Relax,

Isobel. This definitely isn't the Dark Man. The build's all wrong. This guy's about as well-developed as a sparrow. I've seen more muscles on a Leech Street whore.'

'The face is still the same, though,' said Fisher. 'Maybe they're brothers. Twins.'

Hawk frowned. 'Too obvious. Nothing's ever simple, where magic-users are concerned.'

He leant forward, and steeling himself against the smell, he searched the body carefully for the cause of death. It didn't take him long. There was a narrow puncture wound just under the sternum. Someone had stabbed Bode through the heart. Hawk readjusted the sorcerer's clothing, stood back, and frowned thoughtfully. One thrust, right through the heart. Very professional. Or very lucky. But even so, how had the killer got close enough to do it? Even a low-level sorcerer like Bode should have had more than enough magic to deal with a common assassin. Even assuming the killer had somehow got past the house's magical defences. Bode had to have had some defences, or a rival sorcerer would have wiped him out by now. Sorcery was a very competitive business. Particularly in the Northside.

Maybe Bode knew his killer, and invited him in. That would explain a lot. Including why the sorcerer had died sitting quietly in his own study.

'Hawk,' said Fisher suddenly, 'I think you'd better take a look at this.'

Hawk looked round. Fisher had been studying the papers on the desk and was flipping through half a dozen sheets, frowning intently. He moved over to join her.

'Most of this is routine,' said Fisher. 'Reports on experiments, memos to himself not to forget things, dates and addresses and stuff like that. But this is . . . something else.'

Hawk listened intently as Fisher read the pages aloud. It seemed Bode had to travel a lot, to acquire certain ingredients for his experiments. Which meant leaving his house unguarded, apart from the few magical defences he'd been able to put together. Bode was a better alchemist than sorcerer, and he knew his defences wouldn't keep out any really determined sorcerer. Being more than a little paranoid where his work was concerned, he put a lot of thought into protecting his home while he was away. He did think briefly about acquiring a familiar of some kind, but that meant dealing with some very unpleasant Beings, most of which were well out of his league. So he made his own familiar. He used his knowledge of sorcery and alchemy to reach inside himself, extract all the hate and rage and violence, and place them inside a homunculus; a sorcerously created duplicate of himself. The Dark Man. The familiar was bound to the house, and couldn't leave without Bode's permission. It made an excellent watchdog.

Fisher stopped reading, and looked at Hawk. 'Like you said, the Northside brings out the worst in people.'

'It does explain a lot,' said Hawk. 'Presumably the Dark Man was out of the house when Bode was killed, and it's been running loose ever since. Hating and killing because that's all it was ever designed to do. And now there's nothing left to hold it in check.'

'We're going to have to kill it, Hawk,' said Fisher. 'We can't reason with something like this.'

'We've got to find it first. Or wait for it to find us. Dammit, what was a low-level sorcerer like Bode doing, messing around with homunculi? Those things are strictly illegal.'

Fisher looked at him. 'This is Haven, remember?'

'This stuff is heavy, even for the Northside. The creation of a homunculus carries a mandatory death penalty, if they catch you. Research into making homunculi has been banned for centuries. In some places they still hang, draw, and quarter people just for owning books that mention the damn things.'

Fisher frowned. 'What's so important about homunculi?'

'Like a great many other things, it all comes down to inheritance and bloodlines. How are you going to keep the Family bloodlines pure, if exact physical duplicates keep popping up all over the place? Homunculi make a mockery of inheritance laws. On top of that, there's always the possibility of someone important being murdered and then replaced by a duplicate. Not to mention how easy it would be for some sorcerer to create his own army of homunculi, and hire it out to anyone with a grudge against the established order.'

'You've been reading up on this, haven't you?' said Fisher.

'It wouldn't do you any harm to spend a little time in the Guard library. You'd be surprised at some of the stuff they've got there.'

'Can we get back to Bode's murder?' said Fisher. 'These notes aren't just about his research, you know. I saved the best for last. Take a look at this.'

She handed Hawk a sheaf of letters from the desk. He looked quickly through them, his frown gradually deepening. Someone had hired Bode to investigate something to do with the Street of Gods. The details had been left deliberately vague, as though the writer hadn't wanted to commit anything incriminating to paper. Presumably he and the sorcerer had known what they were talking about, at any rate.

'Whatever Bode found out, someone didn't want him passing it on,' said Fisher.

'This is crazy,' said Hawk. 'What was a low-level sorcerer like Bode doing, messing about on the Street of Gods? They'd have eaten him alive. Literally, in some cases.' Hawk shook his head slowly. 'I'm starting to get a really bad feeling about this case, Isobel.'

'You always say that at the beginning of a case, Hawk.'

'And I'm usually right.'

'That's Haven for you.'

The door behind them flew open, and the Dark Man filled the doorway. Hawk and Fisher spun to face him, weapons at the ready. The Dark Man's hand snapped forward, and the severed head flew through the air and struck Hawk on the forehead. Hawk had a brief glimpse of the staring eyes and gaping mouth and then he was staggering backwards, pain blinding him, his thoughts vague and muzzy. Fisher quickly stepped forward to stand between him and the Dark Man. She kicked at the head, and it rolled away across the floor. The Dark Man charged forward, and Fisher thrust at him with her sword. He dodged the blade with inhuman speed, darted inside her reach, and grabbed her by the arm. She struck at him with her fist, but he didn't even notice. He threw her against the wall with sickening force, driving the breath out of her. She started to slide down the wall, but the Dark Man grabbed her by the throat with one hand and lifted her into the air. Her feet kicked helplessly inches above the floor. He was still smiling. And then Hawk stepped forward, swinging his axe double-handed, and buried it in the Dark Man's side.

Ribs splintered and broke under the heavy blade, and the Dark Man staggered to one side, dropping Fisher to the floor. Hawk jerked his blade free, and blood flew on the air. He and the Dark Man stood facing each other for a moment, each judging the other's condition. The Dark Man was bleeding freely, but otherwise showed no weakness from his wound. Hawk had a huge bruise forming on his forehead, and his hands weren't as steady as he would have liked. The Dark Man's smile widened slightly, and he threw himself at Hawk, hands reaching like claws for Hawk's throat. Hawk buried his axe deep in the Dark Man's chest, but he just kept coming.

And then he froze suddenly, and all the hate and savagery went out of his face, to be replaced by something like surprise. He turned his head slowly to look at Fisher, who was leaning against the wall, and then he fell forward onto his face and lay still. Hawk looked at Fisher. The suppressor stone was glowing brightly in her hand like a miniature star. Hawk grinned at her.

'Told you it would come in handy.'

He leant over the Dark Man and pulled his axe free. Fisher came over to join him, and they leaned on each other for a moment.

'I should have worked it out before,' said Fisher. 'If he was a homunculus, he was a magical construct. The suppressor stone took away his magic, and there was nothing left to hold him together.'

Hawk nodded slowly. 'I'm going to have to pay more attention to morning briefings.'

2

The God Squad

Hawk and Fisher were snatching a late breakfast at a fast-food stall when the sound of a struck gong filled their minds, followed by the dry acid voice of the Guard communications sorcerer. Hawk nearly choked on his mouthful of sausage, and Fisher burnt her tongue on the mustard.

Captains Hawk and Fisher, you are to report to the Deity Division on the Street of Gods. Your orders are waiting for you there. You are seconded to the Division until further notice. Message ends.

The rasping voice was suddenly gone from their minds. Hawk spat out his mouthful of sausage, and shook his head gingerly. 'If he doesn't stop using that bloody gong I swear I'm going to pay him a visit and stick it somewhere painful.'

Fisher snorted. 'From what I hear, you'd have to join the queue. This would have to happen now, right in the middle of a murder case. The Deity Division; what the hell does the God Squad want with us?'

'Beats me,' said Hawk. 'Maybe a God's got out of hand, and they want us to lean on him.'

Fisher looked at him. 'I hope you're not going to talk like that on the Street of Gods, Hawk. Because if you are, I'd be obliged if you'd keep well away from me. As I understand it, most Gods don't have a sense of humour. And the few that do have a downright nasty one. After all, we're talking about Beings who tend towards striking down heretics with lightning bolts, and dispensing plagues of boils when Church takings are down on the week before.'

'You worry too much,' said Hawk.

'And it's all because of you,' said Fisher.

The Street of Gods lies in the centre of Haven, right in the middle of the high-rent district. Hundreds of religions crowd side by side up and down the Street, promising hope and salvation, doom and destruction, and whatever else people need to keep them from thinking about the darkness at the end of all life. Everyone needs something to believe in, something that offers comfort in the face of despair, and whatever it is you're looking for, you'll find it somewhere on the Street of Gods. Churches and temples of all kinds stand shoulder to shoulder, each proclaiming the glory of its particular God and ostentatiously ignoring everyone else's. Everywhere you look there's a High Priest claiming to know the Truth of All Existence, and ready to share it with the faithful in return for regular tithes and offerings. Religion is big business in Haven.

According to the official city maps, the Street of Gods is exactly half a mile long. In fact, the Street is as long as it has to be to fit everything in. It's possible to start at one end of the Street, walk all day, and still not reach the far end before night falls. And then there are always the little side streets and back alleys, unmarked on any map, where the persistent enquirer can find the more controversial faiths and religions, the existence of which is often hotly denied in the clear light of day. There are doors that lead to mysteries, to wonders and nightmares, and few of them can be found in the same place twice.

Reality tends to be rather elastic on the Street of Gods.

The Deity Division, commonly known as the God Squad, exists to keep order on the Street. The city Council appoints its members, pays its wages, and does its best to pretend the Squad doesn't exist. Most of the time they try to pretend the whole damned Street doesn't exist. It makes them nervous. On the whole, things tend to be quiet on the Street. The great majority of Beings prefer to believe they're the only ones there, and won't even admit the existence of any other Churches. But there are always the occasional feuds and vendettas, human and inhuman natures being what they are. The God Squad was there to try and head off confrontations before they happened, whenever possible. Sometimes it wasn't possible, and that was when the Squad earned their money.

'You worked with the Squad once, didn't you?' said Hawk to Fisher, as they made their way through the slush-covered streets towards the heart of the city. The sun was starting its slow climb up the sky, and the freezing streets were full of well-wrapped people heading to and from work.

'Briefly,' said Fisher. 'It was while you were working on that werewolf case, the one where young Hightower died. I was teamed with five other Guards on the Shattered Bullion case, and we spent a few days working with the God Squad. Didn't come to anything.'

'What were they like?' said Hawk.

Fisher shrugged. 'Stuck-up bunch, as I recall.'

'Apart from that, what were they like? Give me some details, Isobel. Like it or not, we've got to work with these people, and I want to know what I'm getting into.'

Fisher scowled thoughtfully. 'The Squad is always made up of three people: a sorcerer, a mystic, and a warrior. Individuals come and go, but the mix stays the same. Presumably the Council are so relieved at finally finding a balance that works, they don't want to mess with it. This particular group has been together for four years. They've got a good track record.

'The sorcerer is called Tomb. Cheerful name. He's a bit older than us, quiet, thoughtful, powerful as all hell, and so easygoing it's disgusting. One of those people who prides himself on never raising his voice. A pigeon could crap on his head and he wouldn't ask for a handkerchief. Probably have ulcers by the time he's forty.

'The mystic is called Rowan. She's young, a pleasant enough sort, but crazy as a brewery-rat. Heavily into signs and omens and herbalistic remedies. She gave me a herb tea for my head cold, and I had the runs for two days. She's got the Sight, and a few minor magics, but mostly she earns her keep by figuring out how the various Beings think. She's supposed to be very good at that. Probably because she's just as weird as they are.

'The warrior is Charles Buchan. You must have heard of him. The greatest duellist, intriguer, and womaniser this city's ever known. Mid forties, handsome, daring, and debonair – and about as modest as a peacock. Been getting into scrapes all his life, and talking and fighting his way out of them with equal ease. But he really shouldn't have sneaked past the King's Guards and gone to bed with the King's latest mistress on the same night the King decided to pay her a visit.

'Apparently he was given a straight choice: a career in the Guard or a lifetime in gaol. How he ended up in the God Squad is anybody's guess, but he's taken to it like a politician to bribes.'

'And this is the group we're joining,' said Hawk. 'Great. Just great. I'm going to hate this assignment; I just know it. I was looking forward to working on the dead sorcerer case. How is it that whenever there's a particularly dangerous or unpleasant job that needs doing, our names are always at the top of the list?'

'Because we're the best,' said Fisher. 'And because we're too honest for our own good. The odds are we were getting too close to something sensitive, and someone wanted us out of the way for a while.'

'Someone among our own superiors in the Guard.'

'Probably. That's Haven for you.'

Hawk growled something indistinct under his breath.

They came finally to the Street of Gods and stepped suddenly out of winter and into summer. The snow and slush stopped dead at the entrance to the Street, and the air was dry and warm. A bright midday sun shone overhead in a clear blue sky. Hawk looked at Fisher, but neither of them said anything. The Street of Gods went its own way and followed its own rules. Whatever they were.

Hawk and Fisher made their way down the Street, staring resolutely straight ahead. They'd visited the Street before, while working on their last case, and knew how easy it was to get distracted. Crowds of priests and worshippers bustled back and forth on unknown errands, and the air was full of the clamour of the street preachers, spreading the Word to anyone who would listen. A huge shadow plunged the Street into gloom for a moment as something impossibly massive passed by overhead. Hawk didn't look up. Whatever it was, he didn't want to know. The shadow passed on, and the bright sunlight returned. Hawk began to sweat heavily under his furs and cloak.

Something like a man-sized toad squatted on a street corner and sang sweetly with a young girl's voice. The begging bowl before it was filled with bloody pieces of meat. Something long and spindly with too many legs scuttled up the side of a building, hugging a dead cat to its thorax. A small child with ancient eyes thrust steel pins through its own arms, giggling obscenely. A street preacher was levitating three or four feet above the ground, his head hanging back, his face a mask of ecstasy. Only the tourists paid any attention. It took more than mere exhibitionism to attract a following on the Street of Gods.

The God Squad's headquarters turned out to be a squat little two-storey building tucked away in one of the many quiet backwaters off the Street of Gods. Hawk knocked twice on the discreet front door, and then he and Fisher waited patiently on the front step, keeping a watchful eye on the area, just in case. The narrow back alley seemed calm and quiet, but Hawk wasn't ready to take anything on trust in the Street of Gods. The door finally opened, revealing a short bald man in his early thirties, dressed in sorcerer's black. He beamed at the two Guards like a benevolent uncle, and it took Hawk a moment to realise that this pleasant-looking fellow had to be the sorcerer Tomb.

'Captain Fisher, my dear. How nice to see you again. And you must be Captain Hawk. Delighted. Do come in, do come in. We've been expecting you.'

He ushered the two Guards down a short passage and into a small but comfortably appointed drawing room. He fussed around them as they settled into their chairs, keeping up a pleasant chatter all the while. Hawk took all of this with a pinch of salt. Tomb might like to come across as everyone's favourite relative, but you didn't get to be a first-class sorcerer through good intentions and a charming personality. It took long years of single-minded dedication, and not a little ruthlessness. Hawk smiled politely at Tomb's jokes, and made a mental note not to turn his back on the sorcerer. He didn't trust people who smiled too much. Tomb finally produced an exquisite cut-glass decanter and poured three generous glasses of sherry. Hawk took his and sipped it perfunctorily. He'd never much cared for the syrupy stuff, but he knew Fisher loved it. Tomb stopped talking for a moment as he savoured his sherry, and Hawk took advantage of the pause to get in a few words of his own.

'Pardon me, sir Tomb, but perhaps you could inform us as to what we're doing here. Usually when the God Squad needs help, you call in the Special Wizardry And Tactics team. What good can a couple of ordinary Guards do you?'

Tomb bit his lower lip and looked suddenly furtive. 'If you don't mind, Captain Hawk, I think we ought to wait until both my colleagues are here. They won't be long. The situation is . . . rather complicated.'

The door suddenly flew open, and Hawk and Fisher

looked round, startled, as a stocky young woman strode in, slamming the door shut behind her. She stood glaring at Hawk and Fisher for a long moment, nose in the air and hands on hips. She was short, barely five feet in height, which made her look even heavier than she was, and her round, pleasant face was marred by a perpetual scowl. Her dark hair was cropped short like a helmet, and her heavy eyebrows intensified her fierce demeanour. The dark, shapeless robe she wore was more suited to an older woman. She couldn't have been much into her twenties, but she looked at least ten years older.

'What are they doing here?' she snapped, switching her glare to the sorcerer Tomb. 'I told you I didn't want them here.'

'The Council sent them,' said Tomb easily, apparently unaffected by her angry stare. 'They seem to think we could do with a little help.'

The woman sniffed loudly. 'If we can't work out what the hell's going on with all our experience, I don't see how a couple of strong-arm bullies from the Guard are going to help.'

'That's enough, Rowan,' said Tomb sharply, and there was enough bite in his tone to silence the mystic.

Hawk studied Tomb thoughtfully over his sherry glass. It would seem the sorcerer had hidden depths after all. Hawk was just nerving himself to try another sip of his sherry, when the door flew open again and a tall muscular man strode in, shoulders back, head held high. Hawk didn't need Fisher to tell him that this was the notorious Charles Buchan.

He was handsome in a harsh, brooding way, with a head of close-cropped blond curls and icy blue eyes, and his arms and chest showed the kind of muscle definition you only get from lifting weights. He was supposed to be in his forties, but his superb physique made him look a good ten years younger. He was dressed in the latest fashion and wore it well, which took some doing when you considered that the latest style consisted of tightly cut trousers and a padded jerkin with a chin-high collar. In fact, if the trousers had been cut any more tightly, Hawk would have seriously considered arresting the man for indecent exposure. Buchan's clothes were brightly colored but stopped just short of being garish; so short that the effect had to be intentional. Hawk couldn't help noticing that the outfit had been carefully tailored so that there was plenty of give around the chest and shoulders. Charles Buchan might like to look up-to-the-minute, but clearly he wasn't prepared to let that interfere with his fighting abilities.

Hawk shot a glance at Fisher to see what she made of the man, and was disturbed to find her studying Buchan with a smile on her face. Hawk's eyebrows had just started to descend into a scowl, when Buchan stepped forward and greeted him cheerfully, slapping him just a little too hard on the shoulder. Hawk winced despite himself. Buchan turned to Fisher, who extended a hand to him. He took her hand, raised it to his lips, and kissed it expertly, his eyes on hers. Hawk's scowl deepened. Fisher didn't normally let people kiss her hand. Buchan let go of her hand with becoming reluctance, and straightened up to his full height, pulling back his shoulders a little so as to show off his broad chest and flat stomach.

'So, this is the famous partnership of Hawk and Fisher. I've heard a lot about you, all of it good. Glad to have you with us on this case. I'm sure it's going to be fascinating working with you. But I'm afraid there isn't that much for you to do, actually. I've no doubt we'll solve this case soon enough. We always do, you know. Still, I'm sure we can find something to keep you occupied while you're here.'

His voice was deep, resonant and commanding. *It would be*, thought Hawk dourly. *I'll bet he smokes a pipe as well, and cracks nuts with his bare hands. A devil with the ladies and a natural leader of men. Given a few spare minutes, I think I could learn to hate this guy.*

'Indeed,' said Tomb. 'If you don't mind, Charles, I'd like to take this opportunity to explain to our new friends why they're here.'

'Of course,' said Buchan. 'Don't mind me. Go straight ahead.'

He leaned back against the doorway, took a pipe from his pocket and began cleaning it, whistling softly under his breath. There was a pause, as everyone looked at Tomb. He frowned slightly, as though uncertain where to start.

'We find ourselves in a rather unusual situation, Captain Hawk, Captain Fisher. My associates and I have worked on many strange cases in our time in the Squad, but I have to say we've never encountered anything quite like this. To put it bluntly, someone is killing the Gods of Haven.'

Hawk and Fisher looked at each other. 'Go on,' said Hawk.

'We've lost three Beings so far,' said Tomb. 'The Dread Lord, the Sundered Man, and the Carmadine Stalker. We don't know how they died, or why, but all three have been utterly destroyed. If we don't come up with some explanations soon, the Gods are going to panic, and the Street of Gods could end up as a battleground. There are a lot of old grudges among the Gods, and it wouldn't take much to set them at each other's throats.'

'I didn't think Gods could die,' said Fisher.

'Call them Beings, if it will help,' said the mystic Rowan. 'If you're to be of any help to us, you have to understand how the Street of Gods operates. There are all kinds of religion here – some old, some new, some just fashions of the moment. Most are based around supernatural entities who've gathered a following through displays of power and promises of worldly dominion. Everyone wants to be on the winning side, to have a powerful protector watching out for them. Then there are human preachers whose teachings have developed into a religion. Their Churches tend to last the longest. Ideas are much more powerful and enduring than some magical Being with an ego problem.

'Religions come and go, and we try to keep the peace. Some of them are strange, some of them are beautiful, and some we don't understand at all. People can believe in the weirdest things if they're frightened or desperate enough. We don't take sides. We just try to keep the feuds and vendettas under control, and make sure that whatever troubles there may be don't pass beyond the Street of Gods.'

'How do you do that?' said Hawk.

The sorcerer Tomb smiled. 'Talking things through, playing off one faction against another, and a lot of improvising. If things start to get too out of hand, we call in the SWAT team. If that fails, we turn to the Exorcist Stone. That's our last resort. Essentially it's a much more powerful version of the suppressor stone the Council's been experimenting with. The Exorcist Stone dispels all magic from an area, no matter how powerful, and can even banish a Being from this plane of existence.'

'Banish?' said Fisher. 'You mean destroy?'

The sorcerer shrugged. 'We don't know. They disappear and they don't come back. We settle for that. We use the Stone very sparingly; only when there's a threat to the whole city. If the Beings decided we were a threat to them, they'd band together and destroy us. Stone or no Stone.'

'Is that how the Gods have been dying?' said Hawk. 'Someone's got hold of an Exorcist Stone of their own?'

'That's impossible,' said Rowan flatly. 'There's only one Stone, and no one knows how old it is or how it was created. If by chance there was another, we'd know about it. Every magic-user for hundreds of miles around would know about it; the sheer power involved would blaze like a beacon in their mind's eye. No one but the three of us has access to the Exorcist Stone, and it's impossible for any of us to misuse it. When we join the God Squad, the Council places a geas on us, a spell of compulsion, to prevent any of us using the Exorcist Stone except in the line of duty.'

'But still the Gods keep dying,' said Buchan. 'Their bodies destroyed, their presence dispersed. We've tried to investigate, but we have no experience in such matters. We've got nowhere. We don't even know what to look for. So far, the Gods' followers are still in shock; too dazed to do anything but sit around and pray for their Gods to return. When that doesn't happen, they're going to get angry and start looking for scapegoats.'

'And if that wasn't bad enough,' said Tomb, 'we're starting to hear rumblings from the other Beings. The three unexplained deaths have left them feeling vulnerable and afraid. It's only a matter of time before they decide to take matters into their own hands. We could end up with a God War on the Street. I don't think Haven could survive such a war. I'm not even sure the Low Kingdoms would survive.'

'So we sent to the Council for help,' said Buchan. 'And they sent us you.'

'The notorious Hawk and Fisher,' said Rowan, her voice flat and scathing. 'A pair of thugs in uniform. I know all about your reputation. You're the most violent Guards in Haven. You don't care who you hurt. No one knows how many people you've killed.'

'You should visit the Northside,' said Hawk. 'It might open your eyes to a few things. Northsiders don't believe in reasoned argument or diplomacy. They tend more to poisoning your wine or slipping a dagger between your ribs. Or both. We have the highest murder rate, the worst violence, and the highest general crime rate in all Haven. We're only as hard as we have to be, to get results. That's all the Council cares about.'

'That's as may be,' said Tomb weightily, 'but I feel it only fair to warn you that I won't tolerate such strong-arm tactics here. They'd just get you killed; you and anyone else unfortunate enough to be with you at the time. I must insist that while you're a part of the Squad you follow my orders at all times. Is that clear?'

'Sure,' said Fisher.

'Of course,' said Hawk.

Tomb looked at them both suspiciously. He'd expected to have to argue the point, and their giving in so easily worried him. It wasn't in character. He pursed his lips and decided to let it pass, for the moment. 'There is one other thing we need to discuss,' he said slowly. 'What religion do you both follow? What do you believe in?'

'Death and taxes,' said Fisher promptly. 'Everything else is negotiable.'

'Isobel and I were both raised as Christians,' said Hawk quickly, to deflect Tomb's deepening scowl. 'I've seen a lot of darkness in my time, and I still trust in the light.'

'Christianity,' said Tomb thoughtfully. 'The Old Religion. You're from the Northern countries originally, I take it? Yes, I thought so. I'm afraid your religion isn't much practised in the Low Kingdoms, though of course many of its terms still survive in the language. We really must sit down and discuss this some day.'

'Christians,' said Rowan disdainfully. 'I thought you people believed in love and peace, and turning the other cheek?'

'We're not very orthodox,' said Hawk.

'Well, just remember you're only here on sufferance.' Rowan sniffed disgustedly. 'All the Guards we could have had, and they had to send us a pair of Christians.'

'Apparently you have a friend on the Council,' said Buchan.

'Councillor Adamant, to be exact,' said Tomb. 'I understand you behaved very creditably while working as his bodyguards during the election. Though why he thinks that should qualify you to work on the Street of Gods is beyond me.'

'We fought a God on his behalf,' said Hawk calmly. 'The Abomination, the Lord of the Gulfs. We helped kill it.'

A sudden silence fell across the room. The three members of the God Squad looked at Hawk and Fisher almost respectfully.

'That was you?' said Buchan.

'We had some help,' said Hawk. Fisher's mouth twitched.

'I don't believe it,' said Rowan flatly.

Hawk looked at her calmly. 'That's your problem, lass.' He turned away to look at Tomb and Buchan. 'Fisher and I aren't exactly strangers to the Street of Gods. We've been here before. And whilst we might not have much experience in dealing with Beings, we do know how to track down murderers. That's our job. We're very good at it.'

Rowan started to say something scathing, and then stopped suddenly and looked at Tomb. 'People are gathering out on the Street. They seem angry, disturbed. I don't like the feel of it, Tomb.'

The sorcerer nodded slowly. 'I can See them, Rowan. Two large factions, closing on each other. Damn. There's going to be another riot. Charles, Rowan. Gather your equipment. Hawk and Fisher, come with me. You're about to see what happens when the rules break down on the Street of Gods. You should find it an interesting experience. If you survive it.'

Out on the Street of Gods, everything felt different. There was a vague unfocused tension on the air, and the crowding buildings felt grim and oppressive. Hawk and Fisher hurried along beside the God Squad, weapons drawn and at the ready. Tomb took the point, striding confidently in the lead, his robe of sorcerer's black billowing impressively around his stocky frame. He was smiling calmly, his stance relaxed and at ease.

Rowan hurried along at his side, stretching her legs to keep up with him. She carried a bulging satchel on one shoulder, and her face had taken on an uncomplicated expression of bulldog determination. Away from Tomb's comfortable study, she looked stronger, more focused, almost elemental in her single-mindedness. Charles Buchan strolled along behind them, his long legs easily meeting their pace. He wore a brightly polished chain-mail vest, and a long sword on his left hip. He carried himself well, his bearing calm and controlled. His face was a smiling, pleasant mask, but his eyes were very cold.

Hawk kept a watchful eye on the Squad as they hurried down the Street of Gods. Even with their practised professionalism, he could all but see the tension rising off them. He started to wonder if he ought to feel more worried himself. After all, this was their territory; if they were worried, there was probably a damned good reason for it. The Street itself seemed increasingly uneasy. There were fewer people around than previously, and they hurried on their way with heads bowed and eyes downcast. The street preachers were crying of universal death and destruction. A painted clown with razor blades buried in his bleeding eyes sang a bitter song of love and loss. Two shadows with nothing to cast them tore at each other like maddened animals. A tall angular building began to melt and run away like boiling wax, while the gargoyles on its guttering screamed in agony.

Hawk increased his pace and moved in beside the sorcerer Tomb. 'Pardon me, sir Tomb, but if my partner and I are heading into a dangerous situation, I think we have a right to know what we're getting into.'

'Of course,' said Tomb. 'You'll have to forgive us, Captain, but I'm afraid we're not used to working with strangers. Rowan and I both have the Sight, the ability to see and sense things at a distance. It seems a longstanding rivalry between two religions has boiled over into open fighting on the Street. The way things are, if we don't put a stop to it quickly, it'll develop into a full-blown riot, and the Beings themselves may be tempted to get involved. Normally, things wouldn't get this bad this quickly, but with three dead Gods and the murderer still at large, tempers are running short.'

'Wait a minute,' said Hawk. 'If things are that serious shouldn't we call in the SWAT team?'

'Oh, I don't think so,' said Tomb. 'It's only a riot. We can handle it.'

'Famous last words,' said Fisher behind them.

Hawk gave Tomb a hard look, but the sorcerer seemed perfectly serious. 'All right,' said Hawk, 'Give me some background on this. You said two religions. Which religions?'

'They're based on two lesser Beings,' said Tomb. 'Neither of them especially powerful or important, but both with long-established followings. Dusk the Devourer is head of a no-frills nihilist cult. Everything is vile and awful, the world's going to be destroyed, and only the faithful will be saved and transported to a better world. I can't prove it, but I'm fairly sure Dusk itself is a manic-depressive.

'The other Being is the Chrysalis. It's a huge cocoon about twenty feet long. It's supposed to perform the occasional miracle, but I've never seen any. The Chrysalis' followers believe that eventually the cocoon will open and the God within will emerge in all its glory to purge the world of evil. Whether it wants to be purged or not. They've been watching the cocoon for over four hundred years, but nothing's happened yet.

'Interestingly enough, each religion is the other's particular nemesis. Every God must have its Devil, though I've never been sure why. Good business, I suppose. Anyway, normally the two groups of followers content themselves with blazing sermons, veiled insults in the Street, and the occasional scuffle after the taverns have closed. But with things as they are, nothing's normal anymore. The Street of Gods is like a forest in a drought, waiting for a single spark to set everything alight.'

Hawk nodded. 'Either that, or they heard Fisher and I were coming and wanted to put on a good show to welcome us.'

Rowan muttered something indistinct. It didn't sound complimentary.

They heard the riot before they actually saw it. From up ahead came a roar of massed voices, raised in rage and hatred, and darkened with that animal single-mindedness found only in crowds that are rapidly turning into mobs. Hawk fell back a pace to walk beside Fisher. If they were going into a fight, he wanted someone at his back he could trust. The roar grew louder and more savage as they approached a sharp corner. According to the official maps, the Street of Gods was perfectly straight, but in this, as in so many other ways, the Street of Gods went its own way. They rounded the corner, and there was the riot, spread out before them.

A hundred men and women milled back and forth across the Street, mouths turned down in angry snarls, their eyes wild and furious. They were screaming and shouting and shaking their fists, and glaring in all directions. Some had clubs or staves or lengths of steel chain, while others had bricks or stones. Already there was blood on the cobbles, and several people lay unmoving on the ground, trampled on unnoticed by the mob. The scent of violence was heavy on the air, ready to erupt at any moment.

Hawk came to a halt well short of the mob, and looked the situation over carefully. The setting couldn't have been worse. The Street at this point was long and narrow, with only a few exits. Even if he could persuade the mob to break up and disperse, getting it separated into smaller, more manageable groups was going to be difficult. Breaking up a mob was one thing; keeping them separated was what counted. There had to be somewhere for them to go. The size of the watching crowd worried him as well. There were hundreds of them, filling the Street all around. Presumably they followed other faiths, and were happy at the chance to see two of their rivals knocking the hell out of each other. Even the street preachers had given up trying to spread the Word, and were busying themselves taking bets from the onlookers.

Tomb had come to a halt not far away and was watching the mob narrowly, lips pursed thoughtfully. Rowan was kneeling beside him, ferreting through her satchel. Hawk leaned over to take a look at what she had in there, and then quickly retreated as she glared at him viciously. Buchan was standing close at hand, his arms folded across his mailed chest, staring majestically out over the mob. He looked as though he was only awaiting the word to step forward and generally beat heads together until everyone agreed to see reason. Hawk looked quickly at Fisher, and was relieved to see she didn't appear too impressed. She caught him looking at her, realised why, and grinned broadly. Hawk looked away, and pretended he hadn't noticed. He hefted his axe thoughtfully, and watched the mood of the mob grow worse. This was the God Squad's territory, and he didn't want to interfere, but somebody had better do something soon or there'd be brains spilled on the cobbles and a riot you'd need a small army to contain.

Rowan drew a pair of slender copper rods from her satchel and plunged them into the ground. They sank easily into the solid stone as though it were nothing more than wet mud. The mystic then drew a protective circle around herself and Tomb with blue chalk dust. Hawk frowned slightly as he realised he and Fisher and Buchan weren't included in the protection. Whatever Rowan and Tomb were up to, he hoped they were careful to aim it in the right direction. The mystic and the sorcerer than paused for a technical discussion. Hawk moved over a little to stand beside Buchan, who was still silently studying the mob.

'Who's winning, sir Buchan?'

'Hard to tell. Strategically speaking, this is a mess. There's no cooperation; it's every man for himself and Devil take the hindmost. Quite literally, I suppose, as far as they're concerned.'

'How do you tell the two sides apart?'

'Blue robes are Chrysalis, grey robes are Dusk.'

'Are we going to break this up or not?' said Fisher, moving over to join them. 'I can't just stand around and watch; it's bad for my reputation.'

'It's better not to butt in too early,' said Buchan. 'Let them work off some of their bile on each other first.'

'You mean we're just supposed to stand by and let people die?' said Fisher, her face falling into an ominous scowl.

'It's for the best,' said Buchan. He looked at her and smiled slightly. 'You're new to the Street, my dear. We know what we're doing.' He realised Fisher was still glaring at him, and stirred uncomfortably. 'I suppose you've got a better way?'

'A riot's a riot,' said Fisher. 'Hawk and I have handled a few in our time. You may be an expert in your territory, sir Buchan, but we're not exactly amateurs in ours.'

'Well, if we can't handle this one, you may just get a chance to show us your expertise,' said Buchan, just a little coolly.

Tomb and Rowan suddenly stood together and raised their arms in the stance of summoning. The mystic began to sing, an eerie atonal chant that cut through the din of the riot like a knife. Fights broke up, and people stopped shouting to sway unsteadily on their feet and clutch at their heads. Tomb spoke a Word of Power, and the crowd split suddenly in two, the grey and blue robes separated by some unseen force that left them in two confused crowds on opposite sides of the Street. Hawk shifted uncomfortably from foot to foot, and shook his head to clear it. The magic had only touched him briefly in passing, but he could appreciate how it must feel to those unfortunate enough to have suffered it full blast.

Rowan stopped singing, and the Street of Gods was suddenly quiet. The two crowds took their hands away from their heads and looked uncertainly around them. They spotted the God Squad, and a low rebellious murmur began, only to stop short as Buchan strode briskly forward into the middle of the Street. Hawk and Fisher looked at each other and then strode quickly after him. Whatever was going to happen next, they were determined not to be left out of it. Buchan took up a position between the two crowds, looked left and right, and then beckoned imperiously. There was a pause, and then two men came forward, one from each side. Each man's robe was the colour of his faction, one grey and one blue, but these were gorgeously styled and decorated. From their haughty expressions and bearing, and the amount of jewellery they were wearing, Hawk decided these had to be the respective High Priests of Dusk and the Chrysalis. They came to a halt before Buchan, and bowed very slightly to him, each carefully ignoring the other.

'All right,' said Buchan. 'Who started it this time?'

For a moment, Hawk thought the two priests were going to point at each other and shout 'He did!' like two children caught squabbling in the playground, but the moment passed. Both High Priests drew themselves up to their full height and glared at Buchan.

'Sir Field, sir Stoner,' said Buchan, looking from the grey robe to the blue and back again. 'I'm waiting for an answer.'

'Dusk the Devourer has been insulted,' said Field flatly.

'Dusk insults the Chrysalis by its very existence!' snapped Stoner.

'Blasphemer!'

'Heretic!'

'Liar!'

'Fraud!'

'That's enough!' said Buchan sharply, his hand dropping to the sword at his side.

The two priests quieted reluctantly, and turned their glares on Buchan rather than each other. Hawk frowned slightly. The High Priests were tense, but not cowed. They had their followers watching and neither of them was going to be the first to back down.

'I want you both to go back to your people and get them off the Street,' said Buchan. 'You know the rules. Disturbances like this are bad for business.'

'To hell with your rules and to hell with your Squad,' said Field. 'Cast your spells and be damned. The Lord Dusk will protect his children.'

'Your sorcerer and mystic can chant spells till they're blue in the face,' said Stoner. 'You won't take us by surprise again. We have our own magic-users.'

Field nodded unflinchingly. 'You're not in charge any more, Buchan. The Gods are dying and you've done nothing. From now on we defend ourselves.'

Buchan just stood there, taken aback at being so openly defied, and the silence lengthened ominously.

Hawk glanced at Fisher. 'You take blue, I'll take grey,' he said briskly, and stepped forward axe in hand to face the High Priest of Dusk the Devourer. Field looked at him warily, but held his ground. Hawk grinned unpleasantly. 'I'm Hawk, Captain of the city Guard. That's my partner, Captain Fisher. You may have heard of us. It's all true. Now get yourself and your people off the Street or I'll cut you off at the knees.'

It was Field's turn to look taken aback, but he recovered more quickly than Buchan. 'Lay a hand on me, Guard, and my followers will tear you apart.'

'Maybe,' said Hawk. 'But you'll still be dead.'

'You're bluffing.'

'Try me.'

Field met Hawk's unwavering gaze, and some of the confidence went out of him. A cold breeze touched the back of his neck as he realised the Guard meant exactly what he said. He looked over at Stoner, who was staring at Fisher like a rat mesmerised by a snake. Field looked back at Hawk and nodded slowly. He turned away to face his followers, careful to make no sudden movements that might upset the Guard. Talking slowly and calmly, he told his people the time was not yet right for direct confrontation and they should return to their homes and pray for guidance. Not far away, Stoner was putting the same message across to his people. The crowds stirred and muttered reluctantly, but eventually did as they were told. Field and Stoner turned back reluctantly to face Hawk and Fisher again.

'Very nicely done,' said Hawk. 'Now get the hell out of here. And if there's any more trouble, we'll know it's you, and we'll come looking for you.'

'Right,' said Fisher.

The two High Priests left with what dignity they could muster. Which wasn't much. Hawk looked at Buchan.

'A riot's a riot, sir Buchan. All you have to do is separate out the leaders, and break their authority.'

'You were lucky,' said Buchan tightly. 'Real fanatics would have died rather than give in.'

'But they weren't real fanatics,' said Hawk. 'I could tell.'

'What would you have done if they had turned out to be the real thing?'

Hawk grinned. 'Run like fun and screamed for the SWAT team. I'm not crazy.'

'Right,' said Fisher.

3

Gods and Devils and Other Beings

The sorcerer Tomb led Hawk and Fisher down the Street of Gods, and the crowds parted before them to give them room. Curious eyes watched the Guards pass, but no one wanted to get too close. Word of their arrival on the Street had preceded them. Hawk and Fisher nodded politely to the few brave souls who ventured a greeting, and kept their eyes open for unfriendly faces. Their encounter with the High Priests hadn't made them any friends. And besides, for no reason he could put his finger on, Hawk felt more than usually uneasy about his surroundings. The Street of Gods had changed since the last time he saw it. The buildings pressed more closely together, as though for comfort and support, and the occasional creatures and manifestations had a dangerous, openly threatening air. Even the street preachers seemed wilder, more intent on messages of destruction and damnation. The Street had grown darker, colder, more turned in upon itself. As though it wasn't sure who it could trust anymore. Hawk looked at Fisher to see if she'd noticed the changes, and saw that her hand was back resting on the pommel of her sword. Fisher liked to be prepared.

The last time they'd visited the Street of Gods, Hawk and Fisher had been acting as bodyguards for the political candidate James Adamant, as he made the rounds of sympathetic Beings, looking for support in the elections. Adamant was now Councillor Adamant, though of course that didn't necessarily prove anything. One way or the other. But though even then the Street of Gods had been a strange and eerie place, with its creatures and illusions and uncertain reality, the Street that Hawk walked now seemed somehow more sour, and more defensive. As though it was on its guard . . . Hawk frowned. Presumably even Gods could get scared, with a God killer on the loose.

Hawk scowled, and let his hand fall to the axe at his side. More and more, he was feeling very much out of his depth. He'd faced some strange things in his time, but his experience in Haven was for the most part with human killers, with their everyday schemes and passions and hatreds. He knew how to handle them. But, for better or worse, he was stuck with the God Squad now, until either he found the killer or his superiors relented. He'd just have to get used to the Street, that was all. He'd seen worse, in his time.

A group of monks came striding down the Street of Gods, arms swinging with military precision. Their robes hung loosely about them, the cowls pulled forward to hide their faces. Tomb moved to one side to let them pass, and Hawk and Fisher did the same. Anything could be dangerous on the Street of Gods, and it paid to be careful. The monks went by, looking neither left nor right. Tomb waited until they'd passed, and then continued on his way. Hawk and Fisher followed on behind.

They were on their way to look at the churches of the three murdered Beings. Rowan wasn't with them, because she wasn't feeling well. Apparently she'd been quite ill recently, and spent a lot of time in bed, dosing herself with her herbal remedies. Hawk just hoped it wasn't catching. And Buchan was off somewhere on business of his own. No one asked what. Buchan being Buchan, no one really wanted to know. Which left Tomb to act as their guide.

The first murder site was a huge, solid building right in the middle of the Street. The walls were made of great stone blocks, each of them as big as a man. The church was three storeys high, with narrow slits for windows. There was only one door, made of solid oak, and reinforced with wide steel bands. Hawk studied the building thoughtfully as Tomb fumbled with his key ring. The place looked more like a fortress than a church. Which suggested this was a religion with enemies, in the Church's mind if nowhere else. And it had to be said that worship of the Dread Lord hadn't been an exactly popular religion. Human sacrifice wasn't banned on the Street of Gods, as long as it didn't endanger the tourists, but it was frowned on. Tomb finally located the right key and unlocked the huge padlock affixed to the door. He pushed the door with his fingertips, and it swung silently open on its counterweights. Hawk studied the dark opening suspiciously.

'There's no one in there, Captain Hawk,' said Tomb reassuringly. 'After the murder was discovered I set up protective wards to keep out vandals and souvenir hunters, and they're still in place. No one's been here since I left. Follow me, please.'

Tomb walked confidently into the gloom, and Hawk and Fisher followed him in, hands hovering over their weapons. A bright blue glow appeared around the sorcerer, pushing back the darkness and illuminating the hallway. The hall was grim and oppressive, without ornament or decoration of any kind. Tomb allowed them a few moments to look around, and then led them toward a door at the far end of the hall. The front door slammed shut behind them. Hawk jumped, but wouldn't give Tomb the satisfaction of looking back. The second door opened onto a rough wooden stairway, leading down into darkness.

'Watch the steps,' said Tomb. 'Some of them are slippery, and there's no handrail.'

They followed the stairs down into the darkness for a long time. Hawk tried to keep count, but he kept losing track. By the time they reached the bottom, Hawk realised they had to be uncomfortably far beneath the city, down in the bedrock itself. Tomb gestured abruptly with his left hand, and the bright blue glow flared up, shedding its light over a larger area. Hawk and Fisher looked wonderingly about them. The stairs had brought them to a vast stone chamber, hundreds of feet in diameter. The walls were rough and unfinished, but the sharp edges left by the original cutting tools had been mostly smoothed over by air and moisture in the many years since the cavern had been hewn from the living rock.

Stalactites and stalagmites hung down from the ceiling and jutted up from the cavern floor. There were pools of dark water, and thick white patches of fungi spattered across the walls. There were cobwebs everywhere, shrouding the walls and hanging in tatters between the stalactites and stalagmites. Fisher touched one strand with a fingertip, and it stretched unnaturally before it snapped. Fisher pulled a face, and wiped her hand clean on her cloak. It was very quiet, and the slightest echo seemed to linger uncomfortably before fading away into whispers. In the middle of the cavern, the webbing had thickened and come together to form a huge hammock, hanging suspended above their heads from the thickest stalactites. It was torn and tattered now, but there was enough left to suggest the immense size of the form that had once hung within it.

'Gods come in all shapes and sizes,' said Tomb quietly. 'They can be human or inhuman, both and neither. People don't seem to care much, provided they're promised the right things.'

'You never did say what you believed in, sir Tomb,' said Fisher.

Tomb smiled. 'I'm not sure I believe in anything, anymore, my dear. Working on the Street of Gods will do that to you. It makes you doubt too many things. Or perhaps it just makes you cynical. We need Gods, all of us. They offer hope and comfort and forgiveness, and most of all they offer reassurance. We're all afraid of dying, afraid of going alone into the dark. And perhaps even more than that, we need to believe in something greater than ourselves, something to give our lives meaning and purpose.'

'What happened to the body?' said Hawk. 'I take it the Being did have a body?'

'Oh, yes, Captain Hawk. It's over there. What's left of it.'

Tomb led them across the gloomy cavern to what Hawk had taken for an exceptionally large boulder. It turned out to be a huge pile of sharp-edged objects, dark and glazed, held together in one place by strands of webbing. It took Hawk a while to work out what he was looking at, but eventually some of the shapes took on sense and meaning, and his lip curled in disgust. Going by the size of the carapace segments and the many jointed legs, the Dread Lord had been more insect than anything else. The pile of broken pieces stood nearly ten feet tall, and was easily as broad. The Being itself must have been huge. Hawk shivered involuntarily. He'd never liked insects.

'Was it in pieces like this when you found it?' he said finally.

'More or less,' said Tomb. 'The pieces were strewn across the floor of the chamber. Whatever killed this Being tore the body apart as though it were nothing but paper. Its followers . . . tidied it up.'

'So the killer has to be immensely strong,' said Fisher. She thought for a moment, staring at the pile before her. 'This . . . dismembering – was it done while the Being was still alive, or after it was dead?'

'I don't know,' said Tomb. 'I hadn't really thought about it. How can you tell?'

'By the amount of blood,' said Hawk. 'It stops flowing after you're dead. So if there's not much blood splashed around a dismembered body, it's a safe enough bet the victim was dead at the time. You learn things like that in the Northside.'

'I see,' said Tomb. 'Most interesting. But not much help here, I'm afraid. The Dread Lord didn't have any blood. Its body was hollow.'

Hawk and Fisher looked at each other. 'This case gets better all the time,' said Fisher.

'Do we have any clues as to the motive?' said Hawk. 'Did the Dread Lord have any particular enemies or rivals? Someone who might profit by its death?'

Tomb shook his head. 'There was no feud or vendetta as far as we can tell. The Dread Lord hadn't been on the Street long enough to acquire that kind of enemy.'

'All right,' said Hawk patiently. 'Let's try something simpler. Do we know when the murder took place?'

'Some time during the early hours of the morning, nine days ago. The High Priest came down to consult with his God about whatever nihilists consider important, and found his God scattered across the cavern floor.'

'Can we question him about it?' said Fisher.

'Not easily,' said Tomb. 'The High Priest and all the Dread Lord's followers are dead. Suicide. That's nihilists for you.'

'Great,' said Hawk. 'No witnesses to the murder, no clues at the scene of the crime, and no one left to question. I've only been on this case a few hours, and already it's driving me crazy. Nothing in this damned case makes sense. I mean, how did the killer get down here? I assume the church was well-guarded?'

'Oh, yes,' said Tomb. 'Over a hundred armed guards, supplied by the Brotherhood of Steel. No one saw anything.'

'I hate this case,' said Fisher.

'This is the Street of Gods, Captain Fisher. Normal rules and logic don't apply here.'

Hawk looked at the pile of broken and splintered chitin that had once been worshipped as a God, shook his head slowly, and turned his back on it. 'We're not going to learn anything useful here. I'll call in the forensic sorcerers, and see what they can turn up.' He stopped. Tomb was shaking his head. 'All right. What's wrong now?'

'I don't think the Beings would allow that kind of investigative sorcery on their territory. The Gods must have their mysteries.'

'Even though the sorcerers might come up with something to keep them alive?'

'Even then.'

'Damn. In that case, we'll just have to do it the hard way. Take us to the next murder site, sir Tomb. And let's hope we can dig up something useful there.'

At first glance it was just an ordinary house. Two storeys, slate roof, good brickwork. Windows and brasswork had been recently cleaned. It looked as out of place on the Street of Gods as a lamb in a wolfpack. Tomb knocked politely on the door, and there was a long pause.

'Are you sure this is the right place?' said Fisher. 'This is the closest I've ever seen to archetypal merchant-class housing. All it needs is a rococo boot-scraper and a lion's-head door-knocker and it'd be perfect. What kind of God would live here?'

'The Sundered Man,' said Tomb. 'And he doesn't live here anymore. He was murdered six days ago. Show some respect, Captain, please.'

They waited some more. People passed by on the Street of Gods, going about their business in the warm summer sun, but all of them seemed to have some kind of smile for the people waiting outside the tacky little two up, two down merchant's house. Fisher took to glaring indiscriminately at anyone who even looked in their direction.

'Are you sure there's somebody in there?' said Hawk.

'There's a caretaker,' said Tomb. 'Sister Anna. I contacted her earlier today, and she said she'd be here.'

There was the sound of bolts being drawn back from

inside, and they turned to face the door again. It swung suddenly open, revealing a plain-faced, average-looking woman in her late forties. She was dressed well but not expensively, in a style that had last been fashionable a good ten years ago. She looked tired and drawn, and somehow defeated by life. She smiled briefly at Hawk and Fisher, and bowed politely to Tomb.

'Good day, sir sorcerer, Captains. I'm sorry I took so long, but all the others have left now, and I have to do everything myself. Please, come in.'

She stood back, and Tomb led the two Guards into the hall. It was just as narrow and gloomy as Hawk had expected, with bare floorboards and plain wood panelling on the walls. But everything was neat and tidy, and the simple furniture glowed from recent polishing. Sister Anna shut the door, and slid home four heavy bolts. She caught Hawk looking at her, and smiled self-consciously.

'Our God has been dead barely a week, and already the vultures are gathering on the Street. If sir Tomb hadn't put protective wards round the house on his first visit, they'd have torn the place apart by now, searching for objects of power and whatever loot they could lay their hands on. Not that they'd have found much of either. We were never a rich or powerful Order. We had our God, and his teachings, and that was all. It was enough. As it is, the memory of the wards keep most of them away, and the locks and bolts take care of the rest. This way, please.'

She led them into a pleasant little drawing room, and saw them all comfortably seated before departing for the kitchen to get them some tea. Hawk slipped his hand inside his shirt and felt for the bone amulet that hung from his neck. It was still and quiet to his touch. If there was any magic left inside the house, it was so small the amulet couldn't detect it. Hawk took his hand away from the amulet and looked round the drawing room. It was comfortably appointed, but nothing special. Cups and saucers had been carefully laid out on the table, along with milk and sugar and paper-lace doilies. Hawk looked hard at Tomb.

'What the hell is going on here, sir sorcerer?'

Tomb smiled slightly. 'You'll find all kinds on the Street of Gods, Captain Hawk. Allow me to tell you the story of the Sundered Man. It's really very interesting. His life until his twenty-fourth year was quiet, comfortable, and quite uninteresting to anyone save himself. He was a junior clerk in the shipping offices. A little dull, but good prospects. And then the miracle happened. For reasons we still don't understand, he took it into his head to visit the Street of Gods. And whilst there he started to perform wonders and speak prophecy. For twenty-four hours he walked the Street of Gods, wrapped in Power and dispensing miracles. And then . . . something happened. His followers called it the final miracle. He levitated into the air, smiled at something only he could see, and never moved again. He had somehow become sundered from Time; frozen in a single moment of eternity. Unmoving, unchanging, never ageing. Nothing could reach him, or harm him, or affect him in any way.

'It was never a very big religion, but those who'd been with him on that day, and saw his wonders and heard him preach, proved very loyal. They believed their man had become more than human, a God who had stepped outside of Time to commune with realities beyond our own. One day, he would return and share his knowledge with the faithful. That was twenty-two years ago. They waited all that time, and then somebody killed their God.'

'But why build a house like this on the Street of Gods?' said Hawk. 'Why not a church or temple, like everyone else?'

'This was his house,' said Sister Anna. 'Or as near as we could get to duplicating it. We built it around him, room by room. We wanted him to feel at home when he returned.'

She put her tray down on the table, picked up the china teapot and silver tea-strainer, and poured tea for all of them. She finally sat down facing them, and they all sipped their tea in silence for a while. Hawk studied her over his cup. There were deep lines in her face, and her eyes had a bruised, puffy look, as though she'd been crying recently. Her shoulders were slumped, and her gaze was polite but unfocused. *Delayed shock*, thought Hawk. *The longer you stave it off, the harder it finally hits*. He looked at Tomb and raised an eyebrow, but the sorcerer seemed content to leave the questioning to him. Hawk looked at Sister Anna and cleared his throat.

'When did you first discover your God was dead?' he asked carefully, trying not to sound too officious.

'Four o'clock in the morning, six days ago,' said Sister Anna. Her voice was calm and even. 'One of our people was always with him, so that he wouldn't be alone when he finally returned to us. Brother John was on duty. He went to sleep. He didn't know why. It wasn't like him. When he awoke, the God was no longer standing by the altar we made for him. He was lying crumpled on the floor, a knife in his heart. The blood was everywhere. Brother John spread the alarm, but there was no trace of the killer. We still don't know how he got in or out.'

'Can we speak to this Brother John?' said Hawk.

'I'm afraid not. He took poison, later that day. He wasn't the only one. We all went a little crazy for a while.'

'I understand.'

'No you don't, Captain.' Sister Anna looked at him squarely. 'For twenty-two years we'd waited, devoting our lives to the Sundered Man, only to find it was all a lie. He wasn't a God after all. Gods don't bleed and die. He was just a man; a man with power perhaps, but nothing more. I'm the only one left now. The others are all gone. Some killed themselves. Some went home, to the families they'd given up for their God. Some went to look for a new God to worship. Some went mad. They all left, as the days passed and our God stayed dead.'

For a while, nobody said anything.

'Is the body still there?' said Fisher finally.

'Oh, yes,' said Sister Anna. 'None of us wanted to move him. We didn't even want to touch him.'

She led the way up the narrow stairs to the next floor and ushered them into a small, cosy bedroom. The Sundered Man was lying on the floor, curled around the knife that had killed him. There was dried blood all around the body, but no sign of any struggle. Hawk knelt down beside the dead man. There was only the one wound; no cuts to the hands or arms to suggest he'd tried to fend off his attacker. It was a standard-looking knife hilt; the kind you could buy anywhere in Haven. The dead man's face was calm and peaceful. Hawk got to his feet again, and shook his head slowly.

'There's nothing here to help us. Nothing I can see, anyway. Sister Anna, do you have any objections to our calling in the forensic sorcerers?'

'No,' said Sister Anna. 'Do as you wish, Captain. It really doesn't matter.'

'Why did you stay?' said Fisher. 'All the others left, but you stayed. What keeps you here?'

Sister Anna looked down at the body, and smiled slightly. 'I was there, on the Street of Gods, twenty-two years ago, when it all began. I was just passing through, but he looked at me and smiled, and I stopped to hear him preach. He was magnificent. When he left I went with him, and from that moment on, I was always at his side. After he was taken from us, sundered from Time, I made this place my home, and waited for him to come back to me.

'How could I leave him? It didn't matter to me whether he was a God or a man. I stayed because I loved him, and always have.'

The church of the Carmadine Stalker turned out to be a

door in a wall. To one side of the door stood a pleasant little chapel of the Bright Lady, all flowers and vines and pastel colours. On the other side was an open, airy temple dedicated to the January Man. The door itself didn't look like much. It was six feet high and three feet wide, with peeling paint, splintering wood, and a large discoloured steel padlock. It was the kind of door that in Hawk's experience usually fronted lock-up warehouses down by the docks, specialising in the kind of goods no one would publicly admit to wanting. He studied the door thoughtfully, aware that Tomb was watching him and waiting for him to comment. Obviously Tomb expected him to get all upset again. He was damned if he'd give the sorcerer the satisfaction.

'All right,' he said equably. 'It's a door. Do we knock or go straight in?'

'I'd better lead the way,' said Tomb. 'The Stalkers don't care for uninvited guests, with or without Council authority.'

'Wait a minute,' said Fisher. 'If the Carmadine Stalker has been murdered, why are his followers still hanging around here?'

'They're waiting for him to rise from the dead. With all due respect, Captain Fisher, Captain Hawk, I think we should keep this visit as short and to the point as possible. The Carmadine Stalker was an unpleasant God of an extremely unpleasant Order. If his followers were to take exception to our presence, I'm not at all sure we'd get out of their lair alive.'

'Don't worry,' said Hawk. 'We've been around. It takes a lot to upset us.'

Tomb looked at him for a moment, and then turned to face the door. He gestured at the padlock, and it snapped open. He pushed the door, and it swung back, revealing a sickly green light. Tomb stepped forward into it. Hawk started to follow and then stopped short as the smell hit him. It was a thick, choking smell of corruption and decay. The green light seemed to take on a more sinister aspect, reminding Hawk of the corpse fires that danced on recently built cairns. He braced himself and followed Tomb into the light. Fisher followed close behind, her hand at her sword belt.

The door slammed shut behind them, and they found themselves in a long brick tunnel, slanting downwards, lit only by the eerie green light that came from everywhere and nowhere. The tunnel was only just tall enough for Fisher to stand upright, and no more than three or four feet wide. The brick walls were cracked and crumbling from age and neglect, and the floor was covered with pools of dark, scummy water. Mosses and fungi pockmarked the brick-work, and the smell of death and decay was almost over-powering. Far off in the distance a bell tolled endlessly, like the slow remorseless beating of a great brazen heart.

'What the hell is this place?' said Fisher, glaring warily down the tunnel.

'We're in the Stalkers' domain,' said Tomb quietly. 'A pocket dimension, attached to our reality but not actually a part of it. Follow me, please.'

Tomb led the two Guards through an endless maze of narrow brick tunnels that twisted and turned and folded back upon themselves. The bell tolled on and on in the distance, but never seemed to draw any closer. Moisture dripped from the low ceiling and ran down the walls in sudden little streams. Hawk kept a wary eye on where they were going, but even so, the first priest caught him by surprise. The scrawny figure was sitting cross-legged in a niche set into the tunnel wall. He was old and shrivelled, corpse-pale and quite naked. Bones pushed out against his taut flesh. His breathing was slow and shallow, and his eyes were closed. A length of discoloured steel chain ran from a heavy ring set in the wall to a great steel hook buried in the priest's shoulder. The tip of the hook poked out of the priest's flesh just below the armpit. From the way the puckered skin had healed around the sharp point, the hook had obviously been there a long time.

Tomb and the two Guards moved ahead quietly, trying to make as little noise as possible, but still the priest's eyelids crawled open as they passed. Hawk froze in his tracks, his hand at his axe. The priest had no eyes, only empty sockets, but still his head turned to face Hawk. He smiled slowly, revealing filed pointed teeth, and then his eyelids closed again. Hawk nodded to Fisher and Tomb, and they moved on. They passed more priests, from time to time, sitting unmoving in their niches in the walls. None of them stirred or spoke, but they all watched with empty eye sockets as the intruders passed.

And finally they came to a large, echoing chamber, empty save for a huge brass throne set in the centre of the open space. On the throne sprawled what was left of the Carmadine Stalker. Hawk moved slowly forward, keeping a watchful eye on the other tunnels leading off from the chamber. He stopped before the throne and wrinkled his nose at the remains of the Stalker. The discoloured bones were held together by rotting scraps of muscle, and the grinning skull had been stripped almost clean of flesh. The Carmadine Stalker was an ugly sight in death, and had probably looked even worse when it was alive. It had to have been at least eight feet tall, with a broad chest and a wide flat head. The arms and legs were too long, and much thicker than a man's. There were vicious talons on the hands and feet, and the grinning teeth were long and pointed. Hawk tried to imagine what the thing must have looked like in its prime, and for a moment his breath caught in his throat.

'The Stalker was a grisly kind of God,' said Tomb. His voice was hushed, as though he was afraid of waking . . . something. 'Its religion was based around ritual sacrifice, mutilation, and cannibalism. Let's keep this short, Captain Hawk. This is a bad place to be. It's going to get even worse when the Stalkers realise their God isn't going to rise from the dead.'

'All right,' said Hawk. 'Let's start at the beginning. How was the Stalker killed?'

'Apparently it aged to death overnight, three days ago. According to city records, the Stalker was at least seven hundred years old. From the look of that body, I'd say a lot of those years finally caught up with it.'

'So the killer was a magic-user,' said Fisher.

'Either that, or someone with an object of Power. Such things aren't exactly rare on the Street of Gods.'

Hawk took a quick look round the empty chamber, but no obvious clues leapt to his gaze. 'Is there anyone here we can talk to, about how the killer got in and out?'

'No one here will talk to us, Captain. We're unbelievers.'

'Then let's get the hell out of here. This place looks more like a trap every minute.'

Tomb nodded, and headed quickly for the tunnel mouth that had brought them there. Fisher followed close behind, sword in hand. Hawk backed out of the chamber, keeping a careful watch on the dead God all the way. He had a strong feeling that at any moment the tattered corpse might raise its bony head and look at him . . . He kept watching it until he reached a bend in the tunnel which cut off his view, and then he turned and hurried after Tomb and Fisher. The great brass bell tolled on, its slow sonorous sound prophesying blood and doom.

Tomb led them confidently back through the maze of brick tunnels, and then stopped suddenly and bit his lip. Hawk frowned. By his reckoning, they were barely halfway back to the door on the Street of Gods. Tomb stood very still, his gaze vague and far away. Hawk looked quickly about him. The tunnel stretched off in both directions, silent and empty, bathed in the sickly light of the ubiquitous green glow.

'Something's coming,' said Tomb softly.

Hawk drew his axe and Fisher hefted her sword. 'What kind of something?' said Hawk.

'A group of men. A large group. Maybe as many as twenty. All of them armed. Apparently the Carmadine Stalker's followers don't want us to leave.' Tomb shivered suddenly, and his gaze cleared. 'I may be wrong, but I think it's very likely they're planning on sacrificing us to their God, in the hope it will help him return.'

'All right,' said Hawk. 'You're the sorcerer. Do something.'

'It's not that simple,' said Tomb.

Fisher grimaced. 'I had a feeling he was going to say that.'

'There are things I can do,' said the sorcerer, 'but in this dimension they take time to prepare. You'll just have to hold them off for a while.'

Hawk and Fisher looked at each other. 'Hold them off,' said Hawk.

'Twenty men,' said Fisher.

'All religious fanatics, and armed to the teeth.'

'Piece of cake.'

The two Guards fell silent. In the darkness of one of the side tunnels, someone was moving. Whoever it was, was trying to be quiet, but even the faintest of sounds travelled clearly in the quiet of the tunnels. Hawk and Fisher stood side by side, weapons at the ready. Tomb gave the tunnel a quick glance, and then began muttering something under his breath. The first of the Stalkers came charging out of the side tunnel, and Hawk braced himself to meet him. The Stalker was tall and wiry, with a wide grin and staring eyes. He wore a dark, flapping robe, and carried a vicious-looking scimitar. He threw himself at Hawk, the curved blade reaching for the Guard's throat. Hawk batted the sword aside easily, and buried the axe in the Stalker's face on the backswing. The Stalker fell to his knees, blood coursing down his grinning face, and then he crumpled to the floor as Hawk jerked the axe free.

More Stalkers came boiling out of the side tunnel, their eyes glaring wildly. Swords and axes gleamed in the eerie green light. Hawk and Fisher launched themselves at their attackers. The flood of Stalkers stumbled to a sudden halt as Hawk and Fisher slammed into them. Hawk swung his axe in short, vicious arcs, and Stalkers fell dead and dying to the floor. Fisher stamped and thrust at his side, warding off the few Stalkers with reflexes fast enough to start their own attacks. Blood splashed the tunnel walls and collected in pools on the floor.

The narrow tunnel meant that only a few of the Stalkers could press their attack at one time, and Hawk and Fisher were more than a match for them. But even so, the fanatical hatred and fervour of the Stalkers drove them forward over the bodies of the slain, and step by step Hawk and Fisher were driven back down the tunnel. Tomb retreated behind them, still lost in his muttering.

Hawk swung his axe double-handed, trying to open up some space before him, but the press of bodies was too strong. Everywhere he looked there were darting swords and glaring eyes and pointed teeth bared in snarling smiles. Fisher gutted a Stalker with a quick economical cut, and turned to face the next attacker while the first was still falling. A sharp jolt of surprise went through her as the dying Stalker grabbed her legs with both arms and tried to bring her down. She met a flailing sword with an automatic parry, and tried to kick the Stalker away, but he hung on with grim determination. Blood from his wound soaked her trousers. The first twinges of panic had begun to gnaw at Fisher's self-control, when Hawk spotted her problem and cut through the Stalker's neck with his axe. The Stalker went limp and fell away, and Fisher kicked herself free. The whole thing had only taken a moment or two, but there was a cold sweat on Fisher's forehead as she hurled herself back into the fray.

I must be getting old, she thought sourly, *getting caught like that. Ten-to-one odds never used to bother me, either. Maybe I should get out of this business while I'm still ahead.*

She cut down one Stalker, gutted a second, and blinded a third. Blood flew on the air, and she grinned nastily.

Forget it; I'd be bored in a week.

The Stalker before her paused suddenly, his mouth gaping with surprise, and then his head exploded. Blood and brains spattered the tunnel roof and walls as Fisher jumped back, startled. There was a series of brisk popping sounds, and within the space of a few moments the tunnel floor was littered with headless bodies. Hawk and Fisher lowered their weapons, looked at each other, and then turned to stare at Tomb.

'Sorry it took so long,' said the sorcerer calmly, 'but that kind of spell is rather tricky to work out. You have to be very careful where you put the decimal point.' He stopped suddenly, his head cocked to one side, listening to something only he could hear. 'I think it might be wise to press on. There are more Stalkers on their way. Rather more than I can handle, I'm afraid.'

'Then what the hell are we standing around here for?' snapped Hawk. 'Move it!'

He pushed Tomb ahead of him, and the three of them ran swiftly through the brick tunnels, heading for the outside world. They hadn't gone far when they heard the sound of running feet behind them. Hawk and Fisher ran faster, urging Tomb on. He led them through the maze of tunnels with unwavering confidence, and suddenly they were through the doorway and out on the Street of Gods, blinking dazedly in the bright summer sun. Tomb turned to face the door, gestured sharply, and the door disappeared, leaving a blank wall behind it.

'That should hold them,' said Tomb. 'Long enough for us to make ourselves scarce, anyway. I trust you found the visit useful?'

'Sure,' said Hawk, his breathing slowly getting back to

normal. 'Nothing like being chased by an army of murderous fanatics to give you a good workout.'

'Good,' said Tomb. 'Because I'm afraid I have to leave you now. I do have other work to attend to, you know.' He produced a folded piece of paper from a hidden pocket, and handed it to Hawk. 'This is a list of Beings who may agree to speak to you. It would help you to have an overview of what's happening on the Street of Gods at the moment. Beyond that, I'm afraid I really don't know what else to suggest. Tracking down murderers is a little outside my experience.'

'We'll cope,' said Fisher. 'We're Captains of the Guard; we don't need our hands held. Right, Hawk?'

'Right,' said Hawk.

'I'm relieved to hear it,' said Tomb. 'If you need me again, or any other member of the Squad, just ask around. Someone will always know where we are. It's part of our job to have a high profile. Good day.'

He bowed politely to them both, and then set off down the Street at a pace obviously calculated to prevent any further discussion. Hawk looked at Fisher.

'He knows something. Something he doesn't want us asking him about. I wonder what.'

Fisher shrugged. 'On the Street of Gods, that could cover a whole lot of territory.'

Charles Buchan sat on the edge of his chair, and waited impatiently for them to bring Annette to him. The Sisters of Joy were officially classed as a religion, and had one of the largest establishments on the Street of Gods, but when you got right down to it, their lounge looked like nothing more than an upmarket brothel. Which wasn't really that far from the mark, if you thought about it.

The Sisters of Joy were an old established religion. Older than Haven itself, some said. It had branches all across the Low Kingdoms, to the impotent fury of equally old and established, but more conservative, religions. The Sisters had started out as temple prostitutes for a now forgotten fertility Goddess, probably not unlike the Bright Lady, and had somehow evolved through their discovery of tantric magic into something far more powerful. Not to mention sinister.

Tantric magic is based on sex, or to be more exact, sexuality. Basically, the Sisters of Joy drained people's strength and vitality through sex, leeching at their very life force. The stolen energy gave them greatly extended life spans, and made them powerful magicians, but only as long as the energy level was maintained. They needed a lot of people to maintain their power and their long lives, but human nature being what it was, the Sisters were never short of visitors. Or victims, depending on how you looked at it.

Tantric magic wasn't strictly speaking part of the High Magic at all, having its roots squarely in the older, less reputable Wild Magic, which was partly why most modern sorcerers would have nothing to do with it. The other reason was that women were a hell of a lot better at tantric magic than men, and the High Magic was still largely a male province. So the High Magic was socially acceptable, while tantric magic very definitely was not. The Sisters of Joy didn't give a damn. They went their own way, as they always had. Their doors were always open, day and night, to those who came to them in need or despair. The Sisters offered care and comfort and affection, and in return bound all who came to them in a tightening web of emotional dependency and obligation. There were those who said the Sisters of Joy were addictive, and that those who fell under their influence became little more than slaves. No one said it too loudly, or too publicly, of course. It wouldn't have been wise.

Buchan got up out of his chair, and began to pace up and down. They would bring Annette to him soon.

The lounge was almost indecently luxurious. A thick pile carpet covered the floor, and the walls had disappeared behind a profusion of paintings and hanging tapestries, most of them obscene. Perfumes sweetened the air. There were comfortable chairs and settees and love seats, and delicately crafted tables bearing wines and spirits and cordials, and every kind of drug or potion. Nothing was forbidden here, and it was all free. To begin with. The Sisters of Joy had amassed a considerable fortune over the many centuries, and they still received very generous donations from their grateful clients. No one ever mentioned blackmail, of course. It wouldn't have been wise.

With an effort, Buchan stopped himself pacing. It was a sign of weakness, and he couldn't afford to be weak. He looked again at the brass-bound clock on the mantelpiece, and frowned. He couldn't stay long, or Tomb and Rowan might wonder where he was. They might ask questions. So might Hawk and Fisher. He would have to be careful around the two Guards. They had a reputation for sniffing out secrets and getting to the bottom of things. Buchan was always careful to go disguised when he made his visits to the Sisters of Joy, but no disguise was perfect, especially on the Street of Gods. Still, only the Quality knew for sure of his connection with the Sisters, and they didn't know as much as they thought they did. And when you got right down to it, the chances of the city aristocracy deigning to discuss such matters with the likes of Hawk and Fisher were pretty damned remote.

The Quality wouldn't discuss one of their own with outsiders. Even if they had disowned him.

He smiled slightly. It wasn't that long ago he'd been an important figure in the Quality, a member in good standing and much in demand. No one cared about his reputation then; it just gave them something juicy to gossip about. The Quality do so love their gossip. But even the most sybaritic, most debauched member of the Quality had drawn the line at his associating with the Sisters of Joy. The Sisters were beyond the pale, utterly forbidden. First his friends talked to him about it, and then his enemies. His Family forbade him to visit the Sisters, on pain of disowning him. But he couldn't stay away, and he wouldn't tell them why, so in the end the Quality had turned their back on him, and his Family had cut him off without a penny.

He didn't care. Not really. He had a new life in the God Squad, and he had his Annette.

And then the door opened, and she came in. His breath caught in his throat as it always did, and he stood there for a long moment, just drinking in the sight of her. She was tall and slender and graceful and very lovely. Long blond hair curled down around her shoulders, and her eyes were the same blue as his own. She smiled at him, the special smile she saved for him and him alone, and ran forward into his waiting arms.

Tomb slowly climbed the stairs to Rowan's room, a silver tray floating on the air beside him, bearing a cup of steaming tea. The sorcerer was worried about Rowan. She'd been ill on and off for months now, and she still wouldn't let anyone call in a doctor to see her. She didn't believe in doctors, preferring to dose herself with her own foul mixtures. Tomb didn't know what went into them, but every time Rowan prepared a fresh batch in the kitchen, the cook threatened to quit. Having smelt the fumes himself on more than one occasion, Tomb didn't blame her. If the smell had been any stronger, you could have used it to pebble-dash walls. Tomb's mouth twitched, but he was too worried to smile. Rowan had been taking her vile doses for weeks, and she was still no better. If her condition didn't improve soon, he'd bring in a doctor, no matter what she said. He couldn't stand to see her looking so drawn and tired.

He moved quietly along the landing and stopped outside

Rowan's door. He knocked politely, and glared at the tea tray when it showed signs of wavering. There was no reply, and he knocked again. He looked round vaguely as he waited. Rowan rarely answered the first few knocks. She liked her privacy, and often she didn't care for company. Rowan had never been what you'd call sociable. Tomb sighed quietly, and shifted his weight from one foot to the other.

The house seemed very quiet. Buchan was out, and it was the servants' day off. Tomb had been a member of the God Squad for almost eleven years now, and he knew the house and its moods well. Of late, however, the quiet seemed to have an almost sinister nature; a quiet of unspoken words and too many secrets. Of course, the house was used to secrets. No one came to the God Squad with an entirely clean past. Which was probably why so few of them stayed long. It wasn't everyone who could cope with the eccentric realities of the Street of Gods. Tomb had seen many warriors and mystics come and go down the years. He hoped Rowan would stay. She was special. He knocked on the door again, a little louder.

'Rowan? It's me, Tomb. I thought you might like a nice cup of tea. Can I come in?'

There was still no reply. Tomb opened the door and entered quietly, the tea tray floating uncertainly behind him. Rowan was fast asleep, looking small and helpless and worrisomely frail in the oversized bed. Tomb pushed the door shut, and the tea tray flew forward and settled on the table beside the bed. Rowan stirred slowly without waking, and then settled again. She'd disarrayed the bedclothes in her sleep, like a fretful child, and Tomb moved quietly forward to straighten them. He stood back, looked round the room, and then looked at Rowan again. She seemed to be sleeping peacefully now. There didn't seem to be anything else he could do. There was no reason for him to stay.

He sat down on the chair beside the bed. The room was the same featureless square as his own, but she'd done more to personalise hers in the comparatively short time she'd been there than he had in all his eleven years. There were oil paintings on the walls that she'd executed herself. They showed promise. A cuddly toy with a stitched-on smile lay on the floor beside the bed. Rowan liked to take it to bed with her when the others were away on cases and she was left alone in the house at night. Tomb could understand that. There are times we all need something to cling to in the night. The rug on the floor was a new addition. Tomb had spent a whole afternoon in the markets with her, trying to find one just the right shade to complement the bedclothes.

She stirred again in her sleep, and Tomb looked at her quickly, but she didn't waken. Tomb sat and watched her for a while. He liked to watch her. He could quite happily have sat where he was all day and all night, watching over her, caring for her. Loving her. He smiled slightly. He never used the word love except in his thoughts. He'd told her once how he felt about her, after an hour or so of talking around the subject while he worked up his nerve, and the best he could say of the outcome was that at least she hadn't laughed at him. She just told him that she didn't care for him, and seemed to think that was the end of it. Tomb smiled tiredly. If only it was that easy. He hadn't asked to fall in love with her. She wasn't especially bright or pretty. But she owned his heart and always would, and there wasn't a damn thing he could do about it.

Reluctantly he got to his feet. Rowan could wake up anytime now, and he'd better not be here when she did. He didn't want to upset her. He left the room quietly, and eased the door shut behind him. He made his way back down the stairs, frowning slightly as he tried to work out what he ought to do next. There was a hell of a lot of paperwork that needed seeing to, but then there always was. It could wait a little longer. He supposed he could take a walk down the Street, talk to people, get a feel of how the Street was reacting to Hawk and Fisher's arrival.

Or he could go to see Le Bel Inconnu.

He stopped at the bottom of the stairs. He couldn't go now. It was far too dangerous, with Hawk and Fisher out on the Street. They wouldn't understand. But he couldn't stay away either. It was already too long since his last visit. He glanced back up the stairs. Rowan would be all right. The protective wards around the house would make sure she wasn't disturbed. And if she wanted anything, she only had to call and Tomb would hear her, wherever he was. She knew that.

He hurried down the hall, took his cloak from the rack, and swung it round his shoulders. He pulled the hood forward, adjusting it so that its shadow covered his face. He could have used a disguise spell, but there were too many places on the Street where magic couldn't be relied on.

And this was too important to take unnecessary risks.

The sorcerer Tomb opened the door with a wave of his hand, and went out onto the Street of Gods.

Hawk and Fisher slogged up and down the Street of Gods, working their way through the list of names Tomb had given them. Hours passed, but the sun overhead didn't move. It was noon on the Street of Gods, and had been for several days. Robed acolytes hurried past them on unknown missions, heads bowed to show respect and humility, and to avoid having to see churches and temples more splendid than their own. The street preachers were still working themselves into hysterical rages and setting fire to each other, but no one was paying much attention except the tourists. Hawk and Fisher tramped grimly back and forth, getting what information they could from the Beings that Tomb had named as potentially helpful, and doing their best to ignore the wonders and terrors that thronged the Street.

The Night People were an old necromantic sect, not as well-supported as they had once been. Their High Priest met Hawk and Fisher in the Ossuary, the Cathedral of Bone. Intricate patterns of polished bones formed the floor and walls and ceilings of the Ossuary. Some were recognisably human. Others were so large and grotesque that Hawk preferred not to think about where they might have come from originally. The air smelt of musk and cinnamon, and strange lights flickered in far off windows. All the time they were there, Hawk had a strong feeling they were being watched, as though something awful and implacable lurked just out of sight, waiting patiently for him to drop his guard. He kept his hand near his axe.

The Night People were blind, their eyelids stitched together, but they all moved and spoke with an eerie certainty that bordered on the unnerving. Hawk did his best to ignore the uneasy prickling on the back of his neck, and asked to see the nameless Being the Night People worshipped. The High Priest shook his head slowly. Only the faithful might see God, and that sight was so glorious it burned out the eyes of all who saw. Hawk tried to press the matter further, but the High Priest would not be moved. He wouldn't even ask questions on the Guards' behalf. Neither would he allow them to question the faithful. No one knew anything that might help the Guards. No one knew anything about the God killings. No one knew anything about anything.

Hawk and Fisher went from church to temple to meeting-house, and the message was always the same. The Hanged Man was polite but unhelpful. Sweet Corruption wasn't even polite. The Lord of the New Flesh refused even to see them.

And so it went the length of the Street, until finally they came to the Legion of the Primevil. The Legion's church was a tall building of spires and domes and crenellated towers. There were magnificent stained-glass windows, and flags and banners in a dozen different hues. Some other time Hawk might have been impressed, but as it was, all he could think of was his aching feet. It had been a long day.

The Legion priests, however, were frankly disturbing. Each and every one had a staring alien eye embedded somewhere in his flesh. It was large and crimson with a dark split pupil, and it blazed unblinkingly from forehead, chest, or hand. In a few cases it had displaced one of the priest's original eyes, and it bulged uncomfortably in the too-small socket, glaring balefully at the world. Legend had it that the Legion was the means whereby an ancient Being from another plane of existence was able to observe the world of men.

The High Priest seemed happy enough to talk to Hawk and Fisher, but could do little to help them. With three Beings murdered in a matter of weeks, gossip ran wild on the Street of Gods. But no one knew anything for sure. People were scared. So were some of the Beings. Everyone was looking for a villain; someone to blame and strike back at. No one had mentioned God War yet, but everyone was thinking about it.

Hawk and Fisher talked with the High Priest for some time, trying to avoid staring at the great crimson eye that glared unblinkingly from his forehead. Nothing much came of it until right at the end, when the High Priest suddenly leaned forward on his throne and fixed Hawk with his unnerving stare.

'Tell me, Captain. Have you ever heard of the Hellfire Club?'

'No,' said Hawk cautiously. 'Can't say that I have.' He looked at Fisher, and she shook her head slightly.

The High Priest leaned back on his throne, his expression unreadable beneath the glowing third eye. 'Ask Charles Buchan, Captain. He knows.'

And that was all he would say. In a matter of minutes the two Guards were back on the Street again, not much wiser than when they'd started. It was still midday, and the air was uncomfortably warm. Hawk and Fisher decided simultaneously that what they really needed to help put things in perspective was a stiff drink. Or two. Accordingly, they made their way to the nearest temple dedicated to John Barleycorn, and ordered a ceremonial libation in tall glasses. They took their drinks and settled into a private booth at the back of the temple where the lights were comfortably dim. Hawk stretched out his legs with a luxurious sigh, and propped his aching feet on a nearby chair. Fisher took off one of her boots and massaged her toes. Some moments were just too precious to interrupt, but eventually they turned their attention to their drinks, and the matter at hand.

'All right,' said Hawk. 'Let's run through what we've got. Three Beings are dead. Since they are dead, I think it's safe to call them Beings rather than Gods. The Dread Lord died nine days ago. His body had been torn apart. The Sundered Man was stabbed to death six days ago. And the Carmadine Stalker apparently aged to death three days ago. Doesn't take a genius to spot the pattern, does it?'

'A murder every three days,' said Fisher. 'With another due sometime today, if the pattern continues.'

'Right,' said Hawk. 'And there's nothing we can do to prevent it. We don't have enough information, and no one will talk to us.'

Fisher smiled briefly. 'Why should the Street of Gods be any different from the rest of Haven?'

Hawk sniffed. 'Anywhere else, I could persuade someone to talk to us. But the mystic was right; strong-arm tactics aren't going to work here. If I start shoving my axe in a Being's face, I'll probably end up snapping at flies on a lily pad. Intimidation is very definitely out. That just leaves diplomacy.'

'I'll leave it to you,' said Fisher. 'I don't have the knack.'

'I had noticed,' said Hawk. 'What do we have on the

killer? He comes and goes at will, even when the temples are heavily guarded by well-armed fanatics. Which means he's either invisible, which means a sorcerer, or a master of disguise. Or it's someone they expect to see, someone they don't recognise as a threat.

'Each Being died in a different way, and as far as we can tell, none of them had anything in common. So how does the killer choose his victims? At random? Dammit, I don't even know where to start on this case, Isobel.'

'Don't give up so easily. Look at it this way. The killer has to be immensely strong, and able to pass unseen. So how about a supernatural killer, like a vampire? He could get past the guards by shapeshifting into a bat or a mist, and he'd be more than strong enough to tear apart the Dread Lord. It would even explain why all the killings took place in the early hours of the morning.'

Hawk thought about it. 'It's a possibility, lass, but I can't believe the Beings wouldn't have protective wards specifically designed to keep out supernatural vermin like that. Everybody else does, that can afford them. No, Isobel; I think magic is the key here.'

'You mean a rogue sorcerer?'

'Maybe. An invisibility spell would get him past the wards and the guards, and then he could use magic to blast apart the Dread Lord and age the Stalker to death.'

'But then why use a knife on the Sundered Man?'

'To be misleading.'

'That makes my head hurt,' said Fisher. She took a long drink from her glass, and frowned hard as she concentrated. 'Wait a minute, though . . . Turn it around. You can also see the killings as being linked by a lack of magic. The wards couldn't keep the killer out. The magic keeping the Stalker alive failed. So did the magic keeping the Sundered Man out of time. And maybe it was only magic that was holding the Dread Lord together. He was hollow, remember? So maybe what we're looking for is a sorcerer, or a man with an object of Power, that can dispel magic and leave the Beings vulnerable.'

'An object of Power that dispels magic,' said Hawk slowly. 'The Exorcist Stone?'

'Oh, hell!' said Fisher. 'One of the God Squad as a God killer? Come on, Hawk.'

'They're the only ones that can use the Exorcist Stone.'

'But the Council put a compulsion on them to prevent them from misusing it!'

Hawk smiled sourly. 'If this was an easy case, they wouldn't need us to solve it. It has to be one of the God Squad, Isobel; it's the only theory that fits all the facts. The killer must have found some way to bypass the geas.'

'We don't dare accuse any of them without a hell of a lot of proof,' said Fisher. 'These people have friends in high places. Sometimes literally. Dammit, Hawk, we're supposed to be working with these people. How can we keep something like this from them?'

'Very carefully,' said Hawk. 'Whichever one of them is the killer has already destroyed three Beings. I don't think they'd hesitate to kill a couple of Guards who were getting too close to the truth.'

They sat in silence for a while. 'So what are we going to do?' said Fisher.

'Take things one step at a time,' said Hawk. 'To start with, I think we'll have a word with Charles Buchan, and see what he knows about the Hellfire Club. Whatever that is.'

'He was the only one of the God Squad to be named during our investigation,' said Fisher thoughtfully.

'Yes,' said Hawk. 'Interesting, that. But perhaps just a little too obvious. Unless we're supposed to think that . . .'

Fisher groaned and shook her head, and reached for her glass again.

Hawk and Fisher left the temple of John Barleycorn, and

found that night had fallen without warning. Here and there, streets lamps pushed back the night as best they could, but darkness pooled thickly between them. Unfamiliar stars shone in the night sky, forming alien constellations that bore no resemblance to those seen elsewhere in Haven. There was no moon, and the night air had a feverish, unsettled quality. The Street of Gods was almost deserted. The street preachers had disappeared, and only a few hooded figures still bustled back and forth on their eternal errands. Hawk frowned unhappily. The Street wouldn't normally be this quiet just because it suddenly got dark. But with a God killer on the loose, most people had clearly decided against taking unnecessary risks.

The two Guards headed back down the Street toward the God Squad's headquarters. For once, Hawk's internal clock agreed with the Street's time, and he was quietly looking forward to a good supper. He wondered what kind of cook the Squad had. He usually did the cooking at home. Fisher hadn't the temperament for it.

They'd just passed the mouth of a narrow alleyway when they heard a muffled cry for help. As one, they spun quickly to face the dark opening, weapons in hand, but didn't immediately rush in to see what was happening. In the Northside, a cry for help in a dark place was bait for a trap as often as not. A single lamppost glowed dully at the end of the alley, casting more shadows than light. There was no sign of whoever had called out. Hawk looked at Fisher, and she shrugged briefly. It might just be genuine. Hawk nodded, and stepped cautiously into the alleyway. Fisher moved quietly at his side, the amber lamplight gleaming on her sword blade.

Hawk scowled unhappily as the two of them moved slowly down the alley, alert for any sign of movement. The buildings on each side were dark and silent, with no lights showing at their windows. A low scraping sound cut across the quiet somewhere up ahead, and the two Guards froze where they were, eyes straining at the shadows. Nothing moved. The silence was so deep it was like a physical presence. Fisher gently tapped Hawk's arm to get his attention, and nodded at the structure just ahead and to their right. A window shutter was open just a crack. No light shone from inside. Fisher padded silently forward, and set her back against the wall next to the shutter. She reached up with her sword and eased the shutter open. She waited a moment, and when there was no reaction, she moved away from the wall and peered in through the window. She couldn't see anything but the darkness, and there wasn't a sound anywhere. Fisher looked back at Hawk, and shrugged.

She turned to move away, and the window burst outwards as a dark figure smashed through it. Powerful arms grabbed Fisher from behind and hauled her back through the shattered window. Hawk lunged forward, but she'd already disappeared into the dark building. He took a deep breath, and pulled himself up and through the window in one quick, graceless movement.

He hit the floor rolling and threw himself to one side. He scrambled up into a defensive crouch, axe held out before him, and then froze where he was. He couldn't see a damn thing, and all he could hear was his own carefully controlled breathing. There was always the chance the attacker had already fled, but Hawk didn't think so. This whole thing smelled like a planned ambush. He started to wonder why and then pushed the thought firmly to one side. That didn't matter now. All that mattered was what had happened to Fisher.

He bit his lip angrily. He couldn't just stay put. The attacker's eyes were bound to be more used to the dark than his. For all Hawk knew, the bastard was already creeping up on him from behind. That thought was enough to push Hawk into a decision. Moving quickly but carefully, he put his axe down on the floor, ready to hand, and then eased a box of matches from his pocket. He opened the box and took out a single match. He pressed it against the side of the box and then hesitated. It had to light on the first try. If it didn't, the sound would be enough to give away his position and what he was doing. He'd be an easy target. Hawk took a deep breath, let it out, and struck the match.

Light flared at his hand, illuminating the room. Fisher was down on one knee, on the other side of the room. A dark, hooded figure stood over her, knife in hand. Hawk dropped the match and snatched up his axe.

'Isobel! Hit the floor!'

Fisher threw herself forward without hesitation, and in that brief moment before the match reached the floor and went out, Hawk aimed and threw his axe with all his strength behind it. Darkness filled the room. There was the sound of a body hitting the floor, and then silence. Hawk scrabbled at his box of matches and quickly lit another match. Light flared up again. The hooded figure was lying on its back, the heavy steel blade of the axe buried in its chest. Fisher was in a defensive crouch not far away, unharmed, sword at the ready. Hawk let out a long sigh of relief. He took his emergency stub of candle from his pocket and lit it with the match. He put it down on the floor and walked over to Fisher.

'You all right, lass?'

'A few cuts and scratches, that's all. My cloak protected me from anything worse.'

Hawk nodded, relieved, and leant over the body to retrieve his axe. He grabbed the hilt, and the body came alive.

It surged up off the floor, reaching for Hawk's throat.

He stumbled backwards, trying to pull the axe free, but the blade was tightly wedged in the figure's breastbone. Heavy, powerful hands closed around Hawk's throat.

Fisher loomed up behind the attacker, snarling with rage, and her sword flashed once in the candlelight as it swept round to sink deep into his neck. Hawk pulled at the hands round his throat and felt them loosen. Fisher jerked her sword free in a flurry of blood and struck again, grunting with the effort. Blood flew again as the sword half-severed the head from the body. Hawk pulled free, and with that, all the strength seemed to go out of the hooded figure, and it fell to the floor and lay still. Hawk kicked the body several times, just to be sure, and then tugged his axe free. Fisher knelt down and pulled back the figure's hood. Her hand came away bloody, but that wasn't what made her gasp. Even in the dim light, both she and Hawk recognised the face.

It was the Dark Man. The sorcerer Bode's double.

'Damn me,' said Hawk shakily. 'How many times do we have to kill him before he stays dead?'

'It's not the same man . . .' said Fisher slowly. 'The build's different. Not nearly as muscular. Which suggests that Bode didn't stop with just the one double . . .'

'So there could be any number of them still out there,' said Hawk. 'Just waiting for another chance at us.'

'Great,' said Fisher. 'Just what this case needs. More complications.'

4

Hellfire and Damnation

'The Hellfire Club?' said Charles Buchan. 'Of course I've heard of it. But I don't see what it's got to do with anything.'

'Let us worry about that,' said Hawk. 'You just tell us what you know.'

The God Squad and the two Guards were back in their headquarters' drawing room, catching up on what they'd all been doing. Tomb in particular seemed very interested in Hawk and Fisher's reactions to the various Beings they'd seen, and kept pressing them for details. Rowan looked utterly disinterested, and kept rubbing at her forehead as though bothered by a persistent headache. She'd spent most of the day in bed, sleeping. It didn't seem to have helped her much. Buchan looked calm and completely self-possessed, as always. Hawk's stomach rumbled. The sooner they got this over with and settled down to a good supper, the better.

'The Hellfire Club is the latest craze among the younger Quality,' said Buchan easily. 'They get dressed up in strange costumes, take whatever drugs are fashionable, chant rituals, and try to raise something from the Gulfs so they can sell their souls to it, in return for power and miracles. It's harmless.'

'It doesn't sound harmless,' said Fisher. 'What if they succeed?'

'They won't,' said Buchan. 'It takes more than a few chants and bad intentions to raise a demon. No, Captain, it's just playacting, nothing more. A way to let off some steam and upset their parents at the same time. If it even looked like they were succeeding at raising something nasty, they'd either run a mile or faint from shock.'

'Either way, it's still illegal,' said Hawk flatly. 'Any kind of religious rite or ceremony is expressly forbidden outside the Street of Gods. It's the only way to keep these things under control. Why haven't you reported the Hellfire Club to the Council?'

'We did,' said Rowan, her voice too tired to hold its usual acid. 'We reported it to the Council, they reported it to the Guard, and your superiors filed the report carefully away and ignored it. The Hellfire Club is run by the Quality for the Quality, and the Guard knows better than to try and interfere. The Quality don't give a damn about the law. They don't have to. They own it.'

'Not always,' said Fisher. She looked at Hawk. 'I think we'd better do something about this, Hawk.'

Hawk frowned. 'It's not really our province, Isobel. Our authority is limited to the Street of Gods, for the time being.'

'Come on, Hawk,' said Fisher. 'Doesn't it seem just a little too coincidental to you that soon after the Quality start their rituals, the Beings start dying? There must be a connection, or why would the priest have told us about the Club?'

Hawk looked at Buchan. 'She's got a point.'

'They won't talk to you,' said Buchan. 'The Quality don't talk to outsiders about anything.'

'They'll talk to us,' said Hawk. 'Isobel and I talk very loudly, and we don't take kindly to being ignored.'

Buchan sighed. 'In that case, I'd better come with you. I talk the Quality's language. Maybe I can keep them from killing you. Or vice versa.'

The Quality were throwing a party.

Nothing unusual in that. The city aristocracy based their lives around parties, politics, and the pursuit of pleasure. Not necessarily in that order. But this one looked to be something rather special, and Hawk and Fisher were determined to be there. According to Buchan, at this particular party the Hellfire Club would be in session.

They made their way through High Tory, that part of Haven exclusively reserved for the Quality. While Hawk and Fisher looked interestedly around them at the magnificent halls and mansions, Charles Buchan kept up a running commentary on the Quality, and how they fitted into Haven life. Hawk and Fisher knew most of it already, but let him talk. There was always the chance they'd learn something new; about Buchan, if not the Quality.

There were exactly one hundred families in the Quality, never more, and together they formed a separate little state within the city-state of Haven. The only way in was to be born a part of it, or marry into it. Personal wealth wasn't enough. A man could be poor as a church mouse, and still look down on the wealthiest of merchants, if he had the right blood in his veins. The aristocracy's wealth was mostly inherited, though some of it still came from rents and the like; between them the Quality owned most of Haven and the surrounding lands. They could have been even richer if some of that wealth had been invested in Haven's businesses, but that just wasn't done. Trade was for the lower, merchant classes. Technically, the Quality were subordinate to the elected city Council, which represented King and Parliament, but in reality both sides were careful not to put pressure on the relationship from either direction.

Hawk let Buchan drone on, listening with one ear at most. He had his own problems. The party they were going to gate-crash was being hosted by Lord Louis Hightower, and that might lead to complications. The present Lord Hightower had come to his estate after the tragic deaths of both his father and elder brother. Both men had died violently during the course of enquiries into murders on which Hawk had been the investigating officer. No one blamed him for the deaths. Officially, he'd been cleared of any negligence. It remained to be seen what Lord Louis Hightower felt about the matter. The Quality had its own private ideas on justice and retribution. Officially, the Guard were exempt from the Code Duello, or any other form of vengeance, but that was just officially. In this, as in so many other matters, the Quality went its own way when it suited them.

The cold winter air was brisk and bracing after the artificial summer warmth of the Street of Gods. Hawk kicked moodily at the dirty slush that covered the road and the pavement. The Council was supposed to scatter grit and salt on the road at the first sign of approaching winter, but they always left it too late, with the excuse of not wanting to waste money by acting too soon. So this year, as every year, a gritting that could have been done in an hour or two would now take two or three days, during which business would grind to a halt all over the city. Typical.

Hightower Hall loomed up ahead, dominating the surroundings at the end of Royal Row. It was a long, impressive two-storey building of the best local stone, the great wide windows blazing with light. A high stone wall surrounded the luxurious grounds, topped with iron spikes and broken glass. Four men-at-arms in chain mail manned the tall iron gates. They looked very professional. Hawk slowed his pace, and put a hand on Buchan's arm to stop his monologue.

'Looks like they're expecting trouble,' he said quietly, nodding at the men-at-arms. 'The Quality's security measures aren't usually so ostentatious. And you can bet that if there are four armed men in clear sight, there are a hell of a lot more patrolling the grounds and scattered throughout the Hall. Are you sure this is the right place, Buchan? I'd hate to fight my way in and then find I was at the wrong address.'

Fisher sniggered. 'Wouldn't be the first time.'

'This is the place,' said Buchan. 'I still have a few contacts with High Society. The Hellfire Club meets here tonight. And Captain, please: no violence. The God Squad has its reputation to think of. Besides, we shouldn't have any trouble getting in; I've acquired invitations for all of us.'

'Pity,' said Fisher. 'I was quite looking forward to a good dust-up. There's nothing like kicking a few supercilious backsides to put you in a good mood.'

Buchan looked at her sharply. She didn't appear to be joking. 'Please, Captain Fisher. Promise me you won't kill anyone.'

'Don't worry about it,' said Hawk. 'We'll be on our best behaviour. We'll just ask our questions, get some answers, and leave. Right, Isobel?'

Fisher sniffed. 'You're getting old, Hawk.'

'I'm not even sure what we're doing here,' said Buchan. 'The Hellfire Club may be technically illegal, but there isn't a Court in Haven that would convict a member of the Quality on such a minor charge.'

'You're probably right,' said Hawk. 'Personally, I don't give much of a damn about the Hellfire Club itself; but there's got to be a reason why that priest pointed us in their direction. It may just be professional jealousy, but I don't think so. Somewhere, there's a connection between the Club and the God murders, and I want to know what it is.'

The men-at-arms at the gate looked suspiciously at Buchan's engraved invitations, and passed them back and forth amongst themselves before reluctantly opening the gates and standing back. Buchan retrieved the invitations while Hawk and Fisher strolled casually into the grounds as though they owned the place. Buchan smiled politely at the men-at-arms and then hurried after Hawk and Fisher as they strode off up the gravel pathway that led to Hightower Hall.

'Not the front door,' he said quickly. 'The men-at-arms might have been fooled by the invitations, but no one else will be. Anyone with real authority will take one look at your Guards' cloaks and slam the door in our faces. Only the Quality and their personal servants are allowed into a Quality home. Our only chance of crashing this party is to sneak in through the servants' entrance at the back. Once inside, everyone will just assume you're wearing costumes in rather bad taste.'

Hawk and Fisher looked at each other, and Buchan's heart sank as he took in their expressions. 'We don't sneak in through the back door,' said Hawk firmly. 'We're Captains in the city Guard. We go in through the front door. Always. Right, Isobel?'

'Right, Hawk.' Fisher smiled slowly. 'And anyone who tries to slam the door in my face will regret it.'

The two Guards headed determinedly for the front door, their hands resting on the weapons at their sides. Buchan wished briefly but vehemently that he was somewhere else, anywhere else, and followed them.

Hawk pulled the bell rope and knocked firmly on the front door. Fisher kicked it a few times for good measure. After a discreet pause, the massive oak door swung open, revealing a tall and very dignified butler dressed, as tradition demanded, in slightly out-of-date formal wear. He had a thick mane of carefully groomed grey hair, and a pair of impressively bushy eyebrows that descended slowly into an even more impressive scowl as he took in the two Guards standing before him.

'Yes?' he said, disdainfully, his mouth tucking in at the corners as though he'd just bitten into an especially sour lemon.

'We're here for the party,' said Hawk easily. 'Show him the invites, Buchan.'

Buchan quickly held them forward. The butler didn't even bother to look at them. 'There must be some mistake . . . sir. This gathering is exclusively for the young gentlemen and ladies of the Quality. You have no business here . . . sir.'

'My partner and I are Captains in the city Guard,' said Hawk. 'We're here on official business.'

The butler gestured sharply, and two men-at-arms appeared behind him, swords in hand. The butler smiled slightly, his eyes cold and contemptuous.

'You forget your place, Captain. Your petty rules and regulations have no bearing here, among your betters; your lords and masters. Now kindly remove yourselves from these premises. At once.'

'You're not going to be reasonable about this, are you?' said Hawk.

'Leave now,' said the butler. 'Or I'll have my men set the dogs on you.'

Hawk hit him briskly, well below the belt, waited a moment as the butler folded forward, and then punched him out. By the time the two men-at-arms had reacted, Hawk had drawn his axe and Fisher had drawn her sword, and the two Guards had walked over the butler's unconscious body and into the hallway. The men-at-arms looked at them, and then at Charles Buchan, the most famous duellist in Haven, and quickly sheathed their swords.

'I'm not getting paid enough for this,' said one flatly, and the other nodded. 'The party's that way.'

Hawk and Fisher smiled politely, and strolled unhurriedly in the direction the men-at-arms had indicated. Buchan stepped over the butler and went after them.

'You promised me you'd behave,' he said urgently.

'We haven't killed anyone yet,' said Fisher.

Buchan had a horrible suspicion she wasn't joking.

A footman in a rather garish frock coat appeared from nowhere, and apparently assuming they were official guests, led them to the main ballroom. Servants, laden with trays of food and wine, swarmed back and forth though the wide corridors. Hawk gradually became aware of a growing clamour up ahead, the sound of hundreds of voices raised in talk and laughter and argument. It grew steadily louder as the footman led them to a pair of huge double doors, and then the sound burst over them like a wave as the footman pushed open the doors. Hawk and Fisher and Buchan stood together in the doorway a moment, taking in the sight and sound of the Quality at their play.

Hundreds of bright young things were packed into the huge ballroom, dressed in their finest. There were all sorts of fashions and costumes, ranging from the ridiculous to the grotesque. Hawk wasn't surprised. The younger aristocracy always had a taste for the garish. The whole point of elite fashion was to choose clothes that no one but they would be seen dead in. And yet the crowd wasn't composed of only young people. There were a significant number of older men and women, suggesting that the attractions of the Hellfire Club spread across a larger proportion of the Quality than Hawk had expected. His scowl deepened as he took in some of the more sinister costumes: jaggedly cut leathers and bizarrely dyed furs, metal-studded bracelets and spiked chokers. One striking woman dressed in black rags and tatters carried a live snake wrapped around her bare shoulders.

A band of musicians was playing loudly in the gallery, but no one was dancing. That wasn't what they'd come for. Hawk tore his gaze away from the Quality and looked around the great ballroom. He'd known smaller parade grounds, and the ceiling was uncomfortably high overhead, much of it lost in shadow. Three huge chandeliers of polished brass and cut glass lit the scene below with hundreds of candles. Hawk looked at them uneasily. They had to weigh half a ton each, and the thick ropes used for lifting and positioning them looked almost fragile by comparison. Hawk decided he'd keep an eye on them. He didn't trust chandeliers. They always looked unsafe to him.

He noticed that the footman was still with them, waiting to be dismissed. Hawk nodded briskly, at which the footman bowed and left. Buchan watched this thoughtfully. Hawk and Fisher had surprised him with how comfortable they were with servants. As a rule, it was a knack most people didn't have unless they were born into it. Most people found servants intimidating. Hawk and Fisher didn't. Of course, there was a simple explanation; Hawk and Fisher weren't impressed by servants because they weren't impressed by anything.

Buchan looked out over the ballroom. It was a long time since he'd been welcome here. Almost despite himself, his mind drifted back to his last visit to Hightower Hall. Lord Roderik Hightower had been away on one of his werewolf hunts, and Louis was still in the army then. But Lady Hightower was there, to speak on behalf of the Family. The Hightowers and the Buchans had been friends for generations, but that hadn't prevented the Lady Hightower from informing him in cool, passionless tones that unless he agreed to end his relationship with the Sisters of Joy, he should consider himself banned from High Society from that moment on. Buchan had said nothing. There was nothing he could say.

You're a fool, Lady Hightower had said. *You have good friends, position and wealth, a promising future in politics, and all the advantages your Family have given you. And you've thrown it all away for the sake of those women. You disgust me. Get out.*

He had stood there and taken it all in silence, and when she was finished he nodded once, politely, and left. He'd stayed away from High Tory ever since. Now he was back, among familiar sights and sounds once again. He hadn't realised how much he'd missed it all. He emerged from his reverie, suddenly aware that Hawk was speaking to him.

'We'd better split up,' said Hawk. 'We can cover more

ground that way, and hopefully we'll be less conspicuous on our own.'

'Suits me,' said Fisher. 'What exactly are we looking for?'

'Beats me,' said Hawk. 'Some connection between the Hellfire Club and the God murders. It could be anything. A person, a place, a belief . . . anything.'

Fisher frowned thoughtfully. 'These people, Buchan . . . they worship the Darkness, right?'

'Essentially, yes,' said Buchan.

'They try to make deals with it. Offer it things, in return for power.'

'Yes, Captain.'

'Would they go as far as sacrificing people to the Dark?'

Buchan hesitated. 'I don't know. Some might, if they thought they could get away with it.'

'And it's only a step from killing people to killing Beings,' said Hawk. 'If they have already made a deal with the Darkness, and it's given them enough power to kill Beings . . .'

'Then we could be in a lot of trouble here,' said Fisher.

'Nothing changes,' said Hawk. 'All right, let's make a start. Each of you choose a direction, and start walking. Be discreet, but don't be afraid to ask pointed questions. I'm not leaving here without some answers. Oh, and Isobel; let's try and avoid Lord Hightower. Right?'

She nodded, and Hawk slipped into the milling crowd, letting the ebb and flow of people take him where it would. Everywhere he looked there were flushed faces and over-bright eyes and strained, brittle laughter. The sense of anticipation was almost overwhelming. And yet without Hawk's foreknowledge of what the Hellfire Club was about, it would have been easy to see this as just another party. Most of the Quality here were young, half of them barely out of their teens. Partying desperately, squeezing what joy they could out of their lives before the inevitable time when they would have to take on their duties as part of the Families. There were only a few options open to the Quality: for the men it was either politics or the army, for women it was marriage and children. Perhaps that was why they'd formed the Hellfire Club, in search of pleasure and power with no price to pay. Or at least, no price they believed in.

Hawk knew better. No one encounters the Darkness and comes away unscathed. The scars on his face throbbed briefly with remembered pain.

He moved deeper into the crowd. Hundreds of people filled the huge ballroom from wall to wall, but Hawk wasn't impressed. He'd seen grander gatherings in his time. And the more he looked, the more he became aware of the nervous undercurrent in the party's mood. The laughter was too sudden and too loud, and the general brittle good cheer wasn't fooling anyone but themselves. Many of the Quality were drinking like fish, but no one seemed to be drunk. Hawk frowned slightly. It was as though the Quality were trying to nerve themselves up to something. Something frightening . . . and dangerous.

Buchan wandered aimlessly through the crowd, looking for familiar faces. Most of them here were too young to remember him, and his shame, but clearly there were some who did. They looked the other way, or turned their backs on him. None of them wanted to talk to him. It wouldn't be safe. Some of his shame might rub off on them. Buchan grabbed a glass of wine from a passing servant's tray and drank deeply. Not a bad vintage. A damn sight better than the cheap muck he usually drank.

He hadn't been aware of how lonely he'd been until he came back here, and realised how much he'd had to give up. All the food and wine and comforts. The security of *belonging*. Hawk and Fisher might be contemptuous of High Society, but they couldn't know what it meant, to be a part of it. The Quality were Family and friends and lovers, and more than that. They shared your life from the cradle on.

On good days and bad days and empty days, they were always there. They seduced and protected you, loved you and hated you, and kept you safe from the outside world; made you feel part of a greater whole. It was comforting and reassuring to have the same faces always around you, people who understood you sometimes better than you knew yourself. He hadn't realised how much he missed it all, and how much there was to miss.

The God Squad was his family now, but they were no substitute for what he'd given up. Tomb was a friendly enough sort, but he had no interest in anything save his magics and his books, and he was too sober by far. The sorcerer meant well, but the God Squad was his life, and nothing else really mattered to him. And Rowan was a pain in the posterior. Spent all her time poring over ancient books and papers, and filling the house with chemical stinks. He'd tried to talk to her about her theories and beliefs, but most of the time she just answered his questions with grunts and monosyllables. On the few occasions when she condescended to explain something to him, he was damned if he could follow it, for all his expensive education. All he could grasp was that Rowan didn't believe in anything much but desperately wanted to believe in something. So desperately that there was no room in her life for anything but the search.

Buchan looked slowly around him. It was a long time since he'd considered how much he'd given up for his darling Annette. And though he loved her more than anything else in his life, there were times he hated her too, for what that love had cost him. He pushed the thought firmly aside, and moved on through the crowd of turned backs and averted faces.

Hawk finally spotted a familiar face, and strolled nonchalantly over to join him. Lord Arthur Sinclair was well on his way to being drunk, as usual. The last time Hawk had seen Lord Sinclair, he and Fisher had been clearing up after the Haven elections. Sinclair had stood as a candidate, on the No Tax On Alcohol Party. Also known as the Who's For A Party Party. He never even looked like winning, but he didn't let a little thing like that dissuade him from holding a celebration party long before the results came in. It was two days before he sobered up long enough to ask who'd won.

Sinclair was a short, round little man in his mid thirties, with thinning yellow hair and uncertain blue eyes. He smiled a lot, at nothing in particular, and was rarely without a glass of something in his hand. He was a third son, who'd never expected or been intended to inherit the Family estates. He had no talents, no gifts, no aptitudes, and no interest in anything but parties. His friends thought him a pleasant, harmless little chap. Always ready for a song or a joke or another drink. His Family treated him like dirt for the most part, and tried to pretend he didn't exist. He had no sense of self-esteem, and no chance to build any. And then his father and both his brothers died in the same battle, and the title and estates fell to him, along with the not inconsiderable Family fortune. His mother died soon after, from a broken heart some said, and he was left all alone. He'd been Lord Sinclair for almost five years, and had spent most of that time trying to drink himself to death, for want of anything better to do.

Hawk approached Sinclair and nodded familiarly to him. Sinclair smiled back. He was used to being treated as a friend by people he didn't recognise or remember. There's no one so popular as a drunk with money.

'Good party,' said Hawk.

'Marvellous,' said Sinclair. 'Dear Louis never stints on these affairs. Would you like a drink?'

Hawk nodded, and Sinclair poured him a generous glass of pink champagne from one of the bottles in a nearby ice bucket. Hawk sipped at it cautiously, and refrained from pulling a face. Far too sweet for his taste, but that was the

Quality for you. With their taste for sugar in everything, it was a wonder they had any teeth left at all.

'So, when does the excitement start?' said Hawk, trying not to sound too vague.

'Soon,' said Sinclair. 'Do I know you?'

'We've met briefly, in the past.'

Sinclair smiled sadly. 'That covers rather a lot of ground, I'm afraid.' He emptied his glass, and filled it again. 'You're new here, aren't you?'

'That's right,' said Hawk. 'I'm here about the Club. The Hellfire Club.'

'Aren't we all. My little fancy seems to have caught on. I had no idea it would prove so popular.'

'This was your idea, originally?'

'Indeed. My one and only good idea. Would you like to hear about it? I do so love to talk about it, and everyone else has heard the story by now. You know about me, of course. Everyone does. My parents' generation never tire of holding me up as a Bad Example. Not that I care. I never wanted to be head of the Family. I was happy with my parties and my poetry. I used to write poetry, you know. Some of it was quite passable. But I don't do that anymore. I couldn't see the point. When they all died and left me alone, I couldn't see the point in anything anymore. I mean, they weren't always very nice to me, but they were my Family, and one or other of them was always there, making sure I didn't hurt myself too badly. I do miss them.

'I don't believe in anything much anymore, but I keep looking. There has to be something; something *real* to believe in, apart from just chance. Only sometimes, I think there isn't. I think that rather a lot, actually, but a few drinks usually help. I tried religion for a while. I really thought I was on to something there. But there were so many religions, and I couldn't choose between them. They couldn't all be right, but they all seemed so sure of themselves. I've never been sure of anything. Then I met this fellow on the

Street of Gods. Marvellous young sorcerer chappie; Bode, his name was. He gave me the idea for the Hellfire Club. He was very interested in the power you could get from tapping the darkness within you. Of course, the idea seems to have got a bit muddled since all these other people got involved in the Club . . .

'I liked Bode. He was always good company. Bit too intelligent for his own good, but then, that's sorcerers for you. Had this very intense girlfriend, all sarcasm and deep insights. I was ever so upset when I heard he died just recently.'

He drained his glass, and looked thoughtfully at another bottle in the ice bucket. Hawk's thoughts were racing furiously. He'd come here looking for a connection between the Hellfire Club and the God murders, but he seemed to have stumbled across a connection to a completely different case. Sinclair must have met Bode while the sorcerer was carrying on his mysterious commission on the Street of Gods. But who was this girlfriend Sinclair met? Hawk frowned as another thought came to him. Given the appearance of the second Dark Man on the Street of Gods, maybe the two cases weren't separate after all. Maybe everything was connected . . .

Hawk had just decided he'd better press Sinclair for more details, when someone tapped him hard on the shoulder from behind. He turned round to find himself facing three large and openly menacing members of the Quality. They were all taller than he, and they all looked as though they worked out regularly with heavy weights.

'Can you smell something?' asked the leader of the group loudly. He sniffed at the air and grinned nastily. 'I smell a Guard. No mistaking that stench. But what's a dirty little Guard doing at a private party? A private Quality party?'

'I'm here on official business,' said Hawk, careful to keep his voice calm and unthreatening. It was obvious the three Quality were looking for trouble. Anywhere else he might have obliged them, but not here. The ballroom was full of hundreds of their friends, all of them Quality. They could cripple him or kill him, and nothing would be done. And he daren't lift a finger to defend himself. You could, under very rare circumstances, arrest a member of the Quality, even put them on trial, but it still had to be kid gloves all the way. The Quality were under no such restrictions. At best, they'd give him a good kicking and put him in hospital, just for the fun of it. He didn't want to think what they might do to Fisher.

'An official investigation,' said the group's spokesman. 'Did you hear that? Doesn't it just make you shiver in your boots? I don't give a damn about your investigation, Captain. No one here does. We don't have to. This is our place. We don't allow your sort in here. Is that clear?'

Hawk started to reply, and the leader hit him open-handed across the face. Hawk saw the blow coming and rode most of it, but he took a step backwards despite himself. His cheek flared red from the impact, and a thin trickle of blood ran down his chin from a split lip.

'You're going to have to talk louder, Captain. I can't hear you if you whisper.'

Hawk smiled suddenly, and a fresh rill of blood ran down from his split lip. The leader of the three Quality hesitated, suddenly uncertain. The Guard's smile was cold and unpleasant, and far too confident for his liking. He glanced quickly about him to check his two friends were still there. His confidence quickly returned. The Guard wouldn't dare try anything. The first sign of violence, everyone would turn on him. He opened his mouth to say so, and the Guard's hand shot forward and fastened onto his trouser belt. The Guard took a good hold, and then twisted it suddenly and jerked upwards. The leader's voice disappeared as his throat clamped shut. Tears sprang to his eyes as his trouser crotch rammed up into his groin. He tried to stand on tiptoe to ease the pain, but it was all he could do to get his breath. He grabbed desperately at the Guard's arm, but the thick cords of muscle didn't give an inch. The Guard twisted again, crushing his groin, and a fresh wave of pain welled up through his belly, sickening him.

Hawk brought his scarred face in very close to the Quality leader's. 'You don't talk like that to a Guard. Not now, not ever. Is that clear?'

The leader nodded, and tried to force out an answer. Hawk twisted his hold viciously, and the man's face went white.

'Is that clear?'

The leader nodded frantically, and Hawk let him go. He collapsed into the supporting arms of his friends, who looked just as scared and confused as he did. Hawk fixed each of them in turn with his single cold eye.

'Take your friend and get out of here,' he said calmly. 'I don't want to see your faces again. Is that clear?'

They nodded quickly, and half led, half carried their friend away. Hawk watched them go. The trick to situations like that was to take out the leader as quickly and as painfully as possible. It's not a question of what you do, as what you make them think you're prepared to do. Take control of the situation away from them. Make them sweat. Make them afraid. You learn things like that in Haven. He looked casually around him, but the incident had passed so quickly that no one seemed to have noticed anything. He turned back to Sinclair, who was studying him thoughtfully.

'You know, that really was very impressive,' said Sinclair. 'I wish I could do things like that.'

'You could learn,' said Hawk.

'No, I don't think so. It probably involves a lot of things like practice and discipline and hard work. Not really me, I'm afraid. Did you know you have blood on your chin?'

Hawk took out his handkerchief and wiped carefully at his mouth and chin. 'You have to be able to stand up for yourself. It helps keep the flies off.'

Sinclair smiled. 'Like I said, not really me. It's not important. You see, I don't matter. Not to anyone. Never have and never will.' He stopped, and looked at Hawk. 'Is something wrong, Captain?'

'No. You just reminded me of someone I used to know. Someone who felt like that.'

'What happened to him?'

Hawk looked across at Fisher, on the other side of the room. 'He found someone who believed in him.'

Fisher had found herself to be very popular. Young men gathered around her, plying her with drinks and sweets and smiles, and vying with each other for her attention. The young rakes and blades were always on the lookout for a new pretty face, the more exotic the better. And compared to the carefully groomed and painted flowers of the Quality, the six-foot muscular blonde in the Guard's cloak seemed very exotic indeed. The female members of the Quality seemed caught between ostentatiously ignoring her and glaring at her when her back was turned.

Fisher didn't care much for the Quality, singly or en masse. More money than they knew what to do with, and nothing to give their lives meaning except an endless round of love affairs, duels, and Family vendettas. The ones with any guts went into the army; these here at the party were the ones who'd stayed behind. Which was why they joined the Hellfire Club. Their lives were so empty that there was nothing left but to play at being bad in the hopes of shocking each other, or at least their parents.

Fisher pumped the young men unobtrusively with leading questions, but didn't get much in the way of answers. The Quality were too busy making fools of themselves trying to impress her. They began to get on her nerves after a while, and when hints that she'd prefer to be left alone fell on deaf ears, she started to wonder if punching out one or two of them might help to get her message across. She'd just selected her first target, when a loud confident voice cut across the young men's babble, and quickly sent them all packing.

Fisher looked her rescuer over carefully. He was a little taller than she, elegantly slender, and dressed in well-cut, sombre clothes. He was in his late twenties at most, and good-looking in a dark, traditional way, though there was a self-satisfied look to his eyes and mouth that Fisher didn't like.

'Lord Graham Brunel, at your service,' he said smoothly. 'I do hope those boys weren't bothering you too much. I'm afraid the Club has grown so popular now that we seem to be letting just anyone in. I'll have to speak to Louis about it. Now, may I know your name, dear lady?'

'Isobel,' said Fisher carefully. 'This is my first time here.'

'Yes, I thought it must be,' said Brunel. 'I'm sure I'd have remembered so distinctive a beauty as yourself if we'd met before. That is a Guard's cloak you're wearing, isn't it? Is it the real thing, by any chance?'

'Oh, yes,' said Fisher. 'It's real.'

'You really must tell me how you came by it. I'm sure it's a fascinating story.'

'You wouldn't believe how fascinating,' said Fisher. 'Have you been with the Hellfire Club long?'

'Almost from the beginning, my dear. Arthur Sinclair came up with the idea originally, bless his booze-rotted brain, but it was Louis Hightower and I who brought the Club together and made it what it is.'

'But have you achieved any results?' said Fisher.

'You'd be surprised,' said Brunel. 'We're getting close to something very powerful, Isobel. I can feel it. Something so awful and magnificent it'll tear this dreary little city apart. But there's nothing to be worried about, my dear, I promise you. You just stay close to me, and I'll keep you safe.'

'That's very kind of you,' said Fisher, 'But I already have an escort.'

'Drop him. You're with me now.'

Fisher smiled at him. 'Fancy yourself, don't you?'

Brunel looked at her uncertainly. 'I beg your pardon?'

'You haven't achieved anything, have you, Brunel? In all the time you've been running this Club, have you raised a single demon, contacted a Power, or even managed to make the lights flicker a little?' She paused a moment while Brunel went red in the face and struggled for words. 'I thought not. The Hellfire Club, when you get right down to it, is just another game. Another excuse to get dressed up, drink too much, and have a good time jumping at shadows. Just a bunch of overgrown kids. I don't think I'll be staying.'

Brunel reached out quickly and took her by the arm. 'Oh, but I really must insist, my dear. You've been asking a lot of questions, but you haven't told us anything about yourself. I think it's time you told me who you really are.'

Fisher slowly raised her arm despite his hold, and showed him the silver torc at her wrist. 'Isobel Fisher, Captain of the city Guard. Now get your hand off me or I'll break your fingers.'

Brunel's face was suddenly harsh and ugly, all charm fled. His fingers dug into her arm muscle, trying to hurt her. 'A spy. A dirty stinking Council spy. You're not going anywhere, Captain. We can use you, in the Hellfire Club. Some of us have been wondering if a human sacrifice might not be just what we need, to make the breakthrough we've been looking for. We were going to use one of the servants, someone who wouldn't be missed, but you'll do nicely. No one's going to miss you; no one even knows you're here, right?'

Fisher smiled at him. 'I think this has gone far enough.' She reached out with her free hand and clapped him on the shoulder. Her thumb found the exposed nerve behind the collarbone, and pressed down hard. Brunel's face screwed up as the pain hit him, and his hold on her arm loosened. She shrugged free of him, and pulled his face close to hers.

Brunel tried to pull away, but the stabbing pain paralysed him.

'No human sacrifice, Brunel. Not tonight or any other night. The Guard's going to keep a close watch on you from now on. And if we even suspect you're thinking about a human sacrifice, we'll come back here in force and drag each and every one of you out of here in chains. We've left you alone because you're harmless. Stay that way, or I guarantee you'll spend the rest of your days walking the treadmill under the city gaol. Got it?'

She let him go and he staggered back a pace, clutching at his shoulder. He tried to scowl at her, but couldn't meet her eyes. He turned and disappeared into the crowd, and was swallowed up in a moment. *This is a waste of time*, thought Fisher. *We're not going to find our God killer here.* She looked around her for Hawk and Buchan.

Buchan wandered through a crowd of averted faces, feeling not unlike the ghost at the feast. Word of his arrival had circulated quickly through the gathering. Backs turned at his approach, and murmurs rose and fell as he passed. The Quality, young or old, liked to think of itself as being above petty moralities and restrictions, but when you got right down to it, their affairs and debaucheries still followed very strict guidelines. For all the freedom that wealth and position brings, there remained things that were simply not done. And when it came to matters of Family and inheritance, the Quality were very conservative. Wives and children were important; they continued and preserved the precious bloodlines, without which there would be no hundred Families, no Quality. So for an only son, the last of his line, to turn his back on marriage and make regular visits to the Sisters of Joy was simply unacceptable.

There was a stir in the crowd to his left, and Buchan looked round in mild surprise to find someone approaching him. His first thought was that he was about to be asked to leave, but as the crowd fell away he saw that it was the party's host, Lord Louis Hightower. Buchan winced mentally though his face remained impassive.

The Lord Hightower was of average height and stockily built, much like his late father. As a second son, he had been spending a quiet and not unsuccessful life in the army when his father and mother died in the same night, victims of a werewolf's curse. His elder brother had been murdered some months previously. So he resigned his commission and came home, and now he was the Lord Hightower, one of the leading lights in the Quality and chief organiser of the Hellfire Club. He and Buchan were the same age, and had been friends, once. Buchan waited for Hightower to come to him, and then bowed politely. He was ready for almost anything except the sad, exasperated sigh with which Hightower greeted him.

'What the devil are you doing here, Charles? I wouldn't have thought this Hellfire nonsense was in your line.'

'It isn't,' said Buchan. 'But it may have a connection with a case I'm working on for the Squad. And what do you mean by calling it nonsense? I thought you were one of the people running the Club.'

Hightower shrugged. 'It's amusing. And interesting, sometimes. But I don't get carried away with it, like some people I could mention. I might have known it would take something like this to bring you back here.' Hightower looked at him steadily. 'It's been a long time, Charles. Too long.'

Buchan smiled. 'Not everyone would agree with you, Louis. I don't go where I'm not welcome. I have that much pride left.'

'You're always welcome in my home, Charles. You know that.'

'Yes. But my presence in your house would do you no good at all. People would talk.'

'Let them. You think I care more about my reputation than my friends?'

'You have a position to maintain now,' said Buchan firmly. 'You're not just a second son any longer. You're *the* Hightower, the head of the Family. You have responsibilities to them now, as well as yourself. And to whatever poor woman you eventually decide to marry. You shouldn't even be talking to me, really.'

'As head of the Family, I do have some authority. People may mutter, but they won't say anything. Not in public. It's good to see you again, Charles. I saw your mother last week. She's looking well. Are they still not talking to you?'

'As far as I know. I haven't been back there in a while, either. As far as they're concerned, I don't exist. And perhaps that's for the best.'

'Are you still . . .?'

'Visiting the Sisters? Yes.'

'They'll destroy you, Charles. They destroy all their victims, in the end.' Hightower took in Buchan's face, and raised a hand defensively. 'All right, I know. You don't want to talk about it. And I can't ask you about the case you're working on, because you never talk about that, either. Is there anything you do feel free to discuss?'

'I was sorry to hear about your parents, Louis. It must have been a shock.'

'Yes, it was. The funny thing is, I'd been expecting my father's death for some time. He'd been looking old and tired ever since Paul was murdered. You never knew my brother, did you? He was a good sort, and always too brave for his own good. Father thought the world of him. He took Paul's death hard.

'He hated being retired, too. Didn't know what to do with himself after he left the army. Dabbled in politics for a while, but . . . I was out of town when he and mother died, on manoeuvres. I miss them, you know. Every day there's something that makes me think *I'd better ask Dad about that*, or *I wonder what Mother would say* . . . and then I remember, and the day seems a little colder. I miss them, Charles. I really miss them.'

'You ought to get married,' said Buchan firmly. 'It's not sensible, you and the servants rattling around in this huge old place by yourself. Get yourself a wife and fill the place with children. Do you a world of good.'

Hightower laughed. 'Just like the rest of my Family. Can't wait to see me safely married and settled down. I always said I'd only marry for love, Charles; never just for duty. You can understand that, can't you?'

'Yes,' said Buchan. 'I understand.'

They stood together a moment, wanting to say more, but not sure how. They'd pretty much exhausted the few things they still had in common, and what remained of their lives now was separated by a gulf neither of them could cross.

'So,' said Hightower finally. 'Is there anything you can tell me about the God Squad business that brings you here?'

'You've heard about the God murders, I take it? Well, my associates turned up a lead that suggested there may be a connection between the Hellfire Club and the killings.'

'I don't see how,' said Hightower. 'It's all a lark, nothing more. Just another excuse for a party. The rituals are fun, but no one seriously expects anything to come of them. Well, most of us don't, anyway. There are always a few idiots. But most of the Club are only here to annoy their Families. A sign of rebellion, without having to risk anything that matters.'

'What got you involved?' said Buchan. 'I wouldn't have thought this was your kind of thing.'

'It isn't. But there are a great many young ladies who are interested, so . . .'

Buchan laughed. 'I might have known. Is it true most of your rituals take place in the nude?'

'Quite a few of them, yes.' Hightower grinned. 'And that's not all we do in the rituals that our Families wouldn't approve of.'

They laughed together, and then the double doors burst open and a sudden silence fell across the room as everyone turned to look.

The Dark Man stood in the doorway. Blood splashed his shapeless furs and dripped thickly from both ends of the long wooden staff in his hands. He was grinning broadly, and his eyes were fixed and wild. He looked slowly round the crowded ballroom, and the Quality fell back before his unwavering gaze. Death and violence hung around him like a shroud. In the silence that greeted his arrival they could hear voices moaning and crying out in pain from the corridor outside. Hawk and Fisher pushed their way through the crowd toward him, blades at the ready.

A man-at-arms appeared behind the Dark Man. Bruised and bleeding heavily, he nevertheless flung himself at the Dark Man and tried to get a choke hold on him. They staggered back and forth for a moment, and then the Dark Man twisted suddenly and threw the man-at-arms over his shoulder. He hit the floor hard and lay still, groaning quietly. The Dark Man raised his staff and brought it sweeping down with vicious force, striking his victim again and again and again. Blood flew and bones shattered. The limp body jumped and jerked under the rain of blows, even after the man was clearly dead.

There were stifled screams and moans of horror from the Quality, and a few of the braver men moved forward. Hawk yelled for them to stay back. The Dark Man slowly raised his head and grinned at those advancing on him. There was blood on his face, none of it his. The handful of men slowed to a halt and looked at each other uncertainly.

'Dammit, stay where you are!' yelled Hawk, his voice cutting across the rising babble. 'He's too dangerous! I'm city Guard. My partner and I will take care of him.'

The Quality moved quickly to get out of the Guards' way. The Dark Man grinned bloodily and threw himself at those still between him and his intended victims. He struck out furiously with his staff, not caring who he hit, and men and women alike fell to the polished floor with broken heads and stove-in ribs. The Quality began screaming again, and fought each other in their panic to get out of the Dark Man's way as he headed toward Hawk and Fisher. A handful of men threw themselves at the killer, but he shrugged them off easily, not even feeling their fists. One of them grabbed at the Dark Man's leg from the floor. Without looking down, the Dark Man kicked the man free, and then stamped viciously on his chest. The man lay still, and the Dark Man moved on. The rest of the Quality hung back. It would have been different if they'd had weapons, but wearing weapons in a friend's house wasn't done. So they'd all left their swords at the door.

And then finally Hawk and Fisher reached the Dark Man, and his grin widened. He threw himself forward, swinging his staff in a powerful horizontal arc. Fisher ducked under it and ran the Dark Man through, her sword blade grating between his ribs. His grin never wavered, and he struck at her arm with his staff. Fisher's hand went numb and she had to jump back, leaving her sword wedged in the Dark Man's ribs. Blood ran thickly down his sides, but he took no notice of it, his eyes following Fisher as she backed away.

Hawk stepped in and swung his axe from the killer's blind side. The Dark Man spun round at the last moment and parried the blow with his staff. The impact almost wrenched the axe from Hawk's hand. The two men circled each other warily, searching for an opening. Hawk felt a sudden chill rush through him, as he realised the Dark Man was a better fighter now than he had been the first few times they'd met. It was as though he was learning with each new fight, each new death . . . as though each new Dark Man was the same man . . .

What the hell am I fighting here?

He misjudged a blow with his axe, and the end of the staff clipped him just above the ear in passing. The world rocked around him for an instant, and the Dark Man pressed forward. Hawk backed away quickly, holding his axe more by instinct than anything else. The Dark Man swung his staff, and Hawk ducked at the last moment. He stumbled, off balance, and looked up just in time to see the staff coming round on the backswing for a blow that would crack his skull like an eggshell. There wasn't even time to close his eye.

And then Fisher darted in from behind, and cut at both the Dark Man's legs with her knife, hamstringing him. He fell forward onto his hands and knees as his legs gave out, the muscles half severed. He didn't make a sound, even when Fisher took hold of her sword and jerked it out of his ribs. Instead, he slowly got his feet under him, one at a time, and stood up, still clinging to his staff. Fisher backed away. Hawk gaped at him blankly. It just wasn't possible with wounds like that . . . the leg muscles had to be tearing themselves apart. The pain must be hideous . . .

The Dark Man moved toward Fisher, one step at a time. Blood coursed down his legs. He was still grinning. Hawk looked about for inspiration. His gaze fell upon a heavy rope tied to a wall bracket. He followed the rope upward, and realised it was supporting one of the huge chandeliers. It took him only a moment to see that the Dark Man was standing almost directly underneath the chandelier. Just a few more steps . . .

'Isobel!' he called urgently. 'Hold your ground! Let him come to you!'

Fisher shot him a quick glance and then took up the defensive stance where she was, favouring her bruised arm as best she could. *There had better be a bloody good reason for this, Hawk, because I don't think I can stop him on my own. He's not human.*

The Dark Man shuffled slowly forward, leaving a trail of blood behind him. The Quality were hushed and silent, watching with widened eyes. It was one thing to join the

Hellfire Club for a few easy thrills, but quite another to come face to face with blood and death and suffering at such close quarters. The Dark Man shuffled forward, his grin widening. Fisher braced herself, and Hawk cut the rope with his axe.

The Dark Man just had time to see a shadow gathering around him and look up, and then half a ton of polished brass and cut glass hammered him to the floor. The sound of the crash echoed on and on. He lay still, and for a long moment no one said anything. And then the Dark Man slowly got his hands underneath him and tried to lever himself up. The chandelier lifted an inch or two, and then settled itself more firmly. Blood burst from the Dark Man's mouth, and he fell forward and lay still again. Hawk stepped in, raised his axe, and struck down with all his strength. There were a few shocked cries from the Quality as blood spurted and the Dark Man's head rolled free, but Hawk paid them no heed. He wasn't taking any chances.

Buchan made his way through the crowd to join Hawk and Fisher. 'That was some fight. You might have let it last long enough for me to join in. Do either of you know who he was? What he was doing here?'

'Tracking us, I think,' said Hawk. 'It's to do with a murder case we worked on before we joined the God Squad.'

'I see,' said Buchan. 'Do you want to explain that to these people, or shall I?'

'I think it might be better if none of us did,' said Fisher. 'Hawk, let's get the hell out of here. The regular Guard will be here soon; let them handle it.'

Hawk looked around him. 'All these people hurt, because of us . . .'

'We don't know that,' said Fisher. 'Now let's go.'

Hawk nodded, and let Buchan lead him and Fisher out of the ballroom. Behind them, the Quality had closed in around the Dark Man's body and were kicking it viciously.

Hawk looked back once, and then looked away. Buchan smiled grimly.

'If nothing else, Hawk, you've got to admit the Quality know how to throw a party. You never know what's going to happen next.'

5

Secrets Come to Light

Rowan sat up stiffly in bed and groaned loudly. She hurt all over, and her mouth tasted foul. She felt more tired now than when she'd gone to bed. She reached painfully over to the bedside table and grabbed the cupful of potion she'd prepared earlier. She took a quick sip, then leaned back against the headboard and looked unhappily at the sickly green stuff in the cup. Putting mint in to flavour it had definitely been a mistake. It must have clashed with something. On the other hand, it couldn't taste much worse than her mouth did anyway. She lifted the cup determinedly while her nerve held out, and gulped the horrid stuff down. It tasted even worse than she felt, and she indulged herself by pulling awful faces as she put the cup down on the table. She paused in mid-grimace as she noticed the steaming cup of tea on the silver tray, also resting on the bedside table. Her mouth flattened into a thin line. Tomb had been in her room again. She was going to have to do something about Tomb.

Rowan began to feel a little better as the potion began its work, and she pushed back the bedclothes and swung her legs over the side of the bed. She picked up the cup of tea, looked at it for a moment, and then sipped at it cautiously. It was strong and sweet, and a pleasant warmth moved through her. Say what you would about Tomb, and she could think of a lot, most of it based around the word *irritating*, the fact remained that he made a good cup of tea. Still, she was definitely going to have to do something about him. She'd made it as clear as she could that she had no feelings of any kind for him and would be just as happy if he'd find somebody else to pester, but he seemed determined not to get the point. Maybe she should try something more direct, like hitting him. She didn't really want to be unpleasant about it, but it might be kinder in the long run. It certainly wasn't fair to let him go on hanging around like this.

She smiled sourly as she sipped her tea. Not that she had time for any more complications in her life, but if someone had to fall for her, why couldn't it have been Buchan? All right, he was a few years older than she, but he still had one hell of a body. He was more experienced than Tomb, more sophisticated; he would have understood the situation. They could have had a marvellous, uncomplicated affair that was fun while it lasted but nothing to fret over when it was finished. But no. The dashing, debonair, handsome Charles Buchan couldn't be bothered to look at a dumpy little thing like her. He had to save himself for those stinking bitches at the Sisters of Joy. She sighed wistfully. Such a waste of a good man . . . but then, that was the way the world went. Nothing was what it seemed, nobody could be trusted, and there was no point in believing in anything unless you could hold it in your hand and check it for flaws. A harsh philosophy, but better than nothing.

She looked at the travelling clock on the mantelpiece. Buchan should be back from the Hellfire Club soon, along with the two Guards. She scowled, thinking about Hawk and Fisher. They were going to be trouble; she'd known that from the moment she first met them. They didn't understand what was happening on the Street of Gods, but that wouldn't stop them from charging blindly in, trying to put things right by brute force. They were fools, but they were dangerous fools. She yawned suddenly, and took a long, slow stretch. She looked wistfully at her warm, comfortable bed. Just another half-hour's rest would feel so good . . .

She heard footsteps coming up the stairs, and tensed. Her

head was still too muzzy for her to See who it was. The footsteps came unhurriedly along the landing and stopped outside her door. There was a long pause, followed by a hesitant knock. Rowan relaxed, and let out her breath in a quiet sigh. She knew that knock.

'Come in, Tomb.'

The sorcerer opened the door and came in, shot a quick glance at Rowan to see how she was, and then smiled winningly at her. 'Just thought I'd look in and check you were up. The others will be back soon.'

'Yes, I know. I'm feeling much better, thank you.'

'That's good. I'm glad.'

'Tomb?'

'Yes, Rowan?'

'Do you think you could shut the door? It's rather drafty in here.'

'Oh. Yes. Of course.'

He pushed the door shut, turned back, and tried his winning smile again. Rowan realised she was still holding the teacup and put it down on the tray.

'Thank you for leaving me tea again. That was very sweet of you.'

'You're welcome.' The sorcerer grinned and nodded his head, pleased.

Just like a puppy that's done a trick correctly, and wants to be patted and told he's a good dog, thought Rowan tiredly. *How the hell can a first-class sorcerer like Tomb be such an idiot when it comes to women? I really don't need this. Not now.*

Tomb's smile slowly disappeared, and he shuffled his feet uncertainly. 'You know, Rowan, I really am getting rather concerned about you.'

'You are? Why?'

'Well, this isn't the first time you've been ill like this, is it?'

'There's no need for you to worry. I'll be fine. I know what I'm doing.'

[532]

Tomb visibly braced himself to disagree with her. 'I know you have a lot of faith in your potions, Rowan, but I really would be a lot happier if you'd let me call in a doctor, just to look you over and make sure it's nothing serious.'

Rowan glared at him. 'I do not need a doctor. How many times do I have to tell you, Tomb? My health and how I look after myself are none of your business.'

'But I do worry about you.'

'Don't. There's no reason why you should be so concerned. Just because I'm part of the God Squad doesn't give you the right to hover around me like a broody hen. You're an acquaintance of mine, Tomb; nothing more. Is that clear?'

Tomb nodded slowly. 'Yes, Rowan. Very clear.'

'Now, don't go all sulky on me. How long have I got before the Guards get back with Buchan?'

Tomb's face went blank for a moment as he used the Sight. 'They're just approaching the front door. I'd better go down and greet them. If you're sure you're all right now . . .'

'I'm fine.'

'Then I'll see you in a while.'

He turned and left the room quickly, before she could say anything else. Rowan heaved a quiet but vehement sigh of relief. She knew she shouldn't be so harsh with him, but that damned puppy dog routine of his was getting on her nerves. Always doing her little favours, so she'd have to say something nice to him . . . She got up off the bed, stripped off her nightgown, and reached for her clothes. She was looking forward to hearing Hawk and Fisher tell about what had happened at the Hellfire Club.

Everyone was back in their favourite chairs in the drawing room. Tomb handed round long, narrow glasses of his syrupy sherry, and everyone except Hawk accepted the wine with a smile. Hawk sat back in his chair and tried not to feel like a barbarian. There was a quiet moment as everyone else sipped at their drinks.

'Let's start with the Hellfire Club,' said Rowan finally. 'What did you think of them, Captain Hawk?'

'A bunch of amateurs, playing with magic and jumping at shadows,' said Hawk bluntly. 'No danger to anyone, except maybe themselves.'

'But did you turn up any connection to the God Killings?' asked Tomb, sitting forward on the edge of his chair, as though anxious not to miss a syllable.

'Not really,' said Fisher. 'But we did come across something interesting. Before we were seconded to you, Hawk and I were investigating the murder of a sorcerer named Bode.' She didn't miss the quickly stifled reactions from Buchan and Rowan at Bode's name, but carried on as though she hadn't noticed. 'We didn't have time to find out who killed him, but we did discover that Bode had been hired by some unknown person to carry out a secret mission on the Street of Gods.'

'Did he succeed in this mission?' said Tomb.

'We don't know,' said Fisher. 'We didn't find any evidence directly linking him to the God Killings, but we did discover that Bode had been experimenting with homunculi; that is, magically produced physical duplicates.'

'Yes, yes,' said Rowan impatiently. 'We all know what a homunculus is.'

Fisher gave Rowan a hard look that didn't faze the mystic a bit, and then continued, 'Somehow, Bode invested one of these duplicates with all his rage and hate, and set it to guard his house against intruders. He called it the Dark Man. It was huge, muscular, and very nasty. It murdered at least four people that we know of. Hawk and I killed it.'

'This is all very interesting,' said Rowan, 'but what has it got to do with the Hellfire Club? Or the God Killings?'

Fisher looked at Hawk to see if he'd like to continue with the story, but he was busy looking for some convenient receptacle into which he could surreptitiously empty his sherry glass. Fisher sighed quietly, and continued, 'On our way back from studying the murder sites of the three dead Beings, we were attacked by a second Dark Man. We killed him. The third Dark Man tried to kill us at the Hellfire Club. We killed that one too.'

For a long moment no one said anything. Tomb was frowning deeply. 'Did you notice any differences between the three homunculi?'

'Yeah,' said Fisher. 'They're getting harder to kill.'

'More than that,' said Hawk, putting down his empty sherry glass. 'They were all unnaturally strong, but the muscular development was different each time. There was no way it could have been the same body . . . and yet, each time we met, the Dark Man was much harder to deal with. It's as though he learns from his previous mistakes. I think there's one single mind controlling all the homunculi, jumping from body to body. It's also quite possible that there are more Dark Men out there somewhere, waiting for another chance at us.'

The God Squad looked at each other. 'Can you tell us anything about this sorcerer Bode?' said Rowan.

'Well,' said Hawk, 'apart from his having a mysterious mission on the Street of Gods at the same time as the Gods started dying, he also gave Lord Arthur Sinclair the original inspiration for the Hellfire Club. Bode does seem to get around, doesn't he? Did any of you know him?'

Buchan nodded slowly. 'I met him a few times, on the Street of Gods. Seemed a pleasant enough sort, though I never did find out what he was doing on the Street. I haven't seen him for some time.'

'Was this before or after the God Killings began?' said Fisher.

'Before, I think,' said Buchan.

'Did you ever meet his girlfriend?' said Hawk.

Buchan shook his head. 'Didn't know he had one. Is she important?'

'Beats me,' said Hawk. 'Anyone else here know Bode?'

'I met him once or twice,' said Rowan. 'He was asking questions on the Street, so I checked him out, just to see what he was up to. We get all sorts down here, and it pays to be careful. He was a bit vague about what he was doing on the Street, but that's not unusual. He seemed harmless enough, so I let him be.'

'What kind of questions was he asking?' said Fisher.

Rowan shrugged. 'Questions about the Gods. Their powers, their backgrounds, things like that. The usual tourist stuff. And I didn't see any girlfriend, either.'

Hawk sat quietly a moment, letting his thoughts settle. Bode was turning out to be an important link in the case, but they didn't really know anything about him. Perhaps he should contact the Guards in charge of the Bode killing, and have them send over all the papers found in Bode's house. Maybe there was something in them that would shed more light on the sorcerer . . .

'Assuming all the homunculi have a single mind,' said Tomb slowly, 'the important question must be who is controlling them.'

'Well, Bode, I would assume,' said Rowan. 'After all, the Dark Men are all versions of his own body. Perhaps he knew he was going to die, so he committed suicide and transferred his soul into one of the homunculi. That way he'd be free to continue with his mission. Whatever it is.'

'Suicide?' said Fisher. 'The cause of death was a single stab wound through the heart! If it was suicide, what happened to the knife?'

'That's a good point,' said Buchan. 'But if it isn't Bode, who is it?'

'Presumably the anonymous person who gave him his mission,' said Hawk. 'Whoever it is didn't want to be seen on the Street of Gods in person. Which suggests that somebody would have known him and recognised him.'

'Or her,' said Fisher. 'Remember the girlfriend? That could have been our unknown person, emerging briefly from the shadows to give Bode new orders.'

'This is getting complicated,' said Buchan. 'If we assume the Dark Men aren't really Bode, why are they still after Hawk and Fisher?'

'Because we're dangerous,' said Hawk. 'We're getting closer to the truth, and the Dark Man knows it.'

'Wait a minute,' said Tomb. 'We're overlooking something important. Did I understand you to say that the sorcerer Bode was killed in his own house? Why didn't his magic protect him?'

'Good question,' said Hawk. 'We don't know. When we got there, there was no trace of magic anywhere in the house; no wards, no booby traps, nothing.'

'That's insane,' said Tomb flatly. 'Even after his death, the protective wards should still have been there. They usually have to be dismantled by another sorcerer. Dammit, every sorcerer has wards of some kind; you can't work without them.'

'All right,' said Hawk. 'So it's crazy. Doesn't surprise me. The whole damn case is crazy.'

'But it is definitely looking more and more like one case,' said Fisher.

'It seems to me,' said Buchan, 'that we're not going to get anywhere until we can find out what Bode was doing here on the Street. That's got to be the key to everything.'

'So it would seem,' said Tomb. 'In which case, it's fortunate I asked an acquaintance of mine to join us here this evening. I thought Hawk and Fisher ought to meet him. He's very knowledgeable about the Street of Gods. It's said that nothing happens on the Street that he doesn't know about, often before it happens.'

'Oh, no,' said Buchan. 'You haven't. You haven't called *him* in, have you? Not Lacey?'

'Dirty little sneak,' muttered Rowan.

'He serves a purpose,' said Tomb firmly. He turned to Hawk and Fisher and smiled, almost apologetically. 'In order to do our job here on the Street, we have to be in constant touch with everything that's going on. Given the nature of the Street of Gods, that can be rather difficult. Rowan and I both have the Sight, but there's a limit to how much ground we can cover. So we are forced to depend on various reliable sources for our information.'

'Right,' said Buchan. 'Half our budget goes on bribe money.'

'And most of that goes to Lacey,' said Rowan.

'He's always proved most useful to us,' said Tomb. 'He has his own organisation of informants and eavesdroppers. They bring him all the news, rumour, and gossip, and he puts it all together. He's predicted more trends, business deals, heresies, and conspiracies than all our other sources put together.'

'He's also a nasty, repellent little creep, and he makes my skin crawl,' said Rowan.

'We know the sort,' said Hawk. 'We use informants in our line of work, too.'

'How much do you pay them?' asked Buchan.

Hawk grinned. 'Isobel lets them live. They seem happy to settle for that.'

'Anyway,' said Tomb, 'our man Lacey is waiting just down the hall. With your permission, I'll have him join us.'

He looked around for objections, but no one said anything. Buchan clearly didn't give a damn, and Rowan was sulking. Tomb gestured sharply with his left hand, and the drawing room door swung open on its own.

'Do come in, Lacey. There's a good fellow!' said Tomb loudly.

There was a pause, and then a wide, fleshy figure appeared

in the doorway, smiling ingratiatingly. He was better than average in height, but his great bulk made him look shorter. He moved slowly but with surprising grace, and something in the way he held himself suggested he was no stranger to violence, should it prove necessary. He had a round bland face, the main features of which were his small, dark eyes and constant smile. Fisher didn't like the smile. It looked practised. His hair was dark and greasy, plastered flat and parted neatly down the middle. Just looking at him, you knew immediately that you could trust him completely, provided you kept up the payments, but that the moment you ran out of money he'd disappear in an instant. The smile got worse the more you saw of it; the insincerity of it grated on the nerves like fingernails on a blackboard. All in all, Lacey was the kind of man you didn't want to shake hands with, in case some of his personality rubbed off on you.

'My dear Tomb, how nice to see you again. Looking well, as always. And your charming associates, Buchan and Rowan; two of my favourite people.' His voice sounded exactly the way you'd expect it to. Soft and breathy and thoroughly oily. The kind of sound a toad would make if it was trying to sell you a horse that nobody wanted. 'Always happy to be of service to you, my friends. Now then, I see we have guests present; Captains of our illustrious city Guard, no less. Will you honour me with your names, sir and madam?'

'Captain Hawk and Captain Fisher,' said Hawk. 'We're here on official business.'

Something happened to Lacey's face. He didn't flinch and he didn't stop smiling, but his eyes were suddenly cold and watchful. He looked very much as though he'd like to see how far it was to the door but didn't quite dare look. Apparently even on the Street of Gods, people had heard of Hawk and Fisher.

'The renowned Captains Hawk and Fisher; an honour indeed to make your acquaintance. What can I do for you?'

'We need information,' said Rowan. 'Not long ago, a sorcerer named Bode appeared on the Street, asking questions about the Gods. What can you tell us about him?'

Lacey smiled like a decrepit cherub, lowered himself into the one remaining chair, and laced his fingers across his vast stomach. 'Bode. Yes, I know that name.' He paused a moment, to arrange his weight more comfortably, and the chair creaked loudly. He smiled about him pleasantly, and then began to speak without pause or hesitation, as though he'd only been waiting for permission to speak a piece he'd already prepared. For all Hawk knew, that might just be the case.

'Bode was a low-level sorcerer,' said Lacey. 'Mainly interested in alchemy and the production of homunculi. An expensive interest, which he supported through his extensive knowledge of pills and potions. He was well known in his field, but was never going to be anyone important. He lacked the drive, and the determination. He knew this, but it didn't seem to bother him. He was not, by all accounts, ambitious.

'He first appeared on the Street of Gods just over a month ago, asking questions about the powers and backgrounds of the Gods. Where they came from, what attributes they possessed, why people worshipped them – the usual tourist stuff. Unlike most tourists, however, Bode wasn't prepared to settle for the usual answers. He kept digging for more and more details, refusing to be put off, even when it was made clear to him that some of his questions were not appreciated by the Beings involved. He just pressed even harder for answers, putting things together, despite several quite specific warnings. He was either very brave, very stupid, or lacking in any sense of self-preservation.

'He died quite recently, at his home in the Northside. Accounts of the manner of his death seem confused, but all the accounts agree that the good Captains Hawk and Fisher were somehow involved. As investigating officers.'

Lacey sat back in his chair, smiling serenely in a self-satisfied way. There was a long pause, as everyone digested the information he'd provided.

'Did anyone spot anything . . . unusual, about Bode?' Hawk asked carefully.

'Well, apart from what I've already told you, there were a few interesting occurrences. Several times on the Street Bode was recognised by old friends, who went over to talk to him, as old friends do. It would appear that Bode was very short with them on these occasions. He wouldn't discuss his business, or what he was doing on the Street, and on some occasions even pretended not to know them. All of which was most unlike Bode. Perhaps he thought he was acting undercover, so to speak, but he'd made no effort to disguise himself.'

'Did anyone ever see Bode looking . . . different?' asked Fisher. 'Larger, more muscular?'

Lacey looked at her sharply. 'An interesting question, Captain. It is true that since Bode's death previously reliable sources have reported seeing Bode walking the Street of Gods again, looking . . . somewhat different. Perhaps you can shed a little light on that, Captain?'

'Not right now,' said Fisher. 'According to some reports, Bode sometimes met his girlfriend on the Street. Can you tell us anything about her?'

'Unfortunately I have been able to learn very little about her, Captain. She appeared on only three occasions, each time heavily muffled under a cloak and hood. On the last occasion two of my associates tried to get a close look at her. They both died, right there on the Street.'

Hawk leaned forward in his chair. 'How did they die?'

'Natural causes, Captain. Heart attacks. Simultaneous heart attacks.'

'Sorcery,' said Fisher. Lacey inclined his head in agreement but said nothing.

'So,' said Rowan, 'we have a sorcerer and a sorceress on the Street of Gods, asking questions about the Beings. Questions the Beings don't want to answer. Perhaps that's why the Beings died; because they wouldn't answer the questions.'

'Or because they did.' said Buchan.

Fisher looked at him. 'I'm not sure I follow that.'

'I'm not sure I do myself,' said Buchan. 'What worries me is how the Beings died. You'd need a hell of a lot of power to overcome a Being on his own territory. You'd need a sorcerer the level of the High Warlock. And if someone like that was on the Street, we'd all know about it.'

'Let's move away from Bode for a moment,' said Tomb. 'Lacey, what is the situation on the Street at present? How are the Beings reacting to the murders?'

'Badly, my dear friend. There's a great deal of unease on the Street, both inside and outside the temples. In their own way, the Beings are quite frightened. They all tend to paranoia at the best of times. Right now most of them are busy looking for an enemy they can blame everything on; someone to strike back at. Old rivalries are becoming more intense. Old hatreds are being fuelled afresh. Everyone knows you're doing your best to find the killer, but the Gods aren't known for their patience. I fear it's only a matter of time before some God decides to take matters into its own hands and strikes the first blow. And we all know what that would lead to.'

'You're talking about a God War,' said Tomb.

'Yes, I'm rather afraid I am. Unless something is done soon, something significant, things are going to get worse on the Street very quickly. As it is, we're all waiting for the inevitable spark to set off a conflagration none of us can hope to put out.'

There was another long pause.

'I can't help feeling we're missing something,' said Buchan. 'Something so close we can't see the wood for the trees. Lacey, do you know of any connection between the three dead Beings?'

For the first time, Lacey looked a little uneasy, though his smile never wavered. 'Well, there is one . . . coincidence, my friends, but it may be nothing more than that . . .'

'We'll decide what's important,' said Rowan sharply. 'What is it?'

Lacey braced himself visibly. 'Each of the dead Beings received a visit from the Deity Division, on official business, not long before their death.'

Hawk looked sharply at Tomb. 'Is that right?'

'Well, yes. But we visit Beings all the time. It's part of our job. We've visited so many Beings recently, I hadn't even noticed the dead Beings were included.'

'But it is a connection,' said Fisher.

And then the voice of the Guard's communications sorcerer boomed suddenly in Hawk and Fisher's minds:

Riot on the Street of Gods! Riot on the Street of Gods! All available personnel report to the Street of Gods immediately. This command overrides all other orders and priorities until further notice.

Hawk and Fisher scrambled to their feet, their hands clawing instinctively for their weapons. The God Squad were on their feet too, looking equally shocked. They'd picked up the message, too. Lacey rose uncertainly to his feet.

'My friends, what is it? What has happened?'

'It seems your information came a little too late this time,' said Rowan. 'Someone's just fired the first shot in a God War.'

She ran out of the door, with Tomb close behind her. Lacey made as though to approach Buchan, and then hesitated.

'Pardon my intrusion, my friends, but about my fee . . .'

'Worry about that later,' said Hawk. 'Buchan . . .'

'But . . .'

'I said later!' Hawk glared at Lacey, and the informer backed quickly away. Hawk turned back to Buchan, who was still standing in a daze. 'I think we ought to get moving, sir Buchan. The riot won't wait for us to get there.'

'Of course. I'm sorry. I just never really thought it would happen, that's all. There hasn't been a serious riot on the Street in almost seventy years.'

'Seventy-one,' said Lacey. No one paid any attention.

'You're the expert,' Hawk said to Buchan. 'What's the best thing to do?'

'Pray,' said Buchan. 'But make sure you pick the right God.'

Hawk could hear the riot long before he could see it. Screams of rage and horror and anguish blended into a rising cacophony of sound that permeated the night air. The Street of Gods felt strangely out of synch, as though the various realities that made it up were no longer in alignment. Churches appeared and disappeared, and doors changed shape. Unnatural lights blazed in the starless sky, spread across the night like colours on a madman's palette. A surging vibration trembled in the ground underfoot, like the slow, regular heartbeat of something indescribably huge, buried down below.

Hawk and Fisher ran down the Street, weapons at the ready. They'd been running for some time, but the riot didn't seem to be getting any nearer. The Street was like that, sometimes, but at that moment it wasn't doing a thing for Hawk's nerves. He breathed deeply, trying to get more air into his lungs, and hoped his second wind would kick in soon. Fisher seemed to be struggling a little too, and she could usually run him into the ground. Buchan, on the other hand, was loping effortlessly along beside them, as though he covered this kind of distance every day before breakfast and thought nothing of it. With his physique, maybe he did. Hawk tried to stick with that train of thought, but his mind insisted on bringing him back to what passed for reality on the Street of Gods. The Guard communications sorcerer hadn't been very specific about how bad the riot was, but he wouldn't have sent out a general alarm like that unless his superiors had been sure something extremely nasty was happening up ahead.

He wondered briefly where Tomb and Rowan were. They'd disappeared even before Hawk had left God Squad headquarters, but there was no sign of them on the Street. Maybe they knew a shortcut. Maybe they'd already got to the riot, and had things safely under control. *Yeah*, thought Hawk sourly, *and while I'm wishing, I'd like a fortune in jewels as well, please*. The constant roar of noise was growing louder, uglier and more violent by the minute. Hawk rounded a corner that hadn't been there the last time he'd been this way, and then skidded to a halt, Fisher and Buchan piling up beside him. They'd found the riot.

Hundreds, maybe thousands of gaudily robed priests and acolytes were milling back and forth on the Street, furiously attacking each other with swords and fists and broken bottles. Everywhere there were bloody hands and faces, and unmoving bodies were being trampled blindly under-foot by the savage mob. Old hatreds were running loose and free, as age-old vendettas finally came to a head. Blinding lights flared from churches and temples, and overhead the sky churned sickly with uncontrolled magic. A handful of Guards had got there before Hawk and Fisher, and were fighting back to back on the edges of the crowd, too busy trying to stay alive to do anything about the riot. The Street belonged to the fanatics now, and they didn't care who they killed. A dozen green-robed priests swarmed over a Guard Constable and knocked him to the ground. He disappeared behind a host of swinging boots.

Hawk and Fisher waded in to help. Whatever else was happening, Guards looked after their own. They had to. No one else would. Hawk's axe swept back and forth in short, vicious arcs, and blood flew on the air. The priests scattered, and Fisher cut down those who didn't move fast enough. No one attacked a Guard and got away with it. It might give people ideas. The remaining priests disappeared into the crowd, and Buchan stood guard as Hawk and Fisher got the battered Constable to his feet and led him to the safety of a recessed doorway. There was blood on his face and his legs were shaky, but he seemed more or less intact. He nodded his thanks, and tried to get his thoughts together.

'Have you been here long?' asked Hawk.

'Can't be more than ten, twenty minutes,' said the Constable breathlessly. 'But it seems like forever. Just my luck to be working a beat so close to the Street of Gods when the riot call came . . .'

'Do you know what caused all this?' said Fisher.

'Seems another God has been murdered,' said the Constable. He paused to wipe blood out of his eyes. Buchan passed him an immaculately clean handkerchief, and the Constable pressed it gingerly to his forehead. 'The Lord of the New Flesh is dead. Someone ripped both its hearts right out of its breast. The High Priest found the body less than an hour ago. Didn't take long for word to get around. We don't know who actually started the riot. Could have been anybody.'

'Details can wait,' said Fisher. 'How many more Guards are there already here?'

'There were seventeen. We all got here about the same time, but the crowd separated us. We'd better get some reinforcements here soon. The Beings are mad as hell and scared spitless. It's only a matter of time before one of them decides to take a hand personally. And you can bet your arse if one God comes out onto the Street, they all bloody will.

Where the hell's the God Squad? They're supposed to prevent things like this from happening!'

'They're here somewhere,' said Hawk, carefully not looking at Buchan. 'We'll just have to try and keep the lid on things until they get their act together. Has anybody sent for the SWAT team?'

The Guard smiled sourly. 'First thing we did when we got here was to scream for the SWAT team. But according to the communications sorcerer, they're busy dealing with an emergency on the other side of the city. Typical. They're never bloody around when they're needed. We need them here! We can't cope with this!'

'Take it easy,' said Fisher. 'We're just Guards, not heroes. No one expects us to cope with everything. We just do the best we can.' She broke off to wave urgently at a contingent of Guards running down the Street toward them. 'Look; you join up with this bunch, and fill them in on the situation. We'll do what we can here. Now move it!'

The Constable nodded briefly, and moved off to intercept the newcomers. Hawk and Fisher looked at the growing riot, and then at Buchan.

'If it was up to me,' said Hawk, 'I'd just let them get on with it. With a bit of luck all the fanatics would kill each other off and the Street of Gods would be a far more peaceful place. But, unfortunately, the Constable was right. If we don't break this up, the Gods will get involved. And if that happens, I for one am not hanging around to see who wins. I am going to beg, borrow, or steal a pair of fast horses, and you can wave Fisher and me goodbye as we head for the nearest horizon.'

Buchan looked at Fisher. 'He really would, wouldn't he?'

'No,' said Fisher. 'He's not that sensible. He always did think about his duty too damned much. And since I won't leave without him, it looks like we're here for the duration.' She looked out over the frenzied mob and shook her head disgustedly. 'I've seen smaller armies. You're the expert, Buchan. How do we handle this?'

'Clear the Street,' said Buchan firmly. 'Don't worry about the Gods; Tomb and Rowan will take care of them if necessary. The rioters are our responsibility.'

'Get everyone off the Street,' said Hawk. 'Just like that?'

'It's not difficult,' said Buchan. 'We just have to make them more scared of us than they are of anything else. They may look dangerous, but most of them aren't armed, and those who are probably don't have much combat experience. Either way, they're no match for professionals like us.'

Hawk looked at him steadily. 'So we just wade right in and slaughter everything that moves. Is that it?'

'Pretty much,' said Buchan. 'And watch yourselves; rioting is a capital offence, and they know it. They'll kill you if you give them an opening. Don't make the mistake of thinking they'll respond to reason. They won't. They're beyond that now. So just do what you have to do, and worry about the body count later.'

He walked unhurriedly into the riot, and his sword flashed. Robed bodies fell to the ground and didn't move again.

'The trouble is, he's right,' said Hawk. 'I hate this job sometimes.'

'If we don't stop this riot, hundreds will die,' said Fisher. 'Maybe thousands. What are a few lives, compared to that?'

'I know,' said Hawk. 'But it doesn't make it any easier. I joined the Guard to protect people, not butcher them. Come on, lass. Let's do it.'

Fisher nodded, and together they moved silently into the riot and began the slaughter. They worked back to back, blades swinging, and blood splashed their cloaks. Robes of all shapes and colours surged around Hawk, the fanatics nothing more than angry faces and flailing fists. A few had swords. Some had clubs and lengths of chain. None of them stood a chance against Hawk and Fisher. Hawk swung his axe back and forth in wide, brutal arcs, and bodies crumpled to every side of him. Fisher guarded his back, her blade a silver blur as men and women fell screaming to the ground. The crowd began to fall back around them, and some of the rioters turned to flee rather than face the grim-faced Guards.

More Guards spilled onto the Street of Gods from all directions, drawn from all over the city, and soon the cobbled ground was slippery with blood and gore. An armoured contingent arrived from the Brotherhood of Steel, eager for a fight and determined to restore order. The sound of the crowd changed, fear replacing rage, and it began to crumble and fall apart under the onslaught of so many determined professional fighting men. Priests and acolytes threw down their weapons and ran for the safety of their temples. Piles of dead and injured lay scattered across the Street, mostly ignored. Some of them were Guards. A handful of Guard sorcerers appeared on the scene, and slowly the shifting realities returned to what passed for normal on the Street of Gods.

Hawk slowly lowered his axe and looked about him, panting for breath. The Street was emptying fast, and a slow sullen silence had fallen across the night. Tired-looking Guards were sorting the injured rioters from the dead, and finishing the job. Rioting, as Buchan had said, was a capital offence. Hawk turned his head away, and sat down suddenly, his back to a wall. There were some things he wouldn't do, and to hell with what the law said. Fisher sat down beside him, and leaned against him, her head on his shoulder.

'They're not paying us enough for this,' she said indistinctly.

'They couldn't pay us enough for this,' said Hawk.

'Then why are we doing it?'

'Because someone has to protect the innocent and avenge the wronged. It's a matter of honour. And duty.'

'That argument doesn't sound as convincing as it used to.'

Hawk nodded slowly. 'At least the worst is over now.'

A harsh metallic scream broke the silence, deafeningly loud and utterly inhuman. Hawk and Fisher scrambled to their feet and looked round just in time to see something huge and deadly surging out of a temple doorway not nearly big enough to let it though. Stone and timber broke apart and fell away as the Being emerged onto the Street of Gods. It was at least thirty feet high, a shimmering patchwork of metal fragments held together by rags and strings of rotting flesh. Patches of dark, discoloured skin revealed splintered bone and obscurely connected metal mechanisms. Steel and crystal machine parts thrust through the tattered hide, their razor-sharp edges grinding together as the Being rose to its full height. A roaring crimson fire burned in its steel belly and glowed in its bony eye sockets.

It had slender jagged arms with long-clawed hands that shimmered in its own bloody light. Broken silver chains hung from its wrists. Its steel jaws snapped together like a man-trap. A long tail studded with bony spikes lashed back and forth behind it. The Being threw back its long, wedge-shaped head and screamed defiance at the night. It had got out, and there was nothing anyone could do to stop it. It screamed again, a harsh metallic shriek that sent a sudden shiver through Hawk. There was nothing remotely human in the sound. The creature should never have lived, and was not alive in any way that made sense. But this was the Street of Gods, and it had got out, and not even those who had prayed to it for so long could hope to control it now.

It lowered its massive head, and looked at the Guards and Brothers of Steel gathered before it. There were close on three hundred armed men facing the Being, and Hawk knew with a sickening certainty that they weren't going to be enough. The huge creature darted forward, and its razor-sharp claws raked through a dozen men. More died screaming as the creature surged back and forth, crushing men under its massive bulk. Swords and axes cut uselessly at the Being's patchwork hide. Its long head snapped down to bite a man in half. Blood dripped from the metal jaws like steaming saliva. The Guards and the Brotherhood fell back, only their training keeping them from utter panic. The few Guard sorcerers roared and chanted, but their magics shattered harmlessly against the rogue Being, whose very existence defied the laws of reality.

'Where the hell did that thing come from?' said Fisher, as she and Hawk peered warily at the creature from the shadows of a concealed doorway.

'Must be a God of some kind,' said Hawk.

'You mean there are people crazy enough to worship *that*?'

'This is Haven, Isobel; they'll worship bloody anything here. And if one God's out, it won't be long before more come out to join it. I think this might be a good time to make a strategic retreat.'

Fisher looked at him sharply. 'We're not going anywhere, Hawk. We're God Squad now. And since the rest of the Squad has apparently vanished, that means that thing is our responsibility. It has to be stopped here, before it gets into a more populated part of the city.'

Hawk scowled. 'I hate it when you're right. Okay; you take left, I'll take right. We'll circle round behind the thing and see if we can cut through whatever it has instead of tendons in its legs. That should bring it down to our height if nothing else.'

'And if that doesn't work?'

'Pray really hard that Tomb and Rowan are on their way here, instead of doing the sensible thing and hiding in a storm cellar somewhere.'

'You worry too much, Hawk. After all, we've faced worse, in our time.'

They shared a smile, and then separated, darting silently

from shadow to shadow as they made their way behind the unliving creature. The Being reared up to its full height and glared down at the Guards and Brothers of Steel scattered around it. It screamed again, the inhuman sound echoing on and on. The sound was almost painfully loud as Hawk emerged from the shadows behind the Being, hefting his axe. Up close, the dead flesh smelt of corruption and burning oil. The Being's leg was taller than Hawk and easily twice as broad. There were flat plates of metal sliding against each other, and fraying ropes of muscle that flexed and tore with every movement. Steel cables stretched and hummed, lined with traceries of broken veins. Hawk looked at the axe in his hand and shook his head slowly.

This is probably a really bad idea . . .

He gripped the axe firmly with both hands, and swung it with all his strength at one of the steel cables in the left leg. The heavy axe sheared clean through the cable, and wedged itself between the moving parts inside the leg. The Being screamed deafeningly. Hawk tugged at his axe, but it was stuck tight. The Being lifted its leg, and Hawk was jerked up into the air, still clinging grimly to his axe. The foot slammed down heavily, cracking the cobbled ground, and Hawk was thrown clear. He lay on his back a moment, dazed, and then rolled quickly to one side. The taloned foot slammed down where he'd been lying. He clambered shakily to his feet, and saw his axe protruding from the leg, just in front of him. He grabbed it firmly with both hands, pulled hard, and almost fell down again as it came away easily. The impact of the stamping foot had jarred it loose.

Great, thought Hawk, circling quickly to keep behind the Being. *Now what do I do? Cutting the cable didn't even slow the bloody thing down.*

He caught a glimpse of something moving on the edge of his vision. He spun round, axe at the ready, and then relaxed a little as he saw it was Fisher. He just had time to nod acknowledgement, and then both of them had to throw themselves to the ground as a huge clawed hand slashed through the air where they'd been a moment before. They hit the ground rolling and were up and running before the Being could turn to face them. They ran in different directions to confuse it, but the huge creature paused only briefly before going after Fisher. Hawk swore briefly, and running after the Being, cut at one of its legs with his axe to get the creature's attention. The great wedge head swung down toward him, full of bloody steel teeth over a foot long. Hawk threw himself between the creature's legs and pounded down the Street after Fisher. The Being screamed deafeningly, and started after them.

The two Guards darted into a narrow alleyway, and the Being lurched to a halt at the alley mouth, uncertain how to get at them. Hawk and Fisher backed away down the alley, not taking their eyes off the creature. And then it slowly turned its head and looked away, as though sensing a greater menace close at hand. It looked back down the Street, and turned quickly to face the new threat. Hawk and Fisher watched silently from the protective shadows.

Tomb and Rowan were standing side by side in the middle of the Street of Gods, facing the rogue Being. Everyone else had disappeared. Only the dead remained, scattered over the cobbles like so many crumpled heaps of bloody clothing. The Being stared at Tomb and Rowan with its furnace eyes, and then started slowly, deliberately, toward them. Rowan held up her left hand. A small blue jewel blazed brightly in her grasp, the azure light spilling between her fingers. The Exorcist Stone. Rowan spoke a single Word of Power, and in a moment that seemed to last forever, the world changed.

Reality convulsed, shaking like a plucked harp string, and the rogue Being was suddenly no longer there. There was a sharp clap of thunder as air rushed in to fill the vacuum left by its sudden disappearance. And as quickly as that, it was all over. The night air was still and quiet, and the Street of Gods was calm again. Tomb and Rowan turned away as the Guards and Brothers of Steel reappeared on the Street and moved among them, doing what they could to help the injured. The Exorcist Stone had disappeared, tucked casually away into one of Rowan's pockets.

Hawk and Fisher leaned wearily back against the wall at the alley mouth, eyes closed, letting their aching muscles slowly relax. Tiredness so deep it was more like pain coursed through Hawk's body, tugging at his muscles like a persistent beggar demanding attention.

'So,' he said finally. 'That was the Exorcist Stone.'

'Yeah,' said Fisher. 'Impressive. Pretty colour, too.'

'If nothing else, it should calm things down a bit. Both the Beings and their priests will think twice before getting out of line again.'

'Don't bank on it,' said Fisher. 'That's too sensible, too logical. Nothing on this bloody Street is ever logical.'

'True.'

They moved out onto the Street of Gods to help with the injured. Tomb waved and smiled at them briefly, but he and Rowan were too busy to break away. Buchan appeared from among a group of Guards, caught Hawk and Fisher's attention, and strode quickly toward them. Hawk took in Buchan's face and stance, and his heart sank. Whatever the man had to say, Hawk knew instinctively he didn't want to hear it. Buchan came to a halt before Hawk and Fisher, and nodded briskly. There was blood on his clothes and hands, none of it his.

'Whatever it is, the answer's no,' said Hawk flatly. 'I don't care if someone's planning to destroy the whole Street of Gods. I might even applaud. Isobel and I are exhausted. We've worked too hard too long, and we're way behind on our sleep. That's a dangerous state to be in. It's too easy to make mistakes when you're tired. So, Isobel and I are going to help out here for a while, and then we're going home to get some sleep. Whatever you want will just have to wait.'

'Right,' said Fisher.

'Sleep can wait,' said Buchan. 'This can't. I was just talking to one of the Guard sorcerers. Something nasty is building at Hightower Hall. Something really nasty. Tomb and Rowan can't go. They're needed here. That just leaves us.'

'Read my lips,' said Hawk. 'We're not going. Isobel's out on her feet and I'm not much better. If the Hellfire Club's got their fingers burnt, it's their own damned fault.'

'This is God Squad business,' said Buchan. 'We can't turn our back on people who need us just because we don't like them.'

'Watch me. Isobel's in no state . . .'

'Oh, hell, let's go,' said Fisher. 'The time we spend arguing with Buchan, we could be there and back. Besides, I haven't got the strength to argue.'

'That's the spirit,' said Buchan. 'It's only a mile or so to High Tory from here. We can do it in ten minutes if we hurry. Don't you just love working in the God Squad? Never a dull moment.'

He set off briskly down the Street of Gods, and Hawk and Fisher moved wearily after him.

'If he doesn't stop being so bloody cheerful,' growled Hawk ominously, 'I am personally going to tie both his legs in a square knot.'

'I'll help,' said Fisher.

They hurried after Buchan, muttering mutinously under their breath. From the shadows of a side alley, the Dark Man watched them go but made no move to follow.

6

Needs, Desires, And Other Motives

By the time they reached Hightower Hall, Hawk had found his second wind and was feeling only moderately shattered. The crisp cold air of winter felt refreshing after the close, humid warmth of the Street of Gods, and helped to clear his head. Even so, it was Buchan who noticed the first sign of something amiss. He stopped well short of the tall iron gates and looked uncertainly about him. Hawk and Fisher stopped with him, their hands dropping automatically to their weapons.

'What's wrong?' said Fisher.

'It's too quiet,' said Buchan slowly. 'And there's no one watching the gates. Where are all the men-at-arms? They wouldn't just go off and leave the gates unguarded.' He reached out and pushed at the gates, and they swung slowly open at the pressure. 'Not even locked. Something unexpected must have happened. An emergency, a call for help; something. The men-at-arms went to investigate . . . and never came back.' He looked slowly around him, senses straining and alert. 'There's something else too; a feeling on the air . . .'

Hawk nodded. He could feel it prickling on his skin and scratching at his nerves; a vague pressure, like the building tension on the air that warns of an approaching storm. 'Magic,' he said flatly. 'The Hellfire Club finally found a ritual that worked.'

He hefted his axe once, and then moved cautiously through the gates and into the grounds. The only light came from the half-moon overhead and the wide blazing windows of the Hall. All was still and quiet. There was no sign of men-at-arms anywhere. Hawk padded softly forward, Fisher and Buchan close behind him, swords at the ready. They walked on the grass, avoiding the gravel pathway. Gravel was noisy. The Hall loomed up ahead, silhouetted against the night sky.

Almost halfway there, Hawk found two of the guard dogs. They were lying stretched out on the grass, still and silent, two darker shadows in the gloom. Hawk knelt down beside them, and pushed one gently with his fingertips. The body rolled slightly back and forth, and then was still again. Both dogs were dead. He checked them over quickly, but there was no sign of any wound, no trace to show what had killed them. It was as though they'd just lain down where they were, and the life went out of them.

'Captain Fisher,' said Buchan quietly. 'Do you still have your suppressor stone?'

'Sure,' said Fisher. 'Why?'

'Activate it. Now. And you and Captain Hawk had better stay close together. That way, the stone will protect you both from any general magic in the area.'

'What about you?' said Hawk.

'I have my own stone,' said Buchan. 'Now let's get moving. Something bad has happened at the Hall, and I have a horrible feeling we've got here too late to stop it.'

He and Fisher muttered over their suppressor stones, and then the three of them moved warily forward into the darkness, their eyes fixed on the Hall. There was still no sign of any movement at the brightly blazing windows. Hawk was the first to reach the front door. It was open, standing slightly ajar. Hawk pushed at it with his foot. The door moved back a way, and then stopped as it hit an obstruction. Hawk eased himself through the narrow gap and looked down to see what was blocking the door. As he'd expected, it was a body: one of the men-at-arms. Hawk knelt down and checked quickly for vital signs. The man-at-arms was alive, but only just. His skin was cold and deathly pale, his pulse slow, and his breathing disturbingly shallow. Hawk straightened up and looked along the hallway. More men-at-arms lay scattered and unmoving the length of the entrance hall. Hawk squeezed through the doorway, followed by Fisher and Buchan.

'There was an emergency,' said Buchan quietly. 'Someone called for help. The men-at-arms came running, from the house and from the grounds. This was as far as they got. Whatever the Hellfire Club has called up, it didn't want to be disturbed.'

'But how could they have called up something?' said Fisher. 'They were a bunch of amateurs; you said so yourself.'

'They must have had help.'

Hawk frowned. 'What kind of help?'

'Good question,' said Buchan. 'Let's go and find out.'

He took the lead, and guided Hawk and Fisher unerringly through the maze of corridors that led to the ballroom. The silence was complete, broken only by their own soft footsteps. They found servants here and there, lying crumpled where they fell, struck down by the same deathly sleep. Hawk peered continuously about him, skin crawling in anticipation of the attack that never came, his tiredness burned away by rising adrenalin.

They finally came to the closed double doors that led to the ballroom. Buchan made as though to push the doors open and walk straight in, but Hawk stopped him with a cautious hand on his arm. He looked warily around him, then stepped forward, and pressed his ear against the right-hand door. He couldn't hear anything. Either the wood was too thick, or there wasn't anything to hear. Taking hold of both door-handles, he very carefully eased the doors open an inch or two and then stepped back. He made sure his grip on his axe was secure, looked quickly at Fisher and

Buchan, then stepped forward and kicked the doors open. The three of them surged forward to fill the doorway, weapons at the ready.

The Quality lay strewn across the waxed and polished floor of the ballroom in their brightly coloured finery, like so many broken butterflies. They lay singly or in heaps, wherever they'd been standing when the magic struck them down. Most were awake but unable to move. Some were moaning quietly, as much in horror as in pain. All of them looked withered and ancient, aged long beyond their years, held somehow on the very edge of death as their life drained slowly out of them. Those nearest the blue chalk circle looked almost mummified. And there, in the middle of the ballroom, inside the blue circle, stood the thing the Hellfire Club had called up out of the Gulfs. It looked across at the doorway, and smiled charmingly.

'Well, now,' it said in a soft, pleasant voice. 'Visitors. How nice.'

The figure was six feet fall, quite naked, and aesthetically muscular in a way usually achieved only by statues. Its face was classically handsome and unmarked by time, so flawlessly perfect as to be almost inhuman. A raw sensuality burned around it like an invisible flame, attractive and repellent in its uncaring arrogance, like bitter honey or the smell of an open wound masked by perfume. It was the perfect embodiment of the male form, burning with ruthless vitality.

'What's wrong with the Quality?' said Fisher softly. 'What's happened to them?'

'The creature they called up is draining the life right out of them,' said Buchan. 'Their deaths will make it even more powerful. Even a low-level sorcerer would have known to set wards so this couldn't happen, but these people were amateurs, and they didn't know. At least they had enough sense to draw a restraining circle. That should hold it for a while.'

'How long?' said Hawk, not taking his gaze from the figure before him.

'Only as long as it takes to drain its summoners dry,' said Buchan. 'After that, it'll be powerful enough to break the circle, and there'll be nothing we can do to stop it.'

'What about the Exorcist Stone?' said Fisher.

Buchan smiled tiredly. 'The creature will be gone long before we could get the Stone here, and all the Quality will be dead.'

'Great,' said Hawk. 'Just great.' He moved slowly forward, stopping right at the edge of the chalk circle. The creature watched him intently, still smiling its perfect smile. Hawk looked into its dark unblinking eyes and saw no humour there, or any other emotion he could recognise. 'Who are you?' he said harshly. 'What are you?'

'I'm what they wanted,' said the thing in the circle. 'I'm all the darkness in their souls, all their hidden hates and wants and desires set free at last, given shape and form and substance, in me. I'm strong and beautiful and perfect because that's what they wanted me to be. Or perhaps because that's how they see themselves, in the privacy of their mind's eye. It really doesn't matter. They gave me life, whether they meant to or not, and they'll go on giving me life until they die. Then, when I have fully come into my power, I'll leave them here and go out into the city. A new Being, in all his glory. A new God for the Street of Gods. And men shall worship me as they always have, under one name or another, in blood and suffering and all the hidden darkness of their souls. I shall be very happy here. This city was built with me in mind.'

'I've met your kind before,' said Hawk. 'You're just another Dark Man with delusions of grandeur, that's all.'

'I shall show you blood and horror,' said the creature pleasantly. 'I will break your body and your spirit, and you will praise me before I let you die. You don't understand what I am. What I really am. I'm everything that ever scared you, every dark impulse you tried to hide, your worst nightmare given flesh and blood and bone.'

'You're also stuck in that circle,' said Fisher, moving forward to stand beside Hawk. 'And if you had any power to use against us, you'd have used it by now. You're not leaving this circle. You're not going anywhere. We'll see to that.'

'So brave,' said the creature. 'And so foolish. You are nothing compared to me.'

Fisher grinned. 'Fancies himself, doesn't he? Let's see how he likes half a yard of cold steel rammed through his appendix.'

'No!' said Buchan, moving quickly forward to join the two Guards at the edge of the circle. 'Don't try it, Captain. You can't reach the thing from outside the circle, and once you cross the chalk line your suppressor stone wouldn't be able to protect you anymore. The creature would drain you dry just like the Quality.'

'No problem,' said Fisher. She sheathed her sword, took a throwing knife from her left boot, aimed and let fly with a single rapid movement. The creature's hand moved, too quickly for the eye to follow, and snatched the knife in mid-air. It dropped the knife to the floor and smiled at Fisher. She blinked, and turned to Buchan. 'We might just have a problem here after all. How long do you think we've got before it has enough power to leave the circle?'

'Not long. Half the Quality are at death's door already. Whatever we're going to do, we've got to do it soon.'

'Wait a minute,' said Hawk. 'The Exorcist Stone would get rid of it, right? How about the suppressor stone? That's supposed to work on the same principle, isn't it?'

Buchan frowned. 'Well, yes, but it's nowhere near as powerful. You'd have to get the suppressor stone within an inch or so of the creature, and even then there's no guarantee it would work. And if it didn't . . . the creature would either drain you like the Quality, or tear you apart just for the fun of it.'

'If we wait till it gets out of the circle we're dead anyway,' said Hawk. 'Look, if you've got a better idea, let's hear it. I'm not actually wild about going into that bloody circle unless I have to.'

'There is . . . another alternative,' said Buchan. He turned his back on the creature and looked out over the ballroom. 'It's gathering its power from the life force of the Quality. If they were all to die – before the creature could come into its full power – it would remain helpless within the circle.'

'We can't just kill them!' said Hawk.

'It's inhuman!' said Fisher. 'We can't!'

'You think I like suggesting it?' snapped Buchan. 'I grew up with these people! They're my friends!'

'It's out of the question,' said Hawk flatly.

'No it isn't,' said a quiet voice from among the Quality. 'Kill us. Kill us all. Please. Do you think we want to live like this?'

They found Lord Louis Hightower sitting propped up against the wall. His flesh was pale and blotched and heavily wrinkled, sunk right back to the bone, and Buchan only recognised him by his clothes. His mouth was just a colourless gash, and his breathing barely stirred his chest, but still he fought to force out his words as Buchan knelt beside him.

'If we die, the shock will kill that thing. It's linked to us.'

'Louis . . .'

'Do it, Charles! Please. I can't face living like this.'

'No!' said Hawk. 'If we can kill the thing while it's still in the circle, there's a damn good chance you'll get your life back. The link between you works both ways. Or it should.' He knelt down beside the mummified figure. 'Let us at least try to save you. I've lost two Hightowers already. I don't want to lose a third.'

Hightower looked at him, and his mouth moved in something that might have been a smile. 'All right, Captain. Go ahead. But, this time, get it right.'

Hawk nodded stiffly, then straightened up and headed back to the edge of the circle. Fisher and Buchan went with him.

'I take it you do have some kind of plan,' said Buchan.

'I wouldn't bank on it,' said Fisher. 'Hawk's always been a great one for improvising.'

'Well, basically, I thought I'd cut the creature's heart out and jam the suppressor stone into the hole,' said Hawk. 'That should ruin its day.'

'Sounds good to me,' said Fisher. 'You hit him from the left, I'll hit him from the right.'

'This is crazy,' said Buchan. 'Absolutely bloody crazy. Let's do it, before we get an attack of common sense and change our minds.'

The three of them spread out round the circle, weapons at the ready. The creature smiled at them warmly and spread its arms as though welcoming them. Hawk hesitated a moment at the chalk line, then braced himself and stepped quickly across it. The years hit him like a club, almost forcing him to his knees. He could feel his joints stiffening and his muscles shrivelling as life itself was sucked out of him to feed the creature before him. His axe grew heavier with every movement, and it took all his strength to keep his back straight and his head erect. He heard shocked gasps of pain and horror as Fisher and Buchan entered the circle, but he didn't look round. He didn't want to see what was happening to them. He didn't want to think about what was happening to him. He hefted his axe, and threw himself at the smiling creature.

It dodged the axe easily, and sent Hawk flying across the circle with a casual backhand blow. He hit the ground hard, driving the breath from his lungs, and for a moment he couldn't find the strength to get to his knees. He gritted his teeth and staggered to his feet again, swaying from the effort. Fisher and Buchan were cutting at the creature with their swords, but the thing simply raised its arms to ward off the blows, and the blades sprang away as though they'd met solid metal instead of flesh. The creature's arms weren't even bruised.

Fisher was an old woman, with white hair and a heavily lined face. Buchan was bent and twisted with age, barely able to hold onto his sword. Hawk fought down a rising tide of panic. Their weapons were no use against the creature, but they had nothing else. Except the suppressor stones. *Get the stone close to him.* That was what Buchan had said. *Get it as close as possible, or it won't work.* Hawk scowled. He knew what he'd like to do with the stone . . . The scowl slowly became a smile. When in doubt, be direct. He waited a moment as Buchan and Fisher gathered up their remaining strength and threw themselves at the creature, and then he put away his axe and lurched forward. The creature saw him coming, but since Hawk was empty-handed, ignored him to concentrate on fending off its armed attackers. Hawk moved in behind the creature, took a deep breath, and jumped the thing from behind, locking an arm round the creature's throat. It tried to grab him to throw him off, but couldn't quite reach. Hawk hung on grimly, forcing the head back.

'Isobel!' he yelled harshly. 'Get the stone and ram it down his throat!'

Fisher dropped her sword and clawed the suppressor stone from her pocket. Buchan leapt forward and grabbed both the creature's arms. Fisher seized the creature's chin, yanked it down, and pressed the stone into its mouth. Then she forced the mouth closed with both hands and held on with all her strength. The creature bucked and heaved and threw Hawk off. Buchan let go its arms, stepped back a pace, and punched the creature in the throat. It gagged, swallowed despite itself, and then screamed horribly. There was a small, very localised explosion, and then Hawk, Fisher, and Buchan were alone in the circle.

Hawk blinked dazedly a moment, then looked at Fisher, and smiled widely with relief. She was herself again, the added years gone along with the creature that had tried to force them on her. They hugged each other tightly for a long moment, and then let go and looked around them. There was a rising hum of voices as the Quality discovered that they also had been renewed. Buchan was already moving among them, grinning and laughing and being slapped on the back. Fisher noticed that her sword, her knife, and the suppressor stone were lying on the floor inside the circle, and she bent down to retrieve them.

'One of your better ideas, Hawk,' she said finally, as she sheathed her sword. 'Where did the creature go, do you suppose?'

Hawk shrugged. 'Back where it came from. And good riddance.'

The noise in the ballroom had risen from a babble to a roar, as the Quality tried to figure out what had happened, and exactly who was to blame. Lord Hightower shook Buchan firmly by the hand, and then strode over to join the two Guards. He nodded to them both, and they bowed politely.

'I just wanted to extend my personal thanks and congratulations. I'll see there's a commendation in this for both of you. Going into that circle after the creature was the bravest thing I've ever seen.'

'Thank you, my Lord,' said Hawk. 'It's all part of the job.'

'I didn't get a chance to talk to you the last time you were here. I wanted to assure you and your partner that I don't hold you in any way responsible for the deaths of my father or my brother Paul. I checked you out very thoroughly. It wasn't your fault. You mustn't blame yourselves.'

'Thank you,' said Hawk. 'I'm glad you feel that way. I

never really had the chance to know your father, but I liked your brother. He was a good man to work with.'

'Speaking of blame,' said Buchan, as he joined them, 'how the hell did you manage to raise that creature in the first place?'

Hightower frowned unhappily. 'Lord Brunel came into possession of an old grimoire, and persuaded us that some of its rituals might be adapted to suit our purposes. Yes, I know. We should have known better. But we thought we'd be safe, as long as we stayed outside the circle . . .'

'Oh, that's typical, that is! Put all the blame on me!' Brunel's voice blared out from nearby, and the small group turned to see him stalking toward them. 'You're not laying the blame for all this at my door. We discussed whether or not to use the ritual, and everyone agreed. Including you, Hightower. It wasn't my fault everything went wrong.'

'We can talk about this later,' said Buchan. 'In the meantime, I think you'd better let me have the grimoire for safekeeping. My colleagues in the God Squad will want to examine it.'

Brunel's hand dropped halfway to a square bulge underneath his waistcoat. 'I'm not handing over anything. The grimoire's mine. If I let you have it I'll never see it again. I know your sort. You'd keep it for yourself. But you're not having it. There's power in this book, and it belongs to your betters. All right, things got a bit out of hand this time, but . . .'

'This time?' said Buchan. 'You're not thinking of trying this kind of stunt again?'

'Why not? Next time, we'll get it right. You can't stop us. We're Quality, and you're not – not anymore. What we do is our business and nothing to do with you. You're not one of us anymore, Buchan, and your precious heroics here tonight don't change a thing. You're still nothing more than a dirty little Sister-lover, and we don't want you here.'

Fisher stepped briskly forward, punched Brunel out, and

took the grimoire from his unconscious body. She looked round at the watching crowd.

'Any objections?'

No one said anything, and most of the Quality looked away to avoid catching her eye. Fisher turned her back on them and handed the grimoire to Buchan.

'You have to know how to talk to these people. Shall we go?'

Buchan and Hightower exchanged a brief smile, and then bowed formally to each other. Buchan left the ballroom through the open double doors, followed by Hawk and Fisher. Hawk turned back to shut the doors, and came face to face with the silent, staring Quality. He'd helped save their lives, but all he could see in their faces was resentment, and perhaps even hate. They'd been saved by a social inferior who didn't even have the decency to be apologetic about it. Hawk grinned at them, winked, and closed the doors on their disapproving scowls.

Hawk and Fisher and Buchan returned to God Squad headquarters to find Rowan and Tomb sitting slumped and shattered in their usual chairs in the drawing room. Apparently clearing up the mess left on the Street of Gods had been a major undertaking, and was still continuing even now, but they'd done all they could. The Beings remained in their churches and temples, and their followers had retired to lick their wounds and plot more trouble for the future. Everything was quiet for the moment, but it was a false peace, and everyone knew it. They were just waiting for the next dead Being, and then there would be God War on the Street of Gods. And not even the Exorcist Stone would be enough to stop that. Tomb had sent an urgent message to the Council's circle of sorcerers, bringing them up to date on the situation and asking for help and support, but as usual the circle was split by factions and intrigues, and probably wouldn't even respond till it was too late.

'I don't know why I feel so bitter about it,' said Tomb tiredly. 'This is Haven, after all.'

Rowan's mouth twitched in something that might have been meant as a smile. She didn't just look tired, she looked exhausted. Her face was pale and slack, with dark bruises of fatigue under her eyes.

'Are you feeling all right, lady Rowan?' Hawk asked politely.

'I'm fine,' said Rowan. 'I just need a rest, that's all.'

Her voice was flat and strained, and they could all see the effort it took her just to speak. Tomb cleared his throat uncertainly.

'Rowan, I really think we'd all be a lot happier if you'd let us call in a doctor, just to have a look at you . . .'

'How many more times do I have to tell you?' snapped Rowan. Her anger produced two fiery red spots on her cheeks, but her face remained dull and impassive, as though the facial muscles were simply too tired to respond. 'I don't need a doctor, I don't need fussing over, and most of all I don't need you crawling around me all the time. Why won't you all just leave me in peace?'

There was an awkward pause, and then Buchan rose unhurriedly from his chair. 'Come on, Tomb. Let's raid the kitchen and see what we can find there. I don't know about you, but I'm starving. It's typical we had to have our busiest day in months on the one day in the week our servants have off.'

Tomb nodded without looking at him, and the two men left the drawing room, Buchan pulling the door firmly shut behind them. Hawk and Fisher looked at each other.

'I hate to press you on this, lady Rowan,' said Hawk firmly, 'but if there is something seriously wrong with you, we need to know about it. Things are going from bad to worse out there on the Street, and we have to know if we can depend on you in a crisis.'

Rowan shifted tiredly in her chair. 'Yes. I suppose you do.

And it would feel so good to talk about it to someone. But you have to swear not to tell Buchan and Tomb. Especially Tomb.' She looked at Hawk and Fisher in turn, fixing them with her piercing eyes in her weary face, and waiting until they'd both nodded in agreement. 'I have cancer. It's well-established and very advanced, and there's nothing that can be done about it. I thought for a long time I could cure it myself, with my knowledge of potions. By the time I discovered I couldn't, it was too late. It's spread too far for alchemy to do any good now. I've talked to experts. There are spells that might work, but I don't have that kind of money. I've got a month or so left; maybe a little more.

'You mustn't tell Tomb. It would upset him. He hasn't the power to cure me himself, and the dear fool would bankrupt himself trying to raise the money to buy a cure. It's better that he doesn't know.'

'But surely . . . one of the Gods could do something,' said Fisher uncertainly. 'I mean, they do miracles. Don't they?'

'I used to think that,' said Rowan. 'But if I've learned anything here, it's that there are no Gods on the Street of Gods. I looked really hard, trying to find just one, but all I found were supernatural Beings with no love for the God Squad.'

She broke off as the door opened, and Tomb and Buchan came in bearing trays of cold food. For various reasons no one had much to say while they ate, so the meal passed for the most part in silence. Rowan just picked at her food, pushing it back and forth on her plate, and finally she put it to one side and quietly announced she was going back to bed and didn't want to be disturbed. Everyone nodded, and Tomb wished her good night. She left the room without answering, shutting the door firmly behind her. The others finished their food, and sat for a while in silence, thinking their separate thoughts.

'You mustn't mind Rowan,' said Tomb finally, to Hawk

and Fisher. 'It's just her way. She'll be a lot better once she's had a little rest.'

'Sure,' said Hawk. 'We understand.'

'Now, if you'll excuse me, I have to be going out again.' Tomb pushed his empty plate to one side and stood up.

'Already?' said Fisher. 'We only just finished putting down that riot and clearing up after the Hellfire Club. What else is there that needs doing?'

Tomb smiled. 'Nothing for you to worry about, Captain. This is just some old personal business that I have to attend to. I won't be long. I'll see you again, later.'

He nodded generally to them all, and left. The door was still closing when Buchan got to his feet.

'Afraid I must be off as well. Tomb isn't the only one who's had to neglect his personal life of late. I'll be back in an hour or two. If you have to go out as well, don't worry about Rowan. There are wards around the house to keep her safe and alert Tomb if she needs anything. Now I really must be going.'

And as quickly as that, he was gone. Hawk and Fisher looked at each other. 'I'll follow Tomb,' said Hawk. 'You follow Buchan. Right?'

'Right,' said Fisher. 'There are too many secrets around here for my liking. You know, those have to be two of the flimsiest excuses I've ever heard.'

'I get the feeling they're both under pressure,' said Hawk. 'And I don't just mean the trouble on the Street. They probably intended to go out a lot earlier, but got side-tracked by the riot and the Hellfire Club. Right. They've had enough time to get a good start by now. Let's go.'

They got to their feet and hurried out into the corridor. Hawk spotted one of Tomb's long hooded robes hanging on a wall hook, and slipped it on instead of his own distinctive Guard's cloak. With the hood pulled well forward, he looked like just another priest. He glanced at Fisher.

'Maybe you should try a disguise, too.'

Fisher shook her head. 'Six-foot muscular blond women tend to stand out in a crowd, no matter what they're wearing. I'll just have to be careful, that's all. It's dark out, so as long as I keep well back and stick to the shadows, I should be all right. I'll meet you two hours from now at the Dead Dog tavern. Our usual booth. Sound good to you?'

'Great,' said Hawk. 'Maybe now we'll get a break on this case, and find a motive that makes sense. The way things are going, I'd settle for a motive that doesn't make sense. Now let's move it, before we lose them.'

Hawk had no trouble locating Tomb. The sorcerer was striding down the Street of Gods at a pace that kept threatening to break into a run. People saw the scowl on his face and got out of his way fast. Hawk strode along after him, not even trying to be inconspicuous. Even at this late hour of the evening there were crowds of priests and acolytes and worshippers bustling back and forth, getting on with the business of life that the riot had only briefly interrupted. Hawk was just another robed figure among many. Not that Tomb would have noticed anyway. He shouldered his way through the crowd with utter indifference to the snarls and curses this earned him, apparently entirely preoccupied with wherever he was going. Hawk had been banking on that. If Tomb even suspected he was being followed, he would undoubtedly have any number of spells to deal with the situation, few if any of them pleasant.

Tomb strode on, ignoring the manifestations that haunted the sidewalks and alleyways. Hawk did his best to do the same, but was momentarily thrown when an acolyte in a cheap crimson robe stepped directly in front of him to beg for a blessing. Hawk put a hand on the acolyte's shaven head, muttered something about peace and joy and brotherhood, and hurried after Tomb, hoping fervently that he hadn't inadvertently invoked a nearby Being by accident.

You had to be careful what you said on the Street of Gods. You could never be sure who was listening.

He followed Tomb down into the low-rent section of the Street of Gods, where the twisting back streets and alleyways turned in upon themselves, offering sanctuary to Beings and beliefs who had fallen on hard times. A last harbour for forgotten Gods and fading philosophies. Hawk hung well back as Tomb approached a nondescript, weather-beaten door set into a dirty white wall. The sorcerer produced a heavy iron key from a hidden pocket and unlocked the large iron padlock. The door creaked open under his hand, and he disappeared inside, pulling the door shut behind him.

Hawk quickly took up a position in a shadowed doorway overlooking the street, in case this was only a way stop and the sorcerer might reappear unexpectedly. Long moments passed. No one moved in the narrow back street. Hawk bit his lip, scowling thoughtfully. What the hell was Tomb doing here? It couldn't be anything illegal; the sorcerer had made no attempt to disguise his appearance. But what was so important to Tomb that it could drag him down here at this time of the night, when he was clearly already exhausted from coping with the riot? Hawk left his hiding place and padded silently over to the shabby door. He listened carefully, but everything seemed quiet within. He tried the door handle and raised an eyebrow as it turned easily under his hand, and the door swung open. Hawk froze as the door hinges creaked softly, but no one came to investigate. He slipped inside and eased the door shut behind him.

The narrow hallway was lit by a single lamp on the wall. Hawk tested the glass with his fingertips. It was barely warm. Tomb must have lit the lamp when he came in, which suggested there was no one here but the sorcerer. The walls were bare wood. They might have been waxed or polished a long time ago, but now there was only a thick coating of dust on the dull surfaces. Whatever this place was, no one had lived in it for a long time. There were no doors leading off the hallway. Hawk followed it to its end, where it turned a sharp corner and became a long narrow stairway leading down into darkness. Hawk scowled at the bottomless gloom, and then reached for the stub of candle and box of matches he kept in his cloak pocket for emergencies. His fingers scrabbled futilely against rough cloth for a long moment before he remembered he was wearing one of Tomb's robes instead of his Guard's cloak. He cursed under his breath, and padded back down the hall to fetch the lamp.

The stairway didn't look nearly so menacing in the lamplight, but even so he still hesitated at the top of the stairs. When all was said and done, following a sorcerer into an unknown situation was never a Good Idea. There could well be a magical bodyguard or booby trap waiting for him at the foot of the stairs. The suppressor stone might protect him . . . but it was still in Fisher's pocket. Hawk shook his head quickly, and drew his axe. He'd faced sorcerers before with nothing but cold steel in his hand, and he was damned if he'd let his nerves get the better of him now.

He descended slowly into the dark, lamp in one hand, axe in the other, ears straining for any sound down below. The walls were bare stone, rough and crumbling and splotched here and there with clumps of lichen. What the hell was Tomb doing in a dump like this? It couldn't be anything commonplace or innocent, or he'd have said where he was going. Since he hadn't, that meant Tomb either wouldn't or couldn't explain. Hawk didn't like secrets. Particularly when they left him in the dark in the middle of a murder enquiry. The stairs ended at a simple wooden door, standing slightly ajar. Light shone round its edges. Hawk stayed put on the bottom step and chewed his bottom lip thoughtfully. He seemed to have spent an awful lot of time hovering outside ominous-looking doors recently, and none of them had led him anywhere pleasant. He hefted his axe, took a deep breath and let it go, and kicked the door open.

'Come in, Captain Hawk,' said Tomb. 'I've been waiting for you.'

The sorcerer was sitting on a plain wooden stool, a few yards beyond the doorway. Above and around him loomed a bare stone cavern, maybe twenty feet high and almost as wide. A pale blue light flickered around the sorcerer, gleaming brightly on metallic traces in the rock. There was no one else there, only the sorcerer Tomb. Hawk stayed put in the doorway, looking around him. There had to be someone else there. Tomb wouldn't have come all this way just to sit in a cave by himself.

'How long have you known I was here?' he asked finally, careful to keep his voice calm and relaxed.

'Quite some time, Captain. I wouldn't be much of a sorcerer if I didn't know when I was being spied on, now would I? Don't worry; I'm not angry. In your position, I'd probably have done the same. Probably. I like the robe, by the way. It suits you.'

'Tomb, what are you doing here?'

'It's rather difficult to put into words, Captain. But if you'll stop skulking in the shadows and come and join me, I'll do my best to explain.'

Hawk mentally tossed a coin, shrugged, and stepped forward. He might as well, he wasn't learning anything useful where he was. The moment he crossed the threshold, the Presence washed over him like a wave. It filled the cavern; a vast, implacable but utterly intangible Presence. It was like nothing but itself; a living entity with no physical existence, but so real that Hawk could almost feel its heartbeat against his skin. He looked wonderingly at Tomb, who smiled faintly.

'Le Bel Inconnu; the Fair Unknown. It was worshipped as a God long ago, in another place. My family served as its priests for generations. But we are both far from home now, this God and I. It seems I am the last of my line, and when Le Bel Inconnu discovered it was dying, it had no one else to turn to but me.'

'Dying?' said Hawk. 'How can a God die? It doesn't even have a body!'

'Things are never that simple, Hawk. Especially not here, on the Street of Gods. There is a time for everything, a beginning and an end for all that exists. Le Bel Inconnu was once a great Being, and knew the worship of millions. Now it is almost completely forgotten, nothing more than an obscure footnote in some of the older histories. It has no followers and no priests. It came here to die, Hawk, to fade quietly away into the nothing it came from, and go to whatever afterlife Gods go to. I spend what time with it I can, and never know from one day to the next whether it will still be here the next time I call.'

'But why all the secrecy?' said Hawk.

Tomb sighed tiredly. 'No member of the Deity Division is allowed to worship a God, Captain Hawk. Religion and faith are not for us. It's the law. How else could the Beings on the Street respect our judgements, and be bound by them, unless they could be sure we showed no favour to any of them? But I can't abandon Le Bel Inconnu. No one should have to go into the dark alone, with no one to care or even know they've gone. But if word of my vigil were to get out, I'd have to leave the God Squad. I don't want that. I've given my life to the Squad. Before I took over, it was a mess. No one took it seriously, least of all the Beings. I changed all that. Made the Squad a power to be reckoned with. The Street of Gods had known almost ten years of peace . . . until the God murders began.' He looked unflinchingly at Hawk. 'Are you going to report this, Captain Hawk?'

Hawk looked about him, feeling the Presence beat on the air like the fluttering wings of a dying bird. He shook his head slowly. 'There's nothing to tell, Tomb. Nothing to do with the case I'm working on. I'll see you later.'

He turned away from the sorcerer and his God, and made his way back through the darkness to the life and bustle of the Street of Gods.

Fisher followed Buchan through the crowded Street, elbowing aside people who momentarily blocked her view of the man she was following. No one objected out loud. Even on the Street of Gods, people knew about Captain Fisher. She was careful to stay well back, but Buchan showed no signs of caring if he was being followed. The man was deathly tired; Fisher could see it in the way he walked, the way he held his head too carefully erect. But even so, nobody bothered him. They knew about Buchan's reputation, too.

Buchan, with Fisher still a discreet distance behind him, made his way along the Street, passing through the usual crowd of priests and worshippers. Riot or no riot, business went on as usual on the Street of Gods. From time to time people called out greetings to Buchan, some clearly false and some as clearly not, but he answered them all with the same preoccupied nod and wave of the hand. A few people looked as though they might call out to Fisher, but she glared at them until they changed their minds.

After a while, she began to realise Buchan was heading into the high-rent section of the Street of Gods. The churches and temples became richer and more ornate, works of art in their own right, and there was a much better class of worshippers, most of whom seemed scandalised at Fisher's presence in their midst. Fisher glared at them all impartially. Buchan finally stopped outside one of the more modest buildings. It was three storeys high, with rococo carvings and elegant wrought iron. The building had an anonymous air to it, as though it was a place for those who were just passing through, not staying. The kind of temporary residence popular among people on the way up or on the way down. The management didn't care which, as long as it got cash in advance.

Buchan produced a key and unlocked the front door. He stepped inside, and shut the door firmly behind him. Fisher scowled. What was Buchan doing in a place like this? She hesitated a moment, not sure what to do next. Hawk was the one who usually tailed people. She couldn't just barge in and start asking questions about Buchan. He wasn't supposed to know he was being followed. She frowned. She couldn't just hang about outside the place, either. People would notice. She made her way round the side of the building and down a narrow alleyway she hoped would lead to a back entrance. Maybe she could sneak in that way and find some low-level staff she could intimidate into providing some answers. Fisher always preferred the direct approach.

She hurried down the alleyway, keeping to the shadows when she remembered, rounded the corner, and sighed with relief as she took in the back of the building. It didn't look nearly as impressive as the front, with uneven paint-work and a filthy back yard. Judging by the smell, the drains weren't working too well either. There was one back door, strictly functional and clearly a servants' and tradesman's entrance. Fisher started toward it, only to stop dead as the door suddenly swung open. She darted behind a pile of stacked crates, crouched down, and watched with interest as a hunched and furtive figure pushed the door shut. He was wearing a torn and ratty-looking cloak with the hood pulled forward, but from her angle Fisher could see the face clearly. It was Buchan. He reached up to pull the hood even further forward, looked quickly around him, and then hurried along the alley and out onto the Street.

Fisher grinned broadly, and stayed where she was a moment to give him a good start. Buchan was definitely up to something. Where could he be going, that he couldn't afford to be recognised? Buchan was known and welcomed pretty much everywhere outside of High Society. She slipped out from behind the crates, ran silently down the alley, and emerged on the Street just in time to see him walking unhurriedly away. He was so confident in his disguise he didn't even bother to look behind him. Fisher stayed well back anyway, just in case. She was beginning to get the hang of following people.

Buchan led her through the luxurious high-rent district of the Street of Gods, where the magnificent buildings struggled to outdo each other in splendour and ostentatious opulence. He passed them all by without looking, until he came to the largest and most ornate structure yet. It was as broad as any three churches, and an amazing four storeys high. Fisher didn't even want to think how much money the owners must be paying for spells to protect the place from the violent spring gales. Massive bay windows jutted out onto the Street, and there was gold and silver scrollwork in abundance. And enough intricately carved stonework to have kept entire families of stonemasons busy for generations. There was one door, centrally placed: a huge slab of polished oak, bearing a large brass knocker. Engraved into the stone above the door was a single ornate symbol, known and reviled throughout the Low Kingdoms. Buchan knocked twice, and waited. Even from across the Street, Fisher could feel his impatience. The door opened, and Buchan quickly disappeared inside. Fisher bit her lower lip thoughtfully as the door swung shut behind him. In a way, she was almost disappointed. You didn't expect a man like the legendary Charles Buchan to go sneaking off to the notorious Sisters of Joy.

Fisher didn't approve of the Sisters. They were dangerous. Like a rose with poisoned thorns. In her time as a Guard, Fisher had seen men entrapped by the Sisters and betrayed by their own weaknesses. They lost all strength and dignity, giving up on everything except the object of their obsession. They threw away their jobs, alienated their families, and sold everything they could lay their hands on to make donations to the Sisters. By the time the Sister concerned had sucked them dry, it must almost have come as a relief.

Fisher folded her arms and leaned back against a church wall, staring thoughtfully at the house of the Sisters of Joy. What the hell was Buchan doing here? It wasn't at all in character for the great romantic she'd heard so much about. Of course, she if anyone had good reason to know that people weren't always what their storied personas made them out to be. But still . . . What if there was something else going on here? Something . . . deeper. Fisher pushed herself away from the wall and unfolded her arms. Whatever Buchan was mixed up in, she wanted to know about it. There were too many secrets in this case. She checked her sword moved freely in its scabbard, marched over to the Sisters' door, and knocked loudly. There was a long pause. Passersby looked at Fisher in various ways. Fisher glared at them all impartially.

The door finally opened a few inches. Fisher put her shoulder to the door and shoved it all the way open. She stalked in past the astonished Sister she'd sent flying backwards, and looked around her. There was an understated elegance to the hallway, with delicately fashioned furniture and a deep pile carpet. An ornate glass-and-crystal chandelier hung from the ceiling, and the air was scented with rose petals. It was actually quite impressive in a quiet way. Fisher had been in country mansions that looked less refined. Until you took in the obscene murals on the walls. Fisher had never seen anything like them. She felt a blush rising to her cheeks, and looked quickly away. The Sister had recovered her composure, and took the opportunity to bow respectfully to Fisher. She was very lovely, in an open, healthy way that owed nothing to makeup, with curly russet hair and a heart-shaped face. Her long flowing gown was spotlessly white and hugged her magnificent figure in all the right places. She couldn't have been more than nineteen or twenty. Fisher felt decidedly battered and dowdy in comparison, which didn't do a thing for her temper.

The Sister bowed again, showing off her cleavage, and smiled widely at Fisher. 'Welcome to the house of pleasure and contentment, Captain. In what way may we be of service to you?'

'I'm looking for Buchan,' said Fisher flatly. 'Where is he?'

The Sister shook her head, still smiling. 'We guarantee complete anonymity to all who come here, Captain. Within this house our patrons are free to adopt whatever names or characters they wish. We ask no questions, demand no answers. We offer comfort and security to all who come here, and we protect their privacy. Whatever your business is with the man you seek, it will have to wait until he has left these walls.'

Fisher scowled. She knew a set speech when she heard one. 'All right, we'll do it the hard way.' She reached out, took a handful of the Sister's gown, and pulled her close so that their faces were only inches apart. 'I'm Captain Fisher of the city Guard. I'm here on official business, and I want to see Charles Buchan right now. And if you or anyone else gets in my way, I am going to bounce them off the nearest wall till their ears bleed. Got it?'

The Sister never flinched once. She met Fisher's gaze calmly, and when she spoke, her voice was mild and even and unafraid. 'Kill me, if you wish. My Sisters will avenge me. The secrets of this house are not mine to tell, and I will die rather than divulge them. No Sister here will tell you anything, Captain. We will not betray those who trust us.'

Fisher swore briefly, and let the Sister go. She felt obscurely ashamed, as though she'd been caught bullying a child. She had no doubt the Sister meant what she said. Her voice and face held the unquestioning certainty of the fanatic. Probably brainwashed. Or under a geas' compulsion. Or both. She sighed, and stepped away from the Sister. When in doubt, be direct.

'Buchan!' she roared at the top of her voice. 'Charles Buchan! I know you're here. Either get the hell down here and talk to me or I'll go out into the Street and tell everyone I see that you're in here. What do you think would happen to your reputation as a member of the God Squad if word got out that you were a Sister-lover? Buchan! Talk to me!'

There was a long pause, and then a second Sister appeared from a concealed doorway. She wore the same white gown and was equally lovely, in a cool aristocratic way, but she was nearer Fisher's age, and though she smiled and bowed respectfully, her eyes were cold and hard. 'There's no need for threats, Captain. The person you seek has agreed to see you. Even though he was assured he didn't have to. And Captain; if he hadn't agreed, you would not have got any further in this house. We have spells to ensure our privacy. Very unpleasant spells. Now, if you'll come with me, please . . .'

Fisher gave the Sister one of her best scowls, just to make it clear who was really in charge here, and then followed her through a series of stairs and corridors to a plain anonymous door on the second floor. The Sister bowed deeply and left her there. Fisher knocked once, and walked straight in without waiting for an answer. The room was luxurious without being overbearing, and the furnishings had the understated elegance of old money. Fisher wondered fleetingly just how old the Sisters' establishment was, and then fixed her attention on Charles Buchan. He was standing stiffly beside a chair on which sat a beautiful young woman, a pale willowy blonde barely into her twenties. *Is that it?* thought Fisher. *All this secrecy, just because he's fallen for a girl young enough to be his daughter?* And yet . . . there was something wrong with the scene. She turned and pushed the door shut, to give herself a moment to think. Buchan's attitude; that was what was wrong. As soon as she turned back, she recognised what it was. Buchan didn't look ashamed, or indignant, or obsessed with the girl; he looked protective toward her, as though all that mattered was protecting the Sister from Fisher. If he cared at all about being found out, he was doing an excellent job of hiding it. He met Fisher's gaze unwaveringly.

'Captain Fisher. I should have known you'd find us out, if anyone would.'

Fisher shrugged. 'I don't like secrets. I take it personally when people hide things from me. Particularly when it affects a case we're supposed to be working on together.'

'There's no connection between this and the God murders, Captain. You have my word on that. Annette, I'd like you to meet Captain Fisher, one of my colleagues on the God Squad. Captain, this is Annette. My daughter.'

Annette smiled at Fisher, who just stood there, completely thrown.

'Why don't we all sit down?' Buchan suggested. 'This is going to take some explaining.'

'Yes,' said Fisher. 'I think it is.'

Buchan pulled up a chair beside Annette, and Fisher sat on a chair facing them. Buchan took a deep breath and plunged straight in.

'Annette's mother was a young Lady from a rival Family. The heads of our Families weren't talking to each other, and there had even been a few duels. Nothing unusual, but it was all very tense, and the worst possible time for us to meet and fall in love. But we were young and foolish, and nothing mattered to us except each other. We were going to run away and be married secretly. We even had some naive hopes that our marriage would bring the Families back together again.

'But she became pregnant. Her Family found out, and when she wouldn't name the father, they sent her out of the city to stay with relatives until it was all over. She died giving birth to Annette. Her Family let everyone assume the child was dead, too. They weren't interested in raising some bastard half-breed mongrel, so they gave her to the city orphanage.

'I went a little crazy after I heard my love was dead. I'd do anything, for a laugh or a thrill or just to fill my time. I chased women endlessly, trying to find someone who could replace the one I'd lost. Finally it all got out of hand, and I ended up on the God Squad. It was interesting work, and it passed the time. And then I came here, on business for the Squad, and found Annette. She looked just like her mother. I investigated her background, and worked out who she was. I thought about it for a long time, and then came here and introduced myself.

'She's very precious to me. For all my affairs, Annette is my only child. We sit and talk for hours.

'But somehow word of my visits to this house got out, at least in High Society, and I couldn't explain why I came here. Someday Annette may choose to leave this place and take her rightful place in High Society. The Quality must never know of her time here. They can be very old-fashioned about some things. So, I decided to let people think what they liked about my visits to the Sisters of Joy. My friends and Family disowned me, and the Quality turned their back on me. But Annette's secret was safe. The rest you know.'

Fisher shook her head slowly. 'That is so crazy a story it has to be true.'

'Will you keep our secret?' said Buchan. 'For her sake, if not for mine.'

'Sure,' said Fisher. 'Why not? Hawk will have to know, but I don't see any reason why it should go any further.' She looked at Annette. 'Are you happy here, lass? Really happy? If they've got any kind of hold over you, I can take care of it. No one's stupid enough to upset me and Hawk. If you want to leave, just say the word. I'll escort you out of here right now.'

Annette smiled and shook her head. 'Thank you, Captain, but I'm quite happy here. As I keep telling my father, I wasn't brainwashed into joining the Sisters of Joy, there isn't any geas keeping me here, and if I want to leave I'm perfectly free to do so at any time. The Sisterhood is a vocation, and one I believe in. How many other religions do you know that are simply dedicated to making people happy? Perhaps someday, I'll feel differently, but even then I don't think I'll be joining High Society. From what I've heard of the Quality, I doubt we'd get on. In the meantime, my father and I have each other. No one ever told me who my father was. I never dreamed it would turn out to be the legendary Charles Buchan.'

Buchan stirred uncomfortably. 'You don't want to pay too much attention to those stories, Annette.'

'Why? Aren't they true?'

'Well, yes. Most of them. But I'm a reformed character, now I've found you.'

Annette raised an eyebrow. 'Reformed? You?'

Buchan grinned. 'Partly reformed.'

Father and daughter laughed quietly together. Fisher got to her feet, feeling decidedly superfluous, and wished them both goodbye. They favoured her with a quick smile and a wave. Fisher smiled quickly in return and left them to each other.

The Dead Dog Tavern was a seedy little dive in the Northside, not that far from the Street of Gods. The air was full of smoke, the sawdust on the floor hadn't been changed in weeks, and the only reason the drinks weren't watered was that the patrons would have lynched the innkeeper if he'd tried it. Hawk and Fisher had used the Dead Dog as a meeting place before. It was the kind of place where everyone minded his own business, and expected everyone else to do likewise. Or else. Having Hawk and Fisher around didn't keep people away; the other patrons just kept their voices down and one eye always on the nearest exit. Hawk and Fisher liked the Dead Dog because it was quiet and convenient and nobody bothered them. There weren't many places like that in the Northside.

Hawk glared into his ale, gave a frustrated sigh, and slouched down in his chair. 'Dammit, we're getting nowhere with this case, Isobel. No matter which way we turn, we end up going round and round in bloody circles.'

Fisher took a healthy drink from her mug, and shook her head. 'Don't give up now, Hawk. We're getting close; I can feel it. Look; we know how the God murders took place. Somebody used the Exorcist Stone. That tells us who; it has to be one of the God Squad. Did you notice that when we talked about Bode's death, and the lack of magic at his house, none of them even mentioned the Exorcist Stone as a possible murder weapon? Significant, that. All we have to do is find a way to narrow it down from three suspects to one.'

'It's not that simple, Isobel, and you know it. First, the Council put a geas on all of them, specifically to prevent them misusing the Stone. If the compulsion spell had somehow been broken, the Council would have known immediately. And second, we still don't have a motive for the murders. What do any of them have to gain by killing Gods?'

They sat in silence for a while, nursing their ale.

'Let's go over everybody again, one at a time,' said Hawk. 'The one thing the three of them have in common is that they all have secrets. Buchan has a daughter who's a Sister of Joy. Tomb has broken God Squad rules by worshipping Le Bel Inconnu. And Rowan is dying of cancer and doesn't want the others to know about it. Secrets often make for good motives. People will do desperate things to keep a secret hidden.

'So, suppose the dead Gods knew about Buchan's

daughter. Priests do talk to each other, even when they're supposed to be enemies. They're in the same line of business, after all. Word could have got around. What if the murdered Gods had tried to use that knowledge, to put pressure on Buchan to look the other way on occasion? It could be a very handy thing for a Being to have a member of the God Squad in his pocket.'

'It's a nice idea,' said Fisher. 'But I don't think it's Buchan. In order to come and go without being seen by the Gods' followers, the killer must have had access to some kind of sorcery, and Buchan doesn't have any. He had to use an ordinary disguise when he went to visit his daughter, remember? And besides, if he'd had any magic, he'd have used it against that creature at the Hellfire Club, wouldn't he?'

'Not necessarily,' said Hawk. 'He could be trying to put us off the scent by not using magic when we're around. He might have known you were following him.'

Fisher sniffed. 'Firstly, if he'd known I was following him, he wouldn't have led me to the Sisters and revealed his secret. Secondly, I don't really think Buchan's that clever, to be honest. He's famed for many things, but subtlety's not one of them. I think we'd be better off taking a hard look at Tomb. Now, he has a motive that makes sense. If the Council knew about his private God, they'd throw him off the Squad, and Tomb's put a lot of time and effort into making the God Squad a force to be reckoned with. He might see a threat to himself as a threat to the Squad, and act accordingly. So, if another Being had found out, and threatened to tell on him . . . Hey, wait a minute, I've just had another thought. What if the God killings were some kind of sacrifice to Tomb's God? To make it stronger, more powerful?'

'Could be,' said Hawk, thinking about it. 'Certainly Tomb's got enough sorcery to get in and out of the churches undetected.'

'And he certainly knew his way around when he showed us the murder sites earlier on.'

'No. We can't single him out on that. According to the informer Lacey, all the God Squad had visited the dead Beings previously.'

'All right,' said Fisher. 'Forget that. But the rest fits.'

'It still doesn't explain how he broke the geas without the Council circle of sorcerers knowing. That's supposed to be impossible.'

Fisher nodded reluctantly. 'All right. Let's leave Tomb for a moment and look at Rowan. She's got enough sorcery to move unseen, and she's certainly got no love for the Gods.'

'Sure,' said Hawk. 'But what's her motive?'

'Revenge,' said Fisher. 'She's dying, and she wants to kill as many of the Gods she despises as she can before she dies.'

'That's pushing it a bit, isn't it?'

Fisher shrugged. The two of them drank more ale, their scowls deepening as they struggled with the problem. People around them took in the danger signs, quietly finished their drinks, and made for the exits.

'I don't know,' said Hawk. 'Whatever motives the God Squad have, I keep coming back to the geas. Either one of them's found a way round the compulsion spell, which is supposed to be impossible, or it has to be somebody else. Maybe it's really the sorcerer Bode after all, using the Dark Men as weapons. Remember, two of the Gods had been torn apart, which would seem to indicate that the killer had great physical strength.'

'You may have something there,' said Fisher slowly. 'But have you ever noticed that the Dark Men never attack us except when the God Squad aren't around?'

They looked at each other for a moment. 'Are you suggesting one of the God Squad is the controlling mind behind the Dark Men?' said Hawk finally.

'Why not? It fits!' Fisher leaned forward excitedly. 'That's how someone on the Squad could use the Exorcist

Stone! The geas was placed on a specific person. Once that person was in another body – a Dark Man homunculus – he or she became a different individual, free to use the Exorcist Stone without any restraints!'

'You're right,' said Hawk. 'It does fit. I think we're finally getting somewhere. And it means we can rule out Buchan as the murderer. He was there when the Dark Man attacked us at the Hellfire Club. And anyway, he doesn't have the sorcery needed to transfer his mind from one body to another. You know, more and more makes sense now. Let's assume our God Squad murderer is the same person who hired Bode. That's why Bode sometimes didn't recognise his friends on the Street of Gods: someone else was using a duplicate of Bode's body at the time! Bode's body could ask questions that a member of the God Squad couldn't ask without appearing suspicious. Whoever gave Bode his mission wasn't just hiring Bode as a person, they were also hiring his body! Hell's teeth, that's devious.'

'Don't get too excited,' said Fisher dryly. 'We still haven't got a motive. Let's try it from a different angle. What was Bode, or the person inside Bode's body, looking for on the Street of Gods?'

'Ways of getting to the Beings?'

'No, they already knew how to do that as part of the God Squad.' Fisher scowled, and doodled aimlessly in the spilt ale on the table. 'Bode, or whoever was inside his double, was asking questions about the Gods themselves. Their histories, their powers, their natures. It was the answers to these questions that marked the Beings for death.'

'But what's so important about those questions?' said Hawk. 'Every tourist on the Street asks questions like those.'

'And they end up with tourist answers. But a sorcerer and a member of the God Squad might just get an answer that meant something . . .' Fisher sat up straight suddenly. 'Hawk, I think I've got it! Remember the Being who was stabbed to death – the Sundered Man? That priestess of his, Sister Anna, was really bitter about his death because it meant she'd wasted her life worshipping something that wasn't really a God after all! I don't know about the last death, the Lord of the New Flesh, but both the other dead Beings died when the Exorcist Stone removed all the magic from their vicinity. The Dread Lord fell apart, and the Carmadine Stalker aged to death. That's what Bode and his employer were looking for on the Street of Gods: proof that a Being wasn't a God after all but just a supernatural creature with magic powers and a following.'

'Not quite,' said Hawk suddenly. 'Turn it around. They weren't looking for Beings among the Gods; they were trying to find one real God among the Beings, and killing the ones who failed the test.'

'But why would Tomb or Rowan be so desperate to find a real God?' Fisher's eyes widened suddenly. 'Because one of them needed a miracle cure! It's Rowan; it has to be! It all fits together. The killings only started after she joined the Squad. She went to Bode when her potions couldn't control the cancer, probably hoping he'd have something that would help her. After all, he was an alchemist as well as a sorcerer. He didn't have a cure, but he did have the Dark Men. Which was just what she needed to investigate the Beings. She must have been getting pretty desperate by then. She couldn't ask questions on the street herself, so she got Bode to do it for her, and sometimes did it herself in one of the homunculus bodies. Every time she thought she'd found a real God, she'd go to them and beg for a miracle cure. If they couldn't or wouldn't help her, she destroyed them, using the Exorcist Stone and the strength of the Dark Man. Presumably out of revenge for wasting her limited time.'

'No wonder she's spent so much time in bed recently,' said Hawk. 'Her mind was out and about, attacking us in a Dark Man body. But why did she kill Bode?'

Fisher shrugged. 'Maybe he found out about the God killings, and wanted to call it off. She couldn't allow that. She killed him the same way she killed the Beings. She must really have panicked when she found out the same two Guards who investigated Bode's murder had been seconded to the God Squad. That's why she tried to get rid of us when we first arrived. And why she kept attacking us through the Dark Men. We were so close to the answer all along, and didn't know it . . . But then, why did she tell us she had cancer?'

'Trying for sympathy, I expect,' said Hawk. 'Hoping that would distract us from seeing her as the killer. It almost worked. You don't expect a dying woman to be a murderer. We've got to get back to the Squad and confront her.'

'What's the hurry? She's not going anywhere in her weakened condition.'

'Oh no? What's to stop her leaving her dying body behind and living on in a healthy Dark Man body?'

'A woman living in a man's body?' Fisher wrinkled her nose. 'That's kinky.'

'Don't knock it till you've tried it. Now let's go. I wouldn't put it past Rowan to have a few more tricks up her sleeve. And we can't afford another dead God.'

7

Return of the Dark Man

The Street of Gods was unusually quiet. The riot had cleared the air somewhat, and most people were licking their wounds and waiting to see what would happen next. Guards and sorcerers walked the length of the Street, keeping the peace, backed by armoured contingents from the Brotherhood of Steel. But in the side streets and back alleys, the dark and shadowed places of the Street of Gods, plots were hatched and plans were whispered. The God War drew steadily nearer, awaiting only one last deadly spark. Anticipation filled the air like the smell of spilt blood, feared and desired in equal measure, as man and God looked each to his own position and saw how it could be worse or better. Change had come to the Street of Gods, and whatever happened, nothing would ever be the same again. Four Beings had been proved to be merely mortal, and no God could feel entirely secure after that.

Hawk and Fisher trudged wearily back to God Squad headquarters, following the shortest route the Street allowed. Hawk yawned continuously, too tired even to raise a hand to cover his mouth. Given the Street of Gods' eccentric attitude to the passing of time, he'd long ago lost track of what hour of which day it was, but it had been a hell of a long time since he'd last had any sleep. His feet were like lead, his legs ached, and his back was killing him. *Getting old, Hawk.* He smiled sourly. He always got gloomy when he was tired. Still, the sooner he and Fisher wrapped up this case, the better. The more tired you got, the more likely you were to make mistakes. And making mistakes on a case like this could get you killed.

The few people still out on the Street gave Hawk and Fisher plenty of room. Word of their victory over the rogue Being had spread, and priests and worshippers alike kept to their best behaviour while the two Guards were around. Even the street preachers lowered the volume a little as they passed.

God Squad headquarters finally loomed up ahead, and Hawk allowed himself to relax a little. The small non-descript building, with its old-fashioned lamp shining brightly over the door, looked actually cosy. Almost there, almost over. All they had to do was face Rowan with what they knew, and she'd crack. They always did, when you had them dead to rights. Some villains even seemed relieved as you took them off to gaol, as though they were as tired of the chase as you were. And anyway, Rowan shouldn't be too difficult to handle. When all was said and done, without the Exorcist Stone in her hands she was nothing more than a minor league magic-user with a side line in potions. With the suppressor stone to protect them from her magic, they should be safe enough. As long as they didn't drink any-thing she offered them. A sudden thought struck Hawk, and he stopped dead in his tracks, his mind working furiously. Fisher stopped too, and looked at him.

'Hawk? What's the matter?'

'I just thought of something. We've been assuming Rowan transferred her mind into a Dark Man, then used the Exorcist Stone against the Beings. Right?'

'Right.'

'But if the Exorcist Stone banished all the magic from the area, it should also have affected the homunculus Rowan was inhabiting. After all, that's how we beat the original Dark Man, remember? You fired up the suppressor stone, and he went out like a light. So if Rowan had used the Exorcist Stone, it would have knocked out the Dark Man she was using and thrown her back into her own body. Which means our whole theory has just gone up in smoke!'

'Don't panic,' said Fisher. 'The Stone doesn't work that way. It isn't designed to affect *everything* in the area, or it would end up affecting itself, destroying its own power. It has built-in safety guards, like our suppressor stones, so that they don't affect themselves or the people using them. It's only common sense, after all. If you'd paid attention at the morning briefing when the suppressor stones were handed out, you'd have known that.'

'Sorry,' said Hawk. 'You know I'm never any good with technical stuff.'

'And you have the nerve to complain because I won't let you carry the suppressor stone . . .'

'All right. No need to rub it in. Anything else I ought to remember about the stone?'

'Yes . . .' said Fisher slowly. 'Unlike the Exorcist Stone, our stones have only a limited amount of magic, and we've been using our stone a hell of a lot just recently. And before you ask: no, there's no telling how badly we've drained it, or how much magic there is left in the stone. These things are prototypes, remember?'

'Great,' said Hawk. 'Just great.' They looked at each other. 'If we try and arrest Rowan, and the stone doesn't work, we're going to be in real trouble. Without the stone's magic to counteract hers, she'll just transfer her mind into a Dark Man body and disappear.'

'Then we'll just have to hope there is enough magic left in the stone to hold her,' said Fisher.

Hawk looked at her. 'This case just gets better and better.' He thought hard for a moment. 'Look. How about if we get one of the others to use the Exorcist Stone? That should prevent her leaving her body.'

Fisher nodded. 'All right. Who do we ask?'

'Buchan. We can't trust Tomb. He's too close to Rowan.'

They continued on their way, frowning thoughtfully.

Passersby gave them even more room than usual. The two Guards finally reached God Squad headquarters, and Hawk hammered on the door with his fist. Not the politest way to knock, but Hawk wasn't in a polite mood. There was a long pause, and then Buchan opened the door, sword in hand. He relaxed a little as he saw who it was, sheathed his sword, and nodded politely to them.

'I was wondering what had happened to you two. Officially, we're still on emergency status, but things seem to have calmed down a lot now. The Street's quiet, and the Guard and the Brotherhood of Steel are out in force to make sure it stays that way.'

'I'll drink to that,' said Hawk. 'Is everyone here?'

'Sure. Tomb and Rowan are talking upstairs. Want me to give them a call?'

'Not just yet,' said Hawk. 'I think the three of us ought to have a word first. In the drawing room. It'll be more private.'

Buchan looked at him, and then at Fisher, his face cold but composed. He nodded stiffly, and led the way into the drawing room. Fisher closed the door behind them, and put her back against it so they wouldn't be interrupted before they were finished. Besides, she didn't want Buchan to have the option of leaving. He wasn't going to like what they had to tell him. Fisher couldn't blame him. It always comes hard to find someone you've trusted and fought beside is a traitor. Buchan looked at the two Guards evenly, his gaze firm and unyielding.

'This is about Annette, isn't it?'

'No,' said Hawk. 'Your secret's safe with us. It's irrelevant to our investigation. We need to talk to you, sir Buchan. We know who the God killer is.'

'You do? Who is it?' Buchan looked eagerly from Hawk to Fisher and back again. 'Do you need my help with the arrest? Is that it?'

'In a way,' said Fisher. 'You'd better brace yourself, Buchan. You're not going to like this.'

Buchan frowned uncertainly. 'What's going on here?'

'It's Rowan,' said Hawk. 'She's the God killer. She killed all four Beings, and the sorcerer Bode, too. Probably because he wouldn't go along with her plans.'

For a moment, Buchan's face was absolutely slack and empty. Then he shook his head in a dismissive gesture and laughed shakily. 'You're crazy. You're out of your minds, both of you. It can't be her! She's one of us. Part of the God Squad. Has been for years. Besides, she's been ill; it couldn't be her.'

'It's her,' said Hawk. 'But she's not going to surrender herself easily. There might be trouble. We could use your help.'

'Do you have proof? Hard evidence?'

'Some,' said Hawk. 'Enough. Now, will you help us?'

'I don't really have a choice, do I?' said Buchan. 'If I don't, you'll tell everyone about me and Annette. Right?'

'No,' said Fisher. 'We don't work that way. Your secret's safe, whatever you decide. But we really could use some backup on this.'

'You were right,' said Buchan. 'I don't like this. What do you want me to do?'

'First,' said Hawk, 'go up and tell Rowan and Tomb we're back and want to talk to them. If they ask what about, you don't know. Wait till they're safely downstairs, and then while we're having our little chat, you get hold of the Exorcist Stone and activate it. Hopefully our suppressor stone will be enough to hold her, but I'll feel better knowing you're there.'

'There's not to be any rough stuff,' said Buchan. 'I won't stand for any rough stuff. Rowan's done a lot of good work with the Squad, in her time. She even saved my life once. She deserves better than this.'

'She brought it on herself,' said Fisher. 'How many Guards died out there in the riot tonight, do you suppose? The riot she helped bring about?'

'That's enough, Isobel,' said Hawk. 'He knows.'

Buchan turned and headed for the door. He opened it and stepped out into the hallway, then stopped and looked back at Hawk and Fisher. 'You'd better be right about this. If you're not, if you're only guessing . . . I'll break you. Rowan is God Squad. We look after our own.'

He shut the door firmly behind him, just short of a slam. Hawk and Fisher looked at each other, and then moved as one to the drinks cabinet. They both felt very much in need of a stiff drink, or two.

'He means it, you know,' said Fisher.

'Damn right he means it,' said Hawk. 'This could easily turn very nasty, lass. It wasn't until Buchan asked about proof and evidence that I realised how thin our case actually is. We can show motive and opportunity, and demonstrate how it *could* have been done, but we'd be hard pressed to prove any of it in Court.'

'It's a bit late for second thoughts,' said Fisher. 'We can't put this off; we have to confront her now. All it needs is one more dead Being and all hell will break loose on the Street of Gods. Probably quite literally. We'll just have to face Rowan with what we know, and hope she'll break down and confess.'

'And if she doesn't? If she laughs in our faces, and tells us we're crazy?'

'Then I'll swear blind it was all your idea, and nothing to do with me.'

'Gosh, thanks,' said Hawk. 'What would I do without you?'

Rowan and Tomb faced each other across Rowan's bedroom. Rowan was in a towering rage, her face dangerously flushed, but Tomb stood his ground.

'You did *what*, Tomb?'

'I ran a scanning spell on you,' said Tomb. 'A full body scan. I was worried about you. It seems I had every right to be. You're ill, Rowan, very ill. You have been for some time. Your body's riddled with cancers. I'm amazed you're still able to function as well as you do. I can only assume your potions are effective painkillers, if nothing else.' His voice broke, and his pose broke with it. He looked miserably at her, almost pleading. 'Why didn't you tell me, Rowan? Did you think you couldn't trust me?'

'I didn't tell you,' said Rowan coldly, 'because I wanted to avoid a scene like this. How many times do I have to say it, Tomb? This is none of your business. I'm none of your business. I have no interest in your feelings, and your interest in me is annoying when it isn't intrusive. I want you to stay away from me. Dammit, Tomb, get the hell out of my life and leave me alone!'

'I can't. You're dying, Rowan. You must know that. Your condition is so advanced now there's nothing sorcery can do for you anymore. Healers aren't miracle workers. Why didn't you tell me earlier? I could have helped you . . .'

'I don't want your help! I don't need your help!'

'At least let me tell Buchan. We can handle the God Squad work between us for a while. You have to rest, take things easy. We'll look after you.'

'You'd love that, wouldn't you? You do so love to fuss over me. Well, I haven't time for that nonsense anymore. I have things to do, and not much time to do them in.'

Tomb looked at her blankly. 'Things? What things? What can be more important than this? We're talking about your life, Rowan! If you rest and take things easy, you could have months ahead of you yet. There are still some things I can do, some things I can try. If you don't rest, you'll be dead in a few weeks.'

Rowan looked away from him. 'A few weeks,' she said quietly. 'I didn't realise it had got that close. Are you sure?'

'Yes. I'm sorry, Rowan. My scan was very thorough, and there's no room for doubt. Please. Let me help you.'

'No.' Rowan lifted her head and faced him squarely, perfectly composed. 'I've chosen my way and I'll stick to it.'

'And if you're wrong?'

'Then I'm wrong!' Rowan smiled suddenly. 'Trust me, Tomb. Whatever happens, I'm not going to die.'

'Rowan, you have to face this. You can't just turn your back on it . . .'

'Oh, shut up! Get out of here, Tomb. Find something else to do instead of pestering me. I have some thinking to do.'

There was a knock on the door, polite but firm. Rowan strode past Tomb without looking at him, opened the door, and glared at Buchan. 'What do you want?'

'Hawk and Fisher are back. They're waiting in the drawing room. They want to talk to us immediately. Apparently they've made a breakthrough on the God murders.'

'What kind of breakthrough?' asked Rowan.

'They didn't give me any details. But they seemed quite excited.'

'This had better be important,' Rowan said, sweeping past him. 'I have things to do.'

Tomb and Buchan followed her out of the room, each lost in his own separate thoughts.

Rowan stormed into the drawing room and threw herself into her favourite chair. Hawk and Fisher stood together, their faces professionally calm, their hands resting on their sword belts. Rowan studied them both.

'Buchan said something about a breakthrough. What have you found out?'

'The truth,' said Hawk. 'It took us a while, but we finally got there. We know who the God murderer is.'

Tomb entered the room just in time to hear that, and brightened up a little. 'Well, that is good news, Captain. When can we expect an arrest?'

'I think you'd better sit down, sir Tomb,' said Fisher. 'Our news isn't exactly pleasant.'

Tomb's smile faded away. He made no move to sit down, and studied their faces closely. 'What is this? I don't understand.'

'Rowan does,' said Hawk. 'Don't you, Rowan?'

The mystic met his gaze unflinchingly. 'I don't know what you're talking about, Captain.'

'All right,' said Hawk. 'We'll do it the hard way. Rowan, you're under arrest for the murder of four Beings, and the sorcerer Bode. You will come with us to Guard head-quarters, where arrangements will be made for your trial. If you wish to make a confession, pen and paper will be provided.'

Hawk glanced at Tomb. The sorcerer was staring at him blankly. Rowan hadn't reacted at all, except for a small smile tugging at the corner of her mouth.

'You must really be desperate, if you're reduced to making blind allegations like that,' she said calmly. 'What proof do you have? Where's your evidence? I have a right to know why I'm being charged.'

'There'll be time for that later,' said Fisher.

'We'll talk about it now!' snapped Rowan. 'I'm a member of the God Squad, in good standing. We have friends in high places. They won't stand by and let you lay all the blame on me, just because you're getting nowhere and the pressure's on you to make an arrest.'

'That's right,' said Tomb quickly. 'I think this has gone quite far enough. You must be mad, both of you. How could it be Rowan? She's been very ill, and was actually confined to her bed when the killings took place! I under-stand the pressure you must both be under, but I'm damned if I'll let you get away with this . . .'

'That's enough!' Hawk's voice cut sharply across the sorcerer's bluster. 'That's enough, sir Tomb. We have a job to do, and you're not making this any easier for anyone. We know how the murders were committed, and we know why. And if you weren't so blinded by your feelings for Rowan, you'd have probably worked it out for yourself long ago. Rowan, it's time to go. Is there anything you want to take with you, or anything you want to say?'

'I don't think so,' said Rowan.

'You're not taking her anywhere!' said Tomb. 'I told you; she's ill. She's in no condition to be locked up in some filthy cell. I won't allow it. If she has to be kept somewhere, until she can be proved innocent, she can stay here, under house arrest.'

'I'm afraid we can't allow that,' said Fisher. 'We have to follow procedure.'

'This is all irrelevant anyway,' said Rowan. 'None of you have the power to hold me anywhere.'

'Rowan, dear, let me handle this,' said Tomb quickly.

'Oh, shut up, Tomb.'

Tomb gaped at her as she rose unhurriedly to her feet and smiled defiantly at Hawk and Fisher. Something in the room's atmosphere changed in that moment, and they could all feel it. Without drawing a weapon or moving a muscle, Rowan had suddenly become dangerous.

'That suppressor stone of yours won't stop me, Captain Fisher. It'll protect you and Hawk from my magic, but it's not powerful enough to prevent me leaving any time I choose. I should have killed you both when you first came here. But I made the mistake of going by appearances instead of reputation. I really didn't think you had the brains to work out what was going on. By the time I realised you'd earned your reputation, it was too late to attack you directly. That would have been too obvious. Even Tomb might have noticed something. I tried using the Dark Men against you, but I couldn't match your training as fighters.'

'Rowan, what are you saying?' Tomb's face was pale and slack with shock. He made vague, fluttering movements with his hands, and there was desperation in his voice. 'You mustn't listen to her, Captain Hawk. She's not well, she doesn't know what she's saying . . .'

'Yes I do,' said Rowan, almost cheerfully. 'I'm guilty, Tomb. Guilty as charged, guilty as hell. I killed Bode, and the four Beings, and I'll kill a damn sight more before I'm done. There are no Gods on the Street of Gods, and I'll make them pay for pretending otherwise. I needed them. I needed them to be real, and they let me down. I'll see them all dead and rotting for that.' She smiled at Hawk and Fisher, and it was not a pleasant smile. 'You want to arrest this body? Fine. Take it. I have plenty more, and this one's almost through. I would have had to abandon it soon anyway; you just made the decision a little easier.'

'I'm afraid not,' said Hawk. 'I thought you might try and leave your body for one of your Dark Men homunculi, so I had a word with Buchan earlier. He has the Exorcist Stone, Rowan. Until we decide otherwise, no magic will work in your vicinity. You're stuck in your own body. And you'll stay there until your trial.'

'What are you talking about?' said Tomb. 'Nothing's happened to the magic here. I'd know.' He gestured quickly with his left hand, and a lamp on the wall lit itself. Hawk looked at the bright flame, and his heart sank.

He and Fisher looked at each other. 'That shouldn't be possible,' said Hawk. 'Isobel, go and find Buchan. Make sure he's got the Stone.'

'That won't be necessary,' said a slow, harsh voice from the doorway. Everyone except Rowan looked round in time to see the Dark Man throw Buchan's bloodied form into the drawing room. He hit the floor hard, and lay still. The Dark Man strode into the drawing room, the Exorcist Stone clutched firmly in one large bony hand. Two more Dark Men followed him into the room. They all wore the same shapeless furs, they were all heavily muscled, and they all had the same cold smile. Rowan's smile.

'I've learned a lot since I first started working with Bode,' said Rowan calmly. 'In the beginning, it was all I could do to handle one body at a time. But the more I practised, the easier it got. Now there's no limit to how many homunculi I can control at one time.'

Tomb had knelt beside Buchan, and was checking his injuries with gentle hands. 'Cracked ribs, broken right arm, cracked skull; probably concussion as well. How could you do this, Rowan? He was your friend.'

'He would have used the Stone on me,' said Rowan. 'Luckily, for a famed duellist he was surprisingly easy to sneak up on from behind.'

'We have to get him a doctor, Rowan. I can't heal serious injuries like these. He needs a specialist.'

Rowan looked at Buchan unemotionally. 'He would have used the Stone on me.' She turned and looked at Hawk and Fisher again. 'Keep your hands away from your weapons. I had a feeling you were getting too close to the truth. I had planned to have the Dark Men ambush you as you left here, but this has worked out just as well. Now I have all my enemies in one place.'

'Where did you get all the Dark Men from?' said Fisher, playing for time and mentally measuring the distance between her and the mystic.

Rowan smiled. 'I inherited them from Bode. He really was very talented. After I've had a chance to acquire his notes and study them, I'm sure I'll be able to create even more. I should even be able to produce copies of my original body, without the original's defects. There's a lot to be said for the Dark Men, but I always feel so much more comfortable in my own body.'

'Buchan needs a doctor!' said Tomb. 'He could die!'

'He never liked me,' said Rowan. 'He never even looked at me.'

Tomb got slowly to his feet. 'So. It is all true. Everything they said. And you're going to kill everyone who knows your secret.'

'That's right, Tomb.'

'What about me?'

'What about you?'

They looked at each other, and neither of them would drop their eyes. Hawk drew his axe, aimed, and threw it in one rapid movement while Rowan was distracted. The heavy blade flashed through the air and buried itself between the eyes of the Dark Man holding the Exorcist Stone. Rowan screamed in pain and rage as the homunculus crumpled to the floor. The Stone rolled away from his limp fingers. One of the other Dark Men started toward it, but Fisher moved quickly forward to block his way. She grinned nastily at him, sword at the ready before her. Rowan's mouth set itself in a thin, flat line, and the two Dark Men advanced, one on Hawk and one on Fisher.

Hawk threw himself at the fallen homunculus, put a foot on the head to steady it, and jerked his axe free. He spun round just in time to parry a sword blow from the approaching Dark Man. Sparks flew as steel rang on steel again and again. Hawk was forced back, step by step, from the sheer force of the attack. The Dark Man pressed forward untiringly, and Hawk's arm began to ache from the effort of parrying the blows. The axe was never intended as a defensive weapon. At any other time, he might have been able to turn aside the attack and launch one of his own, but he'd gone too long without rest or sleep and it was starting to catch up with him. His back slammed up against a wall, bringing him to a sudden halt. Finding extra strength from somewhere, he brought his axe across in a short vicious arc that had the Dark Man jumping backwards to avoid it, but he couldn't find the speed to follow it up. He moved away from the wall, and the Dark Man was on him again. Hawk caught a glimpse of the Exorcist Stone lying on the floor, but it was a long way away, and besides, he didn't even know how to activate it. He swung his axe double-handed, and tried to make himself some room to move in.

Fisher attacked her Dark Man head on, and the two of them stamped and lunged, their swords clashing and flying apart almost too quickly for the eye to follow. Rowan obviously didn't know much about swordsmanship, but with the Dark Man's strength and reflexes she didn't have to. All she had to do was keep up her attack and wait for Fisher's strength to run out. They both knew it wouldn't take long. Fisher was already exhausted from the long day, and the Dark Man was fresh and tireless. Fisher held her ground, as much out of pride as anything, but she was beginning to have a bad feeling about this fight.

Tomb faced Rowan squarely. Her face was blank and empty, but her muscles occasionally jumped and twitched in sympathy with the Dark Men.

'Rowan, you've got to stop this. Get out of here while you can.'

'Not now, Tomb. I'm busy.'

'Hawk and Fisher are Guards, experienced fighters. They'll win, in the end. And as long as they've got the suppressor stone, your magic can't hurt them.'

'There are ways round the suppressor stones. I have more magic than you think.'

'I won't let you hurt them, Rowan.'

Life came suddenly to Rowan's eyes, and she fixed him with an unwavering stare. 'Don't interfere, Tomb. It wouldn't be healthy.'

'Your magic's no match for mine, and you know it. There's still time to stop this nonsense, Rowan. We could leave here now, together, and use the Dark Men and our magic to cover our trail. We could leave Haven, start again somewhere else. No one would ever have to know about all this.'

'Yes,' said Rowan slowly. 'I could do that.' She stepped toward him, took hold of his chin, and pulled his face close to hers. 'You'd give up everything, to be with me?'

'Of course,' said Tomb. 'I love you, Rowan.'

'I know.'

She thrust her dagger into Tomb's gut, twisted it once, and then jerked it sharply upwards. Tomb's hands clutched at her shoulders, closed tight, and then released her as he fell clumsily to the floor. His eyes were still open, staring reproachfully at the ceiling. Rowan turned her back on him and slipped the dagger back into its concealed sheath on her arm.

Meanwhile, Hawk had got his second wind. He'd got more than a little annoyed at being beaten by a slab of muscle with no skills, and the anger had given him new strength. He brought his axe across to hold the Dark Man's sword locked in position, and the two of them stood toe to toe, glaring into each other's faces. Without looking away, Hawk stamped down hard on the Dark Man's instep, and felt, as much as heard, bones break in the Dark Man's foot. Pain flared across the homunculus's face, and his sword arm wavered. Hawk spat in his eye, and the Dark Man fell back instinctively. Hawk took advantage of the opening to knee his opponent solidly in the groin. The Dark Man froze, his sword dropping as Rowan's mind tried frantically to deal with so many pains at once, and Hawk swung his axe in a vicious lateral sweep. The heavy blade cut through the Dark Man's throat, almost severing the head from the body. He fell heavily to the floor, twitched uncertainly, and then lay still in a growing pool of his own blood.

Fisher suddenly broke away from her opponent and sprinted across the room toward Rowan. The mystic opened her mouth to begin a spell, but Fisher was already there, her sword point at Rowan's throat. The Dark Man froze where he was.

'Drop his sword, Rowan. Or I swear I'll kill you now and to hell with a fair trial.'

Rowan glared at her. Fisher increased the pressure of her sword. A thin trickle of blood ran down the mystic's neck as the sword-point broke her skin. Hawk stepped in behind the hesitating Dark Man and buried his axe in the back of the creature's skull. The Dark Man crashed to the floor. Some of the strength seemed to go out of Rowan, and her shoulders slumped. Hawk pulled his axe free and wiped it on the Dark Man's clothes. He looked to see Fisher was all right, and nodded, satisfied.

'I trust there are no more surprises in store, Rowan? Isobel, keep an eye on her. I'll take a look at Tomb and Buchan.'

He knelt beside the sorcerer, and winced at the awful wound. Rowan had all but gutted him. Blood had pooled around Tomb and soaked his robes, but incredibly he was still breathing, shallowly. His eyes moved slightly to meet Hawk's gaze.

'Lie still,' said Hawk quickly. 'We'll get you a doctor.'

'No point,' said Tomb, his voice little more than a whisper. 'I'm a sorcerer. I know how bad the wound is. I take it you beat the Dark Men?'

'Sure,' said Hawk. 'We beat them.'

'Is Rowan all right? You didn't hurt her?'

'She's fine.'

'Good.' Tomb closed his eyes. Hawk said the sorcerer's name a few times, but he didn't respond. The man's breathing was so shallow that Hawk was sure each breath would be the last, but somehow Tomb held on. Hawk moved over to Buchan. He was unconscious, but breathing strongly. His wounds looked nasty, but not immediately dangerous. Hawk got to his feet and moved over to join Fisher. She'd taken the sword point away from Rowan's throat but held the sword ready, just in case.

'Tomb's dying,' said Hawk. 'Buchan is badly injured. They were your colleagues, Rowan. Your friends. They cared about you. Doesn't that mean anything to you?'

Rowan smiled briefly, but there was no humour there, only a weary disdain. 'I never wanted their friendship. All I ever wanted was to be left alone. Nobody every really cares for anyone else; they just pretend to, to get what they want from you. They don't fool me. I look out for myself. And you needn't look at me like that. I'm no different from anyone else; it's just that I have the guts to be honest about it.

'You can't hold me, you know. There are more Dark Men, scattered all over Haven. Bode had been creating them for years, selling his potions to subsidise his experiments. He had a horror of dying, you see. He thought he could live forever, through his doubles. But I put a stop to that. I had a better use for them. I still do. You can't stop me. The magic in your suppressor stone is fading, even as we speak. Soon it'll be cold and silent, and I'll leave this defective body behind and live again as a Dark Man. I will have my revenge on the Street of Gods, and there's nothing you can do to prevent it.'

'Maybe they can't,' said a calm, deep voice. 'But I can.'

They all turned, startled, to look at the doorway. A Dark Man stood there smiling, dressed in a cheap grey robe and looking somehow . . . different. He wasn't in the least muscular, being instead slender almost to the point of malnutrition, and his face held none of the anger that was a permanent part of Rowan's expression whatever body she was wearing. Hawk looked quickly at Rowan, but she seemed just as surprised as he was. Hawk looked back at the Dark Man. If she wasn't controlling the body, then who . . . ?

'It can't be,' said Fisher. 'It can't be *him*.'

'It is,' said Hawk. 'It has to be. That's Bode.'

The sorcerer smiled at them all, and bowed politely. 'At your service, Captain.'

'You're dead,' said Rowan harshly. 'I killed you. I watched you die.'

'I'm afraid not,' said Bode, stepping coolly into the drawing room. 'Though you did have a damn good try. Perhaps I should explain. It's a very interesting story, and there's no one else I can tell it to. Besides, I've been starved for company for the past few days. I've been watching you all ever since my death, but I couldn't afford to be recognised. So I stayed in the shadows and waited for the right moment.

'I'm afraid you made a simple but understandable mistake, Rowan, my dear. When you surprised me at my home with the Exorcist Stone, you didn't encounter the real me; just one of my duplicates. I hadn't lived in my own body for months. I kept that somewhere safe, and lived in a series of homunculi. My experiments had become rather danger- ous, you see, and I didn't want to subject my real body to unnecessary risks. So, when you activated the Exorcist Stone in my house after our little disagreement, you des- troyed all the spells I'd set up, including the one that kept my spirit in the duplicate body. The Stone threw me out of the homunculus and back into my own body. All you killed was an empty husk.

'You'd probably have worked it out for yourself, if you'd had time to study my papers, but luckily my Dark Man watchdog returned from the errand I'd sent him on, and you left in something of a hurry, rather than risk being discovered. The watchdog was a rather crude prototype, and unfortunately given to insane rages, but he had his uses. You've really caused me a great deal of difficulty, Rowan. Once the Guard discovered the nature of my researches, I had no choice but to stay dead while I tracked you down. Establishing a new identity and starting over is going to be very difficult. Not to mention expensive. And all because of your obsession with the Street of Gods. I should never have listened to you in the first place. But . . . I needed the money. That's always been my problem.

'Dear me, listen to me talk. Rambling on and on, and all of you too polite to interrupt. That's what comes of being officially dead; you don't dare talk to anyone for fear of being recognised. So, let me get straight to the point. I want my duplicates back under my control, and I want revenge for all the inconvenience I've been put to. So I'm afraid you're going to have to die, Rowan. It's the only way. And of course I can't leave any witnesses . . . Well, I'm sure you all understand. Nothing personal, Captain Hawk, Captain Fisher.'

'Blow it out your ear,' said Hawk. 'You haven't enough magic to get past our suppressor stone, and you don't have the muscles you gave your Dark Men. So you can take your threats and stuff them where the sun doesn't shine. You're under arrest for illegal research on homunculi.'

There was a soft, scuffing sound behind Hawk, and he instinctively threw himself to one side. The dead Dark Man's sword only just missed him, and plunged on to sink deep into Rowan's side. The force of the blow threw her back against the wall, clutching desperately at the sword. Her face was full of pain and horror, as she stared at the risen dead man, but she couldn't find the breath to scream. The Dark Man pulled the sword free, lacerating her hands cruelly, and stabbed her neatly through the heart. She sank slowly down the wall, leaving a bloody trail behind her.

Hawk swung his axe and buried it in the Dark Man's back. The dead body turned slowly to face him, unaffected. Hawk jerked his axe free, and he and Fisher moved quickly to stand back to back. All three Dark Men moved steadily toward them, blood still seeping from their death wounds, their eyes bright and knowing.

'I'd got a lot further in my researches than Rowan ever did,' said Bode easily. 'And I learned a lot more on the Street of Gods than I ever passed on to her. I really shouldn't have let her know as much as I did, but she seemed so keen, so interested . . . and it was a long time since I'd been able to talk to anyone about the advances I'd made . . . Of course, in the end she decided she wanted it all for herself. Which meant I had to be disposed of. I really

[609]

should have known . . . but then, I never was a very good judge of character.

'Still, she's dead now. Really dead. One of the things I never taught her was how to keep someone from leaving their body. But I know how. No more Dark Men for you, Rowan, my dear.'

Hawk listened to the man chatter with one ear, while he concentrated on the approaching Dark Men. They moved slowly but surely, and held their swords with a confident grip. They didn't breathe, and blood no longer ran from their wounds. There was no doubt they were all dead, animated only by the sorcerer's will. Hawk thought quickly, running the possibilities through his mind. He couldn't get to the nearest exit, so he'd have to stand and fight. A lich may be unkillable, but it can still be stopped. Disable them by cutting through the arms and legs, or severing the head, and they'd be helpless. Hawk smiled sourly. Sure. As easy as that. But since he had no other choice; when in doubt, be direct.

He jumped forward and swung his axe in a vicious arc at the nearest Dark Man. Its unblinking eyes never wavered, and its sword flashed up to meet the axe. Hawk changed his grip at the last moment and swept the axe under the sword to slam into the dead man's side. Bones broke and splintered as the heavy axe head punched through the rib cage, throwing the Dark Man off balance. Hawk jerked the axe free and struck savagely at the lich's neck. It sank to one knee under the impact of the blow, and shuddered as Hawk jerked the axe free again. But another Dark Man was already closing in, and although Hawk stepped quickly back, the lich followed him relentlessly, launching a sustained attack with his sword, which took all of Hawk's skill to parry. Behind him, he could hear the clash of steel on steel as Fisher took on the remaining Dark Man. On the floor, the first Dark Man was already getting to his feet again.

Fisher muttered the suppressor stone's activating phrase under her breath again and again, but nothing happened. Either the stone was drained or it wasn't powerful enough to overcome Bode's sorcery. She scowled, and launched a furious attack on her Dark Man, trying to fight her way past it to get at Bode, but the lich stood its ground and parried all her blows with inhuman efficiency. Sweat ran down her face, stinging her eyes, and she had to fight to get her breath. It had been a long hard day, and her second wind had come and gone. Even if she'd been fresh and at her peak, the lich would have been hard to beat, and as it was she had to struggle to make it anything like an equal contest. She had no tricks left up her sleeve, or at least none that would work on a dead man, and she was starting to slow down. Slowly the Dark Man moved from defence to offence, and Fisher began to give ground.

Hawk and Fisher stood back to back, swinging sword and axe with leaden arms and hammering hearts. Their breath rasped in their throats and sweat soaked their clothes. The near misses got closer all the time as the Dark Men pressed steadily forward. Blood flew on the air, and Hawk and Fisher spat curses as here and there a blow struck home. Hawk gathered the last of his strength and prepared for one final lunge to take him past the Dark Man and launch him at Bode's throat. The odds weren't exactly good, but what the hell. It wasn't that far. Maybe he'd get lucky.

And then a brilliant light flared up, filling the room with its glare, and one by one the Dark Men slowed to a halt and fell heavily to the floor. Hawk looked quickly round, gasping for breath. Tomb had dragged himself across the floor, leaving a wide trail of blood behind him, and now sat propped against the wall with the Exorcist Stone in his hands. The Stone blazed like a miniature star, too bright to look at, banishing all magic from the room. Bode looked at Tomb incredulously. Tomb smiled, showing bloody teeth.

'This is for Rowan, you bastard. Hawk, kill him.'

Bode looked back at Hawk, and quickly raised his hands in the air. 'I surrender, Captain.'

'Like hell,' said Hawk, and cut the sorcerer down with one blow. Bode died with the same incredulous look on his face.

'What the hell,' said Fisher, tiredly lowering her sword. 'He'd only have escaped anyway.'

They put away their weapons and moved over to kneel beside Tomb. The Exorcist Stone slipped from his fingers and rolled away. Its light flickered and went out. Tomb's face was deathly pale, the blood at his mouth stark red against the white skin. He looked across at Rowan, lying still and lifeless, and his mouth worked once.

'I loved her, you know. I really loved her.'

He closed his eyes. Hawk felt for a pulse in Tomb's neck. It was there, but so faint he could barely feel it.

'Is he still alive?' asked Fisher quietly.

'Yeah. But don't ask me how. You'd better go for a doctor; I'll try and keep Tomb and Buchan comfortable till you get back.' He looked across at Rowan, and his mouth hardened. 'Do you suppose she ever cared for him at all?'

'I don't know,' said Fisher, getting to her feet. 'Maybe, if things had been different . . .'

'Yeah,' said Hawk. 'Maybe.' He looked away. 'He deserved better than her.'

And then a living Presence exploded in the room, suffusing everything with the glow of its existence. The Presence beat on the air like a giant heartbeat, or the wings of a powerful bird. A deep and desperate sorrow permeated the room, grief beyond bearing, until Hawk felt as though he would break down and weep at any moment.

'What is it?' whispered Fisher, her eyes bright with unshed tears. 'What's happening?'

'It's Le Bel Inconnu,' said Hawk softly. 'The God that Tomb worshipped. The dying God. It's come here to be with its friend, in their last moments. So neither of them would have to go into the dark alone.'

And then, in a moment, the Presence was gone, as though it had never been. The room seemed to echo its loss. Hawk looked down at Tomb, and didn't need to check the man's pulse to know what he was dead, too.

Aftermath

The Street of Gods was back to normal again, or at least as close as it ever got to normal. The sky was a bright and cheerful blue, and reminded Hawk of pleasant summer days. As long as he didn't look at it too closely. The unmoving clouds and lack of a sun tended to spoil the illusion. Priests and worshippers crowded the Street, bustling back and forth and playing out their familiar roles in the never-ending game of salvation and damnation. Seekers for truth rubbed shoulders with wide-eyed tourists, all of them heckled by street preachers and badgered by concession stall-holders. It was all very much business as usual, for mortals and Beings alike.

Guard Constables and Brothers of Steel stood together on street corners, keeping an eye on things and swapping lies about their exploits during the recent unrest. The priests pretended they weren't there, and concentrated on the more important task of sneering at their inferiors and ostentatiously ignoring the rest. There was almost an air of carnival on the Street of Gods; a celebration of life, of chaos narrowly avoided. When you got right down to it, no one had really wanted a God War. It was bad for business.

Hawk and Fisher strolled down the Street, taking their time and enjoying the sights, accompanied by Lord Louis Hightower. People who recognised the two Guards gave them respectful bows and plenty of room. Hawk smiled graciously. It seemed to him he'd never seen the Street so calm and serene. There was still the usual sprinkling of supernatural flotsam and jetsam: a headless man crawling down the Street on hands and knees, a flock of birds that flew in an endless circle overhead, a laughing woman covered with bubbling blood, and burning coals where her eyes should be; but even they seemed content to keep to themselves and not bother anyone.

'I don't think I've ever known the Street so peaceful,' said Lord Hightower. 'One can only hope it'll last.'

'I doubt it,' said Hawk. 'People have short memories, and from what I hear, the Beings aren't much better. Except when it comes to feuds.'

Hightower laughed. 'You're probably right. Still, the Beings have settled down somewhat, now the God killer has been identified and dealt with, and the priests are behaving themselves for the moment. I suppose your work here is pretty much finished.'

'Pretty much,' said Fisher. 'The Guard sorcerers are searching the rest of the city for more of Bode's homunculi, just in case, but that's the only loose end. We're just hanging on here until the Council appoints a new Deity Division. Buchan's the only survivor of the last God Squad, and it'll be some time before he's ready for duty again.'

'Indeed,' said Hightower. 'I looked in on Charles earlier today. He was looking decidedly pale, but much improved. Amazing what they can do with healing spells these days. And the delightful young lady acting as his nurse seemed very competent.'

'She'll take good care of him,' said Hawk. 'Annette's very fond of Buchan.'

They walked a while in silence, each of them waiting for the other to continue. Hawk broke first. 'All right, Lord Hightower. What the hell are you doing here? Not that we aren't pleased to see you, but I can't believe this is the kind of venue you'd normally choose for a pleasant constitutional.'

Hightower chuckled easily. 'I'm here because the

Council has selected me to be part of the next God Squad. I applied some time back, when I realised how bored I was with my life. The Family estate practically runs itself, I've no interest in politics or the romantic intrigues so beloved by High Society, and even the Hellfire Club was starting to seem a bit childish. But Buchan had seemed happy enough with his work in the God Squad, so I applied.

'The Council contacted me last night and gave me the good news. Personally, I think it just goes to show how desperate they are, but that's their problem. I can't wait to see who they're going to choose as sorcerer and mystic. Anyway, in the meantime I have been given the responsibility of keeping the peace on the Street of Gods. If I'm to do that, I'm going to need people to work with I can trust and the priests and Beings will respect. I need you, Captain Hawk, Captain Fisher. What do you say?'

'Sure,' said Hawk, after a quick look at Fisher, 'we'll help you out. But only until the new Squad's ready to take over. The Street of Gods is an interesting place to visit, but I'd hate to have to work here.'